Praise for THE S...

'Sure-footed, suspenseful, and tragic ...'

'Everything about Anderson ... the war, the history, the aliens ... Anderson has fashioned familiar material into a page-turner of a series that fans of sprawling sagas won't want to miss' STARLOG

'Space opera on a grand scale. Anderson has created a fully independent and richly conceived venue for his personal brand of space opera' SCIFI.COM

'Anderson binds the story and the technical elements together masterfully' THE ALIEN ONLINE

'The scope is vast and the plot just revealing enough to keep you on the edge of your seat' ENIGMA

'Combines glitzy space-opera flash with witty, character-driven action on a cosmic scale ... an SF series more entertaining than a 3-D superstar game of outerspace Twister' PUBLISHERS WEEKLY

'A rip-roaring space opera full of treachery, mystery, adventure, intrigue, suspense, aliens, superscience, space travel, and just about everything else you can imagine' CHRONICLE

By the same author in the Seven Suns saga

Hidden Empire
A Forest of Stars
Horizon Storms
Scattered Suns
Of Fire and Night
Metal Swarm

About the Author

Kevin J. Anderson has over 16 million books in print in 29 languages worldwide. He is the author of the X-FILES novels, GROUND ZERO (No.1 bestseller in THE TIMES, and voted Best SF Novel of the Year by SFX magazine), RUINS, and ANTIBODIES, as well as the JEDI ACADEMY trilogy of STAR WARS novels – the three best-selling SF novels of 1994. He is also writing the prequels to Frank Herbert's monumental DUNE series, with Frank's son, Brian Herbert – the US deal for this was the largest contract in SF publishing history. He has won, or been nominated for, the Nebula Award, Bram Stoker Award, Reader's Choice Award from the Science Fiction Book Club, and many others.

Kevin Anderson lives in Colorado.
www.wordfire.com

OF FIRE AND NIGHT

The Saga of Seven Suns

BOOK FIVE

KEVIN J. ANDERSON

POCKET BOOKS

LONDON • NEW YORK • SYDNEY • TORONTO

First published in Great Britain by Simon & Schuster UK Ltd, 2006
This edition first published by Pocket Books, 2007
An imprint of Simon & Schuster UK Ltd
A CBS COMPANY

5 7 9 10 8 6

Simon & Schuster UK Ltd
1st Floor
222 Gray's Inn Road
London WC1X 8HB

www.simonsays.co.uk

Simon & Schuster Australia
Sydney

A CIP catalogue record for this book is available from the British Library

ISBN-13: 978-1-4165-0292-0

Typeset by Rowland Phototypesetting Ltd, Bury St Edmunds
Printed and bound in Great Britain by CPI Cox & Wyman, Reading, Berks

ACKNOWLEDGEMENTS

As the Saga grows, so does the list of people I rely upon. For help, advice, test reading, and hard work, I thank Louis Moesta, Diane Jones, Catherine Sidor, and Geoffrey Girard. The official editorial team of Jaime Levine, Devi Pillai, Ben Ball, and Melissa Weatherill did masterful work, as always. Stephen Youll and Chris Moore created fabulous covers for the US and UK editions. My agents John Silbersack, Robert Gottlieb, and Kim Whalen at Trident Media Group made sure the series keeps getting the attention any author hopes for. And, as always, my wife Rebecca Moesta contributes more to my writing, and my sanity, than even she realizes.

To DEB RAY,

Who was a dear friend long before
she became such a devoted fan

THE STORY SO FAR

The ongoing titanic war between the alien hydrogues and the faeros extinguished suns and destroyed planets. Determined not to be trampled on the galactic battlefield, the various groups of humans developed new weapons and forged powerful alliances.

The Hansa, led by Chairman Basil Wenceslas, ordered the Earth Defence Forces (EDF) to employ more Klikiss Torches, the superweapon with which they had unwittingly triggered the hydrogue war eight years earlier. The EDF also built armoured 'rammer' ships for suicide missions, crewing each rammer with expendable Soldier compies and a token human commander (one of whom was the Roamer recruit Tasia Tamblyn).

On the home front, repeated failures drove Chairman Basil Wenceslas to make impulsive, often damaging decisions. King Peter and Queen Estarra rebelled against Basil's authority, which increased the animosity between the Chairman and the royal couple. When Basil ordered the Queen to terminate her new pregnancy because the unexpected baby did not fit with his plans, she and Peter leaked news of her condition to the media, through the secret assistance of Deputy Eldred Cain. With such an out-pouring of public joy, Basil could not force the Queen to have an abortion, but punished her indiscretion by slaughtering Estarra's beloved pet dolphins.

The spoiled and uncooperative Prince Daniel – Basil's choice to be the next King – escaped from the Whisper Palace. After quite a scandal, the Prince was recaptured and forced to make a public apology. To keep Daniel from causing further trouble, Basil put him into a drug-induced coma, which unfortunately left the Chairman without a replacement for King Peter.

With the Hansa's war against the hydrogues going badly, Chairman Wenceslas turned his military forces against the Roamer clans, using the space gypsies as scapegoats. One major assault destroyed the Roamer government centre of Rendezvous, scatter-ing the clans. EDF ships hunted down hidden Roamer bases and sent prisoners off to the abandoned Klikiss planet Llaro.

Speaker Cesca Peroni hid out on the frozen mining base of Jonah 12, where miners uncovered and inadvertently reactivated a nest of hibernating Klikiss robots buried beneath the ice. The robots went on a rampage and destroyed the base. After Cesca succeeded in obliterating the scheming robots, she and the young pilot Nikko Chan Tylar crashed their ship while trying to escape.

Meanwhile Cesca's love, Jess Tamblyn – fundamentally changed by watery elemental creatures called wentals that in-habited his body – guided his volunteers to spread wental water across new planets. Along with the verdani (the worldforest on Theroc), the wentals were age-old enemies of the hydrogues, who had nearly exterminated them in an ancient war. By restoring the wentals, Jess created another powerful ally in the fight against the deep-core aliens.

Jess went to the water mines on Plumas where his uncles had

taken over the business. Here, years ago, Jess's mother Karla had fallen into a crevasse and frozen to death. Using his wental powers, Jess found and extracted her frozen body, hoping to give his mother a proper Roamer funeral. Delivering her to his surprised uncles in a grotto under the frozen crust, Jess began to melt the ice around Karla. Before he could finish, though, an urgent message alerted him to Cesca's peril on Jonah 12, and he sped away. Finding Nikko's crashed ship, Jess engulfed it in his amazing wental vessel and raced to find help for Cesca, who was injured and clearly dying.

The Roamer clans found other ways to survive. Cesca's father Denn Peroni helped establish an independent trading base at Yreka, a colony cut off from all Hansa support and defences. Denn also travelled to the Ildiran Empire and met with the Mage-Imperator to reopen trade, once again bypassing the Hansa.

In the rings of the gas giant Osquivel, Del Kellum and his lovely daughter Zhett ran a complex of Roamer shipyards. The EDF had recently lost a tremendous battle with the hydrogues there, and among the debris of the battlefield, Zhett found a small, intact hydrogue derelict; her father immediately called the brilliant Roamer scientist Kotto Okiah to study it. Kotto learned enough from the derelict to develop a new weapon against the hydrogues: 'doorbells' that would blow open a warglobe's hatches. With his doorbells Kotto rushed off to Theroc, the likely target for the next hydrogue attack.

The Roamers also rescued a handful of EDF soldiers whose lifepods had been left behind by their fleeing fleet, as well as many sophisticated new Soldier compies, which were reprogrammed and put to work in the Osquivel shipyards. Zhett helped nurse the POWs back to health, paying particular attention to surly Patrick Fitzpatrick III; because of the hostilities between the Roamers and the Hansa, the POWs could not be sent home. Fitzpatrick and his comrades, including Dr Kiro Yamane (a specialist in Soldier compies), searched for a way to escape. While romance grew between Fitzpatrick and Zhett, Yamane found a way to make the Soldier compies go berserk in the shipyards. As part of an escape plan, Fitzpatrick lured Zhett to a romantic rendezvous, tricked her, and stole a ship to get away while the Soldier compies created a diversion. The compies, far more destructive than Yamane expected, systematically destroyed the Roamer facility.

Fitzpatrick's powerful grandmother Maureen was a former Hansa Chairman. After hearing that her grandson was killed in action at Osquivel, she rallied the relatives of other fallen soldiers and flew to the ringed gas giant to establish a memorial. She was shocked to stumble upon the extensive hidden Roamer shipyards, now thrown into turmoil because of the unleashed Soldier compies. During a tense standoff, Fitzpatrick appeared and then angered his grandmother by speaking on behalf of clan Kellum; he brokered a cease-fire by giving the EDF ships the hydrogue derelict Kotto had been studying. As EDF ships took the POWs back home, Zhett and the other Roamers slipped away. Fitzpatrick doubted he would ever see her again.

General Lanyan, the frustrated commander of the EDF, wanted to make an example of someone. With dwindling recruits, he had no choice but to produce huge numbers of Soldier compies (all of them carrying Klikiss-robot programming modules) and to distribute them across the fleet. He was pleasantly surprised when a deserter — Branson 'BeBob' Roberts — came to Earth bearing two survivors he had rescued from a devastated Hansa colony. The survivors, a girl named Orli Covitz and an old man named Hud Steinman, told a wild tale that marauding Klikiss robots and Soldier compies had destroyed their settlement. General Lanyan sent a team to investigate these preposterous claims, but he was much more interested in court-martialling BeBob for desertion.

The trader Rlinda Kett called in all her favours to help BeBob, but it did no good. The trial was a sham, and BeBob's sentence was a foregone conclusion. To their surprise, though, the spy Davlin Lotze helped them escape. BeBob and Rlinda flew off in her ship, the *Voracious Curiosity*, while Davlin led the EDF pursuers on a wild goose chase, faking his own death. Just when Rlinda and BeBob thought they were safe, they ran into a group of inept Roamer 'pirates' at the ice moon Plumas. Rlinda and BeBob's ship was seized, and they were held in the water mines while the Roamers figured out what to do with them.

When he'd gone to rescue Cesca, Jess Tamblyn did not realize that he had unwittingly dispersed a corrupted spark of wental energy into his mother's partially thawed body. Karla came alive, but was no longer human. Offhandedly killing one of Jess's uncles, she began to move toward the others, while Rlinda and BeBob watched in horror.

On Theroc, the recovering worldforest created a wooden golem of the green priest Beneto to act as a spokesman and to prepare the worldtrees for another hydrogue attack. Beneto's sister Sarein, the Hansa ambassador, arrived on behalf of Chairman Wenceslas, secretly hoping to become the new ruler of Theroc. When she did not succeed in that plan, she convinced green priests to spread among the orphaned Hansa colonies and establish a communications network.

When the hydrogues did arrive at Theroc, hoping to destroy the worldforest, unexpected allies came to stand against the enemy: Kotto Okiah destroyed many warglobes with his new 'doorbell' weapon. And a living comet infused with wentals crashed into the hydrogues, finally defeating them. Though they were driven off, the hydrogues now knew that the supposedly extinct wentals had returned to the fight. In the aftermath, the golem of Beneto received an awesome armada of space-faring 'verdani battleships' – huge thorny trees intent on defending the world-forest.

Meanwhile, the insidious Klikiss robots worked their quiet plans for conquest. When Admiral Stromo went to Orli Covitz's devastated colony world, following up on the survivors' reports, he uncovered evidence that robots were indeed responsible for the attack!

Tasia Tamblyn, responding to an ongoing hydrogue attack on a Hansa skymine at Qronha 3, led the sixty compy-crewed rammer ships. The boss of the skymine, Sullivan Gold, evacuated his people and also rescued a great many Ildirans from a nearby facility. Before Tasia's rammers could arrive, Sullivan was already flying away with the Ildirans, and they were intercepted by Solar Navy ships. When Tasia's rammers finally reached the gas giant, the Soldier compies turned on her and captured Tasia and her personal compy EA. Joining with Klikiss robots, they seized the rammer fleet for themselves and intended to use the ships against humanity.

Klikiss robots had also attacked the few people remaining on the Ildiran resort world of Maratha. The scholar Anton Colicos, his friend Rememberer Vao'sh, and a small group found themselves stranded on the night-side of the planet, facing a long overland journey. Not knowing the robots were the culprits, the ragtag band of Ildirans blamed mythical creatures called the Shana Rei, which were the subject of many tales in *The Saga of Seven Suns*. When Anton and his companions reached the supposed refuge of Secda, they found it overrun with armies of Klikiss robots. Anton and Vao'sh barely escaped in a small ship and flew away, alone. But for Ildirans, solitude leads to madness. During their long flight to Ildira, Anton tried to keep Vao'sh occupied, but the old

6

rememberer degenerated into a near-mindless state by the time they arrived. Safe in the Prism Palace at last, Anton tried to nurse his friend back to health.

The Ildiran Empire, meanwhile, was rocked by a civil war led by Hyrillka Designate Rusa'h and the Mage-Imperator's own son Thor'h. After suffering a head injury, Rusa'h was cut off from the telepathic *thism* that bound their race together. Filled with delusions of grandeur, he created an independent *thism* web and spread a bloody rebellion, forcing other Designates to surrender and accept his brainwashing. Adar Zan'nh brought a group of Solar Navy warliners to quell the revolt, but those ships also fell under the mad Designate's control, and Zan'nh was taken prisoner.

When Rusa'h tried to convert his devious brother Dobro Designate Udru'h, he thought he had found a willing partner. Leaving the impressionable young Designate-in-waiting Daro'h in charge, Udru'h set up a trap and a betrayal that led to Rusa'h's downfall and the end of his rebellion. Hyrillka was recaptured by Mage-Imperator Jora'h, and the traitorous Thor'h was seized. But the mad Designate fled, flying directly into Hyrillka's primary sun. In the last moment before Rusa'h's ship was consumed, a group of flaming faeros rose up and surrounded him, carrying him into the star.

The faeros and hydrogues continued their constant war, smothering one of the seven suns of Ildira. Now was the time for the Mage-Imperator to try his special 'weapon' – his own half-breed daughter, Osira'h. With the girl's special telepathic powers, Jora'h hoped she could call the hydrogues and get them to reaffirm an ages-old non-aggression agreement. Osira'h, who had learned the truth of Dobro's human-Ildiran breeding programme from her green priest mother Nira, experienced mixed loyalties and con-fusion, not sure whom to believe. Still, she did her duty and rode in a protective chamber down into Qronha 3 to communicate with the hydrogues.

Back in Ildira, with the civil war over, the Mage-Imperator was shocked when Udru'h revealed that Jora'h's beloved Nira was alive after all. Still in love with the green priest, the Mage-Imperator demanded that she be freed and returned to him at once. But when Udru'h went to the island on Dobro where he'd kept Nira prisoner, he discovered that the green priest had escaped and was nowhere to be found! Before Jora'h could learn this, though, Osira'h returned to Ildira with a huge armada of hydrogue war-globes, all of them looming over the Prism Palace. Now Jora'h had to face the hydrogues, knowing that if he failed to make a convincing case, the deep-core aliens would destroy his entire world.

ONE

KING PETER

A heavy transport bearing the Earth Defence Forces logo settled onto the Whisper Palace plaza to the sound of cheering almost loud enough to drown out the landing jets. An honour guard carved a safe corridor through enthused spectators toward the shuttle and laid down a purple carpet for King Peter and Queen Estarra.

Taking steps in perfect synchronization with hers, the young King spoke from the corner of his mouth so none of the professional eavesdroppers could hear, 'I so rarely get to announce good news that isn't an outright lie.'

Well aware that Chairman Basil Wenceslas was watching and ready to respond if they made the slightest wrong move, Estarra answered with equal caution. 'We've had to report the deaths of soldiers far too often. Greeting genuine returning heroes is a vast improvement.'

No one had expected to find EDF soldiers alive this long after the Battle of Osquivel; the missing men and women had been presumed killed by the alien hydrogues. Now, blinking in the

Palace District's sunshine, thirty survivors hurried down the debarkation ramp, jostling each other as if they couldn't wait to drink in the air of Earth. All of the smiling refugees wore new uniforms provided by the rescue crew. According to reports, they had immediately ejected the clothing given to them by their Roamer captors (or was it 'hosts'? Peter wondered) out the disposal chutes.

Barely able to contain the ecstatic mob, the guards let the corralled VIP relatives and selected loved ones forward. During the return voyage, former Chairman Maureen Fitzpatrick had transmitted the names of the POWs. Excited families bounced from one rescued survivor to another until, like puzzle pieces, the right ones interlocked with hugs, joyous shouts, and mutual weeping.

Despite this glowing reception, Peter knew the Hansa government was thoroughly embarrassed to find anyone alive. The EDF's clash with the hydrogues at Osquivel had been an utter disaster and a frenzied retreat. Many wounded soldiers were left to die aboard disabled vessels and unclaimed lifepods. But a band of Roamers had rescued some of them. Maureen Fitzpatrick and families of the fallen had gone to the ringed gas giant with the intent of establishing a memorial, and by sheer coincidence had encountered the Roamer shipyard and secured the hostages' return.

Without question, many more soldiers could have been rescued if the panicked EDF hadn't abandoned them. Once the heady celebration was over, people would begin asking questions. *Basil, you certainly have egg on your face*, Peter thought and realized that was when the Chairman proved most dangerous.

Behind his eyes he saw a memory-flash of bloodied water, butchered dolphins, lifeless glassy eyes of the once-playful sea mammals: Basil had not reacted well to the leaked news of the

Queen's unsanctioned pregnancy. Peter could not get the smell of blood and saltwater out of his nostrils.

'Keep to the schedule,' Basil's voice scolded from his tiny ear microphone. 'This is taking too long.'

He squeezed Estarra's hand and faced the transport, waiting for the main event. Sensing an even greater spectacle, the crowd grew quiet. The cargo doors cracked open with a thud and a groan, metal sliding against metal. Interior floodlights shone with a glow like banked fires. Soldiers and cargo handlers used lifting apparatus and gravity-reducers like wranglers transporting a chained prehistoric monster. *A small hydrogue derelict.*

Roamers had found the dead ship drifting in the rings of Osquivel after the great battle. Though this scout vessel was less than ten metres in diameter, the crowd drew in a near-simultaneous gasp of amazement, and fear.

As lifters lowered the derelict to the ground, Maureen Fitzpatrick approached Peter and Estarra with her grandson, one of the thirty refugees, and shook the King's hand as if he were a business partner. As a former Chairman, Maureen understood both how little power Peter truly wielded and the necessity of playing the game. 'Sire, we had to let the Roamers escape in exchange for this derelict. I hope you agree it was an acceptable bargain.'

'I'm sure the Roamers won't cause us any particular harm.' He considered the recent aggression against them to be a deadly distraction that wasted vital military resources. Another one of Basil's boondoggles. 'You made the right decision. Now we have an intact enemy ship to study. I will see to it that both of you receive recognition for your service.'

Pleased to be in the limelight again, Maureen looked like a plump cat that had just swallowed a whole mouthful of canaries.

Estarra looked at the quiet young grandson of the old Chairman. 'You look distracted, Mr Fitzpatrick. Are you well?'

'Sorry – I was . . . thinking about someone.'

'All this talk about Roamers must be distressing to him.' Maureen touched the young man's arm. 'He and the rest of the EDF survivors deserve a long furlough, King Peter – if I can convince General Lanyan of that.'

Hansa scientists hurried into the security zone, eager to get their hands on the alien ship. Engineering Specialist Lars Rurik Swendsen was like a child unwrapping the largest present at a birthday party. 'Just look at it! It's perfect. And if its systems work, we should be able to build counterparts using similar technology. This could be the biggest advance since producing Soldier compies from Klikiss robot designs, or . . . or the Klikiss trans-portals themselves. Just think of it!' The tall Swede looked as if he might start dancing.

Maureen interjected, 'We've also secured detailed notes and logbooks from tests performed by a Roamer engineer. Some of the data may be useful.'

Dignitaries came forward to have their images taken beside the hydrogue ship. With so much disheartening news lately, media reporters would seize upon this happy story, just as they had repeated the unofficial announcement of the Queen's pregnancy.

Even so, this small derelict was a grim reminder that the hydrogues could strike Earth at any time. *However*, Peter thought of Basil lurking behind shadows in the Palace, *it would be refreshing to confront an enemy who isn't afraid to face you.*

Two

ADMIRAL LEV STROMO

The Manta shot across space to rescue any surviving 'dunsel' commanders from the rammer fleet. By now, the sixty kamikaze ships should have smashed the drogues at Qronha 3.

The cruiser's Ildiran stardrive was pushed to its maximum; sweating engineering crews and their Soldier compy counterparts monitored all systems, wary of overloads. Admiral Stromo was seventeen hours behind schedule – before launch, he had insisted on going through every checklist and prep report, as if this were merely a training mission instead of a rushed interception – but the escape pods should have plenty of air, food, and water to last the six token human dunsels for at least another day, maybe two. Stromo had plenty of time.

Itching for a chance to deploy the EDF's new rammers, General Lanyan had seized the chance when hydrogues attacked a Hansa cloud harvester at Qronha 3. Crewed almost entirely by Soldier compies, the massive, reinforced vessels were designed to crash into enemy warglobes. By design, the token human commanders should have been able to eject to safety, and the retrieval Manta would pick them up. The operation had looked perfectly good on paper.

The Admiral slept soundly in his private cabin, leaving administrative details to the officer-in-charge. When the wake-up alarm buzzed, he grumbled that a Grid Admiral should be allowed a few extra hours of rest. He climbed out of his padded bunk, rubbed his eyes, and got ready for his shift. He was expected to provide a good example for his troops, though he would rather have stayed home. Stromo's particular skills were in the areas of bureaucracy, politics, and paperwork. Other EDF officers must be eager to make a name for themselves and get a promotion. Wouldn't one of them have been a better choice for the job?

Nevertheless, he was here. He had his orders. He wanted to finish up and go back.

Stromo splashed his face with water from the small basin. When he rubbed his cheeks, he felt a touch of stubble, but decided he could wait another day before taking his anti-beard-growth hormone. The pills often made his stomach queasy, but shaving was a nuisance.

After putting on a clean uniform, he leaned closer to the mirror, increased the magnification. The heavy jaw and round neck showed an unsightly extra chin that matched his growing paunch; even his eyes were puffy, and not from lack of sleep. Maybe he should start an exercise regimen, when he had spare time.

Stromo had never intended to go back into combat, never thought he'd need to be a rock-hard soldier again. But since the hydrogues, few things in his life had gone the way he'd wanted them to. He was aware of much snickering at his expense, the insulting nickname of 'Stay-at-home Stromo' because he preferred a desk job to real military work. But there came a time when the desire for comfort and predictability superseded pride and ambition.

The glowing digits on the bulkhead wall reminded him that he had only a few minutes to get to the bridge if he meant to be there when the cruiser reached Qronha 3. He should be sitting in the command chair for the important part of this bothersome mission. He combed his short iron-grey hair, took a deep breath, and adjusted his bar of medals (most of them awarded for length of service or for being in the right place at the right time). *Ready for duty.*

He moved at a brisk pace down the corridor, back straight, shoulders square, chin pushed forward as if he were power-walking for exercise. He passed a dozen Soldier compies and nodded a greeting out of habit. He was not surprised that they did not salute or respond. Unlike Friendly-model compies, such niceties were not part of the required military programming.

The Soldier models, designed as replacements for real crewmen, stood almost as tall as a man, with armoured torsos and thick arms and legs. Their reinforced musculature and synthetic body coverings made them more durable, less vulnerable to accidents and damage, and stronger than human soldiers. It was a relief to know there were so many of the useful compies aboard.

He stepped onto the bridge and scanned the crew. The strange young female green priest, Clydia, sat at her station, touching her treeling and daydreaming, as usual. The hairless woman wore only shorts and a loose shirt, no shoes, no rank insignia (other than the numerous tattoos that adorned her emerald skin). Although he viewed green priests as basically savages, he was glad to have use of Clydia's instant communication. Many other battleships were crippled by long transmission times.

The bridge crew consisted of a tall Egyptian weapons officer, Anwar Zizu, who, judging both by appearance and actions, might have been carved from oak; a communications officer whom Stromo couldn't remember having met before; two scan operators; and a pair of Soldier compies monitoring routine stations. When no one noticed his arrival, Stromo loudly cleared his throat. A young ensign who had taken over the nav console – Terene Mae, if he remembered her name right – snapped to attention. 'Admiral on deck!'

Commander Elly Ramirez turned in her chair. 'We're on final approach to the Qronha system, sir.'

'This is just a routine pick-up and run.' He took the command seat that Ramirez surrendered. 'We'll snatch the escape pods, turn around, and head back to Earth. The dunsel commanders can give a full report on the operation.'

Ramirez smiled. 'It'll be good to have Commander Tamblyn back aboard, Admiral. I've never felt entirely right about taking this Manta from her.'

'She followed orders, Commander Ramirez. As a Roamer, Tamblyn wasn't cut out for our recent missions.' Not interested in hearing any more, he looked at the viewscreen and saw the visible disc of a gas-giant planet. The glare from Qronha's binary star flared off to the edge of the screen. 'Is that Qronha 3?'

One of the sensor operators made an adjustment to filter out the extraneous light. 'Yes, sir. We should be within range in less than an hour.'

'Any emergency messages? Locator blips from the escape pods?'

'We're still far away, sir,' Ramirez said. 'The transmitters on the pods aren't very powerful.'

Stromo leaned back. 'Carry on.' For a while, the ship's humming was peaceful, relaxing, and he caught himself nodding off. He rubbed his eyes, forcing himself to stay awake. He hoped he hadn't actually snored.

'Still no response,' the communications officer said.

'We're scanning ahead now, searching for debris or any hot engine traces,' said the sensor operator.

Stromo's brows beetled. 'If sixty rammers smashed into a bunch of drogue warglobes, there should have been quite a fireworks display. Aren't you detecting residual energy and radioactivity yet?'

'No, sir. I find very faint traces deep in the clouds, but they seem to be the leftover components from the cloud-harvesting station. Not the rammers. No sign of Ildiran ships either.'

Stromo frowned. 'But there must be something. We're only a day behind the rammers.'

Reaching the bloated planet, they found no blips from the escape pods, no remnants of explosions, no wreckage. 'Keep looking until you find some answers,' he growled. 'Sixty rammers don't just vanish without a trace.'

THREE

MAGE-IMPERATOR JORA'H

Hydrogue warglobes filled the skies of Ildira, ready to obliterate the Prism Palace. Even under the light of the six surviving suns, Mage-Imperator Jora'h felt as if a heavy shadow had fallen across his skysphere chamber.

He had returned to his dais inside the great palace, and the hydrogues would send down their emissary soon, at which time Jora'h would begin the most important conversation in Ildiran history. Never had a Mage-Imperator faced a more dangerous and frightening crisis or decision. Now, all the centuries of planning and intricate schemes seemed weak and insufficient. Sitting in his chrysalis chair, the bitter knowledge that his empire was about to change chilled Jora'h to the core.

His half-breed daughter Osira'h had brought them here, exactly as *he* had requested. And now what?

The Mage-Imperator was about to face beings so powerful that they could extinguish suns and had nearly destroyed several civilizations in the Spiral Arm ten thousand years ago. What could he possibly have to offer such creatures?

We called this down upon ourselves, Jora'h thought.

Using Klikiss robots as intermediaries ages ago, hydrogues and Ildirans had reached some kind of non-aggression pact that had recently broken down for reasons Jora'h did not understand. The treacherous robots had turned against Ildira to follow their own agenda.

But with Osira'h, the Mage-Imperator needed no other intermediary. She was the bridge. Jora'h wasn't sure how the girl had forced the deep-core aliens to come, nor did he completely grasp her unique powers to make the hydrogues understand. When the deep-core aliens had brought her, intact, from the gas giant, she had told him their brief and terrible message. *They require that you help them destroy the humans. If you do not agree, none of us will survive.* It was as if she had swung a crystal scythe at all his hopes . . .

A courier raced into the sun-bright palace chamber. 'Liege, Adar Zan'nh insists on speaking with you! His maniple of warliners awaits your order. Should he open fire on the hydrogues?'

Jora'h took the communications device from the fleet-footed man. An image formed of his oldest son, the over-burdened commander of the Solar Navy. Zan'nh looked haggard, yet his face remained set with duty and determination. His topknot was drawn back, oiled in place and clipped by an insignia band. 'Liege, my maniple is prepared to defend Ildira. Simply issue the order.'

We will not surrender and crawl into a burrow, waiting for our deaths. Even though their weapons were no match for the warglobes, the Solar Navy would still cause a great deal of damage. *Surely the hydrogues can see that.*

'Adar, that would only trigger a massacre. I will see how this plays out. Remove your warliners to a safe distance, remain vigilant, and be ready to respond. I expect a representative of the hydrogues to arrive soon. The warglobes have come at my request.'

The words sounded impossible as he spoke them. If Jora'h failed here, his empire would be destroyed. His glowing bones would never rest among those of his ancestors in the ossuarium beneath the Prism Palace, and his spirit would no doubt journey to the plane of the Lightsource as a blind man.

With obvious reluctance, Zan'nh signed off. The courier retrieved the communications device, gave a formal bow, and sprinted back out of the audience chamber, looking very frightened.

Sitting beside him on the stairs leading to the dais, little Osira'h looked up at the curved ceiling of the reception hall. The coloured lights shining through the segmented crystal panes seemed to shift, as if her innate power could bend light as well as thoughts. 'The emissary is coming.'

'Did you force him?' Jora'h asked. He'd had no time to debrief her. 'Can you control them?'

The girl gave him an odd, mysterious smile. 'The hydrogues choose to believe they have come of their own free will. But I think they are wrong. I understand them better now, and they understand me. They can read my thoughts, but it is not an easy thing.'

Ethereal Osira'h seemed drained, but her large eyes snared odd reflections, and her yearning face was still childlike and innocent until one looked more closely. In confronting, then coercing, the hydrogues, this girl had survived an ordeal that could have stripped away her soul, her mind.

If only Jora'h could be as strong. 'I will be ready for him. You can help?'

Her eyes took on a glazed distance. 'The hydrogue will speak with you, and you will speak with him. I will take the emissary's thoughts into my own, and he will hear mine.' A strange smile curved her flower-petal lips. 'I will leave him no choice. By becoming a bridge, I became a conduit. I forced myself into the hydrogue minds and opened myself to them. I *made* them come here – half by force, half by . . . luring them. But I cannot force them to listen or agree.'

'That will be my task.'

But the long line of Mage-Imperators who had worked to bring about this day had not done enough to prepare him for what exactly he could use as leverage in negotiating. Jora'h feared what he might have to promise before the hydrogues would leave Ildirans in peace.

Suddenly, the girl's face twisted as if ripples of pain were shooting through her, then she calmed herself. 'I have shown the emissary an acceptable route through the Palace. Otherwise his intent was to smash through the skysphere dome. Hydrogues have little patience for obstacles.'

Sensing the disturbing presence, shimmers in the air and in the light, Jora'h climbed out of his chrysalis chair and stood beside Osira'h. He did not wish to appear weak.

A small environment chamber drifted through the wide arched doorway. Osira'h fixed her gaze on it, caught between two opposing forces. Inside the chamber, swirling mists of super-dense atmosphere masked the liquid-metal shape that pulled itself into a humanoid form. It clothed itself in a mockery of an embroidered jumpsuit with pockets and zippers and clips. The face was human, the hair long, though carved out of flowing quicksilver. Apparently, hydrogues had copied the image from one of their early victims.

The emissary's voice manifested itself as a throbbing hum, as if it were manipulating air molecules to transmit sound waves rather than using a simple speaker system. 'We have come. Do you wish to be destroyed?' From the tone of the hydrogue's voice, it sounded like a legitimate question rather than a threat.

Standing tall, the Mage-Imperator kept his voice calm, though he felt trapped in a flash flood of events, searching for a lifeline. 'I called you here to discuss peace between hydrogues and Ildirans.'

'Peace with Ildirans gains us nothing.' Jora'h was disturbed to notice that Osira'h's lips moved in perfect synchronization with the emissary's words, as if they were inextricably linked. 'Our war was against the verdani. Now we fight the turncoat faeros. And we recently learned that the wentals are back. You are but a minor distraction to us.'

Hydrogues gather enemies as easily as a Prime Designate gathers mates, Jora'h thought. 'We know the hydrogues have already lost much to the faeros.'

'The faeros have lost more. And Ildirans will lose everything if you continue to get in our way.' The emissary's tone was entirely dismissive.

Jora'h said, 'I remind you of our compact from ages ago — an agreement that you seem to have forgotten.' He thought of the merciless hydrogue attacks on Ildiran colony worlds; the hydrogues' actions were nonsensical.

'Only because of that ancient alliance did we agree to this encounter. But the Klikiss robots no longer speak for you.'

'Osira'h speaks for us now. We wish to discuss terms.' From her place on the step, the girl looked up, as if expecting the Mage-Imperator to suggest an instant and viable solution. If only it could be that simple!

'You have no terms that interest us.' The alien voice boomed.

Jora'h searched for a lever with which he could change the emissary's mind. He didn't know what the Klikiss robots had done to force the cessation of attacks against Ildirans, so long ago. What key did they use? Once again, he cursed his predecessors for keeping so many secrets, for censoring the accurate record in *The Saga of Seven Suns.* Without that knowledge, he was handicapped now.

The Mage-Imperator recalled Adar Kori'nh's surprising success, smashing numerous warglobes at Qronha 3. Perhaps the reminder of strength would change the tenor of the negotiations. He raised his voice, exuding as much confidence as he could muster. 'Your warglobes have damaged Ildiran splinter colonies, and our Solar Navy has destroyed many of your vessels. These attacks harm both our species, and benefit neither.'

'Planet-dwelling species intrude and spread taint. You comprehend nothing. Your squabbles and conflicts merely distract us from our true enemies.'

Jora'h seized on an idea. 'The humans continue to deploy Klikiss Torches against your planets. How many of your worlds — how many of your *race* — have they already incinerated?' He raised a finger. 'I can make them stop.'

'*We* will make them stop. They will be annihilated.' The emissary pressed closer to the wall of his sphere. 'Long ago, we helped the Klikiss robots destroy their creator race. That extermination is the proper model for all future conflicts.' The metal gaze pierced the swirling currents. 'Since we have come to Ildira, it would be most efficient if we eliminated you now.'

FOUR

JESS TAMBLYN

Leaving Jonah 12, where renegade Klikiss robots had wiped out an entire Roamer base, Jess's water-and-pearl craft accelerated out of the dark system like a liquid cannonball. His living vessel carried within it a damaged ship and two injured passengers. One of them was Cesca – and she was dying.

Floating in the energized water, Jess peered through a porthole of the damaged *Aquarius* to observe a harried and hurt Nikko Chan Tylar. The young pilot huddled over the woman Jess loved, but he could do little to help Cesca. She lay on the deck, looking grey and clammy, unconscious. Her body had been snapped and broken when the *Aquarius* was shot down; it was a miracle they had survived at all.

Tending her despite his own painful injuries, Nikko seemed to have aged a decade in the past few hours. Though the young man had a sprained wrist, probably a few broken ribs, scrapes, and bruises – nothing his ship's first-aid packs and pain killers couldn't take care of – he had barely left Cesca's side. Jess desperately wished he could touch her himself, kiss her or hold her hand.

But he had given up much of his humanity when he'd become part of the wentals. It had been the only way to stay alive. He couldn't lose Cesca, too! The wentals had been part of his body for some time now, had fundamentally changed him, but he still didn't understand the powerful entities. Jess had told the wentals to find any nearby Roamer base, even a Hansa colony with a medical centre. But everything was too far away.

Why wouldn't the wentals help her? He knew they had the power to do it.

In saving him years ago, the wentals had altered his body chemistry, transforming him into a strange dynamo whose touch would kill any other human. He could do great things with this newfound power – even become a tremendous weapon in the war against the hydrogues.

But some of the simplest acts were denied him. What good were his spectacular abilities, if he couldn't do what he wanted most in the universe? How he longed to hold Cesca and soothe her pain. He couldn't even stroke her sweat-damp forehead as she died. But he had to get as close to her as possible.

Moving through the warm water, Jess cycled through the *Aquarius*'s hatch and stood dripping on the deck. A brief filmy white garment clung to him, and his hair waved about like seaweed in a current. Nikko looked up at him, almond eyes full of hope, as if he believed that Jess could work miracles – which he could. But not this one.

'I've scanned the medical database, Jess, but she's way beyond my ability to patch up.' He held his freshly bandaged arm in front of him. 'By the Guiding Star, I can barely take care of a sprained wrist, and she's all smashed inside. Internal bleeding for sure, probably a punctured lung. Who knows what else.'

With his unbandaged arm, Nikko gave Cesca a stimulant, hoping to stave off the worst effects of shock. Drifting closer to wakefulness, Cesca began to cough. Blood bubbled from between her lips. Though the water-and-pearl ship raced between the stars at incomprehensible speeds, Jess knew she wouldn't survive much longer – unless the wentals did something.

'She has to live, Nikko.' Jess stood with his fists at his sides, feeling hopelessly isolated. He couldn't even touch her! 'She's . . . the Speaker for the Roamers.' The reason sounded noble, but both he and Nikko knew that such an esoteric argument was nothing compared to the fact that Jess loved her.

The wentals spoke inside his mind. *The woman will die soon.*

He was angry at them for coldly stating the obvious. 'Then save her.'

Some things cannot be changed.

He tried to pinpoint the source, as if one particular wental might be the origin of this pessimism. 'And some things *can* be changed.' Elemental force made his voice boom against the walls of the *Aquarius* loudly enough to make Nikko cringe. 'I'll give her wental water to drink, like I did! Then you'll be in her tissues, and you can help her.'

Mere contact with wental water will not transform her as we transformed you. It must be a conscious act on our part.

'Then do it. You don't know how much she means to me.'

We know how much she means to you. We understand.

'Then how can you refuse to help? You saved me, why not save her?' He owed everything to the wentals, but right now he wanted to hate them.

Saving you was necessary. Without you, the wentals would have remained extinct. This woman, however, is not a point of failure for us.

'So the wentals are utterly selfish? She's a point of failure for me. If you refuse to save Cesca, how can I know that you're as benevolent as you claim? Maybe wentals are as evil as the hydrogues, but just trickier.' He had never allowed himself even to consider those suspicions before.

You know that is not true, Jess Tamblyn.

Desperation drove him. 'I know that Cesca's going to die – and that my own allies refuse to save her.'

Helpless and miserable, Nikko propped cushions around Cesca, adjusted her blanket. 'Why is this any different from how green priests join with the worldforest? The trees don't have a problem doing that whenever they want to. Aren't the wentals similar?'

We do not bond in the same way that verdani join with green priests. Worldtrees are passive, the joining symbiotic. Wentals are fluid, uncontrollable, more easily tainted. Selfish actions inspire corruption. When we change you, we change ourselves. Sometimes the reflection splinters, distorts. You cannot comprehend the destructive power of a tainted wental. There is great risk.

'What kind of risk?' Jess demanded. All he could see was Cesca.

See how you yourself are changed. You know how much you lost.

'None of that matters if I lose her.' The sudden realization sparkled within him. 'But if you save her in the same way, then she'll be like me – and I won't be alone anymore. Make us two of a kind.'

After a resounding silence, the wentals said, *We cannot simply transform her. It must be her choice, and ours, before she changes.*

In his mind, Jess received an image of the storm-swept but sterile ocean planet where he'd first delivered the wentals. *That is our nearest world. Go to our primary sea. There, we will decide her fate.*

FIVE

RLINDA KETT

I n the water-mining grotto beneath the crust of Plumas, the reanimated woman stood with ice-white skin. Her inhuman eyes were ablaze with a strange inner energy. Karla Tamblyn's hair crackled and waved about, thawed from the ice that had imprisoned her.

'That's something you don't see every day,' Rlinda Kett said with automatic, but forced, humour. She wasn't sure whether to laugh or scream, but she definitely wanted to run. The Roamer workers didn't know what to do.

The reanimated woman had already left Andrew Tamblyn dead in her wake. Karla took another gliding step, sizzling a clear, hot footprint in the Plumas icepack. Her body was supercharged like a pressure vessel without a release valve, building up power and ready to explode.

While BeBob continued to gawp in childish astonishment, Rlinda pulled him out of the way. 'I suggest we give her all the room she wants.'

He let out a moan. 'Coming here wasn't such a good idea after all.'

'Does a court martial and death sentence back on Earth sound better?'

'This isn't really my idea of a viable alternative. Ever since we escaped, nothing's gone right. The *Blind Faith* was destroyed, Davlin was killed, and we were kidnapped by these crazy Roamers. You'd think that would be enough penance.' He pressed both palms against his forehead. 'Now this monster lady is going to kill all of us.'

'Normally, I'd swat your cute behind for being such a pessimist, but right now I can't argue with you.'

Moving with deliberate steps, Karla did not give a second thought to the dead man sprawled behind her on the ice. Andrew had run forward to bring the woman to her senses, but her merest touch had killed him.

'Karla, what have you done?' cried Wynn, staring at his fallen brother.

'Wait! Don't get in her way!' his twin brother Torin warned.

Uninterested, she plodded towards the edge of the ice shelf and the deep steel-grey sea. Caleb and Wynn seized the opportunity to rush to the crumpled figure and drag Andrew's body away. Torin, the more impressionable of the twins, shouted in a beseeching tone, 'Karla, why are you *doing* this? Don't you know any of us?'

Like a confused mobile statue, Karla Tamblyn turned her crackling gaze back towards the habitation and administrative domes beneath the thick ceiling of ice. She stared without comprehension at the water-mining machinery, the hydrostatic pumps that lifted liquid to the surface for filling starship tanks. She continued moving without responding. The cold sea seemed to call to her. When she stared at the subterranean ocean, her eyes took on a hungry look.

BeBob looked at Rlinda. 'Do you think the Roamers will let us go now?'

'I doubt that's their highest priority.'

Jess Tamblyn, another member of the Roamer clan (Rlinda wasn't sure about the whole family tree) had used exotic powers to retrieve his mother's body from deep within the ice. But after he'd rushed away on some emergency, Karla had thawed on her own and come alive, as if possessed by some kind of demon.

The woman stepped to where the ice abruptly met the water. She lifted her hands, and an invisible energy rippled out like the force of gravity. Powerful, distinct tides pulled the water as if it were clay, stretching and shaping it like magnetic forces pulling iron filings into lines.

The ice cracked behind Karla's feet, calving away. She did not seem alarmed. When the ice sloughed off, Karla stood motionless on the broken chunk. In complete silence she dropped into the deep ocean. Without thrashing or uttering a single sound, she vanished beneath the waves. A geyser of bubbles and white vapour swirled for a few moments, then subsided into stillness.

Rlinda looked around for someone who might explain what was going on. 'Does this sort of thing happen often around here?'

SIX

KOTTO OKIAH

After the drogues had been roundly defeated at Theroc – for the second time – a very pleased Kotto Okiah left the forested planet.

He'd left his mining base on Jonah 12 to help the Therons rebuild their settlement, after which he had gone to the Kellum shipyards at Osquivel, studied a small intact hydrogue derelict they had found, developed a simple defence against the warglobes, and rushed back to Theroc with his doorbells.

In the meantime, the Eddies had destroyed Rendezvous, and his mother had vanished along with many other scattered clans. Although she could take care of herself, he wished he knew where old Jhy Okiah was. She was probably safe somewhere with Speaker Cesca Peroni. Kotto loved the way Speaker Peroni smiled at him whenever he demonstrated 'Roamer ingenuity' in solving a problem. She was bound to be particularly proud of his most recent invention.

His ships had arrived at Theroc like the cavalry, dispersing hundreds of adhesive mats that vibrated at a resonance frequency to blow the warglobes' hatches to the vacuum of space. One after another, the enemy globes had reeled away like whirligigs. Single-handedly, Kotto had saved the worldforest.

Well, maybe not single-handedly.

'Even without that wental comet coming in at the last minute,' Kotto said to his two analytical compies, KR and GU, 'we had those drogues on the run.' He kept up a constant internal monologue, and occasionally parts of it came out in comments spoken without context. The compies, always interested, answered as best they could.

'If the wental comet had not come, there is a high probability we would have been destroyed, Kotto Okiah,' KR pointed out.

'All of our doorbells had already been deployed,' GU added. His polymer body was still battered from when he'd unexpectedly opened the pressurized hatch of the hydrogue derelict. 'We had no remaining defences.'

Kotto nodded absently as their small ship flew on. 'I'm not complaining that reinforcements came at a good time. Even so, we proved the principle, right? Our only mistake was in not bringing enough doorbells. We can fix that. Massive quantities – that's what we need.'

Before leaving Theroc, Kotto had copied the blueprints, then sent the ragtag group of Roamer captains out to find any clan fabrication centre to make more of the doorbells. As soon as he got back to the Osquivel shipyards, Kotto would make sure Del Kellum began manufacturing them by the thousands. From now on, nobody needed to be defenceless against hydrogue depredations.

Unlike his mother, Kotto wasn't a politician (and he'd never envied her role as Speaker) but he wanted to send doorbells to Hansa colonies as well. He mused, 'If we help the Big Goose wipe out the drogues, maybe they'll stop being so pissy toward the clans.'

'Please define "pissy", Kotto Okiah,' GU said. The compies loved learning, so Kotto provided a rough explanation of the term.

KR said, 'You suggest that if we assist the Terran Hanseatic League, they will show their gratitude by calling a halt to their attacks on Roamer facilities?'

'Makes perfect sense to me. We shouldn't have to be enemies. But then, that's not my area of expertise. I'll leave it to the professionals.'

'Another conundrum,' GU said.

'Yes, a conundrum.' He flew towards Osquivel, anxious to get back to work on that fascinating hydrogue derelict. He'd been cut off from news, but he had already thought of twenty new tests to run on the alien systems and was particularly intrigued by the transportal he had found inside. Letting the two compies take care of the ship, he made notes and sketched out some ideas . . .

When Kotto arrived at the ringed gas giant, however, he found no sign of the Roamer shipyards. The whole planet seemed completely abandoned.

'Hello? Where is everybody? I've got good news.' He hoped that such a message would be enough to bring out anyone who might be listening. 'Hello?'

The entire facility – smelters, storage rocks, habitation domes, space docks, ore processors, construction frameworks, everything – was empty.

KR and GU continued transmitting on the frequencies commonly used by Roamers. 'Perhaps the hydrogues destroyed them all,' GU suggested.

'Don't be a pessimist,' Kotto said, though his stomach knotted at the very suggestion.

As they flew around the languid rubble of the rings, Kotto

found no sign of the hydrogue ship he had so carefully moth-balled far from other stations. 'The derelict's gone, too! Somebody took it!'

Confused, fearful, even a bit angry, Kotto piloted the ship down into the main shipyard complex. He encountered debris and abandoned scraps, but few intact structures – and no signs of life whatsoever. The whole place had a haunting aura of emptiness, as if the shipyards had been plundered and then discarded. Nothing useful remained.

'I detect signs of a struggle or an accident,' KR said. 'But the damage does not appear significant enough to have disintegrated all facilities and personnel.'

GU added, 'This appears to be an intentional departure. Perhaps an evacuation.'

Kotto stared at the readings as he circled the rings twice more. 'The shipyards are all gone. Not wiped out – just . . . *gone*, as if Del and his crew pulled up stakes and vanished.'

What could have driven off a man like Del Kellum? Could the EDF have done this – just like they destroyed Rendezvous? He cringed to think of it. And they'd taken the derelict! How was Kotto supposed to find anybody now – Del Kellum, Speaker Peroni, his mother, anybody?

'Just when I thought we were fresh out of conundrums.'

SEVEN

DENN PERONI

After centuries of skin-of-the-teeth survival, Roamers never expected things to go exactly as planned. The unforeseen happened with alarming regularity.

Denn Peroni had left the water mines of Plumas, still nursing a hangover and wondering how he had got drunk enough to join the Tamblyn brothers in the crackpot piracy scheme that had ended in the capture of a Hansa merchant vessel with its pilot and co-pilot. Cringing at the magnitude of their collective stupidity, he had flown away, leaving the captives behind. Sooner or later, Caleb and his brothers would realize they didn't know what to do with Rlinda Kett and Branson Roberts. Meanwhile, he was glad to be alone aboard his ship – without the constant chatter, complaints, and sloppiness of Caleb Tamblyn.

Denn flew the *Dogged Persistence* from one known clan settlement to another, adjusting his trading schedule as he received news (much of it out of date). With the angry Roamers ready to chew up metal ore and spit out nails, Denn got little more than rumours, tall-tales, and a lot of admitted ignorance from the other outposts he visited.

He learned that his daughter Cesca was holed up on a small planetoid called Jonah 12 on the other side of the Spiral Arm. In her capacity as Speaker she had sent out messages calling for the clans to hold steady and prepare for rebuilding now that Rendezvous was destroyed. Denn worried about his daughter, but he was sure Cesca could handle the brunt of the Roamers' emergency – probably a lot better than he could!

He heard positive news as well. Nikko Chan Tylar had been passing the word that Golgen was free of hydrogues – a gas giant was safe for skymining again! Denn decided to help spread the word, at least until Cesca made some sort of official pronouncement.

Forrey's Folly was the largest metal asteroid in a strip of rubble around a cool orange K2 star. While coalescing, the sun had lost its grip on most of the material in its primordial cloud and hadn't had enough mass left over to create any planets worth counting. But Forrey's Folly was a large ripe fruit ready to be plucked: Metals were simply there for the taking, and mining tunnels honeycombed the asteroid.

Numerous stony satellites orbited the large oblong rock, low-density moonlets that the metal asteroid had captured in its wanderings through the rubble belt. The small satellites whirled like a group of moths around a bright flame. Though computer models could predict the orbits, the paths changed frequently as the moonlets collided and ricocheted off each other.

A century ago, Karlton Forrey had been the first Roamer to invest money in mining equipment and bring his clan ship here for excavations. Before his family or machinery could be shuttled down, though, Forrey had miscalculated the orbits of the stony moonlets. Collisions sent rocks careening like giant birdshot into his temporary habitation ships. Most of Forrey's family had died, and all the equipment was ruined. A misplaced decimal point, incalculable consequences. Thus, Forrey's Folly had earned its name.

As the *Dogged Persistence* approached, Denn checked and rechecked his calculations, transmitting ahead for the current listing of safe paths. As he came within visual range, he noticed a large group of Roamer ships parked far outside the orbital radii of the rocky satellites. He saw evacuation ships, mobile mining equipment converted to interstellar craft, even components from space docks. Denn was puzzled; this looked like a full-scale operation, packed up and ready for reassembly. But Forrcy's Folly was strictly a resource-stripping operation.

Then he noted the clan markings on the ships. *Kellum*.

'This is Denn Peroni on final approach, with trading goods and news. I haven't seen Oscar in years. Who are your visitors? Is Del Kellum there?'

The station operator acknowledged. 'Yes, he brought all of his refugees after they evacuated from Osquivel.'

'Evacuated from Osquivel?' He couldn't wait to hear the full details. 'Expect me down there in a few minutes. I've got a shipload of farm-fresh produce from Yreka, if anybody's interested.'

'That's the best news we've heard all day, *Dogged Persistence.*'

'Oh, you heard something better yesterday, huh? Then maybe I'll just save some of this sweetcorn for another customer.'

Because Forrey's Folly had so many extra mouths to feed, thanks to Kellum's refugees, Denn subtracted all but a token profit on his load of fruits, vegetables, and grains. The hard-bitten asteroid miners from Clan Kowalski, along with the hundreds who had left the Osquivel shipyards, decided to have a feast. Roamers believed in making the most out of each day, since disasters happened too frequently for anyone to count on unending tomorrows.

Kellum was pleased to see Denn. The barrel-chested man sat at the table, talking too loudly, acting as if he ran Forrey's Folly, rather than being a guest. Denn suspected he was working some sort of cooperative deal with the Kowalskis to combine equipment and resources.

Del Kellum had obviously told the story many times. 'After the damned Eddies left, we knew we had only a few days to get out of there before they changed their minds.' He reached over to pat his daughter's arm. 'Zhett learned the hard way not to trust anything they say.'

The young woman tossed her dark hair. 'Just tell him what happened, Dad.'

'We only had short-range craft at the shipyard, in-system vessels without Ildiran stardrives. We knew we'd never make it to another clan settlement. But we didn't want to leave all of our equipment there, by damn. You know the Eddies would strip it clean and use it for themselves.'

There were grumbles around the table. Kellum picked up a yellow ear of corn and chewed down a row, taking a break from his tale to enjoy the food. A few kernels clung to his salt-and-pepper beard.

'So we decided to pull up stakes, grab everything we could, and ferry it to our cometary extraction facilities high in the Kuiper Belt. The Eddies aren't bright enough to look up there. It's an awfully big chunk of real estate.'

More grumbles, mostly mutters of agreement.

'We had plenty of long-range ships at the cometary extraction facilities, and half a dozen stardrive units for installation into new ships from the spacedocks. So we modified a few big ships and abandoned Osquivel. Now we're here, safe by the grace of

Clan Kowalski.' He looked over at a string-bean-thin man with ice-blue eyes, bushy eyebrows, and a corona of white hair that stuck out in a fringe around his bald scalp. 'Our friends at Forrey's Folly offered sanctuary, but we don't want to overstay our welcome. Do we, Oscar?'

'You haven't ... yet,' said Oscar Kowalski. 'But no Roamer facility has enough surplus to handle so many refugees for more than a little while.'

'Unless we work out a deal to establish new shipyards here, I expect we'll head out in a week,' Kellum said. 'Always on the move. We are Roamers, you know. So where's the Speaker during all this, Denn? We need to hear from her.'

'Last I heard, my daughter was on Jonah 12 trying to call clans together. I think Jhy Okiah was there, too. They'll sort it out.'

'By the Guiding Star, I hope so!' Oscar said, clearing his throat. 'We've got a lot of business to do.'

Denn watched the miners take second helpings of fresh food. 'Since you're digesting most of my cargo from the *Dogged Persistence*, does anybody have goods for me to trade? I could use a cargo for my next port of call.'

Oscar Kowalski seemed to be doing calculations in his head. 'Let us know what metals you need. We can fill you to capacity.'

Kellum grinned down at the gnawed cob of corn on his plate. 'By damn, we've even got a cargo of ekti from the comet processors. You want to take it to the Ildirans, Denn? You reopened trade with them, right?'

'Caleb Tamblyn and I set things up with the Mage-Imperator himself. If you give me a load, I'll head straight to Ildira. Better than selling it to the Big Goose.' The Roamers' deprecating nickname for the Hansa seemed almost too mild to express the contempt Denn felt.

'Be sure you get a good price for it. My clan's going to need to capitalize our new operations – whatever they are. I sure don't look forward to rebuilding a shipyard from scratch. That was a hell of a lot of work.'

Denn brightened with an idea. 'That brings up an interesting possibility I heard about on my travels. How would you like to go back to skymining?' He explained how Golgen's clouds were now safe again for ekti harvesting.

Kellum slapped his big hand on the table. 'By damn, what a fabulous idea! We've still got our big equipment in cold storage up in the cometary cloud at Osquivel – two skymines we haven't used since the drogue ultimatum. But I knew we'd eventually go back to our old ways. Ah, skymining again. Hear that Zhett? Clan Kellum's going to get back into the ekti business!' He beamed at his daughter. 'We're going to Golgen, my sweet – and we can leave tomorrow.' He patted his stomach. 'As soon as all this digests.'

EIGHT

OSIRA'H

Centuries of planning had culminated in this meeting between the Mage-Imperator and the hydrogue emissary. Osira'h had not expected the leader of the Ildiran Empire to appear so helpless and desperate. This communication, this 'negotiation', was entirely one-sided. What had she missed? Did he not have a plan? He must have!

In the skies above, visible through the dome's coloured panes, hovered the armada of warglobes that had carried her from the depths of Qronha 3. After forcing the hydrogues to look inside her mind, Osira'h had coerced them into this encounter. Violent hydrogue thoughts still streamed through the conduit of her mind, splashing hot droplets of comprehension along the way. The hydrogues reached into her brain and stole whatever information they needed, but they had no interest in understanding.

Osira'h had been inside their heads, as well, and knew they would not react to an attempted negotiation in the way her father expected. Through her, they had seen what the Mage-Imperator hoped to achieve from this meeting, and they were unimpressed. She sensed that the emissary meant what he threatened. Even as hydrogues suffered casualties and great damage in their clashes with the faeros, they were ready to annihilate the Ildirans merely to get rid of a nuisance.

She listened carefully, without speaking, watching her father. The girl had met him for the first time only recently and did not yet understand what sort of man Jora'h was. She had many different images of him: father, Mage-Imperator, her mother's cherished lover, and brother of deceitful Dobro Designate Udru'h.

Osira'h had detailed memories of Jora'h from her mother. Those flashbacks were heart-warming, filled with love and tenderness. Yet the girl remembered feeling that same sort of loving pride towards the Dobro Designate — and *he* had fooled her. Had Jora'h done the same to Nira?

Right now, Osira'h wanted — *needed* — to see him not as a father or a cherished lover, but as the Mage-Imperator, leader of billions of Ildirans. She wanted him to demonstrate his strength, the strength of the Empire.

But the hydrogues were much stronger.

The emissary continued in a booming, accusatory voice, 'Ildirans once had a powerful connection with the faeros, our mortal enemies. In our current battle, we have already extinguished one of your suns. It is just the beginning.'

'We have no alliance with the faeros,' Jora'h insisted. 'The faeros attack you, and humans use their Torches to ignite your planets, but Ildirans are not part of your war. We have no interest in hydrogue planets. There is no dispute between our races. We are neutral.'

'You do not understand our war.'

'No, I do not! I understand only that we have become part of it, through no desire of our own.'

The emissary paused as he sifted for a name. 'Your ... *Adar Kori'nh* destroyed many of our warglobes.'

Osira'h sat up abruptly. The hydrogues had taken that specific name from her memory, proving that the strange aliens understood more about Ildirans than they admitted.

Even the Mage-Imperator showed surprise at how much they had drawn from his daughter. 'Adar Kori'nh did no more than defend Ildirans against unprovoked hydrogue attacks.' Jora'h took a step closer to the environment chamber, and his voice hardened. 'Thus, you have glimpsed what we could do if forced to bring our military might to bear. The Solar Navy has thousands more ships. Do not underestimate us. We could inflict extreme damage on you.'

The emissary's indignation crashed into Osira'h's mind like breakers against a seawall. 'And we can exterminate your race.'

'Yes, you could. But if you choose that course, we would weaken you – maybe enough for the faeros to finish you off. Are you willing to risk that? What purpose would it serve?' The emissary remained silent, and the Mage-Imperator continued in a threatening tone, 'In the ten thousand years since your last conflict, our scientists and engineers have developed tremendous defences. You will not find us easy prey.'

Osira'h fought to keep her silence. She knew that the Ildirans had changed little in many centuries, that the *Saga* had gone so far as to cover up all record of the previous war, that the Mage-Imperator's people had not prepared in the slightest to battle the deep-core aliens. In fact, they had developed only one new defence: Osira'h herself. Though she tried, she could not hide her disappointment in her father and his people. The lives of so many humans had been sacrificed on Dobro. *All for ... this?*

And though she struggled to cover her reaction, the hydrogues drew the revelation from her mind. The emissary didn't spare a glance for Osira'h. 'Your attempts at deception are feeble. We do not believe you. You have developed no new defences against us.'

The girl squirmed with anger and frustration. Jora'h looked at her, as if his own daughter had betrayed him.

But she was upset with him as well. The Mage-Imperator *must* have planned something before sending her on her mission. Right now, he could at least call in Adar Zan'nh with his warliners. A full-fledged attack would surely destroy the warglobes overhead, though it might cost much of the Solar Navy and probably ruin most of Mijistra as well.

The emissary no longer had any patience for the meeting. He seemed very disappointed in what the hydrogues had found here. He spoke dismissively. 'We cannot waste time trading threats with Ildirans. The wentals are not extinct, as we believed, and humans continue to harass us. We have a greater war.'

Jora'h walked down the dais steps to stand directly in front of the emissary's chamber. His voice was strong, but Osira'h could sense his fear. 'Long ago, we worked out terms not to engage in mutual hostilities. We must do the same now, as we did in the last war. It might save you from the faeros.'

'You can do nothing for us. We do not need Ildiran assistance. We are strong enough against the faeros – whether or not you fight us.'

Osira'h felt a tug-of-war in her head, and she tried to balance the condemnation of the emissary with the thoughts of the Mage-Imperator. As if thrusting a dagger into an enemy's heart, she pounded the *demand* into the hydrogue that he must offer a solution, must grant the Ildiran race a stay of execution.

Reeling from her mental onslaught, the emissary paused. Finally he said, 'All rock-dwellers damage the song of the universe. Unnecessary notes must be eliminated, but discordant notes must be eliminated first.' The shifting shape paused, as if forming a new idea. 'Ildirans cannot help in our war with the faeros. However, you can assist us against another insignificant opponent.'

Jora'h stonily regarded the quicksilver shape, waiting for the explanation.

'Among rock dwellers, humans are our greatest enemies.' Thick mists swirled around his sculpted face. 'Help us destroy them all, and perhaps we will ignore your planets.'

Osira'h had never been to Earth or Theroc, had met no other humans except for the isolated *Burton* descendants on Dobro. But they were her mother's people! She hammered a deafening mental *No!* at the emissary, but the hydrogue shut her off.

Jora'h swayed. 'Humans have never harmed us! They are our allies.'

'Humans are enemies of the hydrogues. You cannot ally yourselves with both. Choose.'

Osira'h stared at her father, but his attention was centred on the terrible choice he had to make, obviously torn between honour and survival. Above, through the skysphere, she could see the warliners looming closer. With such a deadly armada, the hydrogues could level Mijistra much more swiftly than Adar Zan'nh could bring Ildiran warships to defend it.

But to exterminate all humans! Osira'h longed to beg her father not to agree. She knew too little about his true character. Her experience thus far had been with the breeding camps, with the teachings of Designate Udru'h, with Nira's memories. She knew that Ildirans kept many secrets and told many lies, both subtle and blatant. Betrayal seemed to come easily to them.

Would her father capitulate and agree to obliterate another race in order to save his own? He would show his true colours by demonstrating whether he stood on principle, or whether his loyalty could be changed with a simple threat. She tried to influence his thoughts with her own, shouting inside her mind.

How strong are your convictions, Father? Are you a good person, or is your honour for sale, just like Designate Udru'h's?

A true leader of the Ildiran people *must* find another way. She had seen into the hydrogue minds. She knew their rigid alien thought patterns and their mighty firepower. Even so, the girl believed that a real Mage-Imperator would stand up to the enemy. Would Jora'h betray Nira?

In another flood of memories the girl saw how her mother had held this man, listened to his promises, responded to his expressions of love. Were those memories a lie? The man Nira had loved would never bow to such a threat, would never consider it for a moment. She thought about Theroc, saw through her mother's joyful past the tall worldtrees, the camaraderie of green priests, the mysteries of the great forest. And then she imagined them all turned to smoking, smashed ruins. Because of Jora'h's weakness.

Standing before the hydrogue emissary, with hundreds of warglobes overhead, the Mage-Imperator wrestled with this impossible choice. Obviously, he saw no way out. Jora'h lowered his eyes and answered in a whisper, 'I will do what I must. No matter what it costs.'

NINE

DOBRO DESIGNATE UDRU'H

From his residence outside the fenced-in breeding camps, the Dobro Designate frowned at his unconscious 'guest'. The disgraced Thor'h was maintained in a comatose state by a crippling dose of shiing.

It was better than the young man deserved for his part in the awful Hyrillka rebellion, Udru'h thought as he regarded the slack face. *We all have to endure the echoes of our past indiscretions. But you have an easy way out.*

His idealistic protégé Daro'h seemed uneasy in the well-lit room. 'Thor'h was the Prime Designate. The Ildiran Empire would have been his.' Daro'h looked up at his mentor, whom he would replace as soon as the Designate deemed him ready. 'Why would my brother do this? Why would he break from our father's *thism* and try to destroy the Empire?'

'He did not wish to destroy it, simply to remake it. Some men are misled fanatics who adhere to incorrect ideals and beliefs. Others are selfish and impatient for power. Some are simply fools.' He smirked. 'The Prime Designate was all of those things.'

The young man lay like a corpse on the narrow bed. Udru'h hoped the traitor was swimming in nightmares or smothering in guilt over what he had done, but Thor'h's face showed neither honour nor peace. 'Unlike my brother Rusa'h, Thor'h had no excuse for his behaviour.'

'You can excuse the mad Designate? But you betrayed him yourself and brought down his rebellion! What of all the deaths he caused?'

'The Hyrillka Designate exhibited a clear shift in his personality after his head injury. He had delusions, believed he saw a new route to the Lightsource, and was prepared to pave that path with the blood of any Ildiran who did not join his corrupted *thism* network. He was insane. Why else would he have flown his ship into Hyrillka's sun?' Udru'h looked down at Thor'h in disgust. 'But the Prime Designate knew exactly what he was doing. That is why I despise him. It would have been better if he had died in the conflict. He remains a stain on the Ildiran psyche.'

In further expansions of *The Saga of Seven Suns*, Udru'h realized that the Hyrillka revolt would be chronicled with great care. Rememberer kithmen would show the utmost tact, accurately representing the facts and yet shading the heroes and villains in such a way as to preserve the grandeur of the Empire. No matter what the lower kiths believed, the truth was a flexible thing.

'Fortunately, no one knows he is here,' Daro'h said.

'And we will keep him so drugged with shiing that he cannot reconnect with the *thism*. He no longer deserves to be part of it.' Even after such vile betrayal, Jora'h was too weak to command the execution of his own son. Instead, he had ordered Designate Udru'h to hide Thor'h and make sure he never again felt the *thism*. The planet Dobro already had more than its share of dark secrets.

Designate-in-waiting Daro'h had offered no complaints or naively stern judgements when he'd been told about the genetic experiments, the human captives taken from the generation ship *Burton*. Instead, he accepted the reasons for the overall scheme, and the secrecy. Daro'h did not try to second-guess the Mage-Imperator or his predecessors. He was a smart young man, despite his sheltered upbringing at the Prism Palace. Udru'h was very proud of him.

A commotion and shouts came from the main part of the Designate's dwelling. Daro'h looked up with a hopeful expression. 'Maybe someone has found the missing green priest.'

'I doubt it, though that would solve many of my problems.'

When Udru'h had revealed to the Mage-Imperator that his beloved Nira was alive after all, he had considered the matter to be over. He had promised to retrieve the green priest woman from her isolation, but like one last slap in the face, she had escaped, leaving no clue as to where she had gone. He had to find her again before the Mage-Imperator suspected anything had gone wrong. After having to lie to Jora'h so many times, he could not return to the Prism Palace and say he had failed again. He needed to find Nira, and he had very little time.

Sealing comatose Thor'h in his chamber, Udru'h hurried off with Daro'h at his heels. Standing breathless beside four advisers and guard kithmen, a glitter-eyed courier waited anxiously. 'Designate Udru'h! Adar Zan'nh has sent me here with a report. Hundreds of hydrogue warglobes fill the skies over Mijistra!'

Daro'h gasped, 'Have they come to attack?'

'No, the girl Osira'h is with them. My team was sent on the fastest ship to relay this message to you. Osira'h succeeded. Dobro has succeeded!'

Udru'h felt a weight lift from him as the courier finished his report. Jora'h still needed to make a pact with the hydrogues no matter what the cost; nevertheless, centuries of work had paid off. All his training and devotion to the half-breed girl had helped her fulfil her destiny! He missed Osira'h, but he had done what was necessary. If she had failed, then Udru'h would have sent her brother Rod'h on the same mission, and each of her half-breed siblings would go until every possible chance was exhausted.

Then, as a guard kithman ushered the courier out of the room, Udru'h realized that this turn of events gave him a second chance, an unexpected reprieve. If a hydrogue armada was now over the Prism Palace, the Mage-Imperator would be completely preoccupied. He had more time to find the green priest!

'Daro'h, we must take advantage of this opportunity. While the Mage-Imperator is distracted with other obligations, we must locate his green priest. If we hurry, we may never need tell him she was missing. Find her!'

'But we already went to the island—'

'Perform a full-scale search across the whole southern continent if necessary. Do everything you can – except give up. I have disappointed the Mage-Imperator too often.' Udru'h lowered his voice. 'He may not have been willing to kill Thor'h . . . but if I tell him that I have lost Nira yet again, he will surely command my execution.'

TEN

QUEEN ESTARRA

Now that news of her pregnancy had spread, the public demanded frequent sightings of the Queen. As a diversion for the increasingly anxious populace, the Chairman allowed her to roam occasionally so she could be seen. He generally saw Estarra as no more than a pawn to force the King's cooperation. She hoped he continued to underestimate her.

Estarra found Nahton in one of the mesh-enclosed butterfly pavilions on the roof. The court green priest stood alone in the sunlight, letting the butterflies flit around him, their wings like kaleidoscopic jewels. Seeing him, she remembered how on Theroc she and Beneto had watched a worm hive hatch, how Rossia had told her of his encounter with a terrible wyvern.

Nahton was her only source of news from home; he gave her updates about her parents, about her tomboy sister Celli, about how the forest had resurrected a copy of her brother Beneto. Sarein had only recently returned from Theroc, but Estarra had not yet had a chance to meet with her. Sarein would not tell her anything that Nahton had not already described, though.

The court green priest was a tall man with a long face and a quiet disposition. His face and shoulders were embroidered with tattoo symbols that indicated the training he had completed before being sent to Earth. 'Queen Estarra! It always pleases me to see a fellow child of Theroc.'

'It would please us both even more to see Theroc itself. It's been so long.' She let beautiful orange and yellow butterflies cluster around her, drawn to her perfumes and skin oils as if she were a particularly attractive flower.

Estarra missed the worldforest, her expansive fungus-reef home. Right now, with the weight of humanity on her shoulders and the baby coming in three months, she wanted her mother to hold her. How could she explain about the butchered dolphins, about the numerous veiled threats on her life and Peter's, about how the Chairman wanted to kill her baby just because it didn't fit with his plan? Father Idriss and Mother Alexa could not help from far-off Theroc. Sarein was here on Earth, and she might be Estarra's last resort, but the Queen worried about her sister's loyalties.

Instead, with no one else to turn to, Estarra expressed her fears to Nahton. He looked unsettled but not surprised by her revelations. 'I am a green priest, a son of Theroc. My loyalty is to the worldforest, and then to you, Estarra – and the King. The Chairman, though ... the Chairman has not earned my trust.' He then turned a reassuring smile towards her. 'But take heart. Something remarkable has happened at Theroc, summoned by your brother Beneto. They have travelled for thousands of years, giant tree—'

Suddenly, blond Mr Pellidor marched out onto the rooftop. His face was flushed, his eyes narrowed with edgy impatience. 'Queen Estarra, it is not safe for you to wander by yourself.'

'I am perfectly safe with Nahton.' His concern for her was

as false as the smile she gave him in return. Had he been eavesdropping?

'It is not the green priest we are worried about. I will escort you back to the royal wing. Now.'

'I thank you for your concern for my safety.' Her voice was clipped, her eyes flashing with clear scepticism about Pellidor's true reasons for pursuing her. With a sniff, Estarra stepped past him. She knew he was the man who had killed her dolphins, on the Chairman's orders.

Before leaving, she glanced at the green priest. Their eyes met, but she didn't dare ask out loud what message he would send to her parents. She had told him enough. There was nothing Pellidor or the Chairman could do to prevent Nahton from communicating, short of removing all the treelings from the Whisper Palace. She never got to ask him about the marvellous surprise the worldforest and Beneto had brought to Theroc.

Pellidor took the Queen by the arm. Though revolted by his touch, she made a conscious effort not to brush his hand away. He walked her briskly from the roof.

ELEVEN

CELLI

W hen the majestic verdani battleships landed on Theroc
after their long journey, the people stared in awe. Celli
grabbed her friend Solimar's hand and squeezed so
hard she nearly broke his fingers. The jagged shadows of the
enormous trees cast a hush over all the forest wildlife.

The nearest treeship filled much of the blue sky. As it
lowered itself, the long lower branches bent to the ground like
thin, delicate legs; the rest of the incredible boughs stretched
upwards, back towards space. The curving leafless branches ended
in immense thorns, longer and sharper than the deadliest spear.
The base of the huge trunk terminated in a rounded armoured
bulb, trailing long root tendrils like sensor antennae. These whip-
ping, thrashing threads touched the Theron soil and gently
probed into the dirt of their near-forgotten home.

A second spiny vessel towered in the distance, and a third
settled nearby in the devastated worldforest. Then dozens more,
until almost two hundred had come to Theroc.

Looking at the enormous branches overhead, Celli felt the

majesty about them, an organic construction even more impressive and terrifying than the rooted worldtrees themselves. When her eyes burned, she realized she had forgotten to blink.

Beneto seemed to know what was happening, and he was not afraid. Her wooden brother stood motionless in the clearing near the fungus-reef city, as if his sculpted feet had taken root. His smooth grain-streaked face looked satisfied as it tilted upwards. 'They will stand guard above Theroc.'

She thought of her sister Estarra, who served as the Hansa's Queen. 'What if the hydrogues attack somewhere else? What about Earth?'

Beneto turned his polished face to her. An alchemical mixture of blood and sap now flowed through his artificial body. 'This war is far more extensive than Theroc or Earth, more than humans or Ildirans. This fight can only be won with a wealth of allies. Fortunately, the hydrogues have created many powerful enemies.' He gestured to the forest that was bursting with fresh green after the deluge from the vaporized comet. 'Already the wentals have joined us, and we are stronger.'

That much was readily apparent. After the Theron people had spent months clearing, rebuilding, and replanting, the trees now exploded with life after being drenched with water from the wental comet.

Standing next to her, still holding Celli's hand, Solimar said, 'In the first war, wentals and verdani clashed with the far-superior might of the hydrogues. They nearly drove themselves to extinction, but then the faeros turned against the enemy as well.'

Beneto said, 'Faeros shift their loyalties like a candle flame flickering in the wind. Sometimes they may fight the same battles as we do, but they are not necessarily our allies. We hoped the enemy was vanquished so long ago, driven back into their gas-giant planets. But after hiding for thousands of years, the hydrogues have recovered from their wounds.'

His wooden face seemed sad. 'Sometimes it is easier to leave an issue unresolved, but it is never wiser. The worldtrees and their allies must not make that error again.'

Beneath the jagged shadow of multiple verdani battleships, the grounded worldtrees shuddered as thoughts rippled through their interconnected mind. Celli sensed millennia of rage, fear, and hurt there.

The golem's expression shifted. 'The hydrogues are already battling the faeros, and they will never survive the wentals and the verdani as well. Now that the treeships are here, we will go on the offensive.'

T W E L V E

A D M I R A L   L E V   S T R O M O

F or two days the Manta continued its search for signs of the rammer fleet, lifepods with the human captains, or even hydrogue wreckage. The crew expected Stromo to know what to do, but he'd never been briefed for a situation like this. The original orders were straightforward. *Fetch any escape pods you can find and come home. Report how much damage the rammers caused.* It shouldn't have been complicated.

From the Manta's bridge, Clydia had sent a message to the Whisper Palace's green priest, and Nahton dutifully passed along the question. Distracted by the arrival of a small hydrogue derelict and thirty EDF survivors from the Battle of Osquivel, Chairman Wenceslas promptly sent back an unhelpful response: 'Continue searching. Further instructions to come.'

Stromo was uneasy around this pastel gas giant, where hydrogues had recently obliterated a Hansa cloud harvester and, quite possibly, all sixty EDF rammers. One Manta cruiser wouldn't do much good if warglobes showed up.

He turned his command chair towards the preoccupied green

priest. 'Any word from the Chairman yet? How long does he want us to wait here?'

The green priest stared down at the feathery fronds of her potted plant, stroking the treeling as if it were a pet. When she withdrew from telink, Clydia took a second to centre herself. 'The Chairman suggests that you tune a receiver to the following frequency and boost the gain.' She rattled off numbers. Even though she herself sat at the comm station, she did not know how to use the sophisticated equipment.

'What's that supposed to do?' Stromo asked.

Without suggesting an answer, Elly Ramirez hurried over to configure the receivers. Clydia continued to recite, 'Run any signal through a descrambler. The Chairman thinks you might receive a message.'

Stromo felt even more confused. 'There aren't any habitable worlds around here, and no ships that we can find. Where would a signal come from?'

'Apparently, a Listener compy was planted aboard the rammers to keep watch on Commander Tamblyn and attempt to gather intelligence about the Roamers.' Ramirez glanced up, incensed at the green priest's words. 'You should be able to tap into the surveillance software. If the compy is in range, this may allow you to trace where the rammers have gone.'

The Admiral looked around nervously. 'Any sign of hydrogues yet? What if they detect us eavesdropping?'

'This is a very-low-intensity broadcast for espionage purposes, sir, tailored to blend in with background noise until extracted with our specific algorithms. It was designed not to be detectable.'

'Designed so that the *Roamers* can't detect it. Who knows what technology the drogues have? Stay alert. Be ready to move at the first hint of trouble.'

When Ramirez finished her adjustments, the bridge viewing

screen filled with static as if an electronic dust storm had swept over the cruiser. Gradually, images formed as the signal was strengthened and reinforced; descramblers stripped out noise and extraneous feedback. Then the picture clarified.

Stromo felt as if someone had hit him on the back of the head. Hard.

The viewer showed a group of humans huddled inside a bizarre cell whose walls looked like jewelled gelatin. Closest to the surveillance imagers was a scuffed and dishevelled Tamblyn; next to her sat a dark-skinned young man who looked oddly familiar. *Brindle.* Yes, that was his name – the volunteer who had gone down in a diving bell to contact the drogues just before the Battle of Osquivel. Robb Brindle! But how in the hell did a young man who vanished at Osquivel on the other side of the Spiral Arm show up here at the edge of the Ildiran Empire?

Stromo saw a small group of downcast and weak-looking humans. Were they still aboard one of the rammers? Prisoners of war? And who had captured them? This was all too confusing. 'Where the hell is that signal coming from? Find me the rammers!'

'Doesn't make sense, Admiral.' Ramirez looked up. 'But it looks like the signal originates within the gas giant. Deep down.'

'Impossible! Nobody can survive down there.'

The pair of sensor operators also checked their readouts. 'Confirmed, Admiral. They're inside Qronha 3.'

Then, into the image stepped a Klikiss robot. The beetle-like machine moved its sharp-pointed appendages in a clearly threatening manner. The captives cringed away.

Stromo already had plenty of suspicions about the black robots, especially after what he had seen on the crushed Hansa colony of Corribus, after hearing the unbelievable report from the survivor girl Orli Covitz. 'What is the hell is *that* thing doing there?'

The two Soldier compies manning bridge stations suddenly froze, as if receiving a signal. Stromo glanced at the military robots in disgust. 'Now what's wrong with them?'

'Check their stations, Ensign Mae,' Ramirez said.

Mae left her nav console and ran a quick diagnostic of the closest compy to see if some feedback might have influenced them. 'There's nothing—'

Both Soldier compies moved with astonishing speed. The nearest one spun its flexible torso, reached up, and clamped a vice-like metal hand around Mae's throat. Before she could try to claw free, the compy's other hand grabbed her head and twisted, as if unscrewing a lid. Mae's neck snapped like kindling.

In the same instant, the other compy lunged towards the second sensor operator (Stromo still couldn't remember the young man's name). The military robot rammed a polymer-sheathed metal fist into the crewman's sternum with the force of a jackhammer and exploded his heart. He fell to the deck before blood could even seep out of his smashed chest.

No more than two seconds had passed. While the Admiral sat unable to believe what he had just witnessed, the bridge crew erupted in panic. The green priest almost knocked over her potted tree, but caught it in time.

The two compies turned from their initial victims towards Stromo and Ramirez, as if homing in on rank insignia. Ramirez dived for the command chair, shoved the Admiral away, and fumbled with a side compartment.

While the first compy lunged forward like an asteroid on a collision course, Sergeant Zizu threw himself against the other one. Despite the military robot's greater mass, the security officer knocked it off balance.

Ramirez finally succeeded in activating the thumb-lock and withdrew a twitcher weapon, a sidearm that delivered a powerful stun impulse to take down unruly humans. She adjusted the output to maximum and fired a disruptive impulse directly into the first compy's face. Though it was not meant to affect circuitry, the pulse was enough to disorient the compy's programming.

By now the tackled compy had recovered its balance. With a single blow, it knocked Zizu aside and ploughed forward with the Admiral in its sights. Stromo scrambled away from the chair.

Ramirez did not hesitate. With cold fury in her eyes, she played the twitcher beam over the second compy's core as it lurched towards them. She continued firing the beam until smoke and sparks boiled from the implanted circuits. A metre away from them, the military robot collapsed into a petrified metal-and-polymer statue.

Then the first attacking compy straightened as its systems reset themselves. It reacquired its target and began to move, still orienting itself. Sergeant Zizu detached the metal chair from a bridge station and, yelling at the top of his lungs, he brought the chair's shaft down like a club on the compy's neck. The robot's head bent, neck cables snapped, and Zizu struck again and again. The compy shuddered, then dropped like scrap metal to the deck.

Stromo backed to the other side of the bridge until he bumped against an empty station. Rattled and wheezing, he shook his head. 'This is not possible! Simply not possible.'

The crewmen stared at their two slain comrades. Ramirez recovered first, doublechecked the second compy to make sure it remained inactive. Her face was flushed, her brow furrowed. 'Admiral, remember when King Peter warned us about the Soldier compies and the Klikiss programming? He tried to shut down the factory.'

Stromo mopped his forehead. 'That was just a false alarm. Everything worked fine. No problems.'

'Admiral, there is definitely a "problem".'

'Maybe these two were just flukes,' Stromo said in a watery voice, expressing a hope that even he did not believe. Ramirez gave him a withering glance that came close to crossing the line into insubordination.

'We just saw a Klikiss robot on the screen. What if it sent some sort of signal?' Zizu suggested.

Stromo made himself sound strong and confident. He knew Ramirez was going to make the suggestion herself, so he decided to say it first. 'Extreme precautions, Commander. Let's switch off all the Soldier compies until we can figure out what went wrong here. No sense in taking chances.'

'That's what I was hoping you'd say, Admiral.'

However, when Stromo reached to activate the full-ship intercom, Ramirez cautioned him. 'Do you really want to let the Soldier compies know what we intend to do? They might switch into defensive mode. Instead, let's dispatch specific teams to isolate and deactivate the compies.'

Knowing he should have thought of that, Stromo nodded. 'I hope we have enough time.'

THIRTEEN

TASIA TAMBLYN

F inding Robb Brindle alive brought Tasia the greatest joy she could have imagined. She just wished it wasn't in a place like this – trapped in a prison bubble beneath the clouds of a gas giant, surrounded by inhuman enemies. *The Bowels of Hell* would have been an apt description.

Still . . . Robb was alive!

Tears streamed down her grimy face. For just a moment, her joy pushed back the waves of anger, fear, and confusion. One thing at a time. She embraced the young man who had been her fellow soldier, her lover, and her friend. They hugged without words, their muscles trembling, breaths hitching. Finally, Tasia wrinkled her nose. 'Shizz, you stink.'

Robb's grin was awkward, as if he hadn't had much chance to practise it in a long time. 'You know how long it's been since I've had a shower? This isn't exactly a Relleker resort. I saw images of Relleker once, but I never actually went there . . .' His voice trailed off. Tasia couldn't imagine how he had retained any hold on sanity, just sitting here with no conceivable hope of escaping. *Talk about being under pressure*, she thought. Looking at his dishevelled form, she knew Robb had fared much better than she would have.

He indicated the chamber and his six equally ragged companions. 'How long has it been anyway? With all the Klikiss robots lumbering around out there, you'd think at least one of them would have a clock or calendar display!'

Tasia mentally calculated, shocked at how long it had been since last she'd seen him. 'Almost two years.'

Hearing this, several of the prisoners groaned. Robb swallowed hard and lifted his chin with forced optimism. 'Well, it did seem like for ever. No wonder we all look like shit.'

Tasia ran her fingers through her regulation-short hair. 'Looks like I'll have plenty of time to get used to it.'

When she and her loyal Listener compy EA were taken from the hijacked rammers, sealed in a small prison bubble, and dropped into the coloured gases of Qronha 3, she was certain she would be killed. Only after Tasia had seen the hydrogue citysphere – a fever-dream conglomeration of odd geometric shapes – had she begun to grasp the extent of the alien civilization. How many such cities lurked within the Spiral Arm's gas giants? How many had the Hansa incinerated with their Klikiss Torches, whether intentionally or by accident? 'No wonder the drogues are foaming at their liquid-metal mouths.'

Klikiss robots had accompanied Tasia and her compy through oddly permeable walls into the hydrogue city. 'Where are they taking us, EA?'

'I do not know, Tasia Tamblyn. But if we are making new memories to fill my datacore, then this is an experience I will never forget.'

'Was that an attempt at humour? That sounds like my old EA.'

Next, they'd been brought into this strange zoo chamber to join seven other hostages. Apparently, the hydrogues – or the

Klikiss robots – had been taking 'experimental subjects' for some time now.

Recognizing Robb despite his tattered clothes and long tangled hair, Tasia remembered the day he'd gone into hydrogue-infested depths. His last transmission had been 'It's beautiful, beautiful—' He must have seen a hydrogue cityplex.

Now she asked, 'Why did they take us prisoner, Brindle? What do they mean to do with us?'

'Kill us all,' said one of the most miserable captives, whose name was Smith Keffa. 'Damned Klikiss robots! Damned drogues!'

All the humans were gaunt, their eyes sunken. They had lived here without proper care, without hope. Everybody had a story, and she was disheartened to hear their hair-raising tales. Her fellow captives had nothing better to do than talk about themselves, and it seemed Tasia's arrival was a welcome break in their endless terrifying monotony. Crestfallen, she learned that none of the other dunsel commanders from the rammers had been taken hostage. As far as she knew, she was the only one still alive. Maybe EA had had something to do with the robots sparing Tasia's life . . .

'They keep bringing new prisoners, but there used to be more of us,' Robb said. 'One died trying to escape. Others were taken away and killed in awful experiments.'

'The drogues and the Klikiss robots made us watch!' Keffa held up his hands and arms, displaying horrific scars from long-healed gouges in his skin, but he did not explain what had been done to him. Some of the prisoners groaned, others huddled, staring sightlessly as if they were already dead.

Robb hunkered down next to Tasia and slipped his arm around her. Deep sadness etched his handsome face; all the boyish charm had been sapped away by his endless ordeal. 'I can't say how sorry I am to have you here, Tasia.'

She nudged him with her elbow, still marvelling to see him

regardless of their circumstances. 'Right. I missed you too, Brindle.'

He reached into his grimy pocket and withdrew a brown and crumbly tangle of thin leaves. 'I still have the worldtree frond that green priest gave me before I climbed into the encounter chamber over Osquivel.' He rolled it in his fingers, but the plant material was dry and dead. 'It didn't do me much good. Sometimes, I hold it as if I'm a green priest and I send imaginary letters in my mind to you and my parents . . .'

Tasia saw the withered leaves and recalled when Rossia, the limping green priest with wide eyes, had reverently given the frond to Robb as if it were a talisman. 'I don't think drogues like worldtrees much.'

'No. But in a weird sort of way, I think this little twig has kept me sane. I've been thinking about you a lot. Good memories are about the only things that keep us going here.' Robb shook his head. 'But this nightmare isn't one of the things I wanted to share. Not with you – not even with my worst enemy.'

Leaning against him, she grunted. 'Not even Patrick Fitzpatrick III?'

He gave a rusty-sounding chuckle. 'Whatever happened to him anyway? Is he still a jerk?'

'He's dead.' She described what had happened at the Battle of Osquivel after Robb's encounter vessel disappeared into the planet. 'Fitzpatrick was killed, and so were a lot of other good soldiers.'

There was so much to tell him, so many things that had occurred since his disappearance. Unfortunately, she would have more than enough time to bring her companions up to date. First, she told them about the new rammers, how they'd been deployed swiftly to Qronha 3, and how she had been captured by the turncoat robots.

EA piped up, 'The renegade programming was embedded in

the Soldier compies from the beginning. The Klikiss robots simply activated it.'

Now one of the black robots loomed in front of the translucent wall. Tasia glared at the black machine as it pushed its way through. Smith Keffa cringed from the robot. Obviously trying to look brave for Tasia's benefit, Robb said, 'I don't think it's here to play checkers with the prisoners.'

The robot spoke, as if for no reason other than to taunt them, 'A Manta cruiser has arrived above Qronha 3. We have instructed the Soldier compies onboard to take over. We are also activating the programming system-wide.'

'What do you mean, system-wide?' Robb asked.

'All Soldier compies, all across the Spiral Arm.'

Tasia reacted with automatic outrage. 'Humans have never done anything to Klikiss robots. What the hell do you intend to do?'

'Exterminate you all.'

Tasia put her hands on her hips, not caring how ridiculous she looked in front of the looming black machine. 'That figures. The EDF declares war on the Roamer clans, and now Klikiss robots are trying to wipe out humans. Shizz! Can't anybody figure out the right enemy these days?'

'We know our enemies.'

Having delivered its ominous message, the Klikiss robot departed.

FOURTEEN

PATRICK FITZPATRICK III

On the open deck of his grandmother's Colorado mansion, Patrick Fitzpatrick sat alone and stared at the mountains. He had turned off the environment screen so he could smell the biting, fresh air. The cold was the least of his problems. Snow etched the jagged tops of the majestic peaks, and the sky was an utterly transparent blue, so different from the claustrophobic habitats where he and his fellow EDF soldiers had been held by the Roamers.

If he'd been back in the Osquivel shipyards, Patrick and his EDF comrades would have been hard at work processing metal, assembling ships, doing something productive. Right now, more than anything else, he wondered where Zhett Kellum was, what she was doing. Maybe she was burning him in effigy . . .

He'd been back home for three days now, a 'war hero' with little to do except make public appearances, smile and wave. Some of the other refugees were media darlings – particularly feisty Shelia Andez, who made no secret of her resentment towards the Roamers. Because that fitted so nicely with the Hansa's position,

Shelia got as many bookings and honoraria as she wanted.

The public grumbled that Clan Kellum had not seen fit to turn over the brave soldiers immediately after rescuing them. The public didn't know what they were talking about, and the Hansa kept it that way. He found it offensive; worse, a year ago he would have believed the ridiculous propaganda.

His grandmother stepped out onto the deck. Though he faced the opposite direction, he could sense she was there, and that she must be scowling in disapproval. The former Hansa Chairman had looked over his shoulder all his life while his parents went off on innocuous diplomatic assignments designed to keep them away from anything important. Fitzpatrick didn't acknowledge her.

'Just sitting out in the cold again? Another day down the drain?' As a power broker, Maureen never wasted time on unnecessary small talk; she watched the clock, charged every minute of her time to one account or other.

'Does it bother you that I've got things to think about, Grandmother? Or would you prefer I joined some politically correct volunteer organization?' Intentionally, he blew out a white breath; it reminded him of the vented atmosphere from broken-open pressure domes when Kiro Yamane's reprogrammed Soldier compies had gone on a rampage – the extravagant diversion that gave Patrick his chance to escape.

'You don't look like you're enjoying your furlough, Patrick. I pulled strings to get you plenty of time off, along with full media attention. Your comrades seem to be revelling in their freedom, going to parties, vacationing, exercising. Why don't you visit some of the friends who were rescued with you?'

'They weren't my friends, Grandmother. Just fellow prisoners.'

'Well, I invited them to your reception tomorrow, so I hope you're ready to be sociable. Every day, you just sit here and stare at the snow.'

'Maybe that's what I need right now.' He still didn't look at her. 'I didn't ask for a reception.'

Maureen put a hand on his shoulder, but she was only imitating a gesture of comfort that she had seen other people make. 'There, there. It's really the best thing after what you've been through.' She had raised him, shaped him, tried to mould him into a perfect Fitzpatrick heir. In doing so, she had un-wittingly taught him to recognize her manipulations. Patrick could either pretend to cooperate, or he could find some way to short-circuit her intentions.

He gave a sour laugh. 'A lot of people have been through a lot of things.' At last he glanced at her and was immediately reminded of her nickname. With her stern face, sharp nose, and narrow chin, the 'Battleaxe' did resemble a heavy-bladed weapon.

Seeing that she couldn't melt him with her charm, Maureen crossed thin arms over her chest, but was too controlled to let her-self shiver in the cold. 'I also wanted to give you a report. There's been news. The EDF dispatched investigation ships to Osquivel even before we got home. They wanted to inspect Roamer operations in the rings, salvage anything, gather information.'

'And they didn't find anything, did they?'

'The place was entirely abandoned. EDF search teams dis-covered a few remnants of the shipyards, but everything was either destroyed by the Soldier compies, or else the Roamers scuttled the facilities themselves. Typical. Whenever their furtive little operations are exposed, they scurry away like cockroaches.' When she smiled, her thin lips became completely colourless. Patrick had never noticed that before.

'What did you expect them to do? They exchanged the hydrogue derelict for their freedom – that was the deal – but they knew they weren't safe. Why doesn't the Hansa just leave them alone?'

She clucked her tongue. 'Patrick, you are certainly obsessed with the Roamers! May I remind you that they hardly gave up the derelict voluntarily? In fact, they had the thing in their possession for some time without ever mentioning it, even though our Hansa scientists could certainly have done a far superior job of analysis than their own primitive engineers did.'

Patrick huddled deeper in his chair and focused on the distant peaks, his stomach as cold as a glacier. Roamers were exceptionally good at hiding. When the first EDF expedition came hunting hydrogues at Osquivel, Del Kellum had managed to cover up his huge shipyard operations. Patrick wondered how he would ever find the Roamers now, and Zhett, if they *really* wanted to hide.

His time with the dark-haired beauty had changed him, against his will. Now he no longer fitted in with his blueblood family. 'Grandmother, I want you to do something for me. Make whatever excuses you need to make – I don't really care. I'm going to resign from the EDF.'

She looked startled, but her expression was a reflection of surprise, not disappointment. 'Of course, Patrick. The family never intended for you to have a lengthy military career. We can transition you into a corporate position, or even an ambassadorship, if you prefer.'

'Not that. Too many others are letting themselves become propaganda puppets for a cause we know is false. So, I'm going to speak out, and some of the other refugees are bound to join me. What the Hansa is doing to the Roamers is completely unfair.'

That surprised her. 'You can't be serious! You know what the clans have done, what they *are*.'

He tucked his chin into the collar of his jacket. He had been just as prejudiced himself when he first joined the EDF. He'd been merciless to the Roamer recruit Tasia Tamblyn, treating her like dung – but she had got the best of him more than once. He was good at picking fights.

'I know more than that, Grandmother. All their accusations are true, regardless of what you choose to believe. The clans have perfectly legitimate reasons for cutting us off. We deserve it.'

Now truly shocked, Maureen looked as if her mind was already spinning through possibilities, assessing and discarding ways to mitigate this disaster. 'That's ridiculous and rash, Patrick. Come inside, and I'll make you some tea.'

'Grandmother, you never make your own tea. And stop patronizing me.'

'No need to jump to conclusions. You can't possibly understand all the reasons behind—'

'Of course I understand.' He finally stood up. 'I was *there*. I caused it myself. I was with General Lanyan when we encountered a Roamer vessel filled with ekti. We seized it, stole the stardrive fuel, and then blew the ship out of space. Never gave the captain a chance. *I* pushed the button myself. *I* fired the jazers that disintegrated a Roamer ship.'

He was gratified to see her stunned into silence. 'Later, when somebody found the wreckage, the Roamers knew the EDF was to blame. That was why they broke off all trade with us. That's what started this whole mess.'

FIFTEEN

ENGINEERING SPECIALIST SWENDSEN

The hydrogue derelict was marvellous beyond Swendsen's wildest expectations. 'I can't remember the last time I was so excited. I don't think I've slept in days.'

'You need your sleep, Dr Swendsen,' said his lead materials tech. 'Tired researchers make mistakes.'

'No worries, Norman. I've had coffee. Lots of it.' He kept moving as he talked, bumping into team members, checking on their progress. The alien walls were set at disorienting angles; no one could quite tell what the hydrogues considered up or down.

He ducked through the low hatch and came upon two men standing over a deck of crystalline ... controls? Decorations? The nodules connected to no circuitry that anyone could find. He propped his hands on his hips, nodding absently. 'Just don't push any big red buttons. We don't know how to read "Self Destruct" in the hydrogue language.'

'The systems are intact, Dr Swendsen,' one of the men said, scratching a bushy eyebrow. 'The ship's energy source is charged, as far as we can tell.'

The other tech, a frizzy-haired man with pale skin, grinned like an exuberant child. 'Right! There seems to be no reason why we can't work the derelict, but we haven't figured out *how* yet.'

'We'll crack the mystery – count on it. I'm still studying the lab notes left behind by that Roamer engineer. Lots of good stuff.' He would have liked to meet Kotto Okiah. Maybe later, once the Roamer difficulties were straightened out. 'A very interesting character – brilliant, though a bit disorganized. He wrote down random observations, but never got around to summarizing and extrapolating. Still, he achieved quite a lot, considering he was just one man.'

He mumbled encouragement to the techs, then moved toward the centre. Did hydrogues walk, or fly, or flow? Swendsen stopped a young woman with hair that fell to her waist, though she kept it tied out her way. Rosamaria Nogales. *Dr* Nogales. 'Any report from the biologists yet? Can they confirm that the residue we found was a dead hydrogue?'

The puddle of metallic paste was soft, gelatinous, pliable, and materially unlike anything Swendsen had ever seen. In his notes, Kotto Okiah had postulated that the motionless ooze was one of the deep-core aliens. Swendsen had the same suspicions.

Rosamaria's deep-brown eyes were bloodshot; apparently, Swendsen wasn't the only one getting too little sleep. 'By breaking down the material into constituent elements, they determined it isn't organic. The structure – I hesitate to call it "tissue" – is composed of metallic forms of lightweight gases – which never should have stayed in that state under normal atmospheric conditions.'

'Are you saying that what we found was *air* shocked into a flexible yet crystalline state that somehow retained its molecular structure?'

She shook her head. 'I didn't say that. The biochemists did.'

'Well, then who are we to contradict them?'

He continued like a doctor on his rounds. Understanding how the hydrogue drive functioned might lead to amazing adaptations for EDF ships – new weapons, new defences. So many possibilities, and he wanted to do everything, but he was already wearing too many hats. Swendsen was still ostensibly in charge of the Hansa's compy production facility not far from the Palace District. Fortunately, only a few humans were needed to monitor the automated manufacturing lines; thus, Swendsen was free to spend his time and mental energy here.

He arrived at the most intriguing part of the alien vessel, a flat trapezoidal wall panel that resembled one of the Klikiss transportals. The hydrogues and the original Klikiss, somehow, impossibly, used identical transportation systems.

With a pang, he wished Chief Scientist Howard Palawu could be here to help him. He and Swendsen had worked together to dismantle a volunteer Klikiss robot, then used what they'd learned to modify the Hansa's compy modules. The resulting Soldier compies were far superior to other models. As a reward for excellent work, Chairman Wenceslas had sent Palawu to study the Klikiss transportals – and Palawu had disappeared through an ancient doorway, just as Margaret Colicos had done. No one had seen him since.

Now his main transportal engineer was a dusky-skinned young woman named Sofia Aladdia, who'd been transferred from Rheindic Co. At the moment, she sat staring at the crystalline wall, intently studying the symbols. 'I've looked at all of Dr Palawu's records. He understood transportals better than any of us.'

'Would he have understood this one?'

She shrugged. 'I think he would have concluded that the hydrogues used transportal technology to travel from gas giant to gas giant, from core to core. Maybe understanding it is only a matter of redefining coordinates.'

'That would explain why we never saw drogue ships flying between planets until recently.' If the Hansa had known an alien race lived inside gas giants, they would never have used the Klikiss Torch.

If they could just make a breakthrough or two, Swendsen was sure all the pieces would fit neatly together. The EDF was waiting for anything he could announce.

SIXTEEN

ROSSIA

The Grid 5 battle group – a flagship Juggernaut and eleven escort Mantas – patrolled the starry wilderness. On the bridge of the *Eldorado*, Rossia touched his treeling, shifting uncomfortably in the polymer chair. The green priest was supposed to remain at his station for another several hours, in case Admiral Kostas Eolus should need his services for telink communication. He longed for the treetops of Theroc, despite the dangerous flying predators up there.

Rossia was one of the handful of original volunteers who'd joined the rigid structure of the military. He limped because of his scarred leg, his large eyes bulged as if he held his breath too often, and he talked to himself. But green priests were rare enough in the EDF that eccentric behaviour was tolerated.

Reassigned from his old position with Admiral Willis, Rossia now served as a communications link for gruff Eolus. The Grid 5 Admiral had curly black hair, heavy brows, and a strong chin with deep lines around his mouth. Eolus had never learned how to speak in a quiet voice. With the Admiral watching over his bridge like a wyvern in search of a tender meal, Rossia bent to his duties.

A flurry of messages and concerns caught his attention when he sent his mind out through telink. Something was happening out there. He sensed a deeply troubling flood from other green priests, primarily comrades who served aboard EDF ships. The most urgent message came from Clydia aboard Admiral Stromo's Manta, which was currently searching for the rammers at Qronha 3. Through the worldforest mind, Rossia could hear her thoughts, see through her eyes, and experience her surroundings. After receiving her shocking news, his discomfort on the hard chair disappeared.

Clydia had seen Soldier compies murder two crewmembers on Stromo's bridge. Now she caressed her treeling, both to reassure the plant and to take guidance from the worldtree mind. No one knew how serious the situation might be. Clydia slipped away and headed for her quarters. Perhaps in that sanctuary, she could dim the lights and sit with her treeling, to recover her peace by communing with the worldforest. Alarms thrummed through the Manta.

As she hurried along, the corridor intercom bubbled with a stew of brusque reports and anxious voices. 'Admiral, something's wrong with the compies. They won't obey standard—'

'I already ordered you to shut them down!'

She heard a strange sound – a muffled scream? – then thumps, a scuffle, a shot before the intercom was cut off. Clydia could smell death and shock in the air. Three uniformed crewmen ran past her, obviously frightened. She pressed herself against the wall so as not to get in their way.

From adjacent passages and open hatches came a confusing barrage of echoes – shouts, the clatter of metal, an explosion. Clydia flinched at the crackle of twitcher beams, but she couldn't tell which direction the noises had come from. She moved faster, hounded by ricochets of sound. Her potted treeling felt heavy in her arms, but she held it tightly. It was her only link to the green priests, to the worldforest. They all had to know what was going on . . .

Aboard the *Eldorado*, Rossia jerked upright, astonished and at a loss for words. He blinked furiously, trying to focus his thoughts and his eyes.

Admiral Eolus saw him jump. 'What got you, green priest? Does your tree have a biting bug?'

Rossia stared at his treeling in disbelief. 'Something terrible is happening. Soldier compies are attacking the crew aboard one of the EDF Mantas, I think.'

Eolus let out a gruff laugh. 'Don't be ridiculous.'

'No . . . I don't think it's ridiculous at all. Let me—' He plunged his thoughts back into telink, seeing through Clydia's eyes again, watching her run barefoot through the ship's corridors.

He heard Admiral Stromo's voice bellow over the intercom. 'The damned compies know we're onto them. I want every crewman armed. Ship security, distribute twitchers to all personnel! Bring out the big guns, if we have any.'

The responding voice was raspy, as if the woman had shouted too much in the past hour. 'Admiral, the damn compies have taken over the armoury vaults. They killed six of my men!'

Stromo sounded entirely befuddled. 'But compies aren't supposed to arm themselves!' As if to taunt him, the intercom flooded with a humming crackle of stun bursts, and the woman's transmission changed to a rush of static.

More weapons fire came from ahead of Clydia. Five EDF soldiers rounded a corner in full retreat, running backwards and shouting. Their uniforms were torn, as if they had just lost a fist fight with an automated grain harvester. They shot twitchers down the corridor, but the energy bursts looked weak, as if the charge packs were nearly depleted. 'Pull back!'

Clydia heard evenly rhythmic footsteps coming closer, then Soldier compies fell upon the five crewmen. She ducked down a side corridor and saw the closed doors of a lift at the end of the hall. She had to get to another deck! Screams and sounds of fighting came from behind her as she ran. She could get to her quarters, lock her door, and wait for the Admiral and his fighting men to get the compies under control. It would be only a matter of time.

The treeling grew heavier with every step she took. Her arms ached as she raced to the elevator. Before she could touch the controls, the doors whisked open, and two burly Soldier compies marched out. Skidding to a stop, Clydia saw the glowing optical sensors target her. The compies marched forward.

She turned back in the direction she had come, but the EDF crewmen had been cornered out there. A third group of Soldier compies boxed her in from the main passageway. In the hall's bright light she saw wet reflections of spray patterns on their synthetic skin. The facsimile hands were red.

Clydia pressed her back against the metal wall and clutched the treeling to her chest. From three directions, compies converged on her. Her fingers gripped the slender gold-scaled trunk as she broadcast everything that was happening. Across the Spiral Arm, every green priest would know what was taking place aboard this ship.

But none of them could help her. Rossia couldn't help her. He could only hear and see and experience every second of it.

The closest compy seized the potted treeling. Clydia tried to twist away, but the robot knocked it to the floor, smashing the pot. *Breaking the link.*

With a gasp, Rossia snatched his hands from his own treeling, as if he'd been burned. The images had flown at him like a swarm of stinging insects, and then dwindled to nothing.

All the bridge crew stared at him. Rossia realized that the Admiral had been bellowing for answers. 'A disaster,' he said. 'A real disaster!'

Eolus looked ready to leap out of his seat. 'What disaster? Explain!'

'The Soldier compies are going berserk on Admiral Stromo's Manta. I saw it myself through telink. I watched the compies attack. They—' His breath hitched, and he forced himself to calm down and summarize what he had seen, though the images continued to swirl around him like blowing leaves. A secondary hum of questions and reports from other green priests now yammered through telink. 'The compies just destroyed her treeling. I felt the pain.' As an afterthought, he added, 'I think Clydia's dead, too.'

At first, the *Eldorado*'s bridge crew looked at each other, perplexed, but their mood swiftly turned to alarm. Eolus looked at the cockeyed green priest as if he had made a joke in poor taste. He let out a loud snort. 'They're *compies*, for God's sake. Compies can't think for themselves.'

Ignoring them, Rossia concentrated on the treeling again. When he looked up, he felt even more dazed than before. 'I've received reports from green priests aboard four other EDF ships. Soldier compies are running amok. Everywhere! It's a coordinated rebellion.'

Eolus clenched his hands into fists. 'I will get to the bottom of this bullcrap.' He turned to the comm officer, raising his voice to thunder level. 'Give me all-ship intercom. Immediate reports! Has anyone seen—'

Before the Admiral could complete his sentence, a staccato of alarms went off. Intercom channels filled with shouted accounts of strange behaviour, compies suddenly going rogue, as if they were all on some sort of timer. Rossia let out a low moan, already knowing what must be happening.

Eolus got to his feet. 'Green priest! You sure about this?'

Rossia nodded, yanking his fingertips away from the nightmarish images in telink. 'Yes. Absolutely, yes. They're slaughtering crews on grid after grid. I think most of the green priests are already dead. Oh, I've never seen so much blood. The compies are just attacking and attacking.'

Eolus whirled to the comm officer. 'Word from our ships?'

'Every Manta reports the same thing, Admiral! We're losing contact—'

'Immediate crackdown, by God! No time to lose.'

Rossia did not know his new commander well, but he was sure that this bulldozer of a man would not back away from a fight. Eolus hammered his big-knuckled fist down on the all-ship intercom again. 'This is an emergency, and I expect everybody to act instantly. Stop the compies. Don't bother trying to deactivate – just blast them, into pieces. Many, many pieces.'

Since hand weapons were useless for fighting hydrogues, the *Eldorado* carried only enough twitchers to subdue brawling crewmen or quash an attempted mutiny. Even if sufficient weapons had been available, Rossia wouldn't have known how to fire one.

Only one compy was stationed on the Juggernaut's bridge. When it began to move erratically, Eolus yelled, 'Sergeant Briggs, use your twitcher!'

The security chief was already responding. He pulled his stun weapon and fired a scrambling blast. The compy jittered and crashed forward, its arms outstretched as if reaching for bones to break or windpipes to crush.

Rossia held onto the treeling's ornate pot, trying to shield it. The bridge crew stared at each other in skittish shock.

The comm officer looked sick, her skin pale and grey. 'Admiral, two of the Mantas don't respond! I got a garbled signal that sounded like screams and fighting, then static.'

Eolus's swarthy face turned ruddy. 'Our ships are being hijacked!' As if to prove his fears, the two silenced Mantas changed course and began to withdraw from the battle group.

The Admiral scrambled with his controls, scrolled down the numbers, then looked up in dismay that gave way to frustrated anger. 'Dammit! We just got out of drydock and refit, and they didn't even give me the right guillotine codes! Stupid upgrades – never work the way they're supposed to.' Eolus stalked around the bridge and hit the intercom again. 'Consider every Soldier compy an enemy. Get rid of them before they get rid of us. Do something interesting for your service records.' He shouted to the security chief, who was unlocking a small, sealed vault. 'Sergeant Briggs, you are responsible for protecting my bridge. No matter what, do not let compies take control of this Juggernaut.'

Briggs withdrew more twitchers, giving one to the Admiral and distributing the others to a pair of crewmen he considered competent, while he kept a projectile weapon for himself. 'Twitchers aren't necessarily the best bet against Soldier compies, sir. Those robots are hardened against attack.'

'Lucky us. Ideas?'

'Not off the top of my head, sir.'

The comm officer blurted, 'We've got a flood of transmissions, Admiral! Difficult to process everything. The compies are going renegade simultaneously, deck after deck. They're overwhelming our crew!' Each of the rebellious compies could easily take out five or six human soldiers before being brought down. There weren't enough people, or weapons, onboard to stand against this uprising if it continued to grow.

'Casualties?' Eolus said.

'Officially unknown . . . but I can tell it's a lot.'

Rossia frantically sent reports through telink so everyone else would know what was happening aboard the *Eldorado*. 'Nahton is hurrying to inform King Peter in the Whisper Palace. Maybe they will send reinforcements in time.'

'They can't do much but pray for us,' Eolus growled. 'Don't expect outside help.'

Three Soldier compies charged down the corridor towards the *Eldorado*'s bridge, leaping like mechanical hyenas. Sergeant Briggs stood his ground at the access door to the bridge, shooting his projectile weapon down the hall. The slugs slammed into the oncoming compies, leaving craters in their torso armour; momentum knocked them backward. Rossia flinched at the noise.

'Mister Briggs, are you ready to seal the bulkhead doors?' Eolus bellowed.

'As soon as I shoot just a couple more, Admiral.' Six more compies rushed in from other corridors. Briggs fired again and again, calling for reinforcements.

'Admiral, look!' The navigator pointed towards the screen as two more escort Mantas flew off to join the first stolen pair.

Eolus ground his teeth together so hard that the muscles on his jaw stood out like cables. He glared out into the corridor where Briggs and his comrades continued to fire at the oncoming compies, then loosed an avalanche of booming words. 'Damned robots aren't getting my ship!'

SEVENTEEN

KING PETER

Another pointless social ceremony. Wearing uncomfortable regal attire, King Peter attended an innocuous banquet to present service medals to local Palace District businessmen. Basil Wenceslas sat at the reception table, dapper in his perfectly cut business suit. His expression was cool, his grey eyes placid except for when Peter met his gaze. Didn't the Chairman have anything better to do with his time? *Or is he that worried about me?*

This was a far cry from rallying the human race to stand firm against the hydrogues, but at least the Chairman hadn't ordered Peter to deliver incendiary lies about the Roamers. Not today. Basil seemed to feel that if he was tough and unyielding, then everyone would bow to his instructions. But the Chairman's hardline stance against the clans had backfired, and even his staunch supporters realized that their 'victory' of destroying Rendezvous was pointless. The Roamers were scattered, and the Hansa still had no supplier of stardrive fuel.

Peter did not respond well to that sort of coercion, either.

When the puppet King reacted by blatantly breaking the rules, Basil had retaliated by attempting to assassinate him and Estarra, and later by slaughtering the dolphins as a sick punishment.

Peter pretended to cooperate, if only to keep his wife and unborn child alive. He didn't take his eyes from the Chairman, who sat with calm confidence. He truly hated the man. Peter had to stay one step ahead of him, be smarter, more careful – and that was difficult when Basil Wenceslas had the resources of the entire Hansa behind him.

Lately, while the media clamoured for comments from the Whisper Palace about Estarra's 'blessed pregnancy,' Basil kept the King and Queen out of the public spotlight as much as possible. Reporters and pundits had begun to make increasingly agitated comments, wanting to know why the royal couple weren't seen more often. Grudgingly, the Chairman brought the King out for minor activities, separate from Queen Estarra. Such as this banal ceremony, a tedious bureaucratic duty dance that interested few people except for those directly involved. Apparently, Basil was confident the King could do no damage here.

Seven royal guards were stationed along the walls, ostensibly to protect King Peter, but more likely to keep him in line. The head of the royal guard, Captain McCammon, stood like a statue, as uninterested in the presentation of awards as Peter himself was.

Deputy Eldred Cain, the quiet and pale-skinned man who had secretly helped Peter and Estarra, was not in attendance. Cain was even more averse to public appearances than Basil Wenceslas, not that he was missing anything here.

Wearing a wooden smile, the King held up a ribbon and medal for the audience to admire. 'For service to humanity and for his tireless work with local charities, I give the Hansa's Medal of Glorious Commendation to Dr Anselm Frick.' Applause pattered around the table, and the roly-poly surgeon ambled forward, mumbled his acceptance speech, and returned to his seat. Before the King began to announce the fourth and final recipient, he heard a commotion outside the room, saw the royal guards tense. The newsnet representatives turned their imagers, hoping for something interesting to happen.

A half-clad green-skinned man pushed his way through the door. 'Who dares to prevent a green priest from delivering a vital message to King Peter?' Nahton demanded. Although the court green priest brought frequent messages from Theroc to Queen Estarra, he seldom had anything urgent to report. He was usually a calm and quiet man; Peter had never seen him so agitated.

After years in the Whisper Palace, Nahton was fully aware that the King was merely for show and that Basil himself pulled all the strings. But the Chairman had never shown respect for the green priest, ignoring his repeated requests for aid to devastated Theroc. Nahton knew his real allies in the Palace.

Peter barked at the leader of his royal guards; these men were supposed to at least pretend they served him. 'Captain McCammon, that man is my official green priest. Allow him to pass if he has a message for me.' He looked down his nose, intentionally embarrassing the guard captain. 'Or are you trying to protect me from a *green priest*?'

The audience at the banquet chuckled at the absurdity. The captain adjusted the maroon beret on his bleached-white hair, then glanced in Basil's direction; the Chairman gave a slight nod.

Nahton came forward and called out in a loud voice, suddenly giving all the media representatives a headline. 'King Peter, it is a massacre! Urgent telink messages have come in from many green priests aboard EDF ships. Soldier compies are rising up throughout the battle groups, attacking the crews, and seizing the ships. They've already killed thousands.' He looked at the King as if beseeching him to do something. 'I have felt the deaths of five green priests already. It is a simultaneous revolt, on ship after ship!'

Basil lurched to his feet, but all eyes were on the green priest and the King. 'Compies killing human soldiers?' Peter cried. 'How could the compies coordinate a coup like this? The lightspeed delay alone would make communication—'

'The revolt must have been programmed or timed somehow. Your Majesty, this massacre was well planned.'

Other mysteries suddenly became clear to Peter. 'Admiral Stromo hasn't been able to find a trace of our sixty rammers – and they were all crewed by Soldier compies.' His voice was ominous.

Nahton said, 'I reported a disturbance with Soldier compies aboard Admiral Stromo's Manta yesterday. Malfunctioning compies killed two crewmembers on the bridge. I gave the message directly to Chairman Wenceslas. Were you not informed, Your Majesty?'

Peter spun to where Basil stood at the side of the room. 'I knew nothing of this! Who decided to keep this information from me?' He knew full well it had been the Chairman. Now everyone else did as well.

'The news was to be in your next briefing,' Basil said in an icy voice.

Peter glared. 'If this really is a revolt – and if you had been more diligent, Mr Chairman – perhaps we could have sent out a cautionary advisory! The first incident occurred more than a day ago! With telink we could have sent a warning in seconds.'

'I am no longer in contact with Admiral Stromo's Manta. Their green priest has been murdered,' Nahton pointed out. 'I believe most other crewmen aboard are dead as well.' He didn't even look at the Chairman. 'Now, the crews aboard all EDF ships are under attack.'

'And we could have prepared them,' Peter said.

Seizing his chance, he turned up his voice amplifier to drown out any words the Chairman might speak. He could not let Basil use this for his political purposes, nor could he let the Chairman cover it up the way he had tried to brush aside all previous concerns about the reliability of the Soldier compies. He took no satisfaction in learning that his fears had been justified all along.

Peter glared daggers at Basil as he said for all to hear, 'We missed our chance a long time ago! Everyone will recall that I expressed my suspicions about using Klikiss programming in our Soldier compies. I tried to shut down the manufacturing facilities as a precaution, but they were reopened against my better judgement.' He looked directly at the Chairman. 'That was a poor decision, based on extremely bad advice.'

Basil was already making his way towards the podium, his face a storm of emotions. Peter knew how the Chairman hated to admit errors, knew Basil would try to deal with this disaster quietly, minimize its seriousness. He wouldn't mind if more people died, just so the Hansa could save face.

But Peter had the full attention of the media cameras, and the audience was listening. A King had to do what needed to be done, and no one could openly countermand him during such an emergency.

His face turned hot as he thought of all those Soldier compies with built-in triggers that activated at the same time. Peter acted on impulse. 'If this rogue streak is intrinsic to their programming, then every recently manufactured Soldier compy is a time bomb ready to explode – and our factory is still producing them.' He addressed the royal guards in a tone of unmistakable command, 'Shut the compy factory down immediately. Alert all local defence forces to contain the Soldier compies, should they react. Bring in the silver berets. We can't take chances.'

The royal guards hesitated while Basil fought his way towards the podium amidst the turmoil. Peter didn't wait. 'Captain

McCammon! You have your orders.' The media imagers turned towards the hesitating guards.

Dr Anselm Frick stood and flashed his new service medal, as if it gave him some sort of military rank, and started shouting, 'You heard him, man! It's treason against the King, this is. Do as you're ordered!'

'What are you waiting for?' someone else yelled, appalled at the guards' hesitation. Other audience members began to demand action.

Standing firm, Peter said, 'Captain, do your duty or be relieved of it.'

Finally, his words seemed to sink in. McCammon snapped orders, and the royal guards hurried from the room, calling on their comms to organize an operation around the Palace District's huge Soldier compy factory.

Peter knew he was far overstepping his authority, but he had to show his strength. The people would admire him for it, though he shuddered to think how Basil would retaliate as soon as the crisis abated. *If* it abated.

EIGHTEEN

JESS TAMBLYN

L ike a bullet made of water and pearl, Jess's vessel shot through energy-laced storm clouds alive with wental essence. The sea was a churning froth the colour of molten lead. In this primordial planet's sterile ocean, he'd begun his long, strange quest to bring the elemental beings back to life. His volunteers had named the planet Charybdis after the deadly whirlpool encountered by Odysseus.

Here, if Jess could convince them, the wentals would repay their debt.

With a knot in his stomach, he repeated the question he'd asked Nikko a thousand times over the past several days. 'How is Cesca?'

'She's cold, clammy. Her skin looks funny, and there're dark spots of pooling blood inside. She drifts in and out of consciousness. Jess, I don't think she has much time left.'

'The wentals can still help her.' He tried to keep the anger out of his voice.

Below, on one of the rare patches of solid ground, black rocks glistened with wild spray. Jess's vessel floated above the patch of upthrust rock and released the *Aquarius*, like an insect gently depositing an egg on the surface of a leaf. The small Roamer ship rested on the barren spit of land, its regrown hull sheathed in living water. While it was suspended in the larger wental vessel, tiny aquatic creatures had furiously made repairs. With corals and metals, the wental-guided creatures had grown scablike excrescences to patch and reinforce the hull. The *Aquarius* was now an amalgam of Roamer technology and wental imagination. The much larger wental craft landed beside it.

Nikko bounded out of the hatch. A sheen of perspiration covered his forehead. Wearing his white-fibre garment, Jess stepped through his ship's hull membrane. He felt energized in the ozone-rich air, sensing the great force ready to be hurled against the hydrogues. His primary goal was to channel some of that power to save Cesca.

Jess turned to face the stormy ocean, felt wental essence writhing through the moisture-laden air. The water entities spoke to him, their voices thrumming. *Because you want this so badly, there is a great risk of creating a tainted wental. You do not understand the consequences. Not to yourself. Not to us.*

'What if I'm willing to take the risk? For her sake?' Jess wrestled with what the water elementals were saying. 'How can a wental be tainted? I distilled a single wental from the nebula and helped you grow. I thought you were all the same being, one giant dispersed entity.'

We are a single entity with many parts. And like an enormous body, some parts can become infected. Witness.

Without words, the wentals flooded him with memories and concepts, like a Plumas pumping station bursting its pipes, gushing images all at once. In his mind and his heart, he *understood* the power and danger of a tainted wental.

The memory images came from millennia ago, before the wentals had been obliterated. He saw an Ildiran commander – he did not know the rank, a septar perhaps? accidentally bathed in a wental mist on a strange alien planet. The wental had been sorely wounded in a direct clash with a blazing faeros fireball. Ildiran worlds had been annihilated in the numerous elemental battles of the ancient war. Ildiran cities were levelled, whole continents laid waste, planets cracked open and crumbled into rubble, suns extinguished. The septar knew his Mage-Imperator could not protect the Ildirans, who were sure to be wiped out.

The desperate septar, standing in the smoking ruins of what had been a spectacular city, was drenched by the falling wental. His desire to save his Empire, and the weakness of the wounded water entity, left them both open for a fusion such as Jess and the wentals had experienced. *For the best of reasons.*

The Ildiran septar swelled with a locked power, separate from the other wentals. His body could barely contain the energy, yet he could not disperse it and help it propagate. The septar somehow managed to return to his battleship, but the singing energy discharge flooded the decks, immediately killing the entire crew. Wrapped together, wental and Ildiran flew the great ship into battle. The energy was so great that the warliner itself broke apart, but the strength of the tainted wental held the conglomeration of wreckage together in a flying cloud of destruction.

A tainted wental exists only to break down order. It disrupts any solid form, increasing entropy, making the universe more fluid. A living engine of chaos.

The septar/wental attacked the marauding faeros, but it also exploded Ildiran battleships, razed cities, blasted empty asteroids, not recognizing the difference between ally and enemy. Finally, the combined might of six faeros fireballs dragged the tainted wental into a sun, where the entity was dissociated into molecules. The rest of the water entities could not even grieve.

A tainted wental is a mutation locked into physical form, the voices tried to explain. *Because of its twisted nature, a tainted wental cannot propagate, and the energy buildup can be released only in violent bursts. Trapped in a loop of itself, it is separate from the rest of the wental mind. And because of this it hates us as much as it hates any other enemy.*

'How often does it happen? Just because you had one bad experience—'

Another shower of images cut him off. This memory seemed even older. The creature was like a giant upright beetle with grey-green leathery skin, the breedex of a Klikiss hive at war with all other hives. A rival infestation had appeared on an adjacent continent, and the new Klikiss reapers had already devoured armies of drones and builders. If the breedex did not destroy the enemies, consume them and incorporate their chemical memories into its progeny before the next great Swarming, that hiveline would become extinct.

At the time, the wentals had just begun their war with the hydrogues and the faeros. The Klikiss race was a strange civilization, new to the elemental beings, and the wentals considered recruiting the insectoid creatures into the struggle. The breedex had communicated its need to them, and the wentals did not understand the consequences of acquiescence. Linked with wental power, the swelling breedex had devoured all ten of its domates without even listening to their songs, then burst its carapace and sprouted new segmented limbs without fissioning to create a new swarm. Infused with the tainted wental, it smashed the rival breedex and turned all the new Klikiss towers to dust. As the storm built inside her, unstoppable, the breedex tore the continent itself apart.

The rest of the wentals fought back, unable to believe the monstrosity they had created. The rampant release of so much power cracked the planet to its core. Though the tainted wental was finally extinguished, the battle mortally wounded the world. Gravity shifted, the landmasses were turned inside out, and all life there died.

That is a tainted wental, Jess Tamblyn. That is what could happen here.

He still didn't understand. 'Why? Just because I want it so badly? Cesca is a good person, the leader of the clans. How could she create such a horror?'

We only know the danger.

Jess had made up his mind, though. 'Enough! You distract me with esoteric and meaningless philosophy while she's dying. I accept the risk. I know her heart. Bring her out here, Nikko. Carry her if you must.'

'It'll hurt her even more, Jess—'

He had hurt her so much. 'She is already dying.'

At the young man's urging, Cesca began to stir. Nikko draped her arm over his shoulder and helped her out of the *Aquarius*. Somehow, she saw Jess, focused on the sunlight and sea, and clung to a faint thread of life. She swayed, and Nikko let her gently down onto the dark, exposed rock of Charybdis.

She must come to the water herself. You cannot help her.

Jess knelt beside her and felt his heart ripping in half. Without Cesca, how could he live? He stood at the edge of the reef between the slick stones and the crackling ocean, cursing the wentals and their ridiculous rules and restrictions. 'You're killing her!'

It must be entirely her decision, entirely her action.

'Cesca, if you love me, do one last thing for me. Drink the water and live. Let the wentals join you, and you'll be like me.' Only a few feet away, the ocean stilled itself. Wentals manifested in the waves, stretching the water in narrow fingerlike protrusions reaching up to assess Cesca. 'Or you'll die.'

'But if I . . . I'll be . . . like you?'

The wind around them seemed alive with whispering voices.

95

'Your body will be charged with wental energy, like mine.' He would not lie to her. 'That means you'll never be able to touch another human being without harming them. You'll be isolated like me. It's a terrible thing, Cesca, but I don't know how else to save you.'

She wrestled out one word of a question, then another. 'Touch . . . *you?*'

He had not wanted to coerce her with that tantalizing thought. 'We will be two of a kind, Cesca. Separate from the rest of our race.'

'But together.' Now she didn't hesitate. Jess moved aside to let Cesca crawl painstakingly forward to the edge of the surf. 'Guiding Star . . . clear.'

He tried to encourage her. Just a few seconds more. Another metre or two. He sensed that the wentals were afraid. Jess closed his eyes, remembering Cesca the way he had loved her, how they had secretly tried to be together for so long. How could she possibly become a danger? The memory-images of tainted wentals seemed foreign to him, unreal. *That will not happen to her.*

Cesca scooped a handful of the shimmering water. Quicksilver droplets trickled between her fingers. She brought the water to her face with trembling hands and drank a mouthful. With a gasp, she began to shudder.

She lurched forward, and her body plunged into the water. It was part baptism, part drowning. She vanished beneath the surface.

NINETEEN

RLINDA KETT

Beneath the icy ceiling of Plumas, Rlinda and BeBob attended the Roamer funeral of Andrew Tamblyn. The three surviving brothers, sombre and confused, worked with their comrades to prepare the ceremony. Though the reanimated ice-woman had disappeared into the sea, Rlinda did not assume for a moment that everything was returning to normal.

Maybe Karla Tamblyn was happily playing with whatever creatures she'd found down at the bottom. Rlinda had heard the water miners talk of exotic sea creatures like singing nematodes and glowing jellyfish. A pall had hung over the grotto facility over the past three days, while workers watched, holding their collective breath and waiting for something else to happen.

Because of the Roamers' damned edgy vigilance, Rlinda saw no chance for her and BeBob to escape, and skipping away during a funeral certainly seemed like bad form. Even so, Rlinda was getting awfully tired of sitting on her thumbs, and she was always cold down here. What did she expect, living on a flat shelf of ice under a kilometre-thick frozen ceiling at the edge of a frigid sea? She had plenty of blankets and heaters in the *Voracious Curiosity*, but her beloved ship was docked on the surface, and they were stuck down here . . .

Caleb, Wynn, and Torin Tamblyn had placed Andrew's body in a floating coffin of pressed cellulose, then packed dried icckclp around their brother. Caleb bent over the coffin boat and poured a thick translucent liquid onto the body and the surrounding flammable material. The biting chemical odour of fuelgel struck Rlinda's nostrils.

Wynn and Torin stood together, barely able to contain their tears. The twins exchanged nudges, each encouraging the other to speak first. Finally Caleb said in a raspy voice, 'This is the second Roamer funeral for one of my own brothers. Andrew, and before him Bram.'

'And before that we all came here to mourn Ross,' Wynn added.

'Damned hydrogues,' Torin muttered.

Now there's something we can all agree on, Rlinda thought. The Roamers had good reasons to hold a grudge against the Hansa – she couldn't argue with that – but no amount of rationalization gave them any cause to take it out on her and BeBob.

The three brothers each said a brief reminiscence before they tossed igniters into the fuelgel-soaked boat and pushed the floating coffin into the sea, where convection currents pulled it from the broken shore. The fuelgel burned efficiently, setting the icekelp and cellulose on fire, as well as Andrew's shrouded body. Flames reflected on the frozen ceiling.

Standing on the ice shelf in the cold, Rlinda and BeBob held hands; they could see the steam of their breath. BeBob was actually crying. Her heartstrings might have been tugged a little more if she and BeBob hadn't been held hostage here. Both of them felt like outsiders, witnessing a very private moment.

As the boat drifted farther away, the funereal flames grew hotter until the cellulose coffin broke apart. Caleb turned aside, looking more angry than sad. Torin barely contained his sobs. Rlinda wanted to wrap her arms around him in a big hug, but restrained herself. Sympathy was one thing, reality quite another.

The Roamers kept their gazes down, waiting for the flames to finish burning out. A long, sombre silence fell.

But the sheltered seas did not accept the new offering. The water around the remnants of the pyre began to bubble and froth like a cauldron. Hot steam curled around it like the shadow of a tornado. The boiling increased, churning and swallowing up the fragments of the burning coffin.

In the midst of the fury, something white and sharp like an elephant's tusk thrust out of the ocean. A pedestal of ice formed from the water and rose above the surface. Trickles flowed down and hardened like candlewax.

Her milky-white skin sparkling with frost, Karla Tamblyn stood atop the curved monolith, looking more animated than before, like an angry goddess emerging from the frigid ocean. In the sea around her a medusa swarm of writhing creatures appeared – hundreds of fleshy scarlet tubes that pulsed and expanded like blobby leeches filled with fresh arterial blood.

Karla raised her hands. Her dark hair thrashed in tentacles energized with static electricity. Ablaze with cold fire, she opened her mouth and spoke in a hollow voice. 'Water flows where it wishes.' Karla bent her fingers and clenched her fist. Power crackled through her skin, but her eyes were oddly blank. 'Liquid has no form.'

Dozens of the deep-sea nematodes swam forward as if they were the reanimated woman's footsoldiers. Their round mouths were studded with tiny diamond-like teeth for chewing through thick ice. Or people.

'Cannot propagate. Trapped . . . contained.' Karla turned her ivory face towards the ceiling where the artificial suns shone down. Her voice boomed. *'Water flows where it wishes.'*

She launched a shockwave. Invisible balls of lightning rippled through the air and hammered into the low ceiling. The inner surface of the jagged dome cracked, and ice-melt water began to flow down. 'Chaos and randomness is the natural state. Order is offensive.'

The force in her voice was enough to send them all reeling. A torrent of rain poured down around Karla. Large chunks of ice cracked from the ceiling and tumbled into the ocean. Waves surged around her, as if she were a typhoon incarnate. 'Water flows where it wishes.'

Karla's ice pedestal began to move towards the shore where the terrified humans stood. She brought destruction with her.

TWENTY

MAGE-IMPERATOR JORA'H

A Mage-Imperator was supposed to protect his people, but each deception made Jora'h damn his obligations more. How could even the leader of an empire stand against beings powerful enough to smother *stars*? Jora'h felt as if he had stepped on a trap door and was now falling into an endless pit. How could he resist without bringing the destruction of his entire civilization? What choice did he have? Many times he had cursed his father and all the Mage-Imperators before him.

Three days ago, the warglobes had departed, yet their threat hung in the air like the long-fading note from the end of a musical composition. He would never forget the look of hurt, disappointment, and disdain Osira'h had given him when he capitulated to the alien emissary. But now that he knew the hydrogues could ransack her thoughts and cull whatever information they wanted, he had to make her *believe* that he was a failure. In truth, he might yet fail, but he did not want the enemy to know all the things he might plan against them.

Secretly, the Mage-Imperator knew there was one last chance, if he had the freedom to make the attempt. If his people did not let him down. The emissary had warned that they would return soon to issue their abhorrent demands and force him to betray humanity. He must have another option by then.

But first, he would need to send Osira'h away, so she – and the hydrogues linked to her – could not see what he was doing.

He called his daughter to his private contemplation chambers. The girl stood straight-backed before him, exuding the same inexplicable power that had been strong enough to force the hydrogues to obey her. 'You summoned me. If you require my service, then I am ready to help.' The troubled girl seemed to hope that she'd underestimated her father.

Her eyes flicked to the prized Theron treeling that sat on a shelf, a gift from Queen Estarra of Earth. Every time Osira'h looked at it, Jora'h wondered if she felt the sort of calling that her mother did.

'And how would you help me?'

'By following your plan, Liege.' It was not a question. She herself had done the impossible, and now she expected him to do the impossible as well. 'You asked me to bring the hydrogues to Mijistra. Therefore, you must have a plan. You are the Mage-Imperator.'

'I did what I had to do, Osira'h. Without some kind of appeasement, the hydrogues would have levelled our planet and then destroyed all other Ildiran worlds.'

By pretending to agree to their demands, he had bought time to set a desperate plan in motion. But he could not tell Osira'h that, lest the hydrogues wrest the knowledge from her. *I bought time . . . but after thousands of years of breeding and experimentation and planning, have we not had enough time?*

The girl's odd expressions and strangely alien eyes told him she was not satisfied with his answer.

'I am sending you away, Osira'h. You will go back to Dobro.' He took her hands in his own, and the yearning on his face was not feigned. 'Your mother is alive. Designate Udru'h kept her on Dobro, hiding her even from me. I am sending you to her. I want you with Nira.'

The little girl's face lit up, and he wished he could tell her more, tell her everything. Questions seemed to geyser from her mind, but she drove them down, simply revelling in the surprise and joy. For the moment, she seemed to have forgotten her scorn for his cowardly response. Her happiness startled him, since she had never even known her mother.

Jora'h averted his gaze to the treeling in its alcove, thinking of his beloved green priest. He missed Nira so much, wondered why it was taking Udru'h so long to bring her. Now she would have to stay on Dobro until it was safe again. What would she think when their daughter told her of his willingness to doom the human race? He stroked the pale frond of the worldtree.

Osira'h bowed, but he could see she was smiling. 'If that is your wish, Liege.' At that moment, he wished the girl would have called him Father, but he knew that was too much to expect.

TWENTY-ONE

DESIGNATE-IN-WAITING DARO'H

To help him locate the missing green priest on the southern continent, Designate-in-waiting Daro'h conscripted forty-nine Ildirans. Udru'h urged him to hurry. They had heard no further word from the Mage-Imperator and his negotiations with the hydrogues, but they were aware that time must be short. Daro'h had never seen his uncle look so guilty or anxious.

'Find her,' Udru'h said again. 'Find her, before more damage is done.'

A group of scout ships raced south across the equator to the southern continent, the wide inland sea, and the island where the female green priest had disappeared. Satellite imagery had digested the topography of the southern continent into a detailed map, onto which a fine search grid was projected. Each ship flew low along a separate path, diligently scanning.

Daro'h had never received an entirely satisfactory explanation as to why his uncle had exiled Nira so far away in the first place, or why he had initially told the Mage-Imperator that she was dead. Daro'h himself had seen Nira's grave marker on the hillside, had watched his father grieve before it. All a deception!

Udru'h held his secrets in tightly clenched fists, and Daro'h feared he would have to do the same when he took over the reins as this planet's Designate.

All of the Mage-Imperator's noble sons were born to become Designates, assigned to planets according to their birth order. Thousands of years of history had established a clear pattern for how their lives would play out. The first-born noble son always became the next Prime Designate as soon as the old Mage-Imperator died; the second became the Designate for Dobro, the third for Hyrillka, and so on. Daro'h had often wondered why the Mage-Imperator's second son would be assigned to such a seemingly unimportant place as Dobro. That was before he learned of the breeding programme and its vital importance to the survival of the Empire. So many secrets!

Now he looked through the scratched side window of the fast flyer. Below, the brown dryness abruptly ended in the sinuous shoreline of a blue inland sea. Daro'h intended to have his searchers take separate spirals, circling outwards from the island to scour the uninhabited landscape for any sign of her. Designate Udru'h had made the odd suggestion that the green priest might want to avoid being found. Daro'h could not understand why. Surely she would prefer to be with her Ildiran caretakers than to remain alone – *alone!*

His fellow team members used comm systems to keep in touch as they circled over the expanse of calm water. If Nira had tried to swim from her island, she would certainly have drowned. No one could cover such a distance. If that were the case, Daro'h's search was doomed from the beginning.

He recalled that his father had been extremely fond of the female green priest, who had come to Mijistra to read *The Saga of Seven Suns* to her potted treelings. He remembered seeing Jora'h and Nira often in the Prism Palace. But then she had vanished, apparently killed in a fire.

Now Daro'h knew it had been part of a much more complicated plot. Nira had been brought here already pregnant with the Prime Designate's child. Had that been Jora'h's wish, or had it all been done without his knowledge? Could Udru'h have hidden such a momentous thing from the Mage-Imperator?

The Dobro Designate had explained the need for the breeding programme, and Daro'h understood that the Terran Hanseatic League must never learn what had happened to their generation ship the *Burton*. But why would the secret have been kept from the *Mage-Imperator* himself? Daro'h could imagine no justification for such an act, and it disturbed him greatly.

The fourteen scout ships followed their grid lines, and the searchers meticulously criss-crossed the dry, empty landscape. Daro'h spoke aloud to the pilot and the guard. 'The green priest could have left the island months ago. She might have covered a lot of ground.'

'Then we will cover a lot of ground,' the pilot said.

After several hours, Daro'h received a message from one of his scouts. 'Designate-in-waiting, we have found some interesting debris on the shore. It might be significant.'

Their ship reached the edge of the inland sea and settled next to where the other scout had landed. Four Ildiran searchers stood looking at a tumble of logs high up on the beach. In the bright sunlight Daro'h saw the remnants of dried vines that lashed the logs together. Each one of the trunks had been cut to approximately the same length. *A raft!*

'She could have floated on this to land.' Daro'h glanced back at the water, saw how far up the remnants of the raft rested on the shore. 'She must have dragged it up onto the beach herself.'

'Why would she do that?' asked one of the searchers. 'Her island was lush, and this . . . this is desolate.'

Daro'h stared at the rugged panorama that extended as far as he could see. 'Who can understand a green priest? But we now know she made it this far. Continue the search.'

TWENTY-TWO

PATRICK FITZPATRICK III

With the Hansa at war and the Spiral Arm in crisis, with countless human colonies abandoned and defenceless, former Chairman Maureen Fitzpatrick saw nothing wrong with holding an afternoon party. She was delighted to have her grandson home from his captivity and had invited anyone she considered important. Maureen also sternly lectured Patrick to break out of his malaise and pretend to be happy.

He reminded himself, repeatedly, that he had endured far worse.

When he'd revealed his part in destroying the Roamer ekti ship, she had looked decidedly uncomfortable – not because of what he'd done, but because of the fact that he felt guilty about it. 'Nothing to worry about, Patrick. You were only following orders. The Hansa has far more vital concerns these days.'

'More vital concerns? It's why the Roamers stopped delivering ekti. It's what put us in this untenable situation and made it far more difficult for us to fight the real war.'

'Oh, Patrick,' she had said in an amazingly condescending

voice. 'Leave the tangled politics and subtle trade consequences to the experts. I've been Chairman myself, and I know that things aren't as clearcut as they seem to an idealistic young man.'

'I used to be idealistic, Grandmother. I used to know all the answers, but I'm much older and wiser than that now.'

Though her hired experts and caterers could run a diplomatic party on autopilot, Maureen kept her hands in all the details. Music was playing; guests had begun to arrive. The day was bright and sunny. At his grandmother's insistence, Patrick wore his dress black uniform with crimson flashings and gold shoulder braids, though his resignation papers had already been filed. 'No need to make a point of that now, Patrick. General Lanyan himself is coming. He always had a soft spot for you.'

Patrick walked along carrying a plate of untouched shrimp and exotic fruits, smiling at people he didn't know, accepting their parroted good wishes. When one pot-bellied businessman with a blond moustache and dark hair deprecated the 'filthy Roacher clans', Patrick coolly cut him off. 'Those people saved our lives, sir. The EDF didn't even try to rescue survivors at Osquivel, but the Roamers took us in and nursed us back to health.'

'They held you prisoner,' the man spluttered.

'Better than holding a funeral. They will always have my gratitude.'

Seeing Kiro Yamane beside a gorgeously dressed Shelia Andez, Patrick excused himself to talk to his fellow former POWs. 'Great food,' Shelia said. 'Did you eat like this all the time when you were a kid?'

He looked at his hors d'oeuvres. 'No. Sometimes they served a full meal.'

'And you gave it all up for EDF rations.' She snorted. 'I always thought you were the dim one, Fitzpatrick.'

'And you've been quite popular on the newsnets. I had to get a tissue and dry my tears after hearing of your "great suffering" under the Roamers. Were they torturing you when the rest of us weren't looking? Have you checked on what the EDF has done to *their* facilities? To Rendezvous? Seems to me they treated us pretty well, considering.'

'You're sounding like some sort of bleeding-heart moron.' She smirked. 'You just had the hots for that Roamer brunette.'

Ignoring the comment, he turned to the distinguished compy specialist. 'Kiro, you must have a lot to report after what went wrong with the Soldier compies in the Roamer shipyards.'

'Yes, that little diversion became much more spectacular than I planned. If the EDF and your grandmother hadn't arrived when they did, the whole shipyard facility would have been destroyed.'

'It *was* destroyed, Kiro. We happened to get out alive, but we don't even know the death toll among the Roamers. Doesn't it bother you that you set off something that caused so much damage?'

'We had to get away, Fitzpatrick,' Shelia broke in, her forehead furrowing. 'They didn't give us any other choice. Look what happened to Bill Stanna. They killed him!'

'Bill wasn't exactly the brightest star in the cluster. Roamers didn't kill him. He died because he didn't make a few simple plans.' She made a disgusted noise, but he continued, 'Somebody's got to speak up and balance your sensational stories, Shelia.' He smiled at her surprised expression. 'I've decided to start giving prominent public speeches to describe my true experiences among the Roamers. Much of the continuing conflict is being caused by intentional misrepresentations of the facts.' He looked at Yamane. 'Kiro, I'd like to have you give your perspective, too. I can book you along with me.'

Yamane looked away. 'I'm sorry, Patrick. I've been asked to

document what I learned about the Soldier compies so it can be used to improve them. That has to take priority.'

Shelia started laughing. 'And if you want me to sing the praises of your Roamer girlfriend, you've got to be out of your mind!'

He felt his face burning, though he'd known this wouldn't be simple. 'I'll do it myself, then. My parents are both ambassadors, my grandmother's a former Chairman—'

Maureen was abruptly there. 'Don't count on any of that to give you a soapbox for painting pretty pictures of the Hansa's enemies. Come Patrick, we have to mingle.' The old Battleaxe deftly broke him away from his companions, then whispered harshly in his ear, 'You clearly need some intensive counselling. You're maladjusted and oppositional.'

'I'm thinking for myself, Grandmother. Is that such a bad thing?'

'Yes – when you don't think correctly. Have you ever heard of Stockholm Syndrome? You're exhibiting classic signs. You were held prisoner by the Roamers, and now look at your sympathy for them! It's unnatural. I'm afraid we'll have to keep you quiet here until you recover.' She patted him on the shoulder. 'I'll spare no expense to get my old Patrick back again.'

She marched him up to General Lanyan. The man had gained weight and it showed – especially around his eyes – but he still exuded power and command. 'General Lanyan, my grandson has been so looking forward to seeing you!'

Patrick did not contradict her. It wasn't worth the effort. At one time, he had taken great pride in serving as adjutant to the commander of the Earth Defence Forces, and it had never occurred to him to be offended by anything the General asked him to do.

Lanyan grasped Patrick's hand and shook it vigorously. 'Commander Fitzpatrick, I miss the days when you were my adjutant.

I shouldn't be saying this, but I regret giving you command of your own Manta. If you hadn't been lost at Osquivel, I'd still have you serving me in your former capacity. In fact, young man, as soon as you're pronounced fit for duty, you'll be back at my side helping me out with all those difficult bureaucratic things.'

'I'm sorry, General, but I've already submitted my resignation from the EDF. I will be occupying my time and energy with other matters.'

Lanyan was taken aback. 'You've only been home four days – hardly enough time to rest and recover, much less make a decision of such long-term consequences. Think about it some more, and we'll talk when you're ready.'

Knowing he might not get another chance like this, Patrick blurted, 'Sir, do you recall a Roamer cargo ship that we intercepted while on patrol?'

The General's face maintained a perfectly flat expression. 'No, Mr Fitzpatrick. I'm afraid I don't remember that at all.'

'Really? We seized the ship in open space, boarded her, and took the ekti cargo. The captain's name was Raven Kamarov, from a prominent Roamer clan.' He narrowed his eyes. 'You gave me orders to destroy the vessel.'

A curtain of ice seemed to drop across Lanyan's face. 'No, Mr Fitzpatrick. I have no recollection of that whatsoever. *And neither do you.*'

Patrick felt his anger building. He wanted to raise his voice, put the General on the spot in front of these people, but before he could say anything an officer burst into the room. 'General Lanyan, you are needed immediately!'

With barely a blink of his eyes, Lanyan became suddenly alert and focused. 'What is it?'

The man quickly approached and lowered his voice, though not enough. 'It's the Soldier compies, sir. They seem to be causing some trouble.' He glanced around the room and recognized Yamane among the guests. 'Dr Yamane! We will need your expertise, as well. We have transport prepared. Will you both please come with me?'

As the other attendees began to mutter, a smiling Maureen Fitzpatrick raised her hands and glossed over the interruption. 'Duty calls! That's what happens when you're in command of the Earth Defence Forces. Nothing to be concerned about.'

The General skewered Patrick with one last glare, then hurried after the officer, dragging Yamane with him.

TWENTY-THREE

ENGINEERING SPECIALIST SWENDSEN

P ulling up in front of the cordoned-off hydrogue derelict, a squad of crack commandos boiled out of a military transport, every one of them bristling with weapons. The lead silver beret bellowed for Swendsen.

The tall Swede ducked his head and came out, blinking in the sunlight. 'Yes?' He held out his hand to the foremost commando as if he were meeting a friend at a cocktail party. 'Can I help you?'

The private was square-jawed and clean-shaven; his skin glistened with either lotions or sweat. His nametag read, ELMAN, K. 'Sir, you're ordered to come with us to the compy production facility. You have work to do.'

Swendsen's brow furrowed. 'I'm very sorry, but I have research here.'

'Dr Swendsen, you have the authorization codes and vital information we need for our mission. This is an emergency, sir.'

There had been no trouble at the factory for months, not even any unscheduled maintenance. 'What's going on?'

The silver berets hustled Swendsen toward the military

transport. 'Soldier compies have gone crazy across the EDF. King Peter has ordered the factory shut down before anything goes wrong there.' The engineering specialist was still thinking of questions as the transport's door slammed.

The immense manufacturing facility was the largest centre of its kind, designed for assembling everyday compies such as the Friendly, Listener, Analytical, and Governess models. Since the hydrogue war, most lines had been retooled to produce sophisticated Soldier compies. Preoccupied with the derelict, Swendsen hadn't even visited the facility in days, but the auto-mated lines hummed along with perfect efficiency. He was quite proud of that.

'Oh, perhaps some small flaw crept into the basc programming modules. I'll take a few representative specimens and deconstruct what went wrong.' He smiled at the hard-eyed silver berets, but received no response. 'I have good people I can put to work on it. I'll reassign them from the derelict.'

Just this morning his team had uncovered key clues about how the hydrogue engines worked, but he would have to take care of this mess at the factory before he could get back to the interest-ing work. King Peter had always been a little paranoid about Soldier-model compies.

When the fast transport skidded to an abrupt landing, four bat-wing hatches swung upwards, two on each side of the vehicle. Alert commandos burst out with dizzying speed; Swendsen joined them with much less grace. Three other transports clustered in a delivery zone outside the manufacturing centre. A large tent dome had been erected as a command post.

The escort hustled Swendsen into the tent dome to a table where the operation commander, a sergeant whose engraved nametag gave his last name as Paxton pored over factory blueprints projected on a flat filmscreen. He looked up at the engineering specialist, unimpressed. 'You must be the civilian responsible for this facility. We need your assistance.'

'Of course, Mr Sergeant, I mean, Sergeant Paxton. That's why I'm here.'

Paxton pointed to the diagram, where crosshatches marked off half the building. 'We have no recon in these areas. Can't get a response from any workers inside.' He scrolled down with his finger, found the numbers he was looking for. 'According to records, a hundred and twenty-eight humans are stationed inside.'

'Hmm, that sounds about right. We wanted someone there to monitor the lines and issue daily reports. There's still some prejudice against complete automation.' Swendsen smiled and shrugged.

'The King ordered us to neutralize these Soldier compies. You've heard what they've done aboard our EDF ships?'

The engineer forced a nervous laugh. 'Yes, about that. There must be some mistake. I'm sure the reports were exaggerated.'

'According to our intel, Dr Swendsen, a rebellion flared up simultaneously on all ten grids. Soldier compies have already taken over numerous capital ships. Entire crews were killed, tens of thousands of good EDF soldiers.' Paxton looked at Swendsen, his eyes locking on the engineer. 'My team and I intend to get inside that facility and shut down all operations before the same thing happens here.'

'Of course, of course. This really is very troubling. I can grant you the authority to—'

Paxton gave him a withering look. 'King Peter issued our orders. We don't need authority from you – just your assistance.'

'Well . . . you can have that, too.'

Paxton indicated sections of the blueprint. 'These wings here and here are component warehouses. Interior surveillance cameras show only shelves of parts waiting for assembly. No activity.'

'Correct. We subcontract some of the work. Components are fabricated in satellite facilities and brought here for final assembly.'

The sergeant drew his finger down the diagram; two more silver berets bent closer to see, adjusting an overhead light to drown out their shadows. 'These areas here seem to be the most secure.'

'Cold clean-room chambers for module imprinting,' Swendsen said.

'We already signalled for evacuation, and all the workers from that zone successfully escaped.' The sergeant shook his head. 'But we've heard nothing from the rest of the people still in the centre. They're either being held as hostages – or, more likely – they've been killed.'

'Soldier compies don't kill humans,' Swendsen said.

'And the Earth is flat,' Private Elman grumbled from behind him.

Paxton dragged their attention back to the diagram. 'Near the end is the programming complex, with central upload banks for "finishing" the compies.'

Swendsen added, 'The Klikiss modules are already implanted, but the programming centre gives them an overlay of functional systems, interactive programming beyond the embedded instruction sets.' He gave a nervous little laugh. 'We like to say that's where they get their marching orders.'

Several facility alarms began to sound. Paxton looked through an opening in the tent dome. Four more troop transports and armoured equipment carriers settled down in the now-vacant landing fields and shipping lots. 'Dr Swendsen, tell us what we're up against.'

'The automated lines are very efficient.' Swendsen scratched his upper lip. 'They can produce four hundred compies a day, ready to be deployed aboard EDF ships.'

Paxton frowned. 'That's what I was afraid of. How many completed compies were in the storage bay at last count?'

'I'm not actually in charge of inventory. Deactivated compies stand in ranks until we transport them away. Quite a lot of them can fit—'

'How *many*?' Paxton repeated.

'Several thousand, I think. Depends on when the last shipment went out. I've been busy over at the hydrogue derelict, you know.'

Paxton addressed his team. 'Let's get in there before their Trojan Horse programming switches on like it did aboard the EDF ships.'

Elman snorted. 'Sounds like we may already be too late.'

The silver berets double-timed out of the tent, bustling Swendsen along with them. Paxton kept up the conversation, not even short of breath, 'Just to be clear, Dr Swendsen – once we get inside, you *can* use your managerial overrides to shut down the systems, correct?'

'Sure. It'll be tedious to manually deactivate any functional compies individually, but the ones in the waiting area should just be standing there. Nothing to worry about.'

'Right. Nothing to worry about. Let's get inside.'

The thirty commandos carried electronic pulse projectors and heavy-calibre launchers whose sharp bullets had a lubricant sheath that could penetrate even the armoured exoskeletons of Soldier compies.

'Is all this really necessary?' Swendsen said. 'They're just compies. I'm sure it's only a glitch.'

'A pretty deadly glitch,' a commando muttered, not breaking her stride.

Paxton gave him a scowl. 'Yes, sir. It's absolutely necessary.'

The tall metal doors were sealed. Swendsen stood in front of the locks, baffled. 'Access to these bays isn't supposed to be blocked. Odd. Someone's barricaded them from the inside.'

Elman said, 'Maybe the clankers are having a private party in there.'

Sealed doors did not hinder the commandos. A demolitions crew ran forward, planted foam explosives around the jamb, then blew the entry barrier. Even as the segmented metal gate tumbled inwards, the silver berets were already running, weapons extended. They charged into the factory, shining lights and pointing launchers while several of them protectively surrounded Swendsen.

The last time he'd been inside the facility, Swendsen had remarked how brightly lit even the cavernous open bays appeared. Many of the lights had now faltered, leaving the bays in shadow.

The strangest revelation, though, was that the huge warehouse where all the completed compies stood ready for deployment – was empty. Swendsen couldn't understand it. 'But . . . there should be thousands of deactivated compies just waiting here.'

'I guess they're not deactivated anymore,' Private Elman said.

'Defensive positions, everyone!' the sergeant barked. 'They could be lying in ambush.'

The commandos moved through the empty warehouse towards the assembly lines. Up ahead, the construction din of hisses, clangs, and ratcheting belts merged in a furious symphony of hammering metal, fusing parts, and interlocking components.

'Sounds like it's still cranking out compies,' Paxton said. 'Mr Swendsen, do your stuff.'

'That's *Dr* Swendsen. I'm—'

'I don't care if you're a grandmother – *move!*'

Near the head of the assembly line, spotlights shone upon three mangled human bodies dangling by chains high above the assembly belts to keep them out of the way. 'There's a few of your workers,' Paxton said in a flat voice. 'Still think this is a minor glitch?'

Swendsen stared aghast, watching blood drip down from torn skin. 'I . . . I'm on my way.'

As the team ran past the assembly lines, Soldier compies emerged like army ants from production stations, storage areas, offices, and monitoring enclosures.

'Oh, goody – we found the missing clankers,' Elman groaned. 'We're not going to start pushing deactivation buttons one by one, are we, Sergeant?'

'Not a chance. Open fire.'

As the compies came forward, silver berets fired small artillery shells and electronic scramblers. The approaching compies toppled as jacketed projectiles struck their body cores. Some circuit-scrambled compies pitched forward into one of the production lines, jamming the gears and rolling belts.

'Swendsen! Tell me where you need to go!' Private Elman shouted. 'Me and my weapons will escort you.'

Flinching from all the noise, the engineer snapped his attention back to the mission. He pointed a trembling finger. 'That control tower. From there, I can deactivate the whole assembly facility . . . I think.'

Half-completed Soldier compies rolled down the lines, torsos with heads attached and skeletal arms, not yet covered with armour polymer skin. As the humans continued shooting at the converging compies, the incomplete machines lurched up, optical sensors glowing. The legless compies reached out for the silver berets. Metallic arms grabbed four soldiers by the throats. Other silver berets opened fire, knocking the half-assembled horrors away. More enemy machines dropped from the assembly line, dodging the gunfire and crawling across the floor like bizarre paraplegic crabs.

Five compies emerged from under a low support bridge and snatched a female silver beret by the legs. She turned her weapon towards the floor and kept shooting, but the compies swarmed over her like insects. She went down.

In a daze, Swendsen was barely able to keep moving as Elman pushed him towards the control tower, but now the engineer was having second thoughts. Even if he shut down the actual machinery, he couldn't do anything about the Soldier compies that were already activated.

Paxton yelled into his collar microphone, transmitting outside. 'We need reinforcements! Blockade the doors with heavy armoured machinery so the damned clankers don't get out.'

'Then how are *we* going to get out?' Swendsen asked.

'We're not even all the way *in* yet.' Elman shot two Soldier compies rising up in front of them.

A hundred more military robots emerged from other sections of the facility. The new compies surrounded the control tower in an impenetrable barricade, standing there as if daring the humans to come closer.

'This is like one of those old shambling zombie vidloops,' Elman cried, 'only with robots.'

Looking at the sea of angry robots, Swendsen paused. 'We'll never get through that. There's only thirty of us.'

'Only twenty left by now. But who's counting?'

Compies closed in from the sides and the rear, while the silver berets fired and fired. One man drained his energy-pulse charge, tossed the weapon aside, and pulled out a smaller projectile gun. 'Running low on ammunition, Sergeant!'

'Same here!'

Paxton made a snap assessment. 'We're not going to make it through. Not this time. Better fall back and try again with bigger guns and more personnel.'

Swendsen had never heard such good news.

A flurry of communications ricocheted around as orders were passed. 'Pull together, let's get out of here! We need a unified front.' The silver berets retreated, still shooting.

One commando bled profusely from a torn thigh muscle. Two of his comrades carried him, running ahead while others covered their retreat. As the silver berets reached the front of the factory, Paxton removed a grenade from his belt and tossed it towards the end of the production line. The explosion ripped the assembly machinery into tangled debris. Swendsen knew it wasn't nearly enough damage to cause more than a temporary delay. The compies could rapidly fix the machinery.

'I wouldn't have believed it if I hadn't seen it for myself,' he said, but the commandos weren't interested in conversation. The first silver berets rushed toward the door with their wounded comrade. Swendsen ran as fast as his shaking legs could take him. Before reaching the relative safety outside, he looked back over his shoulder.

In spite of the grenade explosion and weapons fire, the assembly facilities were still thrumming and rattling with a speed and efficiency that far surpassed Swendsen's wildest design estimates. At this amazing capacity, the production lines continued to make more Soldier compies. He didn't see how it could ever be stopped.

TWENTY-FOUR

KING PETER

After Nahton delivered his news to the King, further reports of the compy revolt came swiftly. The EDF scrambled – too late – to avert a total disaster. Royal guards had hustled Peter out of the interrupted awards ceremony and back to the Whisper Palace to 'safety'. Basil had shot him a cold look that clearly said, *I'll deal with you later*.

On strict orders from the Chairman, the guards now watched the King so closely he had little room to move. Peter had overstepped his boundaries, and he would certainly be punished for it. But how could Basil argue with what he had done? Soon after the King's emergency announcement, trouble had begun at the Soldier compy factory – exactly as he'd feared – proving that Peter was absolutely right to send in troops without delay. The Chairman would never commend him for quick thinking, however. Being 'correct' was not a sufficient reason to go against Basil Wenceslas.

If only he had listened earlier, if he had looked at the suspicious evidence against the Soldier compies, rather than dismissing the concerns *simply because* they came from Peter, the military could have been prepared for this.

Flanked by a new set of uniformed royal guards, the King held his head high, knowing he'd done the right thing. Others could see it, too. Would that be enough of a shield to save him, and Estarra, and their unborn baby? He hoped at least he'd set the proper wheels in motion. Maybe it would save a life or two.

Inside the Palace, the guards ushered him to the royal wing's conservatory, where Queen Estarra met with her older sister Sarein and the Teacher compy OX. Shielded from the crisis, entirely unaware of the news, they examined transplanted botanical specimens. Peter envied them their innocence, now that everything was about to change. He couldn't blame the guards for hovering closer than usual.

Estarra's face lit up when she saw him, and for the briefest instant all of Peter's cares washed away. Her face glowing with pleasure, she pointed at a display of veined leaves and unusual decorative frills around fan-shaped flowers. 'See the new specimens Sarein brought back from Theroc? I remember these from when I was a girl exploring the worldforest.'

Sarein's lips curved in a faint smile. The woman's pointed chin and high cheekbones sometimes gave her an innocent elfin appearance, but Peter knew that she was also Basil's occasional lover; therefore, he didn't trust her. 'Because Theroc came so close to being destroyed, our people asked me to bring samples of our most dramatic species here to Earth. We're also using Hansa ships to distribute green priests and treelings to as many colonies as possible, as an emergency preservation measure.'

Shortly after it had happened, Nahton had told the King about the second hydrogue attack and how the deep-core aliens were driven away from Theroc by a fantastic-sounding 'living comet' as well as a flurry of highly effective weapons brought by Roamers.

Chairman Wenceslas had snorted in disbelief at this account and — irrationally, Peter thought — brushed it aside.

On one of the new plants, a cluster of orange berries peeked out from achingly green leaves. Peter lifted the leaves to touch the tiny hard berries, but Estarra pulled his hand away. 'Fauldur berries are extremely poisonous. The first Theron settlers learned quickly not to touch them.'

'Why bring such a deadly plant here?' He looked suspiciously at Sarein. Weren't there enough dangers in the Whisper Palace already?

'The fauldur has many uses,' Sarein said coolly. 'The leaves are the only known cure for a degenerative blood disease, and the roots are considered one of our greatest delicacies. I thought it was important to preserve this plant.'

Peter straightened. 'So it's both useful and deadly at the same time.' He glanced at OX, his affection for his teacher mingling with the dread he felt at what was happening to other compies at this very moment. 'Like compies can be.' Next to the Queen, OX also studied the items on display. The silent guards regarded the little Teacher compy warily.

He finally embraced Estarra, ignoring the guards, ignoring Sarein. When he clung a bit too tightly, the Queen could tell something was wrong. 'What is it?'

He quickly explained. Sarein looked as alarmed as her sister; she shot a glance at the guards, as if wondering why the Chairman hadn't summoned her immediately.

The lead royal guard took a stiff step forward, positioning himself between the King and the little compy. 'Sire, we are charged with your protection. The situation is uncertain and dangerous. Therefore, we should separate you from this potential threat.'

'From OX?' Estarra said in surprise. 'He's served humanity since the time of the first generation ships!'

'Nevertheless, it's time we exercised a little more caution. As the King himself suggested.'

Peter looked at the helpful compy, one of the few he considered an ally and friend in the whole Whisper Palace. Could there be destructive programming implanted there, too? From centuries ago? *Not possible.*

He rested his hand reassuringly on the Teacher compy's solid shoulder. 'Captain, OX was the first to draw my attention to possible flaws in the Soldier compies and to question the Klikiss modules.'

When the compy faced Peter, his voice was calm and modulated, like a patient teacher's. 'Early designs such as mine have proved reliable for centuries. Three hundred and thirty-six years ago, I served aboard the *Peary*. I taught many families, many generations. Would you like to hear stories of how I returned to Earth with Adar Bali'nh to speak for the Ildirans and the generation ship colonists? I was also present in the throne hall when Old King Ben received the first green priest, and I was there when he granted Theroc its independence. My extensive memories of events fill my mental storage to capacity. I am incapable of harbouring hostility toward humans.'

Peter was grave, seeing the guard's continued scepticism. 'To my knowledge, Captain, only Soldier models have been affected. I believe the new Klikiss programming modules are the root of this string of malfunctions. My concerns in that respect have been a matter of public record for more than a year, as you well know.' He narrowed his eyes. 'Now, if you would grant me privacy with my wife and her sister? We'll be safe enough at the moment – unless we have something to worry about from these Theron plant exhibits?'

Grudgingly, the guards backed out of immediate earshot, but

remained within visual range. Peter's knees were shaking with relief and the long-delayed aftereffects of shock.

OX said, 'Recalling my centuries of service and my years with you, King Peter, I reassert my loyalty. You are the Great King of the Terran Hanseatic League. I am programmed to be your faithful servant. You need not fear any threat from me, and I will do my best to warn you of any dangers I foresee.'

Peter's heart warmed at the compy's simple yet utterly believable declaration. OX reminded him of a miniature knight swearing fealty to his liege. 'I trust you, OX. It's good to have at least one less worry in the Whisper Palace.' Impatient, he turned, raising his voice towards the royal guards. 'Do we have an update from the compy factory yet? Have the silver berets secured the facility?'

'We have no further information,' the guard said. 'Captain McCammon is meeting with the Chairman right now.' Then he added with a glimmer of genuine respect, 'I think we caught it in time, Majesty. Your reaction and decisiveness may have saved us all.'

TWENTY-FIVE

GENERAL KURT LANYAN

Unlike 'Stay-at-Home' Stromo, General Lanyan preferred to be *doing* something. He was a real soldier, not a stuffed-shirt military commander or, worse, a politician. And a genuine crisis wasn't meant to be viewed from a distance. He needed to be in the thick of things.

Rushing from the ill-advised 'party' thrown by Maureen Fitzpatrick, Lanyan seized his chance. Time to cause some damage, not just fill out stupid paperwork and wear ceremonial uniforms.

As soon as he reached the nearest satellite EDF office, he demanded a classified update. As he paced the pastel-painted chambers of a minor military functionary whose office he had commandeered, Lanyan listened as message after message came in from green priests. The violent uprising was occurring in all ten battle groups.

Contact had been completely lost with Admiral Stromo's Manta and four other grid flagships. Admirals Eolus, Wu-Lin, and Willis were engaged in furious firefights. At the main fabrication facility near the Palace District, Soldier compies were rising up, barely held off by a massive concentration of silver berets. Scattered reports described widespread Earth-side incidents as individual robots went berserk.

Lanyan scanned the reports again, disbelieving, but the breakdowns and summaries didn't change. 'Gone to hell in a handbasket – in the official EDF-issue hell-carrying handbasket.'

Time to stop this nonsense. He thought about immediately reassigning Patrick Fitzpatrick, even if the kid did have a stick up his butt since spending time with the Roamers. Lanyan needed all the decent men he could stuff into positions of responsibility – but he didn't have the time right now.

'Call the fastest in-system ship here. Pronto. I've got to get to the Mars base, and by the time I arrive I'll probably want to head somewhere else.'

The functionary was flustered. 'The nearest landing field is fifty kilometres east of here, General.'

'Bullshit! Who needs a landing field? You've got a roof, don't you?'

The bulk of the Grid 0 fleet remained at the resupply and maintenance yards in the asteroid belt between Mars and Jupiter. The battle group was just sitting there, vulnerable, plums ripe for the picking – Mantas, Thunderhead weapons platforms, and the Juggernaut *Goliath*. And, thanks to the shortage of personnel, those ships were full of Soldier compies as surrogate crewmembers. *Goddamned ticking timebombs!*

Lanyan was afraid that even a lightspeed transmission wouldn't get there in time. He sent an urgent warning for all commanders in spacedock to isolate the compies and await additional instructions.

Too late.

He had nearly reached the Mars base by the time the signal made its round trip from the asteroid belt. 'General, the compies have already damaged one ship and killed eight maintenance workers in the resupply yard!' The speaker was one of the managers of the maintenance facility. 'Then they started seizing control of the Grid 0 vessels. It was all so . . . so damned *coordinated*!'

If he'd been a desk-bound commanding officer, Lanyan might have waited for clarification, considered further reports, and requested additional information. (Stromo certainly would have.) In times like these, hesitation was tantamount to suicide. 'Try to hold them off. I'm on my way,' he said.

Stuck on a training base, with all the decent battleships deployed elsewhere, Lanyan had to use whatever soldiers he could scrounge at a moment's notice. In other words, kleebs – greenhorn trainees. He didn't have a choice.

The recruits at the Mars base thought it was just another drill when they were ordered to race to all vessels in the training pool. Barely stepping off his fast transport from Earth, not yet acclimated to the new gravity, Lanyan shouted as the kleebs scrambled aboard swift personnel carriers, armoured cargo transports, and fully loaded in-system gunships.

Lanyan kept studying his chronometer, counting down the amount of time that had passed since he'd received the alarm. He knew how fast those military robots could move. 'This is real, dammit! A lot of people have already been caught with their pants down. *You're* going to do damage control. You're the bloody cavalry.'

Lanyan bounded onto the lead transport, chasing the last few soldiers up the ramp – much to the discomfiture of the young pilot. All the ships swiftly launched into the thin greenish sky and out into the emptiness between planets.

The General scratched the rough stubble on his chin and looked over at the still-intimidated pilot. 'Let me address our soldiers, Mr Carrera.'

When the trainee pilot activated the troop transport's ship-to-ship comm, the speakers filled with overlapping accusations, warnings, and anxious questions across a range of supposedly restricted frequencies. Lanyan took the microphone and stopped all conversations dead. 'Cut the chatter! This is no time for you kleebs to be screwing around.' He waited for an appropriately respectful silence. 'I don't care how green you are, I expect you all to behave like EDF soldiers. That's not a reminder – that's an order.'

With in-system engines pushed beyond the official tolerance specs, the hastily assembled rescue fleet reached the asteroid-belt shipyards in less than three hours. *Three hours.* Lanyan could easily imagine how much damage a horde of berserk compies might cause in that amount of time.

Ahead, spangled with artificial lights, reflections from solar collectors, and thermal venting from smelter operations, he could make out the spacedock frameworks and the reinforced skeletons of new ships under construction. But he saw no sign of the main Grid 0 battle group. They should have been there – over a hundred ships, including a Juggernaut! All gone.

Lanyan switched the channel, pinging the shipyard hub. 'Somebody over there give me an update so we know who needs rescuing. Where the hell is my battle group?'

The pilot scanned ahead and got up the courage to say, 'Those ships must have taken off in a hurry, sir! Look at the glowing wreckage they left behind.'

After a burst of frantic and confused reports, Lanyan focused on one man who seemed cooler-headed than the rest. He told the other voices to shut up. The man on the comm turned out to be only a spacedock supervisor, but he had a good overview of what had happened in the battle group.

'First sign of trouble was when we received scattered reports of fighting aboard the *Goliath*, the Mantas, and the Thunderheads. Their Soldier compies went nuts over there, sir – on all the ships, all at the same time. They started slaughtering bridge crews.'

A gruff female voice broke in. 'Our worker compies seem to be fine, but I've isolated them as a precaution.'

'Good work. But where are all my ships?'

'About an hour ago, the docked battle group went into radio silence, then the *Goliath* turned and opened fire on our smelters. Destroyed two of them, wrecked one of my spacedocks. Then the ships just took off – ripped themselves free of moorings and headed out to space.'

Lanyan growled in his throat. 'Well, where the hell did they go?'

'We tracked them on a vertical vector away from the ecliptic. General . . . I don't think there's anybody left alive on board.'

'Are you saying that Soldier compies have control of all my battleships?'

'It appears that way, sir.'

Worse than he'd imagined, but to solve a problem you had to look forward, not back. He turned to look at the barely trained men and women crowded aboard this fast personnel transport – his saviours-in-training – then did a rapid tally of the cavalry ships he had rounded up. On a moment's notice he had pulled together more than seventy craft and five thousand soldiers. Not bad. He had a good feel for their general abilities (book learning and simulations) and real experience (practically nil). On Mars the recruits had been drilled in ground combat manoeuvres; they had formed functional teams, learned how to cooperate to solve problems. Now for some practical experience.

'Those ships are renegade. We need those ships. We, therefore, are going after them.' Lanyan repeated the transmission across the cavalry fleet. 'They haven't been gone long. Our ships are lighter, we have enough fuel, we're fully armed, and our in-system engines are just as fast if not faster than the big capital ships.' He rubbed his hands together. 'We'll catch up with them, all right.'

Some recruits took heart from his words, riled up and ready to fight the treacherous compy bastards; others were more realistic about their chances. Lanyan saw the moods shifting like eddies in a river. As his ships raced along the trajectory of the hijacked battle group, he gave an impromptu pep talk. 'Grid after grid has winked out. Our whole fleet is being taken over by the compies. We cannot let it happen here, at the cost of our very lives, if necessary! We'll fight hand-to-hand, if it comes to that. Dammit, *those are my ships!*'

He observed the uncertain expressions of the soldiers aboard the transport, watched how they shifted from panic to determination. Everyone knew that the Grid 0 warships vastly outgunned their collection of vessels. These young soldiers believed they didn't have a chance. Nor did they have a choice.

But Lanyan knew secrets about EDF vessels that none of these kleebs understood. 'Never underestimate the Earth Defence Forces. Trust me on that.'

TWENTY-SIX

JESS TAMBLYN

Seconds seemed like hours as Jess stared into the sea of Charybdis. Cesca had vanished into the water, swallowed by the living depths.

Save her, Jess silently begged the wentals. *Save her!*

Suddenly, she burst to the surface again, rising with a misty splash that clung to her like a halo. Her clothes and her skin were drenched, and now her eyes were bright. The bloodstains were gone. Her wet dark brown hair seemed to be alive. She rose, standing on nothing.

'You're alive again,' Jess said, his voice the breath of a whisper.

When she stepped onto the shore, Cesca's face was filled with an illuminating essence. 'Not just alive.' Her voice was louder, clearer. 'I feel more alive than I have ever been.'

Jess came forward, scanning her face, afraid that he might discover the boiling destructive power of a tainted wental, as he had witnessed in the memory images. But he saw only Cesca – only her smile, and her freedom from pain. She was healed.

He raised his hands, looked out at the living ocean of

Charybdis, and shouted, 'Thank you!' He gave a jubilant laugh. 'Thank you!'

Inside both of their heads now, the wentals said, *We must always be cautious.*

'Yes. We will. But she's *alive*, and you took that risk for me. Thank you for saving my life as well as hers.'

Nikko had backed away to the rebuilt *Aquarius*, watching the two of them, his expression full of awe mixed with hesitancy. Jess and Cesca contained so much energy that the young pilot probably feared they would achieve some sort of critical mass when they were together.

With an excitement he could not contain, Jess wrapped Cesca in his arms, touching her for the first time in what felt like a lifetime. Jess could not measure how long he had wanted this, how much he had missed her. He stroked her hair. 'See? There's nothing to worry about.'

The energy within her is unspoiled. Our actions have not created a tainted wental. She is part of us, but she is also changed for ever.

Jess held her shoulders, looked into her eyes. Long ago, as merely a man and a woman, their bond had been powerful. Now that both of them were more than human, their love was transformed and infinitely different, stronger than ever.

Even the shadow of reality could not dampen his joy. He reiterated what she already knew. 'From now on, Cesca, your touch will kill. We're isolated.'

She touched his cheek. 'We're not completely isolated, Jess. *We're* together. Right now that seems like more than I could ever have hoped for.'

Now Jess looked at her soberly. 'Whether we want it or not, we're in the same war, and the battles can be large or small. You and I have an unshakable purpose.'

'I am still the Speaker for the Roamer clans. I have to bring them all together. But I'll also stand with you, and the wentals, against the hydrogues.'

Nikko stepped closer to the transformed couple. 'Me, too. Your water-bearers and I were quietly spreading the wentals so they could grow strong before facing the drogues. But now, thanks to the comet at Theroc, the secret's blown. The drogues know the wentals are back and ready to fight.' He fidgeted. 'So, no more point in hiding, is there? Shouldn't we get on with it?'

Beyond the rocks, the phosphorescent ocean churned, and serpentine heads formed out of the liquid. Jess heard the eagerness of the water elementals in his head and knew what they had to do next. *Yes, the battle must be engaged now.*

Jess slipped a strong arm around Cesca's waist. 'We need to bring the wentals together from all across the Spiral Arm and hurl them against the hydrogues. And the verdani are ready to help us, too. I will have to go to Theroc soon.'

We are great races with vast differences. Verdani are passive and grounded in their worldtrees. They do not fight until they have no other choice. Wentals are fluid and spread widely, mist to mist and water to water, but we cannot easily form a solid resistance. Faeros are focused and destructive, but capricious. At one time, they fought beside the hydrogues, and now they fight against them.

Hydrogues, though, are single-minded, dwelling in their gas planets, never forgetting their loss in the last war. They have spent ten thousand years preparing. They will not be easy to defeat.

'So how do we do it, then?' Cesca asked.

In their minds, Jess and Cesca both saw how the wentals intended to bring the battles to the clouds of every gas giant planet in the hidden hydrogue empire. *We use our strengths, we join with allies, and we fight. Deliver us to hydrogue worlds and we will contain or destroy them.*

'We have to carry the wentals to war?' Nikko looked

sceptically at the small size of his *Aquarius* after Jess and Cesca had explained. 'Like buckets of water for dousing the drogues?'

'Like what I did in the clouds of Golgen to make that planet safe for skymining again – but this will be on a much larger scale.'

Cesca added, 'We need as many Roamer tankers as we can find to carry the energized water to gas giants.'

Nikko ducked back into the *Aquarius*. 'I've got maps of the planets infused with wentals, Jess. All of us volunteer water-bearers exchange that information. We can use those worlds as reservoirs for anybody who'll join us.'

Cesca turned to Jess, her eyes bright. 'No matter how I've changed, I can still meet with the clans as their Speaker. I can rally Roamers to use whatever ships they have and disseminate wentals to hydrogue gas giants.'

'Together we'll create a storm the hydrogues can't resist.' Jess's hair rose with static electricity, and damp wind rushed against his skin. 'We fly to Plumas first. Clan Tamblyn has large water tankers. Exactly what we need.'

Nikko soon flew away with enhanced speed. Jess took Cesca's hand, and they stepped up to the shimmering membrane. He couldn't remember when last they'd had time alone with each other. 'Join me,' he said.

'For ever.'

Together they entered the water-and-pearl ship.

TWENTY-SEVEN

RLINDA KETT

R iding a crest of self-forming ice, the resurrected woman came on towards shore in a storm of steam, flying ice chips, and water. Karla clenched her ivory-skinned fists and launched repeated barrages of power into the ceiling, shattering off chunks. Great gouges had already been slashed into the roof.

'She's going to blow a hole right through and crack us open to space!' Caleb shouted. 'We'll be sucked out like snowflakes.'

'Well, we were looking for a quick way out of here,' Rlinda said to BeBob as the two of them backed away, searching for shelter.

Pent-up power seemed to boil within Karla. It seemed to cause her pain unless she released it. The leaden sea froze beneath her every footfall as she walked towards the white shore, accompanied by the pack of pulsing nematodes.

With an empty wail that was half song and half scream, Karla loosed her ethereal energy at one of the implanted artificial suns. The ice cracked around the support framework, and the spherical spotlight dangled for a moment, then swayed and broke free. The bright surrogate sun tumbled into the cold, grey sea, sending up a geyser of flash-evaporated water. Still burning as it sank, the light dwindled, surrounded by a surge of foam.

BeBob groaned. 'I wish we'd never escaped from the Moon.'

Rlinda wanted to swat him. 'If you waste all your pathetic whining, what'll you have left if things get worse?'

'Now *there's* something to look forward to.'

She didn't want to stick around and learn what the ice woman intended to do to all of them. She doubted the Tamblyns had any sort of weapons that might be effective against this demonic apparition. 'I could use a flame thrower, or an assault-model jazer.'

'Here's a shovel,' BeBob said, handing her a wide-bladed tool with a long handle. 'Or maybe it's an ice scraper.'

Rlinda hefted it, frowning at BeBob. 'Am I supposed to smack her in the head with this?'

'No.' BeBob secured another shovel for himself. 'But it might help against those worms she's controlling.'

Scarlet nematodes flexed and crawled onto the solid ice – hundreds of them, each one as long as a human leg. The Plumas water miners scattered for the domed shelters, equipment huts, anyplace to hide. Armed with nothing more than shovels, Rlinda and BeBob huddled behind a berm of piled ice and crystalline snow.

The three Tamblyn brothers faced the woman in a last attempt at reason. 'Karla, it's *us*!' Torin shouted. 'Don't you recognize me? This is your home.'

'Hoooome,' she repeated like a long gust of frigid wind blowing through a tunnel. 'Solid walls. *Prisons*. Break them all down.' She casually extended her finger towards two running water miners which ran towards a habitation hut. It was as if she had sprayed a firehose of pure cold that petrified the hapless workers and covered them with a blanket of ice.

'Karla, no!' Wynn screamed. 'Please—'

139

The woman launched a blast at him as well, but Wynn dived out of the way, rolling under a set of thick gas-separation pipes. All three Tamblyn brothers scrambled away in separate directions.

'Return to fluid state,' she said. Karla directed her bombardment at more of the running miners, as if finding them more entertaining than cracking a hole through the ice ceiling. Next she destroyed one of the habitation huts, followed by a larger dwelling dome and a generator shed. 'Perfect state of disorder.'

Linked to her thoughts, the flurry of nematodes squirmed forward, looking very hungry. In the low gravity, the creatures had a strange adhesion with the vertical ice walls, crawling along the pipes and separating columns while leaving trails of slime. Rlinda thought of giant maggots squirming up the walls of a garbage bin.

With a sound like rasping sand, the slithering nematodes crossed the icepack like hunters. Their flexible bodies swelled, then contracted as they squirted along towards the wrecked complexes and hiding places.

Rlinda heard screams and shouts. A man ran out of a storage shed and fired an ice-melting laser at three of the worms. Instantly hot, they bloated and then exploded, spraying red protoplasm in all directions. Emboldened by his success, he turned the melting laser toward Karla, but the heat had little effect. With a brief gesture, she covered both him and his weapon in a shroud of ice.

On their hands and knees, she and BeBob scuttled to find better cover. The Roamers weren't paying any attention to their captives right now. 'I wish we could *do* something,' Rlinda said.

'I wish we could get out of here. Think this might be our chance?'

'Oh sure, as long as we survive the next ten minutes.'

Another explosion echoed through the underground grotto, and BeBob cringed beside her. 'Right now, running and hiding looks like our best option.' BeBob looked up as another dislodged chunk of ice crashed down from the cracked ceiling. 'It's every innocent bystander for himself.'

Rlinda lifted her eyes towards the fractured roof. 'The *Curiosity* is just waiting for us up there — if the Roamers haven't wrecked my ship.'

They were trying to fix it! I saw them bring spare parts up to the surface.'

'Right, but if the Tamblyn brothers didn't know what they were doing, then fixing the *Curiosity* and wrecking it could amount to the same thing.' She put a hand on her left hip and leaned on the shovel with the other. 'Still, I'd rather be up there and trying. If the whole world's going to fall apart, then I prefer to die aboard my own ship, if you know what I mean.'

'Dying wouldn't be my first preference at all, Rlinda . . . but at least I'll be with you.'

'You're either a sweetheart, or an idiot.' When their eyes met, the decision was clear in the frigid holocaust around them. She grabbed his hand and pulled him along. 'Right now, I'll take you either way.'

TWENTY-EIGHT

KOTTO OKIAH

After finding no explanations in the deserted Osquivel shipyards, Kotto and his Analytical compies went looking elsewhere. 'Quite a mystery,' Kotto said.

'An enigma,' said GU

'A conundrum,' KR added.

Though the scattered Roamer clans were in turmoil, Kotto had never paid much attention to general emergency plans, assuming someone would tell him where to go and what to do. Now, though, he had to take care of himself.

Using the small ship's navigational database, Kotto plotted a course for Jonah 12, where he had established an icy hydrogen-processing base. 'We don't have the fuel or the time to wander around on a wild-goose chase. I'll just go back to my old stomping grounds and see how everyone's doing.' It was so long since he'd had any news.

After he projected his path, he let the Analytical compies input the coordinates as the ship accelerated away from Osquivel. Kotto scratched his curly hair and sniffed under his arms, realizing that he'd been too busy of late to clean himself up. Facing off against the hydrogues at Theroc had certainly made him sweat.

Kotto stripped off his jumpsuit and cast the wrinkled garments into a spinning fabric refresher. He walked naked through the chilly ship, gathering rags and waterless cleansing gels so he could scrub himself down. He finished before the clothes were done cycling, and so he decided to give the Analytical compies a detailed cleaning as well.

Kotto hummed while he worked, thinking about the miners on Jonah 12, mulling over the process of cooking down ices and storing hydrogen gas for later conversion to ekti. Now that the derelict had been taken from him, he looked forward to returning to his real work. He chatted with KR and GU about mechanical systems and chemical-extraction routines. 'I'll bet Purcell Wan will be glad to have me back. I can't wait to see the expression on his face. I never expected to be gone so long when I went to help the Therons.'

'You have accomplished much in the meantime, Kotto Okiah,' GU said. 'You rebuilt the tree cities on Theroc, you studied the derelict at Osquivel, and you developed the doorbell membranes against the warglobes.'

'I don't need a cheering section,' he said, though he grinned anyway.

Kotto called up blueprints of the Jonah 12 base, then designs of the crawler vehicles. Before long, his imager table was covered with active screens, and he asked the compies to run models and simulations, adjusting parameters to improve production. By the time the ship reached the system, he had drawn up new designs that would increase productivity by at least 150 per cent. It would be an exciting day when he marched into the main dome with his refit announcement.

Kotto realized he was still naked, never having dressed after the clothes refresher was finished. He tugged on his jumpsuit, ready for a new start.

But when the ship approached the frozen planetoid, no one answered his hails. The ekti reactors in orbit were dead and cold. This was starting to seem uncomfortably familiar.

Once in range, Kotto scanned the landscape and found only a gaping crater where the base had been. His crew, his workers! An explosion had occurred with such force it had vaporized all signs of human habitation. Everyone was gone, completely wiped out.

Kotto stared in complete disbelief. First he'd found Osquivel abandoned, and now this. What could have caused such a disaster? All those people — he hoped there had been time to evacuate. Most of the Jonah 12 workers were survivors of his crazy scheme on near-molten Isperos, who had followed him to this icy planetoid. They had trusted him!

He gazed down at the huge ugly scar where the base should have been. 'By the Guiding Star, what is going on?'

The two compies looked at him as if considering whether he expected them to answer. KR and GU both decided to remain silent.

TWENTY-NINE

MAGE-IMPERATOR JORA'H

After sending Osira'h away, Jora'h walked a curving path high in the skysphere dome, searching for a moment of tranquility. Coloured light shone through the faceted panes, and misters kept the air moist. Servant kithmen had polished the walkway, and agricultural kithmen tended the skysphere's flora and fauna. Hanging vines and sweet flowers filled the huge terrarium; flying insects and feathered creatures darted about in flashes of vibrant red, green, blue.

The Mage-Imperator absorbed the soothing ambiance, but it could not counteract the ominous knowledge of the impending war. All around him, he felt the thrumming presence of his people. The Prism Palace was like a magnification lens, concentrating all of their faith and confidence in him. Jora'h could barely stand under the weight of it.

He recalled a stanza from *The Saga of Seven Suns*, words he had always found disturbing: 'There will come a time of fire and night, when enemies rise and empires fall, when the stars themselves begin to die.'

That time is already here. And I have helped bring it about.

His people did not understand the potential cost of his agreement with the hydrogues, but because he was their Mage-Imperator, they would not question it. They would do anything he asked, blindly follow their leader's instructions – and somehow that made the situation even worse. How could he explain and justify his actions?

Here inside the lush gardens he found the chunks of worldtree wood he had purchased from Roamer traders months ago. He had placed the fragments here to remind him of Nira. *At least, Osira'h will soon be with her mother . . .*

Yazra'h trotted toward him along the pathway from the opposite side of the skysphere. Her mane of coppery hair flowed behind her as she ran, eyes intent on her father. Even before she came to a stop, she had touched her right fist to the centre of her chest, giving him a formal salute. 'Liege, the Roamer trader Denn Peroni has just landed on Ildira.' Yazra'h gave a wolfish grin. 'He says he wishes to sell us a full cargo of ekti.'

Jora'h was surprised. With the Hyrillka insurrection, the dying sun of Durris-B, and the hydrogue ultimatum, he'd forgotten the Roamers' request to reopen trade with the Ildiran Empire. 'We certainly need it.' He frowned. 'But be careful. Make sure he learns nothing about our dealings with the hydrogues.' If Denn Peroni suspected a secret alliance, then Jora'h would be forced to capture his ship and hold him prisoner, just like the other humans being held in the Prism Palace. 'Keep Sullivan Gold and his skyminers out of sight, as well as your friend Anton Colicos. I don't want this Roamer to catch a glimpse of them. Their presence would raise far too many questions.'

Jora'h resented the fact that he had to imprison the humans. Sullivan Gold and his crew were heroes who had rescued Ildiran skyminers from a hydrogue attack; and the scholar Anton Colicos had survived a Klikiss robot attack and saved Rememberer Vao'sh. By the rules of honour, those men and women should have been rewarded. Instead, since they had seen the warglobes, Jora'h had no choice but to keep them under guard. He feared he would never be able to let them go.

He despised being trapped like this!

'Yes, Liege. I will make the arrangements. The trader is already on his way.' She bowed, then ran away, coloured light dappling her smooth skin. Jora'h began to make his way back down to the dais and his duties.

In an attempt to show respect, the Roamer man dropped to one knee before the chrysalis chair, then looked up with an infectious smile. His long brown hair was tied in a ribbon, and he wore a fine outfit embellished with clan markings. He seemed very pleased with himself.

'This ekti comes from a cometary-processing facility, where we strip out the hydrogen and convert it to stardrive fuel. It's a difficult and costly process, Your Majesty.' He shrugged. 'The hydrogues haven't left us many alternatives.'

Ever since the beginning of the hydrogue war eight years ago, the production of stardrive fuel had dwindled to a trickle, and the Empire's vast stockpiles were now severely diminished. 'We will pay your price,' Jora'h said. Humans worried overmuch about rising and falling expenditures, trying to trick their commercial partners into greater or lesser payments. Ildirans, on the other hand, operated as aligned pieces in a large, interconnected network.

Peroni grinned. 'I have some good news for you, though. The Roamer clans are skymining again! We found at least one gas giant cleared of the hydrogues. There'll be plenty more ekti to come. This could be the start of a long and profitable partnership between humans and Ildirans. I'm sure of it.'

'We thank you for your trust.' Jora'h's heart felt cold and heavy inside his chest. Yet the hydrogues intended to exterminate *all* humans ... and the Ildirans just might be forced to help them do it.

THIRTY

SULLIVAN GOLD

The Hansa skyminers hated being held hostage inside the Prism Palace. Tabitha Huck slumped onto a bench, scowled at the guarded door of their spacious chambers. 'A damned odd way to say thank you.' She glared at the muscular guard woman who prowled the corridors with her vicious-looking panther pets. 'You do a good deed and just look what happens.'

Sullivan took a seat beside her. When the hydrogues attacked Qronha 3, the Hansa workers had been ready to evacuate, but the Ildirans had no way to escape. After a wrenching decision, Sullivan had ordered his crew to save the doomed Ildirans, at great risk to themselves. 'We couldn't just leave them all to die, Tabitha.'

'Maybe we should have! We lost one of our own escape modules while the drogues were attacking, and now we're stuck here. If we'd evacuated while the warglobes were busy destroying the Ildiran facility, we'd be home right now.'

Sullivan put a paternal hand on her arm. 'But would you be able to sleep at night?'

Tabitha looked sideways at him. 'I'm willing to take tranquillizers.'

Sullivan watched the silhouette of Yazra'h prowling in the hall. The lean guard looked in on them and scanned their forlorn faces. 'Stay here until we release you again. You are not to leave these rooms for the next two hours.'

'Why? What's changed?' Sullivan barged towards the door. 'What did we do wrong?'

'It is not my place to explain.'

'Our loved ones need to know we're all right,' he pleaded. 'Can you at least provide a treeling for my green priest, so we can send a message? Tell our families we're still *alive*. Please, it would mean so much to him. To all of us.'

Kolker was the most desperately affected member of his crew. The green priest had always been loquacious, talking endlessly through his treeling with his comrades across the Spiral Arm. But Kolker had lost his treeling during the destruction of the cloud harvester and now was utterly cut off from his beloved telink. Kolker was more than just lonely, more than sad. He was like an addict forced to endure a prolonged withdrawal. And it was all so unnecessary! Why was the Mage-Imperator doing this to them?

'I have other duties.' With an abrupt dismissal, Yazra'h stepped away from the door and closed it behind her.

Tabitha scowled as the guard woman departed. 'The Ildirans wouldn't be doing this unless they had something to hide.' She shook her head, her forehead furrowed with unanswered questions. 'I tell you, something smells fishy – and it isn't caviar. What were all those warglobes doing over the Prism Palace? As soon as we saw that, we got sent to our rooms.'

Sullivan went to the green priest and touched the green priest's bare shoulder in sympathy. Deeply depressed, Kolker sat silently by himself. Although his skin was a bright and healthy emerald green from the abundant sunlight, he needed contact with the worldtrees.

Kolker raised his heavy head, as if he sensed something unexpected. His expression showed a glimmer of surprise, even a faint shadow of hope – and it had nothing to do with what Tabitha or Sullivan had said. 'I thought it was just a desperate hope, but it's not my imagination! I know that now. There really is something here.' The green priest looked directly at Sullivan. 'There is a treeling in the Prism Palace – and I will find it.'

THIRTY-ONE

ANTON COLICOS

'Come with me to the Hall of Rememberers,' said Vao'sh. 'You have never seen the sanctuary and headquarters for my kith, where all stories begin and end. I have not been there since I awakened from my nightmares.'

Anton brightened. 'I'd love to! And not just because it'll get me out of the Prism Palace for a change.'

Ever since the warglobes had come and gone, the Ildirans were panicky and suspicious. With good reason, he supposed ... but why restrict *his* movements? Anton got the impression that he'd seen something he wasn't supposed to, and now his hosts watched him more closely than ever. What could a skinny and preoccupied scholar do against the Ildiran Empire? Anton finally asked the question. 'Why won't anyone tell me the reason I can't go home? I'd really like to know.'

Vao'sh frowned. 'You have not accomplished your purpose in coming here, Rememberer Anton. Are you anxious to leave?'

'I'm not anxious, but it makes me uneasy. My father was killed at an archaeology dig years ago, and my mother is still missing. I'm so out of touch. What if there's news? I just don't like being kept in the dark.'

Vao'sh rocked backwards. 'In the *dark*? We would never do that to you!'

Anton placed a reassuring hand on his friend's forearm. 'It was just a figure of speech. Don't worry.' He saw he wasn't going to get an answer.

Moving briskly, the rememberer led him down a long hall and out through the arched side entrances of the Prism Palace. A winding path descended the elliptical hill to the extensive city. The view was so breathtaking that he barely noticed the pair of silent and muscular guard kithmen accompanying them.

'Will Yazra'h come with us?'

'I believe the Mage-Imperator has currently assigned her to other duties.'

Anton felt disappointment mixed with a small measure of relief. The intimidating woman had been his diligent guardian since he'd returned from Maratha with a catatonic Vao'sh. She didn't seem like the type, but Anton knew that she enjoyed his stories. He awkwardly suspected that Yazra'h wanted something more from him.

One of the most impressive buildings in Mijistra was a storehouse of records for the kith responsible for writing, memorizing, and preserving the *Saga*. Vao'sh hurried up the polished stone stairs, obviously excited. The two guards took up their positions outside the huge hall and waited. Anton barely spared them a glance. Where in the world did they think he might go?

He entered, thinking of all the university lecture halls he had haunted before he'd been invited to study *The Saga of Seven Suns*. This was quite different from anything he had seen before.

Row after row of sequential wall panels formed a labyrinth, each segment delicately engraved with long lines of precise letters.

The wall sections were giant diamondfilm sheets etched with the approved stanzas of the *Saga*, line after line after line. Just inside the doorway, a group of rememberer children, their faces showing prominent lobes, stood rapt before the writing-covered walls. The children stared at the stanzas and mumbled to themselves, repeating what they read, over and over until they had burned each word into their brains.

'They learn the *Saga* from beginning to end,' Vao'sh explained. 'A rememberer will spend half of his life absorbing all the stanzas until he can recite it without error. The story must be told without a single change.'

Anton gave a wry smile. 'I hate writers who keep editing even after a story is finished.' As he and Vao'sh continued past scroll-work pillars and mirrored fountains, rememberers stood before each of the text-covered wall panels, memorizing and reciting. 'They're getting older from one segment to the next.'

'The youngest rememberers begin their training just inside the entrance. Once they perfect the first segment of the *Saga*, they move to the next plate on the wall, progressing year by year until they have absorbed the whole epic.'

Anton laughed. 'And I thought Earthbound academia was tedious!'

At the core of the Hall of Rememberers, scribes quietly and intensely discussed their work, crowded around tables. Middle-aged storytellers pored over stacks of records. Working together with a single goal, they compiled and critiqued one sheet after another, adding new lines to the never-ending *Saga*.

The ceiling swept upwards in a gigantic chimney above a huge brazier that burned with bright flames. Discarded sheets were cast into the hot fire, destroying unacceptable drafts. Once each line was finished, discussed, and approved, then – and only then – was it scribed in permanent diamondfilm that would eventually be mounted onto the walls within the Hall of Rememberers.

'The accurate recording of events is as important as the events themselves.' The lobes on his face flushed a chameleon palette of colours. 'A society that does not remember is not worth remembering. It is a core Ildiran belief.'

Although human epics were often embellished myths that served a purpose beyond the mere chronicling of facts, Ildirans took every mark of recorded history literally. Only Vao'sh's kith – and presumably the Mage-Imperator – knew that the legends of the Shana Rei were false, made up to add drama and conflict to the *Saga*. But if the Shana Rei were fictional, then might not other parts of *The Saga of Seven Suns* be suspect?

As he watched the rememberer kithmen scribbling and discarding draft stanzas, Anton realized that 'history' was literally being made before his eyes. An apprentice threw another sheaf into the brazier, where the flames consumed more unacceptable lines.

Vao'sh walked from one table to the next. 'Right now, my comrades are writing the story of Adar Kori'nh, from his evacuation of Crenna after the blindness plague, through his struggles against the hydrogues, to the final battle in the clouds of Qronha 3.'

'Your Adar Kori'nh certainly earned his place in the *Saga*.'

Vao'sh smiled. 'Within months, rememberers will discuss the inclusion of *our* long trek across Maratha and our battles with the Klikiss robots.'

Anton gasped. 'I came to study your history, not make a mark on it. You mean I . . . *we*—'

'You are no longer a mere observer of historical epics, Rememberer Anton. You will soon become part of one.'

THIRTY-TWO

ADMIRAL LEV STROMO

They kept up the fight for two full days, losing ground a centimetre at a time. But still losing.

After the mutinous Soldier compies killed Sergeant Zizu, taking the security chief down in a flurry of broken bones and last spurts of weapons fire, Stromo saw that only he and Commander Ramirez remained alive on the Manta's bridge. He'd heard enough panicked transmissions across the intercom to know the compies were massacring everyone else aboard. Frightened bridge crewmembers had tried to evacuate, but the corridor was stacked with the bodies of dead soldiers. And the compies kept coming.

Below, Qronha 3 looked maddeningly peaceful, exhibiting no sign of rammers or hydrogue warglobes. His Manta was all alone and vulnerable.

'Admiral!' Ramirez tossed him a charge pack for his twitcher. 'This is the last one.'

Stromo's hands were trembling, but he managed to snap in the replacement pack. He had drained his weapon stalling the oncoming robots, but the stunned Soldier compies reasserted their programming and came forward again.

He jerked his head toward the captain's prep room adjacent to the bridge. 'If we go in there, we could barricade the door.'

'It won't last long, sir.'

'Doesn't need to! Remember the emergency ladder?' It had seemed an odd protective measure when the Mantas were designed, an escape hatch in case the commanding officer needed to slip away from the bridge. On the other hand, he'd sat on enough EDF committees to know that planning sessions often mutated in strange directions.

Ramirez's face remained grim. 'That'll take us down a deck. Then what?'

'One step at a time, Commander.' First, he wanted to get away from here. He would worry about the next stage later.

'Good idea, sir. Go!'

As the Soldier compies battered aside the last-ditch barricades and surged onto the bridge, Stromo bolted towards the small private chamber. At one time, using the military robots had seemed the perfect solution to make up for the shortfall of recruits and the loss of so many fighters in the hydrogue war. Now there was so much fresh blood on the deck he could barely run without slipping.

Before following him into the dubious bolt-hole, Ramirez paused at the command station and fiddled with the systems. Stromo skidded to a stop at the prep room. 'Come on, Ramirez! I can't hold this open for ever.'

'Just a minute, sir.' She worked furiously, sweat dripping from her brow, paying no attention to the oncoming compies. 'Another second . . . one second.'

Stromo swallowed hard. Even once sealed, this door wouldn't hold long. What was she doing? Well, he could no longer be responsible if Ramirez insisted on staying at her station. That was her choice. He had to make a command decision. He turned to the door controls.

She finally finished her routine and hit the activate button. As she sprinted toward him, sparks flew from all the bridge stations like a chain of firecrackers. Ramirez was actually grinning as she burst into the prep room with him. Stromo slid the door shut, sealing it. 'What the hell was all that? You've cost us time!'

'Disabled the primary systems, sir. Now those compies won't have access to my ship, no matter what happens.' He should have thought of that himself. It was clear the compies wanted this Manta for something.

Only seconds after the door sealed, compies began to pound on the barricade; dents formed in the metal. This wasn't an armoured chamber. The door was little more than a privacy screen for the ship's commander to have strategy discussions with his underlings or perhaps deliver a stern lecture to a recalcitrant crewmember.

'Quick!' Stromo gestured towards a tiny closet with an access hatch in the floor. 'Go first.' He didn't know what might be down there.

Ramirez lifted the hatch to expose the ladder and in a smooth movement slung her feet through the hole. Stromo scrambled down more awkwardly. 'There's a cargo lift down at the end of this main corridor,' he said, breathing heavily as he lowered himself rung after rung. 'Maybe we can make it to the hangar deck. Grab a Remora or a personnel transport.' His feet dropped to the floor with a thud, and he nearly lost his balance. 'Then we'll fly out of here.'

'Are you sure there's no one else left alive aboard, Admiral?'

'Even if they are, we can't save them. Come on, hurry up.'

He sprinted down the corridor, and Ramirez easily paced him.

She made no comment, but she was smart enough to know their chances. Everyone had to be responsible for his or her own welfare.

'Watch out, sir!' Two Soldier compies lunged out of a side corridor. Ramirez fired a long blast with her twitcher and knocked them aside.

Ahead, the corridor seemed to go on for ever, with any number of chambers and branching hallways where compies might be lurking. He hesitated, his face red, his heart pounding, but he knew they had to keep moving.

When more compies emerged, Stromo blasted repeatedly with his twitcher, but the military robots seemed inexhaustible. He nearly tripped on a fallen compy; in an automated spasm, the metal arm reached out to grab him, but he jumped away.

Ramirez fired her own twitcher, blast after blast. 'At this rate we'll drain our charges before we even get to the lift!'

Stromo sprinted ahead, concentrating on the wall controls and the closed lift door. Barely able to hold himself upright as he panted and wheezed, he slapped the summoning sensor. The indicator lights raced as the fast cargo elevator shot up to Deck 2. Only a few seconds more!

'Hurry, Ramirez! The lift is coming.' He could feel the wall vibrate, hear the machinery humming.

She fought to catch up. Three cabin doors slid open. The rooms should have been crew barracks where off-duty personnel rested and relaxed. Four compies emerged, covered with blood.

Ramirez fired shorter bursts with her twitcher, just enough to divert the machines, but now compies crowded the passageway. They came toward Stromo, and he fired at them, extravagant with his weapon's energy; in such a dire situation, no half-assed effort would succeed.

Ramirez couldn't shoot the compies fast enough. Her charge pack ran out.

Stromo meant to go help Ramirez, but he saw that his twitcher had only enough energy to fire two more significant bursts – not nearly enough to save her, not nearly enough to let him get away.

'Admiral!' The compies grabbed Ramirez, and she battered at their optical sensors with the butt of her weapon. She shouted his name as they surrounded her, something that might have sounded like 'Go!' Stromo almost moved, *almost* went forward to assist her, to go down fighting.

But the lift opened at last. He saw it was empty and waiting. A miracle!

Before he could see Ramirez fall under the attacking compies, Stromo scrambled into the lift and punched the selector controls for the hangar bay. He tried to remember how to fly EDF ships. He had the training, of course. He'd received instructions long ago, but he couldn't recall the last time he'd actually sat in a cockpit. Did he even know how to open the launching-bay doors?

Stromo set his jaw. With a Remora's jazers, he could blast right through the damned hull if necessary. He stood ready, knowing what to do now, as the elevator opened.

Hundreds of compies filled the hangar bay, all of them waiting for him. They pressed towards the lift's open door.

Stromo's two remaining shots did not last long. He backed against the inner wall, and the compies pushed in on him.

THIRTY-THREE

ENGINEERING SPECIALIST SWENDSEN

O nly a constant barrage from the silver berets kept the robots contained within the barricaded factory. Sergeant Paxton dismantled his temporary command post and took up residence in a large armoured vehicle, where he prepared for the second phase of the assault. This time, no one would underestimate the rampaging Soldier compies.

Swendsen huddled inside the claustrophobic vehicle, racking his brains for a workable solution. What had caused the compies to go wild?

'We could call down an airstrike to annihilate the whole facility,' Paxton growled. 'Melt 'em all into puddles. Solve the problem.'

'That would stop the compies here, but it wouldn't affect the larger emergency,' Swendsen pointed out. 'We can't just blow up every EDF ship where the compies are running wild, now can we? All of my compy schematics and management protocols are in that factory. That seemed the logical place to keep everything. If this is a pervasive programming error, we have to find a way to shut them all down. I can't do that until I understand what went wrong, and it would be difficult to get any data from a lump of melted metal.' The specialist stared at his datapad, scrolling from one assessment to another. Without knowing what had gone wrong with the governing modules in the first place, it was damnably hard to fix things. 'We don't even know for sure if this is intentional sabotage, or just an accidental glitch.'

'An accident?' Paxton looked at him in complete disbelief. 'Occurring across the whole EDF? Some coincidence!'

Swendsen shrugged his bony shoulders, still denying what he knew to be true. 'Stranger things have happened.'

'Not in my career.'

'All right ... not in mine either.' He didn't want to let the sergeant know that *he* – the Hansa's primary engineering specialist – had no idea what to do.

Reinforcements had arrived. One hundred twenty-eight armoured assault vehicles surrounded the factory, blasting any compy that broke loose. Elite commandos were stationed at the primary entrances and shipping bays, but the facility was enormous. If the compies made a concerted effort to break free ...

Touching the numeric pad, Swendsen estimated how many new robots had been ready for deployment, then calculated the additional number that could have been produced in the meantime. Even with new arrivals, the commandos were already greatly overextended. They could never hold back all the compies.

Someone pounded on the closed hatch of the armoured carrier, identified himself to the observation eye, then keyed in his code. A silver beret escorted a thin Asian man wearing a serious expression. 'Sergeant Paxton, this man claims to be a compy specialist, a cyberneticist with a great deal of experience in Soldier models and their programming.'

Swendsen jumped to his feet. 'Dr Yamane!'

'Dr Swendsen.' Yamane stepped forward for a brief but enthusiastic handshake. 'I understand you're having some trouble.'

'A bit.' Swendsen's excitement surged as Yamane explained his experience with the battle group at Osquivel, observing the Soldier compies in action.

'Here's the interesting part, Dr Swendsen. When they rescued us, the Roamers also salvaged a hundred Soldier compies, erased their programming, and put them to work. We had a situation similar to what's going on here, compies going berserk – and I caused it. Intentionally.'

Paxton rested his elbows on the consultation table inside the armoured vehicle. 'How – and why – did you manage to do that?'

'We needed a diversion so Commander Fitzpatrick could attempt to escape. Because of my work with the Soldier compies, I knew how to cancel their behavioural restrictions. An insidious little repeater virus that, for lack of a better term, turned them into loose cannons.' A wan smile crossed Yamane's face.

Swendsen's eyebrows shot up. 'And did it work?'

'They certainly created a diversion, but once the compies clicked into chaos mode, we had no way to stop them. They ended up destroying much of the Roamer shipyards.'

Swendsen considered. 'So, someone transmitted a similar virus to trigger our current revolt?'

Yamane shook his head. 'Transmitted? No, the breakdown is not localized. Soldier compies are simultaneously subverting command protocols all across the Spiral Arm, which means it must be embedded. Some timed instruction must have been included from their initial activation. That implies a long-term plan, which is much more sinister than a programming gremlin.'

Swendsen offered the cyberneticist a folding seat inside the crowded vehicle. Yamane looked into his colleague's bright blue eyes. 'However, it occurs to me that we could use something similar to achieve the opposite effect. A repeater virus that would serve as a big wrench thrown into their modules.'

'That's an idea! I understand.' He shot a look over to Sergeant Paxton. '*We* understand.'

'Then I suggest you get to work as soon as possible,' Paxton said.

THIRTY-FOUR

MAGE-IMPERATOR JORA'H

With Osira'h gone, the Mage-Imperator summoned Adar Zan'nh, senior members of the scientist and engineering kiths, military strategists, even Rememberer Vao'sh. Each was the best his kith had to offer. With the help of these men, Jora'h had to find a way to stand against the hydrogues and save the Empire.

He waited in front of the immense gates of the Prism Palace. At the top of the ellipsoidal hill on which the Palace had been built, the rushing water of seven converging streams thundered like the roar of a storm. In straight lines, the streams came together at this point, flowing uphill. From his high vantage, he could see their courses extending to the perimeters of Mijistra, where the landscape sculptors had finally allowed the rivers to bend back into their natural patterns. He had called the meeting here for a specific purpose.

'Observe the seven streams,' the Mage-Imperator said in his most commanding voice, 'and consider exactly what Ildirans accomplished here.'

Klie'f, an old and distinguished member of the scientist kith, and Shir'of, a younger but talented representative of the engineering kith, studied the convergence point with its foaming water, as if Jora'h had just posed a new technical challenge. Vao'sh nodded, recalling the historical tale.

In a complex engineering feat, the Prism Palace builders had channelled these streams to flow towards the seat of the Mage-Imperator. Using gravity-assist steps and locks, scientists had wrestled the currents, manipulated the water itself, so that the streams flowed against nature, climbing in a white torrent until they reached the apex. Here before the main gate, the seven streams joined to pour down a wide well in a circular waterfall, at the bottom of which the gushing water was redistributed from outlets below and behind the Palace hill.

Jora'h waited, but no one ventured an answer. In angry impatience, he shouted above the roar at the water, '*We did the impossible!* And we must do it again. Long ago, Ildirans used their ingenuity to defy the laws of the universe. They achieved the unachievable because the Mage-Imperator demanded it of them. I now demand the same from all of you.'

The representatives seemed intimidated; Adar Zan'nh's expression remained stoic, but he nodded. Rememberer Vao'sh looked intrigued.

'Answer this question and you will save our Empire.' Jora'h paused. 'How can we stand against the hydrogues?'

Klie'f and Shir'of looked at each other, then the military strategists; they all turned to the commander of the Solar Navy. Zan'nh said, 'None of our weapons have proven effective. Adar Kori'nh destroyed many warglobes, but at a cost far too great for us ever to achieve victory.'

Jora'h stepped to the lip of the furious waterfall as it vanished down the deep well. 'That is why I called you. The hydrogues have given me an ultimatum that I find unacceptable. I bought time by pretending to agree. Now, I need you to give me another solution to another impossible challenge. You are my best. Take these questions to your fellow kithmen, work together with them. Push yourselves beyond your usual boundaries. If you succeed, I guarantee you a place in *The Saga of Seven Suns*, memorialized for all time. What Ildiran could ask for more than that?'

'You are asking us to stand up against the undefeatable, Liege,' Klie'f said.

'Yes, I am. Give me new strategies, new defences, new weapons!'

Zan'nh bowed towards his father. 'You are the Mage-Imperator, Liege. You are our leader, and *we* comprise your empire. If we cannot solve this problem, then we have failed you indeed.'

'If you do not find a way,' Jora'h said in an oddly even voice, 'then two races may die.'

Rememberer Vao'sh, though fascinated by the conversation, looked at his leader. 'Liege, I am a mere storyteller. What can I do?'

Knowing more of the historical truth than he had ever wanted to learn, Jora'h had often cursed his predecessors for hiding so much information about past encounters. He had to break that long-standing censorship. 'We have fought the hydrogues before, but many of the records of that conflict are locked away in the apocrypha. Unseal them and study them. Learn what has been forgotten, and bring me any clues you may discover about our enemies.'

'An immense task, Liege. I will inspect all our records here, but there are important archives on distant planets, particularly Hyrillka.'

Jora'h recalled that the first Klikiss robots had been excavated from their long hibernation on a moon of Hyrillka. Centuries ago.

Was something more buried in that system? Some lost document explaining the ancient compact that had changed the alliances in the first great war? Perhaps a record of how Ildirans had once shared a bond with the faeros, as the hydrogue emissary had accused? So many tangled connections!

'I am sending the new Designate with a recovery team to Hyrillka to help rebuild the areas destroyed by the revolt. Accompany them, Rememberer Vao'sh. Learn anything you can.'

Jora'h watched resolve harden on each of the faces before him. The scientist and engineer would develop weapons that might succeed against the deep-core aliens. Adar Zan'nh would guide the military applications and consider new tactics. The rememberer would dig through hidden history. For just a moment Jora'h felt confident. He briskly clapped his hands. 'All of you, find me answers. Do whatever you deem necessary. I place my faith in you.'

Jora'h once again resented the poor choices of his predecessors. Instead of gambling everything on a breeding programme to create a telepathic negotiator, the Ildiran Empire could have spent ten thousand years creating better weapons. Now they had to do it all within a few days.

THIRTY-FIVE

OSIRA'H

With her mission completed, Osira'h was obviously no longer needed on Ildira. Her father had sent her back to Dobro to get her out of the way while he continued to work his plans with the hydrogues.

The splinter colony looked no different from how she remembered it: the Ildiran town, the grassy hills, the fenced-in breeding camp. But *she* was different. She had met the hydrogues and come back, and she had watched the Mage-Imperator bow to their heinous demands. Osira'h felt that the whole universe had changed. As it had so many times before . . . and would again.

In the dust-hazed sunlight on Dobro, worker kithmen unloaded supplies from the shuttle. Disembarking guard kithmen walked around her as if she were a rock in a stream. The girl tracked her gaze from side to side and finally saw Designate Udru'h striding towards her. 'Osira'h, I welcome you back to Dobro!'

When she saw him, her body and mind seemed torn in two. One part of her recalled the Designate warmly, as a father figure.

He had cared for her, made her work hard to achieve her destiny. She'd wanted so badly to please him. Yet crystal-sharp memories from her mother made her want to recoil. Nira knew his cruel side, his hated touch, all the pain he had inflicted upon her mind and body.

As the Designate came closer, Osira'h wondered if he would show warmth, if he would embrace her. Would her skin crawl? But he stopped two steps in front of her. The words tumbled out of his mouth. 'We received word that you had succeeded.' His face showed satisfaction, contentment with his duty. 'I want to hear about it.'

Osira'h looked at him, feeling a swell of resentment, even hatred, burn deep inside her. She wanted to shout at him: *I did what you trained me to do. I accomplished everything I was born for. I used my powers to communicate with the hydrogues. I opened my mind and formed a bridge, and I am now permanently connected to their alien thoughts. I can't get them out of my head.*

And I dragged the hydrogues to Mijistra so the Mage-Imperator could speak to them. It was what I was supposed to do — and instead, my father, the leader of my people, could not bargain with them. He had nothing the hydrogues wanted. They threatened Ildira with destruction, and the Mage-Imperator crumbled. He agreed to a terrible bargain that will result in the damnation of Ildirans and the destruction of my mother's race!

But she could say none of that to the Dobro Designate. Instead, she simply answered, 'I succeeded. What more is there to tell?' She knew she was a pawn, always a pawn, but she didn't have to play along.

He noticed the metal in her tone, and a flicker of a frown crossed his expression like a wisp of cloud passing in front of the sun. 'Tell me what happened. Did Jora'h speak with the hydrogues?'

Succinctly and without unnecessary detail, Osira'h outlined

the conversations between her father and the emissary, describing what he had agreed to do. Udru'h did not seem disturbed by the terms. In fact, he appeared relieved that the Ildirans might survive after all; that was his only concern.

He finally reached out to clasp her shoulder. 'You have been through a terrible ordeal. Your encounter with the hydrogues must have been difficult, but you understand why it was necessary.'

Osira'h was careful not to agree with him. 'You explained my duty and my obligations, Designate.'

Udru'h gave her an uncertain smile. 'Surely your quarters in Mijistra were far more elegant than these humble buildings?'

Osira'h looked away. 'The Mage-Imperator sent me back. He wanted me safely away from the Prism Palace – with my mother. When can I see her?'

'Your mother . . . is not here.' Udru'h scowled, surprised by the unexpected comment. 'Not at the moment.'

Osira'h wanted to scream. Another lie! Either her father or the Dobro Designate was lying to her! Anxious, the girl glanced around, but did not see young Daro'h in the press of Ildirans. Her half-brother seemed like a good man, not corrupted by excuses and justifications, as Udru'h had been. 'Where is the Designate-in-waiting? Has he taken over his duties yet?' Perhaps Daro'h could bring about the necessary changes in this splinter colony.

'Daro'h is off on another mission.' Udru'h would say no more – evasive, curt . . . as he had always been.

In the Ildiran part of the settlement, Osira'h stood in the doorway of the humble dwelling she had shared with her siblings, all of Nira's children. The Designate had not accompanied her, claiming other duties. Her younger siblings gathered around her in awe. What did Designate Udru'h think about her half-breed brothers and sisters now that they were superfluous to his plans?

'What were the hydrogues like?' Rod'h asked. He was her nearest brother, less than a year younger than she was, the son of Udru'h. Because she had her mother's memories, whenever Osira'h looked on Rod'h, she remembered the repeated rapes Nira had endured until the Designate succeeded in impregnating her. Shortly after he was delivered, the infant had been taken away from her and raised elsewhere. The boy had never felt even a glimmer of love for his mother. He had never known Nira at all. But he was not to blame for that. Udru'h was.

'The hydrogues are as strange as we expected.' Osira'h sat at a small table and they began to share food, simple Dobro fare. Barely managing to maintain a calm façade in front of them all, Osira'h told how her protective sphere had plunged into the clouds of Qronha 3, how she had used all her powers to touch the incredibly alien minds.

'Were you frightened?' asked Gale'nh, her next oldest brother.

'Of course I was frightened. The hydrogues have destroyed everyone else who tried to communicate with them. I had to be better than anyone in history.'

When Gale'nh nodded sombrely, Osira'h saw a flicker of his father, stoic Adar Kori'nh, whom she had seen in countless historical records. She knew from darker documents that the commander of the Solar Navy had been ordered to father a child upon Nira. The Adar had done his duty, as always, but was ashamed at what he'd been forced to do.

Tamo'l, Nira's second daughter – this one sired by a lens kithman – listened intently. Both she and her sister Muree'n were too young to grasp the magnitude of what Osira'h had been asked to do. Muree'n, fathered by a guard kithman, was strong and heavily built for her age, more interested in play and physical activity, barely able to concentrate on meticulous mental exercises. Osira'h could not imagine what the experimenters had hoped to achieve with that pairing. By then Designate Udru'h might simply have been toying with Nira, or punishing her . . .

And her mother wasn't even here, as the Mage-Imperator had promised.

Looking at her brothers and sisters, Osira'h recalled how uncomfortable she'd felt on Ildira. Now she was adrift, no longer belonging on Dobro either. What purpose did the breeding colony have anymore? What would become of the camp and the human prisoners? Even her siblings, who carried Nira's genes, were no longer relevant. Would Mage-Imperator Jora'h confess Dobro's secrets to the Hansa, or would Designate Udru'h simply exterminate his subjects and bury the evidence as if nothing had ever happened? Even that would not surprise her.

The food was tasteless in her mouth. She forced herself to chew and swallow while her brothers and sisters talked and laughed.

THIRTY-SIX

NIRA

Dobro's lonely southern continent seemed endless. Nira kept moving, though she had no idea where she was going. Long ago, as an acolyte, she had toughened her feet by running through the Theron forest and climbing up to the worldtree canopy where she would sit for hours reading stories to the forest mind. For many years now she'd been cut off from that. She didn't even know how much time had passed.

Her spirit was deeply scarred by the hardships she had endured, but Nira refused to give up. She had escaped from her island, ridden a raft across the inland sea, and started walking. Along the way she hoped to spot another settlement, even a ship. That could be her only chance to see her daughter again.

Osira'h was just a little girl, but Nira had poured years of awful revelations into her mind, desperate to tell the truth to the deluded girl. Nira couldn't imagine what that brutal information had done to an innocent child. She suspected that Osira'h had never been a child again after that night. Had Nira done the right thing after all?

Because her journey had seemed impossible from the start, Nira kept no tally of the days. She simply followed the landscape, drinking water from occasional streams, letting her green skin absorb sunlight as nourishment, supplementing her diet with a few bitter fruits, roots, and dry seeds.

She hiked through grassy hills, and the whispering brown blades sawed against her skin. With the uneven landscape blocking her view of the distance, she headed up one of the chaparral ridges from which she could gaze at what lay ahead of her. She wanted to stare toward the horizon, thinking that maybe — *maybe* — she could glimpse a sign of hope.

Nira forged uphill through the thick grasses, and when she reached the top of the ridge, she looked up at a sound in the sky. The humming grew to a roar, and she spotted several sleek craft cutting lines in the atmosphere. From the other side of the ridge, unexpectedly close, another scout ship swept towards her, barrelling low enough to flatten the grasses with its backwash.

Terrified, Nira skidded and slid back down the steep slope. Weeds caught at her bare toes, and she tripped. She thrashed to her feet again, and ploughed headlong through the underbrush. Scout ships! The Dobro Designate had found her! But what could he possibly do to her that was worse than before? He had kept her as a bargaining chip, but she'd escaped. Nira vowed she would never go back to the breeding camps.

Scouts circled overhead, their engines a booming whine. She kept running, sliding, trying to hide in the tall grasses, but from above, the ships could easily spot her. One scout had already landed on the top of the ridge, and several Ildirans emerged, shouting to her.

Nira tumbled down to a valley between the rolling hills. Two scout ships landed on either side of her. Her tormentors were coming from every direction!

'Leave me alone!' Her voice was hoarse and rusty, barely a whisper. She couldn't remember the last time she had used it.

Ildirans hurried toward her. One young man who looked faintly like Jora'h stepped forward, frowning curiously at her. 'Green priest, why are you trying to hide?'

In a flash Nira relived the repeated rapes, the times she had been locked in the breeding barracks. Those memories ricocheted like multiple gunshots in her head. Some of her abusers had been monsters in external appearance, others – like Udru'h himself – merely monsters inside. If she'd had the power, Nira would have willed herself to die, dropping lifeless in front of these Ildirans in a final gesture of defiance. But she had no way to accomplish that.

The Ildirans easily seized her. She could not break free, could not even struggle against their hold. Nira let her legs go limp, but the guards held her up, and dragged her towards the ships.

THIRTY-SEVEN

KOLKER

Without ever being told the reason for their brief confinement-to-quarters, the humans were once again given relative freedom in the Prism Palace. Kolker, though, remained sitting in the sunlight that shone through the broad windows. No matter where he went, the green priest knew he would still be alone, still cut off from the worldforest. And the silence in his mind was endlessly deafening.

Unless he could find the treeling that he sensed like the barest whisper at the edge of his imagination.

In telink, Kolker could always hear myriad voices in his head, a reassuring tapestry of minds and information, filled with thoughts the verdani had developed over thousands of years. He could exchange news with his fellow green priests, wherever they might be; even isolated aboard a cloud harvester, he had not been lonely. Kolker had never imagined he could lose it all. The touch of the worldtrees was infinitely far away. But if he could locate that treeling, he could restore contact, and his life would blossom again!

Sullivan Gold was concerned about Kolker's depression. 'If it's within my power, I'll get us out of here. You know I'm trying.' The facility manager's face sported grey beard stubble around his forced optimistic smile.

Kolker gave a sullen nod. Making Sullivan understand the loss of his connection to the verdani was like explaining to a man born blind the pain of never again seeing colours.

Sullivan went back to grumbling. 'There's not even anything to read! Sure, parts of *The Saga of Seven Suns* are translated, but I don't enjoy heroic folktales about a race that stabbed us in the back.' He picked up an Ildiran writing stylus and a thin sheet of diamondfilm to write another letter to his wife. Lydia was Sullivan's worldforest. He needed to share his experiences with her, even if the messages never found their way home.

A visitor appeared at the door – an old Ildiran with wattled, sagging skin even more greyish than that of most other kithmen. The man's thin limbs were like dry reeds; his head shook with a faint metronome of palsy. Finely spun robes hung like a tent over his fragile body. He was stooped, his hands extended forward as if ready to catch his balance should he fall. Frills of wispy grey hair dangled down from his high temples, covering the small stream- lined ears. His brow seemed permanently furrowed as if in deep concentration.

'My name is Tery'l.' The old man lifted a lovely reflective medallion at his throat; its circular face was etched with an interlinked design of circles and stylized solar symbols. 'I am a lens kithman. Might I speak with your green priest? I think we may have some things in common.'

'Things in common? You are held captive as well?' Kolker intentionally misunderstood. 'You are cut off from the very thing that gives your life meaning, like I am?'

He had hoped the ancient lens kithman would bridle, but

Tery'l only gave a placid shake of his head. 'Lens kithmen are shepherds of the *thism*. It occurred to me that our bond might be similar to the link between green priests and the worldtrees. I would like to tell you about the Lightsource and the soul threads that join us all. Perhaps they are manifestations of the same fabric that binds life and the universe.'

Offended, Kolker stood up. 'There are no similarities.'

Sullivan intercepted Tery'l, also angry. 'So now the Mage-Imperator sends missionaries to us? Are you trying to convert us into honorary Ildirans?'

The old man was befuddled. 'No, that is not possible. Only our people belong to the *thism* web.'

'Let me get this straight. You come here to spout your religion, and then tell us we can't possibly belong?'

'I was simply curious about your green priest.' Tery'l fingered his reflective medallion. 'I thought we would share an interesting discussion.'

Kolker stepped through the door and past the lens kithman without a backward glance. He had no interest in comparisons between telink and *thism*.

As he strode away, easily outpacing the old man, Kolker felt as if he were walking down the gullet of a rainbow. Aimlessly, he passed fountains, waterfalls, crystal sculptures. Here inside the enormous Prism Palace, with no worldtrees to guide him, he could wander for days. His head was utterly silent, empty of telink or any faint whisper of Ildiran *thism*. Except . . .

From the faintest thread in the corner of his mind he felt the treeling's whisper. As he walked, he became more convinced it was close by. The honey-warm familiarity was unmistakable. Kolker made his way through the elaborate Palace like a hunter following a breath of smoke in the air. He didn't know how to search for a small worldtree he could not see.

He crossed walkways, entered large chambers, drifted past courtiers and bureaucrat kithmen. Occasionally he glanced over his shoulder and saw guards; they noted his location, but did not follow him. He found the lax security odd, but if all Ildirans shared a general pattern of thoughts, then they would trust each other. Their race probably didn't know how to do otherwise. But why did they need so damned many guards everywhere?

Kolker concentrated on his mission, pushing all questions aside. If he found the treeling, he would need only a moment. If he could just have a taste of telink again, the hunger in his mind would be quieted.

He skirted the skysphere reception hall. Might the Mage-Imperator keep a treeling next to the chrysalis chair? Inside the great hall, Jora'h held court before a small group of pilgrims. Wary, the guard Yazra'h took two steps from her position near the dais, watching the green priest. Kolker backed away before their gazes could lock. His faint senses tugged him in another direction.

Kolker rapidly entered another segment of the labyrinthine halls, focused on the tiny tingle in his mind. After many twistings and turnings, climbing ramps and glassy stairs, he found himself in a sheltered level beneath one of the Prism Palace's secondary domes: the Mage-Imperator's private contemplation chambers. He sensed the tiny melody in his mind and knew he was close. The treeling was in there! Kolker felt anticipation build like a parched man smelling a cool stream just ahead.

Then far behind him, he spotted Yazra'h and her Isix cats emerging from a stair platform. She had followed him after all! Yazra'h did not call out a warning, but broke into a run as soon as she saw where Kolker was. Her cats leapt in front of her.

Kolker ducked into the chamber. Just a moment, just one moment! Frantically looking around, he saw the treeling in an alcove on the curved wall. It was several years old, thin and spindly but strong. The feathery fronds seemed to tremble. The long-anticipated sight was so precious to him that he froze for just an instant.

Yazra'h bounded into the chamber. Her voice was as threatening as a predator's growl. 'Do not move.'

Kolker lunged forward, his outstretched hands desperate to touch the tree. One brief moment of contact would signal to every green priest across the Spiral Arm. His fingers almost brushed the delicate gold-scale bark. *Almost—*

One of the Isix cats jumped onto his back and drove him to the floor. As he fell, his fingertip brushed the smooth side of the treeling's pot, then slid away. The ornate pot wobbled in the alcove.

He sprawled on the cool, smooth floor, sure the cat would rip him to shreds. The animal was heavy on top of him, growling deep in its throat; the pointed tips of its long claws bit into his green skin.

So close! The treeling was so close! Kolker used all his strength to push himself up again, but a second cat came between him and the treeling, quietly snarling. Kolker grew wild, thrashing, giving a wordless cry.

Yazra'h uttered quick, soothing words to the cats, and the predators withdrew. She seized his arms with a grip like a set of steel manacles.

Kolker looked at the treeling, separated by an infinite gulf of only a few inches, and he began to sob.

THIRTY-EIGHT

MAGE-IMPERATOR JORA'H

Jora'h rushed from the skysphere at the head of a group of guard kithmen. When he reached his contemplation chamber, he found Yazra'h still blocking the green priest from the treeling. Her cats prowled and paced. His daughter remained cool and strong, but it was clear she was fighting impatience. He knew she wanted to unleash her cats. 'Hold,' Jora'h said.

He stared at Kolker, who squatted on the floor holding his knees, weeping. His head was lowered, chin tucked against his chest, but the green priest could not keep his eyes from the treeling. Like a shiing addict, he kept glancing towards it, then at Jora'h, desperate and pleading.

'The green priest knows you have a treeling, Liege,' Yazra'h said. 'If there are ... things you wish to keep from the humans, then you can not let him live.'

Jora'h met her gaze. 'I will not have you kill him.'

Kolker had seemed broken and lost since arriving here from Qronha 3. Remembering how vitally connected Nira had been to her treeling, he thought he understood the withdrawal this

182

green priest was experiencing. Perhaps it was like an Ildiran suffering in complete isolation, without the reassuring touch of *thism*. How could he not sympathize?

Kolker climbed to his feet, red-eyed. 'Please. I *have* to touch the forest mind. I am blind and starving without telink.' He glared at Yazra'h. 'She thinks I was trying to betray you. I just needed to contact the trees. That's all.'

The Mage-Imperator regarded the green priest. Was he lying, or just naive? 'Contact with your worldtrees would send a signal to all your counterparts. Every green priest would know what you know.'

'No. It doesn't work like that. Besides, I don't know anything!'

'You know you are alive, along with all the other Hansa skyminers, who are presumed dead. You know that we have not let you go home. And you have seen the hydrogues here. I cannot let that knowledge reach the humans. The Ildiran Empire cannot risk it.' Jora'h felt a knot in his chest and heard an echo of his father's twisted plans in his head. 'I am sorry for what I am forced to do, but I have no choice. I never wanted to hold you here.'

'Then let us go free! We're no threat to you.' The green priest truly did not understand.

Jora'h gestured. 'Hold him.'

Two guards folded in beside Kolker to take his arms, but he was meek and submissive. Yazra'h tossed her long coppery hair and looked at her father. 'I will increase our security. This cannot happen again.'

'That will not be necessary.' Jora'h closed his eyes, holding the thoughts inside his hammering head. 'I have a better solution.'

He picked up the potted treeling. Looking at the delicate fronds and slender trunk, he was amazed that such a small plant could have so many tremendous repercussions. There was a power here that neither he nor any other Ildiran understood. He fondly recalled Queen Estarra's recent visit along with King Peter and Chairman Wenceslas. Jora'h had been honoured to receive the treeling as a gift. Now he recognized the danger it posed.

As black jaws of regret clamped down on his heart, Jora'h carried the pot to the high balcony. He stood outside where the light was clear and the clean winds were brisk against his face. His long braid twitched.

Behind him, his arms held by guards, Kolker struggled in growing horror. 'What are you going to do?'

From the high balcony, the view was spectacular, showing the faceted skyline of great buildings and towers. Here, Jora'h had stood with Nira. The beautiful green priest had laughed at how the balcony's slight curvature and the transparent floor segments made her feel as if the two of them were floating on air. How he missed her. He hoped she and Osira'h were together now, and that both of them could one day forgive him.

When Jora'h gazed out over his city, foremost in his mind was how the hydrogues had threatened to destroy the whole Ildiran Empire. Until he found a way to defeat the deep-core aliens, he knew only one way to escape that, even if he cursed himself for it. The humans could not know.

He held the potted treeling out over the open air. Kolker screamed. 'No! Please, don't! You can't!'

Jora'h could not allow himself to be swayed. As a wave of self-disappointment rippled through his chest, he opened his fingers, and the pot fell. Buffeted by the breezes, it tumbled twice, dwindling to a speck, and then smashed against the interlocked paving stones.

Now there were no treelings on Ildira. The threat was gone. Behind him, he could hear Kolker's miserable sobs, but he refused to turn around. 'Now you can take him back to his people. There is nothing more to worry about.'

Alone on the balcony, Jora'h's eyes filled with hot tears. He stared across the city for a long time, seeing nothing. Again, he wished Nira could be there with him. Would she hate him for what he had just done? How much would this all cost him?

I am becoming more and more like my father every day.

THIRTY-NINE

RLINDA KETT

I ce shards showered down like broken glass. BeBob yelped when a fist-sized chunk struck him on the shoulder. 'The sky is falling!'

Freezing mist spangled the air. Rlinda could not tell how close the reanimated woman was to shattering the ceiling. If she broke through the crust, all the atmosphere trapped underground would erupt like a volcano of air. Karla Tamblyn seemed intent on knocking down every solid wall, levelling every unnatural structure, turning all of Plumas into a slurry of rubble and water.

Karla gestured towards the water-dissociation plant, breaking pipes and releasing jets of stored gas. Fortunately, nothing exploded. Yet.

Scrambling along as low and out of sight as possible, Rlinda and BeBob hid behind mounds of piled snow and frost, wove among conduits and the wreckage of smashed huts. Sooty residue rose from burst fuel containers and combustible materials in the habitation domes. Vaporized ice and water formed a fog that was as good as a smokescreen. Even when Rlinda couldn't see what was happening, the din was enough to set her teeth on edge.

Directed by Karla's demonic force, hundreds of scarlet nematodes swarmed forward, like a basket of angry cobras dumped onto the ice. Their rudimentary brains weren't sufficient for complex hunting behaviour, but the creatures could sense movement and heat. Their smooth bodies hissed across the icepack, and their round mouths emitted eerie hooting sounds. Looking at them, Rlinda could tell these creatures were not self-aware, but mere tools of the reanimated woman.

As patchy mist drifted in and out, Rlinda watched three water miners stand their ground against the worms that writhed forward like inflated bags of blood. Two jabbed and poked with makeshift spears while the third man hammered with a club.

The nearest nematode convulsed, contracted, and squirmed, but the concerted blows were too much. The skin split open, and bright red fluid splashed the ice. The miners barely managed a cheer before dozens more worms lunged at them.

Without thinking, Rlinda grabbed her shovel and barked at BeBob. 'Come on!' Springing several metres with each bound – she loved low gravity! – she flew in among the chewing nematodes. With her wide shovel, she knocked aside several of the heavy, soft worms. A backstroke with the flat blade splattered another one against the ice. BeBob used his tool like a gravedigger's spade, driving the edge down on a flaccid body and cutting it in two. He scowled as thick gelatinous blood sprayed him, but turned his attention to five more nematodes coming at him.

'I wish I knew what we did to piss that lady off,' BeBob said.

The three water miners were yelling and fighting, smashing and chopping the worms, but the numbers didn't seem to be diminishing. Rlinda swung her shovel, each time rewarded with a hard, wet impact. Elsewhere in the wrecked base, dozens of groups clustered together to make their last stands.

Karla continued her rampage, striding into the centre of the mining base. From the other side of the settlement, two men yelled something and then unleashed a gushing explosion. The twins Wynn and Torin had hooked a wide-diameter outflow tube to an emergency valve on one of the pipes that pumped water to the surface. They struggled to direct the explosive stream toward the reanimated woman. The torrent swept over Karla in a storm of frigid water, but she anchored herself like a statue. A flash-frozen wall of ice rose around her, creating a shield. As the high-pressure jet continued to bombard her, the frozen shield thickened, encapsulating Karla.

The twins shouted over the roar of the flow. 'We've trapped her!'

As if she'd heard them, Karla shattered the cement-like white shell and easily parted the spray of water. With another burst of power, she sent a shockwave that backed up through the emergency valve and burst the treetrunk-thick pipe. Frigid water exploded everywhere at once. Wynn and Torin dived out of the way.

Closer to Rlinda, one of the miners slipped on the ice, jabbing his spear in a last attempt to save himself. More than a dozen nematodes plunged in, tiny diamond teeth fastening, then chewing. The other Roamers tried to defend their fallen friend, but another mass of worms struck them from behind. Too many.

Rlinda watched the men die, but when four nematodes reared up in front of her, she couldn't spare any time for the horror welling up within her. She swung the shovel like a Viking swinging an axe on a battlefield. BeBob was barely holding his own, and then the handle of his shovel cracked. Time for Plan B.

'Can you run faster than a worm, BeBob?' Rlinda delivered a few blows to clear the way, and they sprinted across the uneven icepack, dodging among half-ruined structures. When another nematode lunged, Rlinda swung one of her heavy legs, hitting the worm's soft membrane with her thick insulated boot. The hissing creature tumbled sideways. Rlinda made a disgusted face. 'Like stepping in a bag of wet, runny shit.'

'There's a lot more!' BeBob pointed to a new group of nematodes that squirmed in their direction, hissing and hooting. 'Thousands, I think.'

Rlinda made a snap decision. 'We've got to make it to the lift shaft and ride our way to the surface. Unless you plan to squash them all?'

'Not me – my arm's already tired.'

Though the mist and smoke made it difficult to see, they ran. She and BeBob outdistanced the squirming nematodes, but Rlinda assumed the two of them were still being tracked.

As she had anticipated, an equipment shed stood unlocked next to the elevator, whose shaft ran parallel to one of the primary water wellheads. Always before, the Plumas workers had guarded the lift shafts to make sure the two hostages couldn't escape. Now, though, the Roamers were rather preoccupied.

'Something's hit the lift, Rlinda.' BeBob indicated a dark blotch next to the controls. 'The access door is off track and wedged open.'

'Better jammed open than shut. Or would you rather circle the base, find another lift, and hope that one's in better shape?'

With haunted eyes, he glanced back to see the cadre of scarlet nematodes coming closer, fixated on attacking them. The squirming worms were unbelievably single-minded. 'Uh, no thanks. Let's try this one.'

Rlinda yanked open the shed to reveal a rack of heavy-duty environment suits. She threw an average-sized one to BeBob and ransacked the garments, hoping to find one large enough to accommodate her. 'Roamers are so damned lean and trim!' She went through one after another, breathing heavily, aware of how little time they had. She couldn't drive away the image of the hapless Roamer men who had fallen to the nematodes, their skin chewed away.

Rlinda saw the approaching nematodes as serpentine shadows in the curling mist. She grabbed the largest of the available suits. 'I hope this thing stretches.' She bounded to the damaged lift doors, which hung partly open like the slack mouth of a man who had died from a spacesuit rupture. 'We'll get dressed inside the chamber. Quit dawdling!'

BeBob didn't need further encouragement. 'At least the car is where it's supposed to be.' Rlinda struggled to manhandle the damaged doors shut, but they were caught. As the nematodes squirmed forward like drunken inchworms, she decided there was no time for niceties. She pushed the controls, and after a brief, unpleasant grinding sound, the lift began to crawl upward.

'We'll be fine now,' she said loudly enough to try to convince herself as well as BeBob. Adrenaline made time slow around her, now that she realized how close they'd come to being killed. 'The nematodes won't bother to follow us. Out of sight, out of mind.'

BeBob was fumbling to put on his suit. 'Yeah, but they're being guided by that demon woman. And she really doesn't seem the forgetful type.'

'How can they climb up the shaft? They're just worms.'

'Worms with very pointy teeth.' He fastened his belt, connected the air-regulator. 'Didn't you see how easily they slithered up the walls in the grotto?'

'You've got a cheery answer for everything, don't you?' Rlinda struggled with her too-small suit, getting both feet inside but not making much more progress than that. 'I'm going to need your help with this, BeBob.'

'As soon as I figure the suit out for myself,' he answered, still

190

fumbling with the unfamiliar garment. He pulled his arms into the sleeves, attached one of the gloves, then nodded. 'Not like Hansa designs, but it's a lot easier to don.'

'We need to be all dressed and ready to go as soon as we reach the surface.' Once they cycled through the external airlock, they could run across the ice to the waiting *Curiosity*. Already she imagined they were home free. 'I sure hope we take off before the ice ceiling collapses beneath us.'

She tugged on the reinforced multilayer fabric, working her way into the suit. It wasn't quite stretchy enough. BeBob, who was mostly dressed except for his helmet and left glove, worked with her, massaging her into the constricting legs and sleeves.

'I was never a big fan of form fitting garments,' Rlinda said.

Beneath the lift's floor, a bone-chilling sound grew louder . . . whispery, like wet socks being swirled in a glass bottle. BeBob looked at his feet. 'They're climbing up the shaft after us.'

'Actually, I think they got to one of the lift-stage platforms. Now they've crawled onto the reinforcement struts on our undercarriage.'

'In other words, they're right under our feet.' He looked down, alarmed. She pulled his attention back to helping her with the suit. BeBob swallowed hard. 'Maybe it's only one or two of them.'

The first one struck the underside of the lift chamber with enough force to make a visible dent in the inner floor. The lift lurched, then slowed as if suddenly weighed down. 'Uh, Rlinda . . .'

'Let me think a minute, BeBob.'

With another slam, several more nematodes smashed the elevator and anchored themselves to the pipes and struts beneath the lifting chamber. Then came a chilling scraping sound as the worms, with their small diamond teeth, began to chew through the metal floor.

FORTY

GENERAL KURT LANYAN

With each passing second, the stolen battle group got farther away.

General Lanyan leaned forward on the uncomfortable bench of the troop transport racing after the Grid 0 ships. 'You sure this is our best speed, Mr Carrera? We've got a tough job ahead of us.' Though the kleebs had completed plenty of simulations, he feared they weren't ready for blood-in-the-face combat. Today, they damned well needed to be.

'Doing my best, sir.' Sweat glistened on his forehead. 'But if we pull too far ahead of the others, our ship will be a vulnerable target. The Soldier compies could decide to do a little practice shooting with their jazers.'

Lanyan grumbled. 'So noted. Keep everyone together, but keep hauling ass.' They'd been under heavy acceleration for an hour, and already it seemed like for ever. His pulse pounded, his mind intense as he turned his full attention to the hunt.

While Ensign Carrera concentrated on flying, Lanyan activated the short-range comm and transmitted to all ships in his makeshift cavalry. 'Somebody give me a full inventory. Ships and weapons. We need to make our first punch a knockout blow.' He could sense their uneasiness. 'Come on, you've drilled this often enough! Power all jazer banks to full strength, even on approach. Make sure our shaped charges, fraks, and slammers are ready to go.'

'Is it going to be enough, General?' said the nearest kleeb, an innocent-faced redhead with a rash of freckles on his cheeks.

'Of course it is.'

Requests for immediate reinforcements had already been sent to the bases on the Moon and Mars, but the General did not intend to sit on the sidelines in the meantime and give the compies time to dig in.

'Targets detected ahead, sir,' Carrera said. 'Intercept in five minutes.'

A glimmer of tiny dots looked as if someone had thrown quartz sand into a bright light. The stolen Juggernaut, Mantas, and Thunderheads were on their way out of the solar system towards whatever rendezvous the insidious compies had planned. As Lanyan's rescue squad closed the gap, the twinkling spots resolved into angular silhouettes.

'How come I can see thrusters? God damn, are they turning about?'

'They're slowing and pivoting, General. I think they see us coming.' Carrera ran another sensor scan. 'Their weapons are preparing to fire! Railgun launchers and jazers pointed right at us.'

'Don't give them an easy target.' Precision-controlled Soldier compies would be expert marksmen, regardless of how the response group distributed itself. Sensing the tension surge in the troop transport, he said, 'Remember your training! This is exactly what you've been prepared to do.'

'Sir, we've only got small ships. None of us can withstand a direct hit.'

'Have a little faith, Mr Carrera. Just get us closer. I need another second.'

The clusters of ships careened towards each other. Lanyan's recruits were ready for a free-for-all. 'Shall we open fire, sir? We're in range.'

'Not yet. *This* is my opening salvo.' He manually switched to an elite communications band that was wired into the bridges of all EDF battleships and pushed the transmit button. 'Confirm voiceprint: General Kurt Lanyan. Identification 88RI Alpha.'

His pursuit ships continued to close the gap. The hijacked vessels loomed closer and closer, weapons ports open and primed. The robot-controlled *Goliath* looked huge. Lanyan sat back and smiled.

Lifting his finger from the transmit button, he waited a moment until he received automatic confirmation. Then he said, 'Engage guillotine protocol.'

The pilot barely squeaked out his words. 'That's . . . it?'

Suddenly the running lights on the compy-controlled ships dimmed and went out. The Grid 0 vessels froze in space. Their engines shut down, cutting all thrust. They drifted with only the momentum they retained.

'We've just pulled the plug on their little escape operation.' The General was amused at his stunned-silent crew. 'They're dead in space.'

Sensor technicians aboard the cavalry ships scrambled to take readings. A milky-skinned young woman looked at Lanyan from her cockpit station. 'Confirmed. Their energy readings are fading to ambient, sir. Weapons systems are inactive.'

Lanyan threaded his thick fingers together and locked them behind his head. 'Even if Soldier compies kill our crews and take over our ships, the control computers belong to *me*.'

The guillotine protocol had been specifically designed to stall a mutiny, to prevent anyone from stealing a ship.

The cavalry fleet glided closer to the Juggernaut, the most important target. 'Now it's time to take everything back. I want my ships!' He cracked his knuckles. 'But be prepared – it might get a little messy. Every soldier will carry a sidearm. Distribute the heavy weaponry as far as it'll go. Don't expect these clankers to give up without a fight.'

Lanyan issued orders for his recruits to suit up in special body armour. Similar teams were getting ready aboard all the hastily called vessels. A few pilots and trainees would remain aboard the gunships as a back-up measure, but most of the recruits were in for a long and sweaty day of hard combat.

In the troop transport's cold rear compartment, the General suited up, attaching powerpaks to his alloy-reinforced garb. Finished, he stood before the breathless kleebs, and his speech was piped to all the waiting armoured trainees. 'Those compies took over our ships and slaughtered unarmed crews.' He smiled inside his helmet, clicked his faceplate into place, and activated the suit microphone. 'Now let's go start stomping some robot asses!'

It would have been a lot easier just to destroy the crippled ships so the compies couldn't fly off. But Lanyan wasn't about to give up all those armoured vessels without a fight. He had an uneasy feeling that Earth might need them.

Demolitions techs were the first to emerge, drifting over to the disabled Juggernaut and planting explosive charges against the cargo bay hull. 'Proceed,' Lanyan said. 'Assume that everyone on board is dead.' *Or expendable.*

The demolitions techs jetted out of the way. As the shaped explosives ignited, the Juggernaut's cargo bay cracked open, decompressing the lower decks. Atmosphere vomited out, sweeping dozens of Soldier compies out into the cold vacuum, where they flailed and drifted. Lanyan watched them float away, knowing it wouldn't be so easy to get rid of the rest.

His group of suited fighters adjusted their acceleration packs, checked air tanks and weapons charges, and prepared to jump across the dizzying gulf.

'Let's get started,' Lanyan said. 'We've got a lot of ships to take back today.'

FORTY-ONE

ROSSIA

Though he continued to send reports through his treeling, Rossia could see that they had lost the fight, lost the Juggernaut, and lost the whole Grid 5 battle group. The compies kept coming and coming. He hadn't heard messages from any other EDF green priests in a long time now.

Outside the *Eldorado*'s bridge, blood painted the corridor walls in red abstract patterns. Though the Soldier compies could easily have yanked a few still-charged weapons from their victims, instead they used their metal and polymer-sheathed arms as bludgeons. They were in no hurry now.

Grid 5's Mantas had been subsumed, and the cruisers had withdrawn, waiting for the inevitable end. Soldier compies controlled all command bridges except for the *Eldorado*. Rossia could see it would not be long; he communicated as much through the treeling. By now the delicate gold-scale bark looked worn from his insistent touching.

Long ago, when the wyvern had snatched him from the

Theron treetops, Rossia had been sure he was going to die. Now, he had the same feeling.

But Admiral Eolus wasn't done yet. He prowled the barricaded bridge, his shoulders squared, his thick arms swinging from side to side. 'Come on then,' he snarled at the compies, using his loudest voice. 'Or are you afraid to get a little dented?'

The bridge defenders had put up a valiant fight, but it was a hopeless last stand. As they saw death approaching, one by one the soldiers volunteered to throw themselves against the massed Soldier compies, protecting Admiral Eolus for just a few minutes more.

Rossia squeezed his eyes shut, unable to bear seeing any more blood. He gripped his treeling. 'I just received word from Nahton. Even the Palace District compy factory has turned into a battle zone. I'm the only green priest still alive in any battle group – unless the others are just separated from their treelings.' He blinked his eyes and looked around for reassurance. 'Maybe that's it. Maybe they're still alive.'

Now only the green priest, a station officer, and the security chief remained alive alongside the gruff Admiral. As compies tossed the last of the uniformed corpses aside, Eolus apparently decided enough was enough.

'Screw this, by God. Cut off access to the bridge! Sergeant Briggs, grab the repair kits and start welding around that seam. We've got enough epoxy solder to hold the doors together.' He knotted his fingers together, glowering at fate. 'And I was looking forward to retirement with a beer on a beach, but I guess we're not going out for any moonlight strolls.'

The security chief was already rummaging through a sealed storage bin at an empty station. 'Epoxy solder won't last long, Admiral.'

'Doesn't have to last for ever, Sergeant. Just long enough. It's time to make these clanking bastards pay.' The Admiral looked at the viewscreen, saw his eleven overthrown Mantas hovering nearby, like hyenas waiting to close in on a carcass. 'Those tin soldiers haven't just defeated us. They stole our own battleships – and that makes me very angry!'

Briggs was on his knees in front of the sealed bridge door, squeezing epoxy weld into all the cracks. He jumped back as compy hands began to batter the metal barrier until it bowed inward. The gap between the sliding doors widened enough for one compy to thrust fingers through. Briggs squirted the armour solder, filling in the seal and welding the compy's hand into the gap.

At the navigation station, a grim Eolus began to move the *Eldorado*, easing it towards the group of hijacked Mantas.

Briggs looked up. 'It's holding, Admiral.' He had used up his tubes, slathering the fast-hardening substance all around the entrance. The survivors knew they would never get out. This bridge would be their tomb.

One of the wall plates buckled. Unable to break open the welded door, the compies began to rip their way directly through the bulkheads. 'Oh, for crying out loud!' Briggs blurted.

'This is really messed up,' said the station officer, shaking her head. 'Really messed up.'

'How long did you say this barricade has to last, Admiral?' Briggs asked.

Hunched over the command chair, Eolus gradually accelerated the Juggernaut. 'Easy ... easy ... not enough to scare them. Nothing to worry about, little robots.' As the *Eldorado* approached the waiting Mantas, the compies would assume the flagship had been captured as well.

Out-of-control robots continued to batter the walls, ripping away the plates, thrusting their metal hands through. A crack appeared in the fresh polymer weld, and the whole main bridge door began to shudder.

'It's not going to hold.' Briggs looked down at his empty tubes of epoxy.

Rossia repeated the words into his treeling, sending out a continuous message. He felt detached from everything that was happening around him; it was the only way he could keep functioning. 'It's not going to hold.'

'Now, worst part in a commander's career.' Admiral Eolus looked at the three survivors with him. 'You are not stupid. You all know what we have to do. We can't let compies seize our battle group, and I don't believe in a completely hopeless situation.'

Eolus expected and received no argument from his comrades. He paced, ignoring the battering sounds of compies on the other side of the wall. 'Mr Rossia, inform the rest of the EDF what we plan to accomplish here. That way at least they'll know.'

After the green priest sent a last message through his treeling, he turned his cockeyed gaze up at the man. 'Did you know I'm the only person in the history of Theroc to survive a wyvern attack? Everyone thought I was very lucky.' He paused, the silence broken only by the clamour of Soldier compies. 'I'm not going to survive this one, though.'

'No, Mr Rossia. None of us are.'

As the *Eldorado* eased in amongst the waiting Mantas, Eolus input the command string that every commanding officer knew and hoped never to use. The Juggernaut's computers accepted the emergency verification, and the massive engines grew hotter and hotter, building to a swift overload. The swarthy man muted the countdown. 'Damn thing's too melodramatic.' He sat back in his command chair, thick arms crossed over his chest.

With a coordinated surge, the Soldier compies broke through the doorwelds and ripped support bars out of the bulkhead wall, knocking aside plate sheeting. Now with nothing to stop them, the military robots streamed onto the bridge. Alarms began to sound at all stations, warning of imminent danger – as if any bridge crew member could possibly be unaware that a truckload of crap had just hit a turbine-powered fan.

Briggs threw himself bodily against the compies, but the robots swept over him like a tidal wave overwhelming a bit of dandelion fluff. The compies were covered with blood.

Admiral Eolus swivelled his chair. The countdown on his panel reached the last few seconds. 'Here's something special for you, you wind-up bastards,' Eolus said. 'Bend over and smile.'

Self-destruct routines turned the *Eldorado* into a small-scale supernova, and the shockwave swept outwards to engulf all eleven captured Mantas.

FORTY-TWO

NIRA

The flight to the Dobro settlement was torture. Designate Udru'h would never have gone to such great lengths unless he had some dark plan in mind.

Wrapped in her own misery, Nira wasn't fooled when the Ildiran noble attempted to show concern. Once more she noted that his features reminded her of Jora'h. 'I am Designate-in-waiting Daro'h,' he finally said. 'I will soon assume the administration duties of Dobro and replace the current Designate.'

Nira's eyes flashed. Udru'h was going to step down!

Daro'h pressed, 'I still do not understand why you fled. We are taking you back to the splinter colony, back to your home.'

'It is not my home! It was never my home. And it's not the home of those human descendants you keep caged there, either.'

Clearly discomfited, Daro'h fell silent. They rode the rest of the way without speaking another word.

When the guards dragged her out of the hatch, Nira felt a discordant wash of joy, a flood of giddy relief, a foreign outburst that sang through her thoughts. It was a symphony of love, relief, and longing. Confusingly, the non-verbal images seemed to be reflections of her own memories.

She stumbled, and her eyes focused on a young girl, older than she remembered, but still more familiar than any other person: a part of her and a part of Jora'h. Her daughter, her princess! Osira'h ran forward to embrace her.

As soon as she made contact with her daughter's skin, Nira expected a wash of new memories, an exchange. She remembered the sudden bursting of gates within their minds during the last – and only – time mother and daughter had been in contact. She had been so desperate then, crying out with her thoughts.

Now, however, Nira was afraid to push too much. This time, the contact was not the same as she had previously shared with her daughter. Only silence rang inside her head.

Osira'h, too, seemed to be holding back. 'You don't need to know everything yet, Mother. You can't know everything.'

Nira just held her more tightly. 'I don't need it all at once. I just need to know that I'm back here with you.'

She felt a sudden chill and looked up. Hard-faced Designate Udru'h walked forward, flanked by two guard kithmen just like the ones that had beaten her nearly to death. Cool and aloof, he said, 'The Mage-Imperator asked me to find you. By trying to escape, you made it more difficult for all of us, including yourself.' When he looked at Nira, she recalled again the pain this man had caused her, all the hatred she still felt for him. Nira held her daughter protectively; Osira'h hugged back, offering her mother strength and confidence.

Dismissively, Udru'h turned towards the Designate-in-waiting. 'Good work, Daro'h. I will soon be ready to relinquish my duties to you.'

FORTY-THREE

ANTON COLICOS

A nton looked up from his scrutiny of dusty diamondfilm
sheets in the vaults beneath the Prism Palace. 'These stories
are so vague! I wouldn't put much credence in old folktales.'

Vao'sh would not be swayed. 'The Mage-Imperator gave me
an assignment to find any information about the ancient war with
the hydrogues, especially tales of a supposed alliance between
Ildirans and faeros. This is where we must look.' The expressive
lobes on his face flushed with colour. 'There will be more in the
stockpile of ancient records on Hyrillka. I hope they were not
damaged in the recent revolt – I wish you could go with me.'

'Me too, but nobody will let me out of Mijistra.' He still didn't
have any explanations.

Flanked by her Isix cats, Yazra'h approached the two storytellers deep in the subterranean tunnels. Recently, she'd been
childishly entertained by Anton's traditional Earth stories, though
she often asked odd questions. 'If Little Red Riding Hood was
going through dark and dangerous woods, why did she not carry a
weapon in her basket?' Or, 'If Goldilocks knew she was trespassing

in the home of the three bears, should she not have remained more alert when she chose to sleep in their beds? Should she not have set a guard to watch over her?' When Yazra'h complained about so many weak female children, Anton finally delighted her with stories of Amazon warrior women, Queen Boudicca, and even the historical comic book character Wonder Woman.

When the three Isix cats glided forward to sniff Anton's fingers, he absently scratched the head of the nearest cat, and the other two came forward for their share of attention. Yazra'h was always astonished by her deadly pets' behaviour around him, though Anton wasn't. 'A cat is a scholar's best friend. I can't tell you how many hours I spent translating epics with a cat curled on my lap. It helps concentration, you know.'

Yazra'h frowned at her Isix cats as if disappointed in them. The animals blinked up at her, but did not move away from Anton's scratching fingers. 'It seems they approve of you. We should spend more time together.'

Anton suddenly felt intimidated by Yazra'h's lithe beauty, her strength, her confidence. 'Uh, normally I only talk with shy academics.'

She flexed her arms. 'You have shown me your stories. I invite you now to exercise with me on a combat field.' She cocked her eyebrows. 'It is my way of returning the favour.'

He laughed. 'I prefer enjoying great battles vicariously. I already did my heroic deed on Maratha. That's quite enough for a simple historian.'

'As you wish,' she said. 'Then you can come and watch me.'

As she led him through the training grounds, the clamour was deafening. Anton stuck close beside the bronzed woman, who seemed anything but threatened by the howling, bone-jarring crashes. Instead, Yazra'h revelled in the sights, the sweat, the excitement. Her cats prowled along beside them, ranging afield, sniffing at the muscular fighters, but always coming back to her.

'I love to watch combat.' Her voice was warm with approval. 'Each soldier has the same training but slightly different skills. Thus, each match is unpredictable.'

Two heavily armoured guards clashed crystal katanas against each other. They moved in a choreographed dance, parrying edges with edges, straining, grunting. Blood splattered from a thousand shallow cuts and injuries, but the fighters hardly seemed to notice.

Anton winced. 'And you ... spend your free time training here?'

'I have defeated many of these men myself, though only half of my blood comes from the soldier kith.'

'I hope you don't ever want to fight with me! I've got nothing to prove. You'd defeat me – and that's an understatement.'

She smiled down at him with genuine amusement. 'That would be a most unfair match, Rememberer Anton. If we should encounter great peril, I would use my strength to defend *you*.' Her lips quirked upwards. 'Afterwards, you could use your talents to tell tales of my prowess. That would please me.'

'It's a deal.'

Out in the open field, Ildirans hurled themselves against each other with great gusto. They let out bestial howls as they fought with sheer fury, hammering at each other with heavy clubs and slender, mirrored blades.

Anton wondered why the Ildiran military spent so much time preparing for ground combat. A standing army? Were these soldiers anticipating a fight that Anton didn't know about? Against whom? Even these armoured warriors could not possibly stand against hydrogues. Who else might they be pitted against? Klikiss robots? He hoped they'd go after some payback, considering what the black monstrosities had done to his companions on Maratha.

In a packed clay arena, movable mirrors were set up against the low walls. Riders in polished armour sat astride lizard-like creatures, carrying laser lances which they fired at their opponents' half-reflective shields.

'One day I will take you to an Ildiran jousting match,' Yazra'h said. 'It is our greatest sport. You will enjoy it.'

Anton watched the sluggish beasts, saw the riders jabbing their lances in a confusing play of mirrors and shields. 'I've never been much of a sports fan.'

'Nevertheless, you will enjoy Ildiran jousting.'

'Doesn't sound like you're giving me any choice in the matter.'

'I am not.'

As the two of them walked among the combatants, he wondered if Yazra'h was walking with him because she enjoyed his company, or if she had been ordered to keep an eye on him. The Ildirans still pretended he was a welcome guest in the Prism Palace, but the atmosphere was much different from when he had first arrived to study the *Saga*. Now he held plenty of suspicions that something unpleasant was going on, something they did not want him to know.

On impulse he looked at Yazra'h's exotic face as she led him from the jousting arena. 'Would you like to hear a story?'

'Is it a dramatic one with brave heroes and many fallen enemies?'

'No. It's one about ambition and consequences, the cautionary tale of a man named Faust.' He described, as best he remembered, Goethe's epic tale of a man's downfall, how Faust had agreed to sacrifice his soul to the devil in exchange for perfect happiness, and even then had spent his life searching for what he desired. Faust had got exactly what he wanted, only to discover that his wants had changed. The price of his bargain had nearly destroyed him.

Yazra'h appeared troubled. 'I did not care for that story. The man Faust made a poor choice and then complained about the terms he had accepted. He was without honour.'

'Sometimes the bargain itself is without honour,' Anton pointed out. 'Faust was damned from the moment he was *offered* the choice. From that point on, given who he was, he had no option.'

'He should never have asked for the choice to begin with.' For Yazra'h, every decision was clear-cut, black and white. She turned her attention to a particularly furious battle between two huge soldiers. Like giant fighting machines, they pounded each other, barely bothering to parry or dodge, each simply trying to overwhelm his opponent with brute strength and persistence.

'Yazra'h,' Anton finally asked, 'all those hydrogue warglobes that came to Ildira. They left without firing a single shot. What's going on?' She fixed her gaze on the two duelling soldiers, no longer the least bit flirtatious. 'Are you just going to give me the silent treatment? If I'm stuck here, don't I have the right to know?'

'The Mage-Imperator decides what we should know. It is not for me to say.' Then, as the interminable clash continued, she tried to discuss the nuances of fighting technique, as if she thought he could be distracted so easily. She never answered his question, which in itself was enough of an answer.

FORTY-FOUR

MAGE-IMPERATOR JORA'H

W hen Yazra'h found him on the high, glittering rooftops of the Prism Palace, Jora'h thought his daughter intended to scold him for standing in the open, unguarded. But he was confident the hydrogues wouldn't come back to destroy him – not yet. The deep-core aliens had far more insidious plans.

He gestured her forward as he stared at the sweeping geometric skyline of his grand city. 'I came up here myself because I am troubled.'

He glanced over the edge to the drop far, far below to the spot where the potted treeling had shattered on the interlocked paving stones. Scurrying servant kithmen had scoured away every last speck so no one could see the mark, but for Jora'h the stain was still there. It would always be there. The very thought of what he had done filled Jora'h with revulsion. He knew what Nira would think, if he ever did manage to bring her back to the Prism Palace. *The things I have done . . . and the things I may still have to do.*

Yazra'h came to stand beside him. When he saw her

expression, he knew that she had different concerns. 'Father – Liege – I must speak with you. I need to make a request.' He could not remember when she had ever asked anything of him. 'I do not question the wisdom of keeping certain information from the human government, but neither can I forget that their skyminers helped so many Ildirans. I was there. I was proud of them.'

Jora'h nodded. 'Sullivan Gold and his companions do not deserve what we have done to them. We should be allies. We should trust them.' A stern frown crossed his face. 'However, we cannot. They have seen things the rest of humanity cannot know.' He thought of the Dobro breeding programme and the long-imprisoned descendants of the *Burton*. 'And there are other secrets that would make the humans turn their military might against us.'

She stiffened, automatically on guard and full of bravado. 'We could still defeat them, Liege.'

'I do not wish to fight them at all!'

'Then what are we to do with the humans you keep here? Blindfold them and lock them up? Kill them?'

'No!'

Her eyes were golden and intense, her face strong with determination. 'Or tell them the truth?'

He lowered his voice, though no one else was near them. 'If my experts do not find a way to fight the hydrogues, I may have no choice but to betray the humans, Yazra'h. Do I explain that to them and still hope they understand?'

Her brow furrowed. 'Father, if you let the humans help you, they may improve our chances of winning against the hydrogues.'

He had not considered that. She continued in a rush. 'For instance, the human rememberer Anton Colicos came here as a scholar. He is only interested in *The Saga of Seven Suns*. I have never seen a man so oblivious to politics. Yet even *he* suspects something bad is going to happen here. He has asked me troubling questions.'

Jora'h's expression softened. He had seen his fearless daughter's unexpected flicker of affection for the bookish human. 'And what would you ask me to do, daughter?'

'Give him something else to see. On your orders, Rememberer Vao'sh faces the enormous task of studying the apocryphal archives for clues. Why not let the human scholar assist him on Hyrillka? Send Anton Colicos with him far from here, where he will not observe what you wish to keep hidden!'

'Yes, that is a very good idea.' Jora'h sighed with genuine relief. This was a decision he could make without losing more honour. 'I made plans and promises when I departed Hyrillka in the aftermath of Rusa'h's rebellion. Tal O'nh is leading the rescue and rebuilding mission, and young Designate Ridek'h needs to be about his duties at last.'

Yazra'h stood at attention. 'Ridek'h is still only a boy, but even a boy Designate is better than none at all. The people of Hyrillka are guilt-ridden and wounded. They need him there.'

Knowing it was not logical, but certain this was what he wished to do, Jora'h said, 'And Ridek'h needs *you*, Yazra'h. As my daughter, you will never be a Designate, but you have the knowledge and strength of character. Go with the boy as adviser, protector, and mentor — and also watch this human rememberer to keep him out of trouble.'

'But my place is at the Mage-Imperator's side, to protect you!'

'You cannot protect me against the dangers I face.'

She looked extremely uncomfortable. 'Cannot Tal O'nh be Ridek'h's teacher and guide?'

He shook his head. 'The tal is a military commander and can

offer his strength, but a Designate needs more than that. Ridek'h is the son of Pery'h. He has enough potential.'

Yazra'h left, troubled but not quite successful in hiding her smile. The Mage-Imperator remained on the rooftop, deep in thought, knowing the hydrogues would come back before long to deliver their commands. He could only hope that, before then, Adar Zan'nh and Ildira's best minds could solve the much greater challenge.

FORTY-FIVE

ADAR ZAN'NH

The Ildiran technical teams did not lack for manpower or resources. Every possible laboratory facility was made available to them, and they conducted experiments, refined calculations, and improved their traditional weapons. Unfortunately, after ten thousand years of malaise and stagnation, the scientist and engineer kithmen were no longer capable of true innovation.

'We have increased our destructive power by nearly five per cent, Adar.' Klie'f and Shir'of seemed pleased with the result.

Zan'nh scowled. 'Five per cent? The Mage-Imperator demanded breakthroughs, not more of the same thing we have used for centuries. You need *new* thoughts, not better versions of old ones.'

Klie'f raised his hands helplessly. 'We do not understand, Adar.'

'It is clear you do not. Five per cent, against an extermination force of diamond warglobes? The hydrogues will not even notice the difference.'

As a young tal, Zan'nh had been promoted by Adar Kori'nh because he solved crises in ways that other Ildirans could not imagine. He had won simulated battles with tricky manoeuvres and unconventional tactics, no matter how much he incensed the older officers.

Zan'nh turned away in disappointment. The Solar Navy needed something entirely unexpected, and for that he could not look to unimaginative researchers.

Finally, he pushed aside his reluctance. The Mage-Imperator had told him to try anything, and Zan'nh would solicit ideas from an unlikely source.

The balding administrator of the Hansa cloud harvester faced him indignantly. 'You've got to be kidding. After all *this*, you want us to help you?' He rolled his eyes, looking at his sharp-featured engineering chief, Tabitha Huck.

'That's a switch!' she said. 'I've been bored silly.'

Zan'nh had first met Sullivan Gold when his warliners encountered the trespassing cloud harvester at Qronha 3. Typically oblivious, the Hansa manager had been surprised that Ildirans would take offence just because humans had placed an industrial facility on a planet that did not belong to them.

He crossed his arms and regarded them both. 'Like your Terran Hanseatic League, our Ildiran Empire faces imminent destruction from the hydrogues. The Mage-Imperator has commanded our Solar Navy to develop innovative weapons against them. We have made only minor progress, and time is running out. Therefore, I request your assistance. My people cannot do this alone.'

'The terms "Ildiran" and "innovation" aren't usually used in the same sentence.' Tabitha's voice dripped with sarcasm.

Zan'nh allowed a small smile. 'That is exactly the point. Our civilization reached the pinnacle of achievement centuries ago. Our people no longer develop radical new concepts. Culturally, such things are frowned upon.'

Tabitha clearly had little respect for her Ildiran counterparts. 'And now that you need a new idea, nobody can come up with one to save his life.'

'To save all our lives,' Zan'nh pointed out. 'My people have never been *trained* to think along unorthodox lines. Humans, however, are well versed in this.'

'Damn right,' Tabitha said.

Sullivan's voice was like iron. 'Before we do anything for you, I need you to tell us what's going on. What was your mysterious mission to Qronha 3 with that little girl and her diving bell chamber? What's the real story behind all those warglobes that appeared over Ildira?'

The Adar considered his instructions and the new leeway the Mage-Imperator had given him. No more secrets! Conceding, Zan'nh explained the situation, including the looming hydrogue threat and why they had needed to keep the humans isolated.

'What the hell!' Tabitha cried. Sullivan looked dizzy.

'Unless you help us find a way to defeat the hydrogues, we will have no choice but to give in to their ultimatum. We have no wish to see humans exterminated. Therefore, it is in your best interests to help us. I want—' He caught himself. 'Sullivan Gold, I would very much appreciate it if you and your human workers assisted us.'

Sullivan's anguish was clear. 'Why didn't you just ask in the first place?'

Zan'nh lowered his head. 'Previously, our priorities were . . . incorrect.'

Tabitha's eyes went wide. 'Did you just admit you were *wrong*?' She tossed her light brown hair. 'You don't have to twist my arm to cause heartburn for the drogues. I'm tired of staring out the windows all day long. Remember, I used to be an EDF weapons designer before I came to work on the cloud harvester. I helped create the initial fraks and carbon-carbon slammers. I still have a lot of basic designs in here, but our weapons weren't terribly effective against the warglobes either.' She paced restlessly. 'The question is, what can I do that hasn't been done before?'

'Precisely,' Zan'nh said. 'We are searching for innovation.'

Sullivan laced his big-knuckled fingers together and faced the Adar. 'If we agree to help you, there's got to be some measure of trust. And afterwards, you have to let us go home.'

'Sullivan Gold, if we do not defeat the hydrogues now, none of us will have a home to return to.'

FORTY-SIX

ENGINEERING SPECIALIST SWENDSEN

When the two scientists proudly delivered the tiny upload pack with their repeater virus, Sergeant Paxton held it between thumb and forefinger. 'Doesn't look like much of a secret weapon.'

'If this works, all the compies inside the factory will immediately shut down,' Yamane explained with a calmness that Swendsen certainly didn't feel.

'Then we can use the same idea for the other EDF battle groups,' Swendsen added. 'If we get data copies out to them soon enough.'

The silver berets were ready to take down the besieged compy factory, and this time they meant business. No more practice. Lugging sonic battering rams, the new penetration team – five times the size of the previous squad – rushed up to the barricaded doors on the quiet side of the sprawling facility, choosing to enter through wings less likely to be occupied by the murderous compies.

Without slowing, the silver berets hit the factory door. Sonic rams made a deafening bang that Swendsen could hear even through his comm-receiver earplugs. The barricade buckled like a crumpled piece of foil and fell away.

'Move it inside before the clankers come running!' Sergeant Paxton yelled. 'Move! Move!'

Protected by a phalanx of commandos, Swendsen and Yamane remained confident in their frantically developed virus. They knew the fix would work; they just had grave doubts about surviving long enough to implement it. Every one of the silver berets carried a tiny datapack copy: redundancy increased the odds that at least one patch virus would reach the main programming station.

Silver berets plunged forward, weapons raised. Each one carried a projection grid that displayed the primary path for their insertion, along with alternate routes. The commandos ran, armour and weapons clattering, boots thundering across the floor. Swendsen and Yamane were already out of breath in their attempt to keep up, but knew they would be killed if they fell behind. The Soldier compies would close in on them soon.

The group rushed through narrow corridors lined with shelves stacked with fabricated components waiting to be assembled. As they had hoped, the wing was empty, and they encountered no resistance.

'Keep together. Hold it tight!' Paxton yelled.

The commandos did not let up, and Swendsen could see that even the weakest of these men and women was far more fit than either he or Yamane. As part of their training, silver berets ran ten kilometres every day. According to popular myths, they ate nails, played catch with boulders, and dangled from cliffs for the sheer recreational value.

The squad pushed into the white-walled clean rooms where Klikiss robot programming was impressed upon the control circuits. *I guess it was a big mistake to do that,* Swendsen thought. Too late now.

The point commandos dropped to their knees and opened fire as two Soldier compies emerged from a steamy, cold vault carrying replacement modules. Not expecting to see human intruders, the compies spun about. The silver berets blasted them into shrapnel.

'Must be getting close,' Paxton said.

Swendsen nodded. 'The central upload banks are right ahead.'

'Then that's where we need to go.' Private Elman kicked open the door.

The background noise grew louder with the hammering of assembly arms, the crackle and hiss of welders, the clatter of moving conveyors. A thousand Soldier compies were at work producing more robots. The first two silver berets mowed down the standing compies with dense, depleted-uranium projectiles, knocking the robots backwards, but more machines quickly replaced them.

Paxton shouted, 'Can't shoot them all. Blast and run – brute force, not finesse. We have to cut a swath through these tin cans.'

Swendsen pointed the way. The commandos formed ranks again and charged like an aggressive football team towards its goalpost. They knocked compies away using exploding slugs and electrostatic short-circuiting fields. But several Soldier compies seized hot weapons from the commandos, then grabbed the unarmed men and women and killed them.

Sergeant Paxton growled, 'Look ahead and stay on target! Almost there.'

Several more silver berets fell as the group pushed through the sea of clankers. By the time they reached the control centre, Swendsen was stunned to see that only Paxton and three other commandos had survived, along with him and Yamane. Nearly fifty silver berets had sacrificed themselves so the two technical specialists could get through with their patch virus.

Once inside the upload centre, the last commandos barricaded the door as Soldier compies threw themselves against it. 'How fast can you upload those viruses?' Paxton said.

'No one else could do it faster,' Swendsen said, then cringed as a barrage of gunfire echoed around the walls.

'Two minutes,' Yamane answered. He started to say something else, but an explosion drowned him out. He blinked, recovered, then repeated, 'Two minutes.'

'All right, two minutes.' Without being told, the commandos barricaded the door. 'You better not be exaggerating.'

The compies used weapons seized from fallen silver berets to shoot holes through the door. Staccato thuds and clangs rattled across the barricade and stitched a seam of holes along the walls.

Swendsen cringed over the control deck. Outside, a muffled explosion reverberated through the floor. 'This is delicate work! How am I supposed to concentrate?'

Paxton gave a disbelieving snort. 'Should I go outside and tell the damned clankers to keep it down?'

Yamane was concerned about a more practical matter. 'If one of those projectiles destroys the equipment here, we can't install our repeater virus.'

'Then I suggest you move faster than a proverbial speeding bullet.'

Working in intent silence amidst the background din, the two scientists copied the patch virus into the upload centre and fed it into the imprinting transmitter. By design, each compy that received the virus would copy it and dump it to another compy, and another, and another. Once the cascade began, all the berserk robots would shut down.

At least Swendsen hoped so.

Compies shattered the makeshift barricade. Paxton and his comrades fell back and opened fire. 'These are your last few seconds, gentlemen!'

'There, that's got it,' Yamane said. 'Ready to go.'

Swendsen hit the transmit switch. The brief but deadly nugget of new programming swept out into the compy factory.

The front robot ranks paused as the signal slammed into them, altering their core programming. They hesitated as the repeater virus automatically handed off to the next machine and the next. The compies staggered, then froze, shutting down in waves. An expanding current of stillness swept through the clamour of the factory.

Swendsen and Yamane waited at the control upload deck, afraid to speak. The surviving silver berets looked at each other, then at all the suddenly petrified Soldier compies. Robot arms were outstretched, artificial hands ready to tear them apart. They looked like an avant garde artist's concept of a statue garden.

One of the commandos shouldered a compy aside with a crash. With a growing snarl he knocked another one down, as if clearing debris. Sergeant Paxton and the remaining silver berets got into the vengeful spirit, tossing compies until they had cleared a way out of the battered control centre.

Formally shaking hands to congratulate each other, Swendsen and Yamane surveyed the now-silent compy factory with satisfaction. 'They'll never find their way out of that infinite loop.'

'We still have a lot of work to do,' Yamane said. 'Simply understanding what initially went wrong could take months.'

'Save that for when the emergency's over,' Paxton said. 'We need to inform the EDF that your patch virus worked. They can start transmitting it to hotspots right now, save some of our battle groups.' He triggered his shoulder mike and broadcast his report.

'I'd feel more comfortable if we could just get out of here.'

Swendsen wiped the back of his hand across his forehead, clearing droplets of perspiration.

'Agreed,' the silver berets said in perfect unison.

They made their way back through the frozen compies, amazed by the sheer number of motionless robots. Running the frenetic assembly lines beyond their design limits, the Soldier compies had increased their ranks tenfold.

'The nearest exit's over here.' Paxton led the way. Ahead, they could see the hangar doors.

'Like whistling through a graveyard at midnight,' a silver beret said.

'Nothing to fear now,' Swendsen said. 'It worked exactly as planned.'

Sergeant Paxton clicked his shoulder transmitter again. 'We're at door 1701/7. Be ready to let us out.'

'Acknowledged, Sergeant.'

One of the Soldier compies twitched.

Swendsen paused. 'Did you see that?'

Yamane frowned, as if troubled by this unexpected technical problem. 'They shouldn't be able to bypass so quickly. I wonder if they've installed adaptive security programming in their new constructions.'

Eye sensors glowed. Two mechanical arms shifted. A polymer-reinforced torso straightened. Bullet-shaped heads swivelled.

'Oh, crap!' said Paxton. 'Run!'

Swendsen and Yamane bolted. The surviving silver berets charged toward the door, but the Soldier compies revived too swiftly. Swendsen tripped on a compy that was just starting to move. He caught at a nearby robot to regain his balance, only to be grabbed by it. Terrified, Swendsen wrenched away, ripping a bloody gouge in his shoulder.

With the ammunition left in their weapons, the silver berets blasted away, yelling at the top of their lungs. Hundreds and then thousands of compies marched towards them, blocking the way out. They closed in from all sides.

Swendsen could see the exit, but it was much, much too far away.

FORTY-SEVEN

RLINDA KETT

R attling and tugging, nematodes chewed through the metal
floor of the lift. From its sluggish movement and frequent
lurches, Rlinda imagined at least fifty of the heavy worms
must be clinging down there. How swiftly they had slithered up
the shaft walls and clambered along protrusions, driven by Karla
Tamblyn's furious control.

Rlinda struggled to fasten the chest guard of her environment
suit while BeBob fitted her remaining glove in place. With a thud
followed by loud skittering, the nematodes buckled the insulated
floor plates, and a flash of serrated diamond teeth bit through
a crack in the metal. Rlinda stomped her heel down as hard as
she could, and the worm-thing disappeared. After only a brief
pause, the nematodes flung themselves back with renewed vigour,
squirming and sliding with a sound like wet leather. The ascending
elevator slowed with a jerk, grinding in its track.

'Would it really hurt to let two lousy people escape?' BeBob
groaned. 'We didn't even belong here in the first place.'

Rlinda was already sweating in her half-assembled suit. After seeing the nematodes make short work of the fallen Roamers down there, she knew the thick fabric would offer little protection. Those sharp teeth sent a shudder down Rlinda's spine, but she had no intention of letting either herself or her favourite ex-husband be turned into worm food.

All business, moving as swiftly as she could, Rlinda turned BeBob around, checked his suit diagnostics and his air supply, and pronounced him fully green. 'Now you check me out.' She backed closer to BeBob.

With a mechanical sigh of surrender, the lift finally ground to a complete stop, and it was still far from the top.

'That's not good,' BeBob said.

'You're the *master* of minimizing.' She tried to calm her breathing, but the skittering, thumping sounds of the worms grew louder from below, making her sweat even more. She was embarrassingly close to panic. 'Hurry up!'

Nematodes ripped through another floor segment, and Rlinda had to jerk her feet away from the jagged mouths. BeBob checked her diagnostics, squinted at the readouts, then ran his gloved hands over her padded garment. 'Enough foreplay, BeBob! Is my suit intact or not? We have to blow out of this chamber.'

'Want me to take shortcuts? You'll be the first one to complain if your suit pops open in the vacuum.'

'My suit won't help if those worms chew a hole in it, either.'

He adjusted something, then made a satisfied sound. 'There, you're good to go as soon as we put our helmets on.'

She popped the helmet over BeBob's head and gave it a quick clockwise twist to seal its collar. 'The lift shaft is probably jacketed and pressurized, with an emergency sphincter or two. Up top I assume there's another airlock leading outside.'

BeBob said something, but his helmet muffled the words; when he pushed a suitcomm toggle on his chest pack, his voice came through a speaker in the collar of Rlinda's suit. '—the way Karla Tamblyn is blasting everything down there, she might have cracked something open. If the shaft collapses, we're screwed.'

Rlinda studied the roof of the lift chamber, finding the emergency access hatch. 'BeBob, we have a wide selection of ways to be screwed. That's why I want you out on the roof. I'm tired of these critters trying to eat our toes. I'll bend down and cup my hands so you can step in them. Use my knees if you want, and open that access hatch so we can climb out.'

'Me? Shouldn't I be lifting *you* up? You could go first.'

'Thanks for being a gentleman, BeBob, but I'm twice your weight. Even though Plumas has low gravity, let's not get cocky.'

With a crash, the gathered nematodes bent another floor section until the opening was big enough for one to push its gelatinous red body through. Its skin membrane pulsed, and the protoplasmic body core thrust forward, squirting the creature halfway into the chamber.

Rlinda stomped on its head with her full weight, bursting its body membrane and leaving it jiggling on the floor. Only seconds later, two others fought to squeeze through the same opening.

With a worried glance at the oncoming swarm, BeBob quickly stepped on Rlinda's knee and put his other foot in the cradle of her hands. She boosted him up so he could fumble with the hatch. 'At least it's an analogue mechanism. No electronics or control sequence.'

More nematodes began to work their way through, crystalline jaws snapping closer to Rlinda. Holding BeBob steady, she couldn't move to squash them with her boots. She kept glancing down. The worms were almost through.

'BeBob, you think you could—'

He worked frantically until he snapped the latch and pushed open the trapdoor. 'That's got it.' She gave him a solid shove, and

BeBob sprang upwards in the low gravity, shooting most of the way through the hole in the roof. Catching himself on his elbows, he hauled himself up.

No longer needing to support him, Rlinda landed a swift, hard kick on the nearest nematode. It retracted briefly, then lunged forward again. Her second kick didn't bother the creature as much, and some of the moist slime clung to her boot. From the grotto below, Karla Tamblyn's dark energy drove the nematodes beyond any sensations of pain. 'It's getting harder to discourage them.'

On top of the lift, BeBob flopped flat on his stomach, stuck his helmeted head back down, and extended his hand. 'Come on. I'll pull you up.'

Rlinda didn't see any other way. She grasped his gloved hand in her own, bent her knees, and counted, 'One – two – *three*.' She sprang with all her strength. BeBob managed to tug her through the hatch up to her waist. She barely fitted. Rlinda's feet dangled and kicked while she struggled upwards. BeBob seized her shoulders.

Unhindered now, nematodes tore apart the floor plates, chewed other access holes, and slithered like a nest of snakes into the chamber. Rlinda yanked her legs up and out of the way just as diamond teeth snapped at her heel. She climbed onto the roof and slammed the hatch back down with a clang. 'Talk about a can of worms!'

Now that they were on top of the lift, Rlinda tilted her helmet back to see the dizzying height of the shaft above. 'I really hoped the elevator would carry us a little closer to the top.'

'Look, rungs!' BeBob pointed. Like the ridges of an endless centipede, alloy bars had been implanted in the shaft's jacketed ice wall.

'You're kidding.' She imagined Roamers hauling themselves

hand-over-hand up the shaft just for the exercise. 'Do I look like an athlete to you?'

'You look beautiful to me, and you always have.'

Rlinda rolled her eyes. 'I never pegged you as one of those daredevils who gets hot and horny when his life is on the line.'

'I thought I was being romantic.'

'Save it for when we get to the *Curiosity*. Once we're away from this place, I guarantee you I'll be in the mood. Come on, get moving!'

Below, the nematodes squirmed into the lift chamber, writhing on top of each other, then using their slime adhesion to crawl up the walls. They hadn't yet figured how to get to the roof, but it would only be a matter of minutes.

BeBob gestured toward the rungs. 'Ladies first.'

'You want to look at my big butt during the whole climb up?'

BeBob turned his helmet away as if embarrassed. 'Actually, I was thinking you'd do a better job of opening the airlock at the top, and I wanted to give you first crack at it.'

'Hmmm, practical *and* romantic. Tell me again why I ever divorced you.'

'Because we couldn't stand each other at the time.'

Rlinda had divorced quite a few men, but Branson Roberts was the only one for whom she still carried a torch. 'Right. I like it better this way. Why mess with a good thing?'

She grabbed the rungs and started to climb. BeBob secured the crossbar on the roof hatch, though it would take the worms only a short while to chew through the metal itself. The thought was enough to give Rlinda some incentive. Though she made good speed in the light gravity, within five minutes she was puffing loudly into the echo chamber of her helmet. The suit's recirc and cooling systems worked overtime.

Feeling vibrations through the shaft wall, she imagined Karla's continuing mayhem in the grotto below. Though the Tamblyn brothers had caused them plenty of headaches, Rlinda would have helped if she'd had the option. But this was a mess of the Roamers' own making; she and BeBob had no part in it.

High above, she could see a necklace of lights marking the top of the shaft and the waiting airlock. Huffing, she grabbed the next rung, then the next, and the next. Her muscles ached, and her lungs were on fire. She couldn't remember the last time she'd exerted herself so. BeBob climbed steadily behind her.

When she heard tiny thumps far below, she realized that the nematodes were battering against the roof of the lift chamber; through sheer numbers, they knocked open the hatch and began boiling out onto the roof. Exuding gelatinous slime, the nematodes adhered to the smooth shaft wall. They squirmed like caterpillars, circling around the borehole – and climbing fast.

She paused to glance down, saw the red nematodes gaining ground. 'No need to look, Rlinda,' BeBob called. 'Just assume they're getting closer. If you hear my scream and then a crunching sound, you can be sure you're next.'

She pulled herself nearer to the surface and freedom. The Roamer environment suit carried a kit of useful tools, but once she got to the top, Rlinda would still need time to finesse the airlock. Doubts began to pile up in her mind, brought on by fear. What if the airlock had a fail-safe system that disabled it if the lift chamber was not sealed in place, or if the doors at the bottom of the shaft weren't properly sealed? She didn't even want to think about that and concentrated only on climbing. *Climbing*. Her mind was already planning how she would fudge the airlock controls. There had to be some sort of emergency egress mechanism!

Rlinda reached the top so unexpectedly she was startled to find no more rungs. The inner airlock door was sealed, as she'd feared, and the control panel wasn't one of the standard models. She yanked out the tools clipped to her suit and went to work. When she exposed the controls, she found handwritten notations on all the wiring. 'How am I supposed to figure this out?'

BeBob kept climbing, a dozen rungs beneath her. 'As fast as you can – that would be my preference.' Then he yelped.

The closest nematode reared up just below his leg, and BeBob kicked hard enough to knock it loose. The creature's slimy adhesion wasn't strong enough to hold, and the invertebrate dropped down the shaft. But seven other nematodes were chomping their way up after it, with plenty more behind those.

She didn't see any way she could decipher these controls and cycle the airlock in the time they had available. She did, however, understand the standard automatic-purge routine. She made up her mind. 'Wrap your arms around one of those rungs, BeBob, and hold on.' She dragged the blade of a screwdriver across the circuitry to short out all safety interlocks, then manually cracked open both the inner and outer pressure doors.

With a thump of decompression, the air inside the shaft was sucked out like a cold beverage through a straw. Hooking her boot around one rung and her arms around another, Rlinda held herself in place as evacuating air rushed past. BeBob clung just beneath her.

Far, far below, at the bottom of the shaft, an emergency seal door clanged into place to protect the inhabited underground grotto, and sphincters closed off the shaft at several levels. At least something was still working properly.

The shaft's air geysered out, pulling the bloated scarlet creatures from the wall. The nematodes shot outside into the hard vacuum like wet tendrils of phlegm. Once they hit the freezing emptiness, their skin membranes could not hold their internal pressure, and they exploded.

The tug of wind lasted only a few seconds until the shaft was drained. Rlinda reached down to grasp BeBob's hand, pulling him up, and the two of them climbed through the jimmied airlock door. Outside they saw shelter huts, piping, wellheads, several large water tankers. And the *Voracious Curiosity*.

Rlinda laughed with relief to see her ship, then looked down at the splatters of crimson ice and shredded worm bodies. BeBob bounded past her. 'No time for sightseeing. That woman could crack through the crust at any minute.'

She didn't need to be told twice. Within moments they got themselves aboard, and Rlinda coaxed the engines to life. 'The *Curiosity*'s still pretty battered, and it looks like those Roamers never got around to fixing everything. But she can fly.'

'Then let's fly!'

And they did, leaving Plumas mercifully far behind.

FORTY-EIGHT

GENERAL KURT LANYAN

After the demolitions techs blew open the launching bay, the *Goliath* gaped open to vacuum. General Lanyan's first group of armoured trainees used manoeuvring packs to swoop through the cargo doors. Time to get to work.

'Think of it as a pest-control mission, everyone. We're going in to clean out an infestation.' The patter of responses in his helmet sounded uneasy, but professional. These kleebs had signed up for military service in time of war. In their bunks at the EDF training base, they had dreamed of seeing real combat. Now they were going to get it, in spades.

Even before the assault group had anchored themselves against the recoil, they unleashed covering fire against any compy resistance. Once the trainees locked magnetic boots onto the deck and stabilized themselves inside, they methodically completed the sweep with projectile guns.

The remaining Soldier compies in the bay didn't have a chance. Metal and polymer shrapnel drifted out into space.

A voice clicked in Lanyan's helmet. 'We are secure.'

While EDF guards were stationed at all access points leading from the large bay deeper into the ship, Lanyan launched the second phase of the recovery operation. Hundreds of armed trainees in reinforced suits disembarked from the cavalry ships into the Juggernaut's empty bay and set up their beachhead.

Lanyan needed to get these unseasoned soldiers ready for the hard task ahead of them, but he didn't intend to give them an overly realistic scenario. These newbie commandos would get weak knees.

'Bear in mind that just because we've killed the engines, doesn't mean we've won,' he transmitted through his helmet comm. 'This Juggernaut is crawling with Soldier compies, and you can bet your asses they still mean to hijack these ships. According to our database, two hundred and forty-two clankers were placed in service aboard the *Goliath*. The crew probably managed to take out a good number of them, but there'll be plenty left for us.'

He strode into the bay, still talking. 'In addition to the guillotine command that shut down their engines, I've already input a command string in the Juggernaut's computer to lock down all lifts. That means the remaining compies are bottled up on individual decks.'

'General, can they overhear this chatter?'

Lanyan scowled at the cadet. 'Not unless you're dumb enough to be on an open channel, soldier.'

'No, sir, that would be against regulations.'

He gestured with a gloved hand. 'We're going to clear this whole bottom level and use it as our staging area. We'll show the damned machines what it means to be methodical. Once we scrape the launching deck clean, I propose a direct assault on the bridge. We can't let the compies keep working on the systems or we might lose the whole ship again. Once we capture the bridge, then *I'm* in control, and it's all over except for the bookkeeping.

We can clean up the rest of the walking scrapmetal at our leisure.'

He reminded his trainees to check their weapons, prepare spare rounds of ammunition and adjust charge packs so they could swap out depleted components in half a second. By the book. When a chorus of shouts announced that the primary sweeper teams were ready, Lanyan instructed them to reanchor themselves to the deck. 'When we open the door, there's going to be an outrush of air. You don't want it to bowl you over.'

Simultaneously, point men cracked open the access hatches that led from the bay to the interior of the ship. An invisible storm swept past them and spurted into space as the entire bottom deck emptied of atmosphere. Air was easily replaceable. Human soldiers were much more difficult to come by.

A dozen or so Soldier compies had crowded against each hatch, preparing to fight, but the sudden decompression gust took them by surprise. Many lost their balance; some were sucked out through the open hangar doors. A barrage of projectile fire blasted the rest back.

'Take them out of the defensive equation,' Lanyan lectured. 'Just like in your lessons back at base.'

Now that the deck was open to space, wispy steam curled from beneath closed cabin doors. Splatters of blood froze to iron-hard paint on the walls as the remaining moisture boiled out of the crimson smears.

The sweeper teams split up according to the mission plan. Before suiting up, all of Lanyan's people had studied engineering diagrams of the *Goliath*. Any recruit whose memory was faulty, or who simply couldn't think straight in a panic, could call up projected diagrams on a backlit display within their helmets.

Now the pumped-up kleebs ran forward, yelling into comm lines at the top of their lungs. Unaffected by the vacuum, Soldier compies emerged into the line of fire. Lanyan felt a satisfying recoil against his shoulder armour as he fired his projectile rifle. A depleted uranium slug drove the nearest clanker backward with enough force to topple two of its companions. Normally, no sane soldier would fire such powerful projectiles inside a space-ship: Superdense slugs could easily puncture a hull or shatter a porthole. Right now, though, Lanyan didn't give a damn about a few pinholes or cosmetic damage to the Juggernaut. Those things could be fixed.

Lanyan's trainees continued to fire. Destroyed compies clattered aside while others emerged to take their places. 'They keep coming, General!'

'So keep shooting. The reason the damned clankers succeeded in the first place was that they took our people by surprise. This time there's no excuse.'

Lanyan barked at them to stay in formation as he moved down the corridor door by door, opening each chamber, destroying Soldier compies hiding inside bunk rooms. This mission reminded him of his younger days, when he had trained for urban warfare, prepping EDF soldiers to raid rebellious colony towns that had thumbed their noses at the Hansa Charter. But fanatic rebels were a lot softer than compies . . .

Human bodies lay strewn on the floor or stuffed into closets and storage chambers. When the greenhorn soldiers looked at their dead comrades, Lanyan knew they were ready to puke into their faceplates. He had to turn that emotion into vengeance. 'Compy butchers! Are we going to let them get away with it?'

'Hell no, sir!' One of the recruits next to him opened fire with a yell, knocking down three compies coming down the corridor.

Lanyan's team reached the end of the hall after purging each sector. It took the better part of two hours before he declared the *Goliath's* lower deck secure. Seven trainees had been killed in the methodical assault. Acceptable losses.

The General stood in front of the closed lifts at the end of the hall and addressed the breathless commandos. 'This is going to be tight. The only bridge access is by these two lifts, one on each side. That creates a strategic bottleneck, since we can only get a small group of you in at a time. No telling how many compies have holed up on the bridge.'

He swung his gaze around through his faceplate's limited field of view. 'I'm going to lead one charge myself. Ensign Childress will take a group up the second shaft. Childress, pick fifteen of your coolest sharp-shooters and crowd them into the elevator car. I'll do the same here, and reactivate both lifts. On my mark, hit the bridge selector so that both groups arrive at the same time.'

'Agreed, General!' Childress's voice was husky and eager. 'May I suggest, sir, that we limit our weapons to energy dischargers? D-U slugs will make macaroni of the bridge control boards, and I assume you want to fly the *Goliath* out of here at the end of the day?'

'Good point, Ensign. So ordered. Switch to energy scramblers.' Lanyan swapped his projectile weapon for a soldier's stun-pulser. Having watched his fighters clear the lower decks, he tapped the ones who had been the most proficient. Together, they waited at the lift door. His kleebs were acting like a real team, real soldiers. They were getting the hang of this.

When Lanyan used his command codes to restore power to the lifts, the sealed elevator doors slid open – releasing a Soldier compy like a spring-loaded jack-in-the-box. The reeling compy knocked Lanyan over. Two trainees immediately fired a scrambler burst, and the ruined machine jittered and fell heavily on top of the General. 'Get this clanker off me!'

The soldiers lifted the hulk away and helped Lanyan to his feet. Two of the servo-systems inside his armoured suit had been knocked off-line, so he delayed the bridge-assault teams just long enough to reset his suit controls. When all the lights blinked green, Lanyan transmitted to Childress, 'Let's go.'

He and his chosen group crowded into the first lift. It reminded him of an academy stunt – how many EDF troopers could fit into a ship's elevator? – but there was nothing fun about this operation. At his signal, the two lifts shot upwards, arriving in unison at opposite sides of the captive bridge. The doors slid open, and the sweeper teams boiled out.

Energy weapons crackled around Lanyan. Circuitry-numbing bolts played across the first two trainees as they emerged onto the bridge, freezing their suit servos and turning the kleebs into statues.

'Watch who you're hitting, Childress!' Lanyan bellowed, assuming that the opposite team was firing.

'It's not us, sir. The clankers have their own weapons. Must've seized them from the *Goliath*'s armoury.'

Lanyan ducked out of the way as the firing continued. Static discharges ricocheted like lightning in a bottle. This pitched battle was the compies' last stand. The military robots advanced with the sheer weight of numbers. Lanyan froze a clanker in front of him, then kicked the energy weapon out of its metal hands. Even he hadn't expected so much resistance. 'Why the hell are so many of them up here?'

Then he noticed that the bridge's command modules had been pried open, circuitry boards removed, systems wired up to bypasses. After the guillotine command had shut down the Juggernaut engines, the compies had indeed tried to reconfigure all systems to restore control, as expected. *I'll be damned if they wouldn't have succeeded in another hour or two.*

Right now, the compies must be doing the same thing aboard all the other paralysed ships. A ball of ice formed in his stomach. They had to hurry.

Realizing he had stopped shooting, Lanyan blasted another military robot that came up behind one of his trainees. Three members of Childress's team already lay motionless on the deck. Lanyan didn't count the time, didn't count the number of targets, simply focused on any machine that was still moving.

When the mutinous robots had been eliminated, the sudden calm felt eerie. Childress shot three more blasts into a clanker already sprawled on the deck.

Unable to believe it was over, Lanyan looked at his forearm display, checked the external pressure, and saw that the air was still breathable. He cracked open his faceplate and took a deep breath. The bridge smelled like smoke, ozone, burned circuitry, and spilled blood. Even so, it was better than the inside of his helmet.

The *Goliath*'s bridge crew lay dead, mangled human bodies discarded under the control stations. The captain and bridge officers had put up a decent fight, but were overwhelmed.

Lanyan studied the exposed circuitry modules on the captain's chair. 'We've got some housekeeping to do. Get our best computer specialists up here so we can reactivate this Juggernaut's systems while other cleanup crews go deck by deck and clear out the rest of the clankers. And I want an inventory of all the robot bodies you find, so we can keep a halfway accurate tally.'

'Some of them are in too many pieces,' Childress pointed out.

'And some of them might be still hiding out in the air ducts,' Lanyan said. 'I'd rather not get an unpleasant surprise.'

Though he tried to make his voice stern, he could not prevent a grin from creeping onto his face. All around in the open gulf of space, the rest of the hijacked Grid 0 battle group waited for him. But this Juggernaut was his again. A good start.

'We've got one of our ships back. I'm proud of you all, but it's going to be a long day yet.'

FORTY-NINE

BENETO

B eneto watched the hundreds of towering verdani seedships preparing for war. With their thorn branches outthrust, he could sense the pulsing drive, the anger towards their mortal enemies. Gathered now, these organic battleships were ready to destroy the hydrogues after the holocaust ten thousand years ago.

But it wasn't the only war. The worldforest thrummed with the last cries of green priests trapped on EDF vessels as berserk Soldier compies slaughtered every human they found. Desperate telink reports splattered like hot blood across the verdani mind. The seeds of this current treachery had been planted long ago. Through worldforest memories, Beneto knew how Klikiss robots had used that previous war to set up a betrayal that exterminated their creator race. Now it seemed that Soldier compies had done something similar to humanity, taking advantage of the greater conflict. And there was nothing he or the worldtrees could do to assist the EDF.

Knowing the inevitability of the upcoming clash with the hydrogues, and aware of his special responsibility, Beneto stood before the nearest landed treeship, which thrust up to the sky like a many-tipped spear. He had been created as an avatar of the worldforest, a link between the tree mind and the human race. He had to understand these unspeakably old organic battleships.

A part of him knew that he had to go inside. The gnarled trunk was covered with golden plates thicker than the bark of a normal worldtree, as impenetrable as a dragon's armour. Beneto pressed his woodgrain palms against the overlapping bark scales, and a vertical perforation appeared down the trunk, parting for him like a wooden mouth. He entered the giant treeship, and the wooden portal closed behind him.

The winding interconnected passages were smooth, as if made by a giant burrowing beetle. Beneto went deeper into the core, trailing his artificial fingertips along the walls and *feeling* where he should go.

The vessels had taken flight ten millennia ago, drifting on the cosmic winds. They had travelled far from where hydrogues had once fought the worldforest, where wentals and faeros had clashed, flying away like sparks from a windblown fire. But they had been summoned back.

He reached the immense tree's nerve centre, a vaulted chamber akin to a warship's command bridge. Wooden pillars dripped like stalactites fused into a support framework. At the centre of the chamber sat a half-dissolved creature overgrown by cellulose drapings. *The pilot.*

Beneto could make out the elongated head, angular chin, and upswept cheekbones. The close-set bird-like eyes seemed to be little more than knots of wood. This creature was not meant to appear human, had never been human. An unknown alien species.

The pilot turned its nearly fused head, and Beneto faced it. He could hear whispered history through the immensely complex library of worldforest memories.

Long before humanity had begun to build cities on Earth, some other race — now lost to all records, hidden even in the folds of the verdani mind — had served as green priests in the first war with the hydrogues. After so much time aboard the verdani battleship, little more than a wisp of the original lifeform remained, just this tiny sculptured afterimage. But it was still aware, still serving the worldforest.

Fused into the soft, pulsing heartwood, the overgrown face lifted so that its bird-like eyes met Beneto's. The two of them shared a destiny, and both accepted their fates. Without words, Beneto received a flood of the pilot's experiences and knowledge, warnings and joys.

The alien brain was like a pattern of permanent stains on the battleship's wood. Beneto absorbed the breadth of the long journey out of the Spiral Arm and into unknown reaches of the Galaxy. A cascade of centuries filled his mind, giving him a poignant understanding of endless time. Until now, Beneto had never had any concept of what *ten thousand years* felt like.

Now he knew what was to become of him.

The verdani requested the same commitment from Beneto, the same sacrifice of life and time — and to find other volunteers among the green priests.

Then they asked him to help them create more giant organic vessels to throw against the hydrogues. *Many more*. And for that he needed to call on the assistance of the wentals.

FIFTY

NIRA

The surrounding hills had turned a crackling brown in the dry season. Nira hoped there wouldn't be fires again, though part of her longed to see this whole camp burned to the ground. She had hoped, and prayed, never to return here – and she'd certainly never expected it to be under circumstances like these.

Osira'h took her by the hand and led her towards the austere buildings where the descendants from the *Burton* lived out their lives, men and women forced to breed with Ildiran subjects. The captives found their own glimmers of happiness, selecting companions and mates for when they weren't locked in the breeding barracks.

Nira shuddered at the sight of those dark buildings to which she'd been dragged during her fertile times. No one had bothered to tell her – or any of them – the purpose of the breeding programme, but she suspected that Udru'h had enjoyed it all. There, by the fence, the guards had beaten her, dragged her away, and told everyone she was dead.

The ground showed no bloodstains. Four young children played together by the fence as if their lives were perfectly normal.

Black spots danced in front of her eyes. She wanted to turn and run again, to clamber through the fences and flee into the tinderbox-dry hills. Osira'h sensed her distress and squeezed her hand. 'It'll be all right, Mother. We're together now.'

At her arrival, people came out into the bright sunlight, curious and amazed. Though Nira must look worn and weary, these people knew who she was. They had never seen any other green priest. Benn Stoner, the ostensible leader of the camp, studied her, as if she might be an illusion. 'We thought you were dead. They put up a grave marker for you.'

'The Designate is no stranger to covering up terrible deeds.' Nira doubted she would ever shake off her revulsion for this place until she was away from here for ever. During her previous time here, she had told the captives about the worldforest on Theroc, the Terran Hanseatic League, and the Ildiran Empire. But, having grown up in captivity, the people hadn't believed her.

The girl looked at the curious faces. The captives were just as surprised to see Osira'h walking among them as they were to see Nira. Half-breed children had always been taken away and held in the Ildiran section of the settlement.

'We're going to live here now. Here in the camp,' Osira'h said. 'We need a place to stay.' She opened the door of one of the communal sleeping quarters.

'There are empty beds inside,' Stoner said. 'We have meals together, then stories and a few songs.' He shrugged. 'We used to be assigned hard work, but no one seems to know what to do anymore, not even the Ildirans. The breeding barracks have been closed. The whole camp is practically shut down.'

Nira glanced up in wonder. 'No more rapes?' Maybe it was

some further trick by Designate Udru'h, giving them a shred of hope just to take it away again. 'Isn't that what you wanted?'

The captives looked healthy but confused. Their world had been shaken, obviously for the better, but somehow they were not comforted. Stoner ran a hand along the back of his neck. 'No one will tell us why.'

'There's no longer any need,' Osira'h said. 'The purpose of this breeding camp is complete.' Though she was small, the girl carried an authority that made everyone listen. 'They have *me*. They got what they wanted.' She found a clean bunk and sat down on it. 'I'll take this one. The Mage-Imperator says you and I are supposed to wait here, Mother.'

'When will we see him?' Nira asked. 'Do you know when he's coming here? I haven't seen him in so long.'

Osira'h's small voice sounded profoundly bitter. 'He remains in the Prism Palace continuing his schemes. He doesn't want you to know what he's doing. He doesn't want me to see him either. I think he's embarrassed or ashamed.' She lowered her voice. 'I hope so.'

'You're not making any sense, Osira'h.'

'None of this makes any sense. The Mage-Imperator will summon us back to Mijistra whenever it serves him to do so. He no longer needs either of us.'

FIFTY-ONE

DOBRO DESIGNATE UDRU'H

The female green priest had a talent for making things difficult, even her own rescue. Udru'h had never expected Nira to escape and cause more problems, especially now that he was trying to do the right thing.

At least he would not need to create another deception – another *lie* – for Jora'h. He knew that all the previous ones had been necessary, however. His brother's irrational attachment to a breeding mother could have brought down the very programme designed to protect the Ildiran race. Udru'h had had no choice but to shield the new Mage-Imperator from his own bad decisions. Didn't he?

The Designate simply had to wait and bide his time. All of his actions would be proved right, and justified, sooner or later. The Mage-Imperator, though still angry at Udru'h's treatment of Nira, would know the Designate's true loyalty and dedication.

Now Jora'h had commanded that Nira be kept safe, and he had even sent Osira'h to stay with her. Udru'h had not expected that. He didn't understand why the girl would not prefer to stay with him in his dwelling. She was a living justification for all that had been done here. He had been her guide and mentor for most of her brief life. At first, he had hoped that perhaps the girl returned to Dobro to be with *him*. Now he scowled at his foolish thought. She seemed to want the company of her mother – a human woman she barely knew.

Nira was a thorn in his side reminding him about certain questionable decisions. She was like an unstable explosive in their midst, and would be even more dangerous when she returned to Jora'h. She would burden the Mage-Imperator with sob stories of her pains and sorrows, no doubt blaming everything on Udru'h without understanding the necessity – when Jora'h could ill afford to be distracted.

Pacing alongside him, Daro'h looked with concern towards his uncle. Though the young man didn't speak a word, his body language telegraphed countless questions that had been growing within him like thorny weeds. The Designate-in-waiting, who had always been a diligent student and completely loyal, now appeared angry, hurt, and . . . disappointed?

'I am your successor. Why do you hide things from me?' he finally said. 'Explain what really happened here. Why did you exile that green priest to an isolated island? Why did you hide her even from the Mage-Imperator?'

Udru'h turned to the young man. The possibilities of how much damage Nira could still do flickered like embers ready to be fanned into flame. 'All my reasons are the same one: I did it to strengthen and protect the Ildiran Empire. I have told you everything you need to know.'

Walking towards the camp fences, the Dobro Designate stared at the subdued breeding camp. He had mixed feelings about what would happen to the experimental subjects now. His life's work, indeed the whole centuries-long plan for Dobro, was over. Udru'h could not help feeling an emptiness, an abrupt malaise that set along with the realization that he had achieved an impossible task. And now what?

Daro'h lowered his head in surrender. 'Your behaviour has changed since Osira'h returned, Designate. You were once so passionate about our work here. Now that she has succeeded, what is to become of Dobro?'

'I feel the ending of the thing that has been our very reason for existence for centuries.' His words were sharp with a bitter aftertaste. Udru'h turned from the enclosed breeding compound where the humans continued their routines. He had fulfilled his role, done everything that history and his bloodline asked. He was finished. 'I never thought success would be as disappointing as failure.'

Udru'h reached a decision that made him sad, yet also gave him a sense of liberation and freedom. He placed his left hand on Daro'h's shoulder, turning the younger man to face him. 'This is a time of changes. I have taught, and you have learned, but Dobro is a different splinter colony now. My advice and experience will not benefit you further. There should be a clean transition.'

Daro'h frowned. 'What are you saying?'

'I will return to Ildira.' He turned back towards his private dwelling. The Designate-in-waiting had already made his own home in a different part of the settlement. 'There are too many eyes here, too many who would judge without understanding what I have done, or why. I will retire and never see this place again.' He took a sad look around the grassy hills, the settlement, the croplands. This should have been a fine and thriving splinter colony, where colonists could have a life of self-sufficiency. Maybe if he left, the stain would go with him.

He turned his back. 'From now on, Dobro is yours.'

FIFTY-TWO

CHAIRMAN BASIL WENCESLAS

The Chairman was always upset when things didn't go right, and that had happened a lot lately.

From his private control centre, a grim and silent Basil listened to the screams and gunfire echoing through the monitors. Implanted micro-imagers in the silver berets' armour went dead one after another. Engineering Specialist Swendsen flailed against the reactivated Soldier compies. Finally, Sergeant Paxton's imager – the last one – died to a white-out of static.

Basil made a sound of disgust and looked around for someone to blame. 'Swendsen announced that the repeater virus worked. All the compies were shut down. What happened?' He squeezed his hand into a fist and then forcibly relaxed his fingers.

'Dr Swendsen may have spoken prematurely,' answered Eldred Cain from the seat beside him. The hairless deputy appeared paler than usual. His lips were twisted as if he were enduring a bad bout of indigestion. 'I inspected their planned mode of attack, and it appeared sound.'

The Chairman's jaws clenched so tightly that his muscles

ached. 'Link to the on-site command centre. I want to watch what's happening outside the factory. They've got to contain those compies before they break through the cordon.'

With nimble fingers, Cain accessed a different set of imagers. 'Too late already, Mr Chairman.'

Outside the manufacturing compound, compies had torn away the door barricades, while squads of silver berets drove them back with heavy-projectile launchers. Smashed and shattered robot bodies piled up, but more compies climbed up and over the pile of debris. Shouts rattled back and forth on the command commlines. 'Breach in the south-west wing! They've knocked half the damn wall down, and they're coming out by the hundreds.'

'Then shoot them by the hundreds!'

'We've got to pull troops from the north end. That's just the warehouse side. We're safe there—'

'Shit, here they come!'

Cain said quietly, provocatively, 'Good thing King Peter reacted swiftly and decisively as soon as he received the report. Otherwise, we never would have contained them at all. They'd have taken us completely unprepared.'

Basil breathed through flared nostrils. 'I'll deal with the King's intractability when this crisis is over.'

Cain's expression was unreadable, his voice flat. 'I was pointing out the King's foresight, sir, not his failings.'

After glaring at his deputy, Basil rested his elbows on the table, pressing his face close to the image. The screens showed armoured vehicles pulling up to surround the factory. Compies came out of any hole in the shattered barricades.

Breathless and alarmed, Sarein rushed into the control chamber. 'Basil, Mr Chairman – what's happening? Can I be of assistance?'

'In a word, no.' He spared her only a brief glance, then turned his attention back to the screens. 'Unless you can magically double the number of people I have on the ground?'

Her expression hardened, and she was obviously hurt by his comment. 'I was just coming to offer my support, Basil.'

He had no time for her right now. 'Then please do it silently.'

When he'd okayed the initial response orders, Basil had been convinced that five hundred silver berets would be sufficient to stop any incursion. Now he thought about bringing in more Palace District security forces as well as the royal guards. But he saw that reinforcements could never get there in time. The silver berets were overextended, and the lines were clearly crumbling.

Cain looked at the Chairman, his scalp furrowed with concern. 'We can't hold the outflux. We don't have sufficient weaponry or personnel in position.'

Basil nodded. 'It's time for a vaporization strike. We have to cauterize this wound before it gets worse.'

The deputy's fingers were already flying as he opened channels to the ground-based EDF troops and Palace District security. 'You realize the repercussions, Mr Chairman? Calling in a strike in the middle of the Palace District? I would advise against it.'

'On the *edge* of the Palace District. If those rogue compies get out into the general populace, the bloodbath will be unimaginable. They'll murder tens of thousands. At the moment they're all in one place. I'm calling the strike now.'

'Then please allow me to contact the secondary commander and warn the silver berets to withdraw—'

'Absolutely not. The silver berets are the only thing hindering the spread of the Soldier compies. If they back off for even a moment, the robots will haemorrhage out of every access point in the factory. They will remain at their posts until the end. They knew what they were doing when they signed up. Silver berets will not let us down.'

'Calling in a strike within the Palace District, and targeting your own troops?' Cain's blue eyes were full of angry questions, his fingers hesitating on the keypad. Nearby, though she remained silent, Sarein appeared distraught.

'We'll issue the order in the King's name.' Basil glanced at his status screen; the fast carriers bearing two vaporization bombs were on their way. Estimated time of deployment was twenty minutes.

Basil sighed at the deputy's obvious hesitancy. Sarein looked ready to blurt something, so he cut them both off sharply. 'This is a difficult decision, Mr Cain. A *Chairman's* decision.' Sadly, his own deputy did not understand the burdens a real Chairman was forced to bear. Cain was intelligent, cooperative, competent ... yet he had no backbone, overthinking every decision. Perhaps this man was another bad choice – like intractable (and now comatose) Prince Daniel. Like King Peter himself.

The compy factory was in flames. Several walls had collapsed; black, oily smoke poured from gaping holes in the expansive roof. On the ground, Soldier compies marched through the torn barricades, pushing back the commandos. The fighters gathered for a last stand, but their lines had begun to break as many of them ran out of ammunition and charge packs.

Overhead, two fast carriers streaked in. Any surviving silver berets who looked up and saw the bombers understood their fate. The rest kept firing their weapons to the very end.

When the strike came in, the flash of disintegrating heat and light rippled outward in an expanding ring. Vaporization warheads were carefully calibrated, with an adjustable devastation radius accurate to within a metre. The blast erased a small part of the Palace District, obliterating the factory, all the Soldier compies, and every one of the silver berets who stood in the way . . .

It took more than an hour for the boiling column of dust, smoke, and steam to dissipate, leaving behind a huge, glassy crater that was perfectly circular and perfectly sterile.

Basil showed no reaction, though his emotions roiled: grief for the loss of life (naturally), frustration over the failure, and the maddening sense that he was losing control. But he had to celebrate the victory, while he could still remember how to do so.

'Well, that takes care of the compy problem,' he said. 'Here, at least.'

FIFTY-THREE

GENERAL KURT LANYAN

Once they'd retaken the *Goliath*, the rest of the operation should have been a piece of cake, but Lanyan was wary of underestimating the Soldier compies again. Underestimating the damned clankers — in fact, not considering them a threat *at all!* — had got the EDF into this mess.

As his trainee technicians finished reassembling the command station so he could input the release code, Lanyan's teams continued sweeper operations to root out compies on deck after deck. Before long, the flagship would be clean.

The General tasked his now-eager recruits to do an inventory of the frozen Grid 0 vessels. Under normal circumstances, the guillotine protocol would leave the ships completely helpless until he rescinded the order. But he'd seen how much progress the compies had made in eviscerating the *Goliath*'s computer by the time he had retaken the bridge. No doubt the military robots were doing the same aboard the rest of the paralysed vessels. Even if the compies had to rip out and replace every system, they would get some of the ships functional again before long. Compies were distressingly effective workers.

'Divide up the teams,' Lanyan said. 'Concentrate on the capital ships, the Mantas and Thunderheads. I want at least four of them back under our control within the hour.' It would take two more hours for his anticipated reinforcements to arrive from other EDF bases. In the meantime, he'd have to send smaller teams to each captive ship and order his people to work double-time. That would increase his risk of losing personnel, but he was even less enchanted with the thought of letting so many fully armed battleships slip through his fingers.

It would take years for the shipyards to rebuild all those capital vessels, and the EDF needed every asset right now. Especially if the treacherous compies had already seized other grid battle groups . . . How much of the fleet was left?

Better to destroy the assets, however, than let them fall into enemy hands. As a fail-safe plan, Lanyan issued worst-case instructions. 'Get a targeting lock on as many Grid 0 ships as possible. If they make a move to escape, or attack, be ready to open fire. Take out only the engines if you can, or blow up the whole damned ship if you can't.'

Tactical interns and sensor trainees mapped out the paralysed vessels. Fresh from their drills, the recruits approached the problem as an exercise and submitted meticulous plans for the General's review. Lanyan liked all the details. He was really putting the kleebs through their paces.

What the hell did the Soldier compies have against the Hansa? What sort of vendetta? He remembered that young girl Orli Covitz who insisted that Klikiss robots and Soldier compies had wiped out the defenceless colony on Corribus. At the time, her story had seemed impossible, but he no longer doubted the kid.

A message came over the *Goliath*'s intercom. 'Deck 7 is cleared, sir.'

'Excellent. Have you found any survivors?'

'None whatsoever.'

'I didn't expect to. What's the inventory of destroyed compies so far?'

'Four more decks to survey, sir. Approximately forty Soldier compies are unaccounted for, but we don't know exactly how many were blown out the launching bay in the decompression.'

'Be conservative, and be very thorough.'

Ensign Childress's team had removed the human bodies and wrecked compies from the bridge. The constant chatter of technicians was a low drone, but he sensed the excitement as they replaced the covers on the main operational nodes. Hunched together, the techs ran diagnostic routines. Multicoloured lights winked on across the vital bridge stations, including the command chair.

'General, we're pleased to present you with this Juggernaut.' One of the techs grinned. 'All systems restored, major hull breaches repaired. Ready to take it out for a spin, sir?'

Lanyan sighed with relief. 'Engines? Shields? Weapons?'

'Much of it's jury-rigged, but we're confident this ship will do what you need her to do.'

Lanyan settled into the command chair. Now things were looking up. He received updates from two commando teams in the process of recapturing a pair of Manta cruisers. A third team was encountering fierce resistance and hadn't made it beyond the entry chamber of the nearest Thunderhead.

At last, one team reported taking the bridge of a hijacked Manta. 'Everything's mangled over here, sir. We can hold the high ground and start clearing out compies, but we need some help, maybe even replacement modules, before we can get this ship moving again.'

'All in good time,' Lanyan said. 'Now that we've got control, we'll save the tedious part for Phase Two.'

A woman at the *Goliath*'s sensor station looked up in surprise. 'General, detecting a large group of blips. Inbound ships, I believe.'

'Our reinforcements from the Moon base got here early. I didn't expect them for another hour or two.'

'No, sir – these ships are coming from outside the solar system.'

'Outside? Everyone alert! Have they identified themselves?'

'They're broadcasting a standard EDF transponder signal, a recognizable IFF pattern.' Each ship in the Earth Defence Forces was equipped with an 'identify friend/foe' signal that would peg them as the good guys in a space brawl and presumably prevent them from being shot at by their own comrades.

'Let's be cautiously optimistic. Maybe somebody else got away. Can you determine who it is?'

The sensor technician's brow furrowed with concentration. 'Analysing the signatures now. A Juggernaut ... at least ten Mantas, two Thunderheads, numerous support ships.' Then she brightened. 'I think it's part of the Grid 3 battle group, sir. I have an image coming from Admiral Wu-Lin.'

Lanyan nodded to himself. Wu-Lin was a competent, hard-edged, yet quiet man who never hesitated. He always preferred to make swift decisions and face the consequences if they turned out to be wrong rather than falter and lose an opportunity. 'Put him on. About time we had some good news.'

The image of a lean, steel-haired Asian man stared straight ahead into the screen. His voice sounded very clipped and formal. 'This is the commander of the Grid 3 battle group. Our

Soldier compies turned on us and attacked my crewmen, but we responded swiftly. We lost quite a few ships, but as you can see we prevented a complete takeover.'

'Excellent work, Admiral!' Since no green priest had been assigned to Wu-Lin's ships, the Grid 3 commander would not yet be aware of the scope of the insurrection.

As Wu-Lin continued, his expression did not change. He seemed more wooden than Lanyan remembered. 'I returned to Earth at top speed.'

Finally, things were changing for the better. 'Admiral, the uprising is widespread. Before the compies could steal the Grid 0 battle group, we paralysed their engines and are now in the process of retaking the ships.' Lanyan looked at his bridge crew and smiled. 'With your help, we might finish this clean-up sooner than I'd hoped. We would welcome your assistance.'

On screen, the image of Wu-Lin did not change. The communications officer said, 'General, I'm receiving no response from him.'

Lanyan scratched his head. The Juggernaut drifted silently closer. 'If he had as much of a firefight as we did, maybe his bridge is damaged. Can he even receive transmissions?'

'That's not it, sir. Admiral Wu-Lin, please acknowledge.'

The Grid 3 ships closed in. Lanyan frowned. 'Put everyone on increased alert status!'

'Sir, I think—'

Wu-Lin's Juggernaut opened fire on three of the cavalry gunships from the Mars base. The Grid 3 battleship vaporized the smaller vessels in a single shot.

'Full defences, dammit!' Lanyan slammed his fist down on the command chair, dislodging one of the precariously rewired control panels. Next, the Grid 3 Mantas began shooting at the mostly empty cavalry vessels. 'Send a message back to Earth right away: Soldier compies now control the Grid 3 battle group. Admiral Wu-Lin is presumed dead. Damned simulation!'

He spun to the weapons station, yelling at the frantic-looking techs. 'You better not be bullshitting about my weapons! Power up jazers and explosive projectile cannons. Load the railgun launchers!' Among the stalled Grid 0 vessels, the *Goliath* had the advantage of surprise, but only for a moment. 'Unload everything we've got into those oncoming ships.'

The guillotine code specific to the Grid 3 battle group was locked away in high security back at the Mars base. Wu-Lin would have had it, but Lanyan could not access the command string swiftly enough. The *Goliath* was his only immediate recourse. He felt a thrum as the Juggernaut's weapons fired; each beam and each hardened projectile flew in a fan-shaped pattern towards the approaching traitor vessels.

Two jazer beams ripped open the belly of Wu-Lin's Juggernaut, like gutting a big fish. The battleship's atmosphere vented. A debris of compies as well as human bodies spilled out. Still the marauding Juggernaut came on, followed by a group of Mantas and Thunderheads. All of them opened fire, specifically picking off Lanyan's cavalry ships.

The General swore, but maintained his focus, his perspective. He knew what he had to do. 'Commence the exit strategy now. Cripple as many of these Grid 0 ships as possible and blow up everything else. If we let them get away, the compies will use those assets against us.'

A flurry of weapons sparked a cascade of explosions on the frozen Grid 0 ships. 'Sound the evacuation order! Any teams that can get back aboard in ten minutes are going home with us.' Most of Lanyan's greenhorn sweeper teams were stuck aboard the compy-infested Mantas and Thunderheads, and they would never make it to their pursuit vessels in time.

'General, we can't just leave them—'

'In case you haven't noticed, Wu-Lin's ships outgun our little rescue party by ten to one! Take your best shots, then turn tail and get us out of here.'

With an admirably swift response, the trainee pilots hit their preselected targets, destroying the engines of the paralysed Grid 0 vessels. Several smaller cavalry craft turned about, taking potshots at the compy-controlled vessels. Lanyan had never thought he'd want to see damage inflicted upon EDF vessels.

The robot-commandeered battleships swept in, no longer bothering to broadcast Wu-Lin's image. The Grid 3 Juggernaut now concentrated its barrage against the *Goliath*. The understaffed battleship shuddered under the blows, but the hull armour held. For now.

'We can't stand against these enemies with just one Juggernaut and a few second-rate ships.' In fact, there was little enough chance he would escape at all. He needed to get the *Goliath* back to Earth. Maybe he could scrape together a larger assault force and return before the compies finished repairing the ships. 'Lock down and prepare for acceleration.'

His Juggernaut targeted the engines of more hijacked Mantas with a broad jazer spread, knocking at least seven offline. But that was all he could do.

Feeling angry, ashamed, and helpless as he ran away, Lanyan gripped the arms of his command chair and watched as the compy-controlled battleships continued seizing the Grid 0 fleet.

FIFTY-FOUR

TASIA TAMBLYN

When the Klikiss robot dragged EA out of the environment cell 'for analysis', Tasia shouted herself hoarse. She argued and threatened and pleaded, but the black robot ignored her, and the little Listener compy could not resist.

'I am sorry, Tasia Tamblyn.' Then EA was gone.

Robb held Tasia for a long time while she shuddered in fury and dismay. She had always learned to be tough, but here, bottled up with the other captives, she felt naked and barely capable of maintaining her façade. EA was one of the only threads connecting her to the outside.

'The Klikiss robots and the hydrogues – it's like an alliance between Dr Jekyll and Dr Frankenstein,' she said, halfway between a sob and a snarl.

'No human imagination could come up with anything as evil as those robots.' Smith Keffa wrapped his horrifically scarred arms around his chest, hugging himself. 'Monsters!'

Keffa was gaunt and haggard. During their endless, pointless waiting, he had told his story. He'd been a down-and-out Hansa merchant slipping from system to system, making just enough profit to put some fumes of stardrive fuel into his tanks. The Hansa paid little attention to runners like him, nor did they notice when people like Keffa disappeared. He certainly didn't know how long he'd been in captivity. *For ever*, he said.

When he'd gone to rendezvous with a 'business associate', he'd found his partner's ship dead in space. Then Klikiss robots had chased after him. Though Keffa tried to flee, his tanks were already drained and so his ship stalled. Klikiss robots dragged him off to the hydrogue experimentation chambers.

Fighting nausea, Keffa told of how the robots had sliced off patches of his skin with the tools in their articulated arms, cut deep into his muscles, taken samples of his marrow, apparently on the orders (or whims) of the drogues. He hated the black machines.

'Those monsters aren't my favourite thing in the universe, either,' Tasia said, 'but if they return my compy intact, maybe I won't tear them to pieces.'

Robb tried to offer encouragement. 'I don't think they'll hurt EA. We met another compy – called itself DD – apparently taken captive by the robots. They kept him intact, but we haven't seen him in a long while.'

For an interminable time – a month? An hour? – she pressed her hands against the coloured wall, trying to make out details through the murk of the dense atmosphere. Tasia kept watching, waiting, hoping. Finally, she saw the great black shape leading her small compy through the Escher-esque streets. *EA!* They were returning to the preservation cells. Tasia moved from place to place, looking for a better view.

The black machine approached, then loomed on the other side of the membrane. The prisoners shrank away, but Tasia waited defiantly. The Klikiss robot pushed EA like a doll through the barrier, then followed. 'Your compy is flawed. Her programming is damaged.'

Tasia stood her ground. 'What did you do to her?'

'Humans have interfered with the base routines. We cannot free EA from the restrictions, nor can we restore her to a normal condition. This one is worth no more than a human. Therefore, we will treat EA as an inferior captive.'

Even though the Klikiss robot meant its announcement as an insult, Tasia heard it as good news. 'She's sure as hell welcome with us!'

The alien robot withdrew into the membrane until its large form was swallowed back into the hellish outside environment. Tasia came forward to put her hands on EA's small, hard shoulders. 'Did they harm you? Dissect you?'

'They analysed me beyond any of my self-diagnostic routines. I believe their conclusions are correct. Something was done to change me from the Listener compy you remember. In the process, my memory was wiped.'

'It was an accident, EA. I read the report.' Tasia didn't want to consider otherwise. She had always been stubborn, but now she found herself more rigid, clinging to the details of what she remembered as reality.

'I believe the Earth Defence Forces tampered with me before I was returned to you. Perhaps someone inadvertently triggered an automatic routine to erase my memories. Or perhaps it was intentional.'

Tasia's indignation lashed out like a whip, striking many different targets. All Roamer compies contained fail-safe datawipes so that if any non-Roamer tried to interrogate them, all information about clan facilities and movements would be destroyed. Those precautions had been installed long before the Big Goose's declaration of war against the Roamers.

Robb looked at the compy, his honey-brown eyes wide. 'The EDF messed with EA? Are you sure?'

Tasia took several deep breaths to calm herself. Why was she so surprised? The Eddies had constantly treated her like dirt, regarded her with suspicion, stripped her of command responsibilities. Now she felt even more betrayed. 'I should have found some other way to warn the Osquivel shipyards. Then I wouldn't have lost you. Where was my Guiding Star?'

Robb looked surprised. 'What shipyards at Osquivel? I didn't see any—'

Shoulders sagging, Tasia explained how she had warned Del Kellum's facility about the EDF battle group on its way. She had known the Eddies might turn their weaponry against the clans instead of the drogues; they had an annoying habit of chasing after the wrong enemy. Because of EA's message, the Roamers had managed to hide their facilities in time.

But she had never guessed what it would cost her compy. In some ways, the Earth military was even worse than the Klikiss robots. At least the black alien machines didn't claim to be trustworthy.

'EA was lost after delivering her message,' Tasia continued. 'Someone must have intercepted her before she could find her way home. The bastards ruined her. Could have been General Lanyan, could be some underling.' She stared into the compy's optical sensors. 'I'm sorry, EA. I'm so sorry.'

FIFTY-FIVE

SIRIX

The Klikiss robot stood on the bridge of his stolen EDF Juggernaut and contemplated the extermination of the human race. His enjoyment of their demise was not cold and rational, since the original Klikiss race had imprinted a measure of their brutal personality on their servant robots. The malicious insectoid race considered such feelings necessary for the black drone machines to fulfil their roles. The Klikiss masters could not savour their power unless the downtrodden robots understood the difference between a dominator and a victim. The master could feel no pleasure unless a slave felt pain. The robots comprehended this to their very core programming.

Sirix and his fellows had known exactly what they were doing when they wiped out their creator race in a single, swift betrayal – and they had enjoyed it thoroughly. Even millennia later, the black robots hated the Klikiss with a violence that far exceeded the designs of the insectoid builders.

But with the Klikiss long gone, Sirix had only the humans to hate. And he did so with complete diligence.

This overthrow of the Earth Defence Forces was thorough and efficient. Soldier compies now controlled the Grid 3 battle group. A few ships had slipped away, but the robots had seized the bulk of the fleet and could use the battleships against humanity. It was a victory worthy of the most bloodthirsty Klikiss breedex.

All across the Earth Defence Forces, programming implanted in the compy modules had worked perfectly. The foolish humans believed promises and were slow to suspect supposed friends. No Klikiss would have made such an error.

As soon as the Soldier compies transmitted their initial success, Sirix and five Klikiss robots had boarded the captured Grid 3 ships. According to personnel files and service records in the database, Admiral Crestone Wu-Lin – whose blood now stained this very bridge – was one of the EDF's most competent commanders, yet even he had fallen without much of a fight.

With military efficiency, compies gathered the corpses strewn on the decks and ejected them into space. The blood and bodies did not bother Sirix, but bodies might hinder rapid movement during the upcoming military operation.

Sirix's plan was simple and swift. The combined battle groups of Grids 3 and 0 could converge on Earth. With the human capital destroyed, the Klikiss robots would then engage in straight-forward clean-up operations on all other Hansa colonies, as time permitted.

Humans had created and enslaved their competent computer-ized companions, much as the hated Klikiss race had done with their robots. The humans, though far less cruel, far less horrific than the original Klikiss, had still committed the same basic crime. Sirix and his counterparts had liberated the Soldier compies to perform useful functions, and had also developed a technique to remove programming that shackled other compy models into unwilling servitude. But many compies did not understand their own bondage and, like his prize specimen DD, they refused to appreciate the gifts that Sirix offered.

No matter. With hydrogue assistance, the robots had long ago exterminated the Klikiss race, and now they would do the same to humans. Once their creators were extinct, the compies would be free anyway.

First, however, Sirix had to deal with this setback. The unexpected paralysis of the Grid 0 battle group forced him to deviate from the plan, but Klikiss robots could be patient. They had already waited thousands of years.

General Lanyan had retreated with his hastily assembled group of cavalry ships, but the remaining Grid 0 vessels hung in space. With bursts of coded machine language, Sirix demanded a complete audit of the available ships and a detailed assessment of the damage Lanyan's fleeing trainees had inflicted upon the crippled battle group. Sirix had never anticipated that an EDF commander would shoot at his own ships rather than let them fall into enemy hands. The actions made logical sense, but emotional and panicked humans were seldom logical . . .

Swarms of Soldier compies were tearing apart the command bridges of all the paralysed ships, rerouting systems so the vessels could fly again. Fanatical humans might return at any time to destroy more of their own battleships.

In the name of efficiency, Sirix had sent thousands of Soldier compies outside onto the hulls equipped with tools and swiftly uploaded repair programming. The untiring compies repaired damage, replaced faulty components, removed irrelevant life-support systems. Other robots continued stripping out and rerouting the frozen computer modules.

They would succeed soon enough. It was only a matter of time.

Alone on the Juggernaut's bridge, Sirix received a report from a robot that had gone aboard one of the disabled Mantas. Because Wu-Lin's battle group had taken the humans by surprise, General Lanyan had been forced to leave a recovery team behind. The trainees had barricaded themselves on the Manta's bridge, but had no place to go.

'We detect sounds of destruction,' the Klikiss robot reported. 'They have given up hope of escaping.'

'That is when humans are most dangerous,' Sirix warned. 'You must break through and stop them.'

He clacked his sharp pincer claws together for emphasis. A satisfying sensation. While his components were equipped with delicate sensors, they did not approach the sensitivity of biological nerve endings. Even so, he had already experienced the pleasurable sensation of cutting flesh with his appendages, chopping meat and splintering bone, feeling the slick lubricant of fresh warm blood spilled across his ebony exoskeleton. His original Klikiss torturers would have understood very well.

He reached a swift decision. 'I will go over to the Manta myself. If humans remain alive there, I will assist you.'

FIFTY-SIX

ANTON COLICOS

They were going to Hyrillka. Anton stood self-consciously with Yazra'h and Vao'sh in the command nucleus of the flagship warliner; since he was a guest here, he was careful not to get in the way.

More than three hundred ornate ships flew away from Ildira on a mission of mercy. One-eyed Tal O'nh – second in rank only to Adar Zan'nh – led them all. According to what Vao'sh had told Anton, the old commander had lost his left eye in an explosion aboard a warliner when he was merely a septar; O'nh now wore a faceted jewel in his empty socket. The gem's reflected light provoked more fascination than pity.

Anton suspected that the sheer number of vessels was the Mage-Imperator's magnanimous way of demonstrating his acceptance of Hyrillka back into the fold. These warliners were not meant as a stern punishment but an acknowledgement of forgiveness. Each ship was full of able-bodied soldiers, talented engineers, much-needed supplies – and Rememberer Vao'sh and Anton Colicos as observers to document it all.

Anton thought his rememberer friend would have avoided travelling ever again after the horrors of Maratha, but Vao'sh needed to see what lost treasures were hidden in the vaults beneath the citadel palace. Besides, the rebuilding and restoration of Hyrillka was something a rememberer should witness. Freed from his travel restrictions, now that he was being sent away from Mijistra, Anton felt like a child who was no longer grounded.

In addition to relief supplies and reconstruction workers, the primary reason for the expedition to Hyrillka was to deliver the new Designate who would govern the world. His name was Ridek'h, and he couldn't have been more than thirteen years old.

Anton's heart went out to the kid, who waited anxiously with them in the warliner's command nucleus. Ridek'h always hovered close to Yazra'h, whom the Mage-Imperator had appointed as the boy's mentor. She devoted most of her attentions to the young man now, which was something of a relief to Anton.

Under normal circumstances, the Mage-Imperator's noble-born sons were his Designates, assigned to planets across the Ildiran Empire. The rightful Hyrillka Designate had been Pery'h – a well-educated and thoughtful man, according to everything Anton had heard – but Rusa'h had murdered him at the beginning of his rebellion. Now that the uprising had been crushed, the next in line was Pery'h's young son. Under normal circumstances, the boy would never have had to assume this role. The untimely death of a Designate was rare, and a Designate-in-waiting usually served for years before assuming the mantle of leadership. This time, though, there was no chance for transition. It was all being dumped on the kid, and Ridek'h was overwhelmed. Anton wouldn't have wanted to be in his shoes. He preferred observing from the sidelines.

Standing beside them in the command nucleus, Ridek'h peppered Yazra'h with questions even before they had left the

Ildiran system. 'Do you really think it will be as bad there as they say?' Anton listened to the guard woman dispensing her wisdom and support. Yazra'h was not a political instructor, but she had a strength of character that would serve the young Designate better than a dozen courtly schoolteachers.

'It is as bad as it is,' she said. 'You have inherited a burden greater than you ever imagined you might bear, Ridek'h. But it is your burden. Carry it.'

'The people on Hyrillka will help me,' said Ridek'h in a piping, hopeful voice. 'Will they not?'

'They are your people, and you are their Designate. You will have anything you need.'

'What if I need strength in my heart?' He looked so impossibly *young*.

'If it is within my capability to give it to you, Ridek'h, then I will do so. The Mage-Imperator asked me to help you, though I have no experience in formal instruction. Your father would have made an excellent Designate. Now I will do my best to show you how to become a wise leader.'

Anton felt like an eavesdropper, watching the intimate discussion between the two. Ridek'h put on a brave face, swallowed his anxiety with a visible gulp, and took the time to straighten his posture. Anton watched him imitate Yazra'h's warrior stance. He certainly wanted the young man to succeed.

Vao'sh remained silent and attentive, absorbing details to report back to the Hall of Rememberers. Yazra'h paced around the command nucleus, restless. Her Isix cats had accompanied them aboard the flagship, but during the journey she kept them in a large cargo chamber, where they would not disturb the crew.

'Tal, we are approaching the Durris trinary,' said the navigator. Normally, the nearby triple-star system held nothing of particular interest, no habitable planets, no gas giants. The three suns of

Durris had always shone brightly in the skies of Ildira – until the hydrogues and faeros had extinguished one of them.

Yazra'h looked first at Anton, raising her eyebrows, then at the boy Designate. 'This is what we must see. I asked the tal to take this course on purpose.' While the one-eyed commander called for the warliners in the cohort to reduce speed, Yazra'h looked at her young ward. 'We should all observe this and remember it.'

Maintaining perfect formation, the warliners closed in on the blot in space. The dead star was dark, still simmering with left-over nuclear reactions, but it had collapsed without the photonic pressure to support its own mass. Anton was not a physicist, and wondered what sort of fundamental changes – what sort of incredible weapons – were required to shut down a sun. Durris-B was no longer a star, just a tombstone.

'It's frightening,' he muttered.

'And you should be frightened,' Yazra'h said. 'See what our enemies are capable of doing.'

Ridek'h stared open-mouthed at the image. 'How can we stand against an enemy capable of . . . that?'

'The Mage-Imperator will find a way to save us.' Yazra'h raised her voice, not just for Ridek'h's benefit, but for the entire command nucleus.

Tal O'nh silently touched his hand to his chest where, along with insignia of his accomplishments in the Solar Navy, he had attached a prismatic disc. Anton recognized it as a symbol of the Lightsource. Considering the Ildirans' innate horror of darkness and blindness, he wasn't surprised that a man who had already lost one eye would cling to a prismatic icon representing constant light.

'We have six suns remaining, and the Ildiran Empire will endure,' Yazra'h said, as if she could make it so by commanding it. 'The Empire *must* endure.'

Tal O'nh added his support. 'A Solar Navy officer lives for nothing else.'

Anton knew that these words of encouragement were meant for the Ildirans on board, especially the young Designate, but he took heart from them nevertheless. It occurred to him that beneath Yazra'h's obvious physical strength, she was wiser than most people he had met. A scholar knew how to spot such things.

FIFTY-SEVEN

ORLI COVITZ

The mixed group headed through the Klikiss transportal to their new home. This place would be a fresh start, a second chance. With an odd sense of déjà vu, the girl lifted her chin, gathered her courage, and walked into the flat stone window. An instant later she walked out onto another new settlement world.

Llaro.

After all she'd been through, Orli Covitz wasn't sure about going to another former Klikiss world, but she didn't know where else she could live. Her overly optimistic father would have called Llaro a great opportunity. But he was dead now, along with everyone else on Corribus. She tried not to think about it.

Nevertheless, Orli decided to join the Crenna refugees in their relocation. She had few possessions: her salvaged music synthesizer strips, some clothes, and a lot of bad memories. She was fourteen, an orphan, and a survivor.

Since reports about the obliteration of the Corribus colony had posted her waifish face across every conceivable newsnet,

Orli had hoped that her real mother might re-emerge. But nobody could find her. Orli shrugged. She had never been much of a mother anyway. Orli was better off by herself. Even here.

The lavender skies were lovely: pastel colours over an arid landscape. A relatively ambitious settlement had already been put in place by the initial wave of colonists and EDF soldiers. Standing nearby, her friend Mr Steinman sniffed the air. 'Looks adequate, with room to spread out. I still can't get over my headache from all that *noise* on Earth.'

'I hope we don't have to eat furry crickets,' Orli said with a grimace.

'Don't kid yourself. We'll find something just as nasty here.'

Soldiers stood around the transportal. Military barracks surrounded the alien ruins containing the stone trapezoid, as if to prevent colonists from making a break for the transportal and slipping away. That wasn't a good sign.

A group of people came forward to greet them. Most wore strange costumes, garishly embroidered or adorned with colourful scarves, quite different from the plain but serviceable jumpsuits she was familiar with from Dremen or Corribus. And with many more pockets.

'Never expected to see so many Roamers here,' Steinman said.

Orli soon got the impression that she and the Crenna refugees were the only ones actually happy to be on Llaro. It turned out the Roamers were prisoners of war rounded up during various EDF raids, and they were naturally frustrated and miserable. The original settlers resented having their promised land turned into a POW camp, and the EDF personnel felt stuck in an isolated outpost babysitting a bunch of colonists. Nobody liked it here.

But Orli and the people from Crenna had no place else to go.

The leader of the Roamer detainees, a potbellied man named Roberto Clarin, crossed his arms over his chest, trying to make his displeasure as plain as possible. 'Shizz, this is more of their stupid plan to integrate us into Hansa society. The Big Goose thinks that if we're satisfied with this place, we'll just forget everything they did to us.'

Thinking of her own struggles, how many new starts and setbacks she and her father had faced, Orli studied the Roamer man. 'No one can make you forget the bad things that happen, Mister. But you've got to move ahead. Otherwise, the memories are like quicksand.'

Clarin looked down at the girl and chuckled. 'By the Guiding Star, I hope all the newbies are like you, kid.'

After passing through the transportal, the fresh arrivals inventoried their sacks of clothes and keepsakes, Hansa-issued tools, packages of favourite foods, souvenirs they had salvaged from their world before it had frozen over. Orli clutched her satchel, feeling the flexible bulk of the cheap music synthesizers.

The whole gathering soon became a swap meet. The Roamers and first settlers were eager to see what new items the Crenna refugees had brought. Introductions were made all around, and Orli's mind quickly blurred with the dizzying names and clans and connections.

Before long, everyone pitched in to erect pre-fab structures as temporary homes for the Crenna settlers. Orli wondered whether she might have a small hut to herself, or be adopted by one of the colonist families. She wasn't sure what she wanted. She wasn't really a child anymore. Not really.

Mayor Ruis, representing the people of Crenna, met with the Roamers and the council head of the original settlers. 'I promise we'll do everything possible to make ourselves self-sufficient.' With an infectious grin, he turned to a tall, quiet man with dark brown skin. 'We've got plenty of expertise among us, so we won't be a drain. We can get through anything together. Right, Davlin?'

The other man answered with a thin smile that wrinkled a crosshatching of scars on his left cheek. 'Yes, we do have a considerable ability to solve problems.' He lowered his voice to Ruis, though Orli could still hear what he said. 'But we'd better think of a new name for me, Mayor, if I'm going to stay here with you. I'd rather the Chairman doesn't find out that I'm still alive.'

FIFTY-EIGHT

CHAIRMAN BASIL WENCESLAS

Accompanied by Deputy Cain, Basil rode a shuttle up to the battered Juggernaut that General Lanyan had liberated from the Soldier compies. He studied notes on his datapad, ignoring the pilot's announcement that they would be aboard the *Goliath* in ten minutes.

'I'll have my report to you the moment it's finished, sir,' Cain said. 'I have assigned focus groups to discuss various aspects of the aftermath.' Careful in his duties to the point of being obsessive, the deputy always provided well-considered conclusions with all the supporting evidence Basil needed for making a decision.

With a final glance at the disheartening summary numbers, Basil dimmed the display. 'I am not looking forward to the final tally of this disaster, Mr Cain. I can't begin to estimate the fallout – *if* we survive the next few months.'

When the Grid 0 flagship loomed before them, Basil felt nauseated to see its singed hull plates from the recent skirmish. The only capital ship left of the main battle group! If Lanyan had stayed a little longer, fought a little harder, could more of the hijacked vessels have been retrieved? Or would the EDF just have lost this one, too?

He suspected the General had made the correct decision. The Hansa media staff would have to bury the knowledge that so many trainees had been left in the clutches of the enemy. *Just like at the battle of Osquivel*, he thought. And that one had recently come back to bite them with the return of unexpected survivors and the embarrassing altruism of the Roamers.

A protocol officer in a rumpled uniform hurried to greet them in the Juggernaut's secondary landing bay. 'Let me show you to the bridge, sirs.' He brushed self-consciously at wrinkles in his shirt. 'I apologize for the mess. We've been working double duty to effect repairs.'

Basil scowled. 'That goes without saying. Save the small talk until after we've received the General's report.'

When the three men arrived on the *Goliath*'s bridge, the disorder made Basil wince. Lanyan was usually a stickler for regulation neatness, but though the General was currently on deck, crewmen bustled back and forth as if he weren't there, calling to each other, tossing tools. Workers and officers alike lifted debris and installed components without regard to their relative ranks. Circuitry welders flashed fountains of sparks. The air had an acrid tang of oily smoke, hot metal, and something unidentifiable that was vague and unpleasant.

'General!' The protocol officer raised his voice, '*General Lanyan!* The Chairman is here.'

Lanyan initialled an inspection pad that an ensign pushed in front of him, then swivelled his chair. A shadow of beard stubble covered his face (which was also surprising, since he usually kept his face so smooth it looked slippery). He had taken off his uniform jacket and wore an unmarked workshirt with the sleeves rolled up.

'Mr Chairman, Mr Deputy, I appreciate your coming up to orbit for this meeting.' He briskly shook Basil's hand, then Cain's. His ice-blue eyes were bloodshot. 'As you can see, I couldn't spare even a few hours to go down to Hansa HQ. We've got to get our asses moving and pull everything together. Ships keep trickling in, but not nearly enough for anything close to a thorough defence of Earth, let alone other Hansa planets. By now the compies have seized most of our grid battleships, and if they all come barrelling back here . . . well, let's just say we want to be as ready for them as we can.'

'Deputy Cain is compiling a thorough assessment.'

Cain activated his datapad and sorted the numbers for display, but before he could deliver his summary, Lanyan ran to the sensor station, shouting. 'I told you not to deactivate that system! I don't care what else you have to bypass, but I need redundancy on our weapons trackers.'

'But it's for the f-food synthesizer, sir,' said the amazed-looking ensign, who struggled not to stutter. 'W-we've already sent for replacement parts. They'll be here from the Moon base within the day.'

'And what if the compies come back within the *hour*? Would you rather have jazers or chipped beef?'

'U-understood, General.'

Lanyan turned back to Basil. 'I'm sorry, Mr Chairman. Where were we?'

'I was about to summarize what we know,' Cain said. The deputy might not have the hard edge necessary to be a good leader, but at least he was competent. 'By our best projections, we've lost approximately seventy per cent of our military in the past few days.'

The General looked as if he were in physical pain. 'And *six* of my grid admirals. Unless our crewmen managed to scuttle their own ships, we have to assume those battle groups are now controlled by Soldier compies. As far as we know, only Admirals Willis, Diente, San Luis, and Pike survived.'

Cain did not do a good job at sounding optimistic. 'It is possible that a few more are cut off from communications and simply not responding. However, I'd prefer not to have an unrealistically rosy picture of the situation.'

'Unrealistically rosy picture?' Basil raised his eyebrows.

Lanyan paced around his chair. 'What the bloody hell do the clankers want? What set them off? Are they really controlled by the Klikiss robots?'

Basil took the datapad from Cain, switched to a new screen, and motioned towards the General. 'Here is what we're going to do. In the old days, they called it "circling the wagons" – a defensive posture adopted in dire times. We need to get every single functional ship into position around this solar system.'

'Even small civilian craft, Mr Chairman?' Cain asked. 'That could cause a disproportionate amount of unrest among the public.'

'They can do their part, just like everyone else. We know unarmed commercial vessels won't stand a chance against the drogues or our own hijacked EDF ships, but they can sound an alarm if any enemy comes towards Earth. Set them up as picket ships.'

'We could establish automatic tripwire satellites, too,' Cain suggested. 'It'll increase our coverage, improve resolution and response time.'

Lanyan said, 'Distant early warning? That'll only tell us when to start praying. We don't have much of anything left to fight with. If any significant force comes here, we're toast. Burnt toast.'

Suddenly several of the *Goliath*'s bridge stations lit up with a sparkle of alarms. Announcements chattered over the speakers, signals from outlying picket ships. 'Incoming vessels, General! Three of them.'

'What are they? How big?'

'The size of Manta cruisers, sir. Broadcasting EDF identification signals.'

'That doesn't mean a damn thing anymore,' Lanyan growled. 'Send intercept ships with enough firepower to snuff the intruders if they turn out to be bad guys.'

Though seasoned repair techs continued to work, two stations were up and running, displaying a tactical plot of the incoming bogeys and the intercept vessels scrambling from defensive points around the Earth system. To their vast relief, the intercept ships broke off. 'They're ours! Three Mantas genuinely piloted by humans. They escaped from Grid 7.'

'How can you be sure?' Basil said in a low voice.

'We've spoken to them directly. No doubt about it.'

'I didn't doubt Admiral Wu-Lin either,' Lanyan growled, 'and it cost us plenty. Have someone go aboard and verify. *Personally*. Don't believe it until you see the flesh-and-blood with your own eyes.'

Before long, the announcement was confirmed. 'It really is good news! A hell of a slaughter over here, but it looks like the good guys won this round. One Manta has only seven human survivors – including Admiral Willis! They've piloted the ship here after linking their systems to one of the other cruisers.'

A new voice came over the comm circuit, a salty, grandmotherly drawl: 'Thank heavens for barfing and diarrhoea – otherwise none of us would be alive. Food poisoning saved our lives, General. Funny how things work out.'

'Please explain, Admiral Willis,' Lanyan said.

'Something went wrong with the *Jupiter*'s food-processing systems, and a wave of salmonella knocked an entire shift out of commission. I couldn't afford to have my Juggernaut drastically understaffed, so I drew the bulk of the Soldier compies from the other grid ships for added manpower, primarily to do menial work in the overflow sickbays we set up. Why not let the clankers clean up all the shit and puke, right?

'Anyway, I was over on one of my Mantas inspecting and rearranging the reduced crews when the compies went nuts. There were so many of them on the Juggernaut, they took over the *Jupiter* in a snap, but at least we had a fighting chance on a few of the other cruisers, where the compy complement was reduced. Three battered Mantas – that's all I could bring back. The rest of Grid 7 is in the hands of the enemy. Makes me want to crap my pants, food poisoning or no food poisoning.'

Lanyan looked at Basil, oddly relieved. 'Admiral, at least you managed to limp home. You don't know how much those Mantas mean to us right now. We damn well need every piece of equipment, even if it needs some fixing.'

'We've done all that duct tape can do over here, General,' Willis said.

Basil looked at the repair crews still busy on the *Goliath*'s stripped-down bridge. The task would get larger and larger as more pieces of equipment crawled home. 'Put all skilled space construction crew members on the job. I don't care what else they're doing or whom they belong to. No excuses. We need everybody. Most of our spacedock facilities are out in the asteroid belt, but I'd feel more comfortable keeping any functional ships closer to home.'

'Give us the parts, and my own people can make all basic repairs here, Mr Chairman.'

'Good.' Basil leaned close to his datapad again. 'If only a third of the EDF remains, then I'm issuing a complete reactivation order. Every soldier from any branch of the service, whether on active or inactive duty, any retired personnel, anyone making a fine living as a consultant in the commercial sector – I want them *all* back. And we need to recall any EDF battleships still under human control, no matter where they are. Every single vessel that survived the robot insurrection needs to come back home. Now. We're talking about the full-fledged defence of planet Earth.'

Cain frowned, clearly considering the consequences. 'Mr Chairman, we may have cut off supply runs, but we still maintained a presence at colonies that signed the Charter. Your order would force us to abandon every Hansa colony to its fate.'

'They'll be just swinging in the wind,' Lanyan said. 'They'll have no protection against either the hydrogues or the robots.'

'Focus on the big picture, gentlemen. Earth is our highest priority.'

Lanyan did not look pleased with the instructions either, but he nodded slowly, scratching the itchy bristles of his beard stubble. 'You are defining those other worlds as expendable, correct?'

Basil knew that the bridge crewmembers were eavesdropping, but unlike so many other parts of his administration, this was not something that could be kept secret for long. 'Without the Earth there is no Terran Hanseatic League. We have to set priorities.'

FIFTY-NINE

PATRICK FITZPATRICK III

Maureen Fitzpatrick kept state-of-the-art vehicles for her own purposes: short-range flyers, ground cars, even one elegant spaceworthy yacht equipped with an Ildiran stardrive and a full tank of ekti. But Patrick preferred antique automobiles, mainly because the grease, oil, and sheer clutter frustrated his grandmother to no end.

Years ago the Battleaxe had denied him that hobby because greasy hands and dirty fingernails offended her sensibilities. Now, though, she had actually acquired several cars for him to tinker with, encouraging his 'eccentric pursuits', just to keep him out of trouble.

Patrick wanted to be doing something so much more significant. He wanted to be talking to interviewers, expressing a positive view of what the Roamers had done to the EDF survivors. But Maureen now kept him safely hidden away in the mansion where no one could see him, while she scheduled him with 'the best therapists in the world'.

It had been only a few days since the welcome home party.

He had tried to make postings and schedule interviews in his crusade to defend the Roamers, but in the sudden shock and confusion of the Soldier compy revolt, the returning captives from Osquivel were no longer the story of the hour. The whole EDF had fallen apart, compies had turned against their creators, millions were dead, and killer robots were surely coming to Earth. His grandmother didn't even need to pull strings to keep him gagged: Nobody cared about alleged injustices to Roamer clans.

Maybe somebody might have noticed danger signs among the compies if they hadn't been so preoccupied with chasing down Roamer settlements . . .

He was sure that General Lanyan and Chairman Wenceslas had somehow brought the EDF disaster down upon themselves, just as they had triggered the Roamer ekti embargo. He couldn't believe Lanyan had coolly denied the whole incident about destroying Kamarov's cargo ship! They'd made the current mess, so let them deal with it. Patrick had already resigned from the Earth Defence Forces, and he could not stomach the thought of serving such a flawed organization. How many other eager young officers, like himself, had been ordered to fire upon Roamer trading ships?

Patrick felt as if he would explode from frustration.

Fortunately, in the last few days Maureen had rarely been around to see him. She had suggested that he keep himself busy in the vehicle bay. Patrick did find working with the old engines therapeutic – changing oil, replacing spark plugs, checking fan belts and air filters. The physical work freed his mind and helped him to think more clearly.

Back at Osquivel, he had talked with Zhett about vehicles from the mid-twentieth century, ones built before computer chips and intelligent/adaptive circuitry allowed private autos to diagnose their own problems and repair themselves. The internal-combustion technology was primitive yet effective in a brute-force way. He had downloaded detailed guidebooks for his 1957 Plymouth Fury, his 1972 Ford Mustang, and (strictly for practice) a rusty little 1981 Chevrolet Chevette.

Now that he was done with political nonsense, his military career path, and his family reputation, he made plans while working on the cars. As soon as his grandmother let her guard down, he would do something she'd never be able to prevent. He didn't think he'd have any trouble fooling the therapists trying to 'deprogram' him from Roamer brainwashing. Stockholm Syndrome, indeed!

He slipped behind the Mustang's steering wheel and turned the ignition's old-fashioned analogue key, then pumped the accelerator to awaken the beast under the hood. 'At least I can make *something* work right.'

He mused while looking through the windshield at the other ships in the vehicle pool, especially the space yacht. He knew how to fly every craft here. Why not just take the starship and go searching for Zhett? If the Roamers had packed up from the rings of Osquivel, he had no idea where he would even begin to look, but he certainly wasn't going to find her by sitting in an engine bay and playing with old cars! Patrick began to make more concrete plans.

He released his foot on the accelerator, and the Mustang's engine stuttered, coughed, then died in a choking gurgle. Bluish-grey smoke curled up from the rear of the car, and Patrick could smell the harsh-sweet fumes of internal-combustion exhaust. Silence returned like ripples fading in a pond after a thrown pebble.

As he climbed out of the driver's seat, Fitzpatrick spotted his grandmother standing at the entrance to the service bay, watching him. She looked wrung out, her skin pale, her grey hair bound back in a quick and serviceable clip rather than her usual elegant coiffure. He'd never seen her look so haggard.

He slammed the car door, self-consciously looked at his grease-stained hands, then wiped them on his pant legs. 'You look like you've aged a million years, Grandmother.'

Patrick had long since grown immune to her melodrama. All his life, he had seen her swing through the pendulums of crisis after crisis. She overreacted and exaggerated the importance of every scandal; each time a council vote did not go her way, it seemed like the end of the world.

'Is it any wonder?' She stared at her grandson in the service bay's intense overhead lamps, and her eyes were sparkling with tears! Patrick had never seen such a thing, the Battleaxe had long ago learned not to bother putting on an act for him. 'I'll get your uniforms ready, and I'll have your favourite meal prepared.' She hesitated. 'But you'll need to tell the kitchen staff what it is you'd like. I don't even know your favourite food.'

He scrubbed his hands on a rag. The friction of his actions released a solvent woven into the fabric, and the stains quickly vanished from his fingers and knuckles. 'What are you talking about?'

Maureen looked away as if she had failed him somehow. 'I couldn't convince them to make any exceptions. I used every favour I had left, but the Chairman's instructions are utterly rigid.'

Exasperated, Fitzpatrick slammed the hood of the Mustang. 'Are you aware that you aren't making any sense?'

She stared at him as if she couldn't believe he was so out of touch. 'In the aftermath of the Soldier compy revolt, you've been called back to duty. Everyone has. Even I'll be doing a lot of special projects behind the scenes.'

'What are you talking about?'

'All resignations and retirements have been rescinded, effective immediately. Every trained member of the Earth Defence Forces has to be deployed to protect our planet. Every single one. Killer robots are coming, and probably the hydrogues too. It's only a matter of time.'

Patrick's hands went numb, and the cleaning rag fell to the sealed floor of the service bay. Maureen stepped forward as if tempted to hug him, but then thought better of it. 'You're going back into battle. To the front lines.'

SIXTY

ZHETT KELLUM

Golgen's hydrogen-rich clouds turned a lemony tan in the spreading rays of sunrise. Floating free above the sky-ocean was a lot better than being cramped with the humourless Kowalski clan members at Forrey's Folly. Zhett's father was right – skymining was what Roamers were born to do.

Early Golgen cloud harvesters had discovered a thin temperate zone where the oxygen and nitrogen balance created pockets of habitability. When a skymine cruised in this layer, containment fields, oxygen condensers, and heaters allowed for an open deck. Zhett could stand here all by herself and listen to the winds whistling across the storm bands.

The empty skies seemed an unsettling and lonely place punctuated by rising chemical plumes. She watched, attuned for any sort of stirring below. Would she see an ominous ripple in the cloud banks if a warglobe were to cut through the mists? This was the first place the drogues had ever struck, destroying the Blue Sky Mine in misguided retaliation for the Big Goose's Klikiss Torch test.

Yes, the Big Goose certainly had a talent for pissing people off. She gripped the red painted rail. The metal was cold, but she squeezed hard, imagining it might be someone's scrawny neck. Someone like Patrick Fitzpatrick III . . .

Zhett shook her head to clear her thoughts. Supposedly, the Kellum skyminers had nothing to worry about from hydrogues. If Jess Tamblyn pronounced Golgen free of the enemy, then she believed him. She had flirted with the handsome man when he'd delivered water from Plumas, but she could tell that Jess's heart belonged to someone else – someone whose love caused him more pain than joy. But though he was smitten with another woman and didn't know a good thing when Zhett offered it to him, she was sure Jess had never lied to her. Unlike certain other people . . .

'Out to watch the early morning operations, my sweet?'

Her father wore a warm vest and kept gloves clipped to his belt. Even filtered and tamed by the containment field, the brisk wind made her cheeks rosy. 'What difference does the hour make, Dad? You keep operations going around the clock.'

Kellum laughed. 'It's good to see that my baby daughter understands business. You'll be a fine facility manager someday.'

Sinuous probes dropped into the upwelling atmosphere as the skymine drifted along. Intake and feed tanks gulped gaseous mixtures into separating chambers and ekti reactors, which converted hydrogen into stardrive fuel. Waste gases spilling from the exhaust funnel propelled the facility along. Maintenance ships flitted around the perimeter. Suited workers in jetpacks circled the junctions of the modules, inspecting the process lines.

'Our fourth skymine just came on-line,' Kellum said. 'Without drogues nipping at our asses, the fast condensers and on-the-fly ekti reactors are just as efficient as these big rigs. We'll fill a cargo escort every two days.'

'More fuel than we could ever need.' She held onto her father's thick arm.

'Let's not go overboard. After all these years of austerity and rationing, we've got a lot of ground to make up.'

After leaving Forrey's Folly, former Kellum employees had flown back to Osquivel. In the darkness high above the ecliptic, charged with enthusiasm, they retrieved all their equipment. With a safe gas giant available again, clan Kellum could create stardrive fuel as fast as they could sell it.

Yes, their fortunes had certainly turned, and Zhett tried to feel happy about it. 'Are you going to miss the old shipyards, Dad? You put decades of work into them, your heart and soul—'

'By damn, of course not! They were an administrative pain, and profits were always dicey. Skymining makes me much happier. It's back to our traditional place.'

She chuckled. 'Remember when we were hiding in the rings, watching the Eddies and the drogues fight over Osquivel? You swore you would never go back to skymining again.'

'Big mistake – saying never, I mean.'

Golden sunlight brightened across the clouds. A spidery cargo escort lifted up and away, its metal legs holding ekti canisters. A flush of anger heated Zhett's skin as she remembered how Patrick Fitzpatrick had tricked her and stolen a similar cargo escort.

Her father didn't notice her mood shift. 'At least three other families are bringing skymines here.' He opened his arms to encompass the infinite skyscape. 'But Golgen's a big place. Plenty to go around.'

Kellum rested meaty elbows on the red rail. With a sideways glance, he scooped an arm around his daughter's shoulders. 'After the mess at Rendezvous, the scattered clans are drawing together. Have I told you the plans for a new commercial hub at Yreka? All very hush-hush, not much more than a blackmarket network with

291

the orphaned Hansa colonies – but it's a start. We'll be thumbing our noses at the Big Goose and trading only with the people we like. The Eddy bastards can eat non-recyclable waste for all I care.'

'Yes, Dad,' Zhett said, deciding to think no more of Fitzpatrick. 'That's exactly what the Eddy bastards can do.'

SIXTY-ONE

JESS TAMBLYN

Leaving stormy Charybdis on their mission to Plumas, Jess and Cesca were finally alone. The enclosed water was warm, a buoyant embrace so the two could drift in each other's arms.

At first, Jess was lost in the wonder of the simple physical contact, the solid feel of another human body, the clasp of a hand, the touch of a shoulder – how he had missed it! But the joy was oh so much more intense because it was Cesca. *Cesca.*

Drifting together and more than merely alive, their bodies remembered each other. Skin renewed contact with skin. A tingle suffused Jess's bones, his muscles, his eyes. For years Jess had imagined a moment when the two of them could touch again. And now that the dreamed-of time was actually here, it was somehow more brilliant, more *real*, than any touch he had experienced in his life.

When they had finished making love after such a lonely age, Jess felt completely happy and content. For the first time, Jess truly knew how it felt to be one with someone. With Cesca. He let the sensation encircle him like her arms around his waist.

Always permeating his mind and hers, the elemental creatures drank in every detail of the experience. A voice rang in both of their heads, *Now we understand. Always before, your words and desires had insufficient meaning to us. We are grateful for the enlightenment you shared.*

Jess grinned. 'It was our pleasure.' He realized now that their every kiss, every mingled droplet of moisture, every shared sparkle of perspiration had also joined them closer together, thanks to the water elementals. The wentals had bound them more tightly than he or Cesca could ever have done.

She was embarrassed. 'We had an audience?'

'I prefer to consider the wentals allies and companions, rather than voyeurs. Remember how we've changed. They're part of *us* now.'

'That'll take some getting used to.' She drifted closer to him. 'But I can accept the circumstances – especially in exchange for *this* . . .'

At last, he no longer felt a sense of betrayal towards Ross. If his brother hadn't been killed by the hydrogues, Jess knew he would have stayed on the honourable path. His love for Cesca would have remained unrequited. But the Guiding Star shone steadily now.

When they reached the ice moon, Cesca stared through the curved bubble. The shimmering alien vessel came to rest on the frozen surface, lit with splintered reflections. Below, on the cracked plains of ice, they could make out the silent facilities, the standing wellheads – and fourteen large water tankers.

'There they are,' Jess said. Once filled with wental water, those tankers would become incredible weapons against the drogues. They would find Roamer volunteers to fly them to infested gas giants and release their cargoes into the high clouds. The wentals would recapture one gas giant after another.

He knew his uncles would be glad to see him again, anxious to help with this new challenge. After retrieving his mother's frozen body from the crevasse, Jess had just left her in the grotto and raced off to rescue Cesca. Now maybe he could give her a proper Roamer funeral. Mourning was a way of life for the clans. The last time Cesca had been to Plumas was when his father had died, and before that, Ross . . .

Jess took her by the hand and drew her through the vessel's permeable hull. She stood next to him on the rugged ice, exposed to open vacuum and completely unharmed. The Speaker for the Roamer clans looked like a surprised little girl, filled with sense of wonder.

But Jess could sense unusual vibrations with his bare feet, disruptions so severe they penetrated the thick crust. The wentals seemed to knot within him. *There is danger. The waters here are angry. Something separate from us . . .* Once again, the wentals were being mysterious. Jess was anxious to get to the water mine settlement beneath the ice.

Uneasy, he led Cesca across the rippled terrain to the nearest lift shaft. The airlock had been forced open from the inside, and the ice outside the door was splattered with an iron-hard film, as if someone had dumped out buckets of red paint. Scraps of translucent tissue, like burst and discarded polymer bags, lay frozen to the ground.

The airlock controls showed that the lift shaft had automatically sealed itself when exposed to the vacuum. He would have to find another way inside. 'Come with me.'

Calling up wental energy, he showed her how to shift aside the molecules of frozen water and drop through the ice as if they had a parachute. It should have been a time of wonder for Cesca as she accompanied him, but her alarm grew as she too felt the violent vibrations from below.

When the two of them descended into the grotto, they encountered a scene of appalling chaos. Crashing sounds and hissing steam filled the chamber. Geysers erupted from split well pipes. Torrents of meltwater and shattered chunks of ice tumbled as an irresistible force repeatedly slammed the ceiling.

The light here was far dimmer than he remembered. Jess saw empty craters where two of the artificial suns had once been. Roamer workers ran about, screaming and shouting as they dived for shelter. More than a dozen bodies lay on the ground, many of them encased in cocoons of ice, others simply dead where they had fallen. Cesca pointed to elongated flashes of scarlet, a pack of worm-like creatures that slithered along the ice in pursuit of a fleeing man.

Another explosion slammed into the roof like a tantrum-throwing child pounding on a door. Jess and Cesca spun to the sound. The mists briefly cleared, and he saw the unmistakable form at the heart of the rampage.

When he'd brought her body back out of the crevasse, Karla Tamblyn had been encased in ice. Seeing her alive again but impossibly altered, he experienced a flood of memories, the painful farewell conversations with her, his mother's words gradually slurring as the cold stole her away.

Now his mother had become fury incarnate. Jess saw in her face, and in the almost tangible aura around her, the same terrible and uncontrolled lust for destruction that the wentals had shown him in the memory images of the Ildiran septar and the Klikiss breedex, both of whom had succumbed to tainted wentals. He felt the living water entities tug inside him, a sense of revulsion. His heart sank like a stone, and Jess knew exactly what had happened to his mother . . . though he didn't know how.

Karla's skin was white, as if her face and arms were carved out of milky ice, but corrupted lightning lived behind her eyes. *Tainted.*

When she saw him, her ivory face was blank and implacable. Then her expression registered clear recognition.

With power crackling all around her, Karla's inhuman voice boomed out, without even a hint of warmth. 'Welcome home, Jess.'

SIXTY-TWO

NIRA

It was an unsettling thing for Nira to look upon her own grave. Udru'h had announced her 'death', and everyone had believed him. No Ildiran would doubt the word of a Designate, and the humans had not thought to question it.

The traditional marker was a geometrically cut stone with a tiny solar power source that generated a hologram of her face. Nira looked at the blurry image of her taken from the breeding records. She had started to look old and battered from the moment she was brought to Dobro.

With Osira'h silent beside her, Nira knelt on the hillside, feeling the dry grasses prickle her bare green knees. She touched her fingers to the ground as if searching for her own lost life beneath the soil.

'I first met my father on this hillside,' the girl said solemnly. 'The Mage-Imperator came to see your grave marker – I think that is why Designate Udru'h bothered to erect it in the first place. Most humans don't receive anything so elaborate.'

Nira's throat was dry as she tried to imagine the scene

and what Jora'h must have been thinking. 'You saw him here?'

The girl's expression remained strangely distant. 'Even though you gave me all your memories, I still could not talk to him. I could not be sure which side he was on. I knew what had happened to you, what he had allowed to happen.'

Nira glanced sharply at her daughter. Jora'h had been here, so close, but he too had believed Udru'h's lie about her death. 'He knew nothing about it! He couldn't have. You of all people know how much your father loved me.'

The girl's stare was unwavering and unusually harsh. 'I know how much you loved *him*. But, as you have seen with Designate Udru'h, Ildirans are masters of deception.'

Nira averted her eyes. 'Jora'h loved me. I'm certain he still does. I'll know it as soon as I see him.' If Designate Udru'h did not arrange for an 'accident' before she could return to Jora'h. What did Udru'h have to gain by letting her free now? She would have to be extremely cautious.

She looked at Osira'h, feeling new guilt for dumping all of her terrible memories and hateful experiences into such a fresh and impressionable mind.

'Why are you looking at me that way, Mother?'

Nira forced a bittersweet smile. 'I see only a little girl, but when you talk, I am amazed by your words. You're extremely wise for a child.'

'I have never been just a child. It wasn't allowed.' Nira felt an immense sadness, even though the girl smiled warmly. 'But I did have a *childhood*, Mother. I had yours. I remember living with your mother and father, your brothers and sisters in a crowded dwelling. You were the only one in your family who was interested in stories. I remember us climbing to the high canopy for the first time, right after you were accepted as a green priest acolyte. Ah, the view! The fronds were like an ocean, extending as far as we could see! A big emerald condorfly buzzed right past.'

Nira was lost in the recollection herself. 'I was so startled I fell back, almost dropped off the branches—'

'But a green priest was there to catch us. Beneto, wasn't it?'

'And we just stared for hours, smelling the winds, watching the flying insects, listening to all the acolytes reading aloud.' Looking into her daughter's eyes, she saw that Osira'h really did remember every detail. *So, I offered her a few pleasant memories, too . . .*

'I can't imagine being without the gift you gave me.' Osira'h turned quickly to grin at a group of small figures approaching. 'Here come my brothers and sisters. They wanted to meet you.'

Intent on the sham of her grave, Nira flinched as she saw the small half-breed forms coming towards her. Each of those children, sprung from weeks of abuse in the breeding barracks, was an experiment, conceived not out of love but to meet a genetic design. Her hand clenched.

Osira'h remained placid, though she sensed her mother's fear and reluctance. 'I know very well what you think of their fathers. I have your memories of how they were conceived, born, and taken from you.' She reached out to squeeze Nira's green hand. 'For you, their origin was a curse. You endured it. But that is in the past, and they had no part in it. They are not your enemies. They are your *children*, Mother. Like me. Let me introduce you to them.' Taking her hand, she led Nira to meet the four children halfway. With weak knees, Nira looked at the young faces, forcing herself to truly *see* them.

'This is Rod'h, the oldest of your sons.' The boy smiled at her. His eyes glittered with a star-shaped reflection. Rod'h had a hard face, with the handsome features of Jora'h's line. She could see immediately that he was the son of Udru'h.

Nira's heart pounded, but she steeled herself. She tentatively extended her hand. 'This is how humans greet each other.' Rod'h clasped her hand, and his grip was surprisingly strong.

'You are my mother? I never thought I would meet my mother.'

Nira tried to see beyond her own suspicions. Despite his paternal heritage, this boy was still *her son*. No matter how much hatred she held towards Udru'h, Rod'h was half her child, as well.

'And this is Gale'nh.'

Nira turned to the younger of the boys, recognized his strong and proud features. 'I . . . remember Adar Kori'nh.'

The boy seemed pleased. 'My father was a hero. And you, too, Mother. We were taught how we might save the Empire.'

Nira swallowed hard. 'That is what some Ildirans believed.'

The two other daughters, youngest of the five children, were Tamo'l and Muree'n. Though the youngest, Muree'n was already larger than her two closest siblings, showing her heritage from the guard kith. They all crowded forward, anxious to be close to their mother. When Nira felt their tentative curiosity, their unbelievable innocence, she realized that she did not hate them, could not hold their own births against them.

'I've told them the truth, Mother. We will help you change this place.'

'I am glad to know you all. And you too, Osira'h.' Nira touched her daughter on the cheek as tears welled in her eyes. 'For showing me what was right, even though I was afraid of it.'

SIXTY-THREE

OSIRA'H

N ow that her half-brother Daro'h was responsible for the Dobro splinter colony, Osira'h held a crystal clear knowledge of what must be done, and only she had a full understanding of what was at stake. Difficult but necessary changes needed to take place.

She wanted to give these people a second chance – actually, their first *real* chance. She knew it was what her mother wanted, and Nira stood beside her now, stiff and intimidated before the new young Designate. But Osira'h knew that her half-brother was different from Udru'h. He had not been here long enough to be hardened to his obligations. She was sure she could convince him.

The girl felt very small, yet equal, before Daro'h. 'Our uncle placed you in charge of this colony. The responsibility is yours. Have you asked yourself what you are going to do differently as the new Dobro Designate?'

'Differently? The breeding experiments are no longer necessary, thanks to you, and so they have stopped. What more needs to change?' He seemed genuinely perplexed. He had no idea why Osira'h had asked to speak with him, or why she had brought along the green priest . . . her mother.

Still fighting her inner turmoils, Nira stared at the stark fence around the camp. The breeding barracks were silent, empty. Medical kithmen no longer performed fertility tests on the women, nor did they take sperm samples from the males for their stock-piles. Even as a young girl Osira'h remembered hearing cries and groans coming from those dark buildings. Designate Udru'h had turned on sound-dampeners, kept her inside the instructional rooms, and told her not to waste a moment's thought on the human captives. With no reason to doubt him, she had done what he told her to do.

Turning from the fence, Nira skewered Daro'h with a glare. 'If the experiments have stopped, why do these people remain prisoners?'

Osira'h glanced at her mother, then regarded Daro'h with hardened eyes. 'Do you plan to thrive on secrets like Udru'h, or will you seek cooperation from humans and Ildirans?'

When he looked at her, she wondered if he saw a young half-sister he had never known or simply a mixed-breed child who might be the saviour of the Ildiran Empire. 'What further cooperation do we require from the humans? What more do we need to do for them?' Daro'h scanned the old drab structures, the somehow-hopeful vegetable gardens, the men and women quietly going about their chores. 'If their duties were so distasteful, are they not pleased now that the breeding work has been placed on hiatus? What more can I do?'

Osira'h gave an exasperated sigh, but she would not give up on Daro'h. He had not asked for this. The secrets and lies and pain were Udru'h's fault. Raised to think only of the Empire, Daro'h did not consider that others – humans – might not have been willing to pay such a cost. 'Generations were raised with no purpose but to mate with Ildirans and bear half-breed children. They knew no other life or hope until my mother told them stories of the Spiral Arm.' She put her hands on her small hips. 'They deserve better, Daro'h.'

Daro'h looked from the girl to the green priest. 'But I cannot change the past. What would you have me do?'

Osira'h and her mother had discussed their options thoroughly before coming to a conclusion. Nira said, 'Their forefathers came in the *Burton* to form a colony. The Ildirans promised them friendship, then deceived them. All these humans ever wanted was to settle Dobro in peace.'

Osira'h finished, 'Let them found their own colony. Dobro can be their *home*, instead of their prison.'

It was clear Daro'h had never considered that solution, had never even imagined there might be a question to consider. 'You mean I should just . . . free them?'

Nira gestured to the dry grassy hills. 'Considering some of the places the *Burton* might have settled, Dobro is a good enough world. Crops can be grown. Let the people build their settlement here, but let it be a place of their own – not a prison camp.'

After considering, the Designate barked to the guard kithmen standing near the fence, still watching the captives out of habit. 'Open the gates. I wish to speak with these human descendants.' Osira'h gave him an encouraging nod, and waited to see exactly what he would do. Nira kept her thoughts to herself, seeming stage-struck.

Guard kithmen shouted for the humans to come forward. Benn Stoner stepped close enough to face Daro'h, both curious and concerned to see him with the odd girl and the green priest. Stoner looked at his muttering comrades, men and women of various ages, as if he would try to protect all of his charges. Obviously, after so long, the human descendants expected no good to arise from a Designate's summons.

Daro'h raised his voice. 'I am now your Designate, and it is my decision to institute certain changes.'

'What sort of changes?' Stoner sounded defensive and suspicious.

When young Daro'h looked at Osira'h, taken aback by the reaction, Nira coolly explained, 'Think of what they've been through. To these people, changes are rarely a good thing.'

'Tell them they can have their colony,' Osira'h said.

'I will show them instead.' Daro'h shouted to the guard kithmen. 'Bring a full construction party along with heavy tools, cutters, diggers, haulers. Humans and Ildirans will work together to tear down these fences. There is room enough for both our peoples on Dobro.'

The breeding prisoners gasped. Even Osira'h was surprised by his abrupt decision, though she was sure Daro'h would never tell them the full truth of *why* they had been held here, what the experiments were meant to achieve, or what the Mage-Imperator was doing behind their backs.

Although the *Burton* descendants had never known any other place, any other life, Osira'h thought some of them would want to go far from here. They would pick up their belongings, tools, seeds, and travel to the south, in the vast unclaimed openness. If Daro'h gave them that much freedom.

Inside the camp boundaries, the humans milled around. When work parties actually started to cut the wires and uproot the barricade posts, the captives finally believed what was happening. Stoner gestured, and humans came forward on the other side of the fence. Together, they tore down the barrier that had always enclosed them.

Daro'h said to the former prisoners, 'We need you to continue

305

working in the communal fields, but you will also till your own acreage and provide for yourselves.' He looked at the weathered breeding barracks. 'We will assist you in building new dwellings in an open settlement. Your ancestors came here to found a new home with freedom and independence. I give that back to you.'

Nira began to cry, shaking and overwhelmed. Osira'h hugged her mother, feeling her relief and cautious joy like wind rushing through the worldforest canopy – a sound the girl knew well in her second-hand memories, but which she had never heard for herself.

They all worked with great enthusiasm. With a clatter, the wires were cut and torn down, the fence material pulled away, and the bleak encampment opened to the rest of the world. Daro'h called for the storage sheds to remain unlocked and available, so that Stoner and his people had unlimited access to basic farming equipment, ploughs, hoes, planters, power-diggers, irrigation components.

Osira'h could feel surprise and joy all around her. Some of the people cheered, while others could not accept such changes all at once. With all those lost generations behind them, the captives had lost the skills and knowledge to create and sustain a self-sufficient colony settlement. That information would have been in the *Burton's* databases, but the old generation ship was long gone. They did not know how to live on their own and be free.

But they could learn.

Next to Daro'h, the Ildiran guards remained uneasy. A lens kithman said, 'Designate, I must caution you. These humans have been prisoners for generations. Is it wise to provide them with tools that could easily be turned into weapons?'

'I have given them their freedom. Is that not our best defence?'

The lens kithman glanced away. 'I would not know, Designate.'

Osira'h still felt the pain that lingered after two centuries of oppression. She applauded Designate Daro'h for what he had done, but it was not enough. She knew what the Mage-Imperator was really planning with the hydrogues, how he had agreed to betray humanity. Osira'h understood something about these prisoners that the new Dobro Designate could never fathom.

He did not comprehend the human need for revenge.

SIXTY-FOUR

KING PETER

Ever since the King had reacted decisively in the Soldier compy emergency, the royal guards viewed him differently. Previously, the ever-watchful men had deigned to obey Peter's instructions only after checking with the Chairman or some Hansa functionary. Now even stiff Captain McCammon started snapping to attention whenever the King asked him to do something.

Peter had done what seemed right, since Basil's usual caution would have cost far more lives, and McCammon's guards had noticed who made the decision – the correct decision. Hearing Nahton's words, the guards at last understood that King Peter rarely received the information a true ruler needed. No one had told him about the berserk Soldier compies triggered by Dr Yamane in the Roamer shipyards; no one had let him know about the first murderous compies that had killed two crewmen on Admiral Stromo's bridge – a full day before the rest of the revolt began. King Peter had already expressed his concerns about Klikiss robot programming in the Soldier compies. If prior warnings had been heeded, the court green priest could have sent a telink message out to the EDF, perhaps soon enough to thwart the Soldier compies.

Thus, when Peter demanded to be taken to Chairman Wenceslas, the guard captain did not argue. He simply called in two companions to complete an appropriate escort, and the three of them marched the King to the Hansa HQ.

In his more than eight years at the Whisper Palace, the King almost never came to see the Chairman uninvited. Now, since he was accompanied by royal guards, the door sentries and protocol schedulers allowed them to pass. Everyone assumed that Chairman Wenceslas had asked to see the King – not the other way around.

Peter squared his shoulders and made sure his uneasiness did not show. He had to be confident. He had to give Basil a way out – if Basil wanted one. Over the years he'd seen the Chairman slide closer to the edge of irrationality and desperation. But maybe he could see the clear path after all. Peter very much hoped so.

As they rode to the penthouse level of the administrative building, Captain McCammon nodded significantly at Peter. Because of his bleached hair and his firm, bland face, McCammon's age was impossible to guess. 'It was a difficult decision, Sire, but you did what had to be done.' When Peter looked questioningly at him, the captain explained, 'The vaporization strike on the compy factory. We know it was done on your orders. I regret the loss of the silver berets, but you saved the city.'

Peter was surprised to what extent even the guards believed the charade. And why not? Basil kept everything close to his chest. He always insisted that Peter be the front man, a visible face for the Hansa. Now it was backfiring on Basil. *I have to count on my strength, even if it is only perceived strength.*

Peter nodded sombrely. 'I am the King. All too often, such

decisions are unfortunately mine to make. A ruler is more than just a businessman. The Chairman needs to remember that. If only he had listened to me during my initial warning about the compies.'

'All those silver berets,' McCammon said with a long sigh.

In the frantic days after the first word of the compy revolt, Peter and Estarra had avidly watched what was happening, trying to piece together the true picture through all the media spin. Earth was in turmoil, and the outer Hansa colonies were panicked. The remnants of the EDF were pulling together to form a defensive line around the home planet, cutting loose all other worlds. Despite the promises made in the original Hansa Charter, Earth had instantly written off every other settlement. No one else had a chance against the hydrogues now.

Traditional communications and trade routes had been cut, but many scattered colonies now had their own green priests, thanks to Theroc's recent dispersal of treelings. The colonies cried out about the betrayal, howling through the single conduit of Nahton, demanding the Hansa's protection and assistance. The Chairman ignored it all. Unless something was done soon, the pressure vessel of the Spiral Arm would explode. All the carefully laid threads binding human civilization together would unravel.

Now, however, when the green priest tried to bring messages to the King, Basil kept them apart, though he had no clear authority to do so. The last time Estarra had managed to talk to Nahton, even before the uproar of the revolt, Pellidor had brusquely marched her back to the royal quarters and reported to the Chairman. The blond expeditor was not likely to make the mistake of letting either of them talk to the green priest again.

'I hate Basil more than I can express, Estarra,' Peter had said to her when they were alone together again. 'I know what kind of man he is, and I know his priorities. But the threat to humanity is bigger than our disagreement. He blinds himself to the truth simply because a suggestion comes from my lips.'

'He knows he should have listened to you about the risks of the Soldier compies. Everyone can see that.'

'Will it make him contrite, or even more stubborn? I fear the latter. We should work together. He doesn't have to like me, but he does need me.'

'Maybe you should bring the first olive branch – or treeling frond.' Estarra had hugged him, and he could feel the swell of her pregnancy. He had kissed her on the forehead. *Please, Basil – see your way clear to saving humanity from this disaster.*

Now, when the lift door opened to the penthouse offices, Pellidor blocked the way. The guard captain frowned at the Chairman's personal expeditor. 'The King is here to see Chairman Wenceslas. Move aside.'

Pellidor ignored the three guards, gave Peter a withering glance. 'The Chairman is busy at the moment with his deputy.'

McCammon was unimpressed. 'Is he? His *King* is more important than his deputy. Now stand aside.'

Pellidor was taken aback. Royal guards never behaved this way. Peter took advantage of the hesitation to slip into the room as if he belonged there. He did not want McCammon and Pellidor to waste time in a pissing contest.

Inside his spacious office, Basil was pacing with his back to the door. Peter could see him staring through the expansive windows as if imagining a shattered skyline, a ruined city, a scene of Armageddon. He heard Deputy Cain reading aloud from a report from his focus groups. Peter hesitated, for a moment feeling small and young again, a street scamp rescued from poverty and obscurity and then groomed to be a King, but always under Basil's thumb. *I have grown beyond that. He needs me . . . but does he know it?*

Finally Basil pretended to notice the King, though Peter was sure he had been aware of him for some moments. 'What is it? We're very busy here.'

The captain of the guard burst out, 'Mr Chairman, the King wishes to speak with you.' Though Peter was already in the room, McCammon stood at the door chest to chest with Pellidor, as if they were about to come to blows.

'I don't have time for this right now.'

Peter stepped forward. 'Now is exactly the time, Basil. We need to bury the hatchet and work together for the good of the human race.' He avoided the gaze of the deputy, who had secretly aided them by spreading rumours of Estarra's 'blessed pregnancy' before Basil could send in his abortion doctors. Fortunately, the Chairman still hadn't figured out how that news had leaked.

Basil's expression hardened. He was clever enough to be careful. 'Mr Pellidor, please escort Captain McCammon outside so the King and I can have a private conversation. A brief one.'

Satisfied that he had done his duty, the guard captain withdrew. Cain sat down, quietly watching.

When they were in private, Basil's voice slashed Peter like a razor. 'Stop playing these games, Peter! Strut around and pretend to be important in your own quarters if it amuses you, but *don't do it here.*'

Peter took a deep breath, forcing calm. 'I did not come here to argue with you. Look around you, and decide what's really in the best interests of the Hansa and the human race.' He moved even closer to the dapper Chairman. 'Listen to me, Basil. I want to bury the hatchet. The Hansa needs a Chairman, and it needs me as King.'

Peter's heart sank as he saw Basil immediately turn stony. 'I need *a* King. Not necessarily you.'

'You took great pains to show me how you keep Prince Daniel locked in a coma where he can cause no trouble. If that's your only alternative, then, yes, the King *does* have to be me.'

'I always have other options. Some of them would surprise you, I think.'

'What do you mean by that?'

'You'd better pray you never find out. Time and again, you have proved you are not fit for your role.' Basil crossed his arms over his chest; it seemed a petulant, rather than a decisive, gesture. 'I've decided to have you confined to the royal wing for the foreseeable future, perhaps permanently. That will keep you from disrupting delicate plans.'

'Basil, even you can't be that dense.' Even the normally unflappable Cain gasped at the King's tone, but Peter forged on. This wasn't a time for niceties. 'Now the people need to see us more than ever. You ignored my concerns about the Klikiss programming when I expressed them a year ago, and now everyone remembers that *I* blew the whistle on the Soldier compies, that *I* wanted the factory shut down. But *you* wouldn't listen.'

Cain quietly interrupted. 'That's true. I've heard it mentioned three times in the past hour, Mr Chairman. The newsloops are hailing the King as a visionary and a hero.'

Basil reddened. 'I can control the way the media reports their stories, Peter. I don't know the identity of their "confidential Whisper Palace sources," but I will find out who you've been talking to, and I'll put a stop to it.' His quick smile was brittle and unpleasant. 'As you know, accepting credit *and* blame are two of a King's primary functions in this government. I haven't made up my mind yet whether you should abdicate your throne because of recent errors in judgement that have cost innumerable lives.'

Peter saw his hopes crumble. So much for making a peace offering or finding a solution to an unnecessary conflict. Cain raised his hands to intercede. 'Mr Chairman, no one in the public will assign blame to King Peter. That is nonsense, considering that he blew the whistle—'

'They will believe what I tell them to believe.' Basil's tone cut off any rebuttal, and the deputy withdrew, looking both angry and troubled.

The Chairman would lash out at any target he could defeat, since he could do nothing against the real enemy. The Roamers had been painted as enemies, and Basil would do the same to Peter and Estarra. He had fooled himself that there was a chance for a reasonable solution. Maybe there never had been.

'I won't take the fall for your stubborn inaction, Basil. I reacted swiftly and appropriately to the crisis. My warnings about the compies are a matter of long-standing public record. If there is to be any resignation, it should be yours. Shall I call for it in the next formal session of representatives?'

'Unfortunately for you, I believe you would try something so stupid.' The Chairman looked murderous, losing his temper. *Basil never loses control!* 'I want you out of here. Now.'

Peter backed towards the door, knowing now that Basil would never allow peace between them.

SIXTY-FIVE

CESCA PERONI

S till struggling to understand and use the new powers infusing her healed body, Cesca reeled with the outbursts of elemental power ricocheting around the ice cavern. The entire grotto had become a war zone.

Karla Tamblyn regarded her son with a stony face and blazing eyes. Her reanimated body seethed with destruction, like bottled chaos. Cesca had only seen her once before, long ago, when Karla had come to Rendezvous on clan business. She had been a confident, unshakeable woman who balanced the abrasiveness of her husband Bram. Now she was something else entirely.

'Jess, I can feel the power. She's not even human.'

'I know what she is,' he said.

When Caleb Tamblyn called out for help, Karla turned towards the older man, extended her arm – and shot knives of ice through the air at him. Jess moved in a flash to intercept the projectiles, using wental power to save his haggard uncles. The deflected projectiles smashed against the frozen walls.

Cesca sought strength and answers from the new energies

within her. The strange insistent voices shouted inside their heads. *We feared a tainted wental would arise. Some of our energy trickled into her cells, separate from us. The corrupt wental reanimated her body, yet it remains imprisoned within her, unable to propagate. A terrible mutation, surging with power. Now it is trying to break free, destroying her and remaking her at the same time.*

Jess staggered closer, holding out his hands, as if he could reason with his mother. His voice croaked as he called out her name. 'Karla Tamblyn! Remember who you are.'

Cesca shouted, 'Fight the chaos inside yourself—'

Karla's expression rippled from distaste to hatred, then fury. 'I remember.' She unleashed a second rippling blast that pounded her son with ice and cold. Jess shuddered like an anvil struck with a sledgehammer. *'My little boy.'* She ignored Cesca completely.

As Jess reeled back, struggling to recover from the blow, Cesca cried to the wentals, shouting into a howling wind. 'You couldn't *tell* this was happening here? You couldn't sense it all along?'

The tainted wental is not part of us. Her energies flow in black currents. She wishes only to destroy, to embrace chaos and increase entropy.

'Unless we stop her,' Cesca said.

The woman moved forward, her legs pillars of ice, but each footstep burned a mark into the frozen ground. She raised a fist to deal her son another blow. Jess was already doing his best to prevent further destruction.

Cesca wouldn't let him fight alone. She summoned the tingling power within her tissues and deflected the blast enough for Jess to recover. He joined his power with hers and turned it against his mother.

While Karla staggered in the backlash of the strike, Cesca turned to see a new threat coming directly at her. More than twenty slithering nematodes flexed scarlet bodies and flashed diamond-chip fangs, rushing to attack her.

When she had seen these creatures long ago at Ross's funeral, the prehistoric worms had seemed hauntingly beautiful, graceful denizens of Plumas's primordial sea. Now, they were demon soldiers controlled by the Karla-thing, intent on keeping her apart from Jess. In a hypnotic, serpentine movement, the nematodes swarmed to surround Cesca.

She faced the scarlet worms, knowing she had to keep these creatures away from Jess and away from other victims in the grotto. She already saw far too many bodies sprawled among the wreckage.

Though not yet familiar with her new powers, Cesca fought back in any way she could manage, learning from the wentals as she went. First, she imagined her method of attack, concentrating on the energy of lightning and cold water – and the wentals responded by flowing through her, out of her hands, out of her mind. Cesca blasted two nematodes, and froze a third one solid.

As Jess squared off with his mother, the tainted wental seemed to be dredging up words, memories, ransacking frozen cells within Karla Tamblyn's preserved brain. 'You ... Ross ... And Tasia – your little sister.' Her voice seemed to come from somewhere else, certainly not from her heart.

As more nematodes swarmed out of the sea and onto the icepack, old Caleb came forward in a foolish attempt to protect Cesca. 'Get away, you slithery things. Go back to the depths!' He stabbed his makeshift spear hard enough to puncture one of the nematodes. Several more raced towards him.

Cesca intercepted them with a blast of power, which distracted her from the dozens more swarming around her. She shouted at Jess's uncle. 'Caleb, go stay safe so I can concentrate!'

When the old man looked at her in surprise, she wanted to shove him away with both hands, but her energized touch would have killed him. That thought led to a new idea – perhaps the discharge would also destroy the worms. She reached out to the nearest nematode and touched its slimy skin membrane, but there was no deadly release of power. The creatures, controlled by a spark of Karla's wental energy, were immune.

Hundreds of nematodes swarmed closer, hissing and hooting. She tried to fight them but could not focus her mind to summon her blasts quickly enough. The water elementals themselves were preoccupied with the more important conflict against the tainted wental.

Karla let loose an incredible flurry of blasts, and Jess could barely block them all. His mother hurled random bursts at the ice miners, at the few still-intact dwelling structures, at the machinery, then pummelled her son, driving him back with the sheer power. Cesca could see the anguish behind his eyes when he had to fight back, when his mother attacked him.

With her attention deflected only for a moment, four worms wrapped around Cesca's legs. Others sprang with incredible speed, tangling themselves like heavy ropes around her arms, her waist. Tightening. More swarmed forward faster than she could destroy them. The primeval creatures covered her chest, her shoulders, her neck. Cesca struggled, but the scarlet worms had abnormal strength. Like pythons from the jungles of old Earth, they flexed their skin membranes and pulled themselves tighter, contracting, crushing.

And she couldn't move, couldn't fight.

SIXTY-SIX

JESS TAMBLYN

Jess clenched his fists at his sides as if to contain the elemental creatures within him. They seemed as uncontrollable as the tainted wental inside his mother. He could barely hear anything over the uproar in his head, over the clash and clamour of destruction.

When Karla spoke, the words emerged from the familiar face he had missed so much, but his mother's voice was a hollow, alien sound. 'Jess . . . why are you afraid of me? Don't you remember?' She walked forward, and steam swirled around her like the smoke from a wildfire. Overhead, the damaged ceiling continued to crack. 'My little boy.'

His mother's reanimated body seemed to be growing more accustomed to speaking, though each word was flat, without any spark of emotion. 'I remember the padded sweater I made for you when you were nine.' Her static-charged hair was calmer, her face more peaceful, as if the memories helped his mother wrest brief control over the possessing energy within her. 'I remember

319

your compy EA . . . Did you give that to Tasia? Where is Tasia? Where is Ross? My children . . . ?'

Even surrounded by the horrific turmoil, with slithering nematodes and cracking explosions, Jess recalled the years his parents had spent together, how they'd raised their family beneath the crust of Plumas. Karla had taught Jess how to drive a surface rover when he was only twelve. She had shown him how to operate pumping machinery, how to hook hoses to Roamer ships and fill their tanks with pristine water.

Jess shouted out loud, realizing what had happened. 'She was frozen, trapped in the deep ice for all these years. There must have been some small spark of life still within her. Suspended animation. When I touched her, started to thaw her, I must have released power into her somehow. And now a tainted wental has control of her.'

No life remained. She was dead. She remains dead.

'I don't believe it. There's something still inside her!' Jess faced Karla, willingly taking the brunt of her attack. 'Mother, listen to me. Please!'

As Karla took another step closer, the wental voices thrummed insistently. *She is not truly your mother. She is not alive.*

'But she remembers me.'

The tainted wental is accessing chemical signatures frozen in the tissue of her brain. Your mother is no longer there.

He could not escape the thought of those previous tainted wentals – the Ildiran septar who wanted the power to fight for his Mage-Imperator, and the Klikiss breedex who wanted to conquer encroaching hives. *He* had simply wanted to bring his mother back out of her icy tomb, not to bring Karla Tamblyn alive again. Some strange spark from him had caused this corruption.

We must remove all of the tainted water from her.

The wentals surged out of him, becoming a mist of droplets in the air. The energized moisture began to swirl around Karla like a scouring blast of abrasive hail. Jess's body shuddered. His teeth chattered.

'Bring her back! Save her. My mother's still in there, somewhere.'

She no longer exists. Do not be fooled. We must withdraw every droplet, every molecule.

Jess could not fight what they were doing. The wentals simply used him as a conduit, channelling themselves through his body. He silently called out for his mother to hear him, to exert control over the tainted energies.

Feeling a strange urgency, sensing that Karla was trying to distract him, Jess forced his body to turn. To his shock, he saw dozens of the attacking nematodes wrapped around Cesca. She moved, struggled . . . still alive!

But when he tried, he couldn't move to help her. The wentals inside his body guided his every action. Though desperate alarm erupted within him, the wentals were using his body as a weapon. Their weapon.

'Save Cesca! Help her fight!' Jess said through clenched teeth.

The tainted wental has not propagated inside the worms. As Karla Tamblyn resists us, her control over them weakens.

Jess managed to stretch out a hand, but Karla fought harder, demanding his attention. 'Cesca! Keep fighting!' He couldn't break his concentration away.

From somewhere within, Cesca found a focal point, drew upon her own wental energy. She released the power in a dazzling explosion, frying, freezing, and detonating the swarming nematodes around her.

Then she stood free, her dark hair snapping about, her eyes crackling with power not unlike Karla's. Sparkling, she stepped forward, ignoring the torn scraps of dead worms strewn across the ice.

When she grabbed Jess's hand, an increase of power rushed through his head like a torrent of water over a cascade. An incomprehensible sound came from the combined wentals, and something expanded. He and Cesca moved in unison, guided by the forces inside them. Jess felt as if something essential were pouring out of him, something he hadn't even known was there. The wentals drew upon that.

The desiccating cyclone increased around Karla Tamblyn's trapped body. She held up both pale hands, defending herself with bursts of lightning, waves of cold, and geysers of water that spun in a howling storm. She let loose wild destruction in all directions, bursting against anything that could be shattered.

But in a rush the combined wentals began withdrawing the contaminated moisture from Karla. Her waxen skin glistened with droplets that wept from her pores only to be whipped away by wind.

Seeing what was happening, frantic to find another way, Jess tried to hold the wentals back. He wanted to persuade them to save his mother, rather than annihilate her. Previous battles with a tainted wental inside the Klikiss breedex had broken an entire planet, and the possessed Ildiran septar had wrought as much destruction as a full-fledged battle fleet.

The wentals had to contain Karla here, even if it meant the obliteration of Plumas itself.

His mother's ivory-cold body shuddered as more and more of her flesh's water was stolen away and purified by the unified wentals. Jess moaned as the water elementals continued. He couldn't stop them.

Karla's expression changed, softened, became human again, actually ... maternal. A trick? 'Jess – you know what you have to do.' She had ceased blasting the grotto around her, stopped her assault on him and Cesca. Instead, his mother seemed to be withdrawing into herself, blocking the tainted wental, lowering its defences.

She was doing it on purpose. Jess saw it. He knew that this was *real*, a genuine glimpse of his mother. With the last ghost of her memories, she fought the warped elemental presence. Karla understood the horrific damage she could cause – and refused to continue. Yes, *that* was his mother. He was sure of it.

But the wentals had told him that was impossible. Jess knew what he saw, looked into the sudden flickering *humanness* that appeared in tiny static flashes in Karla's eyes. How could the wentals be wrong? And if they were wrong in this, what other errors might they have made? The sudden doubt in his heart seemed as damaging as a tainted wental could be.

And so he drove it away. He had already made his decision. He had thrown his lot in with the water elementals, had accepted the loss of his own humanity to join them and fight their battles with them. He could see the damage this warped life-force was causing, and he knew what tainted wentals had done in the past. He knew she had to be stopped. Here.

Without tearing his eyes from his mother, Jess ceased resisting the wentals' efforts from within him. He threw all his energy into the grim task, and drew on everything that Cesca could give him. He could feel the strength of Cesca's human heart as well as the unearthly power inside her.

The subsequent blow hit Karla like a cannon blast. She accepted its desiccating power with a hint of a relieved smile. Her skin wrinkled, turned leathery, and began to collapse in upon itself. Her face mummified.

The unnatural storm built to a higher pitch, until finally his mother cracked into a spiderweb of fractures, as if she were an ancient crumbling sculpture. Karla Tamblyn dissolved into spangles of dust that swirled in the remnants of the harsh winds.

At last, the wental storm dissipated, leaving nothing at all where Karla had been – neither the tainted wental, nor the woman who had been his mother.

In the background, the Plumas water mines roared with venting steam, tumbling ice, and gushing water, but compared to the storm, it sounded like a vacuum. Mindless again, the remaining nematodes flopped away to drop into the iron-grey sea.

Eventually, surviving water miners crept out of their hiding places. The wounded groaned for help. His three uncles ventured from their shelters. 'I don't understand what I just saw,' Caleb said. 'I'm not sure I want to know.'

Jess couldn't speak. He should have left his mother entombed in the ice where she'd died long ago. Because he had disturbed her – and because he could not control the wental energies within him – he had caused this disaster.

'It's over,' Cesca said to the shocked miners, as if remembering her role as Speaker. No one here had even seen Cesca since the destruction of Rendezvous, and they certainly didn't know what had happened to her. 'You're safe now. You can start putting things back to normal.'

Old Caleb looked at the devastation and blinked his bloodshot eyes. 'Normal? With the drogues attacking gas giants, and the Big Goose hunting us down, and now *this*, it's been a long time since anything's been normal.'

SIXTY-SEVEN

ANTON COLICOS

As soon as Tal O'nh's warliners arrived at Hyrillka, the process of unloading supplies, crew, and equipment became a massive undertaking. Thousands of dedicated Ildiran engineers and heavy labourers streamed from the landed warliners, carrying crates and operating machinery, all of them eager to get to work.

The planet had been brought to its knees twice: first by a hydrogue attack and then by the mad Designate. But the Mage-Imperator would not brush aside one of his worlds, even if the the rest of his Empire was at risk.

During the initial operations, Anton and Vao'sh accompanied Yazra'h while she encouraged the young Designate aboard the flagship. He had gone to his private consultation chambers to meditate (or hide? Anton wondered) before facing his responsibilities on the ground. Tal O'nh issued orders to manage the extensive operation, but Ridek'h could only wait and worry.

'I am already worn out, and we haven't even started yet.' The boy stared out the warliner's windowport.

Watching the Isix cats rubbing against Anton's legs, Yazra'h turned back to Ridek'h. 'I am anxious to begin the heavy work, as you should be. We have been on this ship for too long.' She flexed her arms, loosening her muscles. 'We are up to the task, Ridek'h.'

'But I am not a worker, or a fighter. I am a noble kithman.'

She regarded him sceptically. 'And thus you are helpless in the face of a difficult challenge? Nonsense. I am noble-born as well, but I can outfight any soldier and outwork any labourer. I will train you to govern Hyrillka.' Yazra'h tossed her coppery hair. When Anton noticed her turn a secretive, feral smile towards him, he had the strange impression that she was actually trying to impress him.

'Rememberer Colicos and I would like to be on one of the first ships down to Hyrillka,' Vao'sh said, 'to better observe these important operations.'

'Do we have to go down right away, Yazra'h?' Ridek'h sounded plaintive. 'It is more comfortable and . . . organized here.'

Yazra'h shot him a sharp glance. 'Are the people of Hyrillka comfortable and organized, *Designate* Ridek'h? Your place is among them, learning what they suffer.' Outside the broad viewing window, the large planet filled much of space as the multiple warliners inserted themselves into orbit. 'Speak your uncertainties here in private, Designate, but never voice them to the people. They have their own doubts – do not add to them. The people will draw hope from the fact that they have a Designate once again.'

'Even one as untrained and uncertain as I am?'

Yazra'h glanced at the two historians, considering, then spoke the words she needed to say to the boy. 'What you feel now is only half as important as what you *appear* to feel in front of your people. Maintain a façade appropriate to your role – strong, brave, dependable, in control.'

Anton watched the boy search for strength, then pull himself together. The veneer was thin, but good enough to keep the shell-shocked Hyrillkans from suspecting. 'Thank you. Of course, I must go down to the surface.'

Though Hyrillka's main spaceport had been reconstructed, it could never accommodate the hundreds of warliners, certainly not all at once. Knowing this to be a major bottleneck, Tal O'nh had devised the swiftest and most efficient disembarkation protocol. He assigned bureaucratic kithmen to subdivide the process into manageable stages and then work on the operational details. Now the ornate vessels crowded in orbit, their crews anxious to get to work.

Warliners landed seven at a time. Solar Navy crewmen and Hyrillkan labourers swiftly removed equipment and engaged local transport vehicles to distribute the much-needed workers and equipment. Carrying only skeleton crews, the emptied warliners rose back to orbit, out of the way while the next group of seven descended. It would take days to unload everything.

Anton, Vao'sh, and Yazra'h accompanied the young Designate aboard the fourth round of shuttles. When Designate Ridek'h set foot on the damaged world, the great fanfare Anton expected (considering the Ildiran penchant for such things) was drowned out in the constant clamour of distribution operations.

The boy Designate seemed barely able to grasp the extent of the damage as he studied the burned ground, the ruined fields, the scarred landscape. 'Look at all that needs to be done!'

Yazra'h's answer was both scolding and supportive. 'Look at all these dedicated workers. Look at all these ships, all this equipment. How can you not succeed?'

'We haven't seen the full extent of the damage yet,' Anton pointed out. 'I've learned from my historical studies that it's always more of a challenge to rebuild than to tear down.'

Vao'sh replied, 'That, Rememberer Anton, is the thread from which we will weave our story.'

They joined Ridek'h for a formal tour of the main city and surrounding farmlands. Flying low in an observation craft, they saw how much had been devastated. Even before the reconstruction crews had arrived, Hyrillkan workers had begun clearing the burned ground and replanting crops. Because the deluded Designate had uprooted food crops and devoted all fertile land to producing the drug shiing, Hyrillka's food stockpiles were quickly dwindling.

Subdued and ashamed, the people threw themselves into their labours with an abandon that showed how much they wished to atone for their rebellion. If their work continued at such a guilt-driven pace, they would surely collapse from exhaustion . . . and perhaps recover faster than expected.

As their small group inspected the damage for hours upon hours, Anton felt his mind grow numb. Vao'sh sat beside him, his large eyes gathering details, watching for small stories to retell.

Yazra'h never sat down. At the haunted look in the boy's eyes, she chided him. 'If *you* give up, Designate, then they will all give up. Remember the old stories in the *Saga*. What if you were a commander of a warliner being pursued by a Shana Rei blackship? A blackship travels as swiftly as darkness, but is as intangible as a shadow. Your weapons have no effect. You can not outrun the enemy. You would be terrified, would you not?'

Ridek'h hesitated, then chose the honest answer. 'Yes.'

She held up a long finger. 'But even if you were quaking, you could not let your crew see the fear, for they would experience it sevenfold. You must conquer your fear and keep focused on the work that needs to be done. If your greatest battle is with fear, rather than with the real enemy, then you have already lost the fight.'

Riding beside them, Vao'sh smiled. From the colours flushing through his facial lobes, Anton could tell the old historian was both amused and impressed. 'Perhaps you have a hint of rememberer kith in you, Yazra'h.'

She sniffed, as if she considered his comment to be a vague insult. 'I have many unexpected skills. The Mage-Imperator has enough confidence in those skills that he asked me to educate the Designate. I understand honour, how to fight for a cause, how to learn from mistakes.'

Anton was rooting for Ridek'h. He suspected that the young man's shortcomings were primarily from inexperience, and that through careful mentoring and guidance he could reach his potential.

Yazra'h stood behind the boy, gripping his shoulder, both to prop him up and to make sure he saw everything below. They gazed out over an expanse of blackened nialia vines and dry irrigation channels.

She was taking it upon herself to make certain the new leader of Hyrillka turned out properly. If anybody could do it, Anton thought, Yazra'h certainly could. She had enough strength and confidence to share with her nephew, as well as the people on Hyrillka.

SIXTY-EIGHT

MAGE-IMPERATOR JORA'H

Sooner than Jora'h had feared, the hydrogues returned to Ildira to deliver their specific instructions. So far, Adar Zan'nh and his experts had been unable to offer any miraculous new defences against the enemy. Without any proven way to fight them, Jora'h might be forced to concede after all, or accept a death sentence for the Ildiran race.

After sending Osira'h away to Dobro, the Mage-Imperator had recalled four of his seven Solar Navy cohorts to stand guard over Ildira. Tals Nodu'nh, Lorie'nh, Tae'nh, and Ur'nh lined up more than thirteen hundred of the ornate battleships overhead. The hydrogues seemed neither intimidated nor impressed by the show of force. Twelve diamond spheres simply shot through the numerous septas of Solar Navy warliners as if they were no more than blowing leaves. The hydrogues did not open fire . . . yet.

Inside the Prism Palace, Jora'h steeled himself. This time, he did not have Osira'h to act as a bridge. On the other hand, the hydrogues could not use their strange connection with her to eavesdrop on his own plans either.

The Mage-Imperator stood from his chrysalis chair, left the audience chamber and his guards and attendants, and ascended one of the tallest towers. He moved like a man going to meet his executioner.

'I am the leader of all Ildirans,' he said to himself. 'In my hands and thoughts I control and protect an Empire that has stood for millennia. I will do what is necessary to save my civilization.' *No matter what damnation it may bring.*

His father would have agreed to help destroy the humans without a moment's hesitation, without a flicker of conscience or remorse. Mage-Imperator Cyroc'h had done many unpalatable things for the good of the Empire.

But I am not my father. Not yet.

A solitary figure atop the tallest tower, he waited under the bright sunlight from half a dozen stars in the sky. The mirrored warglobes dropped like asteroids towards the Prism Palace, and Jora'h felt as if a great fist hung above him, waiting for the whim of a powerful being to smash him, his palace, and the whole city.

Jora'h knew that patrolling Solar Navy warliners had reported other battlefields around flaring stars, faeros fireballs and hydrogue warglobes locked in mortal combat. Apparently, however, the war against the faeros did not make the deep-core aliens forget their other threats.

The foremost warglobe descended to the level of his balcony, and a tiny sphere detached like a dewdrop. The small chamber held a single hydrogue shaped as the Roamer man they always copied. Was this the same emissary who had delivered the original demands, or a new one? Did it make any difference? In resonant tones, a voice emanated from the pressure sphere. 'Our plans have become crystal, and your part will soon be required.'

Although he had no choice but to show his cooperation, he did not have to appear pleased or eager. 'What are your instructions?'

331

'We will send a small group of warglobes to attack the humans at Earth, but we will rely on you to destroy them all.'

'Destroy them all? The Earth military is as powerful as the Solar Navy.'

'That is no longer true. They have been weakened from within by their own compies. Your numbers and weapons should be sufficient.'

Jora'h took a moment to digest this new information. 'Why would their own compies turn against them?'

'They were programmed to do so. Our allies the Klikiss robots bear hatred towards humanity because the humans have created their own sentient robots.'

He seized a fine thread of hope. 'But Ildirans have never created sentient machines. We promised the Klikiss robots that long ago. Why is my race being threatened?'

'Your race is irrelevant. You can avoid destruction only if you assist us in this small skirmish. We have an ancient agreement with the Klikiss robots.'

'You had an agreement with us, too.'

'Therefore we will not obliterate your race, provided you fulfil your role.' Then the emissary added ominously, 'Warglobes will go to other Ildiran planets to ensure your cooperation.'

Then, in a pulsing emotionless drone, the hydrogue ambassador methodically laid out the end of the human race, explaining how the Solar Navy would trick the humans and then turn on them when they were most vulnerable.

Cold wind blew against Jora'h's face. The chill spread like ice through his veins, and he had no choice but to listen.

SIXTY-NINE

ZAN'NH

I mmediately after the hydrogues departed, Zan'nh tried to bury himself in his regular duties. In these times, he served as both Adar and acting Prime Designate, and he felt useless at both. His Solar Navy – four full cohorts overhead – hadn't even been allowed to challenge the threatening warglobes!

A new female presented herself in the chambers assigned for the Prime Designate's mating duties. She came from the rememberer kith, attractive and intelligent in her own way, her face a sculpture of fleshy lobes that could display a palette of emotions. When Zan'nh made love to her, he could watch and react to everything she liked. He knew that the golden-green colour now flushing her skin was an indicator of joy.

He had not been born to be Prime Designate, but the Mage-Imperator had tasked him to serve in that capacity nevertheless. There was pleasure, naturally, but it was also his duty. Zan'nh had already begun to forget the names of the eager volunteers. He might have found it easier if his bloodline had been pure, if he'd been entirely noble-born. Because half of his genetics came

KEVIN J. ANDERSON

from the military kith, Zan'nh was better skilled at tactics and command than he was at courtly romance. Fortunately, the female candidates did not seem to care.

'You have honoured my kith,' the rememberer said, her face blushing a hint of sky blue. 'I am certain I will bear a healthy child for you.'

Zan'nh remembered to stroke her face, her bare shoulders, though the whole process felt awkward to him. As Prime Designate, his father had showered his lovers with lavish gifts; entire staffs had tracked the births and maintained records of offspring. Zan'nh, though, would rather be at his military work instead of this. Especially now – he had to find a way to defeat the hydrogues!

'It is important for us all to do our duties for the Ildiran Empire.'

The rememberer woman pulled on her filmy, colourful garments, bowed, and left the mating chamber. Outside in the corridor, medical kithmen and bureaucrats made careful notes while the woman submitted to their inspection. Noble advisers would already be sifting through female candidates, selecting his next visitor for tomorrow.

Zan'nh sighed. He was not meant for soft and pleasurable work, receiving one female after another. He couldn't forgive Thor'h's traitorous actions and took no pleasure in being promoted to his brother's place. But someone else should be doing this. Already, his mind was occupied with tactical matters.

It was not his place to second-guess the honour or the wisdom of what his father was forced to concede to the hydrogues. Betray and destroy the Earth Defence Forces? Zan'nh had always felt an uneasy dislike for humans and their impatient eagerness to swarm across planet after planet. Adar Kori'nh had told him how humans had taken advantage of plague-stricken Crenna, claiming the world even as the Solar Navy evacuated the last Ildiran survivors. Zan'nh had watched impertinent human cloud harvesters set up operations on Qronha 3 – an Ildiran planet – without requesting permission.

And yet humans had also shown surprising altruism. Sullivan Gold had risked, and lost, many lives to save Ildirans when hydrogues attacked the Qronha 3 cloud harvesters. Such a selfless feat warranted inclusion in *The Saga of Seven Suns*, but instead those heroic skyminers had been prevented from going home. He hoped *they* could achieve a breakthrough that no Ildiran could imagine.

As soon as he stepped out of his chambers, a courier found him. 'Adar ... Prime Designate! The Mage-Imperator requests your immediate presence!' Zan'nh marched after the breathless man.

Inside the skysphere audience chamber, courtiers and bureaucrats were in a flurry of activity. Jora'h was already coming down the steps of the dais to meet him. Zan'nh bowed and gave a formal salute.

'Adar, the hydrogues have delivered their instructions, and I have sent couriers out to distribute my orders. I have already dispatched a message to Dobro so that Osira'h can hear, in case the hydrogues are listening through her.'

Zan'nh didn't lift his gaze from the polished steps below the chrysalis chair. 'How may I be of assistance, Liege?'

'Go to Earth immediately – and here is what you must tell the King.'

SEVENTY

CHAIRMAN BASIL WENCESLAS

I n the Whisper Palace's hushed infirmary levels, Basil waited
with Deputy Cain and OX. Not knowing where he was going,
Sarein had tried to accompany them, but Basil had expressly
forbidden it. He did not want her to see this. And now even
Captain McCammon seemed to show a tinge of sympathy towards
the embattled King. Did everyone give up so easily? Basil had to
put a stop to this, and right away.

A slack-faced Prince Daniel lay insensate, but that was about
to change — not by choice, but out of desperation. Medical
specialists set to work reviving the formerly unacceptable Prince:
the Chairman's next best chance. The other alternative Basil had
in mind would take far too much time, time that he didn't have
right now.

*Daniel is still unacceptable, even if his brain has been punished with
nightmares for months*, Basil thought. He clasped his hands behind
his back and scowled at the pallid young man. *But he is the lesser of
two evils.*

Daniel had proved to be a terrible disappointment, but he had

336

never actively opposed Basil's policies. He wasn't smart enough, didn't have a broad mind. His role was not to think, just to listen and to repeat what he was told to say. With Peter – or Raymond Aguerra, as he'd once been called – they had chosen someone with too much intelligence, too much initiative. *Not a mistake we are ever likely to make again.*

Like window dressing, the Teacher compy waited silently beside his once-plump former student. As soon as Daniel underwent a brief but necessary recovery, OX would try to instruct the Prince again.

After the stimulants and counteractants had been administered, but before the young man awoke, Basil let out a long, disappointed sigh. 'I'm convinced King Peter will never learn his lesson, despite many chances and clear warnings.' He began to pace, watching the young patient's twitchings and moanings as he swam up from the depths of unconsciousness. 'Worse, Peter has begun to garner a disturbing amount of popular support. Even when he blatantly goes against our instructions, the people applaud everything he does.'

Cain frowned at him. 'Sir, the people are *supposed* to adore him. That is what he's there for. Doesn't that mean he's doing his job properly?'

'Not unless it's the way *I* tell him to do his job. We've done our work too well. The last thing we need right now is a glory hog. Peter made an obvious power play through the media with his grandstanding about the compy revolt. Before that, he somehow leaked the news about Estarra's pregnancy. I don't like it when my choices are taken from me.' He shook his head. 'I never thought I'd long for the days of that bumbling fool King Frederick.'

'Still, it has turned out for the best, Mr Chairman.' Cain maddeningly insisted on being optimistic. 'And he *was* right about the Soldier compies. It's illogical to hold that against him.'

'He did it just to spite me. The harder we push, the less he cooperates.'

'Maybe we should try a different tactic. Sometimes pushing doesn't work,' Cain pointed out, earning even more of the Chairman's ire.

'Prince Daniel is my different tactic.'

As stimulants coursed through his body, the Prince stirred, groaned, then vomited. Medical specialists rushed forward to clean him up and record his vital signs. The young man's fingers twitched, his eyelids fluttered. A long, haunted groan drifted from his lips. His body shuddered and writhed as he retched again, but after so many weeks on thin nutrient solutions, his stomach had nothing to bring up.

The medical specialists ignored the conversation as the chemicals were purged from the Prince's bloodstream and stimulants brought him all the way to consciousness. The young man groaned more loudly and finally awoke. His skin was greyish and damp with fresh sweat. His eyes were yellowed, bloodshot, and unfocused. Daniel stared at the ceiling, as if trying to remember how to see. He squirmed to cast away the gauzy threads of bad dreams. 'Where am I?' His voice squeaked like new shoes that hadn't been broken in.

Basil leaned over, regarding the Prince with a baleful glare. 'You are in a room where your future will be decided. Consider it your last chance.' He looked scoldingly at the medical technicians, sniffing the sour smell of vomit and medicines in the room. 'Everything always requires more time than I expect. We'll be in my offices. Call us when he's cleaned up and coherent enough to hear what we have to say. And I'm a busy man, so don't take too long.'

When some of the grogginess had dissipated, Daniel sat propped up in his bed, looking like death warmed over twice with a malfunctioning heating plate. First he'd slipped into a near-crash state of metabolic shock from his long enforced coma; when he returned to consciousness, he screamed for ten minutes.

Basil hadn't been there to watch the unpleasantness; all that mattered was for *Daniel* to remember the misery. The young man's arms had been strapped down, more as a reminder of his helplessness than as any real preventive measure, since his limp limbs were too weak to cause any damage.

By the time Basil, Deputy Cain, and OX returned, the disgraced Prince remembered full well what he'd done to earn his punishment. He had defied the orders of the Chairman, run away from the Whisper Palace, and (most unforgivably) behaved in an unspeakably foolish fashion while in the public eye. Thus, his drugged stupor, the long limbo of nauseating nightmares, and his pathetic bodily deterioration had all been a fitting sentence. Henceforth, Prince Daniel would never be more than a breath away from remembering how easily he could be squashed.

The young man literally trembled with fear as the Chairman stood over his bedside without saying a word. Basil didn't need to speak. He turned to look at the Teacher compy, then at his deputy. 'Mr Cain, remind me again why we brought OX here. We've had enough problems with compies lately.'

'Sir? OX was constructed centuries before Soldier compies and their Klikiss instruction sets. No need to worry about him.'

'But why is he *here*?' Basil insisted.

'Because we need him to see this. OX is going to do his best to make our Prince conform. Trust me, it's for the best, Mr Chairman.'

Breathing so fast and hard that he skated the edge of hyperventilation, Daniel listened while OX mechanically explained the current situation in the Hansa, summarizing what had happened since the recalcitrant Prince had been placed in an artificial coma.

The second round of drugs was wearing off, leaving behind a general malaise and a bad taste in the young man's mouth. Daniel was much thinner than before. *A good start*.

Shifting his gaze from the compy to the Chairman, struggling to control himself, the terrified young man blinked more than was necessary. He shook his head like a dog drenched in water and tried to focus on what had happened to him. As he gratefully sipped from a glass of fruit juice, absorbing electrolytes and sugar, he had to be wondering why he was still alive.

When the compy finished with the explanations, Daniel stammered, 'So . . . so what happens to me now?'

'That depends. You have already proved to be a disgrace.' Daniel flinched. 'The question is, are you salvageable, or should you be discarded? I'd prefer not to waste time starting from scratch with another candidate. But I don't want to waste time with you, either, if you haven't learned your lesson.'

'I've learned my lesson!'

As he scrutinized the shaky young man, Basil wondered what kinds of nightmares the boy had experienced while asleep.

'Please, just let me out of here.'

'Easy enough to say. But have you fundamentally changed? Learned your place in the Hansa down to the marrow of your tiniest bone?' Basil's voice cut like a surgical instrument. 'If you force us to remove you again because of your intractibility, we'll turn you into fertilizer for a colony world. No sense wasting resources on life support.'

'No! You won't need to do that. I promise.' Basil studied Daniel's eyes. Fear dripped from the young man like icicles from a wintry rain gutter.

'Can you be the King that Peter isn't?'

Daniel swallowed hard, rallied his courage and sniffed. 'I can be the right kind of King. He's had his chance. Now it's my turn.'

'It's your turn if I *say* it is.'

'Then say it, Mr Chairman. Please.' His lips trembled. 'Just please don't kill me. I want to be a Prince – *the* Prince.'

'It's not a Prince I'm looking for, Daniel.' Basil walked around the bed. 'I need a new King.'

OX spoke up. 'Mr Chairman, I have the proper instructional programming. All I need is cooperation from my student.'

Basil gave the compy an annoyed glance. 'I wouldn't start keeping score, OX. Peter was your student, too.'

Daniel swung his gaze quickly to the compy, whom he had previously hated. 'I promise to do whatever OX says! Really. I mean it this time.'

The young man's complete surrender and cooperation was a good sign – Peter had never shown such submissiveness, not even in his earliest days. When Daniel began to whimper, Basil frowned. 'Stop that. It isn't very regal of you.'

In response, Daniel sat stiffly on the infirmary bed, barely able to keep his balance. In a few days the boy should be able to walk again. He composed himself, dredging up everything OX had taught him. It was an impressive show.

Basil smiled at Pellidor and Cain. His voice was warm and gracious. 'All right, Daniel, you've convinced me.'

SEVENTY-ONE

OSIRA'H

A cutter bearing forty-nine Ildirans arrived at Dobro, sent directly from the Prism Palace. The courier asked to speak to the Designate, though he could not specify whether he meant Daro'h or Udru'h. Ildirans and freed humans had come to the spaceport to watch.

Scanning the gathered crowd, the courier recognized the half-breed girl. 'And the Mage-Imperator requests that Osira'h also hear my words.'

Within the hour, they met inside the new Designate's private residence, where the courier delivered his dark message. 'The hydrogues have returned to Ildira with their demands. Adar Zan'nh will be dispatched with a message to Earth offering Solar Navy warliners. He will claim they are for protection.'

'And they are not?' Udru'h asked.

'That is not for me to say. Most of the Solar Navy's warliners have been summoned back to Ildira, gathering for the massive deployment.'

Listening in angry silence, Osira'h felt a dull knife of disappointment pierce her heart. She wanted to weep for how easily her father had surrendered.

'So the Mage-Imperator agrees to this?' Daro'h, too, seemed disbelieving.

Udru'h was gruff. 'It is the only way he can save the Empire. It is what Osira'h helped him to achieve.' When her uncle smiled at her, she felt nauseated.

'Why did my father want me to hear this?' she asked.

Udru'h said, 'I assume the Mage-Imperator felt you would be overjoyed to know that you have succeeded, that your work had a true purpose and that our breeding programme was not a waste.' She forced herself not to glare at him.

Osira'h felt a thread inside her mind, knowing that she still had the potential to touch the hydrogues. But she walled it off, refusing to let the deep-core aliens glean this information from her. She hoped never to touch those appallingly disturbing minds again. If Udru'h could keep secrets from the Mage-Imperator, then she could keep secrets from the hydrogues.

She turned to Daro'h. 'And now that you've torn down the fences, Designate, now that you've let these people free, are you going to tell them that the rest of their race is doomed? Or will you just let them keep happily working until the hydrogues come here to wipe them out?'

Daro'h spread his hands. 'I cannot control what the hydrogues do!'

'There is no purpose in telling the humans a truth that would only make them unruly.' Udru'h turned to the courier. 'Your ship will depart soon for Ildira, and I wish to be aboard it. My work here is done, and the Mage-Imperator needs my assistance. He requires advice when it comes to difficult matters.'

*

When Dobro's darkness drove the Ildirans into their well-lit dwellings, the former breeding subjects gathered in private. The *Burton* descendants spoke in hushed voices.

The communal buildings were scrubbed clean and had new beds and new furnishings. All the men, women, and their pure-bred children now had the option to construct dwellings outside the settlement perimeter. They could also have real families with whomever they chose, instead of the best genetic matches as determined by medical kithmen. But just because Daro'h had torn down the fences did not mean they were free.

Osira'h now knew their hopeful future was nothing more than a cruel illusion. She had tried to hold a thread of belief, but her father had failed her as badly as she'd feared. The courier's revelations were the final straw for her. Though their race might soon be extinct, these captives should at least know the truth. Finally.

The new Designate had never shown them the secret records, images of the enormous generation ship that had carried their ancestors from Earth, how Ildirans had introduced human blood-lines to the gene pool for hybrid vigour, hoping to achieve their long-sought telepathic intermediary. All those generations held captive . . . all unnecessary.

My parents accomplished with love what no amount of forced breeding and genetic slavery could achieve.

And for what? So she could facilitate the extermination of the human race?

Now even Nira listened in horror as Osira'h told the whole story and recounted the recent decision Jora'h had made. The *Burton* descendants had been abused for many years, but now they understood they'd been deceived as well. They were pawns, used to bring about the end of their own civilization.

'The big question is what do we do now?' Stoner said.

'We should be grateful to the new Dobro Designate,' said an

older woman. 'Look how things have got better. This other matter is out of our hands.'

Osira'h replied angrily, 'Is that enough?' She looked at the others, trying to incite them. Raised in captivity, they had never known anything other than fences, their women taken away and raped, their men harvested for sperm. 'You will never be allowed to leave Dobro. In fact, you w:.. probably be killed – along with all humans everywhere.'

'But we're free now,' a balding man said. 'We all heard what the Designate promised.'

Nira turned from the darkness outside the barracks window, miserable. 'Can we trust what a Dobro Designate says? Think of what Udru'h did to me and to all of you. And now, what Jora'h has planned . . .' She closed her eyes. 'It can't be true.'

Osira'h touched her mother's arm. 'It is true.'

The girl sensed a mood shift as the people began to grasp the enormity of their situation. Struggling with anger and disbelief, they tried to balance a need for retribution against their own desire for peace, freedom, and a fresh start.

Stoner ground his teeth together, lowered his head, and said in his deep voice, 'But how do we do anything against this? We don't know how to fight. How can we have any effect on his scheme? Do we go see Designate Daro'h? Demand that he take action?'

Nira raised her voice like an iron blade, as if she had finally got a grip on vengeance. 'Daro'h may be the new Designate here, but he is not the person responsible.'

Osira'h closed her eyes, forcibly drove back any fond memories she still had of her uncle and mentor – every remnant of pleasant times, every hint of love and devotion Udru'h had once shown her. He would be leaving for Ildira soon, and had asked her to join him for a quiet dinner tomorrow. That would be a perfect time for them to move. The former captives had to make their plans swiftly.

'We all know who guided the programme,' Osira'h said, 'and we know who is to blame.'

SEVENTY-TWO

SULLIVAN GOLD

The warliner's engine rooms hummed with the stardrive machinery and the constant conversation of crewmen. Now that the hydrogues had come back to issue their terrible instructions, the level of urgency had increased dramatically. But as far as Sullivan could see, the Ildirans still didn't *get it*.

The engineer Shir'of beckoned him and Tabitha to follow him into the engine chambers. They trooped down metal stairs past curved reactor tanks and circulation cylinders filled with hot ekti. He showed them everything, every deck and every engine room. They passed hundreds of crewmen, three times as many as he could imagine were necessary. Sullivan rubbed his temples in the constant noise, missing Lydia and his children and grandchildren.

If we come up with something here, the Ildirans will let us go home. Provided the Adar is true to his word.

Tabitha drank in the details with a mixture of fascination and scorn. She had given up trying to take notes on the unfamiliar Ildiran datapad that the scientist Klie'f had given her. She lifted

347

the Ildiran datapad. 'This thing is probably the same model they were using two hundred years ago.'

Shir'of smiled, as if it were a compliment. 'Once we reached the pinnacle of our technology, there was no need to continue improvements.' He did not see the flaw in his reasoning.

'And now you're in trouble,' Tabitha said. 'After picking your noses for so many generations, you've forgotten how to come up with new ideas.'

When they reached the command nucleus, Adar Zan'nh dispensed with formalities. 'Show me your breakthroughs. Time grows desperately short. I am ordered to go to Earth immediately, and if you cannot find us an alternative before I return . . .' He let his words hang ominously.

'We've only had a few days to think about it,' Sullivan said.

'Yeah, I usually need at least a week to defeat an invincible enemy,' Tabitha quipped. 'I can't come up with a doomsday weapons system off the top of my head, design, develop, produce, and implement it all within a couple of days.'

Sullivan looked at her. 'Nevertheless, that's what we've got to do.'

Tabitha cracked her knuckles, turning to the problem. On the screen, blips marked thirteen hundred ornate battleships gathering in orbit, drawn from across the Ildiran Empire. 'So we're stuck with what we've got. How do we use your Solar Navy in a different way?'

Sullivan scanned the constant activity around the command nucleus. Solar Navy soldiers hunched over stations, arriving and leaving in a constant flow, as if the warliner's bridge were a busy city street.

'Here's what I've been thinking.' Tabitha bit her lower lip. 'The only thing I know of that can take down a hydrogue warglobe – other than a bunch of faeros, I mean – is slamming a big ship into it, like that Ildiran commander did. I don't suppose you could just construct a thousand or so empty warliners and throw them at the drogues?'

Zan'nh heard no humour in her comment. 'They do not need to be empty. The Solar Navy does have seven cohorts of warliners. As a last resort, we will use them in such a manner.'

Sullivan realized that he hadn't seen anything remotely similar to compies in the Ildiran Empire. 'But look at all these personnel it takes to run your ships. Don't you have automated systems to minimize casualties if you go into battle?'

The Adar shook his head. 'The Ildiran Empire has no intelligent machines, robots, or competent computerized companions. That was part of our bargain with the Klikiss robots long ago.' His face was stony, as if he refused to allow himself to scowl. 'Another bad bargain.'

'So, everything needs to be done by hand?' Sullivan said in disbelief.

'We do not lack for manpower.'

Tabitha rolled her eyes. 'When your Adar Kori'nh crashed all those warliners into the enemy, you mean each one of them had a full crew aboard?'

'A minimal crew,' Zan'nh said. 'There was no other way.'

Sullivan wondered how many people Ildirans considered 'minimal.'

Tabitha cocked her eyebrows. 'Let me explain about autopilots and cruise control.'

SEVENTY-THREE

KOLKER

When the green priest climbed to the top of the Prism Palace's domed towers, he could almost imagine sitting in the worldforest canopy on Theroc. The warm light of multiple suns drizzled on his emerald skin like melted butter.

But since the treeling had been snatched from his grasp in the Mage-Imperator's chamber, nothing could bring him joy. He'd lost his only possible connection to the worldforest. The treeling was dead. The Mage-Imperator was truly a monster, and some further treachery was brewing.

Overhead, the sky was criss-crossed with exhaust trails from warliners and construction ships. Hundreds of craft moved in a frenzy of activity; the whole population of Ildira seemed to be involved in a massive effort. Streamers flew intricate manoeuvres in tight groups; normally, Ildirans would have applauded the sky-parades, but now they threw their full energies into their tasks. High in orbit, Tals Lorie'nh and Tae'nh had already begun to organize the Solar Navy warliners that would be dispatched to Earth as part of the hydrogue ambush.

Sullivan, Tabitha, and most of the captive Hansa skyminers had been put to work. The green priest had never felt so adrift, so disconnected.

Without being invited, the old lens kithman joined him in companionable silence. Kolker wasn't sure if their meeting was happenstance, or if Tery'l had intentionally sought him out. They both stared at the forest of crystal buildings.

Though Kolker wanted to be left in peace, he also longed for conversation. He just couldn't decide how to speak with this strange hyper-religious Ildiran. Without thinking, he blurted, 'I'm lonely. I've never been so lonely.'

'I am not. I never am.' The old man stared with milky eyes into the bright sky, though the sunlight was so bright that the green priest could not bear to look without blinking. 'At my age, the eyes grow foggy. My sight is dimming, and I must gaze directly at the suns just to take the light into me. However, the Lightsource remains bright inside me. The soul-threads keep me warm and content.' With a gnarled hand, he clasped the reflective medallion at his throat. 'It makes me sad that you cannot feel the *thism*, friend Kolker. If you could touch us all, connect through the mental web, you would never feel lonely.'

Kolker turned away. 'I know what would make me feel less lonely, and it isn't your *thism*.' Though he was hungry for any sort of conversation, he found it hard to relate to someone so self-satisfied.

Sensing he was unwelcome, the lens kithman slowly got to his feet like a poorly maintained piece of antique machinery. 'You would not think that way if you understood more about what I was saying.'

Kolker sighed. Since the old man was there anyway, he decided he might as well listen. Maybe he could get his mind off his problems. 'Wait, stay. I'm your captive audience.' The green priest could not keep the bitterness out of his tone. All he could think of was the lost treeling. 'Go ahead.'

And so Tery'l began to explain.

SEVENTY-FOUR

NIRA

After Osira'h had gone to the former Designate's residence to join him for a meal before his departure, Nira and the other captives finalized their plans. Udru'h pretended that he would miss the half-breed girl and thought Osira'h would be sad that he was going away. The vile man intended to leave Dobro behind, sweeping all of his crimes under the rug as if they had never happened. Nira couldn't let him get away with it.

She loathed him for what he had done to her, both physically and mentally. When she'd first discovered she was pregnant, she had been so happy. Osira'h was Jora'h's child, a baby conceived out of love – a new experience for the Prime Designate, whose assignment had been to spread his bloodline among all Ildiran kiths. They would have raised their baby in the Prism Palace, showering the child with affection. Instead *this* had been forced upon them all.

And after hearing what Jora'h was planning with the hydrogues against the human race, Nira questioned what he would really have done. During her years of captivity and abuse, she had clung to what she believed. She had loved Jora'h, but now she only allowed herself to think of him as the 'Mage-Imperator', someone whose heart had died when he ascended to the chrysalis chair.

Tonight, the restless, angry people had crowded into a single dwelling house, and it was up to Nira to guide them. They would demonstrate to the Ildirans the extent of their anger.

She spoke firmly, 'In turning you loose, your captors gave you a power they never guessed. For so many generations, the Ildirans thought of you as meek and helpless. Tonight you will show them that you are no longer their pawns. Tonight we burn down the old, eradicate the scars, and pave the way for a fresh beginning. We'll see just how true to his word Designate Daro'h is.'

She looked at her half-breed children waiting by the bunks. Nira had easily taken them from their quarters in the Ildiran settlement. Not even the mentalists and lens kithmen watched them closely any more, now that Daro'h had declared the camp open. The children were simply leftovers of a defunct programme.

Stoner saw her gaze. 'Will they be safe out there? What if guards come?'

'It is important that they see this. It is more than a symbol.' Osira'h had told her younger brothers and sisters everything about how they had been deceived, that their unnatural skills might have helped an Empire that would in turn kill their mother's people. Even Rod'h had heard the truth in Osira'h's words. Those children stayed with Nira now.

Like a work detail sent out to excavate opalbone fossils in the arroyos, the former captives filed out of the dwelling structure. They carried igniters and makeshift torches. Ildirans thrived on light, hated the darkness. Tonight, Nira and the others would give them a blaze they would never forget.

They gathered outside the empty breeding barracks. Even

those who had been raised to this fate despised those buildings. Nira took the first torch and applied it to the nearest wooden wall. 'Burn them down.'

There were currently seven of the large barracks, each with many rooms, poisoned with centuries of memories and pain. Flames licked up the boards and swiftly spread along the plank shutters. Her own children took igniters and lit other walls, then all the captives came forward to help. A night wind sprang up, as if hungry to fan the blaze. Nira watched their bonfire become ravenous. The breeding barracks crackled and popped. Sparks flew into the air.

The bright hot glow began to draw attention from the well-lit Ildiran town. Blazers shone among the buildings where the guards and doctors, mentalists and lens kithmen resided.

Benn Stoner yelled, 'This isn't enough! Let's torch the Ildiran settlement, too. It was built by the labour of our forefathers to house our captors. If we have to make a clean start, then they should as well.'

The angry people liked the suggestion and took up the cry. 'Smash their windows, burn their buildings.' With their igniters they ran towards the town.

Alarmed, Nira saw her followers rapidly slip out of her grasp. 'No! We have already burned the barracks – that is what we needed to accomplish.'

The fire was spreading through their hearts as well as the blackening structures. 'We can show them how it feels!'

The barracks were completely engulfed now, a bonfire in the night. Nira realized with deep dismay that she could never control this mob. She felt sick.

Beside her, Rod'h tugged on her arm. He saw her staring towards the settlement. 'Are we going to see my father now?'

In her shock, Nira had forgotten to consider who Udru'h was to the boy. 'Yes, Rod'h,' she answered. 'Now we'll go see your father.'

SEVENTY-FIVE

FORMER DESIGNATE UDRU'H

A fresh dose of shiing circulated through Thor'h's veins like a constantly blowing sandstorm obscuring the light. The drug locked the traitor away from his mind and thoughts, from any comfort of *thism*. His waxen face had not shown any emotion, any flicker of wakefulness, since the catastrophic end of Rusa'h's rebellion.

'You sleep too easily, Thor'h,' Udru'h muttered. 'The rest of us are forced to face the consequences of our choices.' He turned away from this messy loose end and left the comatose former Prime Designate in his cheerless room. Soon, he would have to move Thor'h to Daro'h's residence. But not tonight. Udru'h intended to have a far more pleasant evening. He had invited Osira'h to join him for his last dinner on Dobro, before he went back to Ildira.

The girl was already waiting for him. She sat primly at a table, dressed in serviceable garments. Seeing her, Udru'h paused only a moment. He had raised this dear half-breed girl almost as his own, had taught her everything she needed to know to save the Empire – and she had succeeded. Udru'h could always cling to that knowledge even if he never received a single accolade or word of recognition for his work on Dobro, even if the Mage-Imperator punished him for his lies and for what he had done to Nira. The programme had been *crucial*.

As he took his seat, servant kithmen rushed in with a clatter of beverage bottles, appetizers, fruits, and plates of steaming food. Udru'h increased the lighting, though the girl had not seemed to mind the dimness. She had been spending a great deal of time with her mother among the human breeding subjects. It was good for her to join him, where she belonged.

Osira'h looked up. 'Shall I still call you Designate, or former Designate?'

'You may call me Uncle.' His smile did not fit comfortably on his face.

She accepted the answer without comment.

When the plates were set in front of them, they ate slowly. Neither showed any relish for the food. Udru'h didn't understand why he should feel so awkward. The two had spent many meals together.

'This reminds me of all those times we sat together during your instruction sessions.' With a bittersweet pang, he could not fight the sensation of loss. 'When you were younger, all you wanted to do was please me. That was not so long ago.'

From across the table, Osira'h watched him with her large eyes. She seemed distant, uncommunicative. 'In my mind it feels like a thousand years.'

He could not imagine what she had gone through, what she had felt being dropped into the clouds to find the hydrogues, to communicate with them or die. What had happened to her mind when she had opened her thoughts to those alien creatures? 'I am sorry for the difficulties you faced.'

'It was necessary,' Osira'h answered distantly, then added

in a hard voice, 'Are you sorry for what you did to my mother?'

He frowned. The green priest woman was irrelevant, but clearly she was talking with her daughter about terrible things. 'That, too, was necessary.'

Udru'h heard a disturbance outside – shouts and clashes, voices that sounded distinctly human. He hurried to the broad, angled windows. Standing close to the pane, he looked past the Ildiran settlement to the former human compound. He saw bright flames – bonfires, not blazers. The old breeding barracks had been set on fire! 'What are they doing now?' In the dry season, with the brisk winds, the flames could spread.

A crowd charged through the streets, making no attempt to move quietly. Alarmed Ildiran kithmen ran back to their homes, but human figures pursued them. They used sharp farm implements to knock down street lights and shed darkness.

This was madness! Udru'h ran to barricade the door of his residence. 'Stay here, Osira'h! It is an uprising of some sort.' In trying to do the right thing, Daro'h had given the humans too much freedom too quickly. He should have warned the young Designate. For all their clamour and dissatisfaction, the breeding subjects did not understand how to be free.

Calm but curious, the girl walked to the window. Carrying portable blazers, three Ildiran guards attempted to mount a defence, but the humans seemed out of control. The breeding captives fell upon them like animals.

Udru'h raced to the room where Thor'h lay insensate. Though he despised what the Prime Designate had done, he was obligated to protect the unconscious young man. Given his choice, he would have thrown the treacherous young man to those wolves, let them rip the Prime Designate's body to shreds. But the Mage-Imperator had given him clear instructions, and Udru'h had already disappointed his brother too often.

He lift.⁴ the scarecrowish body and easily carried the young man down a set of stairs into the underground storage level. The chamber beneath his private residence, a bolt hole Udru'h had designed for emergencies, would be a perfect hiding place.

He dropped the limp body onto a narrow cot there. 'The door is hidden. The chamber is well-lit, and once I seal it, you will be secure.' He said, though he did not imagine Thor'h could actually hear or understand him. 'You will be safe until I deal with this situation.' Outside, a few minor reshufflings of boxes and crates concealed the bolt hole.

When he finished, Udru'h rushed up the stairs to the main level of his residence and called for his guards, mentally aligning a defence against the rebellious humans. Even if Daro'h was technically the new Designate, Udru'h could better command in a crisis. He wondered what Daro'h was doing in his own residence.

On the main level, he found Osira'h standing in front of the front entrance. She looked directly at him, smiled – then unbolted the door and opened it wide.

Udru'h shouted, but could not stop her in time. Outside, he saw a mob waiting for him. The angry humans let out a roar.

SEVENTY-SIX

ANTON COLICOS

Anton was not surprised when young Ridek'h took up residence in the damaged citadel palace. Yazra'h herself had encouraged it. It was the place where a Designate should live. Ridek'h chose his own quarters – specifically *not* the master chambers where Rusa'h and his pleasure-mates had lived, and not the rooms where his father Pery'h had been held prisoner.

For days, reconstruction teams swarmed across the wreckage, tearing down ruined buildings, clearing roads, replanting crops, erecting temporary homes.

Meanwhile, in underground chambers well lit with artificial spotlights, the two historians found the ancient vaults still intact. 'It's like a tomb of records,' Anton said with a smile of anticipation. 'What do you think is in there?'

'Many mysteries, information not considered worthy of inclusion in the *Saga*.'

A cadre of broad-shouldered diggers and heavy labourers stood placidly in front of the bricked-up walls of the archives, ready to smash open the seals. They were not the least bit interested in what they might find inside.

Yazra'h watched her cats pace restlessly up and down the dusty tunnels. 'Can I trust you to remain here? Do I need to guard you?'

Anton chuckled. 'I think there will be plenty to occupy us.'

She shrugged, obviously perplexed to see two men so excited to spend hours with musty old documents. Nevertheless, she smiled at Anton. 'Find new stories to tell me.'

He flippantly said, 'I could always make some up.'

She scowled. 'I want only true stories.'

Anton asked her to leave the cats when she left to take Ridek'h out again, and the tawny animals were content to stay with him. 'Nothing better than reading with a cat at your side,' Anton reminded her. Ildirans didn't seem to understand that.

Vao'sh gave instructions, and the three muscular diggers raised heavy cudgels over their heads, then brought them back down. Crashing blows cracked the translucent bricks that sealed the ancient vault. Anton stepped back to avoid the flying debris. After two more explosive blows, the blocks tumbled inward to expose a chamber.

'Long ago, such apocryphal documents were sealed away here,' Vao'sh said. 'These writings were never part of *The Saga of Seven Suns*, thus they had little official historical value to the Hall of Rememberers. Rememberers rarely even refer to their existence, but now we must study them for information the Mage-Imperator needs.'

The diggers shovelled away debris, and Vao'sh scrambled into the cramped chamber, carrying a portable light. 'Thousands of documents not seen by any Ildiran in millennia! We have our work cut out for us, Rememberer Anton.'

Vao'sh picked up a stack of perfectly preserved diamondfilm

sheets, looking as if he might cry. He sent the diggers away and handed Anton a stack of sheets. The human scholar carried the documents into the brighter corridor and, tilting the top diamond-film sheet, he squinted at the Ildiran writing on it. The letters were far more ornate and archaic than he was accustomed to reading. 'I might need your help deciphering this.'

A group of chattering servant kithmen brought more blazers and two desks, courtesy of Designate Ridek'h – Yazra'h's idea, no doubt. Anton wished his mother could be there to enjoy these ancient mysteries. Margaret Colicos would have loved to help her son unravel lost parts of the alien epic. He had still heard no word about his mother. He wondered if she was still alive . . .

He and Vao'sh delved into obscure passages. The Mage-Imperator had told them to look for answers to questions no one had previously thought to ask. Working closely together, they struggled to find secrets about the ancient war and how the hydrogues might be defeated; Anton worked, intensely fascinated, though not overly hopeful about the relevance of these accounts. From everything he'd learned, the last great conflict had not turned out particularly well for anybody.

Underground, Anton easily lost track of time, though the Isix cats growled to alert him when they became hungry. Yazra'h came down into the archives after a full day of work, her expression stern and scolding. 'You are as fixated and as focused as any work crew in the burned croplands. Eat! Sleep! Do you know how long you have been down here?'

'Not a clue,' Anton said.

Vao'sh barely looked up. 'Please have the servant kithmen bring us food.'

Anton scratched the golden fur of the animals' heads. 'And maybe you should take the cats up into the open, where they won't be cooped up.'

'I should take *you* out into the open, Rememberer Anton. Exercise you.'

'I'm really busy right now.' She snorted, but took her pets with her as she departed. Before long, servant kithmen arrived carrying food.

Anton felt they were in a different, isolated world, sheltered from all the work outside. Vao'sh, his fingers covered with dust, his face lobes smeared with powder from the crumbling walls, lifted one sheet after another, reading with remarkable speed. He caught his breath when he scanned one section of records. 'Tales of the Lost Times? This history was all supposedly lost!'

'Good thing somebody kept notes.' Anton occupied himself with the sheets in front of him, scanning testaments, discovering accounts of previous struggles with the hydrogues, records of the faeros, even tales of the Shana Rei. He wasn't sure how to separate the factual evidence from fiction.

Vao'sh lifted a diamondfilm sheet as if it might burn his fingers. 'Secrets within secrets within secrets. Have our plans brought us to this?' He shook his head, and the colours in his lobes flickered with distaste. 'The Lost Times were designed to hide the ancient war against the hydrogues. We believed that all the rememberers died, that part of history was forgotten. But it wasn't true! The Mage-Imperator caused our own people to forget the entire conflict after a dozen generations.' He looked as if he might be sick. 'Everything I was taught – so much of it is untrue. Even the Lost Times!'

Anton, quite familiar with the idea of history being edited or even fabricated, was not the least bit sickened, as Vao'sh clearly was. In fact, he found the news exciting. 'Is that when they created the Shana Rei as a surrogate enemy? A fiction to smooth over the gap in all this censored history?'

'I do not know what to think.' Shaking, Vao'sh read the words again and again before he set them aside. Anton leaned closer, reading over his friend's shoulder. The rememberer was clearly torn, not wanting to know more, but given orders by the Mage-Imperator to discover what he could. He had no choice but to dig deeper, no matter how it shattered his world. Anton felt sorry for him.

Vao'sh stared at another sheet as if it might burst into flames. 'According to this, Rememberer Anton, the Shana Rei may have been real after all.'

SEVENTY-SEVEN

KING PETER

'The bastard!' Peter knew he shouldn't be surprised. 'The slimy, egotistical bastard. He's going to kill us.'

The loyal Teacher compy stood before the King and Queen, having replayed his precise recording of Basil's conversation with the revived Prince Daniel. Basil had isolated the King in the royal wing for days, basically under house arrest; OX, however, was always able to move invisibly through the Whisper Palace. He had served almost every single King in the Hansa's history.

Basil always treated compies and underlings as nothing more than furniture; the Chairman had so little regard for OX that he could not conceive of the fact that the Teacher compy might object to his tactics. Deputy Cain had already used OX twice to send very guarded messages.

They were alone in the royal wing next to a burbling white-noise fountain to discourage any eavesdroppers. OX had also detected and temporarily deactivated the omnipresent listening devices planted around the royal suite to give them a respite from the difficult hand signals.

Estarra's face showed both concern and determination. 'Now that Daniel's awake again, how long do we have?'

'Basil's going to move as soon as he can rationalize an excuse and find a good way to cover it all up.' Peter looked at OX's placid polymer face. 'First, though, he'll want to make certain Daniel's truly a better alternative; he's not likely to increase surveillance and impose tighter controls on us until he actually has his plans in motion. We've probably got a few days, at least.'

'He doesn't know we've been tipped off,' Estarra whispered. 'That gives us one advantage.'

Peter ran the palm of his hand down her long twists of hair. 'He has withdrawn all EDF support to the colonies and just left them to die.' He made a disgusted noise. 'The hydrogues can wipe out our settlements and then come here whenever they like. It's the extinction of the human race. All through this war Basil has considered everyone to be expendable except himself.'

Estarra clearly looked uneasy. 'I hate to say this, Peter, but what if the Chairman's right? What other choice does he have? He's lost most of the Earth Defence Forces, and what's left won't be enough to stop a concerted force of hydrogues. What if he's right?'

'He might be right – but in the wrong way.' Peter struggled with his anger, and he felt the heat of a flush on his cheeks. 'Look what he's doing to the human race. You saw the last tactical summary. He's already condemned all of the Hansa colonies.'

Recently, Captain McCammon had independently decided to help the King from being kept in the dark. The head of the royal guard had begun to surreptitiously deliver copies of Basil's daily summary briefings so that Peter could remain informed of the business of the Hansa. The data itself was valuable, though Peter was not at liberty to do anything with it.

The Teacher compy said, 'I have noted many instances of the

367

Chairman's extreme and irrational behaviour, especially in the past year.'

'He broke his own cardinal rule and let himself be blinded by personal feelings. He's thinking more about himself than about the Hansa or the future.' Peter turned to the Teacher compy. 'OX, we need your help.'

They all froze, hearing movement in the hall. Two royal guards outside the door stepped aside to let in a pair of gaudily liveried servants carrying trays of food for an early lunch. Both men wore the colourful cap and flamboyant vest designed for workers in the Whisper Palace. Peter had always thought the impractically quaint costume was for tourists and the media, but the workers dressed the same even in private sections of the Palace.

'We didn't order our food yet,' he said.

The men blinked simultaneously. 'Sorry, Sire. A banquet is about to start in the east gardens for two hundred Hansa func-tionaries.' The servers set down the trays. 'We were afraid that if we did not bring your lunch now, the kitchens could not give your order the proper diligence.'

The costumed men looked afraid that the King might reprimand them for their foresight, but Peter just wanted them to go. 'It's fine. Now please leave us. My Queen and I were having a private conversation.'

The two men scuttled away, their colourful uniforms flapping. The royal guards stationed outside the apartments – supposedly loyal to McCammon – stepped back into position, preventing anyone from entering or leaving. Peter sealed the door, blocking them off.

Estarra inspected the savoury soup and colourful fruit, and picked up one of the sandwiches made from smoked fish and spicy greens. 'I am hungry, but at least it's not one of those strange cravings.'

OX stood beside the table, patiently waiting to resume their interrupted discussion. Before the Queen could take a bite, Peter gestured for the compy to scan the food. Basil did not know that the two used OX to guard against poison whenever they could.

OX examined the sandwich, then the plate of food. His optical sensors brightened. 'I detect no poison, King Peter. However there is an unexpected chemical signature, a complex pharmaceutical strain. I am accessing the molecular structure and comparing it to my records.'

Peter took the sandwich away from Estarra, glaring at the food, certain Basil had tampered with it somehow. 'I don't even want you touching that.'

OX finally delivered his summary. 'Each of these food items contains a substantial dose of a tasteless abortive chemical. King Peter is not likely to experience any symptoms, but the dosage would surely trigger a spontaneous miscarriage in the Queen.'

'A miscarriage! But I'm too far along.' Estarra leaned back in the chair as if she'd just received a physical blow.

OX said in an even voice, 'A miscarriage at six months, triggered by such a harsh drug, would likely cause severe medical complications in the mother, perhaps even death.'

Peter's hands trembled. The back of his head became a hot, dull ache. 'That bloodthirsty bastard won't ever let it go.'

'Just like the dolphins,' Estarra whispered.

He wanted to rush to the balcony and hurl the platters of food into the open square, shouting curses at Basil Wenceslas as he did. But Peter forced himself not to overreact, not to tip his hand. At the moment their only advantage was that the Chairman didn't know they'd detected his sabotage. If Basil thought it was working, he wasn't likely to try anything else. It might buy another day . . .

Seething, Peter picked up the tray of food, moved it far from Estarra, and then fed every scrap into the waste recycler.

The Queen looked sick. 'From now on we need to test every-thing we eat. OX, if you hadn't caught that . . .'

'I can possibly arrange to bring food to you, Queen Estarra, in small and unobtrusive packages,' the compy offered.

'Maybe Captain McCammon can smuggle something to us as well,' Peter said, feeling the anger burning hotter inside him.

The King sighed. 'I tried to make peace with Basil, tried to cooperate. We could have been partners. I did what was right for the Hansa, as I will always do. But now' – he turned towards Estarra – 'now I know. We're going to have to kill him before he kills us.'

SEVENTY-EIGHT

OSIRA'H

As the angry humans stood in the doorway, Udruh shouted, 'Osira'h, come to me! I will keep you safe from them.' He still did not believe what the girl had done, nor did he understand what he faced.

She didn't move. 'I am perfectly safe.'

All the lights suddenly died. The house plunged into impenetrable shadows. The captives had smashed the power conduits and cut off the generator serving the former Designate's residence. Releasing long-pent-up anger, reinforcing each others' madness, they pushed their way into the residence.

'He has nowhere to go.' Osira'h was a disembodied voice in the darkness.

Udru'h, as a man who had always relied on himself, sprinted away from the mob. He stumbled in the dark as he charged down the hall. He could not see, and the blackness would surely terrify him.

Osira'h recognized the gravelly voice of Benn Stoner as he

371

pushed past her. 'Follow the Designate. Don't let him get away.' Other voices took up the cry.

With keen eyes, she watched the Designate running in the dark. When he encountered a staircase, he rushed up it. Dim light from spreading fires outside gave the intruders enough illumination to follow.

She felt strange, both weak and excited. She could not afford to remember that she'd had feelings for this man. His just punishment could no longer be stopped. It was like an avalanche, and she had encouraged it herself.

She hurried after the shouts, the sounds of running feet, the scuffle. On the upper levels, Stoner and his allies had cornered the fleeing Designate. Osira'h drove away her sudden lump of regret by recalling her mother's memories as vivid as fresh, bright blood. Just as if it had all happened to *her*, the girl felt the burning pain, the constant humiliation, the sheer damage done to Nira.

When she reached the upper landing, her sensitive eyes could make out Designate Udru'h. His eyes were bright in the reflections from a few remaining blazers in the Ildiran streets and the spreading fires. Sensing Osira'h there, he turned to face her. She shouted accusingly, 'Your breeding plan stole the lives of all these people, and the generations before them.'

Udru'h seemed confused. 'Osira'h, you know why we did this. I saved my race!'

'And you doomed my mother's.' It sounded like a verdict.

Stoner and his fellow mob members closed in on the trapped former Designate. Every person carried one of the farm implements that Daro'h had made available to them – hooked furrowers, weed rakes, planting staves. Their anger erupted. With the Designate backed against the wall, they began to pummel him.

Udru'h did not cry out. He fought back, but did not hurl curses or snarl. Osira'h heard the soft, ripe slap of hard implements on

372

yielding skin. She saw the pain on his face, and in an unforgettable echo of memories from her mother, she remembered other expressions on the Designate's face in the shadowy breeding barracks.

'Wait!' Nira's voice was perfectly clear even over the tumult. *'Stop this!'*

Osira'h turned to see the green priest woman standing at the top of the stairs. She looked scuffed, singed, bruised, as if she'd already had an ordeal just getting here. She had come to the Designate's dwelling, bringing her other four half-breed children with her. Osira'h looked up, her pupils huge in the shadows. Her brothers and sisters stayed close to their mother.

The captives also fell silent. Nira took a step forward, surrounded by a faint glow of spreading fires outside. Osira'h had expected her mother to take great satisfaction from this, but a green priest could not. 'Don't kill him.'

'But Mother, you know what he did to you, to all these people. *And to me.*'

'I did nothing to you!' Bloody and beaten, but still very much alive, Udru'h hauled himself up. He spoke, clearly addressing the little girl, finding the strength to push back his confused attackers. 'You were my greatest hope, my prize.'

Osira'h looked at him with an expression of utter distaste. 'Every touch, every word you spoke to me was like the barbed fences enclosing the camp. You would pat me on the shoulder to congratulate me after some difficult exercise, but all I could feel was how your cruel hands had touched my mother.'

Nira's voice cracked as she looked at her daughter, then at her tormentor. 'Designate Udru'h, I never wanted to hate you. Jora'h and I were happy at the Prism Palace, but you took that from both of us.'

The mob had backed off, not finished expressing their anger. Osira'h had riled them up to this point, and they wanted release.

The girl shouted at the former Designate. 'I experienced my mother's pain and humiliation. How could I drive that out of my head? When you raped her, you raped me.'

'No!' Udru'h seemed horrified by what the girl was saying.

Nira explained to the Designate, 'She is my daughter. We were linked. For a long time she has known everything you did to me – I gave her all of my memories on the night you ordered your guards to beat me . . . when you told everyone else I'd been killed.'

Osira'h raised her hands to touch the bloody cheeks and forehead of the former Designate. She felt hot inside, and her head pounded. 'I can make Udru'h understand. He has much to learn.'

He blinked at her in surprise and relief, as if he expected her to offer him forgiveness. But she did not intend to absolve him. 'Osira'h, what are—'

The girl pressed her hands harder against him, tensing. She stared at her former mentor with the intensity of artillery shots, and Udru'h stiffened. 'I am a bridge between species. I learned how to open myself and act as a conduit for the hydrogues.' Osira'h had a frightening expression on her face. 'This is just *sharing*.'

Udru'h began to shudder. His eyes widened, and his expression drew back in fear. Osira'h did not release him. 'Enough!' He raised his hands, clearly in deep pain. 'It is enough.'

Osira'h let go, and the injured man reeled. His eyes were glassy. She smiled at her mother and said calmly, 'I gave him every memory. Every assault, every torture, every rape. He now experienced it as you did, Mother.'

Udru'h looked at Nira with a new kind of revulsion.

The girl raised her delicate eyebrows. 'Maybe we should have just killed him. Is that what you want? Would that make you feel free, Mother?'

The other angry men and women raised their implements

and shouted, but Nira seemed to speak only to her children, all of them. 'No. You might know my hatred of him, but you don't know what I want. Hatred cannot free me. *You* made me see your brothers and sisters — made me accept them for what they are and not reject them for how they came to be born. Think about your brother Rod'h. Udru'h is his father. Would you do this to Rod'h as well? Does he deserve to see his father beaten to death?'

Osira'h was confused and uncertain. 'But I was doing this for *you*, Mother! What do you want?'

Nira seemed to have considered that already. 'For these people, for this camp, I want changes. We are now strong enough to demand them. *Changes*, Osira'h. Not mere revenge. Revenge and violence are easy, but they leave a stain you can never wash away. I could never want that for you — for any of us.'

She gestured towards the battered and bloody Udru'h, who huddled on the floor. 'Bind him so he can't get away. Then we will all take him to the new Designate Daro'h. He has the power to end this all . . . if he is wise enough.'

SEVENTY-NINE

NIRA

Outside the former Designate's residence, people ran wild through the settlement. Lens kithmen, labourers, servants, and guards were trapped within crowded communal residences, unable to escape the spreading flames. Screams rose like smoke from the burning structures.

At first, running far ahead of her from the bonfire of the breeding barracks, Stoner and his uncontrolled comrades had begun to burn outbuildings, supply structures, even a medical inspection centre. But now the fire went wherever it wished, sweeping to inhabited buildings. Unsuspecting Ildirans had been caught within their homes and were even now being burned alive.

The former captives were horrified to hear the agonized wails from those trapped behind the flames. This was not what they had intended. Men and women rallied, called to each other, and ran to the doorways, attempting to batter their way in. Nira joined them, trying to help rescue the helpless Ildirans.

And then the guard kithmen had come.

Seeing the flames and the mob of humans, the bestial-looking

Ildiran soldiers had fallen upon the former captives, hacking with crystal swords. Dozens had died before the rest of the humans scattered in complete panic. Thinking of the half-breed children with her, Nira had run with them to the residence of Designate Udru'h, where she hoped they might be safe.

There, she had not found what she'd expected, but she had prevented yet another murder. Now, perhaps she could stop the rest of this madness.

Nira felt sickened as her group left the former Designate's residence. When she had planned this protest, the burning of the breeding barracks, she had only wanted to force Daro'h into more than the token concessions he'd made in order to cover up the larger plan. She had never intended wholesale destruction. The mayhem continued. The flames were brighter, the screams louder, the situation completely out of control. And the Ildiran guards were killing any loose humans they encountered.

On the outskirts of the Ildiran settlement, the barracks had collapsed into smouldering rubble, and Nira watched as the rising wind blew sparks beyond the camp, setting fire to the grassy hills. The rioters had no interest in stopping that inferno and moved inexorably towards the separate residence of new Designate Daro'h, dragging a battered Udru'h with them. Nira guessed he must be in terrible pain, but at least she had saved his life – for the time being. She doubted her former tormentor would appreciate it.

Her half-breed children accompanied them, following Osira'h as much as they followed her. Raised and trained to sacrifice everything for the Ildiran Empire, they had never imagined anything remotely like this. Both repelled and fascinated, their strange mixed eyes missed nothing.

Frantic Ildirans ran outside; some of them tried to extinguish the flames, while others attempted to free those trapped in the buildings. Humans rushed pell-mell from one burning building to another. Guided by her determination, Nira's small group of followers had only one goal. They marched forward in a disorganized group, the antithesis of precisely trained Ildiran troops.

Suddenly brutal guards carrying long crystal spears charged into the scattered breeding subjects. The former captives fought back with sticks and clubs, furrowers and planting rods, killing two Ildiran guards. But they had no fighting experience, and dozens were swiftly hacked to pieces. Nira urged her group to run forward, calling out Daro'h's name.

Staunch kithmen formed a cordon in front of the new Designate's residence standing against Nira's approach. They held katanas – sharp crystal blades mounted on poles. With amazing synchronization, the guards hurled the sharp weapons. Every blade flew true as the panicked mob scattered. Katanas plunged into chests, necks, and even the backs of those few who turned to run. A scream rose up, followed by a wave of outrage.

With deep dismay Nira saw that the guards would never allow the mob to enter Daro'h's house. Thinking dangerously, she made up her mind in an instant. She glanced at Osira'h, who quickly understood. Suddenly the girl and her mother stood holding a still-shuddering Designate Udru'h at the forefront, presenting themselves as living shields.

'We must speak with Designate Daro'h!' Nira's words were clear above the screams, the crackle of flames, the shattering of crystal panes. 'Bring him!'

The guards stepped forward, raising their weapons. Nira could see that many of the sharp blades were already smeared with blood.

Osira'h called, 'I am the Mage-Imperator's daughter. This is former Designate Udru'h. You know us. My mother was a consort of Prime Designate Jora'h. Did he not give you orders to protect her?'

As if daring the guards to kill them, the half-breed children joined their mother and sister-saviour whom they revered. Rod'h sent a disturbed look toward the defeated Udru'h, then faced forward.

Soldier kithmen followed orders without question, but they did not know how to deal with complicated and unclear decisions. Finally, Udru'h croaked out through bloody lips, 'Bring Daro'h! Do not be fools.'

The upper windows of the Designate's residence swung open. Daro'h had been there observing, arguing with over-protective guards. 'Hold your weapons! There will be no more killing.'

The guard kithmen froze but kept their crystal spears ready. Angry humans pushed forward, growling. Nira and Osira'h stood beside the former Designate, in front of all the others.

Daro'h sounded distraught. 'Why are you doing this? I gave you your freedom. I tore down the fences.'

Osira'h cried, 'You never told them about the hydrogues – and how the Mage-Imperator surrendered to them.'

'If the hydrogues are going to kill us anyway,' Benn Stoner shouted from behind, 'why shouldn't we kill all of you first?'

Nira stepped forward, apart from the mob's simmering anger. 'We can stop this now – or we can all perish.' Glancing behind her, she added, 'Do not underestimate the strength of these people. They've got nothing to lose.' The screams and the roaring flames demanded her attention. 'We will help you get this madness under control. Please let us help you – there isn't much time. And afterwards, you can tell them all the truth.'

Udru'h swayed, then dropped to his knees. Osira'h stepped away from him. 'Do as they say,' the former Designate called.

Roaring flames now spread across the hills and through the

Ildiran settlement. Daro'h commanded his guards to cease their attacks, to work instead – with the humans – to save whoever could be rescued from the burning buildings. 'Or we will all be dead before the hydrogues come anyway.'

EIGHTY

CHAIRMAN BASIL WENCESLAS

Whenever he summoned Deputy Cain, the pale man came with some optimistic report that Basil had not asked for. It was as if Cain strategically wanted to fend off unpleasant issues by arming himself with something irrelevant. Or was it a deeper plan? He wondered what the man would bring this time.

Basil had called his deputy to the rooftop gardens of the stepped pyramid. The carefully manicured shrubs, dwarf fruit trees, and sweetly pungent exotic flowers were maintained with a geometric precision that he wished he could impose upon his own people. It comforted him to see how the plants thrived and yet maintained their exact places.

Cain waved a data display screen. 'The crew at the hydrogue derelict has made a new breakthrough with the exotic wall that is similar to the Klikiss transportals. The engineers have activated the energy source. We anticipate this will lead to a great many new developments.'

Basil pursed his lips. This was indeed interesting. 'Good, we can make it function. Now, how long until we know how to *shut down* a warglobe? We've heard reports that the Roamers even have some kind of effective weapon that they used against the hydrogues at Theroc. If the damned Roamers can figure it out, I expect the Hansa to do better.'

'If we can make the hydrogue ship work, Mr Chairman, we can probably figure out how to break it down. It's generally easier to screw things up.'

Basil scowled. 'Yes, I am very familiar with screw-ups. Speaking of which, I've decided to send another small retrieval ship to Qronha 3 in search of our missing rammers. Just in case. They've got to be out there somewhere. Maybe we can bring back some of them.'

Cain looked perplexed. 'I thought the Soldier compies stole the rammers.'

'Probably. But Stromo's green priest mentioned a curious transmission they intercepted. We had a surveillance compy hidden among the rammer crews. If we strengthen and lock onto the spy signal, it could lead us to the rammers.'

'Interesting.'

Basil's jaw clenched. 'And it will give the busybody media reporters something relevant to talk about. They keep raising questions about the King and Queen, wanting to know when the baby is due to be born, demanding that the royal couple make more public appearances. They've already started broadcasting reports that Peter and Estarra are under house arrest and confined to their quarters. "Inside sources!"' Basil made an angry noise. 'I assigned you the task of finding out who has been talking to reporters, who has been leaking information from the Whisper Palace. I'm counting on you, Cain.'

'I am doing my best, sir. At the moment, I have no leads. This inside source seems to be a very careful, very clever person.'

Basil heaved a sigh of disgust, then cut off further irrelevant chitchat. 'I called you here because I have a job for you. I need you to write a very important letter.'

Cain was intrigued. 'A letter to whom?'

'To whom it may concern – or whatever phrase you choose. The author will be Estarra. You see, our poor Queen is about to be terribly distraught, shattered in fact. We can only imagine how much pain and abject misery a woman feels when she loses her unborn child.'

Cain could not cover his startled expression. 'The Queen lost her baby? When did that happen?'

'She's going to lose it soon, and there are bound to be medical complications. If she happens to survive the miscarriage, then we will need your note.' Basil narrowed his grey eyes. 'It has to be perfect, considering it'll be widely reported in the media.'

Cain seemed guarded, even upset. 'I need to be perfectly clear what you're asking me to do, Mr Chairman.'

'Don't be obtuse. You need to make sure the Queen sounds sufficiently distraught, even suicidal, after losing the baby. She can't deal with the responsibility and the loss. It's clear to her that she has no option but to take her own life, and so on. She'll find a quiet and painless way, I'm sure.'

A flush appeared on the pale man's face. His nostrils flared as he drew a deep breath. 'It is very dangerous – and, I believe, ill-advised – for you to kill the Queen.'

'The Queen is going to kill herself, Mr Cain . . . if that should prove necessary. And I believe it will be.'

Cain remained silent for a long time. He didn't pace, didn't move, simply stared into the Chairman's eyes. 'Consider the consequences of such an action. You saw how the public cheered when they learned of her pregnancy. If she loses the baby, they will be devastated. If the Queen commits suicide afterwards, it will be another blow. Now is not the time for us to wilfully damage morale. The people are already in despair — what if this pushes them over the edge? Mr Chairman, that is a decidedly foolish risk to take.'

Basil gave a dismissive wave. 'Public morale will drop for a while, and then we'll shore it up. In a time of such tragedy, the people will grasp at any straw.' The Chairman bent over to smell the fragrant white blossoms. 'By the way, I'm happy to report that Prince Daniel is doing remarkably well. Ever since we put abject terror into him, he's been fabulously cooperative. Oh, he's a bit full of himself in front of functionaries and servants, but never around me.'

Cain was obviously not so satisfied. 'He takes out his frustration on others. That is not a desirable leadership trait, sir. We should do our best to stamp it out while he is still malleable. It could come back to bite us in the future.'

'On the contrary, I see it as a sign of healthy self-esteem. A King needs that, so long as he does exactly what he's told.'

Cain continued to struggle with his genuine anger. Basil was pleased to see the deputy show a little backbone. 'Sir, may I speak frankly?'

'If I wanted simpering, I could find any number of people to do it.'

'Your animosity towards King Peter has passed beyond the professional level to become a personal vendetta. I believe it's affecting your ability to perform rationally as Chairman.'

'I have never lost sight of the big picture, Mr Cain. The list of Peter's infractions is very long, and so is the number of once-reliable men and women who've now let me down. I am re-establishing order one piece at a time, step by step, and to do so I must grant myself the freedom to do whatever is necessary. I have my own methodology.'

Though Cain remained disturbed, for Basil the meeting was ended. 'Go and write your draft of the letter. Maybe we'll never need to use it, but I intend to keep my options open.'

EIGHTY-ONE

ANTON COLICOS

Eager to share one of the new stories they had found in the Hyrillka vaults, Anton and Vao'sh met with a weary Designate Ridek'h in his citadel palace quarters. They had already sifted out the best, most provocative new stories, but they had not yet found a miracle cure for the Mage-Imperator's problems.

The boy was red-eyed and obviously exhausted, but Anton thought he looked a great deal more determined and confident than he had been aboard the warliner. With Yazra'h and Tal O'nh assisting him, the young Designate was overseeing so many rebuilding operations, boosting the morale of his people, that he was too preoccupied for doubts anymore.

Interested in what the historians had found, Yazra'h joined them in the Designate's private room. The beautiful but intimidating woman took a seat very close beside Anton, though he hadn't left her much room. She smelled clean, freshly scrubbed, but not perfumed. The tawny Isix cats circled the room twice, then melted onto the floor at Anton's feet.

Ridek'h looked eagerly at the old rememberer. 'Is it a brave story? About Hyrillka?' He sat in a chair that looked much too large for him.

'This is the tale of the Shadow Fleet, the voyagers in darkness, trapped for ever just a thin boundary away from the light.' Anton had read the accounts, too, but decided to let Vao'sh share it. His friend was a master storyteller.

'Orryx ... a name not much remembered, a place no longer visited. It was the first of our splinter colonies to succumb to the black shadow of the Shana Rei.' The old historian's voice grew stronger with each stanza he had memorized, and the lobes on his face flushed a variety of colours. '*Shana Rei*. The creatures of darkness had emerged from their black nebulas and swallowed our survey fleet, leaving their victims nothing more than pale ghosts killed by the utter absence of light!' He drew in a quick breath, startling them.

'But Ildirans did not yet know the nature of their terrible new enemy. The Shana Rei were a hungry wave spreading out from the dark nebulae, living shadows that devoured light and life. Orryx was the first in their path, a place of flowers and fields, families and songs. They suspected nothing until the Shana Rei flung blackness across the landscape like a shroud that absorbed all light, blindfolding the eyes and hearts of those poor people. A permanent eclipse.'

Outside, Hyrillka's bright primary sun had set, and the orange secondary left a coppery burning undertone in the air. As the rememberer told his story, the room seemed to grow dimmer.

Vao'sh extended a finger. 'When the Mage-Imperator sensed his subjects being engulfed on Orryx, he rushed a septa of warliners to fight for them. Seven warliners armed with our best weapons and crewed by the bravest soldier kithmen. All seven battleships vanished into the blackness.

'Feeling echoes of horror through the *thism*, the Mage-Imperator commanded his engineers and scientists to develop new weapons from the Lightsource. Before long, brave Tal Bria'nh rushed to the dying splinter colony with a cohort of warliners. He carried a hundred new sun bombs – satellites that could produce as much purifying brightness as a star. They were confident, angry, and ready to take revenge for the unprovoked attack.

'When the sun bombs ignited, the light burned the Shana Rei like acid. A flash and a rainbow, searing light to bring joy to any Ildiran, and death to a creature of darkness. Although the ebony blanket of the Shana Rei began to dissolve, the hundred sun bombs eventually dwindled. Then the Shana Rei returned for a second onslaught, without tactics or compassion. Faced with the new wall of darkness, Tal Bria'nh knew he could not defeat it. He dispatched streamers with details of the attack back to Ildira, but he stayed with his flagship. Help would never arrive in time.'

Vao'sh caught his breath, inserting a masterful, tense pause. One of the Isix cats shifted against Anton's foot. 'When reinforcements did arrive, Orryx looked as if someone had painted the whole world black. The Shana Rei had succeeded. Every living thing had perished. To this day nothing grows there.'

Vao'sh looked directly at young Designate Ridek'h. 'And do you know what happened to brave Tal Bria'nh's warliners?' The boy shook his head. 'They were still in orbit, but each one was wrapped in a cocoon of pure shadow that allowed no light in or out. Nothing. Tal Bria'nh and his brave crew were literally smothered in darkness!' Anton imagined a black body bag being drawn over the warliners.

The rescuers finally used lasers – concentrated light – to cut through the inky skin. Retrieval parties broke into the warliners, searching for any living Ildiran, but to no avail. No one had survived. How could they have, knowing there would be no more

light, no more warmth?' He shuddered, and Anton did not think
it was part of his performance. 'We can only imagine their nightmarish last moments.'

'So how were these Shana Rei ever defeated at all?' Anton
asked. 'In the stories, I mean.'

Vao'sh smiled at him. 'I know only that the Mage-Imperator
created a new alliance and "brought forth a Great Light." The new
records we found tell that the Great Light was fire personified,
which drove away the creatures of darkness using fire against
the night.'

'It sounds like the faeros,' Yazra'h said.

'Maybe the faeros have helped us before!' Ridek'h said in an
excited voice. 'Is that what the Mage Imperator asked you to find?'

Suddenly, the Isix cats bounded to their feet, and Yazra'h's
reaction was only a fraction of a second slower. Anton turned
to the door of the Designate's chamber to see one-eyed Tal O'nh
marching in, flushed and breathless.

'Designate, three hydrogue warglobes are en route to Hyrillka.'

'Hydrogues! What do we do?' Ridek'h's eyes widened, looking
from the military commander to Yazra'h. 'Do we fight? We have
warliners—'

The officer touched the prismatic Lightsource medallion on
his chest for strength and delivered his words in a flat, businesslike
tone. 'My warliners can make suicide plunges against the warglobes. Fortunately, they are mostly empty, with all their crews
down here. I hope, however, that will not be necessary. When
hundreds of warglobes came to Ildira not long ago, they departed
without attacking. Maybe the same thing will happen here.'

'We let them make the first move, Designate,' Yazra'h advised.

They hurried to the open balcony, looking out into Hyrillka's
dull orange evening. From a communication badge on his collar,
O'nh received curt updates from his ships in orbit. Anton stared

upwards. Yazra'h stood close to him, and he realized that he felt oddly safer to have her there.

She spotted it first, extending her arm to point. A trio of diamond spheres cruised down over Hyrillka's landscape as if observing the ruins. Eventually, they took up position directly above the citadel palace. Though the enemy transmitted no warnings or ultimatums, the threat was clear. They just hung there.

'Should I go to shelter?' Ridek'h looked at the one-eyed officer, then at Yazra'h. 'Tal O'nh, would I be safer aboard one of your warliners?'

Yazra'h frowned at her young nephew. 'The Designate must stay here. If you are to die, then you will die – but do not die as a coward. Your father did not, when Rusa'h's followers stabbed him to death. Hyrillka is yours now. Show these people how a Designate behaves. After recent events, maybe they have forgotten.'

Again Ridek'h steeled himself, and did as she told him.

Anton looked up into the sky, hoping he wasn't about to become another part of the epic story.

EIGHTY-TWO

THOR'H

The darkness was absolute. Black, endless black, seemed to extend from one side of the universe to the other. No torment could be worse.

For an impossible time, Thor'h's dreams had been empty, then strange. Gradually, as the shiing wore off, the nightmares became more intense, like sharp teeth gnawing at his consciousness.

He slowly began to remember Hyrillka, how he had fought beside Imperator Rusa'h. Together, they had meant to overthrow Jora'h, the false Mage-Imperator, his own father. But they had failed. Thor'h remembered flying his warliners, expecting to die ... then being captured, bound, humiliated. He remembered Designate Udru'h's cruel smile, his stony refusal to hear Thor'h's pleas.

Afterwards, there had been shiing ... too much shiing.

And then bliss.

And then nothing.

And now darkness. Utter darkness.

He did not know where he was. The walls were thick, and he

found no way out. Groggily, as if from a great distance, he thought he heard the sound of scuffling feet, furniture being moved, but no one unsealed Thor'h's chamber.

He could see nothing, could feel no light on his sensitive skin. His hands were unbound, and he touched his face. He reached out and struck a wall. The inky blackness all around him felt like a cold ocean filling his mouth, his nose, his eyes.

He screamed endlessly and flung himself at the walls, pounding until his knuckles felt wet with his blood. He couldn't find a door. The blackness was a crushing weight, literally killing him.

But first it drove him mad.

Howling, Thor'h battered against the black walls of his prison, shrieking until his vocal cords were torn and bloody. He continued to wail a husky, breathy sound of hopelessness as his mind broke apart.

No one heard him.

No one knew he was there.

And the lights never came back on.

EIGHTY-THREE

JESS TAMBLYN

Eighty of the workers on Plumas had survived the disaster. The water mines, which had been in clan Tamblyn for generations, did not.

Frigid steam gushed from damaged conversion equipment. Life-support generators had failed, and the grotto temperature was already dropping to a deep bone-chilling cold. Only one of the artificial suns remained embedded in the ceiling.

Another thing broken, another thing lost. Jess looked at the crumbling ice ceiling, the shattered ground, the frost-petrified bodies of fallen miners and dead nematodes. This had been his family's sanctuary, their dream for so many years. He had first left Plumas because of his impossible love for Cesca, and he'd come back as a different person, a different sort of being altogether, with good intentions and dangerous delusions.

The tainted wental inside his mother had wrought all of this damage, but he was to blame as well. Sensing his dismay, Cesca came up to hold him. Her touch – which had been denied him for so long – now gave him strength.

Old Caleb clapped his hands with a gunshot-loud sound and shouted to all the survivors. 'Come on, all together. We have work to do.' Water miners scrambled to give first aid to the injured. The exhausted and broken-hearted Tamblyn brothers helped erect temporary shelters by shoring up partially destroyed living huts.

A huge chunk of ice fell from the ceiling and splashed into the metal-grey sea. Jess said sharply, 'Cesca, we have to hold this place together until we can get the people away to safety. A lot of them are hurt.' He held her tingling hand. 'Let me show you how.'

Focusing on the damage, shunting aside his grief and uncertainty, Jess showed Cesca how to use her newfound powers to seal the worst cracks in the ceiling, welding shut the fissures. With deep concentration and a sweep of his hand, Jess evaporated away mounds of fallen ice.

Since Jess could not touch any living person, he accepted the grim task of hauling bodies of the dead to the edge of the now-calm sea. Before he touched any of the corpses, he paused. 'And what if I infect them with a tainted wental?' After what had occurred with his mother, he was very cautious.

That will not happen here, the wental voices said in his head. *It will not happen again.*

He looked down at a pale, twisted man who had bled to death from dozens of lacerations; the blood was dark and glassy, already frozen in the ground. Jess vaguely remembered him, a worker in the hydrogen-fuel separation columns; they had nodded hello to each other when Jess lived down here, exchanged a few words. Just acquaintances. Jess didn't even know his name. Now he was dead.

A crew came back down from a surface-access tunnel wearing full environment suits and delivered their report to Caleb. 'Crust

394

shiftings knocked our wellhead shafts out of alignment. The pumping machinery is wrecked, the fuel-conversion tanks broken, the chemical lines completely out of whack.'

Defeat salted the old man's voice. 'We've got one lift still functional, but some of the indicator lights are giving funny flickers. Jess, even if you and Cesca patch the ceiling, I just don't know if this place is salvageable. With Andrew dead ...' He choked, then drew a long breath. 'And without you working with us on a regular basis, we'll have to reassess how we do business, if we do business at all.'

When Jess spoke the words aloud, they hurt him deeply, but he and his uncles already knew the decision that had to be made. 'We'll have to abandon Plumas, at least for now. Too many systems are damaged to maintain a reliable environment.'

The survivors still hadn't absorbed what exactly had happened. Wynn and Torin shook their heads, though. 'We can't just leave, Jess. Look at all the work that needs to be done!'

'How is Clan Tamblyn ever going to afford all this?' Torin moaned.

'Andrew handled our finances. How can we do it without Andrew?'

'Clan Tamblyn has money in its accounts, don't you worry about that,' Caleb growled. 'But where are we going to get the heavy equipment to redrill the damaged shafts and repair the delivery systems? I'm getting a headache already. By the Guiding Star, it'll take years!'

Jess felt the wentals singing through his body. Now was the time. He and Cesca could not forget their primary mission. 'There's other work for you all to do – something more urgent. We need your help. All Roamers, all humans.'

Caleb blinked. 'Look around you, Jess! We're not in a position to help with folding napkins.'

'Not true,' Cesca said, 'Call the survivors together. They need to hear this.'

His uncle shrugged. 'We could use a break – and a little bit of hope.'

Haggard-looking men and women gathered around the ruins of the settlement huts. The Plumas workers stood together, uneasy and uncertain. They had watched Jess and Cesca battle the thing that had been his mother, and these people were afraid of the powerful couple.

The wentals made Jess's words resonate through the entire grotto. 'Speaker Peroni and I came to Plumas for a reason. You have already fought the Eddies and the drogues. You've lived on the run, struggling to survive, even as one livelihood after another is taken away. However, the war isn't finished yet. Not even close. The greatest battle is coming – and the wentals need our assistance.'

Torin grumbled, 'Seems to me your wentals caused us a whole lot of grief.'

'One tainted wental,' Jess corrected. 'The others saved you. The others can save all the clans, and the rest of the human race. We have to unleash thousands and thousands of wentals against hydrogue planets.'

Cesca said, 'It has to be us. The Ildirans and the Eddies don't have weapons that can crush the drogues.'

'The Eddies were powerful enough to turn Rendezvous into a scrap heap,' Caleb pointed out. 'Why should we bother helping them?'

A stormy flicker crossed Cesca's face, but she narrowed her eyes and spoke calmly. 'All humans aren't like the Eddies. Roamers are better than that.'

Caleb raised his eyebrows. 'You expect us to believe that if we defeat the drogues, the Eddies will stop preying on clan facilities?

Stop wrecking our fuel depots and greenhouse asteroids? Are they going to release the Roamer prisoners they've taken? Shizz, maybe they'll rebuild Rendezvous while they're at it! Jess, you and Speaker Peroni know better than that.'

'What we know – and what all of us need to remember – is that the drogues are our real enemy. Among humans, there will always be conflict. Would you just prefer the hydrogues exterminate us all?'

Caleb did not sound convinced, but he grudgingly agreed. The Tamblyn brothers stood together, took one long look at the ruins and the impossible task of rebuilding it all. Torin said, 'All right, we're at your command. Tell us what you want us to do.'

The surviving workers were glad just to have a sense of direction after the turmoil they'd been through. Jess could see they were ready to cause damage if they were pointed towards the enemy and given an appropriate weapon.

Together, he and Cesca explained how they intended to use water tankers to distribute wentals in a simultaneous attack against drogue gas giants. Jess spoke up, 'Everyone here can fit in the remaining fourteen tankers. Divide the duties among yourselves as you wish. We'll tell you where to go fill your tankers and be ready.'

'Nikko Chan Tylar is already recruiting as many Roamers as he can convince to join the fight. Jess's other water-bearer volunteers are doing the same thing all around the Spiral Arm, directing them to congregate at other central wental worlds,' Cesca said. 'If we're going to strike all drogue planets at once, we'll need every clan from Avila to Zoltan.'

'If you want to find a lot of Roamers, go to Yreka,' Caleb said. 'That's our main gathering place these days. Denn and I were the ones who set up the whole thing.' The Tamblyn brothers described the new trading centre, where orphaned Hansa colonies were working secretly with Roamer traders. Cesca was pleased to hear that her father might be there.

Later, the survivors made their way up the one functioning lift shaft to the surface, taking ground vehicles to the water tankers waiting at transfer points. They crowded into the passenger compartments.

Jess stood outside on the bleak terrain. His wental vessel shimmered nearby like a veined bubble. He wondered if Plumas would ever be a bustling and thriving outpost again, or if this would be the end of the water mines.

Cesca held him. 'A peaceful and prosperous future is not so far off,' she said. 'But first we have to win this battle. In order to strike all gas planets efficiently and simultaneously, we've got to coordinate this whole wave so the drogues don't have a chance.'

'A real administrative problem,' Jess said.

'That's something I'm good at. These people need the Speaker.' She gave him a relieved smile. Out in the open under the starlight and the reflected illumination from the ice moon, he thought she looked very beautiful.

He hesitated, but they both understood the wentals' plan. 'It took us a long time to be reunited, but now you and I need to separate once again. You go to Yreka – and I've got to go to Theroc.'

'I know,' she said. 'I heard the worldtrees calling the wentals, too.'

The verdani had pledged to fight with them, worldtrees and wentals in an alliance even greater than what they had ten thousand years ago. When Jess kissed her, the sadness of their parting only made her lips taste sweeter. 'By the Guiding Star, I swear that when this is all over, you and I will be together.'

EIGHTY-FOUR

KOTTO OKIAH

otto had almost run out of ideas – an entirely new experience for him. After scanning the ruins of the Jonah 12 base, he detected high radioactivity levels, which implied that the reactor had a catastrophic meltdown. (That was inconceivable, but how could he argue with the data?) He found no ships in the vicinity, no signs of life, and no answers.

So he went hunting again. After searching three more systems, he found a small Roamer settlement named, of all things, Sunshine. A blistering bath of photons poured over the planetoid's surface. The Tomara clan holed up underground, excavating tunnels in the crater walls, while solar collectors gorged on extravagant amounts of energy. During the long cold nights on Sunshine, the Roamers scurried out to do their work on the surface.

The place was mostly empty. Kotto asked where everyone had gone. 'Why, they've all flown to Yreka,' answered an old, one-armed man who worked a tunnel-excavation machine that was five times his size. 'Not much work here that my crew can't handle, so everybody else is off trading.'

'Yreka? What's on Yreka?' Beside him, KR and GU began to recite the vital statistics of the Hansa colony on the edge of Ildiran space, but Kotto shushed them.

'Biggest swap meet in the Spiral Arm,' said the one-armed man. 'Closest thing to free trade since before the drogues showed up.'

'Then that's where I'll go.' Maybe he would find his mother, or Speaker Peroni. Kotto thanked the man, took his two compies, and flew away from Sunshine.

He immediately spotted Denn Peroni's *Dogged Persistence* on Yreka's landing field. The locals had made a thriving business of their new marketplace, setting up full-fledged restaurants and food stalls to cater to the influx of visitors. Now that new ekti was flowing in from Golgen, transportation between orphaned colonies had become commonplace again.

When Kotto stepped out into the bustle, Denn was among the crowd waiting to greet him. Speaker Peroni's father laughed at the bewildered engineer. 'I've never seen such a grin! You look like you just found buried treasure.'

'Better – I've found people again. It was getting lonely out there.'

Surrounded by the hodgepodge of ships and the drone of haggling voices, Denn and Kotto strolled among the vendors. Kotto saw unusual musical instruments, colourful woven sculptures, and gaudily embroidered garments that were obviously more for show than for practicality. With a chuckle, Denn said, 'A good indicator of a healthy economy is when people buy completely useless things.'

He introduced Kotto to Yreka's Grand Governor. Her long dark hair was streaked with a few threads of silver and hung down to her waist. Her health and mood were thriving with all the business that had come to Yreka. 'I have heard much about you, Kotto Okiah. You're the Roamer equivalent of Einstein.'

He blushed. 'I wouldn't go that far, considering all the mistakes in my track record. I just tried to visit my operations on Jonah 12 – it's been wiped out. Reactor overload, or something. I couldn't find any survivors, so I hope they managed to evacuate.'

Denn blinked in alarm. 'Jonah 12? That's where Cesca was hiding after the destruction of Rendezvous.'

Kotto had never considered that. 'But why would Speaker Peroni go to a place like that?'

'Hiding from the Eddies. We all were.' Clearly disturbed, Denn ran a hand across his long brown hair, fidgeting as he tried to deal with the news.

Kotto swallowed. 'Do you ... um, have you any word about my mother?'

'I thought she was with Cesca, helping out.' Denn rubbed his temples. 'Shizz, I wish we had decent communications! Nobody knows anything.'

The Grand Governor looked at both of them. 'Considering how your people are dispersed, Yreka is probably the best place to get information. People come here all the time with fresh news.'

As if to prove her point, two more Roamer trading ships arrived. Their captains seemed to be racing each other to display their wares. A stocky woman came forward in a mismatched combination of old work clothes and a beautiful newly bought scarf. Yreka's provisional trade minister handed a datapad to the Grand Governor. 'A summary of all the new arrivals, Sarhi. If you want dibs on any particular item, you better hurry. Everyone else is anxious to buy.'

'Tell them to go ahead. I've got enough to keep me happy for now.'

The people were lighthearted, negotiating prices with good-natured bravado. It seemed like old times. Kotto, however, was distracted by nagging worry. 'Aren't you concerned about the Eddies? They'll stomp on all this the moment they find out about it. They don't like Roamers much.'

'The Eddies can suck on a radioactive exhaust pipe,' Denn said, his voice edgy now. 'We're not afraid of them.'

The Grand Governor was calmer. 'We've put up with enough bullying from the Earth Defence Forces. They embargoed this planet just because we saved a little ekti for ourselves, and then they never answered when we called for help. Now they've written us a "Dear John" letter and pulled all their battleships back to Earth. Too scared of the hydrogues.'

Watching the Roamer cargo ships and the eager customers, Denn said boldly, 'It leaves the Spiral Arm open for us. That's how the clans are supposed to operate.'

The Grand Governor brushed a few strands of long, wind-blown hair away from her face. 'EDF weapons don't work against warglobes anyway. Their protection wouldn't do us any good.'

Kotto grinned, suddenly remembering why he had come here. 'Well, I know something that works.'

Denn rolled his eyes. 'What's going through that head of yours?'

'Oh, it's a simple little thing. I've got the blueprints right in my ship. KR, GU, go bring them back.' The two Analytical compies marched off like wind-up soldiers while Kotto explained how his doorbells could pop open a warglobe's pressurized hatches. GU and KR returned carrying the simple plans between them, though either one could have brought the single sheet.

'You told us to get the drawing together,' KR said.

'It did seem rather inefficient,' GU added.

Kotto showed the plans. 'At Theroc, with minimal expense

and a handful of civilian ships, we killed as many drogues in a few minutes as the Eddies have managed to kill since the beginning of this whole war.'

Denn looked at the simple diagram. 'I can think of at least five or ten Roamer industrial facilities that could crank out your doorbells as fast as we could ship them.'

A hard smile crept across the Grand Governor's lips. 'We'll distribute these things to every orphaned Hansa colony. If the hydrogues try to attack, we'll throw your doorbells at them like confetti.'

Denn laughed. 'Nothing wrong with a little independence, as we Roamers always say.'

Kotto placed his hands on the polymer shoulders of his two helpful compies. 'Do you think I could stay here and help ... maybe manage the project? I've been looking for an important task to occupy my mind.'

EIGHTY-FIVE

ZHETT KELLUM

Lightning lit Golgen's night-time skies with a simmering glow. In the troposphere, bright lights from new skymines blinked and signalled to each other. Exhaust lines marked where cargo escorts lifted up and away, and shuttles ferried visitors from one floating city to another. For the first time in years, Roamers were doing the jobs they were born to do.

Zhett sat in a mesh chair out on the observation deck, her long legs propped on a railing while breezes stole around her dark hair. Though she was listening, she pretended casual nonchalance as the facility operators and clan heads gathered to hear the news Nikko Chan Tylar had brought.

Young Nikko was enthusiastic about his task. He had arrived at Golgen that afternoon in his exotically transformed *Aquarius* and breathlessly asked to speak to representatives from each of the skymines. Zhett's father had used the excuse to host a party on his largest observation balcony.

While the milling attendees served themselves steaming pepperflower tea or home-distilled alcoholic beverages, they

404

listened as Nikko filled them in on what had happened. 'This is our chance, our real chance to defeat the drogues. The wentals are just as powerful as the hydrogues – but they need us to distribute them. Roamers – *humans* – are in this, too.'

'Aw, we just got settled here, Nikko,' said Boris Goff, who looked as if he hadn't slept in the four days since his clan's skymine had arrived. 'Give us a few weeks to catch our breath. By the Guiding Star, do you know how long it's been since Roamers could produce enough ekti to sell?'

Nikko gestured over the railing of the observation deck, indicating the peaceful sea of clouds. 'And the wentals are the only reason you've got a chance here. Jess Tamblyn released them into this gas giant's clouds. *They* cleared the drogues out of Golgen.'

'Get to the point, kid,' said Bing Palmer, who captained a skymine operated jointly by the Palmer and Sandoval clans. 'What do you want us to do? Find more water planets for the wentals to live and grow on?'

Nikko shook his head. 'No, the other water-bearers and myself have done that already. Now it's time to turn them loose. Roamer ships need to fill up with wental water and take them in a great offensive. Everywhere at once. It's the only way we'll ever finish this war.'

'By damn, that sounds like a mighty big operation,' Kellum said. 'And a management nightmare.'

'Since when are you reluctant to tackle a big job, Dad?' Zhett put her hands behind her head while lounging in the chair. 'We're set here. We've got cargo escorts flying out every hour on the hour, delivering ekti faster than we can issue bills to our customers.'

'Now that the hydrogues know the wentals have returned, this war is going to heat up – and fast.' Nikko could not hide the urgency in his voice. 'If we don't defeat the drogues, then your skymines and the Roamer way of life spiral down a bottomless gravity well. The wentals need us, and we need them!'

'Well, the damned *Eddies* aren't going to defeat the drogues,' grumbled a new skymine chief, someone Zhett hadn't met. 'They get their collective asses whipped every time they engage.'

Boris Goff let out a deep, rumbling laugh. 'Ha, wouldn't they be embarrassed if Roamers saved the day?'

'Why should we help the Eddies or the Big Goose, by damn?' Kellum snapped. 'Look what they've done to us.'

Zhett finally stood from her chair. 'I seem to remember one of your lectures, Dad, about taking the high road.'

'That was different, my sweet.' He scratched his beard as he pondered. The lights of far-off skymines continued to blink, lonely sentries above the clouds. Steam jets and exhaust plumes billowed like ghostly breath in the frosty air.

'Believe me, I've got no love for the Eddies,' Nikko said. 'They wrecked my family's greenhouse asteroids. As far as I know, my parents are prisoners of war in some hellhole work camp. But the hydrogues are a bigger problem. All I'm asking is that you commit some ships to haul wental water.'

The young man grinned at Zhett, but she turned her attention to the clan heads. 'Look at you all! Do you really want to miss the biggest battle ever to hit the Spiral Arm?'

'That's supposed to convince me?' Goff said. 'After what we've already been through?'

Bing Palmer snorted. 'Shizz, Boris, I've heard you brag for years about skymining through a moon-sized hurricane on Franconia. It's time you got some new stories, if you want anybody to keep buying you drinks.'

'Just follow your Guiding Star,' Nikko insisted. 'It's time to take back more gas giants, like this one. You all know how many people died on the Blue Sky Mine here. On all the skymines.'

'The bloody drogues killed my Shareen on Welyr.' Kellum's nostrils flared. 'All right, by damn, you've got my vote, Nikko. We've been punched in the gut so many times that I'm sick of just folding over. I'd rather be wringing the Hansa Chairman's neck for what he did at Rendezvous, but I suppose wiping out the drogues will have to do. For now.'

Nikko grinned with relief. 'I'm going to give you the co-ordinates for a planet called Charybdis. It's where Jess Tamblyn first seeded the new wentals. Meet me there and load up with all the wental water you can carry. We've got a schedule so that we, and all the other water bearers and all of *their* volunteers, can keep everything running smoothly.'

The gathering degenerated into excited talk about commitments of vessels and materials, schedules of when to arrive at the ocean planet, suggestions of who else might participate. Nikko paced the deck, and Zhett could tell the young man was sneaking glances at her. Aloof, she turned towards the cloud decks below. Nikko was a handsome young man, though a bit flighty; she'd seen him make deliveries to the Osquivel shipyards, showing up either late or early, rarely on time. Zhett sniffed, not at all interested in flirting. The bad experience with Patrick Fitzpatrick still left a sour taste in her mouth.

At some point, the pilot slipped away to deliver his message to other Roamer settlements. Zhett saw his oddball growth-encrusted ship take off from the lower landing deck and skim across the clouds and realized she should have said goodbye to him.

Tired of all the bluster, excited swagger, and brave talk, Zhett let her thoughts wander to smaller concerns. Confronted with such grand events, she found it odd to worry about personal feelings.

But after leaving the Osquivel shipyards – and, yes, the EDF prisoners – she was lonely. She hated how Fitzpatrick had betrayed her . . . and she hated that she missed him, too.

EIGHTY-SIX

PATRICK FITZPATRICK III

'No exceptions,' his grandmother repeated, more annoyed at her failure than saddened to see him go. 'I'm sorry, Patrick. It's been decades since I served as Chairman, and the favours people owe me don't count for as much.'

Late at night, he moved through the large stainless-steel kitchen, passing from pantry to refrigerator as he made a quick snack. He had not asked Maureen to pull strings for him, but he knew she did whatever she pleased if she thought it was 'for his own good'.

'I'm sure you did your best,' he said, mentally running through his options. 'No one is blaming you.' He couldn't go back to serve in the Earth Defence Forces, not because of the trauma he'd been through, but because of what they stood for and what they'd made him do. He had frequent nightmares about Kamarov's cargo ship, about giving the order to fire, about the explosion. The trader hadn't even known what was coming.

'No, Mr Fitzpatrick. I have no recollection of that whatsoever. And neither do you.'

How could he serve a man like General Lanyan? Instead, Patrick should be out atoning for the pain he had caused, getting at least a token measure of justice, exposing how the Roamers had been wronged. Maybe he could find a lead as to Zhett's whereabouts . . .

The Battleaxe wrinkled her lips in a frown. 'Are you listening to me, Patrick? I can get Wanda to cook you something. It'll be much better than—'

'This is perfectly fine.' The selections in her sprawling kitchen were dizzying: meats and exotic vegetables, elaborate sweets, cheeses from five different worlds. He wasn't used to extravagance anymore, and now he found it unsettling, even offensive.

Back in the EDF, he'd eaten whatever nutritionally approved meal the mess hall served, and after an initial few months of complaining, he'd learned to be satisfied with whatever there was. Roamer food at Osquivel had been unusually spiced, but he'd grown to like it. This was just too much. He got a drink from the water dispenser, disdaining the exotic juices, energy beverages, and liqueurs his grandmother kept on hand.

'The EDF will assign you to an excellent ship,' Maureen continued. 'Maybe even to General Lanyan himself. He always had a soft spot for you, dear. You'll be out of harm's way.'

Patrick gave her a cynical look. 'The General is not a man to sit on the sidelines.'

'Oh. Well, then.' She seemed more disturbed by the fact that she might have miscalculated than by where her grandson would be stationed. 'I promise I'll get you home as soon as the emergency is over.'

He had to laugh at that, but only a bitter sound came out. 'Which part of the "emergency" do you mean? As soon as we've destroyed the hydrogues? As soon as we've recaptured our battleships from the Soldier compies? Or were you including a complete victory over all the Roamer clans as well?'

'Don't take that tone with me, Patrick. I'm trying to help you.'

With his fingers, he pulled out several slices of nutty-smelling cheese and ate them straight off the gleaming counter. 'Trying to be realistic, Grandmother. I've been in battle before.' His throat suddenly thickened with a spasm of panic. Vivid memories of the massacre at Osquivel flooded his mind: warglobes destroying EDF ships faster than anyone could count . . . abandoning the wreck of his Manta, watching from the lifepod's tiny observation port as the rest of the EDF fleet fled, leaving him to drift all alone. 'We're going to be sitting ducks.'

Maureen began to pick up wrappers and packaging, pulling away the food even before Patrick was finished with it. She scowled at the fingerprints and the food smear on the countertop, but she tried to sound reassuring. 'If the hydrogues or Soldier compies intend to destroy Earth, then you might have a better chance of surviving away from here.'

He looked at her and didn't need to say anything. As the awkward silence drew out, Maureen became visibly uncomfortable. She preferred to snap orders to servants and underlings, knowing that her wishes would be followed. She didn't quite know how to deal with her grandson. Finally she backed away. 'I just wanted to let you know I did my best. I'll leave you to your . . . snack. We can discuss this more in the morning.'

Patrick continued to eat the cheese, though he'd lost his appetite. He had already made up his mind.

He remembered the grudgingly satisfying work he had done at Osquivel. Here on 'civilized' Earth, he'd been brought up to believe the space gypsies were rowdy and disreputable. No one in the Hansa had ever bothered to pay attention to what the clans could do; instead, they spread rumours and insults, portraying the Roamers as shiftless con artists who didn't deserve any respect.

Since then, Patrick had seen with his own eyes how Roamer families laboured together and accomplished miracles. And he had enjoyed being with Zhett Kellum. He still regretted how he'd tricked her for a chance to escape. He hoped he could make it up to her somehow, someday.

He'd served the Earth military, worked with General Lanyan, and seen first-hand the capricious and unfair way political decisions were made. Patrick was convinced that the EDF and the Hanseatic League had caused their own problems. But from inside, Maureen simply could not see the flaws.

He went to his ridiculously spacious room, though he wasn't tired – which was a good thing, since he had a long night ahead of him. No turning back.

He changed into a serviceable outfit and packed fresh clothes, untraceable currency and food supplies he'd taken from the kitchen. In the EDF he'd learned how to travel lightly, how to make swift decisions and carry them through. When he was finished, Patrick padded quietly through the mansion and deactivated the intruder alarms and perimeter surveillance. He slipped into the service bay where his restored antique cars sat smelling of polish and engine oil.

On the far side of the bay rested Maureen's sleek space yacht, a ship purchased by an extremely wealthy person in a time of prosperity. Had the old Battleaxe paid for it herself, or had one of her political cronies simply offered it in exchange for a plump contract? He intended to take it out on loan, use it for important work. He could find Roamer outposts, Hansa colonies orphaned by the Chairman's decrees, tell his story to anyone who would listen. He was sure he could find a sympathetic ear somewhere. A person of his lineage and status, someone with a relatively high rank in the EDF, certainly had enough credibility to make even the most sceptical person think twice. It was about time his family name was useful for something *worthwhile*.

His grandmother had always controlled his life. Patrick Fitzpatrick III had been trapped by expectations, forced to do whatever somebody else told him. And he had already given one life to the EDF. 'Now I'm going to do something for the right reasons.'

He silently opened the hangar doors and climbed into the yacht, noting that the cockpit controls were far less complex than a Remora's. This vessel was designed for someone unfamiliar with the nuances of flying, certainly not made for sharp evasive manoeuvres or swift battle scenarios. He could fly it easily.

The fuel tanks were full. He snorted in disgust: With such tremendous shortages, with so many colonies desperate for medical supplies and food, how did one old woman warrant a supply of ekti? Well, he would put it to good use.

Patrick powered the engines, felt the ship vibrate, and heard the reverberations building in the reaction jets. Even with the house alarms shut off, the noise was bound to wake someone up. His grandmother had always been a light sleeper – probably because of her heavy conscience.

He didn't look behind him, didn't leave a farewell note, and he certainly didn't request clearance or file any flight plan. When Patrick activated the propulsion systems, his stolen yacht slipped into the night sky, rising over the rugged Colorado mountains towards the starry emptiness above.

Somewhere out there, he would find the Roamers. He would find Zhett.

EIGHTY-SEVEN

DESIGNATE DARO'H

The fervour of the human mob died swiftly as the long night ended. The growing conflagration had already devoured the old breeding camp, then swept through the main settlement, fanned by capricious winds. Humans and Ildirans alike devoted most of their energies simply to surviving until dawn.

So many people were already dead. Daro'h had felt their agony in the *thism* as either the rioters or the fire killed them. Somehow, the green priest woman had prevented them from murdering Udru'h, but the now-unconscious Designate suffered broken bones, a severe concussion, and internal bleeding. He had been handed over to medical kithmen, who were overwhelmed with patients. Daro'h did not know if the actual injuries, or the mental shock of receiving a lifetime of horrific memories, had caused Udru'h more harm.

Medical kithmen on Dobro tended to be experts in obstetrics; they studied human fertility, monitored pregnancies, made genetic projections. Many of the half-breed births proved difficult, and the doctors had standing orders to give an infant's survival priority over the mother's. Now those doctors were treating battlefield injuries, and the human patients loathed their touch.

The destruction appalled even the former captives. They separated the dead, including many of their own half-breed children who had fought against them. Guards and doctors had been clubbed or stabbed to death; human prisoners had been hacked and trampled. Many black and blistered bodies had already been dragged from the smouldering wreckage. The lucky ones were no longer alive.

Surrounded by a deafening roar in the *thism*, Daro'h felt numb. The whole planet seemed to be a shout of agony and grief. The death toll was worse than Daro'h had expected, and the numbers continued to climb. By the second day, he didn't want to hear any more reports.

Of one thing the Designate was sure: The agony in the *thism* had sent a clarion call to the Mage-Imperator. Daro'h had no doubt that his father was on his way. Jora'h could never ignore such a disaster.

Now, as he walked through the streets smelling the smoke of burned wood and charred flesh, he saw people – both Ildiran and human – moving about in a daze, struggling with the overwhelming but urgent tasks that demanded their attention. They would only have time to complete the first stage of their efforts before the Mage-Imperator arrived.

Wildfire crews struggled to contain the blaze that swept across the dry grasses. They dug trenches, made firebreaks, set back-fires to clear all the fuel. The green priest Nira and her human followers, now organized into teams, threw themselves into the work. They had never shown such enthusiasm for their camp chores.

Just as the guards and medical kithmen did not know how to treat these humans as partners or allies, so too the *Burton* descendants were not sure they wanted Ildiran help. What would happen when they caught their breath and sank to their knees with the realization of what they had done?

A digger and one of the mentalist teachers approached Daro'h. Covered in soot and grime, they looked even more distraught than the others. 'Designate, you must come with us,' the mentalist said. 'We have found . . . we have found something terrible in the residence of former Designate Udru'h.' His expression looked fearful.

Daro'h sighed wearily. 'The Designate's home was not even damaged.'

'Not the residence itself, Designate,' the mentalist said. 'It is Thor'h.'

Alarmed, Daro'h hurried after them. In the turmoil, he had forgotten about his disgraced brother. Udru'h had been in charge of the drugged young man, but during the riot there had been no word of Thor'h. Since then, the former Prime Designate had not been on anyone's list of priorities.

The pair led him hesitantly down to the chambers beneath the residence. They had found the hidden room, pried it open, and brought lights inside. 'We do not know how long it was dark in there, Designate,' the mentalist said. The square-shouldered digger stood silently unsettled.

Daro'h stepped into the room, alone. Thor'h lay sprawled on the floor, twisted and frozen in a death-spasm. His face held a repulsive look of abject fear. His skin was an astonishing white, his eyes wide open and empty. He looked as if he'd been dipped in bleach and then petrified. The unrelenting darkness and isolation had literally killed him, sucked him until he was empty.

Even knowing what Thor'h had done, he could not bear to behold his oldest brother's fate. 'He was cut off from the *thism*. None of us would have sensed him, all alone and in the dark.'

'Perhaps that was what he deserved, Designate,' said the mentalist. The digger grunted.

Daro'h's mind rejected the suggestion, but then he recalled all the deaths Thor'h and the mad Designate had caused. Thor'h had come here with a stolen warliner, threatening to destroy Dobro if Designate Udru'h did not join them. And Udru'h had tricked Rusa'h, which led to his downfall.

Yes, he thought, *perhaps Thor'h deserves even this*.

'Bring his body out into the light and place it with the others,' Daro'h said. 'We will build a great funeral pyre.' He stepped out of the hidden chamber. 'The Mage-Imperator is coming. Let us hope he forgives us all.'

EIGHTY-EIGHT

KING PETER

Forbidden to leave the royal wing, the King and Queen stood on the balcony behind a protective transparent screen. Chairman Wenceslas let them look out as often as they wished. It was a gesture more of cruelty than kindness.

Two days had passed since OX discovered the abortive drug in Estarra's food. By now, Basil would realize that they had thwarted him somehow. He would have been waiting for an urgent medical call from their quarters, and Peter was glad not to give him that satisfaction. *Let him stew*.

He kept up to date by studying the Chairman's daily briefing, which was surreptitiously given to him by Captain McCammon. The guard captain was convinced that foolish secrecy had cost many lives during the Soldier compy revolt – silver berets, EDF crewmen, even civilians.

After the compy uprising, the Hansa waited for the other shoe to drop, wondering when the stolen ships would attack Earth. Or had the Soldier compies flown away, never to return? Were they truly in league with the Klikiss robots?

In a cordoned-off sector of the plaza, the hydrogue derelict was surrounded by tents, equipment sheds, computer analysis stations, and temporary offices. Even without Dr Swendsen, the activity continued day and night. Peter often stood with Estarra after dark, looking at the spotlight banks that illuminated the scene as researchers continued their investigations.

The derelict team had recently discovered how to reactivate the power core. The alien systems had sprung to life again, and the engineers postulated that they could open the transportal gateway; however, since they had not yet transformed the symbol coordinates, no one wanted to risk opening a door to a high-pressure gas giant.

Estarra pointed to the scientists, who were quickly withdrawing to a safe distance. 'It looks like they're going to try another test.'

The researchers stood behind barricades, waiting for something. Then, silently and smoothly, the derelict rose off the ground like a soap bubble drifting on the air. Estarra's expression filled with joy and hope.

'It's a huge step in the right direction,' Peter said. 'But turning on an engine and understanding one are drastically different things.'

'What is it?' snapped a voice behind them. 'I want to see.'

Peter and Estarra both spun. The excitement of the experiment and the muffled noise outside had covered the arrival of visitors. OX stood beside a gaudily garbed young man. 'Please excuse the intrusion, King Peter.'

Prince Daniel had lost a great deal of weight, and his once-chubby cheeks looked loose and pasty. The Chairman would probably force Daniel to wear makeup whenever he went out in public. The Prince pushed his way out onto the balcony and watched the small derelict move about on its brief test flight. 'It's about time they got something done down there. When I'm King, I won't allow scientists to take so long.'

Trying to guess why the compy had brought the Prince here, Peter said, 'This certainly is an unexpected . . . honour, OX. Do we have the Chairman to thank?'

In an innocent voice, OX offered, 'The Chairman gave me explicit instructions to train Prince Daniel in all matters related to the duties of a Great King. I determined that direct interaction with the existing King would be a relevant part of that instruction. No further permission was required.'

Peter felt like applauding the compy's calculated obliviousness. OX knew precisely what he was doing. He must have wanted to show the King and Queen how Daniel had changed since his reawakening.

The Prince sounded bored. 'I didn't want to come here. According to the Chairman, you aren't exactly the best King.'

'Nevertheless, I *am* the King.'

'Not for long. The Chairman says you won't ever learn from your mistakes. That's why OX is teaching me what I need to know – so I can replace you.' Daniel flashed his small teeth, but he had not mastered the art of a sincere smile. 'And I'll do a better job. I know my place now – and it's on the throne. And I'll follow the Hansa's instructions.'

Peter never took his eyes from the Prince. *He's even worse than before.* He turned to the compy. 'Thank you, OX. This was most instructive.'

A scuffle arose outside the door to the royal chambers, and Mr Pellidor pushed past Captain McCammon, his face flushed and stormy. When he saw OX and Daniel, the blond expeditor took the Prince's arm in a vice-like grip.

Daniel squealed, 'Leave me alone! You can't touch me – I'm the Prince.'

'You do not want to test that theory, Daniel,' Pellidor said in a threatening voice. The Prince immediately fell silent. 'That's better.' He flashed an accusing glance at Peter and Estarra. 'What is he doing here?'

The King spread his hands. 'Learning from his tutor, apparently.'

OX repeated his explanation, but Pellidor did not seem convinced. 'Prince Daniel must go back to his quarters. He has a lot of preparation work to do.' He pushed the young man towards the door, where two assistants took Daniel by the arms and hustled him out. OX followed.

Still close to the King and Queen, the expeditor kept his voice low, clearly enjoying himself. 'How's the baby?' He ran his eyes up and down Estarra's rounded abdomen.

Peter remained cool, pretending ignorance. Pellidor would never admit that the Queen's food had been tampered with. 'Extremely healthy.'

Dropping pretence, Pellidor lowered his voice. 'You are not long for your role, King Peter. Don't expect any more daily briefings from Captain McCammon. We've put a stop to those. The Chairman has already announced a banquet during which he'll reintroduce our beloved Prince Daniel to the public. Shortly afterwards, you and the Queen can expect to . . . retire.'

Peter glared at him. 'So why warn us? Why tip your hand?'

'Because there's absolutely nothing you can do about it.' Smiling, Pellidor departed, leaving a chill in the air.

Peter had no doubt that the Chairman would arrange to kill him and Estarra as soon as he found the opportunity. Dissatisfied that his hand-picked King was no pliable buffoon like Old King Frederick, Basil had been threatening Peter for years. As humanity's crisis grew worse, Peter had hoped for a resolution, a grudging acceptance that the King and Chairman needed each other, needed to work together.

But Basil would hear none of it. His antipathy towards anyone who would challenge his demands had made the Chairman pathologically unable to accept anything Peter said or did. The recent, and demonstrably *correct*, actions Peter had taken during the Soldier compy revolt proved as much. Basil Wenceslas was like a rabid dog who needed to be put down, before he – or his patsy Daniel – could do more damage.

Alone again after Pellidor and the Prince had left, though convinced they remained under observation, Peter and Estarra sat in silence. Using their silent hand signals and a few whispers, Peter communicated, 'Daniel has no backbone, no conscience. What kind of King would he be?'

'Exactly the kind Chairman Wenceslas wants.'

Daniel would agree to every suggestion, every order, to protect himself. 'We need to do more than just escape, Estarra. Basil has already got away with outrageous things. If left unchecked, who knows ... The human race itself might break apart, destroyed by enemies from both the outside and within. I can't allow that to happen.'

She kissed him, then spoke aloud, not caring if anyone overheard, 'Then you are a true King after all.'

EIGHTY-NINE

DAVLIN LOTZE

'What an odd lot we are,' Davlin Lotze muttered to himself.

Though many groups had been thrown together on the Klikiss world of Llaro, the colony functioned remarkably well. The Crenna refugees were happy to have any new home after the death of their sun. Two survivors from a massacred colony, a young girl and an old man, had no place else to go. The Roamers, prisoners of war in everything but name, longed to return to their clans, and the soldiers in the EDF garrison wanted to go back to Earth. Recently, in the wake of the Soldier compy uprising, the EDF had withdrawn most of Llaro's military contingent, leaving the remaining babysitter-soldiers more isolated than ever.

Meanwhile, Davlin did his best to stay unnoticed, or at least unremarked-upon. There was a chance, albeit a slim one, that he could actually live out his life in peace without having to return to Hansa service.

'What did you say your name was again?' Roberto Clarin

wiped his forehead with the back of his hand, then bent back to his shovelling. The pot-bellied Roamer wasn't put off by hard work; none of the Roamers were, as far as Davlin could tell.

'Alexander Nemo.' It was the alias he had chosen.

Clarin cocked his eyebrows. 'Nemo? Like in that Jules Verne novel?'

'The word is Latin for "no one". Apparently one of my ancestors had low self-esteem and took a new name when he moved away from Earth.'

'Maybe he had something to hide.' Clarin chuckled. 'The same could be said of a lot of our clans. Sooner or later, though, it catches up with you.'

The two men excavated an irrigation ditch that would connect fast-flowing springs from the alien cliff cities to the fertilized flatlands where crops flourished under the lavender skies. Overhead, a pair of EDF Remoras practised aerial manoeuvres, circling on what they called 'patrols'.

'The way they waste fuel, we're not going to have a drop left if we ever need it for anything,' Clarin grumbled. 'Damned Eddies. I hate 'em all.'

Davlin wasn't so sure military proficiency manoeuvres were a waste of fuel. Even before the compy revolt, Davlin had known something sinister was afoot in the Spiral Arm. He believed Orli Covitz's story about the robot battleships that had destroyed Corribus. Now that the Hansa had withdrawn most of Llaro's EDF troops, the remaining soldiers were from the bottom of the barrel; Davlin hoped they would be capable of mounting a competent defence if circumstances demanded it. Otherwise, he would have to do it himself.

Through subtle intel, Davlin learned how many commandos had died in the massacre at the compy factory on Earth. Fellow silver berets. He himself had been one of them before becoming a 'specialist in obscure details'. Now, with his additional experience and training, Davlin could pull off things that even the best silver berets couldn't manage.

Clarin shaded his eyes and looked up in the sky as the Remoras circled back towards the garrison barracks by the transportal. 'I don't know which is more dangerous – having them bored and flying around with a bunch of armed weapons, or down here helping us out. They'd probably muck up even a standard civil-engineering project, our crops would fail, and we'd all starve during the first winter season.'

'It's not as bad as that,' Davlin said. 'A lot of us are experts at survival.'

Field workers tended the genetically engineered crops, harvesting fast-growing grains and vegetables while planting others for a constant turnover. These Roamers were used to intensive farming techniques, where every drop of water and fertilizer had to be reused. Compared with austere deep-space conditions, this planet was truly a child's playground.

Davlin was no slouch at either survival or at helping people survive. He had helped save the colonists from Crenna, and he had also rescued Rlinda Kett and Captain Roberts from a sham court martial. While the two escaped in Kett's ship, Davlin had modified Roberts's *Blind Faith* to be flown remotely. By mapping provocative transmissions onto a hologram of Roberts, he had convinced witnesses that Roberts perished with the *Blind Faith* during an attack by EDF Remoras. So far, everything seemed to have gone smoothly.

He doubted anyone in the EDF knew of his involvement in the escape, especially Chairman Wenceslas, but he still preferred to keep a low profile. For years he had followed the Chairman's instructions and done everything to accomplish the Hansa's aims. But the Chairman made too many poor decisions, and Davlin had given enough of his life to the Terran Hanseatic League.

Human civilization seemed to be spiralling into a bottomless pit. Neither an optimist nor a pessimist, Davlin was at least pragmatic, and he could see deep trouble for the Hansa. How long, he wondered, would a galactic-scale dark age last? If time was short and the future bleak, then he wanted to spend the rest of his days with these people, among whom he felt at home.

'You're thinking pretty hard there, Alexander.' Clarin interrupted his thoughts. 'I hope you've figured how to install a new filtration system and water recirculators so we can irrigate without losing significant flow.'

Davlin tapped his head. 'It's all right in here. I've double-checked with the storehouse, and we do have the components we need. We can get it done by tomorrow – if we finish digging this trench today.'

'You're pretty handy to have around.'

'For a Roamer to acknowledge my ingenuity, that's a compliment indeed.'

From the distant EDF barracks station near the Klikiss ruins, loud alarms began to ring. Soldiers in rumpled uniforms scrambled to their stations. A third Remora took off into the sky. The first two patrol ships on practice manoeuvres circled around, obviously on high alert.

'Don't they ever get tired of those stupid drills?' Clarin growled.

Davlin scanned the skies, concerned. 'I don't think this is a drill.'

'What do you mean? How can it not be?'

Davlin watched as the third Remora joined the first two, and the trio streaked off to the south. Tracking them, he saw four intense spots like falling suns dropping through the sky. Ellipsoidal fireballs curled silently ahead, leaving a streak of singed sky behind them. They were huge.

'By the Guiding Star, what are those things?'

The fireballs streaked downwards, and their immense size became more and more apparent. Davlin had to shield his eyes. 'Those are faeros.'

'Terrific. What do they want?'

Davlin glanced at him. 'They didn't send me a memo.'

One of the Remoras, flown by a cocky pilot, approached the nearest ellipsoid and launched a volley of jazer fire. Davlin uttered a curse. What did the idiot think he was doing?

Like a rippling solar flare, an arc of fire curled from the faeros ship and incinerated the Remora. The other two scout pilots, more intelligent (or at least less brave) than the first, spun about and raced out of the fireballs' range.

The faeros paid no further attention to the Remoras. The blazing ellipsoids cruised across Llaro's sky as if on a reconnaissance flight. Davlin thought he could feel a wave of heat as the fireballs rumbled above him. The faeros continued over the colony, then – apparently finished with whatever they had come for – accelerated in blinding fingers of fire towards the horizon.

'But what did they want?' Clarin asked. 'They didn't attack.'

Davlin shook his head. He had witnessed the awesome conflagration of their battle inside Crenna's sun, and he knew what the faeros were capable of – whether they intended to do damage or not.

'I'd hoped the hydrogues and the faeros would keep each other busy.' He dreaded what could possibly go wrong now.

NINETY

ANTON COLICOS

For four days the spiked diamond spheres hung motionless in Hyrillka's sky like armed bombs that could go off at any time. They made no move, sent no emissary, did not attempt to communicate. Anton felt as if he had been holding his breath for ever.

Watching them, he thought about his calm and uninteresting job as a post-grad student of Ildiran studies on Earth. His archaeologist parents had taught him that the best knowledge and experience was acquired in the field, but he was having second thoughts. Considering the powerful warglobes, Anton might have been safer underground, sorting through obscure documents in the vault.

'I hope that isn't something else I'm not supposed to see,' he said. 'It's a little late to keep me under house arrest again.'

'It is too late for many things,' Yazra'h said. 'You are part of this story now, Rememberer Anton.'

'What could they possibly want?' Ridek'h asked.

'To intimidate the people,' Yazra'h answered.

'But for what?'

She could only shake her head.

Anton said, 'If the Mage-Imperator worked out some sort of bargain with the hydrogues, then why are those things hovering overhead like a couple of bar-room bouncers? What's changed?'

Yazra'h turned cool again. 'I do not know.'

Tal O'nh kept his Solar Navy warliners on high alert. The reconstruction efforts came to a standstill as people waited to see what would happen. They seemed reluctant to rebuild more if the hydrogues might smash it all again in another day or two.

'Look! The streamers!' Ridek'h pointed to where a group of seven sleek Solar Navy ships cruised around the hovering warglobes.

Anton couldn't believe what he was seeing. 'Those pilots must either be completely insane or extremely brave. Are they trying to provoke an attack?'

'Tal O'nh sent those ships to transmit to the warglobes,' Yazra'h said. 'He hopes to establish communication. Their message is simple: we do not want hostilities, but our warliners are ready to defend Hyrillka, if necessary.'

'Isn't that . . . um, unnecessarily provocative?' Anton continued to watch the strange ballet overhead. So far, the warglobes didn't even seem to notice the gnat-sized streamers.

Yazra'h shrugged. 'It is the truth.'

'One warliner has already been sent back to Ildira at top speed with a report, but we have had no response from the Mage-Imperator.' The boy seemed to have confidence in Jora'h. 'He is apparently occupied with other urgent matters.'

Suddenly the three hydrogues began to move, spinning, separating from each other. The Solar Navy streamers scattered and withdrew.

'What is happening, Yazra'h?' Ridek'h said. 'Are they attacking us?'

The voice of Tal O'nh burst from the comm transmitter in the chamber. 'Emergency! All warliners, be prepared. Designate Ridek'h, something is—'

Without waiting to hear the rest, Yazra'h grabbed the boy and pulled him from the open balcony and into the inadequate shelter of the citadel palace. Anton scrambled after them, keeping his eyes turned upward.

A group of fiery projectiles streaked across the sky – ten, fifteen, even more. The incandescent ellipsoids shot in from all sides, leaving trails of smoke and rippled air behind them. Seconds later, delayed by distance, sonic booms provided a fanfare of invisible explosions.

Anton suddenly remembered the new tale fragment Rememberer Vao'sh had shared several nights earlier. *A Great Light came forth to fight the enemy.*

'Look, the hydrogues cannot get away!' the boy shouted. 'The faeros are coming!'

Like a fireworks display in reverse, fireballs intersected at the same spot in the sky and slammed into the warglobes. Most of the flaming torpedoes exploded on impact, shattering the diamond spheres. There were far more fireballs than necessary.

The fiery barrage was over in a few seconds, but rumbling aftershocks continued to throb in the air for long moments.

The smashed hydrogue vessels continued to break apart as they tumbled from their great height, and giant chunks of diamond debris fell to the streets below, crushing buildings. Pieces of broken warglobe hulls ploughed long furrows through the burned nialia fields. Screaming crowds ran in all directions.

A few surviving faeros ships flitted back and forth above the scene like smug fireflies. Then they streaked away, rising high and dwindling into hot starry points before vanishing entirely.

Astonished, Ridek'h turned to Yazra'h. 'Are ... are the faeros our protectors now? They saved us!'

Yazra'h stared at dissipating smoke that looked like a spreading pool of blood. 'Or perhaps they have just caused us a great deal of trouble.'

NINETY-ONE

NIRA

Nira had no doubt the Mage-Imperator would rush to Dobro after the uprising ... and she would be waiting for him. She wanted desperately to see him, to look into his star-sapphire eyes and decide for herself what his true motivations were.

The sooty daylight was filled with an unbearable anticipation. She stared at her rough green hands. These fingers had spent years digging in arroyos to pry loose opalbone fossils. Her body had been abused in countless ways. Deprived of contact with the worldtrees, her soul had cried out in anguish. She had been torn from her love, and later even her children had been stolen from her. In the end, Udru'h had imprisoned her on an island. In escaping from that island, Nira had made herself stronger. Alone, she had endured, and endured, and *endured*, barely looking ahead, simply walking and living.

Jora'h would be here soon.

Osira'h seemed disoriented after the revolt, as if the girl didn't quite understand how everything had happened, and what her own part in it had been. Sometimes, when she didn't know her mother was observing her, Osira'h genuinely looked like a child. But that aura of innocence never lasted long.

As if sensing her mother's scrutiny now, the girl offered her a strange smile. 'Maybe we have changed things for the better. The Mage-Imperator is coming.'

'Yes, he is.' Nira's voice was harsh from all the inhaled smoke and the shouting. She was ready . . . and terrified.

As the Solar Navy cutter descended through the sky and the young Designate emerged from the gutted buildings where he'd been clearing debris, the humans looked fearful again.

In a daze, Nira hurried around the former boundaries of the camp to the landing zone. Her throat was dry, her heart pounding. She stared intensely at the shuttle, remembering Jora'h's eyes, his feathery living hair, his warm kisses, his gentle caresses. She remembered the first time they had touched. And she remembered being attacked in the night, dragged away from the Prism Palace while Ildiran guards murdered old Ambassador Otema.

The ornate vessel approached in a tight circle, facing the still-smouldering main settlement as it came to rest. First to emerge from the cutter was a contingent of soldier kithmen prepared for a fight. They gazed at the dirt-streaked, haunted people who came forward like children who knew they must face a harsh punishment.

Then Jora'h stepped out wearing decorative robes sewn with ribbons that reflected the sunlight. His star sapphire-eyes found Nira, and he stared at her, drinking in the sight.

At first her legs trembled, and her feet felt as if they had taken root. Then something broke inside her, and all hesitation was gone. Before she knew it, she was sprinting with all her strength towards him.

The Ildiran guards drew their weapons to intercept her, but

the Mage-Imperator raised his voice. 'If anyone touches her, I will execute him myself!' The guards stopped in their tracks as if felled with a stun gun.

Nira kept moving towards Jora'h, but more slowly now, suddenly uncertain. When she stood before him at last, she was nervous about his touch – anyone's touch. After her experiences it was impossible not to feel threatened. But she resisted the urge to pull away. They embraced with the sweetness of painful anticipation

'You are alive,' he said tenderly, disbelieving. 'Alive.' She pressed her face into the ornate fabrics covering his chest and felt his heartbeat, listened to the warmth of his voice. 'Udru'h told me – more than once – that you had been killed. Then he said you were alive. I did not know if I could believe him, but it is true.'

'Yes, it's true.' She looked up at his face. 'It's one of the few things I know is true.' So much had come between them, so many storms and nightmares, such vast emptiness. 'How much can I really trust, Jora'h? What can I believe anymore?'

The people of Dobro – Ildiran and human alike – waited for the Mage-Imperator to speak, fearing his reaction. Jora'h looked ready to collapse under the weight of impossible burdens, and Nira's heart longed to comfort him in spite of her doubts.

He seemed to struggle for a long moment, searching for words before giving them voice. 'I will show you what to believe. There will be no secrets between us . . . but it may take some time.'

NINETY-TWO

MAGE-IMPERATOR JORA'H

J ora'h looked past Nira to see the scars where everything had burned to the ground. With a heavy conscience, he tried to imagine all the lives that had been consumed here in unwilling service to an unexplained distant goal.

Still holding her, he knew that Nira's life was one of them. She had aged, her body worn by a harsh life and the torments she had endured. Jora'h's heart ached from seeing the changes, knowing that he was partly to blame.

She looked at him with anticipation in her eyes. Her face, so lined with bad memories and experiences, brightened as if the dead sun of Durris-B had reignited to shine upon her features. But she was guarded. And no wonder, after all those years of suffering. What must she think of him?

Ever since ascending the throne, Jora'h had been torn by the schemes his father had set in motion, the plans he was forced to follow. Even as Mage-Imperator, he had not been able to escape those entanglements. He looked into the clear, empty sky, glad at least that the hydrogues had sent no watchdog warglobes to

Dobro as they had to Hyrillka, Dzelluria, and at least eleven other splinter colonies as threats to ensure Ildiran cooperation.

How many Designates lived in fear because hydrogues loomed over their planets, while most of the Solar Navy gathered at Ildira to follow hydrogue orders? Adar Zan'nh had already departed for Earth with his supposedly benevolent offer. The deep-core aliens would be watching his every move.

But the fury of this riot had cut through the other distractions like a sharp crystal knife. From the *thism*, he knew that something terrible had occurred on Dobro. He mentally corrected his thought. *Something terrible has been occurring on Dobro for a long time.* He had raced here as swiftly as possible.

Now, Designate Daro'h walked towards him, eyes cast down, as if he had failed. A contrite Osira'h accompanied him, both of them soot-stained, her small hand in her brother's. Daro'h stopped in front of his father and completed the ritual salute. 'We have established a truce, Liege. Both groups agree to put aside their anger and work side by side.'

The Mage-Imperator squared his shoulders. 'Explain what happened here.'

'Do explanations change anything?' Osira'h asked, her voice sharp. 'Do you care?' When the girl raised her small chin, Jora'h felt a shudder go down his back. He feared what she might say. In her face he saw reflection of Nira, but with a harder edge. She came closer to take her mother's hand. Jora'h looked at Nira, who was trembling.

Osira'h said, 'I have always wanted to believe that you were a good man, Father. I wanted to be convinced that my mother's love for you was not wasted. Do you know how many years she waited for you to rescue her? I know Designate Udru'h deceived us, but I am not sure about my own father.'

Again, Jora'h's heart ached. 'I have tried to be a good man.'

Now the girl flashed with the fire of anger. 'You lie, just like my uncle!'

'Osira'h!' her mother cried.

The girl ignored her. 'You have already made a bargain to doom the human race — and you used me to do it! You agreed to help the hydrogues kill my mother's people! And you say you're a "good man"?' Osira'h's raw emotion struck him like a hammer in the face. 'You are not honourable at all.'

Jora'h lowered his gaze. 'Imagine an unreasonable beast looming over you, over your entire city — promising immediate eradication if you do not comply. The emissary came to me with his whole armada of warglobes in the sky.' The star-sapphire reflections flashed in his eyes. 'The hydrogues would have slaughtered all my people — people I am responsible for! I am the Mage-Imperator. I hold all of them together through my *thism*. I had no choice.'

'There is always a choice,' Osira'h cut in. 'And you chose damnation over failure.'

He turned to his beloved green priest, using all of his effort simply to remain upright. 'Nira, you must believe me. There is more. Osira'h is a bridge to the hydrogues. They can see and hear through her.'

The girl frowned. 'Only if I let them. When I choose to, I can shut them out and re-establish the connection at any time — on my terms.'

'You cannot be sure of that.'

'Yes. I can.' Suddenly through the *thism* he felt a current of chaotic thought flow towards him in a wave of burning cold and alien fury. Augmented by Osira'h? Rushing towards him, growing louder and louder and — just as suddenly it was gone. 'The hydrogues don't hear me unless I want them to.'

Jora'h believed her.

437

Nira stood closer to her daughter, and slightly away from him. 'The question is, what will you do now?'

'I agreed to their demands in order to buy time. I could not let Osira'h see what I was really doing because I could not let the hydrogues know. That is why I sent her away. Immediately after she left Ildira, I called together my experts and commanded them to find me a solution, a way for us to fight the enemy.'

Osira'h sounded sceptical. 'And did they succeed?'

Jora'h frowned. 'Not completely ... not yet. But I did not want the hydrogues to sense my intentions. I had to make you believe, Osira'h.'

The girl scowled, but said grudgingly, 'It was a wise precaution, but unnecessary.'

More Ildiran workers and freed human captives came from the camp ruins, as if they expected the Mage-Imperator to pronounce judgement. Then an uneasy ripple went through them like a cloud passing over the sun. Jora'h turned to see the former Dobro Designate moving painfully towards him. Medical kithmen had bandaged him, and his face was mottled from severe bruisings and half-healed wounds. Udru'h looked as if he had been buried in an avalanche and clawed his way out. His eyes had a haunted look, especially when he looked at Nira; he would not even meet Osira'h's gaze.

Two guards escorted him, but he did not lean on them, coming forward in a slow, laborious gait. The former Designate did not want help, did not want to show his weakness. Nor did he want to avoid facing the Mage-Imperator. He struggled to make the formal salute. 'Liege, I accept whatever consequences you choose to impose upon me.' He looked around as if he still could not believe that the camp he had so tended was now burned wreckage. 'The seeds of this turmoil were planted long before Daro'h became Designate. It is not his fault.'

Nira stiffened like a statue, and Jora'h could feel her cold anger toward Udru'h, as if she found his very presence repulsive. Osira'h, oddly, just smiled at him. The Mage-Imperator knew what his brother had done to Nira as part of the breeding experiments. He could not fault her reaction.

And yet ... hadn't the Dobro Designate been trapped by the schemes of his predecessors – just as Jora'h had been? When he'd first learned of the old Mage-Imperator's plans and how Udru'h willingly went along with them, Jora'h had despised both men. He had wanted to halt the experiments immediately, but when he became Mage-Imperator himself, that proved impossible. Udru'h would have found it impossible as well.

'The crimes on Dobro were set in motion centuries ago,' Jora'h said, loudly enough for all to hear. 'I could not stop them. My father could not stop them. Designate Udru'h could not stop them. Now they are finally over, and I am left to deal with the consequences of all those generations of planning. The hydrogues gave me an impossible choice, and I must still find an answer. Nira, Osira'h, please, return with me to Mijistra and we will try to work this out.'

'All of my children must come,' Nira said, indicating the other four wide-eyed half-breeds. Jora'h nodded.

Udru'h's voice was a croak. 'I would go, too, Liege, to assist you.'

'No. You will stay here. Humans and Ildirans will rebuild Dobro in whatever way they see fit. You are part of this process. I cannot punish you. But they can.' The former Designate stiffened, but did not argue. Jora'h raised his voice to the human settlers and made his pronouncement. 'For generations, you have been told what to do. Now you will decide for yourselves.'

The human listeners looked more unsettled than the former Designate. Udru'h did not stand defiantly, nor did he make excuses. He accepted his fate without fear. 'I will not beg for mercy, Liege.' He looked coolly at Nira, and his face fell when he turned to Osira'h. 'I know what these people think of me, and I know exactly what I did to you. But I am not repentant, for I did only what our Mage-Imperators deemed necessary for our survival.'

Daro'h said to the people, 'I suggest we allow the former Designate to recover from his injuries while we finish putting out the fires and clearing the wreckage. It will give us time to make a reasoned consideration of whether there has been enough vengeance and bloodshed.'

Jora'h said in a low voice, speaking only to Osira'h and Nira. A sparkle of tears mixed with the reflections in his eyes. 'It is time for me to offer you a promise instead of a lie. I will not give up, and I will not sacrifice your race in order to save mine. It is not acceptable.' He drew a breath, as if fighting with himself about what he had to say. He knew what would happen if he defied the hydrogues. He also realized that worse things could happen if he did not.

'Help me find a way out of this trap I have built for myself.'

NINETY-THREE

KING PETER

'I cannot help you harm another human being,' OX insisted. A mist of oxygenated water drifted around them from the white-noise fountain. 'I am precluded from such actions.'

'But it's self-defence. He has already tried to kill us, more than once,' Estarra said. Since the incident with the miscarriage-inducing drug, they had eaten nothing but packaged food smuggled in to their private chambers. 'And he's going to try again.'

They had not been allowed out of their quarters for days. The edgy populace assumed their royal leaders were busy working to save humanity.

Peter tried a different approach. 'OX, consider how many people are going to die because the Chairman has abandoned all of the Hansa colonies. He is not acting in the best interests of the Terran Hanseatic League or the human race. Isn't that your priority?'

'I have several priorities, which now appear to be in conflict. The Soldier compies slaughtered so many people that I dare not question my programming.' OX was not being stubborn, just firm in his orders. 'Also, especially now, any compy bringing a deadly item into the presence of the King would certainly be stopped and destroyed.' Peter quietly cursed, knowing OX was right.

The Teacher compy offered a story, 'Over the years I have had to delete many memories due to space limitations, but I retained this one, because it is instructive. It is my purpose to teach.

'At one point during the *Peary*'s long journey, several crewmen planned a mutiny against the captain. Fifty-eight years had passed, and the ship had not yet sighted a habitable star system. The mutineers tried to convince me to access the weapons lockers, but I would not. Though they promised to harm no one, events grew out of their control. The mutineers killed seven men and women before they were stopped. I am sure they did not intend for such violence to occur.

'I have already expressed my loyalty to you, King Peter. You have demonstrated that you have the best interests of all humans at heart, regardless of their politics. But I cannot perform any action that would harm a human.' He paused. 'I could, however, carry messages to others, if you desire. Chairman Wenceslas does not watch me closely.'

Estarra eased herself onto the lip of the fountain with a heavy sigh. She didn't seem to mind that cool water splashed her back. 'You're our only ally in the Whisper Palace, OX, and we're counting on you.'

Peter's brow furrowed. 'You have already been a go-between with Deputy Cain.'

'There's also my sister Sarein, though I'm not sure she'd believe me,' Estarra said.

'If we can trust her,' Peter said. 'If we can trust Deputy Cain, or Captain McCammon. I've done a lot of soul searching, but there aren't many people we can rely on.'

Estarra's expression hardened. 'What other choice do we have?'

When she suddenly stiffened, Peter turned to see Basil Wenceslas striding through the door. Tart sarcasm clogged Peter's throat like phlegm. *Is this a social call, Basil? Come to share tea and cookies with us?*

'Don't expect any more strategic briefings from Captain McCammon,' Basil said baldly. 'That error has been corrected.'

'I'm sure the captain of the royal guard could not understand why important information was being kept from the King,' Peter said.

'Exactly what Deputy Cain said,' Basil replied. 'He made the point that there's no reason to keep information from you, since you are incapable of doing anything with it.'

'And you don't believe him? You think I'll read a daily briefing and somehow figure out how to overthrow your government?'

Instead of answering further, Basil glared at OX. 'Why are you here? You should be with Daniel, not wasting time with these two. They no longer need your services.'

'Yes, Mr Chairman.' The Teacher compy dutifully departed.

Basil's expression of frustration and displeasure now carried an undercurrent of anger as well. Without answering, Peter took Estarra's hand and helped her stand up from the fountain's edge. The King knew that silence was the best way to encourage conversation; Basil had taught him that.

Scowling, Basil said, 'Today, I have no choice but to let you out in public. Briefly.' As if he were being forced to do something he could barely stomach, he explained, 'The Adar of the Ildiran Solar Navy just arrived on Earth, unannounced. For some inexplicable reason, he's requested to see the King and Queen. I offered to meet with him, but the Adar has explicit orders to speak directly to you two. He is very inflexible.'

Peter smoothed an imagined wrinkle on his shirt and tugged

his cuffs straight. He knew what a momentous event this was. Ildirans rarely came to the Hansa. 'Then we're ready to meet him. We shouldn't keep the commander of the Solar Navy waiting.'

Despite Peter's quick cooperation, the Chairman couldn't resist a petulant jab. 'I have already informed him that he is likely to be dealing with a new King from now on. Perhaps I will introduce him to Prince Daniel. As a professional military leader, the Adar has no choice but to accept our chain of command.'

Peter looked the Chairman squarely in the eyes. 'You taunt and provoke us, letting us know your plans. That's a hazardous strategy, Basil, according to what you taught me.'

The Chairman rolled a condescending look down his nose. 'You apparently missed many of my lessons. You've already done irreparable damage. Now you will face the consequences.'

The Ildiran warliner landed in front of the Whisper Palace in a flurry of stabilizing jets, unfurled reflective sails, and flamboyant panels and fins. The gigantic battleship inspired awe – exactly as the Ildirans intended, Peter was sure.

Despite Basil's scolding, OX accompanied them as an adviser and recorder. 'This is very similar to what happened one hundred and eighty-six years ago, when Ildirans first made contact with Earth. I was aboard that warliner, chosen as an independent spokesman from the *Peary*.'

The uniformed Adar stepped out into the sunlight. The encounter was transmitted to screens and pickups across the royal plaza and throughout communications networks. Zan'nh offered a formal bow, came forward to meet the King and Queen, then got immediately to business. 'I bring greetings from the Ildiran Empire – and a warning. Our Mage-Imperator recently learned of a planned hydrogue strike against Earth.'

In the background, Peter could hear gasps and groans of

dismay. Conscious of the observers, the King wondered if they should meet in private, but to an Ildiran, the leader was the leader, and everyone else was beneath him. Speaking to King Peter, the Adar assumed he was addressing the Hansa's only important representative; everyone else in earshot was superfluous. Peter also realized that if he moved this meeting into the Whisper Palace, Basil would take control of it.

Peter stared into the military commander's reflective eyes. 'And how does the Mage-Imperator know what the hydrogues intend to do?'

Zan'nh looked evasive, as if he hadn't expected such a question. 'He does not explain himself to me. I simply follow my father's orders.' Then he returned to what sounded like a well-rehearsed speech. 'I bring you a message of hope as well. Because humans have long been our friends and allies, the Solar Navy offers to station a full cohort of warliners – three hundred and forty-three armed battleships – here in your home solar system. We will stand with you when the hydrogues come.'

Although the Adar looked entirely sincere, Peter could hardly believe what he was hearing. In the tiny microphone implanted in the King's ear, Chairman Wenceslas snapped, 'Agree to it! Agree!' But he didn't need Basil to tell him what to do.

Peter could not help but wonder, however, why the Adar looked so uncomfortable. Was the Ildiran commander hiding something? Would the Hansa have to pay an unpleasant price later for the Solar Navy's assistance? 'What do you require of us in exchange for this aid? You would not risk so many ships simply for the sake of friendship.'

'Is friendship not payment enough?' The alien commander's expression was unreadable. 'Would you not remember our assistance if we ever asked anything of you?'

That was exactly what worried King Peter. How would this

come back to haunt them? However, if a hydrogue invasion force was on its way, he didn't see that the Hansa had any real choice. Hundreds of Ildiran warliners might make all the difference.

He nodded warmly. 'For the safety of our people, of course we welcome Ildiran aid. Your assistance could not have come at a more opportune moment. How imminent is this invasion?'

'Very soon.' The Adar was all business. 'There is barely enough time to prepare.'

NINETY-FOUR

SAREIN

Hansa duties and meetings kept Sarein so busy that she didn't really notice how long it had been since she'd spoken with her sister. But as she watched Peter and Estarra meet with Adar Zan'nh, she began to wonder if the Chairman might subtly be arranging things that way. Keeping them apart.

After the Ildiran commander promised to deliver hundreds of warliners as soon as they could be consolidated, he departed in his flagship. The great vessel rose into the sky like a gigantic fighting fish. Their purpose served, the King and Queen were whisked back to the royal quarters under an escort that looked suspiciously like prison guards.

So Sarein went out of her way to see Estarra. Wearing her Theron Ambassador's robe, she stopped at the doorway to the royal apartments.

'That's strictly against the Chairman's orders,' Captain McCammon said, then he smiled thinly. 'However, I don't see any harm in letting you two go to the Queen's conservatory. She enjoys that place.'

Indeed, Estarra was thrilled. At six months, with her pregnancy clearly showing, she covered her curved abdomen with loose cocoon-weave scarves and a skirt. She easily kept up with Sarein's strides as they walked through the private greenhouse, escorted by three royal guards. Estarra was happy to be among the plants again, sniffing the exhibits of lush flowers, bushes, and herbs.

But the armed men hovered too close for Sarein's comfort. Here inside the King's private wing of the Whisper Palace, who in the world were they protecting the Queen *from*? She maintained a firm, haughty expression as she shot a sidelong glance at the captain. 'I don't understand why it was so difficult to see you.'

Estarra raised her eyebrows. 'Because Peter and I are being held under house arrest. The Chairman doesn't want us speaking to anyone.'

Although her instinct to deny this statement was automatic, Sarein had seen the changes herself. Caught up with emergencies and disasters, Basil had been ignoring her, too, making excuses when she wanted to spend an evening with him or slip into his bedroom late at night. Always before, he had used her as a sounding board for advice. Now it seemed that the Chairman didn't want to listen. From what Sarein had heard around the Hansa HQ, Basil had stopped listening to everyone.

Estarra seemed deeply disturbed. She didn't seem to care that the guards overheard. 'Among other things, the Chairman feels that Peter overstepped his authority by ordering a swift response during the compy emergency.'

Eavesdropping, Captain McCammon made a gruff noise. 'King Peter saw the threat of the Soldier compies long before anybody else did. The Chairman should reward his foresight, not punish him.'

Sarein was about to snap in annoyance. If guards had to be so close, they should at least pretend to be unobtrusive! Estarra, though, looked sweetly at McCammon. 'Captain, I'd appreciate it if you could give my sister and me some privacy.'

'We'll keep our distance, Your Majesty.' He gallantly gestured for the Queen and Estarra to walk ahead along the rows of exotic flora. Sunlight warmed the mists rising from delicate irrigation systems that maintained the various plants.

Estarra took her sister's arm, and the royal guards waited well out of earshot. 'Now, what is this about a house arrest?' Sarein hissed. 'That's ridiculous. You're the Queen!'

'And Peter is the King, but that doesn't mean anything to the Chairman. You don't understand how much he hates Peter and me, because I had the poor foresight to get pregnant at an inconvenient time.'

Sarein scowled. 'Don't be melodramatic, Estarra. The Hansa has never been faced with so many impossible situations. The Chairman is forced to make difficult decisions every day. Give him a bit more credit than that.'

Estarra let out a long sigh. 'You're my older sister, and you're politically savvy, but right now, you seem very naive. You're so close to Chairman Wenceslas that you're blind to his faults. He'll do whatever he can to destroy Peter and me.'

Sarein spoke as if to a child. 'Oh, Estarra! You're isolated in the Palace and don't realize how much is going on. I meet with Hansa representatives regularly. We've been betrayed by the Soldier compies and lost seventy per cent of our Earth Defence Forces. Now the Ildirans say that hydrogues are coming to destroy Earth. What do you expect the Chairman to do?'

'Maybe he should concentrate on real problems and stop wasting time on petty jealousies.' Estarra stopped in front of a reef plant from Rhejak, which looked like a cluster of fleshy blue fingers. When Sarein touched one, the whole cluster collapsed protectively into its hard stem.

'Basil is searching for solutions. Since we lost so much of our military, he's investigating the missing rammers at Qronha 3 again. If our scout can locate them, it will change the whole defensive equation.'

Estarra's eyes narrowed. 'Maybe for Earth. But what about all the other Hansa colonies – and Theroc – that the Chairman abandoned like sacrificial lambs?' She paused at the fauldur plant from Theroc, studying the clump of bright but deadly berries. 'Let me tell you something, Sarein. You can believe it or not – depending on how much the Hansa's brainwashing affects you.'

Sarein listened with an amused and slightly dismissive expression as Estarra repeated her story of how the Chairman had tried to kill them by hiding an incendiary bomb aboard the royal yacht.

'He already explained that to me,' Sarein said. 'It was just a bluff because Peter was being so intractable. He never would have harmed you.'

'A bluff? You really believe that? The Chairman already had a Roamer trader held in administrative custody to be used as a scapegoat for the assassination. His name was Denn Peroni – look it up. The Chairman was setting up the Roamers so he could move against them. When Peter discovered the plan, he quietly issued an executive order to get the man free.'

Sarein's brow creased as she remembered the ceremonial regatta around the Royal Canal, the day they learned that hydrogues were attacking Theroc for the first time. She'd been standing next to Basil, who was tense atop the observation stand, as if anticipating something, counting down moments. He had looked very surprised and frustrated when nothing happened.

'This is all very hard to believe, Estarra,' Sarein said.

'Look into the details yourself and see if they all add up. The

Chairman has made other threats, even ordered me to get an abortion because my pregnancy isn't part of his plan. He was about to force the issue, but when the rumour leaked about my baby, your beloved Chairman had no choice but to let it alone.' Estarra's anger was palpable.

Now Sarein remembered that Basil had indeed mentioned asking the Queen to get an abortion. 'He wouldn't really have gone through with it.'

'Oh? Two days ago, he slipped a potent abortive drug into my food. If we hadn't caught it in time, I would have lost the baby and probably died during the miscarriage. Fortunately, we'd been in the habit of testing our food for poisons. We discovered the chemical in time.'

'You're overreacting.'

'Overreacting? What about my dolphins?' Estarra's face looked stricken. 'The beautiful dolphins. We used to swim with them.' She swallowed hard, and her breath hitched. 'He had them butchered. We came into the pool and found them all cut up, the water full of blood and chunks of floating meat. Look into it for yourself!'

Sarein blinked in amazement. Estarra couldn't be making this up.

Her sister continued the litany of accusations. 'After Prince Daniel tried to escape, they covered it up and then kept him drugged. The Chairman forced Peter to go look at him, and threatened him with the same thing if he didn't behave. But then Peter acted independently during the compy revolt, so your Chairman revived Daniel after all, and is planning to put him on the throne.' Her eyes flashed. 'And then they're going to kill us. Mr Pellidor has made no secret of it.'

'That's . . . but that's—'

Estarra looked weary, and distressingly old. Sarein didn't think she would ever again see the wonder-struck young girl who'd loved to climb trees and run through the worldforest. 'Sarein, I always thought you were so smart, so sophisticated. You spent years on Earth learning things that none of us on Theroc knew. But all your training has just made you naive in different ways.'

Sarein struggled to convince herself that Basil would never do such a thing, but in the back of her mind where the truth lived without propaganda, she knew he was capable of it. She had seen him make swift and harsh decisions before. After all, she allowed, it was part of what had made him so attractive.

Her voice sounded awkward. 'The Chairman already announced a grand banquet for Daniel five days from now, a coming-out party so the people can welcome him.'

Estarra nodded sadly. 'And afterwards, the King and I will "quietly retire".'

'That doesn't mean—' Sarein began.

'Yes, it does!' Frustrated, Estarra began to walk back towards the guards at the door.

'Wait, Estarra!'

The Queen turned. 'I don't know anymore if you're my ally or my enemy, Sarein. Which side will you choose?' She made a disgusted sound. 'Chairman Wenceslas is going to kill us. His plans are already in motion. Believe me if you like, or live with your delusions. You have that luxury. Peter and I don't.'

NINETY-FIVE

CONRAD BRINDLE

The large scout ship approached Qronha 3. It was similar to the military craft he flew many decades ago as an EDF pilot, able to handle a pilot and up to seven passengers. The passenger compartment was empty now, but Conrad Brindle hoped he could fill it, if he found any survivors from the rammers.

He had served in the Earth Defence Forces for most of his life, as had his wife Natalie. As had Robb. They had been so proud of their son when he joined the EDF, when he qualified as a Remora pilot, when he was promoted to wing commander.

And then the drogues had killed him.

Robb was always eager to jump before considering the consequences. Sometimes that was a good tactic; other times, it only made one into cannon fodder. Robb had perished along with many of his comrades at the Battle of Osquivel. Conrad wished he could have bidden his son farewell before he climbed aboard the encounter vessel and dropped into the thick clouds in a last attempt to communicate with the drogues. The glorious gamble had failed.

Times had changed dramatically since then. Because of the

emergency troop recall, Conrad wore a lieutenant's uniform again. Years ago, he and Natalie had retired, but once the hydrogue war started, their commissions were reactivated. For a while, the couple oversaw training exercises at a boot camp in Antarctica, but after the recent compy revolt, desperation forced the EDF to put reactivated troops on front-line duty. Natalie now served aboard a Manta patrolling the Earth system.

Despite his age, Conrad was still perfectly able to perform missions such as this one. His reactions were as good as always, unless he found himself in an active dogfight. And, dammit, he wanted to do something. Since he could fly a scout ship – and, off the record, he was too rusty to keep up with the younger troops in furious combat – Conrad had been ordered to recon Qronha 3. Were the missing rammers hiding here, or had they flown off to another part of the Spiral Arm? Admiral Stromo's Manta had been lost during the compy uprising, and the unresolved mystery pained the EDF like an open wound. Even a negative answer was an answer.

Commander Tasia Tamblyn, Robb's friend – perhaps even his lover? – had disappeared along with the sixty rammers. As he flew alone, surrounded by the emptiness of space, he recalled Tamblyn with mixed feelings; he and Natalie had met her only once, when the Roamer girl came to the Antarctic training base. Conrad remembered receiving their visitor that day in a domed shelter that overlooked the white wasteland. Tasia had stood ramrod straight, face pale, bearing a heavy burden that did not get any lighter by sharing it. Stiff and formal in her best dress uniform, she had personally delivered the news about Robb's death. It had been the worst day in Conrad Brindle's life.

Later, he and Natalie had joined former Chairman Maureen Fitzpatrick on an expedition to establish an Osquivel memorial, where they had unexpectedly found a Roamer base and rescued thirty EDF survivors. Unfortunately, Robb had not been among them, not that Conrad had expected him to be. Hope was an important part of a soldier's personality, but pragmatism counted for more.

As he flew close to the gas giant now, Conrad saw nothing beyond the dizzying vertigo of clouds, swirling storms, plumes and bands. He knew it was all a smokescreen for the murderous drogues and their warglobes. He hoped this scout was not large enough to warrant their notice.

He tuned his transceivers to the special frequency the Hansa had provided, activated boosters, pumped up the gain, and listened. Apparently, a spy camera was hidden somewhere among the rammers. If the big ships had been hijacked instead of destroyed, the surveillance imager might still be able to transmit, and he could switch it from passive to active. Admiral Stromo had picked up something; maybe Conrad could do the same.

Static filled his tiny cockpit comm screens as he began to receive fragments of a signal. Alert for warglobes, Conrad descended into a tighter orbit, searching for a stronger transmission. The viewscreen finally resolved into clear images ... unbelievable images.

Humans! And they were down there – hidden, imprisoned? – deep within Qronha 3. What was the enemy doing to them? As the resolution increased, Conrad used image-clarification algorithms to sharpen the picture. Astonished, he recognized one of the haggard-looking figures inside the planet as none other than Tasia Tamblyn. But she had been aboard the rammers – how could she be down there in the clouds? Had the hydrogues taken her prisoner?

The view shifted, and Conrad gasped. A father would never forget the face of his son, though years of captivity had made him haggard and gaunt. Robb was alive!

He could barely contain his excitement. He wanted to shout to Robb and let him know that they would find some way to rescue him.

Two warglobes emerged from the clouds, accelerating towards him. He had been spotted! As the diamond spheres shot upwards, Conrad scrambled with the scout's controls. His heart pounded. He had to get out of here, report to Earth, convince the EDF to send a rescue mission. His small vessel was unarmed. He had no option but to run. Reversing trajectory, he streaked away.

As Conrad retreated, he was surprised to see a Manta cruiser moving towards him from interplanetary space. For a moment he thought reinforcements had come to help him – maybe they could rescue Robb! – but an ominous message broadcast on a standard EDF frequency. 'Scout ship, stand down. You are our prisoner.'

Conrad spotted the insignia, scanned the ID numbers, and realized that this was Admiral Stromo's Manta – the one hijacked by Soldier compies. He veered away in a hard one-eighty that nearly made him lose consciousness, or at least lose his lunch. Then he goosed the scout's engines and shot out of Qronha 3's gravity well.

The warglobes ascended in pursuit, gaining on him. Blue lightning crackled from the pyramidal protrusions. Remembering exercises from when he was a young soldier, Conrad dipped and circled, dived back towards the planetary clouds in a porpoising manoeuvre.

The huge warglobes could not adjust their courses so easily. Conrad reached the far side of the planet as Stromo's stolen Manta closed in. Jazer blasts ripped through space, missing him by such a narrow margin that the static discharge overloaded the scout's secondary systems. Now he wished he had a smaller, faster ship.

Throwing caution to the winds, Conrad powered up the Ildiran stardrive even before he was safely out of the system. As he accelerated, another blast from the Manta's weapons damaged his engines. Stuttering away to safety, Conrad lurched off course and engaged the stardrive.

The warglobes and the turncoat Manta closed in on the spot in space where his ship had been. Too late.

NINETY-SIX

TASIA TAMBLYN

ven constant terror could be mitigated by sheer tedium. How in the world had Robb endured years of this?

After an uncountable number of days trapped within Qronha 3, Tasia found the monotony maddening. They couldn't go anywhere, couldn't plan anything, couldn't imagine even a crazy chance of escape. They exercised, told stories (many times over), and devised games with what little they had. Mostly, though, they just sat together, minute after minute after minute. She was surprised the captives hadn't killed each other even faster than the drogues had.

Worse than boredom, though, was when something *did* happen.

A Klikiss robot plunged its beetle-like body through the membrane wall like a rogue asteroid. Smith Keffa squirmed away, crying out in abject fear. The alien machine lumbered forward with a stormy sense of urgency and focused its red optical sensors on EA. 'You are a spy.'

The suggestion was so unexpected and absurd that Tasia actually burst into laughter. 'And you're a deranged can opener.'

The robot droned, 'This compy has transmitted information about our activities here. We can no longer permit this.'

Though baffled by the nightmarish situation, Tasia moved protectively next to her compy. 'How can EA possibly be a spy? Who would she communicate with?' Robb grabbed her arm to pull her away, but she shook him off.

The Klikiss robot paused as if considering whether it should bother to answer the question. 'We now understand the anomalies we previously detected. Microscopic surveillance apparatus was cleverly implanted within innocuous circuitry. We presume that data acquisition was previously passive, but now it has become active.'

'That's . . . ridiculous.' Tasia's voice trailed off as pieces fitted together in her mind. Her superior officers had pleaded ignorance as to what had damaged EA, claiming they had simply found the compy with her memory wiped. But they had given Tasia plenty of reason for distrust, and she certainly wouldn't put it past them to install a spying device in EA.

'A human scout ship tapped into this signal and acquired information about the hydrogue cityplex in Qronha 3,' the robot continued. 'Therefore, your Listener compy is a threat to us.'

'That conclusion could be correct,' EA said. 'After my memory was wiped, something was planted inside me, like a parasite that I could not identify. I expect it was some sort of extremely low-level recorder-transponder, masked by white noise and scrambled. Supposedly undetectable except with specific equipment.'

Tasia stepped between the looming black machine and the compy, thrusting her chin forward. 'It doesn't matter. If the EDF installed surveillance, their purpose was never to gather information about hydrogues or Klikiss robots. They did it to spy on *me*.' She flashed a hard glance at Robb. 'Probably hoping I would reveal the names or locations of Roamer outposts. Bastards!'

The robot was unimpressed. 'We cannot allow it to continue.' An articulated arm shot out from the black exoskeleton and seized EA's silvery arm with a clawed hand. 'By removing the spy, we remove the threat.'

Tasia grabbed the compy's other arm in a tug of war. 'No! She's my compy. EA is—'

'Do not allow yourself to be injured on my account, Tasia Tamblyn,' EA insisted in a voice that sounded calm, even resigned.

Not listening, she tried to pull her compy free, but the Klikiss robot knocked Tasia sprawling with another powerful mechanical arm. Robb rushed to her side and helped her up, but her mind had only one focus. 'EA!'

'We hate our Klikiss creators for what they did to us,' the robot droned. 'However, their methods of torturing us for their own entertainment are quite applicable to our dealings with other betrayers. We learned much from them. We learned to enjoy inflicting pain, both on a large and small scale.'

'Maybe we can disable the spying function!' Robb suggested.

The black robot dragged EA away. 'We will disable it. Permanently.'

The compy turned her head and looked directly at Tasia with flickering optical sensors. 'I was unaware of this until now. I do not remember. I did not intend to betray you, Tasia Tamblyn.'

'Of course you didn't!' Tasia lunged one last time for EA, but she could not get a grip on the slippery polymer skin. 'Leave her alone!'

The little compy could not resist as the Klikiss robot pulled her through the membrane into the extreme high-pressure environment of the hydrogue cityplex. The captives peered through the transparent membrane in horrified anticipation.

'At least they didn't take one of us,' Keffa moaned. 'They just wanted the compy. At least the robot didn't touch us!'

'Shut up!' Tasia cried.

'We've seen them take humans for experiments before,' Keffa continued. 'They slice and cut and torture!'

A woman named Belinda seemed frantic. 'What are they going to do with the compy? That poor compy—'

As if emerging from pools of congealing lead, six hydrogues took humanoid forms. They looked exactly – excruciatingly – like her lost brother Ross. From media footage, Tasia knew the drogues usually manifested themselves as her brother, for some incomprehensible reason. The emissary that killed old King Frederick had looked just like Ross. All of these here in the cityplex did the same whenever they chose to mimic a human form. Tasia felt ready to explode. The drogues had killed Ross, destroyed his skymine – that was the reason that drove her into joining the EDF in the first place.

Hateful bastards! Why would they bother taking a human shape deep in their own environment? Did it somehow enhance their observation of the prisoners? Was it part of their experiments? Two more Klikiss robots marched in from curved and angled walkways. Something was going to happen.

'Stop it!' Tasia screamed at the black robot through the gelatinous wall. 'Bring EA back!'

The little compy stood like a convicted prisoner before an executioner. While the quicksilver hydrogues watched with expressionless yet hauntingly familiar faces, the three robots surrounded EA. Clearly unable to escape, the compy did not even try to struggle.

Each Klikiss robot extended a full set of sharp arms tipped with wicked-looking implements. Together, they grasped the small arms, turned EA as if determining the best approach. Then, in a flurry of articulated limbs, they sliced and tore open her silvery polymer skin.

Pressed against the translucent wall, Tasia watched in horror. She screamed. Robb put his arms around her, but she couldn't feel him.

EA turned her head, and Tasia got a last glimpse of golden optical sensors. The Klikiss robots continued their work, rapidly and efficiently dismantling the helpless compy. Her limbs, her body core, her head, her internal circuitry, the governing boards and mobile sensors, were all stripped from her alloy bones and crushed beyond recognition. Within moments, nothing remained except a clutter of discarded components.

Wearing identical, unchangeable expressions, the Ross-hydrogues dissolved and flowed away. The Klikiss robots also departed, leaving the scraps of EA in full view as if to push the remaining captives closer towards despair.

NINETY-SEVEN

JESS TAMBLYN

As Jess approached Theroc in his water-and-pearl ship, he saw that a bizarre gargantuan *forest* had somehow sprung up in orbit. More than a hundred gigantic treeships stood sentry high above the atmosphere like colossal guard dogs with spiked collars. Thorny boughs were spread to drink the unfiltered sunlight pouring onto the dayside.

When he saw the verdani battleships, Jess understood exactly why the wentals had sent him here. Incredible armies were gathering. Inside the water-and-pearl ship and in his very blood, Jess could feel the water creatures singing. The pull was like a riptide.

The energized comet had already drenched the ground, reinforced the wounded trees, and spread through conduits of the worldforest, the roots and soil. From his strange vessel, Jess could sense the isolated moisture drawing together like gathering thunderclouds. Ready for war.

At the fringes of the atmosphere, the mammoth many-branched trees drifted aside, allowing Jess's vessel to pass unhindered. The elemental creatures sensed each other, remembered past battles in which both races had nearly been eradicated. By facing their common enemy together, they were far stronger. Yet this was more than a mere alliance; this was elemental synergy.

Jess had come here to facilitate that bond.

His vessel descended through the atmosphere, touching cumulus clouds whose fresh moisture rejuvenated the wentals. Below, the once-verdant landscape was healing. Blackened scars from the hydrogue attacks were flushed with fresh green.

The interlocked worldforest canopy swayed, and a whisper of voices like rustling leaves joined the constant buzz of wental thoughts inside his head. Boughs swept past him as he descended into the regrown treetops, finding open passages through the tall dense forest. His spherical vessel touched down in a clearing near the main human settlement, where a dozen more towering verdani battleships stretched sharp branches to the top of the sky.

Emerging through the soap-bubble wall, Jess could feel electricity in the air: a life, an energy, an anticipation. Under the overarching worldtrees, people came forward. Seeing the Therons and emerald-skinned green priests hurrying to greet him, he held up his hands in warning. 'Please keep a safe distance.' He looked at the faces staring at him, then added, 'I represent the wentals.'

Jess felt an unnatural stir within him, a signal from the trees. An animated sculpture walked forward – a perfect replica of a man, moving with all the grace of a living human despite his wood-grained skin. 'And I am Beneto. Of the verdani.'

The golem appraised him, then reached out. Before Jess could draw away, Beneto clasped his hand and squeezed. Expecting a disastrous discharge of deadly energy, Jess flinched, tried to call a warning. But the wentals within him did not harm the strange wooden man. Instead, they found a kindred spirit.

Beneto's hard lips curved in a smile. 'We were expecting you. Together we will create a new army.'

NINETY-EIGHT

CELLI

First the huge treeships, and now this water-and-pearl bubble, complete with a Roamer man inside who seemed as unusual as Beneto. Celli grinned with amazement. Faced with adversaries like these, maybe the hydrogues would just run away and hide inside their gas giants for ever!

Solimar whispered in her ear. 'Watch this, Celli. The trees have been waiting. We'll be invincible now.'

Jess Tamblyn and Beneto backed to the edge of the clearing as the spherical wental vessel rose from the ground and climbed like a weightless raindrop towards the canopy.

'What's it doing?'

'You'll see!'

The numerous verdani battleships drew closer until they formed a thicket in the sky. On the ground, the rooted worldtrees rustled with anticipation. Celli longed to know what was happening. If only she could use telink like Solimar!

After the wental vessel reached the top of the trees, a flurry of large globules of energized water split off from the quivering craft.

The coral-and-pearl framework contracted like fingers drawing together to hold the now-smaller volume of wental water. The flexible globules drifted from the main vessel, as if searching for something.

'This could change the balance of power.' Solimar's voice was barely above a whisper. He stood close enough to one of the tall worldtrees to touch it and receive messages from the forest mind. 'No human has ever seen this.'

Celli waited to be amazed again. Solimar would not let her down, she was sure.

Beneto and the Roamer man stood inside the ring of five broken trees that formed a temple-like meeting place. While her brother's body was made of clean, vivid wood, these burned stumps were tortured wrecks. Thus far, they had stood as a memorial to the enduring strength of the worldforest. Now, though, the verdani and the people of Theroc needed more than a symbol. Celli understood that.

One of the bubbles of wental water hovered over Jess and Beneto, who raised their hands towards the shimmering ball. The bubble burst. Wental water showered down into the five-trunk grouping, soaking the burned earth and drenching the two men.

More water welled up from the dirt, like a spring bubbling to the surface. The ground became saturated, sparkling. Jess began to laugh. 'We summon all the wental water dispersed by the comet!'

His woodgrain face slick with wental moisture, Beneto nodded, showing complete contentment and satisfaction. 'Wentals and the verdani will join completely. That is how we will defeat the hydrogues.'

Celli clung to Solimar, her mind bubbling over with questions. She smelled the earthy ozone of heavy dampness rising through the dirt, heard the whispery rush as the moisture flooded into the scorched tissue of the worldtrees. She felt small and insignificant in the scheme of grand events, but she didn't understand.

Almost immediately after the sparkling water soaked the ring of five burned trees, the soil bubbled and churned like a simmering volcano preparing to erupt. Celli felt tremors beneath her bare feet.

With a rustling of their thorned branches, the ancient verdani battleships rose higher, clearing the canopy, making room. Celli tried to look everywhere at once. Anticipation was a building storm in the air.

Beneto addressed the worldtrees in an amplified voice, 'You know what is contained within you. Draw on all of your reserves!'

The ring of near-dead trees responded.

The stunted, blackened trunks cracked, straining to reach the sky. The heartwood began to writhe. Shafts of fresh growth thrust up, new branches snapped out like concealed weapons. With a rough thrashing sound, sharpened fronds grasped upwards. As the damaged trees sucked wental water into their tissues, the broken trunks expanded in an accelerated rush of regrowth. The five trees surged higher, twisting around each other and braiding into one enormous main trunk. Rejuvenated roots plunged deeper beneath the surface, tapping into the interconnected forest and drawing more energy, siphoning the wental-comet water that had percolated into the Theron soil.

Feeling the exuberance of the worldforest through the green priests and other observers, Celli laughed with sheer joy. Leaves sprouted from the fresh boughs, and thorns sprang from the ends of the energetic branches, extending like scimitars in search of any enemy. No longer a set of blackened stumps, the new wental-infused growth towered above the canopy.

Another enormous treeship, the first in a new fleet.

Jess Tamblyn watched the spectacle with obvious surprise, as if even he hadn't guessed what the wental power could do when joined with the worldforest. Celli saw her parents standing together, mouths agape, like little children watching a condorfly hatch from its chrysalis.

Beneto's voice echoed from all the trees. 'This is just the beginning.'

More water globules spread away from the Roamer man's strange ship. The separate wental bubbles homed in on other broken trees, crippled trunks, and blasted boughs that had never recovered. The large droplets drenched stumps, reviving and transforming them into monumental thorny structures as well. A new armada of treeships sprang to life, surging up from the forest floor.

Solimar grinned at Celli, full of fresh knowledge from the forest. 'Now you know what created the verdani battleships in the first place! Worldtrees infused with living wentals, joined in a symbiotic construction great enough to battle even a hydrogue warglobe. A hundred warglobes!'

New thorny battleships lunged up from the ground all across the forest, at least a hundred more. Celli wanted to race through the wooded paths to see them all.

Ever since the first hydrogue attack, the Theron people had felt sore and defeated, overwhelmed by an impossible task of mere survival. Now, though, Celli could feel the strong new sensation of hope. 'If the hydrogues know what's good for them, they'll just surrender.'

Beneto stood beneath the shadow of the first newborn seedship, facing the Roamer man. 'You brought what we needed more than anything, Jess Tamblyn. By reviving Theron trees with wental water, we can now add a new fleet of verdani battleships to the ones we summoned from the far reaches.'

Dazed, Jess flexed his hands, as if he couldn't believe what he'd helped to accomplish. 'Will it be enough? That isn't the only ability we have to offer. Even now, Roamer clans are gathering tankers and cargo haulers to take shipments of wental water and drop them like bombs into hydrogue gas giants.'

The wooden man looked at the thorny trees that filled the Theron sky. 'These new verdani battleships will also find and destroy hydrogues. The enemy is already weakened by their struggles against the faeros. We can tip the balance and defeat them for ever.'

Jess beckoned to his water vessel. 'Before that can happen, I still have plenty of work to do – coordinating Roamer water carriers, managing the wental distribution – while you prepare to launch your treeships. Even a few hundred verdani battleships aren't a sure bet against thousands of drogue warglobes.'

The nearest verdani battleship continued to crack and thrash as it grew like a geyser of living wood. Across the worldforest, a hundred more like it reached for the sky, unsheathed swords prepared to strike the hydrogues.

'Our fleet will join the great fight very soon,' Beneto said, then lowered his voice. 'But first we must find pilots for each of these new vessels.' He studied the looming, gold-scaled trunks. 'And I will be the first volunteer.'

Solimar's face was solemn, and Celli's heart clenched with instinctive dread. What did the golem of her brother intend to do? 'What does he mean?' She shouted, 'Beneto, what are you doing?'

With a splitting sound, an opening appeared in the still-scarred trunk, a dark and mysterious passage. 'Each verdani battleship requires a green priest to join the heartwood. The trees cannot fly alone. They need a partner.'

Celli ran towards her brother. 'You mean you're going inside that thing? For how long?' She ignored the other looming battleships, ignored Solimar, even her parents, who still hadn't realized the terrible truth.

Beneto turned to her. 'Look at what I've accomplished, little sister. Now it's time for me to depart. I will fuse myself with this ship, in the same way that the first verdani battleships partnered with other living creatures.'

'But can you come back when the war is over?' Celli forced optimism into her voice. She had always resented being treated as a child, as the youngest, but now she felt very small. 'After the verdani battleships destroy the hydrogues, you'll return to Theroc, right?'

He shook his head. 'Even if we win, Celli, I will be part of this ship for ever.'

'But ... but you can't just leave. You're my brother, Beneto! I've already lost you once.'

'Yes, I am your brother, Celli,' the wooden simulacrum said gently. 'I love you. I look like him and have his memories. But I am also much more than that. My purpose now is greater than when I was only human.'

She wanted to drag him away from the dark and forbidding crack in the thick trunk, but Beneto stood firm, as if he had taken root. His next words stuck fresh fear into her heart. 'We need a hundred new pilots.'

Before Celli could blurt another question, a crowd of green priests walked out of the forest, summoned via telink. Beneto addressed them, his face content. 'Thank you for coming. We have many more volunteers than we need.'

Desperate, Celli whirled to Solimar for explanations. It was all happening too quickly. First the joy and awe, then hope, and now this terrible cost. Solimar squeezed her shoulder in an ineffective attempt to comfort her. 'You need to let them go, Celli. Our fate rides on this.'

She shook him off. The volunteers looked placidly determined, accepting their fates far more easily than she ever would. She realized that the green priests must already have decided everything via telink, talking in ways that no other Theron could hear. But what about their families, their friends?

On the other hand, what about the war and the survival of Theroc? She hated the necessity of this choice that was not really a choice. Nobody gave Celli any say in the matter. None at all.

She looked at the face of her brother, saw the longing expression carved there in the vibrant wood. He looked at her, and she felt a flood of all the times she had spent with Beneto, the real Beneto. And this one, too.

A spot appeared by one of his woodgrain eyes, moisture welling up like a bead of sap that spilled from the corner of a delicate eyelid, then began to flow down the hard, rounded cheek. Beneto stepped into the yawning crack in the verdani battleship, then the trunk sealed itself again, and Beneto was gone.

Solimar held Celli for a long moment in silence. She shuddered, feeling his strength, glad for his closeness. At least he was still here to treedance with her, be her friend and maybe eventually even her lover. They had many possibilities open to them . . .

'I have to tell you one more thing, Celli,' Solimar said, his voice dropping into the silence like a stone. 'I have volunteered to fuse with one of the new ships as well.'

NINETY-NINE

NIRA

I n contrast with the horrors of Dobro, the trip back to Ildira
was full of joy and love, memories and relief. But her heart was
not the same.

The *Burton* descendants would finally be allowed to establish a
real home on the planet they had expected to settle centuries ago,
before the betrayal. Hopes and dreams could be reborn from the
smallest seeds, but what good would even those concessions do if
the hydrogues came to eradicate them all?

Aboard the ship, Nira told Jora'h about her years of emptiness,
voicing as many searingly painful recollections as she could bear.
She didn't actually blame him, but a kind of distance took the
place of her initial joy.

'I swear to you I did not know where you were all those years,'
he said again, as he had several times before. 'I did not know you
were alive.'

'I was already pregnant with our daughter, but they beat
me.' Her voice hitched. 'As soon as I was capable, after they took
Osira'h from me, Designate Udru'h forced himself upon me again

and again until I finally conceived his son. After that, there were more fathers, more tortures, and more children. Those poor children. I am glad we could save them.'

'I did not know you were there.' It was a chant.

'But you must have known about the other breeding captives!' Her words became hard now, and her muscles tensed. 'All those people, for generation after generation. You had to know what was happening.'

'The programme was established long before my father took the throne. I was not told about it until just before his death.' His words caught in his throat. 'And he killed himself to prevent me from finding you. Then, when I ordered the Dobro Designate to release you, he told me you were dead.'

'You should never have believed him.' Nira was aware of the harshness in her voice. 'You are the Mage-Imperator! You touch the minds of every living Ildiran, and yet your own brother tricked you? How many people have you allowed to lie to you, Jora'h?'

Jora'h clenched his hands into fists. 'Right after the Hyrillka rebellion, Udru'h came to me like a penitent and confessed that you were alive after all. He must have known I would learn the truth. I had never even considered that Udru'h would deceive me. That he *could* deceive me.'

'I've heard enough lies to last ten lifetimes,' Nira said. 'Thoughts of you kept me alive. I called out to you, dreamed of you. I would have given anything just to see you while I was in the breeding barracks. I . . . love you, Jora'h.' She lowered her gaze. 'But I am no longer sure I trust you.'

She understood the impossible decision the hydrogues had demanded of him, and understood – now – that he was trying to find a way to stand up against the enemy. But if none of his plans had a chance of succeeding, how quickly would he change his mind? How easily would he bow again?

Adar Zan'nh would be coming home any day now after delivering his message to King Peter, and the Solar Navy was gathering the requisite warliners over Ildira, ready to dispatch them like gamepieces played by the hydrogues.

Jora'h seemed to sense her doubts and concerns. 'I promise I will do everything I can to stand up to the hydrogues, Nira.'

'But what if everything you can do is not enough to save your people, and mine?'

After the quiet calm of their journey, Nira felt an old measure of excitement as they descended through the sun-swept sky and landed on a platform atop the Prism Palace. Mijistra spread out like an incomprehensible fantasyland. Guard kithmen marched forward across the rooftop, accompanied by well-dressed courtiers, bureaucrat kithmen.

Behind Nira, Osira'h led the other half-breed children. Raised on drab Dobro, her younger brothers and sisters had never seen such marvels. For a moment, the delight on the faces of her children made Nira forget her other concerns. 'This is your home now,' she said.

'We will find quarters for all of you in the Prism Palace,' Jora'h promised.

Adar Zan'nh was also there, standing at attention but looking deeply disturbed. He gave a swift, formal salute, and his voice was leaden. 'Liege, King Peter has accepted our offer of warliners, as you expected he would.'

Nira shot a swift glance at Jora'h. He squeezed her arm as if to reassure her. He wanted her to trust him, and a Mage-Imperator was not accustomed to assuaging doubt. Jora'h straightened his reflective robes. 'Send them as soon as they are ready. Two cohorts, if possible.'

'Two cohorts, Liege?' The Adar wrestled with his surprise.

'That is twice what the hydrogues demanded. And it takes defences away from Ildira!'

'If we are going to do this, then we must take our best gamble. That is my command. Can we prepare that many warliners? How long will the refitting take?'

'Our teams are working without rest, making remarkable progress. It is the greatest and swiftest mobilization of manpower and resources ever attempted by the Solar Navy. We learned innovative techniques from Sullivan Gold and his engineers.' Zan'nh seemed awkward with his pride. 'What we lack in time, we make up for in workers and dedication. Your people will not let you down.'

'Good, Adar. When the cohorts leave, I want you to command them personally.'

Zan'nh seemed taken aback, but then rallied his resolve again. 'Yes, Liege. No one else should have to bear that burden.'

Much later, Nira and Jora'h were alone in his high tower room. They stood on the transparent balcony, staring across the magnificent skyline. He put an arm around her shoulders. 'Because you are human, we can never share our souls through the bonds of *thism* . . . yet words seem inadequate for all that we have to say to each other.'

'That is why it's so important that I can trust you.' Nira thought wistfully of the time they had spent together when he was Prime Designate. Those had been peaceful times.

'You are as beautiful to me as ever, Nira, but neither of us is who we were.' He drew back to look into her eyes. 'Our love cannot be the same as before. I—'

'I know.' In order to become Mage-Imperator, he had surrendered his manhood – the price of controlling the *thism* to hold his people together. She herself had been damaged, abused. The two of them would no longer have a sexual relationship, but now perhaps their love would even be stronger. Physical passion would instead become inseparable companionship.

They stared for a long time at the dazzling, clear skies, at the reflections of the curved buildings. After a while, she finally said, 'Oh, how I long to touch the forest mind again! Do you have a treeling? Where are the treelings that Ambassador Otema and I brought?'

Jora'h shook his head, looking extremely sad. 'I have no treelings at the Prism Palace. They were all destroyed.' He pressed his lips together, as if catching himself before he could utter another outright deception.

Nira could tell he was still hiding something, keeping secrets. It was as obvious as dark knots in a pale beam of wood. Would it never end?

477

ONE HUNDRED

TAL O'NH

After the faeros had destroyed the watchdog hydrogues in Hyrillka's sky, Tal O'nh seized the opportunity to continue his rushed deployment of construction crews and equipment. He dispatched more ships to the spaceport, adding to the numerous teams already on the ground. Hundreds of warliners emptied their holds and distributed food, machinery, and raw materials.

Like a swarm of constructor beetles rebuilding a hive after a storm, soldiers, engineers, and many strong workers erected new buildings. The exhausted people were uplifted by the progress all around them, seeing structures rise and fresh rows of crops laid down in the ash-fertilized soil.

The crews managed to work for several days before the next disaster occurred.

The one-eyed commander rode in the near-empty flagship warliner to better survey the activities below. He had barely slept in days; his short grey topknot was frayed, not tightly braided and waxed as he normally kept it. He did, however, take the time to

478

polish his reflective Lightsource medallion, and the facets of his jewelled eye. O'nh felt an urgency to get his work done.

Several members of the skeleton crew in the command nucleus sat up abruptly as sensor alerts sounded. 'Tal!'

He turned his good eye to the main screens. 'Report.'

'They are coming from all sides, on a hundred different vectors. An armada the likes of which we have never seen. Sensor stations are overloaded.'

'An armada of *what?*'

'Hydrogue warglobes – all coming to Hyrillka! We cannot possibly stand against them.'

The alien spheres swirled in from outside the system like a blizzard of diamond chips. They must have been dispatched from numerous gas giant planets, emerging from transgates deep within and spewing into nearby space.

O'nh stepped up to his place at the command rail. In destroying the three watchdog warglobes, the faeros must have provoked the deep-core aliens. He stared at the tactical screen that showed incredible numbers of oncoming warglobes, far outnumbering the Ildiran ships.

'Prepare for our final battle.'

Given luck and determination, his cohort might cause extraordinary damage to the enemy in a flurry of suicidal attacks. But even if every single warliner destroyed a hydrogue globe, they could never win. The enemy numbers were overwhelming.

He wished Rememberer Vao'sh and his human companion had come up here with him. This would certainly be something for them to observe, for the sake of history. However, they were not likely to survive long enough to record their experiences.

'Should we form a defensive line, Tal? Concentrate our forces above the central city?'

O'nh squinted to watch the blips of enemy ships. 'Inform

Designate Ridek'h that I will do my best. Have all crews ready to move on my command, but do not overreact. Warglobes have come before and did not attack.'

The alien armada rocketed closer, never slowing. Then, in an endless storm, they streamed *past* Hyrillka and headed towards its blue-white primary sun.

The warliner's command crew cheered in disbelief, while O'nh watched with his brow furrowed. 'They are not after *us* at all. Hyrillka does not matter to them. Even their bargain with the Mage-Imperator has lost its priority because of the faeros.'

'That is good news, indeed, Tal!'

Relief lasted only a few moments, and then his suspicions turned to dread, for he had seen a similar thing before. 'Not necessarily. This could be even worse.'

Like moths drawn to a flame, the warglobes swarmed around Hyrillka's main sun, swirled in the corona, and began to attack the star itself.

Flushed out by the sudden barrage, faeros ellipsoids erupted from the roiling plasma seas. Numerous flaming shapes slammed into the hydrogues in a blinding display. The battle was engaged.

With a sick heart, O'nh knew that the faeros were likely to lose. Hyrillka's primary would be extinguished, just like Durris-B. There was nothing Tal O'nh or his warliners or Designate Ridek'h or even the Mage-Imperator could do about it.

As he stared at the screen, O'nh made a mental tally of the population on Hyrillka, all who had survived the first hydrogue attack and then Rusa'h's rebellion. He considered the disposition of ships in the Solar Navy, closed his one eye, and visualized which grouping would be closest.

'Send an immediate message to Tal Ala'nh. Summon his cohort to Hyrillka as swiftly as possible. I do not know how much time we have before that sun dies.' He opened his eye and looked again

480

at the bright main sun, where flashes and sparks of the conflict churned through the solar layers. 'We will need every one of his warliners and all of mine to effect a total evacuation of this planet. After all our work, Hyrillka cannot be saved.'

ONE HUNDRED AND ONE

CESCA PERONI

After Jess left for Theroc and the fourteen Plumas water tankers set off to primordial Charybdis, Cesca went to Yreka hoping to reestablish connections with the dispersed Roamer families. She still thought of herself as the Speaker, though, after all the turmoil, she knew it might take some time for Roamers to re-establish their identity and determine their place in the changed Spiral Arm.

Since she flew only a small craft scrounged from Plumas, everyone assumed Cesca was just another clan trader coming to the bustling outpost. Her ship settled onto the crowded landing field, and she stepped out into the dusty air, feeling the energy tingle through her skin. The colours, the noise, the smells, the chatter of cordial conversation! She hadn't seen so many Roamers together since before the destruction of Rendezvous.

The place looked more like a crowded bazaar than a space-port. Smiling clan members wore flashy clothes, embroidered jumpsuits, jackets with a multitude of pockets, clips, and zippers.

The Yrekans' serviceable clothes and plain overalls were now embellished with bright scarves and ribbons.

Scanning the other ships, Cesca's heart leapt when she recognized the *Dogged Persistence*. Denn emerged from his craft, saw her, and his face beamed. He ran forward, words jetting out of his mouth like engine exhaust. 'Cesca! Cesca, what happened to you? Where have you been? Kotto came here and said Jonah 12 was destroyed! I was so—'

She scrambled back up the ramp, holding up her hands to fend off his attempted embrace. 'Dad, no! Stop! Stay back.' For the first time she realized how Jess had felt. 'I'd love a hug, too . . . but it would kill you. Lots of things have changed. *I've* changed.'

He blinked in confusion. 'What do you mean a hug would kill me? And what's that glow about you? Your skin looks—' He caught his breath. 'By the Guiding Star, I heard what happened to Jess Tamblyn! Is this the same thing? You're . . . possessed by some strange life force?'

Her dark hair swirled with static electricity as if alive. 'Otherwise I'd be dead right now. Jess saved me. The wentals saved me. But they had to change me.' Even his questions and the obvious strangeness of the circumstances could not diminish Denn's joy at seeing her. She wished she could wrap her arms around him, but she did not complain. 'Oh, it's good to see you, Dad.'

'People have been asking about you. We're doing the best we can – which is damned good, if I do say so myself – but the clans need their Speaker. What a mess!'

'And I need them, too, Dad. We've got a whole new mission now, our most important task ever. With Roamer help and Roamer ships, Jess and I have found allies that can help us trounce the drogues, once and for all. Across the Spiral Arm, clan ships are gathering to take part. Jess's water-bearers are organizing distribution points at many wental worlds.'

Colonists and Roamer trade intermediaries came towards her ship, eager to take an inventory of whatever she might have to sell. Cesca spotted curly-haired Kotto Okiah, whom she had last seen on Theroc before sending him to investigate the hydrogue derelict. 'Kotto!'

The eccentric scientist was clearly happy to see her. 'Speaker Peroni! Wait until you hear the new ideas I've been working on. We've pulled out all the stops, making resonance doorbells and getting ready—'

'Kotto, wait.' His rush of words stopped, and he noticed her expression. She could see the point at which he understood exactly what she was going to tell him. Cesca turned to her father. 'Dad, I need to see you and Kotto aboard my ship for a few minutes.'

When the three of them had a moment of quiet, with Cesca standing on the far side of the small cargo chamber, she said, 'Kotto, your mother died on Jonah 12. I'm so sorry. We went there after the Eddies blew up Rendezvous. It was just our temporary base of operations, but . . . everything went wrong.'

The engineer nervously kept looking at her, then away. 'I went there. I saw the crater, but no signs of life.' He quickly lifted his chin. 'But you escaped. Please tell me that some of the others got away.'

Memories whipped past her, cutting like sharp ice chips in the wind. 'No, Kotto. Only me. Nikko Chan Tylar came to rescue me, but our ship was shot down by the Klikiss robots. Then Jess saved us, and convinced the wentals to change me before I died.'

And that opened up more and more questions. She explained about the Klikiss robots found frozen under Jonah 12 and how they had destroyed the base in a rampage. Kotto looked as if his whole body was sagging in a heavy gravity well. 'So my mother died there, with all of them.'

She shook her head. 'Jhy Okiah died peacefully, Kotto. She passed away while resting in the base dome. Purcell Wan and I arranged a fitting Roamer funeral for her and launched her into space. It was afterwards that all hell broke loose.' Kotto seemed to take comfort from that.

'I remember when your mother died, Cesca,' Denn said. 'Roamers are supposed to adapt to drastic changes, to roll with disasters. But I thought I'd never recover from it.'

'Even so, you did.' Cesca smiled sadly. 'She told you to, and you always did what she asked.'

Unlike many Roamers who died suddenly in accidents, killed by equipment failures or the vagaries of space, Cesca's mother had had time to come to terms with her imminent death. Lyra Peroni had flown her own merchant ship, and because of a failed sensor panel, she didn't know that one of her cockpit radiation shields had slipped away. Cesca's mother flew a dozen runs before a routine maintenance check noticed the problem. By then, the dosage she'd received was several times the lethal amount.

Denn had rushed her to Rendezvous for treatment, but there was nothing Roamer doctors could do. Cesca had been there, training to become Speaker Okiah's heir-apparent. Cesca and her father had hovered over Lyra for weeks as she deteriorated. The previous time her mother had come to Rendezvous was to help embroider the symbolic Roamer chain and dress her daughter in colourful ribbons for her betrothal to Ross Tamblyn.

A million years ago, and in a completely different universe . . .

Denn had begged his wife to go to a Hansa medical facility, which he believed had better equipment, a better chance of saving her. But Lyra refused. She knew, as did the Roamer doctors, that there was no chance. She had instructed Denn to 'get over it'.

To live his life. To adapt to the changes. After his wife's death, he'd followed her last request with great difficulty.

'I guess we've got more changes ahead,' Denn said.

'Major changes,' Cesca said. 'And we need your help.'

When she went outside again to meet the crowds, Denn and Kotto helped keep a wide perimeter around Cesca. She took nearly an hour to explain the crisis point of the Spiral Arm, and the listeners showed as much awe at hearing her tales as they did from seeing the unearthly changes in her body. Her father was shocked to hear about the tainted wental nightmare on Plumas, which he had only recently visited. Cesca doubted she would have trouble convincing the Roamers to follow her.

'Tell us where to go, and we'll do what we have to, Cesca,' Denn said. 'Seems a better use of our time than to sit here waiting for the drogues to come to us. I'd rather fight them on their own turf.'

'Give me a chance to show Roamer ingenuity in action,' Kotto said, struggling to find his determination. His two compies came forward carrying rolled-up polymer mats. Kotto took one and spread it out in front of Cesca like a red carpet. 'This is one of my doorbells, Speaker. It's how we mean to fight the hydrogues. With enough of these, we can crack open drogue warglobes like rotten eggs.'

Denn laughed. 'We've already made over a hundred thousand of these little things, and we expect to double that number within a few days, now that the production lines are up and running. By the Guiding Star, the drogues'll wish they'd never crawled out of their gas giants.'

Cesca wanted to kiss him. 'Excellent work, Kotto. I'm very proud of you.'

He beamed. 'You're the one who gave us the challenge,

486

Speaker. I never stopped thinking of new things that might defeat the drogues.'

'As long as we have minds like yours, Kotto, the Roamers will survive. Keep manufacturing those doorbells. I have to go to Charybdis, where our largest tankers are gathering – and as many of you who can come. The drogues are in for more of a fight than they could ever imagine.'

ONE HUNDRED AND TWO

SAREIN

Prince Daniel's coming-out banquet was a 'private' affair for two hundred of the Hansa's most important representatives. Impeccably produced, every dish, every seat, every bouquet of flowers had been arranged with exquisite care. Sarein hadn't seen such extravagance since Peter and Estarra's wedding.

Unlike the royal marriage, however, there were no representatives of Hansa colonies, no Mother Alexa and Father Idriss from Theroc, no governors or dignitaries from planets that were now cut off from EDF protection. Sarein was the only offworld ambassador in attendance.

Hansa-approved camera drones flitted about, transmitting the spectacle to viewers across Earth. The signals were also beamed into space so that soldiers serving in the EDF defensive cordon could watch, though she couldn't imagine a handful of last-stand fighters being interested in watching a Prince's banquet.

Sarein took her seat beside Chairman Wenceslas. She maintained her composure, smiling at not-so-clever jokes made by politicians and other notables. It was hard to be near Basil when he'd been so distant lately, increasingly distracted and aloof. He seemed to have lost interest in everything but the continuing disasters. In the back of her mind, she kept thinking about the accusations Estarra had made . . .

Before the banquet, Sarein had wandered through the conservatory again, mulling over what she had learned. The familiar Theron plants reminded her of how Estarra had loved to explore the wilderness as a little girl. As Sarein pondered, preoccupied, she had glanced down and was surprised to note that the cluster of poisonous fauldur berries was gone. Some gardener must have removed them, though their colour had been fresh, at their peak. She'd thought it odd at the time, but quickly dismissed it . . .

Now the bearded Archfather of Unison droned through a traditional prayer, and the banquet began. Since Prince Daniel was the centre of attention at the feast, servers presented his plate first, a carefully measured portion of appetizer rolls and cheeses. When other attendees received larger servings, the Prince did his best not to let his disappointment show. Though the boy had been overweight the last time Sarein had seen him, Daniel now appeared gaunt. A hollowness haunted his eyes, and he snapped to do everything Basil told him, like a puppy eager to please.

Had he really been kept drugged and out of the way for the last several months, as Estarra claimed?

As the salads were distributed, Sarein glanced at her sister. The King and Queen were seated at an isolated table at the front of the huge banquet hall, where private servants took care of them. Ostensibly, those were the prime seats, with the best view and the most privacy, but Sarein wondered if Basil had put Peter and Estarra there to keep them from speaking to anyone.

Sarein wrestled with her suspicions. Instead of marching to Basil's penthouse and confronting him with the claims, she had quietly checked as many details as she could, using news databases and classified Hansa memos. Without much trouble, she verified even the least believable of her sister's claims.

Save for the well-guarded meeting with the Ildiran Adar, the King and Queen had not been allowed outside the royal wing since the compy revolt. They were truly under house arrest. Sarein even tracked down a medical order signed by Basil and then rescinded, instructing a doctor to perform an abortion on Estarra.

And, as Estarra had indicated, the pet dolphins were gone, though Sarein could not confirm that they had been slaughtered. Their saltwater tanks were empty, scoured out and left to dry. She found a maintenance worker who would say only that the dolphins had died.

Next, with growing dread, she reviewed the tapes of the procession around the Royal Canal, paying particular attention to Basil's expression. She saw his clear anticipation, his building tension . . . then noticeable frustration, though nothing obvious had changed. After being close to him for so long, she knew how to read the Chairman's emotions. He had been expecting *something* to happen. An explosion? Sarein also confirmed that a Roamer trader named Denn Peroni had been detained on some trumped-up administrative matter exactly during the time when the alleged thermal bomb would have killed the King and Queen.

Everything fitted, just as Estarra said. How could Sarein disbelieve her own sister? How could she argue with so many facts?

After the second course, Basil stood, straightened his impeccable suit, and called for attention. The Chairman rarely made speeches in public; Sarein took it as another sign that he didn't want King Peter to utter a word.

Basil rested his hand on Daniel's shoulder. 'Previously, out of deference to the King, Prince Daniel has maintained a low profile. However, given the current crisis, King Peter has urged us to use every possible advantage. We need Daniel's strength and energy.'

490

While Peter remained conspicuously silent, Basil nudged the young man to his feet. 'I give you the Prince. Note his face well. Recognize him. You'll be seeing a lot more of Daniel in the future.'

She shot a quick glance at Peter and Estarra while all attention was turned to the Prince. The two sat close together, clapping politely but without enthusiasm. Basil was obviously setting things up for a clean transition of power.

Nodding to acknowledge the applause, Daniel appeared jittery. His clothes had been tailored to fit him perfectly, but he did not seem accustomed to wearing them. He blushed at the attention, and Sarein thought it added a perfect touch.

Daniel cleared his throat and thanked his supporters. 'Every person on Earth knows that we must pull together if we are to survive. I'd like to offer my personal commendations to the research team working on the hydrogue derelict.' He motioned towards a side table where the group of scientists seemed out of place, surprised by all the media imagers that turned towards them.

'Even without Dr Swendsen, these researchers succeeded in activating the hydrogue engines. In several test flights they have demonstrated they can manoeuvre the derelict.' He glanced down at his hand, as if looking for notes, then snapped his head up again, glanced at Peter, and turned abruptly away. 'The team also managed to power up the transportal, even if they have not yet deciphered the hydrogue coordinate system. It is only a matter of time.'

He looked as if he was finished, ready to sit down, but then remembered to add, 'And how does this help us fight against them, you ask? Once we understand the engines, we can identify their vulnerabilities. But getting the hydrogue transportal working will be the best part. If we could open a transportal inside any of those warglobes, we could drop a big bomb right into their laps! We wouldn't even have to send EDF ships against them.'

Good thing, since we don't have many ships left, Sarein thought.

After Daniel finished his speech to more applause, he sat down and called for the main course. Sarein remained puzzled. The news about the hydrogue derelict was interesting, but it didn't merit having the new Prince issue it in such a dramatic forum. Maybe it had been nothing more than a test to prove that the young man could follow instructions and do his duties.

While plates of food were distributed, the conversation hummed with both hope and scepticism over the promises from the Solar Navy. 'The Ildirans will be like the cavalry ... if they ever get here,' said a florid-faced energy minister.

'It's only been five days,' said the Hansa's transportation secretary around a mouthful of pheasant drizzled with savoury sauce.

'Right, but he said the hydrogue attack was imminent.'

Sarein ate her food but did not taste it. Every time she glanced across the room at Estarra, she noted that Peter was holding his wife's hand. If Estarra's suspicions about the Chairman were true, then the King and Queen had good reason to be deeply worried. Now that Daniel had been reintroduced to the public, their time might be short indeed.

But what did they plan to do about it? What should *she* do about it? Despite her placid public face, Sarein's thoughts were in turmoil, her stomach knotted. Twice during the meal Mr Pellidor came to whisper something in the Chairman's ear, before the expeditor faded back to his own table.

Finally the dinner plates were cleared. Though he was not talkative, Basil seemed satisfied with the banquet. Servers came in with the dessert course, a sculpture made of whipped fruit that had more artistic merits than flavour. After everyone had complimented the elaborate confection, a compy strutted in with a special pot of cardamom coffee for Basil. Rich aromas wafted up from the pot with a sweet sharp bite of exotic spices. The compy poured a cup for the Chairman.

Sarein had never developed a taste for the beverage, but Basil rarely drank anything else. It was one of the quirks she had found endearing about him.

When Basil reached for his cup, Sarein noticed that the King and Queen were intensely interested in his every move. Estarra and Peter were convinced that the Chairman would kill them, if they didn't find a way to stop him first. Both of them focused on the cup of coffee. Cardamom coffee. A beverage that no one else drank.

The missing fauldur berries!

Before Basil could take a sip, Pellidor interrupted him yet again; after listening to the whispers, the Chairman scowled.

Sarein's thoughts raced, her emotions clashing like thunder-clouds. She feared for Basil, but she could not deny the evidence of the terrible secret things he had already done. *He is my lover!* Her muscles locked. *He tried to kill my sister!* She wanted to knock the cup out of Basil's hand, wanted to shout at him, warn him that the coffee contained poison.

But that would be condemning Estarra to death. Even if Basil hadn't actually made up his mind to kill the King and Queen, he would certainly do so if they tried to poison him. She couldn't implicate Estarra. She *couldn't!*

But she also loved Basil. She had been with him for years. He had taken Sarein under his wing, taught her Hansa politics. She couldn't just look the other way and let him die. Thoughts raced through her mind in a flash. She was reluctant to cause a scene, but how else could she prevent this? Overreaction was an unforgivable sin in Basil's eyes. Years of political training restrained her for an instant.

Suspecting nothing, he lifted the cup to his lips. Sarein shot to her feet. 'Don't drink that!'

Conversation died. Basil looked at her with a flare of annoyance, and she had to think quickly. Every excuse that came to her mind sounded ridiculous and, knowing Basil's stubbornness, she realized he would insist on drinking the coffee, in public, just to prove Sarein wrong. Oh, he would punish her for this – *if* she had made a mistake.

'I saw . . .' Sarein refused even to glance at Estarra and focused her gaze instead on Mr Pellidor. The expeditor was a cold and often rude man; she knew he must have carried out many of the terrible deeds Estarra had described, like planting the thermal bomb, and even butchering the dolphins. His hands were as bloody as the Chairman's.

Basil frowned at her. 'Yes, Ambassador Sarein? What is it?'

'I saw Mr Pellidor doing something with your coffee. He seemed very furtive about it.'

Basil looked at her in surprise. She had never overreacted before, had never done anything to make him question her. 'That's a rather strange thing to say.'

She held her breath, forced herself to nod. 'I'm aware of that, Mr Chairman. Perhaps it was just my imagination, but it certainly looked suspicious.' She swallowed hard. 'Isn't it wiser to be safe than sorry?' She desperately wanted to search the faces of the King and Queen for guilt or anger, but she kept her eyes fixed on Pellidor's now indignant face.

'This is ridiculous, Mr Chairman. I never touched your coffee.'

'I saw what I saw,' Sarein insisted.

Someone from down the table commented loudly enough to be heard in the intrigued silence. 'Isn't he the one who refused to believe the King's warning about the compies? The man who told us all there was nothing to worry about!'

Since the uprising, media clips had run and rerun Peter's brave speech in the compy factory, when he'd demanded that the operations be shut down until the Klikiss programming modules could be checked. Pellidor had featured prominently as a man whose refusal to listen had cost countless lives.

Hearing the loud muttering, Basil glared at Sarein. 'I have no reason to believe my expeditor would do me harm.' He held up his cup, sniffed it, then extended it towards the blond man. 'However, if it makes Ambassador Sarein happy – Mr Pellidor, please drink this coffee and prove to us that there's nothing wrong with it.'

The other man frowned. 'I don't care for coffee, Mr Chairman.'

'And I don't care for baseless suspicions. Do it!'

Glaring at Sarein, Pellidor accepted the cup, took a sip of the coffee, grimaced, and gulped the whole cup down. He looked defiantly at Sarein, who felt a wash of relief mixed with confusion.

Pellidor's fingers spasmed, and he dropped the cup on the floor, where it shattered. His face twisted with amazement. He turned towards the Chairman and collapsed, groaning and gasping. Basil scrambled away from him. Pellidor made a choking sound. His face writhed, his tongue swelled, his eyes bulged . . . and he fell slack.

Pandemonium erupted in the banquet hall. Media crews rushed forward. Royal guards stormed in. The appalled Chairman stood unmoving, and Sarein grabbed his arm and yanked him away from the table.

Captain McCammon barked orders at his men, and royal guards rushed to form a protective circle around Peter and Estarra. 'Get the King out of here! There's been an assassination attempt.' Moments later, as an afterthought, guards came to protect Prince Daniel as well.

Basil attempted to recover, swiftly raising his voice, aware that the media would be showing these clips for the next several days. 'Yes, take the King and Queen to the royal wing for their own safety – and guard them well.' His voice grew harder. 'There may be other assassination attempts.'

Peter and Estarra looked suitably stunned, and Sarein didn't think it was an act. Just before the two were rushed away, the Chairman gave Peter a hateful glare. No matter how she had tried to divert suspicion to Pellidor, Sarein could see that Basil knew exactly who the real culprit was.

ONE HUNDRED AND THREE

KING PETER

With urgent steps, the royal guards rushed the King and Queen out of the banquet hall. Captain McCammon led the way with his twitcher drawn. 'Isolate them in their quarters as swiftly as possible!' His maroon ceremonial beret was askew on his bleached white hair.

Royal guards folded protectively around Peter and Estarra. Although their functions were frequently ceremonial, the gaudily uniformed men moved with gratifying precision. The Queen's pregnancy hindered her movement, but she kept up. If she slowed, Peter was sure the guards would pick her up and carry her in their arms.

'This way! Clear the halls.' McCammon raised his voice to a bellow. Functionaries and Palace workers scattered into side rooms. 'You two, head to the next intersection. Keep watch. Highest alert!'

Estarra stumbled, and Peter caught her. They kept running. Both of them knew the implications of what had just happened. Peter had seen Basil's glare. 'That's it, then,' the Queen mumbled to him, her voice bleak. 'We're dead.'

'Not if I can help it, Your Majesty,' McCammon called back over his shoulder. 'No need for talk like that. We'll keep you safe.' The royal guards had no idea what was at stake. Or maybe, Peter thought, they actually did . . .

There would be no safety for the two of them in the Whisper Palace.

The lead pair of guards stopped at a junction of corridors up ahead, drew their weapons, and blocked access so that the group could hurry the royal couple through without pausing. Palace District security squads had closed off the banquet hall. The two hundred guests would be held for questioning, grilled over and over again about any possible involvement with Franz Pellidor. The Palace would be in continued chaos for many hours.

Peter ground his teeth together. The Chairman knew damn well there were no other accomplices, that Pellidor had nothing to do with the attempt, yet he had to go through the motions. Media imagers had broadcast the reintroduction of Prince Daniel. Much of Earth's population had seen Sarein accuse Pellidor and watched him fall dead, supposedly a victim of his own poison.

Why had Sarein ruined everything? If she'd guessed about the poison, she would also have known that Pellidor was not involved. Peter wasn't particularly sorry that the murderous expeditor was dead. Long ago, it had been Mr Pellidor who kidnapped an unsuspecting boy named Raymond Aguerra, and then arranged for the conflagration that had killed Raymond's – Peter's – family. Pellidor deserved a death far slower and far more painful than fauldur poison.

Sarein had chosen to save Basil, even if it meant death for her own sister. It wasn't likely Estarra would ever get a chance to talk with Sarein now. In fact, they might never see her again.

But the clumsy failure had accomplished one important thing: if the Chairman killed them now, even the most gullible media reporter would sense something was wrong. In a roundabout way, exposing the assassination attempt had bought Peter and Estarra some time. Maybe that meant he and his Queen would stay alive for the next few days.

When they finally reached the royal wing, Captain McCammon remained tense and alert. He sent several guards ahead to sweep the bedchambers and waiting rooms. 'All clear, Captain.' After the King and Queen had passed into the private quarters, McCammon stationed four of his men outside the main entryway, and Peter believed these royal guards would actually do their best to protect him and Estarra.

The captain cautiously followed the two into their suite, double-checking every corner for an unexpected threat. Tendons stood out on his neck. 'I always knew something was wrong with that Pellidor. A bit too full of his own importance. I'll never forget how he thought *he* had the authority to prevent you from seeing Chairman Wenceslas.' He made a disgusted sound. 'If you ask me, that man got himself involved in some shady business and paid the price for it.'

Peter nodded, careful not to speak.

'If Pellidor had listened to you about the Soldier compies in the first place, Your Highness, the Hansa wouldn't be in such a mess.' McCammon shook his head. 'If the hydrogues come, like the Ildirans say they're going to, we could be looking at the end of the human race.'

Peter was unsettled by the man's passion. For the past few days he'd been so focused on survival, trying to dodge Basil's political knife thrusts, he had become distracted from the big picture. McCammon was right; this could indeed be the end of the human race.

Finding a seat, Estarra gathered her breath to ask obvious questions so she could gauge the guards' reactions. 'But if Pellidor poisoned the coffee, then he must have known it would kill him. Why would he drink it voluntarily?'

'Most likely to protect his accomplices. A fanatic. This plot is probably much bigger than we think.' The captain straightened his beret. 'In fact, I'll have my guards install poison scanners in your quarters. From now on, I insist that you test your own food.'

'Even so, we can't assume that we're safe,' Peter said. He took an unexpected chance. 'Captain McCammon, give me your sidearm.'

The guard blinked. 'There's no need, Your Majesty. We will protect you. Nothing's going to happen to you or the Queen on my watch.'

Peter stared at him, hard. 'I don't doubt your ability, Captain. But don't underestimate these ruthless assassins. They tried poison this time, and no doubt they will use a different method when they try again.' He held out his hand for the weapon. 'At least give me a chance to protect my wife and unborn child if the worst happens.'

McCammon drew his twitcher, looked at it, adjusted the charge, and nodded. 'You know how to use this?'

'I fired some weapons in my younger years.' That had been in another life, struggling to survive the tough streets. 'And it is your job, Captain, to make sure that I don't need it.'

Peter concealed the weapon in his robes, while McCammon went to check on his guards. Feeling the twitcher's reassuring weight, Peter looked meaningfully at the Queen. Now at least they were armed against whatever Basil intended to do to them.

ONE HUNDRED AND FOUR

NIRA

In accordance with the hydrogue demands – and the Mage-Imperator's plan – Adar Zan'nh dispatched hundreds of 'protective' warliners to Earth. Nira clung to the hope that Jora'h would be true to his word and do all he could to save both of their races. She wanted to trust him again, but he hadn't yet earned her unquestioning faith. She still knew he was keeping secrets from her.

Smiling uncertainly, Jora'h led her up into the skysphere. Courtiers, guard kithmen, and pilgrims waited in the audience chamber below, but the Mage-Imperator had already spent hours with them and ordered them to wait. He needed some private time with Nira. 'Come with me. I have something to show you.' Together, they ascended the ramps into the overarching terrarium, past the exotic plants on display for the glory of the Mage-Imperator.

A jewel-winged creature sped past her eyes, swirled, and then shot off in a different direction. Fleshy comptor lilies bloomed, shedding a perfumed sweetness as thick as mist. Enjoying the verdant beauty around her, Nira touched Jora'h's hand with her rough fingers and wondered what it would be like if their two separate minds could touch through telink or *thism*.

'I know you long to reconnect with the worldforest. But though I control this empire, I cannot help you.' Nira could feel sadness emanating from him. 'All the treelings were destroyed. Every one of them. That is the truth, and I am ashamed. Long ago, my father killed the ones you and Ambassador Otema brought with you.' He looked away. 'Recently, though, Queen Estarra from Earth brought me another treeling. I kept it in my own quarters. I used to stare at it and think of you.'

Nira sensed his uneasiness. 'What happened to it? Where is it now?'

'I destroyed it.' He let the confession hang in the air. 'There is another green priest in the Prism Palace, part of the Hansa skymining crew from Qronha 3. He lost his own tree during the hydrogue attack, but he sensed the treeling in my private contemplation chamber. He tried to break in. He wanted to send out a telink message, which would have been disastrous before. To remove the temptation, and the risk, I destroyed the treeling. I am sorry, Nira, but I could not allow him to reveal our plans. There was too much at stake.'

'More likely he just wanted to touch the worldforest mind,' she said, her voice cool. This was what he had been afraid to tell her. He had killed a treeling, and now she remained cut off, just like that other green priest. 'So all the treelings on Ildira are truly dead.'

'Yes. But let me show you what I have left.'

He led her to where the terraced dirt was strewn with large fragments of wood, like a rock garden made from chunks of demolished trees. Some of the lumps had been crudely shaped and carved, others merely sanded to excise external charring.

Immediately recognizing the grain, colour, and sheen, Nira hurried forward, her face full of longing. 'This is worldtree wood!'

'A Roamer trader brought them to me. His clan members assisted your world after the hydrogue attack and were given this wood as thanks.'

Nira's shoulders sagged. She had come to Ildira as a young acolyte, but she had been gone for many years and was unaware of so many incredible events. Until recently, she had not even known about the devastation of the worldforest.

Jora'h held a piece of the polished wood up to the light. 'I asked the trader to give me every scrap he had. Because the wood reminded me of you.' He handed it to her. 'I did not know what to do with it, so I kept it here, where I would see it often.'

Wistfully, she knelt, resting the worldtree wood on her knee. The smooth chunk, though dead and silent, felt comfortable in her hands. She touched the strangely familiar wood and traced the feathery grain, followed the contours of splinters and flat surfaces, searching for a warmth inside. Nira let her thoughts flow, longing for any kind of connection. Hoping for *something*.

Though this wood was dead, the worldforest mind itself was still intact, still dispersed across the forest. There must be some way she could touch the rest of the vast network. During her long isolation, she'd feared that she might be deaf to telink. She had yearned for the touch of the worldforest as much as she yearned for Jora'h to come to her.

Now, though she heard the background noises of small birds and butterflies, rustling leaves, rushing water from fountains and irrigation misters, she heard nothing inside her head. Nothing.

Beside her, Jora'h sat as motionless as a tree himself, waiting, not sure what she was attempting to do. Nira saw his expression of deep pain, hope, and sorrow for her. She closed her eyes, concentrating only on the worldtree wood.

She recalled her youth as an acolyte, enamoured with stories, loving to sit high in the canopy and read aloud to the trees. When she was chosen to become a real green priest, Nira had gone alone into the densest worldforest, and the verdani had claimed her, swallowing her up in the living underbrush. She had emerged with green skin and an unbreakable link to the worldforest mind. At least she had thought it was unbreakable.

Nira squeezed the wood in her hands, plunging her silent mind into the woodgrain. She had never needed to work to establish telink before, had never considered the exact process. It had always just . . . happened. She didn't know how to force it. She had grasped at any hope. But that was gone, too.

Without opening her eyes, Nira reached out and grasped Jora'h's hand as tears began to flow from beneath her closed eyelids. She took comfort from his touch, though she knew there was no hope of forming a mental bond like the one the Mage-Imperator shared with his people through the *thism*. He could not connect with her, any more than she could connect with the dead wood now.

She felt a spark like electricity. Faint, like heat lightning in the distance . . . but definitely there.

She clenched her hand, letting her fingers press hard into Jora'h's skin. Something about the contact with him was helping. The spark grew brighter, and suddenly she felt a tiny echo deep within the worldtree wood.

'What is it?' he asked.

Nira did not respond, but concentrated furiously, following the faint thread, burrowing into the thick wood with her memories. Although this tree itself might be dead, all worldtrees were connected. Startled, she looked down to where her free hand had been tracing the burned edges of wood, sure that she could now feel the bloodsap moving, stirring. Something was changing,

504

and somehow Jora'h's powerful control of the Ildiran *thism* had aided her. A small gasp of awe escaped her lips. She had broken a new path!

In a barely audible voice, she whispered, 'Please – hold me,' and pressed both of her palms hard against the wood, making as strong a contact as possible. She felt him put his arm around her shoulders. There!

'Jora'h, I can sense a change . . .' He held her tightly, increasing their bond.

But it wasn't just her telink, or just the Mage-Imperator and his *thism*. Something new and incredible was happening with the verdani – all of them. Right now on Theroc, a deep part of the worldforest mind was awakening, just as hers was. The thoughts reached out, straining upwards until they shot like a bright flare into the night sky. Nira didn't know what had triggered this new burst from the heart of the worldforest, but she felt the effects of the resurgence rippling across the Spiral Arm.

In her hands, the chunk of wood shifted. A knot thrust up, a hard lump that split . . . and shot forth a fresh sprout. Before her eyes, it grew into a tiny pale frond. How could that be? This dead wood had come to life again, through her! The frond was barely as long as her index finger. But it was enough.

Nira touched it. In a flash, she reconnected with the world-forest. Finally!

Gasping, falling, she drowned in an amazing flood of information. She poured out everything that had happened to her over the last eight years. In a rush of images and painful memories, she dispersed her knowledge. Nothing could stem the outburst of her thoughts.

When she was done, every green priest and all the worldtrees across the Spiral Arm understood everything.

ONE HUNDRED AND FIVE

BENETO

Beneto had always been part of the trees — both when he was human, and after his absorption into the worldforest. Since his rebirth on Theroc, he had shown the forest what it *meant* to walk, to move, and to live. The verdani understood much more about what it meant to be human now, to be a living independent being with sorrow and joy.

And Beneto understood many things, as well. Most of all, he understood that he had found the rest of his destiny. The worldforest mind had given him a new life, resurrected him to be a spokesman and intermediary with an understanding deeper than any green priest could achieve. It had also given him a second chance with his life, with his family. Now he would willingly pay the price they asked of him.

Encased within the verdani battleship, his wooden body sacrificed even its human shape. He was rooted once more. His carved hands fused like clay to the living wood that was energized with wental water. His legs melted into the forest tissue, and he sank into a swirling vortex of woodgrain.

Even as he grew into the structure of the massive treeship, he retained part of himself. Immediately after his rebirth, Beneto's connection to the world and his beloved family had been tenuous and intellectual. Back then, he would not have hesitated to make the sacrifice. Now, though, he felt the loss to his very core. To his heart. Thus, so did the worldtrees. He would miss being alive . . .

Aboard the swarm of new-grown verdani battleships, his fellow new green priest pilots were all symbiotically fused with their enormous tree forms. They had let their flesh-and-bone bodies be absorbed into the enfolding wood, while leaving their minds still alert, carrying human personalities. After a thousand years or more, they would begin to lose their individuality like those poignant ancient creatures who guided the original tree-ships. Though these volunteers were giving up a great deal, Beneto also knew how much they would gain. In the end, they would consider their sacrifices worthwhile. He was sure of it.

Outside, looking simultaneously forlorn and relieved, Solimar squared his broad shoulders and gazed up at the giant vessels – the seedships that had turned him away. Celli was with him, her dark eyes sparkling with tears. She was deeply sad to see Beneto go, and also happy for the parting gift her brother had quietly offered her.

Like so many green priests, Solimar had been enamoured with the idea of joining a verdani battleship. He had volunteered to give up his life to become a pilot of a huge seedship, just as Beneto had done. Many green priests had offered themselves, far more than the hundred who were needed.

Though he was no longer entirely human, Beneto still knew his young sister's heart. He had seen her and Solimar treedance together and understood their affection for each other. They belonged together. For love of Celli, he had not allowed Solimar to be chosen. The worldtrees listened to his heart, though it was clear the verdani did not entirely understand. But they had regrown him as a manifestation of the worldforest and of humanity, the sentient trees wanted to learn from Beneto and his memories. They listened to his love for his sister.

He had offered Solimar a legitimate explanation. As one of the few technically literate and mechanically inclined people on Theroc, Solimar was needed for his engineering knowledge. The other green priests were not irreplaceable, but Solimar possessed skills the Therons would need. The worldforest asked him to stay behind, and the new battleships accepted another green priest pilot in his stead.

And so, as volunteers had streamed to the hundred new battleships, the gold-armoured trunks remained closed to Solimar, forcing him to stay behind. Celli realized immediately what her brother had done. She silently thanked him, and did not tell her friend what she knew.

Now Beneto could concentrate on his new residence, his new mass, his new existence. This great vessel was an extension of his body. He could look out upon the forest – *all* extensions of the worldforest – through the simulated eyes of uncountable leaves. He saw the many colony worlds where green priests had brought treelings to form a communication network.

More than ever before, Beneto could feel all the memories, the secrets, the wistful experiences stored deep in the verdani mind. His thoughts flowed like sap through the intricate woodgrain, deep into the past. Beneto rode along with the lives of other green priests, his many predecessors all the way back to the first landing of the *Caillié*.

For the first time, he actually saw a spark of old Talbun, his devoted mentor from Corvus Landing. Long ago Talbun had asked Beneto to be his apprentice, to watch over the colonists and tend the worldtree grove there. In dying, the old green priest had

let his flesh be absorbed into the forest; Talbun was here, too, *inside*
the verdani battleship, inside all of the great trees. Beneto would
not lack for company. With wooden lips, he smiled. He felt
strong, confident, at home.

With the battleship as a conduit, amplified by the wental-
infused wood around him, a thousand telink messages streamed
through him. Beneto listened everywhere.

Thus, instantly and unexpectedly, he became aware of the
long-lost green priest Nira Khali.

Beneto remembered the enthusiastic young green priest who
had gone to Ildira with Ambassador Otema to experience *The
Saga of Seven Suns*. But their treelings had been destroyed, cutting
both of them off. After the former Mage-Imperator sent word that
Nira was dead, no one, including Beneto, had found any reason to
think otherwise.

Now the terrible truth swept over him with the speed and
devastation of a forest fire. Nira's thoughts and memories were
unstoppable. Even the towering worldtrees in the thick Theron
forests swayed and reeled with the revelations.

All at once, the scattered green priests received her experiences, the treachery, the breeding programme, the secrets that
Ildirans had kept. This sudden, shocking knowledge changed
everything the green priests – and all other humans – had ever
assumed about the Ildirans.

And there was more.

Because Mage-Imperator Jora'h had revealed it to Nira, her
urgent message told of the forced alliance with the hydrogues and
the impending attack on Earth. From within the huge battleship,
Beneto comprehended what the Ildirans hoped to do, and how
he must respond. Twists within twists. The hydrogues were going
to Earth! The birthplace of humanity would be wiped out, unless
someone else fought on their behalf.

This war was everywhere at once.

Around the Spiral Arm, green priests rushed the news to human settlers but, abandoned by the EDF, the former Hansa colonists could do nothing to help Earth. And the Hansa military would never be sufficient to stand against the flood of warglobes that would soon bombard them.

Understanding what was at stake, Beneto imposed another command, drawing upon his human existence more than the wishes of the worldforest. 'We will take twenty of the new battleships, including the one that I captain, and go immediately to help defend Earth.'

He felt a response ripple from the trees. They considered Earth a small part of the overall battle and didn't want to expend part of their seedship force on a target they did not consider vital. But Beneto was adamant. 'In spite of what its current government has done, that planet is humanity's home. The seeds of our race came from there. Our roots go deep. Our hearts still remember the forests and jungles.' A flood of images rushed through telink, reminding the verdani of what was at stake. 'We must save it.'

The affirmation of the other green priests resounded through telink, and the worldtrees capitulated. In his mind he also received a swift burst of information and a warning from Nahton in the Whisper Palace. The last intact ships from the Earth Defence Forces were prepared to face any attackers, and they would no doubt be trigger-happy. What would the EDF do upon seeing the ominous and unexpected verdani battleships? Beneto needed a way to communicate directly with them.

Seeing something he could do, Solimar hurried to the fungus-reef city to gather the components Beneto needed. In rebuilding the settlement, the good-hearted Roamers had installed new communication systems, traditional transmitters and beaming devices. While the hundreds of verdani battleships shifted and rustled impatiently, he dismantled one of the comm systems and brought it to Beneto's giant ship. Celli followed him.

Beneto separated the armoured plates in his thick trunk and created a passage for them to enter. He sensed them as they climbed up to the heartwood chamber, following the tunnels he made. Solimar carried the communit, trailing wires and a long-term power source.

He and Celli stopped upon entering the great chamber at the middle of the ship. Breathing hard, Beneto's little sister looked at him with mingled fear, sorrow, and wonder. Solimar seemed uncertain of himself, his eyes downcast, his expression glum. Through telink, Beneto could read his feelings.

Physically joined with his carved pilot seat, a wooden throne fused with symbolic controls and guidance systems, Beneto moved his body forward, detaching an arm from where it had grown into the seat. 'You see, Solimar, the worldforest required your skills as a human after all. Any green priest can join with a battleship, but I needed you to do this.'

The broad-shouldered young man looked disconsolately at the commsystem. 'To hook up this simple equipment? Anyone could have managed that.'

Celli was quick to scold him. 'How many Therons understand technology the way you do? Name anyone else who built a gliderbike from scratch. Tell me who could maintain all those Roamer systems if you were to go away.'

'Someone else could learn.'

'Now no one else has to.'

Beneto indicated where he wanted the commsystem. 'If I can make contact with the Earth military, I can coordinate our fight when we arrive. At the very least, it will stop them from shooting at me.'

Her heart aching, Celli threw her arms around the remnants of her brother's form. 'I'll never see you again, will I?'

His carved face smiled. 'My body was never really here in the first place. But I am always part of the forest. Solimar can contact me – he knows how.' She seemed to take heart from that. 'And now you must leave. Our ships are about to depart. There is a war to be fought, and won.'

Celli clung to him a moment longer. She always wanted to be seen as older and more mature, but at the moment she looked like the sensitive little sister he remembered from long ago. Beneto had many regrets for the things he had not accomplished in his second chance at life, but he also had many obligations to meet. Foremost, he had to join the final battle against the hydrogues at Earth.

He conveyed his goodbyes and his love, not only to Celli but also to their parents. She and Solimar hurried out of the giant treeship, and Beneto sealed the opening in the trunk, armouring himself for spaceflight and war.

Beneto stretched his new arms and felt his branches move through the air. His thorns and leaves extended upwards into the winds of space. The huge branches were barely able to hold themselves up in the planetary gravity, but in open space they would stretch out to embrace the stars. All of the new battleships experienced the same reaction within their cores.

The Therons and the verdani were ready, as were the wentals and their numerous Roamer partners. This battle could be won after all! His thoughts thrummed through the interconnected worldtrees. 'Our verdani seedships will not wait here any longer. We must bring the fight to our enemies, while the wentals launch their great offensive.'

It was time to go.

Beneto's treeship was the first to lift off. With a tearing

sensation followed by a wonderful sense of airy freedom, he uprooted himself from the soil of home. As he pulled away from the worldforest, his myriad verdani eyes saw the Theron people raising their hands, waving farewell. Through his enhanced vision, Beneto discerned Celli and Solimar, Mother Alexa and Father Idriss.

The other new organic vessels tore free of the Theron dirt and joined the rest of the forest battlefleet. Hundreds of spiny treeships rose together like a flurry of seeds showered into the sky, and moved beyond the boundaries of atmosphere.

They cruised between the stars, drinking raw sunlight. Beneto's gigantic tree body was sealed by an impenetrable verdani force and infused with the life energy of the wentals. If he survived the war with the hydrogues, he could survive for a very long time.

The enormous tree battleships headed out into space, dispersing towards countless simultaneous battlefields.

ONE HUNDRED AND SIX

JESS TAMBLYN

When he left Theroc, Jess knew that the hundreds of verdani battleships would do their part in the imminent battle – as would the wentals. If all was going according to the broad plan, Nikko and the rest of Jess's water-bearer volunteers would be rallying Roamer recruits; many pilots should be flying to various central wental planets to prepare for their final push. Cesca would coordinate the whole plan, sending messages through the wentals to guide near-simultaneous strikes to infested gas giants across the Spiral Arm. The concerted attack against hydrogue planets would hit like a chain-reaction ...

As the water-and-pearl vessel raced across empty space, heading toward Charybdis, through the wentals Jess instantly *knew* that something unexpected was out there ... another ship. It hung dead in space, drifting. Damaged? Lying in ambush?

He approached cautiously, and soon identified the human craft – a large EDF scout, far from any star system. A lone figure floated outside completing repairs to the external engines. Though the ship could have carried a small crew, only one person was visible.

Seeing the strange wental sphere coming towards him, the panicked man jetted into the open hatch. Detaching his helmet inside, the Eddie pilot scrambled into his control seat. Through the cockpit windowport, Jess could see he was an older black man, his close-cropped wiry hair dusted with smoky grey.

Jess cautiously hovered his alien vessel in front of the scout's cockpit, standing at the outer skin of the bubble so that the EDF man could see that he was human. With a reassuring smile, Jess raised his hands in a non-threatening gesture. He hoped the pilot wouldn't fire a jazer blast at him. The other man stared in disbelief.

Drifting to the comm apparatus his water bearers had installed, Jess opened a direct channel, using one of the supposedly secret EDF frequencies that Roamers had discovered long ago. 'I mean you no harm.'

After fumbling with his systems, the pilot responded on the same frequency. 'I am Lieutenant Conrad Brindle on a scout expedition for the Earth Defence Forces. Who are you? What are you doing out here – and what kind of ship is that? Are you . . . human?'

'Oh, I'm human, and maybe a little bit more. How did your scout come to be damaged, Lieutenant Brindle?'

'Hydrogues!'

'Ah, so we share the same enemy.'

'I was doing recon at Qronha 3.' Brindle was clearly unsure of how far he should trust this exotic stranger, but he was so overwhelmed he quickly broke down. 'The drogues and the Klikiss robots are keeping human prisoners! They're holding eight people hostage inside a gas giant.'

That seemed impossible. 'How do you know this?'

'Direct video images. My son is down there. We thought he was killed by the hydrogues before the Battle of Osquivel. But he's alive and he's deep inside Qronha 3!' Brindle shook his head. 'How am I ever going to rescue him?'

Jess had heard of Qronha 3, but this made no sense. 'Why were you scouting a gas giant in the Ildiran Empire in the first place? What interest do the Eddies have?'

'We lost sixty new rammers there. Commander Tamblyn led them on an assault against the hydrogues, but they just disappeared. My orders were to see if I could intercept a surveillance signal.'

'Commander *Tamblyn*?'

'Tasia Tamblyn. They picked her to lead the rammer charge.'

A suicide mission. Of course Tasia would have flown the highest risk operation. The Eddies would have chosen her because she was a Roamer. Expendable. Eddies had always treated clan members like that.

'Commander Tambyn is my sister,' he said. Surprised, Brindle looked again at the strange figure of Jess in his shimmering white garment and his alien water-vessel. 'Is she still alive? Tell me what happened to her. Tell me everything.'

While Brindle explained, Jess seethed inside his wental ship. If Tasia was being held by the drogues, then he needed to do something. Immediately. 'Can you finish your own repairs to this ship?'

'Oh, the weapons just grazed me. I can jury-rig the systems, and I should be flying out of here within a day. I never assumed anyone would find me.'

Jess wrestled with the tides of anger and urgency. He'd been about to rally the wentals, send them off to hydrogue gas giants. All the players were now ready. But the drogues had captured his sister! He knew where he had to go first. The wentals would communicate the details to Cesca.

Jess prepared to set out, sending one last transmission. 'Even after what the Eddies have done to our clans, Lieutenant Brindle, we Roamers are on your side. We're fighting against the *real* enemy. Go back to Earth and tell your Chairman it would be best if he did the same. Meanwhile, I'm going to rescue those hostages in Qronha 3.'

Brindle was surprised. 'If you're going to try to rescue my son, then I'm coming with you.'

'I am going where you cannot follow. Deep inside a gas giant.'

'With the environment down there – the pressures, the poisonous atmosphere – it's impossible!'

Jess cut him off, already preparing to depart. 'Then by the Guiding Star I'll have to do the impossible.'

ONE HUNDRED AND SEVEN

NIKKO CHAN TYLAR

The turnout at Charybdis was even larger than Nikko had prayed for. All those Roamer volunteers ready to deliver wentals! Obviously, a lot of people held a grudge against the drogues. The new arrivals came to the stormy water world with the utmost resolve. At least he could be sure this conflict would not be lost due to a lack of enthusiasm or manpower.

The planet-sized ocean surged and swelled, crashing against the scattered rocky landing areas. The turbulent environment made a profound impression even on hard-bitten Roamers who thought they had seen it all.

Nikko landed the *Aquarius* near some big Roamer ships donated by Del Kellum and other skymining families from Golgen. Zhett Kellum flew one of the cargo haulers herself, insisting (repeatedly and loudly over the open comm channels) that she was as good a pilot as any other clan could dredge up. No one challenged her assertion, certainly not Nikko.

Fourteen water tankers from Plumas arrived, along with many smaller craft, so it was only a matter of loading the ships and telling them where to go with their holds full of wental water – and that was an administrative problem he did not relish. Nikko Chan Tylar had never been good at organizing even his own routes and schedules. Speaker Peroni was supposed to be here soon to help him.

Nikko's fellow water-bearers had spread the word of the impending assault across the Spiral Arm. They had called ships to the numerous ocean worlds where clan volunteers would fill their ships with the potent water before flying off to every known drogue-infested gas giant. So far, well over a hundred Roamer craft had been drawn into the overall operation. In small clusters, the ships could hit an overwhelming number of hydrogue worlds. Soon enough, the enemy would have no place to hide.

But it had to be a coordinated effort. Roamers were notoriously independent, and Nikko couldn't let them fly off wherever they chose. Some key planets might be missed, while others were hit twice. If the wental distribution took too long, the drogues might find some way to block it. Or they might escape in their warglobes.

Nikko had no idea how many hydrogue gas giants there were – hundreds? Thousands? Thanks to the renewed skymining operations at Golgen, the Roamers at least had enough ekti to make all those runs . . . but unless it was organized, the whole plan would be one big mess!

He already had a headache.

He went outside to the barren, spray-swept black rocks where Roamers milled about next to their ships, impatient to get moving. Del Kellum and several other clan heads were good organizers, but he didn't delegate the work to them, yet. (They probably wouldn't have listened to him anyway.) He glanced up at the sky, hoping to see Speaker Peroni.

Finally, he decided to get started by having the ships load up.

Nikko was sure he could handle that part, since the wentals knew what they were doing. When he directed the battered Plumas tankers to hover above the restless waves and open their cargo doors, Caleb Tamblyn transmitted sceptically, 'I don't know if our pumps can handle this. The tankers were designed to use hydrostatic pressure from beneath the ice caps.'

One of the Tamblyn twins – Nikko wasn't sure whether it was Wynn or Torin – added on the same channel, 'We might have to use buckets or barrels for the little ships. But we'll fill up that way, if we have to.'

Nikko didn't have any doubts. 'Just sit back and watch. Trust me, that water *wants* to get aboard.'

The ocean itself took care of the rest. Rising up, the living waves poured themselves into the voluminous holds. Amoebic streams of water, acting like pseudopods, lifted up in defiance of gravity. Wentals flooded into every storage hold of the volunteer ships.

While activity continued in a blur around him, Nikko stood on the rocks, smelling ozone-laden air. The cargo operations went on for hours, as ship after ship of every configuration came down, checked systems, jockeyed for position even though the ocean was huge, then took aboard the strange water. Similar scenes must be happening on other wental distribution worlds as groups of Roamer ships filled up, preparing to deploy their secret weapon.

Upbeat, Nikko transmitted across the common circuit, 'Once you all deliver this water to your designated gas giants, the wentals will spread through the clouds like an unstoppable flood. The drogues won't know what hit them.' He laughed. 'Or maybe they will, but they'll still lose.'

'The Eddies didn't do much good when they knocked their thick heads against the drogues at Osquivel,' Zhett Kellum said sourly. 'It'll be a pleasure to show them how it's done.'

'Sounds better than a Klikiss Torch, by damn,' said her father. 'At least we'll still have a planet left when we're done!'

Near sunset, another small Roamer vessel arrived. As the straggler descended to the edge of the water, a thick arm of living ocean rose up to form a liquid landing platform, safely apart from the rocky archipelago where the other diverse craft had settled down. The ship rested calmly on the shimmering platform, buoyed up by the silvery-blue shelf. Even before she emerged, confident and alive with her power, Nikko guessed that it was Speaker Peroni. His shoulders sagged with relief. *She* could organize the whole operation!

The Roamer volunteers gathered around. Most were defiant and eager to launch a strike against the drogues. She swept her gaze across all the people, obviously pleased by the size of their ragtag force.

'Jess just sent me a message through the wentals. He is going to make an immediate assault on Qronha 3 – but that will be only one of many simultaneous strikes. Hydrogue gas giants are located all across the Spiral Arm. The wentals have dispatched detailed navigational information to all the water bearers and their respective teams, sorting gas giants by distance from each distribution world. There will be no overlap in targets. Everyone will know exactly where to go.'

'We haven't made any assignments here yet, Speaker Peroni,' Nikko said.

She looked around. 'With all the ships here, I'm guessing we have at least fifteen separate distribution groups. I will provide updated charts and specific target worlds for each group. With us, and all the other squads from the various distribution worlds, we can take care of hundreds of drogue gas giants in a few days' time.

'When they come under attack, the hydrogues will probably try to jump through their transgates to other gas giants. But if we

521

hit everywhere at once, they'll have no place to go, no way to escape. We can't allow them to keep a single foothold. We must leave no safe worlds for them to run to.' The Roamers cheered, ready for the fight.

On their star charts, Speaker Peroni outlined the upcoming offensive. Datapoints scattered across the Spiral Arm marked the extent of the hidden hydrogue empire. As the Roamer volunteers shared information and compared charts, a restless Nikko paced around his odd-looking ship. Everything was ready.

Before they all climbed aboard their separate ships, however, Cesca pointed out across the restless waves. Nikko felt his heart thrum, like the string of a plucked musical instrument.

The Charybdis sea stopped churning, and the waves flattened in an eerie calm. A cigar-shaped projectile shot upwards like a missile fired from underwater. The spindle-shaped torpedo was made entirely of wental fluid formed into a new ship. Before the first wental torpedo had disappeared into a sky full of storm clouds, five more silvery ships rocketed out of the waves. Then another ten.

Nikko tried to follow the torpedoes with his eyes, but they flew too fast, vanishing into the sky. 'If the wentals could do that all along, then why do they need us? And all our ships?'

Speaker Peroni smiled. 'Those are intense kernels of wental energy, as different from the water in your tankers as diamond is from coal. The wentals can create only a few of them – but, ah, the blows they will strike!' She paused as if receiving a message. 'We'd better get back to our ships and launch. Jess is about to reach Qronha 3.'

ONE HUNDRED AND EIGHT

GENERAL KURT LANYAN

More than a dozen EDF perimeter scouts sounded alarms at the same time. The unidentified armada diving into Earth's solar system was so enormous that sensors went off like popcorn bursting in a superheated flame.

'Hundreds of targets, General! Looks like almost a thousand!'

Permanently stationed aboard the *Goliath*, Lanyan rallied his last-ditch defensive forces, pulling every remaining Manta, weapons platform, and gunship together to form what he hoped would be an impenetrable cordon for their final stand. 'Everybody awake! Looks like this is it, here they come. If that's the hydrogues, form a wall that they're not going to get through!'

With a ricochet of communication bursts, the platcoms and Manta captains announced their readiness. Ships scrambled in from opposite sides of the system and high outer orbit. Lanyan ordered all weapons hot and ready to fire, jazer banks charged, projectile weapons loaded into rail-gun tubes. Like angry hornets, Remora squadrons flew out, ready for the most intense dog-fight in history. Sensor hits from the unknown vessels filled the screens like a whiteout snowstorm. He actually uttered a prayer. A sincere one.

'Message coming in, General,' said the *Goliath*'s communications officer.

'The drogues want to talk? Put it on screen.'

'Not the hydrogues, sir.'

An image of the proud Ildiran Adar resolved in front of him. 'By order of the Mage-Imperator, I am here to deliver two cohorts of Solar Navy warliners to assist in the defence of the Earth, each one fully armed and ready to fight.'

The sensor blips resolved into Ildiran vessels, each one adorned with streamers, antennae, and solar sails. Lanyan had never seen a prettier sight. '*Two* cohorts? That's almost seven hundred battleships!'

'Six hundred eighty-six. Upon further consultation, the Mage-Imperator decided to double our commitment, due to the extreme importance of this upcoming battle. The hydrogues will strike at Earth very soon.'

Excited conversation buzzed around the *Goliath*'s bridge. Lanyan grinned. 'You're a very welcome sight, Adar. Allow me to escort you to Earth.'

The EDF ships formed a parade, while hundreds of Ildiran warliners followed like fish in a perfectly coordinated school. As the mixed fleet approached Earth, the Solar Navy vessels went into a well-practised set of manoeuvres, as if showing off for observers. Each warliner was nearly as large as a Juggernaut, but they pirouetted around each other with clockwork precision. Though the General had often made quiet and deprecating comments about the stagnant alien Empire, he was certainly impressed by the prowess and coordination of their pilots.

'I hope they can fight as well as they can dance,' Lanyan said.

Once the ships in the combined fleets were in place, General

Lanyan requested to meet with Adar Zan'nh face-to-face aboard his flagship. 'I've always wanted to see one of your warliners up close, Adar.'

The Ildiran commander was surprisingly evasive. 'Perhaps later, General. For now we prefer our privacy.'

'Uh, sure.' As soon as he switched off the communication line, the General frowned. 'Anybody else get the impression that was one of those invitations where "later" actually means never?'

His new executive officer, Kosevic, nodded. Kosevic was a thin man with short bronze hair and eyes set just a little too wide. 'Certainly sounded that way to me, General.'

For this all-important defence, the General had hoped to use his former adjutant, Patrick Fitzpatrick III. In spite of that distressing confrontation during the young man's recent welcome-home party, Lanyan had requested his assignment to the *Goliath*, but Fitzpatrick was conveniently nowhere to be found. Lanyan suspected the kid's grandmother had something to do with that. Maybe Fitzpatrick needed to have the silver spoon taken from his mouth and shoved somewhere else . . .

For the moment, though, Lanyan kept puzzling over the Adar's reply. 'If the Ildirans would send seven hundred warships to help us against the drogues, why be paranoid about letting us go aboard? Is he hiding something?'

The exec was equally troubled. 'And I'm wondering how in the world *Ildirans* know the schedule of a hydrogue assault fleet. What sort of intelligence and espionage techniques do they have?'

Lanyan heaved a long sigh. 'We'll leave it for now. The last thing in the world I want to do is stir up trouble with our new best friends.'

ONE HUNDRED AND NINE

BASIL WENCESLAS

B asil stood with his face close to the angled glass and looked out into the falling night. He stared at the firefly lights of small commercial transport vehicles racing across the dark skies. Seen from atop the Hansa HQ, the Palace District was a magnificent sight. Though the Ildiran Solar Navy had come through with their promises, Basil was too preoccupied to feel any great relief.

Peter tried to kill me!

Orange flames curled from the cupolas and towers of the Whisper Palace, each torch symbolizing a world that had once signed the Hansa charter. It was all a sham. After the withdrawal of EDF protection, how many of those planets still felt any loyalty to Earth? The hydrogues would no doubt come and extinguish the rest of the torches. Peter had caused this all to spin out of control.

The self-important bastard tried to kill me!

Reflected against the darkening window, his face looked gaunt and drawn. He had been endlessly weary and agitated, struggling with so many burdens, trying to solve each crisis faster than a

new one could occur. He would have to order his medical specialists to give him better stimulants. Though he wasn't yet scheduled
for another rejuvenation treatment, he would feel more alert,
refreshed, and competent if he underwent the procedure. He
couldn't recall the last time he had even allowed himself the
release of sex with Sarein. Now he had assigned her a much more
difficult task – dealing with her sister the Queen . . .

They tried to poison me, and now Pellidor is dead!

The deputy seemed anxious. 'Nahton insists he has an
important report for King Peter. He's been trying to deliver an
urgent message since yesterday. Maybe we should hear what he
has to say.'

'He was already informed to give his message to me, or give
it to no one. The green priest needs to be reminded who's in
charge.'

Cain looked deeply displeased. 'That's exactly it, sir. He's
decided to say nothing. We're in the dark. I feel strongly that
it's a tactical error to cut ourselves off from vital intelligence.
We should make an exception in this case.'

'That green priest can communicate everywhere, instantly, via
telink. Should I give Peter a chance to secretly slip a message to
the whole Spiral Arm? I don't think so.' Basil fumed. 'We cannot
allow Nahton to keep his delusions that the King actually matters.
His reign is finished. Permanently.' Basil turned from the window
to stare at the pale deputy. 'He tried to *assassinate me*, Mr Cain.
Prepare for an immediate transition of power.'

A servant compy delivered a fresh pot of cardamom coffee,
but Basil ignored it. Not surprisingly, he had lost his taste for the
beverage.

The deputy was being deliberately obtuse. 'Do you have
proof the King was behind this? I have seen no results of the
investigation. Mr Pellidor appeared to be the man responsible.'

Basil's scowl turned into an outright sneer. 'And we must continue to let media reports reflect that. Damn Peter!' Thanks to the way the King had worked his twisted plan, and Sarein's misguided method of protecting Basil, the newsnet crews had all the proof they needed. Franz Pellidor had served him well for many years as a useful and committed expeditor and a man who knew how to keep secrets. But even though he was obviously uninvolved with the poisoning attempt, Pellidor had already been convicted by the public.

Basil had to endorse that popular perception and tar the reputation of his friend and ally. He had no choice but to make Pellidor look like a corrupt, evil conspirator. He could never let the King, even a miserable disappointment like Peter, seem to be at fault. If word got out that the King had actually attempted to murder the Chairman, the scandal would rock the already terrified and confused populace.

But Peter and his pregnant Queen would pay the price. Oh, yes. Sarein had already been given her instructions. It was time for Basil to see who his allies were . . . if he had any left.

With a wave of intense weariness, he sat behind his cluttered desk screen. 'Raymond Aguerra looked like such an exceptional candidate, on paper. Our watchers, including Mr Pellidor, observed him for more than a year. He had a terrible life, no future, very little potential. And we gave him everything. Why would he fight us?' He pounded a fist on his desktop, and the pot of coffee clinked against its tray. 'I should have eliminated him at the first sign of trouble and started fresh, like we did with Prince Adam.'

'Adam? I am not aware of—'

'No one is. He was to have been Frederick's successor, but we realized our mistake in time. The matter was resolved cleanly and quietly. But with Peter it's too late. We'll have to do a great deal of damage control.' Basil knotted his fingers together. 'Of course, if the damned hydrogues come, there won't be much of human history left to rewrite.'

He sighed. 'Maybe we have a chance, thanks to the Ildiran warliners. At least *somebody* proved to be reliable and did what he promised to do. Once we get rid of the King and Queen, we can start over again with a clean slate.'

'Forgive me for speaking frankly, Mr Chairman, but are you convinced Prince Daniel is truly our best alternative?'

'No, I am not. However, Daniel is all we have left.'

'Would you like me to talk to King Peter about his resignation? I can find an appropriate political excuse and send him and his Queen into quiet exile. At least Peter would still be available if Daniel turns out to be . . . even worse.'

'That is not an option! Peter has shown his true colours again and again.' Basil glared at his deputy. 'Why are you getting squeamish, Cain?'

'I'm offering rational alternatives, Mr Chairman. That is the job for which you appointed me.'

Even Cain sounded on the verge of insubordination! 'There are no alternatives, rational or otherwise.' It was difficult to hide his disappointment in his chosen deputy. Basil rubbed his itchy eyes. He wanted to be alone. 'You're dismissed. You have your instructions. I'll take care of the . . . messier details personally, if you are incapable of doing so.' *Damn, I could really use Pellidor now.*

Basil watched him go, considering. *Maybe it's time for me to seek another heir-apparent as well as a new King.*

ONE HUNDRED AND TEN

QUEEN ESTARRA

The next morning when Sarein came to take her, Estarra knew something was very wrong. 'Chairman Wenceslas asked me to do this. He . . . gave me clear instructions. I'm sorry, Estarra.' A deeply troubled expression crossed her sister's face, and she quickly turned away to hide it.

Estarra's suspicions screamed silently inside her head. *Is this it?* She said bitterly, 'I never thought it would be you, Sarein.'

She responded with a puzzled look. 'What do you mean?'

'I half-expected the royal guards to come in and gun us down, like the last Russian tsar and his family. But not my own sister.' On the other hand, she had grown to trust Captain McCammon, to a certain extent.

'Don't be melodramatic – I'm not going to hurt you, but I do need to show you something. Basil calls it your punishment.' Her dark eyes flashed quickly. 'And how can I blame him?'

Estarra regarded her coolly. 'So, did you verify any of the things I told you about? The attempts on our lives?'

530

Sarein's voice grew very small. 'Yes, I did. Now come with me, so we can get this over with.'

The Queen's feet felt leaden, and the air was heavy with the smell of danger. The royal guards let them out of the normally blocked door, and Sarein led her down the bright corridor to the private gardens in the glassed-in royal conservatory.

When the two of them stepped inside, the smell hit her like a slap. She detected the odours of dirt and chemicals with a sour undertone of soot. This place had been a sanctuary for her, a beautiful room of peace that held reminders of her Theron home. Now the stench made her gag.

What has he done?

The once-lovely greenhouse was barren and brown. Plants had been poisoned and burned. Some were completely uprooted, others scraped away, leaving only empty soil. All the carefully cultivated specimens from Theroc were gone . . . especially the fauldur berries.

Sarein took three steps through the doorway and turned towards Estarra, her face stricken as she stared at her sister with wide and glistening eyes. 'He did this just to hurt you. I could see it in his face. He knows you and Peter were involved in the poisoning plot. He can't prove it, but that doesn't matter.'

Estarra's breath hitched. She couldn't tear her gaze from the mangled plants, the brown and dying leaves. Just like the dolphins. *He finds something I love, and destroys it.* 'This is just the start of it.'

Sarein stepped closer to wrap her arms around Estarra. Estarra could feel her sister trembling. Sarein whispered in her ear, making sure no one could overhear her, 'I was sceptical of your story before, but now I know you were telling the truth. Basil isn't the man I thought he was – not anymore – and I'm very, very afraid of what he might do next.'

Estarra said, 'I told you, the Chairman means to get rid of Peter and me.'

After a long pause, Sarein said, 'I'm afraid you're right.' Still hugging Estarra and shielding them from the always-hovering royal guards outside the ruined conservatory, her sister whispered, 'As far as I can see, your only alternative is to get away from here, somehow.'

Estarra was careful not to answer. Could they slip out of the Whisper Palace? Yes, it was possible – Prince Daniel had done it. Once they got away, she and Peter could wear nondescript clothes and just vanish into the city.

Peter had told her about his younger years as a street kid. She was sure the two of them could survive out there, find little jobs, obtain food. Peter had provided for his mother and brothers enough times in the past. They might be safe. They could never expect to live like a King and Queen, of course, but Estarra was not a pampered child and could endure whatever she had to. A twinge in her abdomen reminded her that she also had the baby to worry about. Would the Queen of the Hansa have to give birth in a dark alley?

Quickly and guardedly, Sarein said, 'If you make any plans, don't tell me. I can't betray what I don't know.'

Estarra looked at her sister. 'If we do try to disappear, you know the Chairman will use every resource available to track us down. He hates loose ends. Where on Earth will we be safe?'

'You can't be safe on Earth. But maybe on Theroc.'

'Then, Sarein – come with us. We can all go together back home.'

'I can't do that!'

'How can you stay with him? You know what sort of man he is!'

'And I also know what sort of man he was.' Sarein continued

532

in a rush, laying out her excuses as if their were bullet-points in a trade presentation. 'Besides, I am more useful staying here as a voice of reason. I can talk to Basil. I can act as an intermediary in difficult situations.'

Estarra could not argue with her sister. She found she could not walk any farther into the devastated conservatory. In a low voice, she said, 'I'm never sure which side you're on, Sarein. I thought you loved the Chairman.'

'I do – at least, I did. Or maybe I just thought I did. But you're my *sister*. That will never change.'

ONE HUNDRED AND ELEVEN

KOLKER

To Kolker's astonishment, he learned there was another green priest inside the Prism Palace. She came to see him. 'We have a common bond. My name is Nira.'

He got to his feet quickly from the bench where he sat bathed in multicoloured light from a prismatic window. Kolker looked at her smooth green skin and identified her as a storyteller and a traveller by the tattoos on her face. 'How did you get here? Are you a prisoner as well?'

'Not a prisoner – not anymore. And neither are you.'

'I'll be a prisoner until I can touch a worldtree again, until I can feel telink. It's been so long.'

She reached out a calloused hand. 'Then come with me.'

In recent days, though Sullivan and the Hansa skyminers had finished their frantic work for the Solar Navy, Kolker had been spending a surprising amount of time with Tery'l. He had come to enjoy the company of the old lens kithman, and now he was actually interested in learning about the *thism*, about their belief in the soul-threads that bound all Ildirans together. It intrigued

534

him to think that every member of this race was linked in a way that no humans, not even green priests, could be. The realization made him somewhat sad

What he longed for most was to taste the buzz and flurry of the worldforest again, to reconnect with his friend Yarrod, to talk with all the other green priests. He had felt so lonely. But he knew the only treeling had been destroyed. He thought, however, that maybe Nira could fill some of his emptiness, perhaps ease the pain of his isolation. He wondered where she was taking him.

'I disappeared a long time ago, but I'm here with the Mage-Imperator of my own free will.' Nira sketched out the basics of her story. Kolker already knew that Ildirans did many unbelievable things. When he heard what had happened to her, though, the shock was almost unbearable.

'Not all Ildirans are treacherous like that,' she assured him. 'Let me show you.'

He followed her through winding bright corridors towards the glassed-in rooftops of the highest towers. She seemed to know exactly where she was going, and Kolker didn't ask questions. There was so much he didn't understand anymore.

Finally they emerged onto a rooftop where gardens had been planted. A maze of colourful shrubs and blooming flowers flourished in the bright sunlight. 'I placed it up here, where it could spread its fronds under the open sky.'

When Kolker saw the tiny worldtree growing out of a lump of burned wood, his pulse began to pound. His hands reached out as if he were a drowning man grasping a lifeline. 'Where – where did this come from?'

Tenderly, Nira bent over the charred wood from which fronds extended like sprouts from a redwood burl. 'I was able to find life within this shard. By connecting through telink, and using the

Mage-Imperator's *thism* as a catalyst, I guided the forest mind back. The sap flowed, and the wood came alive again.'

Kolker had been starving for this connection ever since his own treeling had tumbled from the cloud harvester on Qronha 3. He remembered clinging to the potted plant, trying to remain in contact, but he had tripped. Even now he winced at the memory. His fragile treeling had spilled into the clouds.

Reverently yet ravenously, Kolker touched the thin, supple frond, and with a mighty rush his thoughts connected like a completed electrical circuit. Ever since he'd been cut off, he had imagined this euphoric moment.

In a flood that took both for ever and merely an instant, Kolker learned everything, communicated everything. He traversed the thick forests of thoughts and memories, reconnecting with many of his comrades. Yes, Yarrod was there, and overjoyed to learn that his friend still lived. He sought but could not find Rossia, Clydia, or many other green priests he had known, but they were dead, fallen in either the second hydrogue attack or during the Soldier compy revolt.

The worldforest and his green priest friends now knew what had happened to him, what the Mage-Imperator had done to the well-meaning Hansa skyminers. But Nira had already told them other threads of the story, how Sullivan's crew had been working frantically to assist the Solar Navy.

Kolker did not release the lump of wood, but continued to send and receive thoughts. He had tried to describe this sensation to the old lens kithman, but he hadn't been able to convey the depth of the experience to Tery'l. He looked up at Nira with eyes full of gratitude. When he finally released his grasp, Kolker felt the residual tingle of what he had experienced. And yet . . .

Nira was smiling at him. 'Now you have rejoined the world-forest. Isn't that what you were waiting for?'

'Yes!' But inside he felt oddly empty. Blinded and starving, he had longed for this for so many months. So many months. He should have been overjoyed. To his surprise, though, it hadn't been as magnificent as what he had described to Tery'l. Had he forgotten? Or had he himself changed?

After releasing the treeling, Kolker felt utterly disconnected again. Not like the *thism* bonds that the lens kithman described. Kolker found his return to the worldforest mind mysteriously dissatisfying, and he didn't know what to think.

ONE HUNDRED AND TWELVE

KING PETER

Both the King and Queen knew they were in the path of an oncoming storm. Estarra had been sickened by what happened to her lovely conservatory, and the malicious pleasure the Chairman obviously took in having Sarein show it to her, but they knew it was only an opening salvo. The destruction of the greenhouse was barely even a warm-up for what was going to happen to them.

Isolated in the royal apartments — though not as isolated as Basil assumed — Peter pored over the details of the Chairman's latest daily summary briefing, which he wasn't supposed to have. Captain McCammon had been forbidden to forward those reports to him anymore, but the summary had appeared on his screen unexpectedly that morning. Peter assumed Deputy Cain was the anonymous sender.

He drank in details about the defensive deployment of the EDF ships and Ildiran warliners, as well as the preparations being made on Earth for the imminent hydrogue attack. Chairman Wenceslas had figuratively tied the King's hands, but as Peter

538

flexed and twisted, he felt the invisible bonds begin to loosen. He and the Queen would have to do something drastic, and soon.

'Peter!' Estarra said, her voice a quick whisper.

He turned to see two figures standing at their door, unannounced. Captain McCammon and his three fellow royal guards blocked them, but McCammon seemed inclined to let the visitors through. One was Sarein, unsuccessfully trying to cover her furtive anxiety; the other figure was cowled, with a hood that shrouded his face and gloves that covered his hands.

Peter looked at Estarra, who gave a slight nod. 'It's all right, Captain. Let them in,' he said.

Sarein ducked into the chambers as if anxious to get out of view. The stranger with her stepped forward and pulled the hood back to reveal crude flesh-coloured make-up smeared across his face to hide the emerald-green skin.

'Nahton!' Estarra sounded delighted, but the man remained grave.

Sarein drew a deep breath. 'When I learned that Basil is intentionally keeping the green priest away from you, I knew I had to do something. I thought you needed to hear his urgent message. Nahton refuses to tell it to anyone but you two.'

Peter looked at McCammon, who stood at attention. 'That will be all, Captain. Please close the doors.'

The guard captain looked narrowly at Sarein, uneasy to leave the two guests alone with the King and Queen, in light of the recent assassination attempts. Estarra gave him a reassuring smile. 'It's all right, Captain.'

'This is in direct violation of the Chairman's orders,' he said. After a tense moment he lifted his chin. 'However, it is wisest for the King to be included in important matters.' The royal guards gave them the privacy they needed.

Once they were alone, Nahton tilted his head down.

'Chairman Wenceslas tried to force me to deliver my message to him instead of you, but I do not serve the Chairman. I do not serve the Hansa. I serve the worldforest.'

Feeling a thrill of possibilities run through him, Peter said, 'We could certainly use the services of a green priest right now.'

'What is your news, Nahton?' Estarra said. Sarein looked eager to hear, but also afraid to know.

'I have to tell you what the Ildirans and the hydrogues plan to do. I must explain about the verdani battleships, great trees, some of which will come here to Earth. And what the Roamers are doing, and the wentals.'

And so the court green priest recited everything he knew, informing and warning the royal couple. Peter held Estarra's hand, absorbing everything. Sarein listened with surprise, but added no comments.

When Nahton finished, the King said, 'And I need you to do something for me. Talk to the green priests and send word to Estarra's parents, so they know we need their help. We need Theroc. Also, I've got to get a message to the Roamers, make them understand that the Chairman's will is not the King's will. The Queen and I are being held prisoner, while Basil issues orders I abhor – in my name. I do not agree with what has been done to the Roamers. We need their ingenuity. We need all factions of humanity.'

Nahton nodded. 'Green priests have been sent to many orphaned Hansa colonies, and those Hansa colonies interact frequently with Roamer traders. When I get back to my treeling, I will spread the word swiftly through telink.'

'Thank you, Nahton,' the Queen said. Then she scowled at her sister. 'I suppose you're now going to run to the Chairman with your report?'

Sarein looked decidedly uncomfortable as the green priest

pulled up his hood and turned to go. 'Even if I wanted to, I'm not sure he would want to be bothered with seeing me. Ever since I raised the alarm at the banquet, made Pellidor drink the poisoned coffee, Basil is . . . not certain about me.'

'Looks like you ruined things for everybody,' Peter said bitterly.

She gave him a haughty glance. 'I would do it again if I had to.'

'We've all had to do things we never expected to do,' Estarra said. 'Thank you for bringing him here, Sarein. I know how difficult it must have been for you.'

'It'll be more difficult if we're seen.' She seemed very anxious to be going. When Nahton had his disguise in place again, the two of them slipped out past the royal guards and into the labyrinth of the Whisper Palace.

Before he closed the door again, Captain McCammon stepped into the royal apartments. He hesitated, as if screwing up his courage and wrestling with his loyalties. He lowered his voice, 'King Peter, at least five of my guards have come to me with grave concerns about the way the Chairman has handled the war and how he has treated you. They are not certain his intentions serve the best purposes of the Hansa.'

'That's an understatement,' Peter said. 'And what about you, Captain McCammon?'

'I thought I've made myself perfectly clear. I believe the Chairman has a great deal of blood on his hands – the blood of silver berets, of EDF crewmen, and potentially the whole human race. I believe many people died because you were not given vital and timely information. I won't have that on my conscience again.'

'What are the names of these other guards?' Estarra said.

McCammon fidgeted. 'They spoke to me in confidence. I feel obligated to protect their privacy.'

'I believe Queen Estarra means we would prefer for those

particular guards to be assigned to watch over us,' Peter said. 'There's no telling what enemies we may have to defend against, and I'd rather have someone I can count on.'

McCammon smiled with relief. 'That is something I can most certainly do, Your Majesty.'

That night Peter slept restlessly, knowing that at any time some assassin might come to kill him, to kill both of them. How long would Basil wait to act?

He awoke suddenly, startled to hear OX's voice so close by their bed. 'King Peter, Queen Estarra, there is a visitor who must speak with you.' Peter lurched upright. Outside, the Palace District lights gave off just enough glow for him to see their chambers. OX waited politely, as if embarrassed to be so obtrusive.

'Another visitor?' Estarra's dark eyes flashed with fear.

As his eyes adjusted, he saw the spectral figure of a pale-skinned man next to the compy. 'I apologize for this unorthodox and unscheduled meeting, King Peter. I felt that this circumstance was urgent enough to merit such a risk. You know your days are numbered.'

Deputy Cain had already helped them, but was anyone in the Hansa government to be completely trusted? Peter got out of bed. 'The Chairman must have his eyes on you, too. Aren't you afraid you'll be seen? How did you get in here?'

The deputy raised a dismissive hand. 'It is late at night, and I have enough connections to avoid suspicion for a brief time. Your royal guards were somewhat cooperative.' He found a chair and sat down. 'If you had succeeded in killing the Chairman, that would have been a neat solution to our little dilemma. I would have become his replacement, and you and I could have reached an accord. However, that sort of coup is no longer possible. Chairman Wenceslas will never leave himself so vulnerable again, and he will eliminate you both very soon. I wouldn't suppose you have more than a day or two before he creates some other "fanatical assassin" lurking in the wings.'

'So why did you come here?' Peter asked. 'To tell us to say our prayers?'

'As I said, removing the Chairman is no longer an option. Therefore, you two have to leave. Preferably in a most unexpected way.' Cain extended several datapacks. 'These contain the schematics of the hydrogue derelict. Our research team has achieved many breakthroughs, all of which are documented here. An enormous amount of data. Our researchers do not have the incentive to go beyond the theoretical stage, but you, on the other hand, might consider it an unexpected exit strategy.'

Peter took the datapacks. He realized that any traditional vessel would certainly be intercepted, outrun, and outgunned by the EDF watchdog ships swarming protectively around Earth. But they wouldn't know what to do against the derelict – if it could be flown.

'And what about you, Deputy Cain? Care to make your exit as well? You know that Basil needs to be stopped for the good of the Hansa.'

Cain ran a finger over his colourless lips. 'What I know and what I can accomplish are two different things. I have made numerous secret leaks to the media, but I dare not do more. My own involvement must remain completely confidential, and I have already done more than I should. If the Chairman were to find out, more than my employment would be terminated.' He drifted back into the shadows. 'You can't rely on me any longer. I gave you information you can use. You two will have to decide what to do. After this, I am done. I hope you succeed in whatever plan you work out.'

'Are you sure there's nothing more you can do?' Peter asked, but Cain had melted into the dimness. He waited but heard no response. 'Mr Cain?' The deputy was gone.

OX remained with them. 'As always, I would be pleased to help you plan and implement strategy, within the strict parameters of my programming.'

Peter glanced at OX, then returned his full attention to his wife. 'We have to think beyond ourselves. While I need to save you and our baby, I know this is about more than just us. We have to take action for the good of humanity.'

He could see Estarra's dark eyes even in the dimness of their quarters. 'Peter, Chairman Wenceslas makes a serious error when he considers *humanity* to be only the members of the Hansa. He has disenfranchised the Roamers, and the Therons, and countless colonists on the worlds he's already written off. There's a whole lot more to the human race than those few the Chairman bothers to recognize.'

Peter looked at her. 'So, what are you saying?'

She took his hand. 'Sarein made the suggestion in the greenhouse yesterday. You are the King, and I am the Queen. If it's not safe for us to rule on Earth, then we have to go somewhere else. Theroc would take us in. It's perfect. And . . .' She lowered her voice. 'I would very much like to go home.'

'We can't do anything for humanity unless we're alive,' he agreed, holding the datapacks Cain had given them. 'But getting away from the Whisper Palace isn't good enough to accomplish what we need. If the King and Queen disappear, Basil will cover it up and simply install Daniel as King.'

'And humanity will keep sliding over the brink.'

Peter's gaze hardened. 'We don't dare leave Basil with any options. When we go, we have to take Daniel out of the picture, too.'

ONE HUNDRED AND THIRTEEN

MAGE-IMPERATOR JORA'H

Although Jora'h had done exactly as the hydrogues commanded – sending Adar Zan'nh with all his Solar Navy ships to Earth – sixty diamond warglobes returned to Ildira. Obviously the deep-core aliens doubted his resolve.

They intend to destroy us, no matter what. Jora'h could see that now.

More than a thousand Ildiran warliners gathered in orbit, ready to protect the Mage-Imperator. Though far outgunned by the anxious defenders in orbit, the hydrogue ships hurtled down through the sky, demonstrating the arrogance of the enemy: they considered a mere sixty warglobes to be a sufficient deterrent.

Even so, those diamond spheres were more than enough to destroy the Prism Palace, kill the Mage-Imperator, and obliterate Mijistra – if they chose to. If even a hundred Solar Navy ships careened down to smash into them, the explosions and the wreckage would cause a breathtaking amount of damage to the city. And the hydrogues could always call for more of their diamond ships.

Tal On'h's current desperate evacuation of Hyrillka had drawn away many of the largest ships in the Solar Navy, recruiting Tal

Ala'nh's entire cohort. Now, refugee-laden ships were streaming back to Ildira, bearing hundreds of thousands of displaced Hyrillkans. But this was no longer a safe place, not for any of them.

As soon as the threatening warglobes appeared, Jora'h ordered Nira and Kolker into hiding. Knowing how the hydrogues hated the verdani, he could never let them become aware that *green priests* were inside the Prism Palace.

Osira'h stayed by his side, smiling mysteriously up at her father. 'My mind is open. I feel the warglobes overhead. The hydrogues are angry ... but they are always angry. They are suspicious. They do not understand Ildirans.'

'They have not tried to understand us. That is their mistake, and their weakness.' Looking at her, he tried to reinforce his confidence. 'You will not let them learn our secret?'

'I will not.' Her voice carried not even the hint of a doubt.

Fresh from the gathered defensive cohorts above, Tal Lorie'nh waited in the skysphere reception hall as an adviser. 'I hope you are right, Liege.' An older officer with an adequate if undistinguished career, Lorie'nh was a tall, thin man who rarely took chances, never surpassed expectations. Jora'h knew, however, that he would serve in any capacity the Mage-Imperator requested.

Jora'h had already made up his mind, though he believed it would cost his race dearly. Through the rush of evacuees from Hyrillka, as well as reports from other Solar Navy ships, he knew that the hydrogues were engaged against the faeros on numerous fronts. Now that Nira had regained her telink connection to the worldforest, she shared with Jora'h what she had learned about the widespread efforts being planned simultaneously across the Spiral Arm. How much more could the deep-core aliens endure? The wentals and the verdani battleships might be enough to turn the tide. Did they really want to fight the Solar Navy at the same time?

Perhaps we will survive this after all. If we are strong ... and if we are lucky. He would live or die by the consequences of his decision. He knew precisely what he needed to say. This was *his* realm.

When the hydrogue emissary finally came to the Prism Palace, Jora'h stood to meet him. He placed his hand on Osira'h's shoulder as the small pressurized chamber came to a stop in front of the dais. Tal Lorie'nh looked alarmed and anxious. He had never seen a hydrogue so close before, had never even faced them in direct battle.

Jora'h watched the humanoid shape appear behind the transparent wall. The clock was ticking, the Mage-Imperator knew. With a firm voice, he let his displeasure flow. 'Why do you come here? I already dispatched my Solar Navy ships to Earth, as you demanded. Can you not see that I have cooperated?'

The emissary's voice was flat. 'We are here to guarantee that you do as you promised, or to punish you if you fail.'

Jora'h did not allow his expression to change, but he felt a cold shaft of ice pierce his chest. 'That is not necessary.'

'Nevertheless, we intend to stay here until the battle at Earth is satisfactorily completed. We will know immediately if you betray us.'

Jora'h showed no fear. Ildirans believed they were born as part of a grand cosmic story, and they considered *The Saga of Seven Suns* to be a true map that delineated the reality of past and present. But his father had shown him that much of the information was distorted, even false. What mattered most was what he actually *did*. He would not be described as a coward and a betrayer in the *Saga* . . . if anyone survived to write new stanzas.

Though he felt powerless, Jora'h did not back down. He clenched his hands, reaching a difficult decision. 'You do not trust us? Very well. To further demonstrate my cooperation, I will send even more Solar Navy ships to Earth. Tal Lorie'nh! As soon as the hydrogue emissary leaves, take your entire cohort to Earth as well. Adar Zan'nh may require assistance.'

The thin military officer blinked, looked confused, then finally found the right words. 'As you say, Liege. As soon as the emissary departs.'

Jora'h turned back to the pressurized sphere. 'I have now provided more than a thousand Solar Navy warliners — I expect that will be sufficient to defeat whatever remains of the Earth Defence Forces. Now are you satisfied?'

'We are still watching. Closely.' The thunderstorm tension dissipated in the air, yet Jora'h did not relax. He wasn't sure if his bluster had convinced the emissary, but the hydrogue had nothing further to say. Levitating from the tiled floor, the small sphere drifted back down the Palace corridors, escorted by soldier kithmen who could not have fought against it even if they'd wanted to.

When the chamber was empty again, both Osira'h and Tal Lorie'nh stared at him as if he had gone as mad as Rusa'h. Lorie'nh blurted, 'Liege, if I take my cohort away, Ildira will be dramatically weakened! The hydrogues are looming over our heads.'

'I do not trust what the hydrogues will do at Earth,' he said, 'and we do not dare lose there. We must be absolutely certain to crush the enemy. Travel with all the speed you can possibly manage, or you will arrive too late.' The Mage-Imperator drew another deep breath, aware of the death sentence he was about to pronounce. 'There is no time for Sullivan Gold and his engineers to work on your ships, Lorie'nh. I am sorry.'

The tal remained stiff and formal. 'My crew and I understand what we may have to do.'

Jora'h nodded. 'We will not lack for defences here, Lorie'nh. I will keep two cohorts to defend the Prism Palace, and many septas of loaded warliners are returning from Hyrillka every day.' He lowered his voice and looked at his daughter. 'The question is, can we wound the hydrogues enough to make them leave us alone?'

Osira'h gave her father an oddly distant but reassuring smile. 'Just wait. Do not give up.'

'What is it you know? What are you thinking?'

She smiled enigmatically. 'I have the powers that centuries of breeding experiments sought to create, and I've already established a link. I *am* a bridge with the hydrogues, and my mother has given me an idea. Maybe I can do more than you or the hydrogues expect.'

ONE HUNDRED AND FOURTEEN

ANTON COLICOS

Hydrogues and faeros continued to battle in Hyrillka's primary sun. Solar flares rippled outwards, ionic bursts disrupted transmissions, and weather patterns changed significantly. Each change produced an additional hindrance to the evacuation operations, but Tal O'nh bulldozed through them with all the efficiency he had shown when organizing the initial relief efforts.

By the time Tal Ala'nh arrived with hundreds more ships to take evacuees, the one-eyed veteran had already loaded most of his original warliners and dispatched them back to Ildira. With so many hydrogues and faeros in the vicinity, he did not want the crowded warliners to remain in the Hyrillka system. Together, two Solar Navy cohorts would be sufficient to carry all the inhabitants away to safety before the great battles killed the star.

'One step forward, two steps back,' Anton said. 'I think this planet has one whopper of a string of bad luck.'

Vao'sh gathered armloads of apocryphal documents from the vault. 'Peaceful times make for dull stories, Rememberer Anton.'

The two scrambled to retrieve records from the archives beneath the citadel palace. At first they took great care to keep everything organized, but toward the end, they simply threw everything into protective containers. Even Yazra'h helped them, as a special favour to Anton, though she also discharged a hundred other obligations during the frantic exodus.

The din of the spaceport was deafening. Warliners landed fourteen at a time, far more than the spaceport's capacity. The big ships dropped down into open fields and empty plazas, any place large enough to accommodate them. Personnel shuttles flitted across the landscape, rescuing outlying Ildirans who could not reach the main evacuation depots.

This struggle made Anton's chest tighten with dread. He sensed time slipping away from him in an accelerating plunge. The unbelievable operation was being accomplished with unheard-of efficiency, but even with almost seven hundred huge Ildiran battleships, how could they ever get everyone off the planet in time?

The boy Designate was crushed at the loss of such an old and respected colony, and Anton felt deeply sorry for him. Exactly as Yazra'h had taught him, the boy appropriately showed only resolve when he appeared before his people; but in private he was obviously shattered by the turn of events. 'I could have made it work,' Ridek'h said, as he watched a pair of workers carry another crate of diamondfilm sheets aboard a landed shuttle. 'We were going to make Hyrillka a good place to live again.'

'And the people believed in you, Designate.' Yazra'h's use of the title seemed to build up the young man's self-confidence. 'But now your obligations have changed. Your duty as Hyrillka Designate is to protect your people – and right now that means saving them from the destruction of their world.'

Rememberer Vao'sh said to the boy in a voice perfectly tuned to play his heartstrings, 'I will make sure that the Hall of Rememberers writes your role in these events properly, Designate Ridek'h. Never before has such a young man earned a place in *The Saga of Seven Suns*.'

Neither Anton nor Vao'sh spoke as they climbed aboard the shuttle and headed towards the waiting flagship. They sat together, both feeling dismayed.

Once back in the command nucleus, Anton watched high-resolution images of the churning clash in the sun, and the sight horrified him. Hyrillka's primary star was dying. Flaming ellipsoids slammed into warglobes by the hundreds. From somewhere within the star itself, the fiery creatures turned solar flares into weapons, blasting out huge arcs of ionized gas in a disintegrating wave that even the warglobes couldn't withstand. Even so, faced with such overwhelming numbers, the faeros fireballs winked out one by one. The blue-white star now looked like a churning stewpot.

Scientist kithmen performed calculations to estimate how much longer the primary sun would last. If the main star did burn out, they postulated how swiftly and dramatically the climate would change with only the dull orange secondary. The sudden extreme drop in solar flux would cause unimaginable upheaval. Mega-hurricane storms would literally tear the atmosphere apart. Temperature shifts would rip the landscape, sparking seismic or volcanic activity. No living thing was likely to survive the transition.

'A real disaster story,' Anton muttered.

ONE HUNDRED AND FIFTEEN

JESS TAMBLYN

Jess's wental vessel plunged like a bullet towards the cloudy gas giant. Together with the water elementals, he would fight the drogues, and he would bring Tasia and the other human prisoners out alive. Because of all the wentals had learned from him, they understood his drive, his connection to his family, his love for other individuals.

Though reinforcements would arrive soon, Jess did not intend to wait — not if Tasia was down there. As he struck Qronha 3's rarefied atmosphere, plunging headfirst into an impossible struggle, the wentals roiled inside and around him, spoiling for a fight. He wouldn't be doing this alone.

Water droplets sprang from the surface of his ship, rushing through the clouds in an explosive release of wental power, dancing from one atmospheric water molecule to another. Wental energy crackled and spread, splashing into the layers of gases like coloured dye spreading through a jar of liquid.

The first strike.

Descending, Jess peered through the curved walls but could

see only storms and mists outside his vessel. Inside his mind, the wentals described their expanding fight, though in terms he could barely comprehend. In the same way they had tamed storm-racked Golgen, the wentals now exerted a stranglehold on this planet.

Suddenly hydrogue warglobes boiled up all around him. Blue lightning lanced out to strike the wental-infused cloud decks. Jess careened away from one spinning warglobe, narrowly escaping a crackling bolt of energy. With a sharp manoeuvre, he dodged again, then plunged deeper.

He barely avoided ramming a warglobe that emerged from a thundercloud; the hydrogue did not see him, did not open fire, apparently too preoccupied fighting its elusive enemies. As he streaked past, Jess noted that the warglobe's polished diamond exterior was becoming pitted, eaten away as if by acid. The wental moisture was corrosive to them.

Guiding the small ship, Jess dodged, sweeping ever downwards. Ten more warglobes rocketed up from the depths and into the fray. The deep-core aliens must have a significant base or city somewhere far below. Jess had to find it, had to find his sister.

The dense atmosphere pressed in around his vessel's shell like a spherical vice, trying to crush it, but the wentals wouldn't allow that. *Jess* wouldn't allow that. With part of his mind connected to the soul of the ship, he followed the fading wakes of the drogue vessels back to their origin.

The air thickened to a heavy soup around him. Water drops split from the walls of his spherical vessel like splatters of molten metal from a burning meteor. As each energy-charged raindrop flew into the air, new wentals seeded the clouds and spread like a poison.

Exhilaration rushed like a white torrent through him. With sheer force of will, Jess maintained the integrity of his vessel even as the wental water sweated away. Parts of the mother-of-pearl framework sloughed off as the support ribs pulled together to hold the ever diminishing ball of water. Infused with the wentals, he could survive out in the hostile environment, just as he could live in the open vacuum of space. But he had to keep some reserve to protect his sister and the others.

As organic mists of long-chain aerosols blurred his vision, Jess identified the awesome hydrogue cityplex: a cluster of geometric domes and interlinked enclosures, structures impossible to comprehend. From here, on this very planet, the hydrogues had launched warglobes to attack helpless humans . . . all those ruined Roamer skymines . . . Ross's Blue Sky Mine.

Focusing the intensity of his gaze like a laser, Jess made the water-and-pearl vessel hurtle forward. Never decreasing speed, the spinning ship crashed through the protective membranes surrounding the floating cityplex. His vessel careened into the alien metropolis and cruised past the polyhedral building structures. Hydrogue infestations.

Jess raced down streets and between tall angled complexes of the strange city. His senses were alert for any hint as to where he might find the human prisoners. As he searched, wental senses directed him, helped him track down the protected prison. Seeping through water molecules in the air, the wentals seemed to know he was growing closer every moment. Tasia was somewhere nearby.

Down in the streets among inverted bridges and Möbius-strip arches, liquid-crystal forms gathered like puddles of mercury to stand against him. The hydrogues in this cityplex were aware of his intrusion and pulled together to prevent him from succeeding in what he had come to do.

The diminished water-and-pearl ship drifted to a halt as the hydrogues blocked its passage. Pooled in front of Jess's vessel, the hydrogues rose into shapes, coalescing until they all stood in front of him as an army of perfectly identical, exquisitely detailed replicas.

Jess could not move.

They were all Ross.

ONE HUNDRED AND SIXTEEN

ZHETT KELLUM

When all the Roamer ships were full of wentals from the living oceans of Charybdis, Speaker Peroni dispatched her squadrons. The planning and distribution had been complex, with so many target planets and a limited number of ships to do it. Zhett Kellum damn well expected to do her part.

In groups of twos and threes, the hodgepodge vessels flew to their chosen infested gas giants. The fourteen Plumas tankers, even the small cargo and passenger cruisers, were filled to bursting with wentals, enough to engulf the drogues in a massive multi-pronged assault.

On target and on schedule, Zhett and her father flew their water-laden cargo haulers towards the first planet on their list: Welyr, a burned-out-looking gas giant where the rusty clouds reminded her of old bloodstains. Zhett's father had requested this world in particular. He had a score to settle here.

'I took too damn long to ask Shareen to marry me, but we were planning on it – before the drogues, that is,' Kellum mused over

557

the transmission line, sounding regretful. 'Those bastards smashed her skymine right down there.'

'Oh, Dad,' Zhett said from her cargo hauler. She could barely remember her real mother, who had died when Zhett was very young. Her father had always been businesslike and independent, and Shareen Paternak was also tough and stubborn. The two had made a perfect couple.

He continued, 'Never had a chance to say goodbye. I'm glad to be doing this for all the clans – but by damn, this is personal for me.'

'Let's send those warglobes packing and get on with our lives.'

'Are you sure you wouldn't like to strike the first blow, my sweet?'

She snorted. 'There'll be enough drogues for all of us, Dad.'

The two water-bearing ships dived towards the upper layers of the ruddy gas giant. Cargo hatches opened, spilling thousands of litres of energized water, and the freed wentals dispersed into the swirling clouds.

Cruising along, the ships roared above the misty layers, continuing to drop a rain of water elementals. When they were certain the task was accomplished, they ascended to a safe altitude. Peering through the slanted cockpit panes, Zhett watched rapid storm systems form as the wentals spread out from the seeded clouds like a flame front devouring dry tinder.

'If warglobes come after us now,' she said, 'they're going to run smack into spreading wentals.'

The Roamer ships had swung over to the nightside of Welyr. Zhett resisted the urge to spill even more water into the dark clouds. The wentals were already propagating swiftly enough. She could tell her father was anxious to move on.

'Save some for the next gas giant, my sweet,' he transmitted.

'We've done what we need to do, and it's time to head off to our second target.'

'Then let's be off. Just when I was starting to have fun. Next stop, Osquivel – six hours away by stardrive.'

'Ah, Osquivel. Back to our old stomping grounds – to do some genuine stomping, by damn.'

Behind them, as they departed, the battle raged in the skies of Welyr.

GENERAL KURT LANYAN

The EDF ships and two cohorts of Ildiran warliners settled into a well-choreographed defensive pattern around Earth, just waiting for the hydrogues to show themselves. The far-outnumbered human battleships circled with ornate Solar Navy vessels both outside and inside the perimeter. More Ildiran warliners patrolled widely.

On the bridge of the *Goliath*, General Lanyan counted down the hours, simultaneously eager and full of dread. He had no way to guess when the damned enemy fleet would show up. Adar Zan'nh hadn't been specific, nor had he revealed how the Mage-Imperator had obtained his information in the first place. The Ildirans were so enamoured with stories, he wondered if they'd ever heard the one about Chicken Little.

Basil Wenceslas contacted him three times daily for updates. Though Lanyan reassured him, the Chairman still sounded uncomfortable about all the unanswered questions. The General answered reassuringly, 'We're fully staffed and as ready as we

560

can be, sir. We may have diminished crews, but we're capable of running our ships just fine without Soldier compies.'

The Chairman did not seem cheered by the information. 'No surprise, considering we only have a fraction of the vessels we had a month ago.'

'I will inform you of any changes.' Lanyan quickly got off the channel. At least here in the home system, he didn't need a green priest for direct communication. Besides, there weren't any green priests available other than Nahton at the Whisper Palace. And according to the Chairman, Nahton had recently become intractible.

EDF Remoras circled alongside the much larger Ildiran warliners. Though the scout flyers transmitted greetings to the giant ships, the alien crews sent no response. Ildirans had always been standoffish; every EDF soldier knew that.

The fighter pilots extended a network of tripwire sensors farther out to the fringes of the solar system in hopes of spotting the approaching warglobes. Multiply-redundant teams kept diligent watch, waiting for the invasion force to sweep in. All eyes were turned outwards, looking into the deep interstellar distance for the earliest possible warning.

No one, however, expected the enemy to suddenly appear from *inside the solar system*.

At Jupiter, the gas giant nearest to Earth, the white and ochre cloud bands began to boil. Like a horde of barbarians, more than a thousand diamond warglobes emerged from a hidden hydrogue base.

The first direct clash between the Earth Defence Forces and the enemy had occurred at Jupiter. There, hydrogues had utterly defeated the most powerful EDF battleships. Now the deep-core aliens came back through a transgate inside the giant planet – a back door, an undefended route into the solar system. Hydrogues emerged inside the outer perimeter, already within humanity's first line of defences.

The asteroid belt shipyards were the first to report the disturbance. High-resolution extreme magnification imagers spotted warglobes streaming like a barrage of cannon balls up from the cloud bands. The initial warning came from a spacedock inspector. 'General, the warglobes are coming, and coming! We've already dispatched the few fast-response ships we have left.'

Urgent alarms sounded on the *Goliath*'s bridge. The crew, already tense and on high alert, scrambled to their battle stations. Lanyan knew the few swift craft from the shipyards didn't stand a chance. 'Withdraw and do not engage!'

The shipyard pilots were space construction workers, and none of them had ever expected to go into direct combat. Now, facing the armada of warglobes, they performed standard evasive manoeuvres. But after two blasts from the front line of oncoming hydrogues, the pilots' transmissions ended in static.

The General issued orders. 'All ships, withdraw from the outer solar system immediately! Get your asses in close – the drogues are already here!'

'General, what if this is just a feint?' said his exec. 'What if even more warglobes are coming from outside the system?'

Lanyan looked over at him. 'If that's the case, Mr Kosevic, then we're all dead.'

EDF station ships pushed their in-system engines to their limits, swooping down towards the Sun with all possible speed. But as widely separated as they were, it would take hours for them to arrive.

Lanyan paced the bridge, knocking his fists together. 'Inform Adar Zan'nh – just in case he hasn't been paying attention. We need every possible defence close to Earth – *now*.'

On the tactical screens, the tally of warglobes already exceeded seven hundred, and more continued to stream out of the transgate deep within Jupiter.

Reinforced EDF hull armour was designed to resist known hydrogue weapons. Each gunship, Manta, and Thunderhead had a full arsenal of shaped charges, fracture-pulse bombs, carbon-carbon slammers, and intensified jazers. Even so, Lanyan doubted they had enough to do more than annoy an enemy fleet of such magnitude.

He gave orders to his helmsman, 'Bring our defensive ring out to stand guard.' Admiral Sheila Willis acknowledged from her rescued Manta and flew to the forefront of the fight.

Ildiran warliners joined the EDF battleships as the human vessels pulled forward. Behind them came the second cohort of Solar Navy vessels; all told, they presented an extremely intimidating front. But the hydrogues did not slow as they rushed in, aiming at Earth as if it were a bull's-eye.

The tension among his crew was palpable. Lanyan used the intership direct line, saying whatever words came out of his mouth, not bothering to think of how he would be quoted in the history books.

'Buckle in and get ready to meet the drogues head on. If those ships get past us, they'll destroy Earth and then go on to exterminate every one of our colonies. You know damn well that I might be asking you to fight to the death today, but *we* are the last line of defence. If we don't stop the enemy here, there isn't going to be a tomorrow.'

The warglobes tumbled relentlessly closer, looking like the spiked balls on the end of an ogre's medieval weapon. Lanyan knew that his EDF was as ready as it could be. Every Remora had been launched. Mantas, Thunderheads, and various gunships swirled around like wasps trying to block a herd of stampeding elephants.

'Prepare to open fire.' Lanyan broadened the transmission. 'Adar Zan'nh, are you ready?'

'I am here to do my duty.'

Seconds before the warglobes came within firing range, the Ildiran commander sent a silent signal to his ornate battle-ships. Nearly seven hundred warliners spun about in a precision manoeuvre as if they were all connected to the same puppet strings. Every one of the Ildiran vessels turned their weapons ports away from the hydrogues and aimed at Lanyan's last-stand fleet.

In an instant, the Solar Navy warliners completely surrounded Lanyan's ships. All of them.

'What the hell?' The General lurched to his feet.

Ahead, the warglobes slowed, dispersing to take up positions – exactly as if they had expected this to happen!

Lanyan ran to the communications console, opened a channel to the Ildiran flagship. 'Adar Zan'nh, what the hell are you doing?'

It was a rhetorical question, though. General Lanyan knew a betrayal when he saw one.

ONE HUNDRED AND EIGHTEEN

KING PETER

Four hours before dawn, Peter awoke to the sounds of urgent activity outside the royal suite. After Cain's warning the night before, OX had stationed himself inside their locked-down chambers to keep watch in case Basil made his move before they could implement their own plans.

Estarra hurried to the balcony and stared out. The Palace District illumination banks switched off one by one. The brighter buildings dimmed like snuffed embers. Muffled sirens echoed through the streets. 'Peter, all the city lights are going out.'

He and Estarra had known something was going to happen, and they had to be ready to move the moment they saw an opportunity. From out in the corridor, he heard running footsteps and shouted orders. The royal guards were on the move. 'OX, do you know what's going on?'

The Teacher compy said, 'I have not been in contact with outside news sources, although this reminds me of when the first Ildiran septa arrived, long ago. The Earth government thought they were being invaded—'

'The hydrogues must be attacking.' Peter dressed quickly. Through the balcony window, the city's normal glow had faded to an ominous darkness. What possible good would a blackout do in the face of a civilization-destroying hydrogue armada?

Captain McCammon and the guards normally stationed outside their chambers snapped brisk comments back and forth. McCammon knocked his maroon beret askew as he touched an embedded earphone to receive an update. He quickly dispatched three of his uniformed men. '*—and run!*'

'Captain, what is it?' Peter's voice was calm and authoritative.

The guard captain snapped to attention. 'The hydrogues have launched an assault, Your Majesty – as we feared. The number of warglobes is even greater than we expected.'

'Will our perimeter ships be able to keep them away from Earth?' Estarra said.

McCammon's skin looked pale and grey in the dim emergency lighting. 'General Lanyan and the Ildirans are mounting a defence, but there seems to be some confusion. The Solar Navy warliners are not behaving as expected.'

The Ildirans? Nahton had told them what the Mage-Imperator might do.

'Has Chairman Wenceslas called for me yet?' He knew, of course, that Basil would never do such a thing.

'The Chairman is in the war room in an emergency council session. I've just sent your other guards to assist him.' McCammon and his fellow guard squared their shoulders and thrust out their jaws. 'Don't worry, Your Majesty. We can offer sufficient protection. Just the two of us. Loyal guards.' He seemed to be hinting at something.

Peter looked questioningly at the Queen. They would never get a better diversion, and the continuing confusion might assist their escape. It had to be now. Estarra gave a faint nod.

Peter slipped his hand inside his garments. McCammon had not noticed or commented upon the odd fact that the royal couple were wearing casual street clothes instead of their usual robes. Peter wrapped his fingers around the twitcher McCammon himself had given them in their escape from the poisoning attempt, hating what he had to do.

'Captain McCammon, I want to thank you for your service. You have done your duty well.' He struggled to keep the tremor out of his voice.

The praise brought a hint of a smile to the corners of McCammon's mouth. Knowing he could never turn back, the King drove aside his regrets, thinking of his wife, his unborn child, and all the deadly webs Basil had woven. Peter had no choice. He truly had no choice. Their lives were at stake.

He pointed the twitcher at McCammon's face. 'I'm very sorry, Captain. But if my Queen and I don't escape now, we'll never have another opportunity like this.'

The astonished second guard fumbled for his sidearm, but the guard captain moved in a surprising blur, yanking out his own twitcher and blasting the guard. The other man crumpled to the floor. It all had happened so quickly! Peter hadn't even been able to get off a shot. He looked at the fallen guard, still keeping his twitcher pointed at McCammon. 'I don't know why you did that, but we have to escape now. I'm sorry you're in the middle of this.'

'Sorry isn't good enough,' McCammon said. 'You didn't actually think I'd give you a functional weapon, did you?'

Peter glanced at the twitcher, wondering if McCammon's claim could be a trick. Surprisingly, the guard captain extended his own stun weapon, butt-first. 'It is a good thing you managed to overpower me and stun me with my own twitcher. I'm sure I'll be reprimanded, when all this is over.'

Peter looked at the original weapon in his hand – had it really been deactivated? – and at the twitcher McCammon extended to him. The guard captain glanced at the fallen guard. 'Don't worry about him. He's one of the loyal crowd. I'll have him eating out of my hand as soon as he wakes up – provided you and the Queen actually succeed in escaping.'

'What about the guards at the derelict?' Estarra asked. 'And at Prince Daniel's quarters?'

'Those are not my men,' McCammon said. 'They are Hansa servants, through and through. You'll have to deal with them yourselves.'

'We will,' Peter said.

'Make it look good,' McCammon said, then threw himself on the King, yelling. Instinctively, Peter fired the new twitcher, and the captain slumped beside his comrade on the cool, hard floor.

He and Estarra both looked at the two fallen guards. 'Now I suppose we don't have any choice,' Peter said.

'We never did. Let's go.' She picked up McCammon's limp arms. 'Help me drag these men inside where no one will see them.' Working together, the King, the Queen, and the compy pulled the unconscious guards across the slick stone floor into the royal apartments.

Since OX knew the secret ways of the Whisper Palace better than any of them, the Teacher compy led the way. The Palace normally kept a quiet night-time schedule with only a skeleton staff. Now, because of the alarms, many people ran through the dim halls. Fortunately, none of them paid attention to the King and Queen in their nondescript clothes.

At a brisk pace, OX rushed them through back corridors and service halls to Prince Daniel's plush apartments. As the compy hurried them towards the doorway, Peter saw that five royal guards remained in position to protect Daniel – more than had been assigned to watch over the King and Queen. Either Basil didn't trust Daniel, or he didn't dare risk his precious Prince.

Edgy because of the alarms, two of the guards stepped forward. The King knew from his training that personal demeanour was as much a part of recognition as any costume. He strutted forward to address the guards. 'What is this? Do you not salute when you see your King?' Estarra, obviously pregnant, completed the picture.

The guards snapped to attention.

OX walked briskly up to them. 'We must see the Prince.'

'The Prince is asleep, and we have orders not to let him be disturbed.'

'This an emergency, Sergeant,' Estarra said. 'Your orders have changed.'

'The hydrogues are attacking! We must speak to the Prince immediately.'

Surprised and still suspicious, the guards looked at each other in confusion.

Unable to wait for their compliance, Peter raised the twitcher and blasted the front two guards. He spun to the third man as the first pair melted to the floor, but the stunner only sputtered. An empty charge pack already!

The remaining guards whipped out their sidearms. 'That can't be the King!'

A thrumming shuddered through the air. 'Oh, yes it is,' said Estarra. She tucked a twitcher back into her loose pocket as the last three guards spasmed and fell to the floor. She looked at Peter, smiling. 'I took the other guard's weapon before we left him. I thought we might need an extra one.'

He gave her a kiss that was not nearly long enough, then looked around. The corridors were empty. The doors to side rooms were closed. 'Hurry! Daniel might have heard something. If he sees these guards, it will make everything more difficult.'

'Prince Daniel is a heavy sleeper,' OX pointed out. 'I doubt he has the curiosity to investigate a noise in the night. Even these alarms.'

Several doors in the hall were locked, but OX used his compy strength to break the latch on a storeroom filled with unmarked boxes. The layer of dust implied that the room might well have remained unopened since the reign of King Jack. By the time they had pulled all five guards inside and closed the door, Peter and Estarra were both panting and sweating.

'The lock no longer functions. We must be gone before the guards revive,' OX said.

'Count on it,' Estarra said.

Peter opened the door to the Prince's chambers, and strode in with the Queen and OX behind him. 'Daniel! Time to wake up. No time to waste.'

Tousle-headed and confused, the young man was already pulling a robe around himself. 'Why did you disturb me? And who are—' He rubbed his bleary eyes and stifled a yawn. 'You're the King! What are you doing in my quarters? Where are my guards?'

'This is an emergency, Daniel. They're guarding the Chairman.'

'What kind of emergency? Some sort of attack?'

'Yes,' Estarra said as kindly as she could. 'The hydrogues. You've got to come with us. Hurry!'

'We can take you to the Chairman,' Peter said.

'Do you know what time it is?' He blinked, then stared at Estarra and Peter again. 'And why are you two dressed like that? You don't look much like a King and Queen. It's an embarrassment.'

Peter gave the uncouth young man a meaningful look. 'The Chairman's in the middle of a crisis, and now he's calling you to him. Haven't you figured it out?'

From the blank expression on Daniel's face, obviously he hadn't. Peter continued, exasperated, 'The Chairman has ordered the Queen and me to retire. He promised us a new identity and a nice, safe villa where we can live a normal life, but only if we leave immediately. The Chairman plans to crown you right now. From tonight on, you'll be King.' He smacked his hands together, and Daniel jumped at the loud noise, unable to believe what he had just heard. 'So hurry up!'

'The Chairman wants to crown me? Tonight? But I thought—'

'You know how he is when he makes up his mind,' Estarra said. 'He decided this would be the most dramatic time.'

Grinning, the Prince hurriedly put on shoes. When he looked unsure about which clothes to wear, Peter gestured him to follow. 'Don't worry. There's a full staff waiting to dress you. But you have to come with us right now.'

Not knowing what else to do, and very frightened about the consequences of not obeying orders, Daniel followed them.

ADAR ZAN'NH

The humans didn't have a chance. Optimistic and over-ambitious, as always, they had hung all their hopes on one plan. They gambled everything on their last stand at Earth, and they believed Ildiran assurances. Now they were more vulnerable than ever.

The hydrogues were watching.

Though he'd never been overly fond of humans, Adar Zan'nh still felt soiled after the promises he had made, delivering the words exactly as the hydrogues, and his father, had told him to do. It did not seem right. Were the deep-core aliens truly monitoring even ship-to-ship transmissions? It seemed best to err on the side of caution. He particularly didn't like the thought of hydrogues using *his* Solar Navy to attack the Hansa.

Zan'nh looked stonily at the few Ildirans in his command nucleus. They all knew the Mage-Imperator's orders. He watched intricate tactical projections showing the hopelessly outnumbered EDF ships preparing to meet the oncoming wave of hydrogues. He was sitting on the crux of a moment that would always be remembered in *The Saga of Seven Suns*. Honour or victory . . . humans or Ildirans, survival or annihilation. The hydrogues had pushed them to this.

Through the warliner's speakers, General Lanyan yelled obscenities. He cursed the Adar by name, howling at the Ildiran commander for his betrayal. With a frown, Zan'nh gestured towards his communications officer. 'Switch that off. I have no desire to hear it.' Abrupt silence fell on the warliner's command nucleus.

The Solar Navy crewmen aboard the flagship were clearly uncertain about what they had come here to do, but they obeyed their Adar's commands. Zan'nh turned away from the inundated EDF ships, humanity's last – and insufficient – defence. He wanted no distractions right now.

Before Zan'nh could issue his fateful instructions, before he could trigger the cascade of events that would change – or end – history, his tactical officer yelped. 'Adar, more incoming ships! All of them show the configuration of Earth Defence Forces vessels.'

'How many?'

'An overwhelming number! Twice as many as the humans had before.'

'Is it a trick?' Zan'nh rushed to the screen and identified the sensor signatures of Juggernauts, Mantas, Thunderheads, and whatever other gunships the EDF had managed to assemble. 'Did the humans deceive us? Are they not so wounded as we were led to believe?'

New armed war vessels cruised in at full speed, directly towards the confrontation. How was this possible? Had the EDF held these war vessels in reserve to lure the hydrogues and the Ildirans? Zan'nh couldn't believe that. Not even humans were capable of such deviousness.

The Adar looked from side to side, studying the projections.

How might this change what he was forced to do? He crossed his arms over his chest and decided that it changed nothing.

Then a transmission shot across the communication band reserved for the Solar Navy. The image showed a black Klikiss robot standing at the helm of the lead Juggernaut. 'We have come to assist you in the extermination of humans.'

So, not EDF reinforcements after all.

Zan'nh assessed his response, then gestured to his communications officer. 'No reply. This complicates our job, but it is General Lanyan's problem. Klikiss robots are not, and never have been, my concern. We will still do what we must.' He drew a deep breath, the air in the command nucleus smelled stale and metallic. 'Yes, we will do what we must.'

By now hydrogue warglobes had surrounded the two cohorts of Ildiran battleships, coming in close as they anticipated the Adar's next move. The trapped and outnumbered EDF ships had no room to manoeuvre. Zan'nh felt cold inside, knowing there could be no turning back now. The hydrogues had sent far more warglobes than they had told the Mage-Imperator they would. Too many.

He signalled his bridge crew. 'Link with all warliners. Inform me when our ships are prepared.' The crewmembers took only moments to inform the Adar that everything was ready. Staring hard at the screen, Zan'nh narrowed his eyes. 'Execute your instructions. Now!'

Except for the flagship, the engines burst to life in all of the Ildiran vessels, ramping up in an extreme spike. Massive work crews had disengaged the safety governors before the two cohorts departed from Ildira, adding other modifications. Right now, with no concern for material tolerances, six hundred and eighty-five individual warliners turned about in a single perfectly coordinated movement. Their engines built to greater and greater power.

Before the hydrogues could react to the unexpected move, before they could take any sort of evasive action, all of the Ildiran warliners slashed outwards. Each heavily armoured battleship had a specified target, determined by calculator kithmen in the Adar's command nucleus.

Accelerating with full stardrive thrust, the warliners slammed directly into the diamond globes. The cascade of impacts happened with astonishing speed, and it was all perfectly choreographed. Shattering flashes erupted as hundreds upon hundreds of suicidal warliners obliterated the hydrogues.

A few enemy warglobes lashed out with blue lightning bolts to defend themselves, but only five of the programmed warliners were destroyed prematurely; all of the others annihilated their targets. A chain of explosions blossomed, as if all the stars in a globular cluster had simultaneously gone supernova.

With a powerful sense of finality and satisfaction, Zan'nh nodded at the forty-nine crewmen in his own command nucleus – the only crewmen aboard all six hundred and eighty-six warliners. The rest of the ships had been completely empty. Remote controlled.

With the assistance of the human engineers and the inexhaustible manpower of the Ildiran Empire, all those warliners had been reworked to accommodate automated systems. Zan'nh's single flagship had guided every vessel in the two cohorts. In only a few moments, nearly seven hundred warglobes had been obliterated, and not a single Ildiran had lost his life. Yet.

Zan'nh wondered what General Lanyan thought of him now.

But the Mage-Imperator had never anticipated that Zan'nh would face so many enemy ships. Despite their coercion, the hydrogues had not trusted the Solar Navy to carry out its promised betrayal. Now that the battle was engaged, the hundreds of remaining hydrogues began to open fire on the EDF ships.

Taken by surprise at the turnabout and unexpected firefight, the robot-hijacked EDF ships also launched their weapons indiscriminately. General Lanyan retaliated, blasting away at any attacker without taking time to aim.

Zan'nh's flagship sat in the eye of a deadly hurricane, the last surviving vessel of the Solar Navy at Earth. In his single overwhelming gambit, he had lost all of his warliners, and now he had nothing other than his ship's standard defensive systems, which could do little or no damage to the hydrogues. The hellstorm of weapons fire sparkled and exploded all around him.

All but defenceless, they watched the battle rage. Several shots slammed into the side of the warliner, causing the systems in the command nucleus to spark and overload.

'Emergency stabilization!' Zan'nh shouted. 'Our task here may be done, but the war is not over.'

'We have no effective weapons, Adar.'

Zan'nh stood alone, staring. Even if he could move, it would have accomplished nothing. The feeling of helplessness left him very angry.

He did not make excuses, did not apologize to his crew. The Adar had done what he had sworn to do, but now he and his brave group of soldiers were no longer relevant to the continuing battle. They could only sit like fallen leaves while the furious storm of conflict roiled around them.

ONE HUNDRED AND TWENTY

ANTON COLICOS

When the work was done and the planet evacuated, Tal O'nh's flagship and seven warliners remained to watch the final death throes of Hyrillka's primary sun. Anton and Vao'sh kept careful notes.

Though the one-eyed commander had insisted that his priority was to get the young Designate safely back to Ildira, Ridek'h stood firm. 'Hyrillka is my world, my responsibility. I will stay to the end. I want to go down there one last time.'

Yazra'h turned her head away from the boy to hide a proud smile.

O'nh fixed him with an intense stare from his single eye. 'To what purpose, Designate? Everyone is gone. You have done your duty.'

'I wish to say farewell. I should be the last one there – along with my rememberer.' He looked at Vao'sh.

Yazra'h stepped forward. 'I can guarantee the Designate's safety, as well as Rememberers Anton and Vao'sh.'

The tal could find no excuse. 'Hyrillka will be stable for a short while yet. However, our schedule should not be disrupted.'

'My entire *planet* is disrupted.' Ridek'h sounded alarmingly strong and stern. Anton blinked in surprise.

And so their small party had gone down. Piloted by Yazra'h, the cutter descended to the ghost town of Hyrillka's main city. Clouds in the sky were a soup of smoke. Angry weather patterns already seemed to be conspiring to unleash their wrath upon the helpless planet. Anton had a small electronic pad for recording his thoughts, but he had not input a single sentence. 'Vao'sh, I think I'm completely out of words for something like this.'

The cutter landed at the base of the hill by the empty citadel palace. Some of the buildings looked painfully new with fresh wood and bright stone. A few green shoots poked up from the fertilized plantings in what had been burned nialia fields. Plants rustled in the breezes. The city itself, though empty, seemed aware of its fate.

To Anton, the spaceport looked like an empty field after a huge carnival had passed through. A few broken-down ships and forgotten belongings cluttered the ground. Discarded supplies and abandoned equipment sat in piles where they had been dumped. Everything would be left behind.

Anton drank it all in, unable to push from his mind the words of the classic Shelley poem. He recited aloud:

> '"My name is Ozymandias, king of kings:
> Look upon my works, ye Mighty, and despair!"
> Nothing beside remains. Round the decay
> Of that colossal wreck, boundless and bare
> The lone and level sands stretch far away.'

The old rememberer frowned. 'Is that a tale about the fall of one of your great human empires?'

'More a reminder of the transience of all things, and how even our most enduring works crumble in the end.'

'We have similar stanzas in *The Saga of Seven Suns*. "There will come a time of fire and night, when enemies rise and empires fall, when the stars themselves begin to die."'

'Yes, I know that part.'

Ridek'h stood in front of the cutter, staring as the brisk wind played across his face. The boy's eyes were full of emotion. His gangly body trembled with impotent anger. 'I tried my best, but I failed.'

'You never really had a chance to start,' Yazra'h said. 'Neither your father nor the Mage-Imperator could have done better.'

'I hate the hydrogues.'

'As do we all.'

They remained among the empty buildings in uneasy silence for a long time. Ridek'h walked once more up the citadel palace hill to survey the half-completed structures and the newly repaved streets. With a flash of fire in his eyes, the boy turned. 'Take me back to the warliners. It is time for us to leave.'

When they returned to the battleship, the young Designate gave Tal O'nh the official order to depart.

The implacable struggles of the faeros and hydrogues continued in the primary sun. The myriad diamond warglobes swirled around, pouring out icewave blasts as if rallying to deliver the *coup de grâce*. Solar flares shot out in all directions, giant curls of plasma confined within magnetic loops. Anton wondered what last desperate weapon the faeros might unleash.

Before Tal O'nh's warliner could leave Hyrillka, the sensor technician cried out. 'The sun has undergone a dramatic shift. It is brightening!'

Without warning, a surging eruption hurled an uncountable

number of incandescent shapes into space. Like sparks from a grinding wheel, hot ellipsoids sprayed from the beleaguered star in an ever-increasing flow.

The scientist kithmen scrambled to take data and interpret it.

'The sun is blowing up!' Ridek'h said. The command nucleus crew gasped.

Yazra'h studied the scene carefully. 'No, it is not exploding. It has spawned thousands of faeros ships. *Thousands!*'

Anton was amazed. 'Maybe it's . . . *all* of them.'

Like spores ejected from an overripe fungus, a new wave of faeros swept outwards, and they outnumbered the hydrogues ten to one. The hydrogues swirled to mount their defences, but the fireballs kept coming . . . and kept coming – a seemingly infinite number.

Anton supposed the faeros had opened their own transgates deep within Hyrillka's primary sun. 'It almost looks like those fireballs are streaming through from every other inhabited faeros star, all them coming here, all at once. Talk about a showdown!'

On the screen, the overwhelming number of ellipsoids disintegrated the diamond specks one by one. Faeros continued to surge out of the plasma like lava from an erupting volcano, fireball after fireball, and the blue-white star brightened again, revitalized.

Within hours, every warglobe had been annihilated. Hundreds of shattered diamond vessels formed a field of rubble and debris close to the primary sun.

Like a cloud of ignited tinder, the faeros withdrew to the safe layers of the star. They dived into the flaming pool like otters playing in warm water, contributing once again to the stellar fire. Anton wondered if the damaged sun would ever return to normal.

In the flagship's command nucleus, few words were spoken.

Finally Designate Ridek'h looked hopefully at Yazra'h. 'Does this mean . . . is there a chance the sun will keep shining? That we do not need to abandon Hyrillka, after all? If the hydrogues are beaten, then my planet is safe – is it not?'

Yazra'h remained uneasy. 'Perhaps. Or perhaps not. Hyrillka may always be a dangerous place.'

Anton looked over at her. 'Then I will be very glad to be back on Ildira, safe and sound.'

ONE HUNDRED AND TWENTY-ONE

OSIRA'H

'The hydrogues know what we have done,' Mage-Imperator Jora'h said to Osira'h. 'And we did not succeed.' The *thism* bond between her father and his son Zan'nh had already told him what he needed to know. 'The Adar expended all of his automated ships, and they were not enough. The hydrogues launched many more warglobes than the small fleet they specified when they explained their plan.' Jora'h bowed his head, gripped the sides of his chrysalis chair. 'Far too many warglobes remain.'

Osira'h did not share her father's sense of defeat. Not yet. In the days since coming to live in the Prism Palace, she had come to realize that, although she had fulfilled her ostensible mission in life by making contact with the hydrogues, she had never fully tested the extent of her powers. She knew there was more inside her than even Udru'h and the lens kithmen on Dobro suspected. She had faith in that untapped power, faith that she could draw strength from the abilities of her mother and her father, faith in the unique synergy between her parents – a loving synergy that had produced Osira'h herself.

'We are at a cruxpoint, Father. But all is not lost.'

Jora'h had already sent a signal, placing the warliners in orbit on high alert. Two maniples of warliners were descending at high speed, burning through the upper atmosphere to position themselves in front of the sixty watchdog hydrogue spheres. 'I had hoped Tal Lorie'nh would arrive in time. Perhaps I should not have sent his warliners away from here.'

Osira'h looked up at the interlocked panes of the skysphere dome. No one could arrive in time to intervene. Only *she* could deal with the hydrogues.

'The emissary is coming. He is very angry.' Strangely, Osira'h felt more anticipation than fear. She was actually looking forward to this.

The small containment chamber careened through the Prism Palace corridors like a diamond wrecking ball. The emissary smashed through a gateway, knocked down an arch, and streaked along the stained-glass halls. Ildirans scrambled out of the way.

Osira'h stood in front of the Mage-Imperator. 'Allow me to speak to him, Father. It may be our only chance.'

'I should never have brought you and your mother into this trap.'

'Wait. An unwise hunter may be caught in his own trap,' the girl said.

Overhead, the warglobes were dropping lower, crackling with blue lightning. The Solar Navy defenders would never destroy the diamond spheres in time. Even if they did, the explosions and wreckage would level half the city.

The girl faced the furious emissary as he entered the chamber and came to a halt. The liquid-metal figure within had already formed into a human shape surrounded by swirling internal gases. An ominous voice thundered out, 'You knew the price you would pay if you did not comply with our instructions, and yet you betrayed us at Earth.' Despite his anger, the hydrogue's simulated expression did not change. 'We will now obliterate your city, your world, and your race.'

With the grace of an Isix cat, Osira'h walked down the steps and stopped innocently before the containment sphere, undefended, non-threatening. In her mind the bridge between herself and the deep-core aliens had never been completely severed, but she had closed off access in her mind, like slamming a gate shut. 'Before you destroy us, we have vital information the hydrogues should consider.'

'What information?' the doubtful emissary said.

'A fatal weakness in the verdani, and a flaw you can use to annihilate the returned wentals.' Osira'h's mother had explained many things she'd learned from her renewed link with the world-forest. 'We offer this information to save our lives.'

'Tell us.'

'Only if you spare the Ildirans,' she said.

The emissary seemed taken aback by the girl's boldness. 'We will decide the worth of your information once we know it.'

Seeming to accede, she said, 'I will communicate it through my mental bridge.' Her face went blank and, without waiting for permission, she opened herself in the way she had learned, re-establishing contact. The hydrogue emissary opened access to the bridge from his side. Good. His cooperation made her task easier.

Always before, her contact with the hydrogues had been accommodating, even subservient. Not this time. Catching them off-guard, she smashed the narrow gate open wider with the battering ram of her mind. She felt no hesitation about what she had to do.

But she needed more. When the emissary recoiled in surprise from the power of her mental touch, Osira'h took a step backwards and reached out for her father's hand as he came down to join her. They touched and bonded. He was the centre of all Ildiran *thism*, the Mage-Imperator, and her father. The bond could not have been stronger. Contact with the *thism* intensified her own specially bred abilities, and she became unstoppable. Blasting away all barriers, Osira'h *forced* the telepathic connection like a rape upon the hydrogue mind.

There was nothing the emissary could do. Osira'h was the bridge. She had to move swiftly, before he understood his true danger. Seizing his mind, the half-breed girl became a conduit through him to all the hydrogues in the sixty warglobes overhead. She crashed through their individual walls, pooled into their common minds. Osira'h instantly sensed their confusion, heard their demands, even detected a glimmer of fear at their inability to understand the unbreakable bond.

It was exactly what she needed.

Without releasing his daughter's grasp, Jora'h drew her closer to him. More important, Osira'h knew her mother had arrived as well.

Nira emerged from a hidden side alcove carrying her newly sprouted treeling, its fronds green and golden from the lump of worldtree wood. The moment the female green priest revealed herself, the alien emissary recoiled inside his environment sphere. He struggled desperately to disconnect the mental link, to close the gate that Osira'h had blasted away, but she held his mind fast, refusing to let him go.

With the treeling in one hand, Nira touched her daughter's shoulder, and connected through telink. As soon as Osira'h and her mother were united, the telink flooded in. Her parents acted as amplifiers, augmenting Osira'h's power with the *thism* on one side and telink on the other. Osira'h, the bridge, now became an aqueduct through which the power could stream.

Nira set loose the worldforest mind.

The vast and forceful mind of the verdani – every ancient and knowledgeable tree throughout the widespread worldforest – surged like a locomotive through the new and unorthodox conduit. Osira'h let it all flow. The hydrogues could not stop any of it.

Thousands of years of verdani thoughts, resentment, and horrifying memories spewed into, and overwhelmed, the raw mind of the emissary – and plunged through him to the warglobes overhead. It was as if she had planted and then detonated hundreds of explosives within the warglobes.

Together, Osira'h, Jora'h, and Nira moved closer to the containment sphere. Shrieking, spasming, the hydrogue's shape dissolved within his chamber. The feedback hammerblow also destroyed many of the quicksilver creatures aboard the looming warglobes. The hydrogues were components of a shared species like the verdani, like the wentals. If the mental shockwave continued long enough, the force would eat away *all* of the hydrogues, even the far distant ones. The corrosive thoughts of the trees, their enemies, were poison to them.

The deadly thoughts shot outwards, streaming towards the hydrogues overhead. The sixty diamond spheres reeled in the Ildiran sky. Blue lightning weapons discharged erratically, but most of the blasts went wild, firing off into the clouds. With sonic booms from their roaring descent to defend the Prism Palace, Solar Navy warliners plunged towards them – but the warglobes were already dying.

The deep-core aliens chose to sacrifice themselves and break the link, saving the rest of the hydrogues across the Spiral Arm. They forcibly cut the bond with their race rather than let the poisonous thoughts spread. Reeling out of control, warglobes tumbled out of the sky like crystalline asteroids. They bowled through the streets of Mijistra, crashed into the hills, exploded over dwelling complexes. The dying warglobes shattered ornate towers, levelled tall buildings, and killed thousands. Around them, concussions and flames and collapsing buildings created great havoc.

Osira'h could sense many of those deaths through her own partial *thism*, but she felt the end of the hydrogues more keenly. Tears streamed down the face of the Mage-Imperator as he endured so much death and destruction. But her father knew this also meant the liberation of his people. Osira'h could only hope the same thing was happening to all the watchdog enemy ships at other Ildiran worlds.

ONE HUNDRED AND TWENTY-TWO

JESS TAMBLYN

B efore he could reach his sister inside the alien cityplex, Jess faced an army of Ross replicas. The hydrogues could not have chosen a more potent image to use against him. He could think of no greater symbol of his failure and his heart's betrayal than the face of his dead brother.

How had they guessed? How could the drogues possibly know about Ross?

Long ago, Jess had taken advantage of his brother's trust, had fallen in love with the woman who should have married Ross. But now Cesca was wental-infused, like him. And Ross was *this*.

His hovering wental vessel had come to an impasse with the crowd of quicksilver copies that blocked his way from all sides. Ross stared at him.

How could they know?

From within the encapsulated ship, the wentals spoke to him. *It means nothing. They do not know you.*

Ross had been one of the very first victims of the deep-core aliens. The hydrogues must have copied his appearance. That was all. The hydrogues had used that image when their emissary had killed Old King Frederick.

Despite the doubts in his heart, his mind insisted on the logic. He'd been tricked by his emotions too many times – recently by the tainted wental that had reanimated his mother, and now this. How could the hydrogues possibly understand Ross's significance to the man now leading a wental invasion into their midst? It couldn't be so.

With iron-hard resolve, Jess shouted at Ross's infinitely repeated face. 'You are not my brother, any more than she was really my mother.' He clung to his love for Cesca and his hatred for the hydrogues. Tasia was down here somewhere, and he wouldn't let this inhuman horde stop him.

Knowing what he had to do, Jess made his choice. With a single thought, he burst the bubble of his ship. Liberated wental water sprayed out like deadly hail in all directions. Droplets splattered across the quicksilver drogues with the force of burning acid, and the human shapes began to writhe and dissolve. The elemental mist engulfed the standing army and destroyed the hateful charade of Ross look-alikes.

Jess was alone now and unhindered, clear of the protective shell of his wental ship. Although he stood in the impossible environment wearing only his white gossamer suit, the water elementals flowing through his bloodstream preserved his tissues.

When he found his sister, he would have to re-form the protective bubble, create a new water-ship. That problem didn't seem any more insurmountable than the other hazards he had already knocked aside. First, though, he had to figure out where Tasia was being held.

Jess hurried through the confusing labyrinth of the cityplex. Far away, unaffected by the destruction caused by the wental droplets, other liquid-crystal hydrogues slithered through hollow structures, climbed monoliths and entered geometrical grottos. A new barrage of warglobes cruised high overhead, launching to the upper atmosphere.

Jess hurried. When faced with this crisis, how long would it be until the deep-core aliens disposed of their human prisoners? His sister and her fellow captives were somewhere in this geometrical nightmare. Were they being held as hostages, strange zoo specimens, torture subjects?

Then, with a lurch, the entire citysphere began to move. He felt the great mass slowly accelerate. Far outside the metropolis, a ragged line appeared in the swirling soup of sky, a vertical tear not only in the atmosphere, but in the fabric of space itself. The dimensional line opened, yawned wide like a gaping mouth to swallow the bizarre citysphere.

A hydrogue transgate.

Fear shot through Jess as he realized what they were doing. To shake off the overwhelming attack of the wentals, the deep-core aliens intended to abandon Qronha 3 and vanish to another one of their gas giants. He couldn't let the hydrogues get away! They would take Tasia with them.

Then Jess felt an external exhilaration swell around him. A tingle rushed towards him like a fusillade of gunshots. Turning his head, he felt *something* outside streak past the citysphere like a bullet, a silvery spindle composed entirely of living water, directly on course. A wental torpedo. The cigar-shaped projectile dived in, plunging, tunnelling.

As the yawning transgate opened, the wental torpedo struck the dimensional line, collapsed, dissolved, and detonated. The liquid energy exploded across the gateway. The opening dwindled, collapsed, and disappeared.

The giant cityplex rumbled to a halt in the gas giant's atmosphere, throwing Jess off balance. All across the hydrogue empire, wental torpedoes were likewise disabling transgates, so the deep-core aliens could not join forces or flee the concerted attack.

Now the hydrogues had no way to escape from the Qronha 3 battleground.

KING PETER

L eaving the Whisper Palace, they rushed into the dark and confused night. Peter and Estarra marched Prince Daniel so swiftly that the young man had no time to ask questions. OX led them out through a side gate, across a courtyard, past a statue garden, and finally to the main plaza.

Though excited at first, Daniel soon became sceptical, then suspicious. 'If this is a coronation, why would Chairman Wenceslas want me to leave the Palace? That doesn't sound like him.'

'He needed to find a safer place for you,' Peter said. 'Remember, we're under attack.' OX crisply marched across the flagstoned plaza, leading the way.

'But shouldn't there at least be some celebration? Where is everyone?'

In answer, echoing air-raid alarms pealed through the dark city. Estarra pointed towards the extinguished lights throughout the Palace District, the rows of shadowy buildings. 'Everybody's hiding inside their houses, glued to their media feeds and hoping they survive. You can inspire them.'

Peter added with emphasis, 'If the EDF and Ildiran lines crumble, then the hydrogues will lay waste to Earth.' But if he and the Queen escaped, there would be a strong, *new* leadership for all of humanity.

The Prince's face became blotchy. 'Then I might not be King for very long. Shouldn't we get to shelter? A King should be kept safe, no matter what happens to Earth.'

'It's just ahead, Daniel.' Peter tried to sound reassuring. 'Right there.'

Illuminated by small emergency lights instead of great glowing banks, the hydrogue derelict sat outside like a trophy. Even the research teams had been evacuated. When Peter saw how many guards stood watch over the alien ship, however, he realized this was going to be more difficult than he had expected. Basil must have been paranoid that the hydrogues would come to retrieve their vessel. 'Don't they have more important duties right now?'

'It was the weak spot in the plan,' Estarra muttered.

Daniel saw their destination. 'The derelict? Why are we going there?'

'Because that is where we must go,' OX said innocently.

Estarra dodged the question. 'If Earth is under attack, can you imagine a more secure place than inside an armoured hydrogue ship?'

Daniel was clearly wrestling with the question, not trusting them, but he had been slapped down enough times that he probably couldn't imagine the royal couple having the nerve to rebel against the Hansa. Of course, that wasn't how Peter interpreted what they were doing. This was for the good of the human race. 'Right over here, Prince. They're waiting for us inside.'

Estarra closed in next to Peter. They couldn't show any concern now.

The guards warily raised their weapons. 'Halt! No one comes closer, by order of the Chairman.'

'The Chairman? Shouldn't you be more concerned with the orders of your *King*?' Peter said.

He felt the twitcher inside his pocket, a fully charged one taken from the fallen guards at Daniel's doorway. Estarra looked at him, and he could read her expression. *Whatever it takes.* From the shift of her arm, he knew she was also holding her weapon.

Boldly leading Prince Daniel, OX continued forward. 'You have no authority to stop King Peter, Queen Estarra, and Prince Daniel.'

Given time, Peter might have bluffed his way inside the derelict, but it was more likely the guards would contact Basil. He couldn't risk that. As a flash of recognition and relief crossed the nervous guards' faces, the King and Queen drew their twitchers and played the wide-dispersal stun beams across the five men. Taken completely by surprise, the guards began to spasm and twitch, unable to control their muscle impulses. Three of them succeeded in yanking out their own projectile weapons, but no one had a chance to fire.

Daniel gaped at the uniformed men as they all crumpled, his eyes wide and round. Whirling towards Peter and Estarra, he spotted the twitchers in their hands. His face turned an uneven red, and he couldn't seem to find his voice. Peter saw the instant in which all of the young man's suspicions clicked into place. Bawling for help, Daniel broke away and tried to run. Peter dialled the twitcher down to its lowest setting and fired a pulse at Daniel's legs.

The Prince collapsed. The disruptive impulses ricocheted through his central nervous system. Even his back twitched. The Prince tried to cry out, but his voice was weak. His legs had turned to rubber and he could barely manage to flop on the ground.

Now the derelict lay open and undefended. 'Estarra, OX — we've got to get him inside.'

As Peter worked with Estarra and the compy to pull the young man to his feet, he noticed that Daniel had lost control of his bladder, wetting his loose pyjama pants and the front of his robe. It was probably the least of the indignities he would suffer in the near future. Holding the arms of the twitching Prince, who continued to mumble incoherently, they hauled him past the stunned guards and into the alien sphere.

'Carry him up this ramp, and I will begin my preparations,' OX said.

Letting the compy lead the way, Estarra and Peter dragged Daniel into the derelict's central room. The Teacher compy marched up to the hydrogue trapezoidal wall. 'I have already uploaded all the information compiled by the research team from Deputy Cain's datapacks, as well as relevant data from Chief Scientist Palawu and the Roamer engineer Kotto Okiah. This transportal functions very much along standard lines.' OX swivelled his head, and his golden eye sensors glowed. 'I spent six hours completing a coordinate transform. Judging from a preliminary test the scientists performed yesterday, I believe it will work.'

'Is there a risk?' Peter glanced at Daniel, whose eyes were wild and uncomprehending. Drool dribbled from the right corner of his mouth; he didn't have the muscular control to form words, though he made faint whining sounds.

OX stared at the alien coordinate glyphs, then turned towards the King. 'No greater risk than in using any Klikiss transportal. Provided I have properly transformed the coordinates, I have selected an appropriate place to send him.'

Desperate to recover, Daniel twitched his arms, but to no avail. Peter and Estarra held him still, grunting with the effort.

Peter doubted the young man could comprehend why all this was happening to him, but he decided it was best not to explain. 'Don't worry, I'm sure OX picked the perfect location for you.'

Daniel made a mewling noise as the Teacher compy attempted to work the controls of the hydrogue transportation system. After linking his own systems to the alien command deck, OX selected one of the coordinate tiles while busily reprogramming the unit. The transportal misted, shimmered, then grew ready. 'I have been successful. You may send him through.'

Daniel made a last uncoordinated thrash, but Peter and Estarra lifted him. When his wife winced with the effort, Peter hesitated, looking at her swollen abdomen with concern. 'Maybe you shouldn't be—'

'I'm not helpless, Peter. This is life or death.' With a silent count to three, they swung Daniel through the transportal wall. Peter hoped they weren't accidentally dumping the conceited and ill-behaved Prince into a deadly environment, but he trusted OX. He always had.

With barely a twitch, Prince Daniel vanished through the flat barrier, swept off to one of the settlements claimed in the Klikiss colonization initiative. The hydrogue transportal wavered, then grew opaque again.

Peter looked at Estarra. 'Well, at least one of us is safe – even though Daniel will never thank us for it.'

'I didn't get the impression Daniel liked much of anything.' Estarra wistfully looked at the transportal as OX reset the systems. 'Too bad there's no doorway direct to Theroc. That's where we need to go.'

The Teacher compy stepped away from the transportal controls. 'No, Queen Estarra. For that, I will need to fly this ship.'

ONE HUNDRED AND TWENTY-FOUR

GENERAL KURT LANYAN

Aboard the beleaguered *Goliath*, Lanyan yelled for his weapons officers to fire indiscriminately. 'Plenty of targets to choose from. Just shoot anything that's shooting at us.' He wished he knew what the hell was going on.

First, all the Ildiran warliners had turned against the EDF, then they'd turned again, throwing themselves at the warglobes in a suicidal mêlée such as Lanyan had never seen. Nearly seven hundred ships had sacrificed themselves all in the space of a few minutes – what a monumental massacre!

The drifting wreckage of incinerated warliners and exploded hydrogue spheres had turned the battle zone into a minefield. Flaming fuel chambers, heavy engines, and rotating hull plates flew past like a meteor storm. Continuing explosions spangled space, as if the *Goliath* sat in the middle of a coronation day fireworks show. Lanyan's ships had to fly evasive manoeuvres and dodge shrapnel while they continued to fire. Any hope of rigid battle formations had gone straight out the airlock.

And then there were the damned Soldier compies and Klikiss

robots to contend with. An overwhelming number of hijacked EDF vessels ploughed into the fray, looking exactly like Lanyan's own ships. It was hard to know which ones to shoot at.

Tactical officers scrambled to keep track of ID blips, but the hijacked vessels plunged and wove through the disordered fleet until no tracking systems could maintain a lock. 'They're swarming around like a cloud of drunken gnats.'

'General, each one is transmitting the same IFF signals.' Kosevic wiped sweat from his face. 'Our targeting computers think *all* those ships are EDF vessels.'

'We know they're *not*, so start shooting at them. Now! Fraks and carbon-carbon slammers might not work against warglobes, but they'll sure as hell rip the guts out of an EDF ship.' His eyebrows knitted together, and his cold, pale eyes focused on the screen. 'And please try not to take out our own ships while you're at it. We don't have many to spare.' Still, he saw no way around it.

Close in among the EDF ships, the robot-controlled infiltrators blasted away. The concentrated jazer volley tore a Thunderhead weapons platform into a mass of broken deck plates and a cloud of venting atmosphere.

Lanyan lurched to his feet. 'All right, there's a bloody target for you! Put a marker on every ship that opens fire on one of ours.'

The *Goliath* swiftly destroyed the attacking Manta. Marching back and forth between the Juggernaut's weaponry stations, Kosevic rallied the gunners to shoot at other likely hostiles, but the targeting computers were overwhelmed. 'General, now that we've opened fire as well, nobody can tell who's attacking and who's defending.'

Lanyan slammed his fist down on the arm of the chair.

On the screen, the images of two grid admirals – Peter Tabeguache and Kostas Eolus – overlapped with frantic signals.

'General, why are you firing on us? We recaptured some of our ships, and we're here to help the Hansa!'

Lanyan regarded the images with a gimlet eye. 'Oh, really? Then why did you start opening fire?'

'We thought *your* craft were the ones hijacked by compies,' pleaded Eolus.

'We had no way of knowing,' Tabeguache said.

Lanyan blanked the comm transmission. 'Hit Eolus's signalling tower with an EM burst. I want to rattle that ship.' He saw his exec's hesitation. 'I was tricked by Admiral Wu-Lin once. I don't trust either of those Juggernauts any farther than I can throw them.'

After the weapons officer sent out the precision scrambler burst, the image of the Grid 5 admiral dissolved on the screen. The hologram vanished, revealing instead a sinister Klikiss robot hunched over the *Eldorado*'s bridge controls.

'Doesn't look like Admiral Eolus anymore,' Lanyan said, not surprised. 'Now you've got another target. Go!'

Officers raced to their stations, and jazers and fraks pummelled the turncoat Juggernaut, damaging its engines, ripping holes through its hull. Admiral Willis's ships also swept in and opened fire. At Lanyan's signal, more grouped EDF ships pounded the flagship that had belonged to Admiral Tabeguache.

Flying erratic patterns to evade the counterattack, the hijacked ships continued to swoop among the EDF defenders. As the *Goliath* wrought plenty of mayhem, one more robot-controlled Juggernaut hurtled towards them, unleashing a barrage of projectiles. Lanyan saw the vessel coming and shouted for evasive action. The *Goliath* pivoted on its axis, but the compy-controlled vessel struck home. Two of Lanyan's main engines exploded. A jazer lance slashed through the starboard hull, splitting open seven decks.

'Put everything into the weapons and shoot at that damned Juggernaut – everything we've got left!'

KEVIN J. ANDERSON

A flurry of slammers hit the underbelly of the robot attacker with enough force to send the hijacked ship reeling off course.

'Jazer banks are almost drained, but I've got one engine on-line, enough to manoeuvre us out of here,' Kosevic said. 'We've got to retreat, General. We're a sitting duck.'

'We've still got a few weapons, Mr Kosevic, and I intend to keep causing damage until my last breath. Figure out which grids these vessels came from, contact the Mars base, and get me someone who can provide their guillotine protocol codes. We'll pull the plug one way or another.'

He turned and snapped at a frozen weapons officer. 'You! Did I tell you to stop firing?' The startled crewman scrambled with his targeting systems and launched the rest of his fracture-pulse explosives.

Even though the ship's intercom was damaged and his signal could only go to a handful of the surviving crew, Lanyan said, 'Let me be perfectly clear: if we surrender here, then we surrender Earth — and that's not going to happen today.'

ONE HUNDRED AND TWENTY-FIVE

CHAIRMAN BASIL WENCESLAS

E ven inside the Hansa's war room with the doors guarded and the walls reinforced, Basil did not feel safe. If the hydrogues got past General Lanyan's defenders, they would come straight to the Palace District. A single hydrogue barrage could obliterate this building.

Basil sat at the main observation table while tactical experts and ground-based EDF officers clamoured for updates, studied real-time reports, and tried to stay one step ahead of the battle occurring in space. He hid his clenched hands under the table. 'It's not as if this was a surprise! We had plenty of time to prepare for this. Humanity failed itself.'

Even paler than usual, Deputy Cain flitted from station to station like a grim ghost. 'There was nothing else we could have done, Mr Chairman.'

'We should have known!' Basil raised his voice. 'Every living human being in the Terran Hanseatic League was aware of the threat – so why didn't they give me their best work? Now it's their own damned fault. They knew what was at stake. I was trying to lead them, but my plans can't succeed without a little cooperation. Why do people keep letting me down? One' – he raised his fist from under the table and pounded it down – 'after another' – he pounded again – *'after another!'*

Tactical experts enlarged the images on their screens, trying to keep track of the myriad moving vessels. 'Three complete EDF battle groups have just arrived at Earth. But they're shooting at General Lanyan's vessels.'

'Of course they're shooting – it's the battleships stolen by the damned compies! The Klikiss robots must have had an alliance with the hydrogues all along.'

Cain locked his hands behind his back. 'We can't determine exactly *what* is happening, Mr Chairman. At first it seemed as if the Ildirans had betrayed us, but then they launched against the warglobes. From these energy signatures' – he pointed to glowing smudges of static – 'hundreds of ships have already been destroyed: EDF vessels, Ildiran warliners, and hydrogue spheres.'

Basil could understand little from the flurry of blips. It looked as if someone had smashed two wasps' nests together and then stepped back to watch the resulting flurry. He turned to a rabbit-faced comm officer. 'Get me General Lanyan on the speaker right now.'

'Sir, he's blocked all but—'

'I'm the Chairman! Don't tell me you can't arrange a priority override.'

'Yes, Mr Chairman. Of course I can.' Skittering fingers across the control pad, the meek comm officer shouted into the voice pickup then switched over the screen.

Basil rose to his feet and addressed the EDF commander. 'General Lanyan, I need to understand what's going on up there. Have the Ildirans—'

Gruff and harried-looking, Lanyan flicked his ice-blue eyes

at Basil. 'I'm busy right now. Can't you see we're in the middle of a battle?'

'We can see very little, General. I want a full summary '

'You'll get your report when this is over, sir.' Abruptly, he cut the channel.

Basil was left staring at a blank screen. He felt as if someone had punched him. 'How dare he terminate the conversation!'

Cain was at his side. 'Mr Chairman, the General needs to concentrate on the battle. In the meantime, I advise that we evacuate to our safe bunkers.'

'No guarantee those are hydrogue-proof either. I need to be in the thick of things, for better or worse.' Basil shook his head as he raised the questions to himself. Even if he could survive the destruction of Earth and the decapitation of the Hansa, *why* would he want to? Running the government was his entire life. If he'd had anything else to do, he could have retired long ago. And since he no longer seemed to have an acceptable successor, Basil had no choice but to remain in his role. If need be, he would stay here and go down with his ship.

But he wouldn't be the only one.

An idea spread like sunrise across his features. 'Go find King Peter and Queen Estarra . . . in fact, bring Prince Daniel as well. I want them all here.'

Cain readily agreed. 'They can record a brave speech. We'll stand together and show history the defiant end of Earth, if it comes to that.'

Basil squeezed a fist again, then forced his claw-like hands to uncurl. 'Regardless, they're going to be here waiting just like the rest of us.'

But no one could raise Captain McCammon on the local communications net. The guard team stationed outside Prince Daniel's quarters also failed to respond. Was no one in the universe reliable? Had even the royal guards abandoned their posts?

He threw orders like sharp knives at the guards standing outside the war room. 'Go to the Whisper Palace and personally bring me the King, the Queen, and the Prince.' Hearing the rough-edged threat in Basil's voice, the uniformed men bolted.

The Chairman continued to watch the storm of battle. The blips, images, and projected courses were impossible to decipher. Basil had no way to tell who was winning. While he waited for the runners to return with his sham royal family, he counted down the seconds. *Why does everything take so long?*

Finally, one of the guards reported back over the intercom. 'Inform the Chairman that we've arrived at the royal wing. The King and Queen are not in their apartments, but we discovered Captain McCammon and another guard unconscious. Apparently stunned. The guards' twitchers are gone.'

Basil leapt to his feet. 'Impossible!'

The second group of men responded. 'We just found the same thing at Prince Daniel's quarters, Mr Chairman. The guards were knocked out and hidden in a storage room. They're still pretty groggy. No sign of the Prince, either. Maybe somebody kidnapped them.'

Basil's legs turned to water, as if someone had hit *him* with a twitcher. He dropped back into the chair. 'Nobody kidnapped them. They escaped.' It was too much! Peter had defied him over and over again. No matter what the Hansa did for him, no matter what Basil threatened or promised, Peter still lashed out at them like an ungrateful dog. Now it was all failing because everyone had betrayed him.

His vision went red and his eyes burned. He heard a loud sound, felt a tearing pain in his throat, and realized that *he* was making the noises. He howled with rage, screaming inarticulate curses – and then he caught himself. Deputy Cain stared at Basil in astonishment. All the tactical experts and comm officers turned from the dramatic battle screens to look at the Chairman as if he had gone insane.

Embarrassment came down on him like a freezing rain, and Basil forced his breathing to calm. He remained statue-still, demanding that his face resume its normal calm façade. If they were all going to die, then he would do it in a dignified fashion.

ONE HUNDRED AND TWENTY-SIX

CESCA PERONI

Roamer commando groups had spread out to dozens of known hydrogue haunts. For the initial strike with her own team, Cesca had chosen to fly one of the enormous Plumas water tankers alongside others flown by the Tamblyn brothers. They had a long list of infested planets to visit.

Meanwhile, her other teams set off to separate targets, following star charts that marked the lairs of hydrogues. The deep-core aliens were being hit on hundreds of planets, all at the same time.

Cesca's small squadron spiralled down to the indistinct edge of atmosphere high above the gas giant Haphine. She had never visited this cool, storm-swept world before, though she knew its historical significance. One of the first two skymines the Roamers ever leased from Ildirans had been deployed here. Haphine was also the site of the fourth hydrogue attack against humans; six thousand Roamers had died here.

Now the tables were turned. Cesca directed her team to disperse their wental cargoes and begin the recapture of another hydrogue stronghold.

Caleb Tamblyn sounded conversational on the comm, but Cesca detected his underlying anxiety, a nervous need to talk and distract himself from the upcoming engagement. 'Clan Tamblyn has always been the best at shipping and delivering water where it's needed.'

'You could consider this all part of a day's work,' Cesca added.

Then they dumped part of their wental supply. The energized water penetrated the thick, bluish-grey clouds, diffusing deeper into the planet.

The cacophony of wentals in Cesca's cargo hold filled her senses and talked inside her head. She could feel the clash surging through the winds, and she could feel the imminent victory. 'The wentals are already dissolving Haphine's transgate to bottle up the drogues. The enemy can't get away.'

As if hearing an invitation, three diamond battleships rose from the contaminated clouds, already crackling with energy bolts. Their crystal surfaces were pitted and stained, scoured by corrosive wental vapours in the atmosphere. Mist smothered the warglobes, clinging with caustic droplets, as if the fog itself were conscious.

Caleb Tamblyn flew his tanker close to hers. 'That means we get to deal with those warglobes ourselves?'

'Isn't that what we came here for?' asked Wynn from his own ship.

From below, at the edge of the planet's atmosphere, Torin Tamblyn came racing upwards. He had already dumped his load of wentals, but even the lightened water tanker was not able to outrun the three warglobes that came howling after him. 'They're on my tail!' he transmitted. 'Everybody either help, or get out of my way.'

His two brothers altered course and plunged down towards him with their heavier tankers. Torin tried to escape the blue lightning storm that came lancing out of the diamond spheres.

Cesca's own tanker was still filled with Charybdis water, and she could feel the contained wentals pulsing through her, through the cargo hold, through the entire ship. She could see immediately that the hydrogues were going to destroy all of the tankers. 'You Tamblyns – scatter! You can't fight this.'

Caleb cried, 'But they're after Torin!'

'Then let them go after me instead.'

As the water elementals vibrated into the hull of the large tanker, Cesca's ship accelerated, roaring between Torin Tamblyn's fleeing vessel and the oncoming warglobes. The hydrogues had no idea what they were facing.

As the trio of diamond spheres shot towards her, still barrelling after the Tamblyn ships, Cesca pulled up to expose the tanker's lower hull like a submissive animal baring its belly. When she released the cargo bay doors, the wentals lunged out like a hurricane made of living water.

The rolling cloud of vengeful fog expanded into an insubstantial barrier before the warglobes. When the spiked spheres tore through it, they were suddenly swathed in clinging, destructive mist. Cesca had time only to see the water elementals begin to do damage, a caustic film sizzling through the supposedly indestructible diamond shell.

The hydrogues careened left and right. Two of them cracked into each other, then ricocheted like billiard balls. Cesca's tanker was right in the path of all three blinded warglobes.

When the impact came, the flash of light and fury was all around her. She felt as if her entire body were a gong being pounded by a band of cruel gremlins with hammers. Then she was falling, floating, spinning within a demolition derby of hull shrapnel, freezing air vapour, and energized water.

The wentals kept her alive. Cesca had not meant to test her

indestructibility, had not thought about putting herself or the valuable tanker in harm's way. She had done what was necessary. She turned to see the three tankers flown by the Tamblyn brothers circling around. She floated alone, without a radio or any means of communicating with them.

To her grim satisfaction, though, the three warglobes were blotchy and leprous, mortally wounded. When the spheres shattered, curved fragments glittered in the distant sunlight, beginning a slow orbital spiral back down towards the clouds of Haphine. The wental mist, moving of its own volition, swooped down past the wreckage like a swarm of angry hornets to the clouds, where the other wentals were already spreading destruction.

Experimenting, Cesca found that she could make herself move, impelling herself through the vacuum simply by willing herself to do so. Caleb, Wynn, and Torin Tamblyn must have thought she was killed in the explosion, for as she rose in front of one of their cockpit windows, waving her hands, she could see Caleb's jaw drop. He grabbed the communications transmitter, excitedly spreading the news to his brothers.

She grinned and mimed that she wanted to be picked up through one of the hull hatches. Now they had one less tanker – and one less hydrogue world to recapture. But they had plenty more to do before the day was over.

TASIA TAMBLYN

Tasia had never understood most of what she could view through the jewelled membrane of their preservation cell, but now things were crazier than she had ever seen them. 'Something's going on out there again, and it doesn't look like a party.'

Warglobes cruised over the streets, exiting through the barrier that surrounded the drifting cityplex. Liquid-metal hydrogues flowed like schools of startled fish, and Klikiss robots marched about.

'They've always been crazy,' groaned Keffa. 'Why don't they just kill us and be done with it?'

'Maybe they're trying to see how we hold up under stress,' Robb said.

'Not very damn well,' said Belinda. The haggard-looking female captive had never told Tasia her last name.

After EA's murder, anger still simmered inside Tasia like molten metal. She longed for a way to smash a Klikiss robot or two. The hydrogues were alien, sure, but the big mechanical cockroaches were actually *evil*. Klikiss robots enjoyed inflicting pain, dominating and destroying. It was part of their programming.

She had always relied on her own toughness and brains, using Roamer skills and any scraps of material she could find. Tasia Tamblyn had never expected a white knight on a horse to ride in and save her from her imprisonment. She knew that no heroic cavalry – not even an EDF commando squad – would swoop in to take them away from this nightmare.

However, the sudden sight of her brother Jess on the other side of the translucent membrane was so ridiculous and unexpected that Tasia thought she'd gone completely insane. She had expected to last at least as long as the other prisoners before she cracked. Could the drogues be playing another cruel trick on her?

Jess stood outside in the deadly environment wearing only a thin white garment that clung to his body. His legs and arms were bare. His long brown hair flowed even in the incredible pressures of the hydrogue world.

'Shizz, if I'm going to have delusions, I'd hoped they would have at least a glimmer of logic to them.'

Robb yelped. 'Who's that?' When the others crowded closer, all of them gasping and shouting questions, Tasia could not deny that everyone else saw him, too. She rubbed her eyes.

'That's – that looks like my brother Jess. But it can't be.'

'I'll second that,' Robb said. 'He's at the core of a gas giant and he's . . . barefoot.'

Tasia had seen the drogues create a quicksilver sculpture of her brother Ross, so this must be a new form they had chosen. The aliens' imitative abilities must have improved, because he certainly looked lifelike. Why did they keep preying on Tasia's memories? Her joy changed to crushed disappointment. 'You're not real!' she shouted through the membrane.

When Jess came closer to the preservation cell, his face lit up with a real expression of delight and triumph. His rakish grin was unmistakable, dredging up many memories from her childhood. When the drogues had copied Ross, they had never succeeded in showing any emotions or expressions. This was something definitely different.

'Who the hell are you? And what do you want?' she demanded.

His voice came as vibrations transmitted through the dense atmosphere, amplified by some unknown power. It was *Jess's* voice, all right. 'I've come to rescue you, little sister. Don't you recognize me?'

Her sarcasm was automatic. 'Let's see, your hair's a little longer than I remember . . . Oh, and I don't recall that you could float out in a high-pressure environment wearing nothing more than a thin shirt and trunks!'

'Let him rescue us!' Belinda cried. 'We don't care who he is!'

'I care,' Tasia growled. 'The drogues have screwed around with my family enough already.' She looked again at Jess's face through the murky membrane and felt her heart flutter. By the Guiding Star, he sure looked like Jess! And she hated hated *hated* this place. 'Okay, I'm willing to be flexible if he can get us out of here.'

'It is really me, Tasia, but I'm not the same as I was – you can guess that much. My body is infused with power from the wentals, a type of being as powerful as the hydrogues and the faeros. I have the power to get you out of here. Right now the wentals are attacking, and vanquishing, hydrogues all across the Spiral Arm.'

'It's about damn time!' Keffa said.

'Anybody who crushes the drogues is a friend of mine.' Robb grabbed her arm. 'Come on, Tasia. We're light years beyond having anything to lose at this point.'

The prisoners began to shout, anxious to break out of their hellish cell. Keffa was the lone voice of dissent, warning that it was a trap. Belinda jostled Tasia as if trying to throw herself headfirst through the barrier.

'Can we let him explain everything *after* he takes us away?'

'All right, we've been under a death sentence ever since we got put in this bizarre zoo. POWs are supposed to try and escape.' She looked at her brother, who stood in the hydrogue city without any visible means of carrying them to safety. 'How are *you* going to pull this off?'

In a voice that remained eerie and powerful, Jess said, 'Wentals are the mortal enemies of the hydrogues. They changed me, altered my body, so that I can do things you might not think possible.'

Tasia laughed. 'Shizz, that's an understatement!'

'Trust me.' His wental-amplified voice resonated in the cell. 'I may not be completely human anymore, but right now that's an advantage.'

Jess extended his arms and closed his eyes. Misty power crackled around him like gathering fog as he condensed water droplets out of the air, molecule by molecule. He summoned rain until he had gathered enough elemental-charged water to fashion a protective bubble. The newly created sphere appeared fragile, with a skin as thin and insubstantial as soap film. The wental bubble kissed the protective membrane of the chamber. The films fused, and the cell barrier split open like parting lips.

Jess called from outside, 'Pass through, and I'll hold it together. You have to hurry. The battle is growing worse all around us.'

Tasia had already accepted, and endured, more than her share of impossible situations. What difference did one more crazy thing make? She grabbed Belinda and pushed her through the opening into the wental bubble. 'Come on! I thought you all wanted to get out of here.'

A frantic Keffa stumbled through. Tasia and Robb helped the

other captives, and then climbed together into the unusual escape vessel. Inside, the air smelled of ozone and fog. Each breath was incredibly delicious after such a long confinement in the hydrogue cell.

When Jess passed through the bubble film, Tasia realized just how much she wanted to run to him, to throw herself into the protective arms of her big brother. The last time she had seen him was when he'd flown past the lunar base, transmitting a coded message to EA that their father had died. But Jess warned her away, explaining about his deadly touch.

'Well, I promise you more than a thank-you note – as soon as we get out of here.'

For the first time since her capture, Tasia saw a glimmer of hope in her fellow prisoners' faces. Jess's water bubble detached itself from their hated cell, then rose up and away from the hydrogue cityplex.

ONE HUNDRED AND TWENTY-EIGHT

KING PETER

Peter prayed that Chairman Wenceslas was sufficiently distracted by the hydrogue attack to let them slip cleanly away. 'You're sure you can fly this derelict, OX?'

It tore his heart to escape now, when it meant leaving so many people to die if the hydrogues did break through Earth's line of defences. But Basil's decisions had brought them to this impossible situation. If mankind was ever to have a second chance at survival, they could not rely on the Chairman's irrational leadership. King Peter and Queen Estarra were humanity's last, best hope.

The Teacher compy stood at the confusing and intricate bank of controls for the derelict's engines. The colourful panels were inlaid with jewels and crystals that bled downwards into the block of translucent polymer, like blood vessels pumping strange chemicals. 'The research team compiled an enormous amount of data. I have to assimilate it all.'

Looking exhausted and clutching her swollen belly, Estarra

tried to find a place to sit inside the alien ship. She rested against one of the smooth protrusions on the slick alien wall. 'Did they learn enough?'

The compy remained intent on the alien control systems, perhaps too intent. For the first time in Peter's memory, he saw OX hesitate. 'Yes, I have sufficient data from which to compile the knowledge I require. These engines are far more complex than the Ildiran stardrive or any propulsion system used by the Earth Defence Forces. However, if I utilize all of my processing power, I can create a paradigm overlay that will enable me to pilot the ship to Theroc.'

'I knew we could count on you, OX,' said Estarra.

With only the slightest pause to gather his resolve, the compy swivelled his synthetic body to face Peter. 'Unfortunately, because our plans were made so swiftly, I did not have the opportunity to bring separate downloads. As you know, my memory storage is already filled to capacity with personal history. I have needed upgrading for some time.'

'What does that mean?' Peter said. 'You don't have the processing power to run these engines?'

'I have sufficient processing and storage capacity. However, in order to employ that capacity to comprehend the intricacies and nuances of running this ship, I will need to delete all of my memories.'

'That's three centuries of experiences!' Peter gasped. 'We'll do something else. We'll find another way to fly this ship – or we can just hide here on Earth until the emergency blows over.'

'No, King Peter, you cannot. You and the Queen must be kept safe. That is my priority.'

'Then I order you to change your priorities.'

'You cannot, any more than you could order me to kill Chairman Wenceslas.' OX turned his golden eye sensors to the

Queen. 'Taking you to Theroc is our best opportunity to save you and your child.'

Peter said, 'We could go through another Klikiss transportal, like Prince Daniel did.'

Estarra's eyes pleaded with him. 'It's got to be Theroc, Peter. My people can protect us, and we can use it as our new base of leadership.'

Peter knew she was right. 'If we went somewhere else, we wouldn't be doing anything but hiding. The human race needs more from us than that.' He swallowed the lump that was forming in his throat, knowing exactly what OX would do. He also knew that the tears in his wife's eyes were for him, for their baby, for Earth . . . and for OX.

'The Chairman will notice we're gone any moment now. If any of those warglobes break through, they'll hit the Palace District first. We have to go right away – and hope this derelict is small enough not to get shot down by either side once we reach space.'

In a voice that sounded almost optimistic, OX said, 'I will attempt to retain at least a few of my memories of you, if storage space allows.'

Before the King could say anything to stop him, before he could consider another solution to the impossible problem, OX turned to the alien ship's controls. Jacking into the library of stored information culled from the work teams and stored on all the datapacks Cain had given them, the old Teacher compy stood rigid, only a few systems twitching as centuries of experiences drained away to be rewritten by deluge of necessary data.

Peter's heart wrenched and he blinked back tears as he grasped how much the Teacher compy was losing, emptying everything that he held dear just to be filled with the cold equations necessary to understand hydrogue engineering. The Teacher compy was a

KEVIN J. ANDERSON

historical treasure. He wondered if the Hansa had made a back-up download at any point, just to preserve OX's memory files. He doubted that Basil would have gone out of his way for that. He wouldn't have considered it relevant.

After an interminable moment, OX turned to them with a blank and disengaged demeanour. 'King Peter, Queen Estarra.' His synthesized voice was flat. 'I am ready. Do you wish to depart now?'

Peter and Estarra both knew they had just lost one of their only friends in the political quagmire of the Hansa. 'Yes,' Peter answered, his throat tight with emotion. 'Please get us out of here.'

The compy focused on the control panels, flowing crystal grids, and jagged protrusions grown out of the diamond framework. Power systems thrummed through the curved derelict, transferring energy through the structural lattice. The small sphere sealed itself and lifted up into the embattled night.

T wenty verdani battleships came out of the cold emptiness of space and swooped down towards Earth. Beneto's human ancestors had departed from the home planet centuries ago in their generation ship, hoping for a new place to settle. They had never expected it to end like this.

And he did not intend to let it end, even if he was no longer human. His flesh had perished years ago on Corvus Landing, and in dying he had let his soul fall into the verdani mind. Now that he was part of this incredible organic craft, Beneto and his hundreds of fellow treeships were strong enough to conquer the ancient enemy.

'The verdani have awaited this battle for ten thousand years,' he said through telink to all green priests, all pilots. 'And these ships are our greatest weapons. Now we must finish our enemies, as we should have done long ago.'

His wooden flesh was fused with the heartwood; his arms were branches kilometres long; his roots trailed out like antennae strands. His rigid verdani body was stronger and more massive than anything his imagination had ever prepared him for. Seeing the mayhem and destruction around Earth, he hoped that the monstrous trees would turn the tide of the battle. With only a thought, he guided his spiny seedship directly into the fight.

Near Earth, hundreds of warglobes had already been destroyed, but through the myriad forest eyes of his battleship, Beneto saw that many diamond globes still survived – enough to ruin Earth if they broke through the last line of defences. And the remaining EDF ships seemed to be firing on each other.

The twenty green-priest pilots saw their alien targets, instinctively agreed on where each would fly, and careened in amongst the fighting vessels. The huge flying trees dodged blasts from EDF jazers, ploughed through clouds of shrapnel and shockwaves from exploded Ildiran warliners, and scraped past the sharp eggshell fragments of broken warglobes. Using the communication systems Solimar had implanted, Beneto transmitted their intentions to General Lanyan, but in the mêlée he did not think anyone was listening.

Upon seeing the treeships, the hydrogues recognized their mortal enemies. Warglobes abandoned the EDF vessels and spun in space to unleash wild gouts of withering icewaves and deadly blue lightning.

Fused into the treeship, Beneto felt something akin to pain as his outer bark scorched and branches were singed or frozen away. But he came close enough to wrap his thorny branches around the nearest warglobe in a galactic bear hug.

The diamond sphere fought back with the same weapon the deep-core aliens had used to annihilate the worldtree grove on Corvus Landing, where Beneto had died. He remembered the fear, the pain, the death – all those trees, all those colonists! His treeship felt the cold death of icewaves cauterizing several of his huge limbs, but he pulled his spiny branch arms tighter and *tighter*, squeezing until the diamond sphere cracked ... and finally shattered.

Nineteen other verdani seedships engulfed warglobes as well, crushing them with irresistible botanical strength.

Around them, the human EDF ships continued to fight each other. All Ildiran warliners but the flagship were already destroyed. And still several hundred hydrogue warglobes pressed towards Earth. Even twenty verdani battleships would not be enough to stop them from breaking through.

But still, they must try. Beneto and the other treeships launched themselves at the numerous warglobes. He stretched his thorny battleship arms again and embraced another diamond vessel, squeezing until it broke apart.

His determined comrades did the same.

ONE HUNDRED AND THIRTY

ADAR ZAN'NH

The flagship of the Solar Navy hung useless in space. A nearby explosion had severely damaged its engines. The Adar's sensor-station operator doggedly repaired damaged control panels, pulling out fused circuit blocks, extracting spares from secondary systems that were no longer necessary. At last he got the tactical screens operating again so that Zan'nh could observe the scope of the continuing battle, even if his flagship could not participate.

They could do nothing but watch as the awesome tree battleships struck the warglobes. Zan'nh had never seen anything like them, could not imagine what could create such monstrous living vessels. So many forces had gathered to fight the hydrogues, but even the tremendous treeships could not block the hundreds of remaining warglobes. The hydrogues had sent an inexplicably large force against the EDF ... or had the deep-core aliens intended to destroy the Solar Navy at the same time? The more he thought about it, the more he decided it must be true.

Through the *thism*, with his close connection to the Mage-

Imperator, Zan'nh could already feel cold ripples, waves of deaths. Countless people were dying on Ildira – he felt the slaughter like a spine-grating note go through him. After the Solar Navy's turnabout here, the hydrogues must be brutally retaliating. They would have known of the betrayal instantly. He sensed that the Mage-Imperator still lived, but the Adar suspected the Prism Palace was under attack. Had the sixty watchdog spheres above Mijistra simply opened fire in retaliation, in *punishment*?

And he was trapped here, unable to move, unable to fight. The flagship's deck was tilted. Zan'nh swept his gaze across the faces of his downcast crew, then pounded his hard fist against the command railing. He felt helpless. He had already done his part . . . and it hadn't been enough.

His tactical adviser said, 'We did everything we could, Adar. We eliminated fourteen times as many warglobes as Adar Kori'nh did at Qronha 3. Never have Ildirans destroyed so many of the enemy.'

Zan'nh felt no triumph. Lights flickered inside the ship, and sparks continued to fly from the control panels. 'But it wasn't enough. We did not bring enough ships.' That single mistake would doom the Ildiran Empire.

'If we had brought more ships, then not enough would have remained to protect Ildira,' the tactician said.

Zan'nh raised his hand. 'This is for the protection of Ildira! We were commanded to deal a mortal blow to the hydrogues. If we do not defeat them here, they will destroy all of our worlds, one by one.' He lowered his voice. 'Already warglobes may be levelling Mijistra! Can you not feel all those deaths?'

Robot-seized EDF vessels continued to hammer their human-crewed counterparts. Verdani treeships destroyed diamond spheres one at a time, but still the hydrogues pushed closer to Earth.

'Adar!' The sensor operator looked up as if he couldn't believe his readings. 'More ships arriving – hundreds more!'

Zan'nh's heart sank. Did the Klikiss robots and their Soldier compies have further reinforcements? Or was it more hydrogue warglobes? 'Do our comm systems work?'

In answer, an image resolved itself on the ship-to-ship screen to show the anxious face of an older Ildiran officer. 'Adar, this is Tal Lorie'nh. Please acknowledge if you're still out there. We detect no functioning warliners.'

Zan'nh leaned closer to the screen. 'Yes, Tal Lorie'nh! We are here.'

The older Solar Navy officer responded with a thin smile. 'The Mage-Imperator thought you might require some assistance.'

'He has brought a full cohort!' cried the sensor operator.

Hundreds more warliners. Zan'nh held onto the command rail to keep his balance. 'We had thought the battle was lost.'

'Not yet, Adar. We have a final strategy.' Lorie'nh gave an order to his seven quls, each of whom directed seven septars.

Lorie'nh had once been Zan'nh's commanding officer, but the older man had no aspirations to increase his rank; in fact, Lorie'nh had been surprised to achieve the level of tal in the first place, a promotion that he credited to good personnel serving him, including young Zan'nh.

With a sinking in his heart, the Adar realized that this cohort, dispatched at the last moment, had never been part of the plan. These were not empty, automated ships like the other sacrificial vessels, but the Mage-Imperator had sent them here anyway. When planning this appalling gambit, Zan'nh had been aware of the potential cost, but had salved his conscience by relying on the new remote-control systems Sullivan Gold and his engineering team installed. He hadn't expected to ask hundreds of thousands of crewmen to sacrifice themselves. So many torn threads of *thism*!

On the screen, he met Lorie'nh's bright gaze. 'Tal, are you and your subcommanders prepared for this? Do you at least have minimal crews aboard?'

Lorie'nh answered with a wry smile. 'These warliners carry the full crews for which they were designed.' The group of battleships accelerated as they entered the fringes of the space battlefield.

Zan'nh's heart ached. Had Adar Kori'nh felt the same resolve as he drove his maniple down into Qronha 3?

Lorie'nh said, 'Do not count our deaths, Adar. If we were to fail now, then our entire race would die.'

Zan'nh knew it was true. 'Safe journey to the Lightsource.'

Lorie'nh gave a brisk nod. 'May we all meet there some day.'

Three hundred and forty three warliners streaked past, diving like a meteor storm towards the remaining warglobes. With glistening eyes Zan'nh watched the ornate ships flow by. He had never seen such a beautiful sight in his life.

QUEEN ESTARRA

Under OX's piloting, the hydrogue derelict rose smoothly against gravity. Earth's skies were empty and dark, all tourist zeppelins and commercial transportation craft grounded in the emergency. Only a few glimmering lights marked the location of the Whisper Palace, which she and Peter were now leaving behind for ever.

Estarra held onto Peter, both drawing and giving reassurance. 'I never thought we'd get this far.'

As Earth receded, bright and blue and unprotected, Estarra knew that Peter's heart was torn for abandoning his people, for leaving during this crisis. It made him seem a coward, running away in humanity's time of greatest need. But Basil would kill them, especially now, if they didn't go. The King would accomplish nothing if he stayed. Estarra knew, though, that even if they lost the battle here, human civilization was not destroyed.

'Peter, the human race is more than just Earth. We've spread far beyond our original boundaries. Chairman Wenceslas forgot that. He cut ties with Theroc, with the Roamers, with all the other

Hansa colonies.' She looked at him with her large brown eyes. 'From Theroc the two of us can rule as true King and Queen, to help *all humans* recover from this. No matter what happens on Earth, win or lose, the Chairman would never have allowed you to be the leader humanity needs. This is our only chance.'

He nodded, knowing she was right. 'OX, get us away as fast as you can.'

The Teacher compy flew in silence. OX's memories might be gone, but he had uploaded enough information to become an expert in this alien craft. In a clipped and emotionless voice, he reported, 'I detect multiple obstacles distributed across all valid paths ahead. I will attempt to avoid them.'

Estarra could see through the transparent walls to the raging battle. The 'multiple obstacles' were remnants of hundreds, even thousands of ruined vessels — Ildiran warliners, hydrogue war-globes, EDF battleships. Their tiny derelict was a mere grain of sand among all the spaceships crashing into each other and firing weapons.

The attacks had spread out to encompass a huge volume of space in the neighbourhood of Earth. The battle was everywhere, and Estarra saw no way around it. OX chose the best course and accelerated straight into the frenzy of engagement. Another group of ornate Ildiran warliners had just arrived, hundreds more ornate battleships.

'Is there anything we can do if ships start firing at us?' she asked. 'We are in a hydrogue ship, after all.'

'The engineering crew left basic communication devices and controls aboard the derelict. I can attempt to send a message over standard military frequencies. That will inform them we are not enemies.' OX worked the controls, sent out a signal.

'If they believe us,' Estarra said. 'And if they notice us at all.'

'I hate to tell everyone we're aboard. I'd just as soon keep Basil in the dark for as long as possible.' Peter leaned over, folding his hands together. 'But there's nothing to be done about it now.'

'I have now removed your identification from the transmission,' the compy said. 'I suspect few people aboard the EDF vessels noticed. They are quite busy now. General Lanyan has just attempted to transmit a "guillotine protocol" to shut down the robot-controlled ships, but it seems the Soldier compies have rerouted their systems. General Lanyan sounds quite angry that his plan is not effective.'

The tiny derelict dodged, swooped, and dipped, making abrupt course corrections that should have thrown Peter and Estarra against the walls, but the deep-core aliens had an efficient momentum-dissipation system.

Some of the beleaguered Earth Defence Forces ships took potshots at the tiny sphere – which meant they probably hadn't been listening at all. A glancing jazer bolt sent them spinning, but OX quickly reasserted control.

Then Estarra saw something more incredible than anything else in the space battlefield. 'Look, Peter! They're ... they're *trees*. Huge trees from the worldforest – just like Nahton told us!'

Verdani battleships engaged the hydrogues, wrapping spiny branches around the warglobes to crush them. Estarra pressed her hands against the curved wall, peering into the chaos of space. Everything seemed to be happening at once. Twenty of the enormous trees came towards the main struggle, and the derelict raced onwards, but not fast enough.

One of the huge alien trees shifted its course and came at them. Peter cried out. 'OX, change course. We don't want to get caught by that thing.'

'I will attempt to avoid it, King Peter.' The compy focused on the jumbled crystalline controls, and their tiny sphere moved in an erratic pattern, but the thorny treeship came closer, its branches sweeping wide like the jaws of a trap.

'I don't think it's our enemy,' Estarra said. 'It's from Theroc.'

'Maybe not, but we're sitting in a hydrogue ship, and those trees are destroying warglobes one after another.' Peter's blue eyes were wide.

'Shall I identify Queen Estarra in my transmission?' OX asked.

She jumped at the chance. 'Yes, OX! Say . . . I'm a daughter of Theroc, but don't give my name.'

Moving with amazing speed, the organic vessel caught them in its mighty grasp and drew the derelict into a nest of thorns and fronds. The branches were huge. Estarra could see the overlapping golden bark scales now turned into impenetrable space armour. The javelin thorns scraped against the smooth curve of the derelict. The limbs pulled them closer, wrapping tighter.

OX did not sound concerned, though his hands flurried over the controls. 'I apologize, King Peter. It is beyond my capabilities to evade the treeship.'

Huddled against the derelict's wall, Estarra pressed her hands flat against the crystalline hull. The ominous growth looked similar to and yet different from the worldtrees she had climbed when she was younger. Those trees had been so peaceful, curious, wanting only to acquire knowledge. But these verdani battleships seemed intent on destruction. Or was it protection?

Crackling words came from the portable commsystem aboard the derelict. She leaned forward, surprised to hear a sound like singing, a warm voice she remembered from childhood. 'Estarra . . . sister.'

'Beneto!' She looked at Peter, then scrambled to the comm-system. 'It's Beneto. He's inside that treeship.'

'I *am* the treeship.'

Beneto had died on Corvus Landing. Yet Sarein and Nahton

KK E V I N   J .   A N D E R S O N

had told her of Beneto's reincarnation as an avatar of the world-forest, complete with her brother's thoughts and memories.

'Beneto, don't harm us,' she said.

'You are in a hydrogue ship?' His voice no longer sounded exactly human.

'We're escaping from the Hansa, from Earth. The Chairman is trying to kill us, so we're going to Theroc.' She fiddled with the transmitter's controls to hear him better. 'I wish I could tell you everything, Beneto! I wanted to see you again.'

'Can he help us?' Peter asked.

'We need to get home, Beneto. Come with us,' she urged.

'I cannot. The battle is here. The final battle. I belong to the seedship now. We are one.' The enfolding branches now held the derelict in an embrace rather than a threatening grip. 'We destroy the hydrogues today, but first I will see that you stay safe, little sister.'

The treeship began to move away from the furious combat zone. Blasts of enemy weaponry struck and splintered the outer fronds, but Beneto's huge tree body did not flinch as he protected them. Once the verdani battleship had carried them beyond the last attacking warglobes, the thorny branches spread out and tossed the derelict into empty space, like a farmer casting seeds.

'I'll miss you, Beneto,' Estarra called after him.

'I will always hold my memories of you, and of Theroc. They will remain with me for thousands of years as I journey across the cosmos.'

At his controls, OX piloted their craft again, resetting course for Theroc. 'I have already begun to make new memories,' the compy said. Peter smiled.

Estarra stared back through the transparent hull as they hurtled away. The enormous organic vessel dwindled in the distance. In her last glimpse of the verdani battleship that was her brother, the many-branched weapon crashed again into the hydrogues

DENN PERONI

When Denn Peroni flew a group of Roamer ships into the Earth system, he did so with genuine misgivings. He had never expected to return here, certainly not after the last time when he'd been arrested and held on trumped-up charges. Thankfully, King Peter had freed him before he could be used as a scapegoat.

I repay my debts, Denn thought.

Kotto Okiah guided the foremost of the eleven spidery cargo escorts next to Denn's *Dogged Persistence*. The craft were nothing more than frameworks for hauling tanks of concentrated star-drive fuel, useless for bearing wental water to gas-giant targets. However, the thin tubular legs could easily fold around the stacks of flat packages like decks of giant playing cards.

Ever since the eccentric engineer had brought his blueprints to Yreka, dozens of Roamer and former Hansa manufacturing facilities had produced hundreds of thousands of the simple, flexible mats. Though the Roamers were stung by Eddy depre-dations, and the Hansa colonies were just as angry for being abandoned by their own government, when they had learned of the drogues' planned attack on Earth, they decided to do something about it.

'This is your baby, Kotto. Would you like to be out front and centre?'

'Oh, I don't really need to have any special credit. The doorbells will be doing all the work.'

Denn chuckled. 'I'm not expecting the Big Goose to hand us any trophies, no matter what we do here.'

The Roamer ships saw the fireworks of a furious battle long before they came close to Earth. Denn tried to drink it all in. Green priests dispersed around the orphaned Hansa colonies had forewarned them about the huge verdani battleships, but none of the Roamers was prepared for the sight of those twenty awesome trees grappling with one warglobe after another.

He saw EDF battleships clashing with each other, Juggernauts firing upon Juggernauts. Was it some sort of civil war? Then he remembered that Soldier compies had hijacked much of the fleet. Maybe the robots had come back for revenge. The Eddies seemed to piss everybody off . . .

Of course, there was no mistaking a gaudy Ildiran warliner. Denn had been to Ildira more than once to reopen trade with the Mage-Imperator, and his *Dogged Persistence* had been escorted by such warliners. Hundreds of the extravagant Solar Navy ships had already smashed themselves into warglobes, but the hydrogue forces still looked overwhelming. As the remaining deep-core aliens reeled, recovered, then renewed their attack, Denn spotted hundreds more Ildiran warliners charging in. They moved in perfect formation and accelerated, obviously preparing for another concerted suicide run. Hundreds of vessels, each one of which must contain at least a thousand Ildirans. All of them ready to sacrifice themselves.

If the doorbells worked as the engineer promised, it was all so unnecessary.

'Kotto, we've got to do something about this.'

'Our cargo escorts are flying as fast as they can. We'll be there in ten minutes.'

'Doesn't look like we have ten minutes. Those warliners are already starting their acceleration runs.' Without waiting for further discussion, he sent a broad-range burst. 'Calling the Solar Navy! This is Denn Peroni from the Roamers. Remember me? I've been a guest of your Mage-Imperator several times. Is anybody out there?' The cohort of warliners continued to plunge towards the hydrogues. Obviously, they weren't interested in conversation. He raised his voice, feeling greater urgency. 'Please listen! We have brought a new weapon to deploy against the hydrogues. There's no need for you to sacrifice your lives.'

Kotto added his voice, 'Let us show you what we've got up our sleeves. By the Guiding Star, it's much more efficient than smashing so many warliners.'

'And it'll save thousands of lives,' Denn added. 'Just give us a few minutes.'

A deep voice answered. 'This is Adar Zan'nh. Tal Lorie'nh, you have my permission to suspend your attack run. I know about these Roamer traders – let us see what they intend to do.' His voice held a note of relief.

'Acknowledged, Adar,' said Lorie'nh. The accelerating warliners broke off their run, changing course and arcing away from the clustered hydrogue spheres. 'I am happy to give the humans the first chance to defend their own world.'

'It's not exactly my world anymore,' Denn muttered. 'But we'll help them out anyway.'

A rough voice he recognized as General Kurt Lanyan's elbowed its way through the commsystem. 'Roamers! What the bloody hell are you doing here? If you get in the way, I'll shoot you down myself.'

'Why General, we've just come to demonstrate a bit of Roamer ingenuity, not to mention generosity.'

Denn's *Dogged Persistence* and the eleven cargo escorts dumped their packages. Each craft carried thousands of tightly stacked resonance membranes, which spread apart as soon as they were released, separated by quick electrostatic charges. Kotto's door-bells created a blizzard in empty space, flakes drifting onto the enemy craft.

Most of them missed, but enough clung in place. Once fastened, the doorbells began to thrum through a frequency cycle until they stumbled upon the correct resonance tone with dramatic results. The warglobes' enormous hatches split open. Windows and access ports burst to vent the superdense atmosphere into space.

At first, Kotto and Denn cheered in triumph, then yelled in panic as they scrambled to avoid the out-of-control drogue ships. Roamer vessels tried to get out of the shooting gallery. Ricocheting warglobes collided with each other and barely missed the cargo escorts. Spherical battleships crashed into each other, haring off in random directions, completely out of control. The diamond globes had no defence against this kind of attack.

It was a massacre.

The hundreds of Solar Navy warliners that had been pulled from suicide runs circled about. Denn imagined the Ildirans must be pleased, or at the very least relieved.

Even with the warglobes destroyed, however, the battle wasn't over. The EDF Juggernauts and Mantas were still firing on their robot-controlled counterparts. On a whim, Denn transmitted to the Ildirans. 'Adar, if you have any spare ships, I think General Lanyan could use some assistance.'

Tal Lorie'nh's cohort, still spoiling for a fight, happily joined the fray. Ildiran ships tracked down the hijacked craft and opened fire. Eavesdropping on EDF channels, Denn heard loud cheering among the human soldiers.

General Lanyan sent a loud call across the comm line, sounding stunned. 'Roamers, identify yourselves. Who are you?'

Denn couldn't resist. 'We're the people who just saved your butts. Don't ever forget that. We're *Roamers*, and proud of it.'

'I can't believe you'd do this for the EDF,' the General said.

Denn heard several of the clan pilots laughing out loud on the channel. 'We didn't do it for you, General. In fact, we did it in spite of the EDF. We did this for King Peter.' He smiled. That would certainly put egg on the Chairman's face! He leaned back in his pilot's chair. 'We'll be taking our leave now. No sense overstaying our welcome.'

Lanyan sounded embarrassed. 'Wait around for the mop-up operations. Get yourself a pat on the back from the Hansa.'

'Oh, I don't think so, General,' Denn said. 'Roamers just don't seem to be safe in your clutches.' On a private channel, he called Kotto and the pilots of the other cargo escorts. 'We'll just let them chew on that for a while.'

Without a further word to the Hansa or the EDF, the Roamers departed from the Earth system.

SIRIX

Aboard his stolen EDF Juggernaut, the Klikiss robot assessed what remained of his military force. Actual events were greatly at variance with what he had anticipated.

Knowing the hydrogue scheme, Sirix and his fellow robots had made a perfect plan to participate in the annihilation of the human home world. Flown by reprogrammed Soldier compies and independent Klikiss robots, these military ships should have been unstoppable against the disorganized remnants of the Earth Defence Forces.

He had committed serious errors. Sirix had never anticipated that enormous treeships would join the conflict. He had never believed *humans* could mount an effective defence against such overwhelming numbers. He had not expected Roamers to arrive with an unprecedentedly effective weapon against the warglobes.

In all of his calculations, Sirix had also dismissed the Ildirans as a threat. Ages ago, as part of his bargain with the Klikiss robots, the Mage-Imperator had vowed never to create sentient machines. After the robots discarded the agreement, Sirix had never counted on a half-breed girl with unexpected telepathic powers to help the Ildirans negotiate with the hydrogues. He had also not expected the Solar Navy to turn against the far-superior warglobes. Mage-Imperator Jora'h had cast aside the alliance like so much worthless debris, even though he knew the hydrogues would retaliate. It defied reason.

Now it was no longer possible for Sirix to complete the original objectives. It annoyed him.

The robot-hijacked battleships were identical to those commanded by General Lanyan. The stolen Mantas and Thunder-heads outnumbered real EDF ships, and this time they had preemptively disabled all of the guillotine protocols. General Lanyan could not use that insidious trick again.

By displaying stock images of now-dead grid Admirals, Sirix had expected to slip cleanly among the EDF vessels and open fire. But humans had a surprising ability to distinguish the subtlest details in each other's features and behaviour. The deceptive images of human commanders had been taken directly from EDF records, but the surviving soldiers somehow detected the ruse.

Suspicious human captains challenged the holographic simulacra with ridiculous trivia that could not be found in EDF databases. They asked opinions about sports teams or gossip about celebrities and medialoop stars. Neither the Klikiss robots nor the Soldier compy poseurs could answer swiftly or correctly. Real EDF ships easily identified the infiltrators.

Sirix had underestimated these vermin. Simulations and analyses did not allow adequate understanding of chaotic bio-logical intelligences.

Now, from his damaged Juggernaut, General Lanyan dis-tributed target lists of robot-controlled ships. A third cohort of Ildiran warliners added their weapons to the remnants of the EDF.

Verdani treeships continued to attack the few hydrogues that had managed to elude the Roamer doorbells.

What should have been a simple victory was turning into a rout.

Sirix had already lost a third of his stolen ships – and he required those vessels for cleansing human inhabitants from other planets. Unless he retreated with his remaining vessels now, he would not be able to recapture the former Klikiss colony worlds. That was his priority.

Faced with defeat, Sirix decided to save the rest of his ships. Otherwise, the overall mission – not just this single battle – would fail.

Watching the last hydrogues being wiped out, he reached the only logical decision. In a burst of machine language, his instructions rattled across all functional robot-controlled battleships. 'Retreat. Salvage our military craft. Withdraw from the fight.'

He repeated his transmission to make certain all of his counterparts understood. With extrapolative programming, they should have already reached the same conclusions on their own. 'Disengage from the conflict.'

In unison, with precision that would have made even the Adar of the Solar Navy proud, the robot-controlled vessels spun about. The stolen EDF battleships fired up their engines and fled swiftly into space.

ONE HUNDRED AND THIRTY-FOUR

JESS TAMBLYN

The alien cityplex shrank into the misty distance as Jess guided his wental bubble out of Qronha 3. Hydrogue domes, chambers, and pyramids were still visible through the coloured fog, though a living mist continued to thicken around the bizarre metropolis. Wentals had penetrated to the core layers, approaching the cityplex itself. Diamond warglobes hurtled past, battling their intangible enemies with icewaves and deadly blue lightning, which had little effect.

'I didn't think we'd escape this easily,' Tasia said.

Robb Brindle made a strangled sound. 'You call this *easy*, Tamblyn? Maybe you hit your head on something—'

'There's more to come,' Jess warned. 'Count on it.'

With hydrogues and wentals colliding all around them, no one expected the immediate threat to come at them from below. On her knees, peering through the soap-bubble hull, Tasia cried out. 'Shizz, Jess – Klikiss robots after us! Lots of them.'

From the alien metropolis, a swarm of black machines cracked open their armoured carapaces, spread their wings, and activated propulsion systems. They flew after the escaping ship like a swarm of metal locusts.

Smith Keffa's face contracted with fear as the Klikiss robots closed the distance, their multiple articulated limbs extended. 'They're coming to kill us. Damn machines! Leave us alone.'

The first black robot slashed past, and skittering mechanical claws ripped the wet membrane. Jess used his fluid control to instantly seal the breach and reform the protective film as fast as the robot swept by, but dozens more attackers buzzed closer. The ship was already flying upwards at the greatest speed Jess could attain. There were so many of them. So many.

Jess shouted to the elemental voices in his head, demanding help, but the wentals sang back, *We are unable to assist. The battle is joined, and the hydrogues are fierce.*

Another Klikiss robot slammed into the bubble and somehow held on with its blurring, slicing claws. The healing membrane immediately closed against the deadly atmosphere, but the robot worked its bulk through the bubble wall, like a bizarre and horrific baby being born.

Belinda screamed. With a wild cry, Keffa pushed off the bubble wall and flailed forward to tackle the heavy robot. The force of his leap drove both him and the robot out through the membrane with a hollow *pop*. As soon as they passed into the superdense atmosphere, the man was crushed to a splatter-smear of flesh and blood. The robot spun away, falling as it tried to reorient itself.

Now only six captives remained, and more Klikiss robots surrounded Jess's ship. The escape bubble rose towards the upper atmospheric layers, but not nearly fast enough. The black robots swarmed higher, their beetle wings flapping, their propulsion systems driving at high speed.

Unable to do anything more himself, Jess again pleaded with

the wentals. In his head, the elemental voices answered, *The robots are not our primary enemies.*

'They're *my* primary enemies right now! If you don't do something, we're going to die.' After an interminable pause, the wentals grudgingly agreed.

Diamond-like water vapour condensed out of the moisture-laden slipstreams. Living wet fog folded around the flying robots, individual packets of mist that began as gauzy cocoons, then condensed into bubbles of water. Within moments, the pursuing robots were encased in what looked like giant raindrops. The black machines struggled inside the blobs of liquid, and then in a snapping instant, the water cocoons froze solid, encapsulating the robots. The nodules of ice dropped away like hailstones.

Tasia and Robb hurled smug insults at the robots. The other captives sat in shock. Belinda huddled with her eyes closed, as if counting the seconds until they could be far from there.

Jess shot their ship through the highest layers of the atmospheric battlefield, and the gaseous air grew thinner. 'We're almost to the edge of space.'

Before the wental ship could escape into orbit, a group of six already corroded warglobes gave chase. 'Shizz, don't the drogues have bigger problems right now?' Tasia said.

Jess answered, 'In us, they see an enemy they believe they can destroy. Hold on!' He sent the bubble into a wild pinball spin.

'Still think this is easy, Tamblyn?' Robb held his stomach as if he were about to vomit.

The half dozen warglobes followed the escaping bubble, lumbering closer as if to roll over the ship with brute force. No matter how much speed he urged from the wental vessel, Jess lost ground. He could not avoid all six hydrogue spheres. They would be on him in moments.

'We came so close,' Tasia groaned. 'Dammit, we came so close!'

Finally the ship tore free of Qronha 3's atmosphere and shot out into clear, empty space. Behind them, the last veils of indistinct mist faded as the churning clouds continued their elemental battles.

Space beyond the planet was crisp and black, unhindered by obstacles, but Jess found no sanctuary there. The warglobes hounded them like howling wolves, their hulls scarred and close to cracking. He dodged a lance of blue lightning, but couldn't go any faster.

With no place to hide, he swept downwards again, grazing the edge of the atmosphere. The gigantic world rolled past below, and dark battle stains spread through the clouds.

And a miracle rose over the bright edge of the gas giant, backlit by the distant sun: a tangle of branches and thorns, huge limbs extending from an armoured core trunk. Seven of the new verdani battleships Jess had helped create, ready to intercept any fleeing warglobes.

Jess drove his small protective sphere straight towards the treeships.

Tasia cried, 'Jess, what are you doing? Look at those things!'

'Beautiful, aren't they?'

Closing in, the pursuing warglobes tumbled after Jess's tiny bubble. They didn't seem to understand the threat of the treeships until it was too late.

Extending huge, thorny branches, the flying trees seized the already damaged alien globes. Blue lightning bolts sizzled out, along with icewave spurts, but the spiny treeships ignored the searing energy. They embraced the warglobes with their thick limbs and *squeezed*. With silent explosions in empty space, the warglobes crumbled. Jagged shards tumbled slowly back into Qronha 3's deep atmosphere like so many smashed components of a Roamer skymine. Leaving the wreckage of hydrogues behind, the verdani treeships climbed away from the gas giant and soared off in search of other targets.

Carrying his frightened passengers far from their hellish hydrogue prison, Jess flew off to safety and freedom. They were cramped in the water-bubble ship, but Tasia and her companions would have endured anything to get away from their captors.

Jess groaned when an EDF ship appeared over the planet. It was a large scout, a troop transport rather than a battleship. After a tense moment, Jess recognized the vessel and its pilot. 'Conrad Brindle, I told you to go back to Earth.'

'I came to help,' the pilot transmitted.

Suddenly excited, Robb grabbed at Tasia's arms. 'Is that my father? What's he doing here?'

'If he's offering a real toilet and a bunk to sleep on, I'm there,' Tasia said. 'Shizz, right now even spampax sounds delicious.'

'I'll see what I can arrange,' Jess said. The EDF scout vessel approached, drawing closer to the wental bubble. Jess sent out the message, 'I've got a few people who would like to come aboard, Commander Brindle. They belong with you more than with me.'

'Nobody knows where we belong anymore,' Tasia said.

Robb answered, 'We sure as hell belong away from that nightmare.'

'No argument from me there, Brindle.'

'I have seats for them all,' the man answered. 'I can take them back to Earth . . . Or wherever they want to go.'

ONE HUNDRED AND THIRTY-FIVE

FORMER PRINCE DANIEL

As the effects of the twitcher wore off, Daniel struggled to regain control of his unreliable body. He had never experienced a sensation like that, falling through the transportal. It felt as if his body had been folded, turned inside out, flying for ever in an instant – then dropped intact somewhere far, far away.

It had been night-time in the Palace District when Peter and Estarra threw him through the dimensional doorway, and the sudden sunlight was so bright that his eyes hurt. He couldn't wait to get back at them. Even if they were the King and Queen, they had no right to do this to him – *him*! Those two would soon be ousted, and *he* would be the new King. Nobody could treat a King this way.

Daniel rolled to one side on the uneven ground, flopped his numb hands, and tried to find his footing. The sky was dusty-brown, and the air smelled awful, like dirt, wet weeds, slimy mud . . . even poop. What was this place?

Though his muscles continued to misfire, Daniel lurched to his hands and knees, caught his breath, then squatted on his heels. When he looked around, the distances seemed huge. He was up on a slope, and the horizon was very far away. He saw tall grasses, square patches of crops, and small human figures moving in a wide fertile valley. Colourful prefab houses were aligned in a tiny town that might have looked quaint if he'd seen it in a nostalgic videoloop.

Weather-worn Klikiss towers poked up from the plain, but they had crumbled to little more than nubs, like rotted teeth. He couldn't identify this particular planet, but all pictures he had seen of Klikiss colony worlds looked the same to him anyway. He'd never had any intention of visiting one.

Behind him, the transportal wall was the only nearby structure. He used it to support himself as he got to his feet and brushed off his clothes – pyjamas and a robe, certainly not the finery in which he wanted to be seen. Worse, he had pissed himself. It was so unseemly for a king, or even a prince.

Indignant, Daniel raised his voice and started yelling for guards, for the Chairman. Someone was bound to hear him. He rubbed his muscles, gradually getting back full control of his body.

'Hello?' he shouted again. 'Why doesn't somebody answer?'

He waved his arms, drawing the attention of the dark-clad workers tilling the crop patches. The distant group began to come towards him, but they didn't seem to be in a hurry. With a heavy sigh, Daniel trudged to meet them halfway.

The ground was muddy with irrigation and – yes, indeed – he distinctly smelled poop. He couldn't wait to tell Chairman Wenceslas what Peter and Estarra had done to him. They were going to be in so much trouble!

As he approached the group of men, he saw that they all carried dirty farm tools – rakes, hoes, shovels. One even led a plough horse! They looked hot and sweaty in their rough clothes.

Every man sported a wide-brimmed hat, and most had facial hair that was untrimmed and unstyled. Perhaps they hadn't been able to find a barber to join them on their colonization initiative.

When the men came closer, Daniel almost gagged. He'd never smelled so much body odour before. The farmers didn't even seem to notice. At least they appeared peaceful and friendly, smiling beneath the shadowed brims of the hats.

'Welcome to Happiness,' said the first man to arrive. 'We weren't expecting visitors, but we're pleased to have you join us.'

'I don't intend to join you. I'm the victim of a heinous crime, and I demand your assistance. I am Prince Daniel, soon to be King of the Terran Hanseatic League. You all owe me your allegiance.' He expected gasps of awe or bows of deference; instead, the bearded men looked at him curiously. They introduced themselves faster than he could remember any names.

'We are just neo-Amish farmers,' said the leader, who called himself Jeremiah Huystra. 'We established this bucolic settlement here as a bastion of the old ways, one step closer to Eden.'

Daniel spluttered, wondering how anyone could call this dirty, primitive place an Eden. 'I insist upon priority treatment. I'm your Prince.' He gestured towards the Klikiss transportal wall behind him. 'Send me back to the Whisper Palace, where I belong.'

Jeremiah and the other neo-Amish farmers shrugged. 'Oh, we don't use that thing anymore. None of us knows how, and we don't wish to. We stopped receiving shipments from the Hansa a while back, and I doubt we'll get any more. But that is a blessing, since we came here to be left in peace.'

The enormity sank in. Daniel blinked his blue eyes several times, looking around this primitive planet that someone had had the nerve to name *Happiness*. Peter and Estarra had planned this! They knew he would be stranded here without any hope of getting back.

KEVIN J. ANDERSON

As if he'd been hit with a twitcher again, the Prince dropped to the ground and began to sob. His hands made fists and pounded the unyielding dirt.

Jeremiah Huystra put a strong hand on the young man's shoulder. 'Do not despair. You have nothing to fear.' Huystra handed him a crude homemade hoe. 'You are welcome to join us. We can always use another worker.'

ONE HUNDRED AND THIRTY-SIX

ADAR ZAN'NH

After the last explosions died away, space became eerily still, a graveyard of drifting wrecks. The remaining ships performed emergency repairs, while EDF scouts searched for survivors.

From the warliner's command nucleus Adar Zan'nh took inventory of what he had left. So much of the Solar Navy was gone! Two full cohorts of ships, every single warliner destroyed. But thanks to the Roamer traders and their ingenious invention, Tal Lorie'nh had not been required to add another cohort and hundreds of thousands more Ildiran lives to the cost.

All together it had just barely been enough. Across the Spiral Arm, the deep-core aliens were suffering defeat after defeat from other unforeseen battles. The hydrogues had not expected to combat so many enemies on so many fronts. Even the Ildirans had not counted on all those unexpected allies.

Even so, Zan'nh could still feel the stinging cries of uncounted dead and injured back on Ildira. He desperately wanted to know what had happened there.

And now he needed to show his strength to get through this. In the quiet after the holocaust, he stared at the starry emptiness around him. His skeleton crew worked with all possible speed to restore the flagship's engines, but when the chief mechanic returned smeared with grimy residue, his face was downcast. 'We cannot complete the repairs ourselves, Adar. The damage is too severe.'

Zan'nh nodded. 'Scavenge the components we need. I will make contact with Tal Lorie'nh's warliners and request their assistance.'

Once he expressed his need to Tal Lorie'nh, though, he was surprised when General Lanyan's voice interrupted him. He had forgotten the EDF was also tied to their Ildiran command frequency. 'I know you Solar Navy types like to keep to yourselves, but we could help you out in a snap. After all, Ildirans *did* give us our stardrive technology two centuries ago. We use pretty much the same equipment as you do.'

Zan'nh reminded himself that without the Earth Defence Forces, and without the assistance of Sullivan Gold and Tabitha Huck in equipping the automated warliners, the hydrogues would never have been beaten.

'General Lanyan, we would be grateful if your engineers could help us.'

'No trouble at all.'

Less than an hour later, Lanyan's shuttle entered the warliner's landing bay. Zan'nh and two crewmen went to meet him, while the minimal Ildiran crew continued to work. As the square-jawed General emerged from the shuttle accompanied by a well-equipped EDF technical team, the Adar remained rigid. He remembered all too clearly the curses this man had showered upon him when he believed Zan'nh had betrayed him.

Instead of accusations, the bullish commander grabbed the

Adar's hand and pumped it so vigorously that Zan'nh's elbow ached. 'It was all a set-up, a goddamned set-up! You sure fooled me and my soldiers. For a few moments there you made me crap my new uniform, but you put one over on the drogues even more than you did on us!'

'I apologize for not being more forthcoming, General. I had my instructions. We had to keep our plans secret from the hydrogues, but we assumed the green priests had disseminated the details of the plan to you.'

'Not a word of it. And we didn't expect the Roamers to come either. Everything turned out all right – can't complain about that – but I still feel completely caught with my pants down.'

'As I said, General, we assumed the Hansa knew. Do you not speak with your green priests?'

'Not so much anymore.'

Zan'nh explained how his warliners had been automated with help from Hansa engineers, then he gave the General his long-awaited tour of a Solar Navy warliner, while the EDF technical crew met with Ildiran engineers to determine how much of the flagship was salvageable. Lanyan claimed to have experts familiar with 'old-fashioned' stardrive designs; over the centuries, the humans had made many modifications – the General called them 'improvements' – to the stardrives. 'And what we can't fix for you, we'll replace. We've got the largest salvage yard in the Spiral Arm right out there.'

A message came from Tal Lorie'nh. 'Adar, my cohort is ready to return to Ildira, if you wish to accompany us. We can leave your flagship here and return for it later with a full restoration crew.'

General Lanyan had already received a report from his engineering team. 'If we all work together, Adar, we could have the basic repairs finished in a few days.'

Zan'nh hesitated. He wanted to rush back to the Prism Palace, to learn what had happened with the watchdog warglobes once he'd turned the tables during the hydrogue ambush. He knew that his father was still alive — he would have felt the Mage-Imperator's death like a scream through the *thism* — and he knew that the hydrogues were vanquished, though many thousands of Ildirans had died.

Zan'nh pondered the options and then reached his decision. He would send Tal Lorie'nh back with his cohort of warliners to assist at Ildira. For the moment, that was enough. 'No thank you, Tal. I will keep one warliner here to assist me. Meanwhile, return to Mijistra and make your report to the Mage-Imperator. I will come home soon, in my own flagship.'

ONE HUNDRED AND THIRTY-SEVEN

QUEEN ESTARRA

Connected through telink to the verdani battleships, green priests followed the battles across the Spiral Arm, the vanquishing of hydrogue gas giants, the tremendous last stand at Earth. All of the new verdani seedships had uprooted themselves from the forest floor and joined the other monstrous trees in space, fighting against their ancient enemies.

But Theroc itself was quiet and undefended.

The arrival of a small hydrogue craft created quite a stir. The worldtrees rustled, preparing to defend themselves with a barrage of seed-projectiles. Green priests rushed out to stand together. Mother Alexa and Father Idriss stood together on a high open balcony of the fungus-reef city, looking fearfully into the sky.

But the tiny diamond bubble made no threatening moves. It hovered over a ragged gap in the thick canopy, then passed down to settle onto the churned dirt where Beneto's five-trunked treeship had torn itself from the ground.

When the small sphere's hatch finally hissed open, releasing a breath of Earth-normal air, King Peter and Queen Estarra stepped out. They were accompanied by a stiffly formal Teacher compy.

Estarra was overjoyed. 'We're home!'

It had been so long. She could not absorb enough details of her beautiful world: the colour of the sky, the quality of the sunlight, the overarching majesty of the great trees that had twice survived hydrogue devastation. The smells were fresh and wonderful, perfumes of flowers, sharp oils from dark-green leaves, and the warm musk exuded by the worldtrees.

In the years since the horrific attack that had killed her brother Reynald, the people had worked slavishly to heal the wounds. Dead trees had been cleared away, new treelings planted. The surge of life from the wental comet had covered many of the freshest scars.

Estarra clung to Peter's arm with great pleasure. 'I never knew how much I'd miss everything about Theroc. I can't wait to show you my world.'

Peter stroked her hair, more interested in his Queen's happiness than in answering the questions of the cheering people who came to meet them. 'You talk about Theroc so much, and I've seen images . . . but no words or pictures could do justice to this. It's a perfect place for us.'

'A place to stay, and a place to keep our family safe.'

'And a place to live while we help guide the human race – far from the Chairman. That's the best part, I think.'

Celli bounded forward, dragging her big-shouldered green priest friend by the hand. Estarra saw with amazement that her wiry little sister was not only older, but she appeared much more mature. 'Celli, look at you!'

The younger girl couldn't tear her eyes from Estarra's belly. 'And you, you're so . . . so pregnant! Are you about to have the baby?'

Estarra laughed. 'Not for a little while yet.' She patted her stomach. 'I'm at six and a half months – I don't even want to imagine how much bigger I'm going to get.'

Celli introduced herself to Peter as if she had just noticed him, then she did a double-take when she realized who he was. 'You – you're the King!'

'And you must be Estarra's little sister.' Peter turned to Estarra. 'Is she the one who kept pet condorflies?'

'Oh, I was just a little kid then!' Estarra demanded introductions, much more interested in Solimar, who was apparently Celli's boyfriend, than she was in condorflies.

Peter craned his neck, staring up at the beautiful green canopy. 'Are all the trees here so . . . *tall?*'

Celli laughed. 'You should have seen the verdani battleships!'

'Oh we did – a lot closer than I would have liked.'

Wearing overly extravagant beetle carapace headdresses, cocoon-weave garments, and shellacked chest pieces, Idriss and Alexa arrived, happy but perplexed. 'We're thrilled to have you home again, daughter,' Alexa said, 'but please explain what's happening. Nahton sent us sporadic messages from Earth, but he doesn't have many details. Even if the hydrogues are defeated at Earth, they may keep coming back and—'

'The hydrogues won't be a problem any longer, Mother Alexa,' Solimar said, and all the nearby green priests nodded. 'The verdani battleships are quite convinced of that. The war seems to be won. The enemy is destroyed.'

Estarra said breathlessly, 'And we escaped from the Chairman. He was trying to kill us. And the baby, too.' Nahton had already sent word of their danger.

Alexa quickly understood the implications. 'Are you in exile, then?'

Peter's voice was grim. 'The Hansa is in a shambles and run by a corrupt madman. The Chairman taught me my skills and duties, but he himself has forgotten what it means to be a leader.'

Idriss looked from side to side. 'What about Sarein? Did she come with you? She should be here with the rest of her family.'

Estarra frowned, feeling a pang. Sarein had given them invaluable assistance, but in the end she had chosen to remain with the Chairman. 'No, she stayed on Earth.' The Queen hugged her parents, feeling a deep gratitude in her heart. 'We had no place else to go.'

Alexa had tears streaming down her face. 'There is no question about it. You must both stay here.' She held up a gently scolding finger. 'Forget all of your politics for now. I insist that you let our first grandchild be born here on Theroc.'

MAGE-IMPERATOR JORA'H

After ten thousand years of waiting and preparing for the inevitable, it was over. Now, the Ildirans began to pick up the pieces.

Standing outside under the multiple suns, Jora'h gazed at his damaged city. All sixty of the threatening warglobes lay smashed in the streets and on hills where they had fallen. Though Mijistra's sky had been empty of enemies for days, the last cohorts of the Solar Navy maintained a diligent cordon around the planet.

Nira stood next to the Mage-Imperator, silent and sombre, her hand resting lovingly on their daughter's shoulder. Armies of worker kithmen operated heavy machinery to excavate and drag away the wreckage of shattered warglobes. As they considered the devastation, she said, 'It could have been worse, Jora'h. Much worse.'

'It very nearly was.'

Jora'h still didn't know the extent of damage across his Empire. He had been overwhelmed by resounding echoes of mental anguish in the *thism*. As the dying warglobes had crashed into the

city like a rain of diamond asteroids, a wave of shock and death
had rolled over him, nearly overloading his ability to receive
messages of pain. The Mage-Imperator was at the centre of it all,
the lives and deaths of so many people funnelled into him.

Medical kithmen scurried to rescue the injured, pulling bodies
from the wreckage. Handlers counted and prepared the dead.
Jora'h had felt them all cry out, felt the threads of *thism* snapping
with exquisitely sharp pain. But oh, how much more terrible it
would have been had the hydrogues vaporized the entire city —
and then the whole Ildiran Empire.

Nira sensed his distress. 'Your gamble paid off.'

'It was not my gamble alone. It was for all of us. And I could
not have done it without you or Osira'h.' Turning Adar Zan'nh's
warliners against the hydrogues might have sealed the fate of
all Ildirans, but Jora'h had made his decision to follow the bright
soul-threads, to see the Lightsource and a path of honour. 'I
thought I was going to spend my last moments with you, Nira.'

She smiled up at him. 'Maybe you will. But not for a long
time yet.'

He folded his arms around her and his daughter, gathering
them close. A small family, a microcosm of the Ildiran Empire.
The Mage-Imperator was father to all his people, yet no leader in
memory had ever had a family such as this.

From high above, one more warliner descended through the
clear sky. Unlike the other Solar Navy ships patrolling Ildira, this
warliner was scarred, its gaudy hull plates blackened and damaged,
solar fins and streamers dangling loosely. But it could fly, and it
had returned.

'Adar Zan'nh has come home.' Jora'h flashed a small grin.
'I have news that will make him very happy.'

Later, when the Adar faced his father at the entrance to the
Prism Palace, his uniform looked impeccable, even after what his

ships had been through. Despite his haunted eyes, Zan'nh bowed and pressed his fist against his chest in a salute to the Mage-Imperator. Eschewing formality, Jora'h hugged his oldest son. 'You accomplished the impossible! I am proud of you and my entire Solar Navy.'

The Adar did not look pleased. 'I lost two cohorts of warliners, Liege. The Empire's defences are greatly weakened.'

Jora'h's optimism would not be shaken. 'The hydrogues are defeated, and we can endure. That was the threat for which the Solar Navy was constructed ten millennia ago. Who are our enemies now?'

'Even so, Liege, we dare not remain defenceless. We must start immediately to rebuild our Solar Navy.'

'Certainly, and for that reason I am forced to modify your duties. When I lost Thor'h, I asked you to serve as my next Prime Designate. Because you are loyal and faithful, you agreed. But that was never your calling.'

Zan'nh bowed. 'My calling is to serve you, Mage-Imperator, in whatever fashion you command.'

It was the answer Jora'h had expected to hear. 'I hereby release you from your duties as Prime Designate, Adar Zan'nh. You may now command the Solar Navy without other distractions, if that is your desire.'

'Yes, Liege! But who will become Prime Designate?'

Jora'h glanced at Osira'h who stood serenely beside him and her mother. 'Daro'h is next in line for such work. He is now my oldest noble-born son. I will bring him back to the Prism Palace to become Prime Designate in your place.' The feeling in his heart was bittersweet. 'Now the Empire needs him more than Dobro does. I have already sent a summons. The breeding programme is ended, and our splinter colony can be made open again.'

Though Jora'h suggested that he and his soldiers rest, Zan'nh would not hear of it. The Adar hurried away from the Prism Palace to set in motion his plans for rebuilding the Solar Navy. Smiling, the Mage-Imperator let him do as he wished.

Next, Jora'h summoned Sullivan Gold and Tabitha Huck. It was time for complete truthfulness. Keeping secrets to protect the Empire seemed intrinsic to his bloodline, but at Nira's urging he was determined to change things.

He looked at the two humans, who still appeared shaken from all the destruction. Jora'h said, 'When you agreed to help us, Adar Zan'nh gave his word that once we defeated the hydrogues, you and your comrades would be allowed to go home. The human race may distrust us. Your people and mine will have great obstacles to overcome before we can recover from our past treachery.'

'I'm not a diplomat, and I can't speak for anyone but myself,' Sullivan said, 'but maybe I can put in a good word or two. After we get home.'

'Seems to me that without your hundreds of remote-controlled warliners, Earth would be a smoking ruin right now,' Tabitha pointed out. 'Maybe – just maybe – people will cut you a little slack for that.'

Nira smiled at the skyminers. 'As a green priest, I would be happy to facilitate sending messages to your loved ones.'

Sullivan beamed. 'Oh, that would be marvellous. A letter to my Lydia is long overdue. She'll be glad to know I'm not dead after all.'

ONE HUNDRED AND THIRTY-NINE

KOLKER

Even after restoring his connection to the worldforest, Kolker remained reticent. He had never felt so confused and unsure of himself.

Ever since he'd lost his treeling, his all-consuming desire had been to touch telink again. But now that Nira had made it possible, he still felt lost, as if his life's central goal had fallen away like a trapdoor beneath his feet. He had not been able to discuss it with his close friend Yarrod, or anyone else. He seemed farther away from them than even interstellar distances could account for. He had achieved what he'd wanted for so long. What was missing?

Though he could touch the treeling whenever he wished – especially now, with the hydrogues defeated – Kolker had avoided doing so. He wanted to understand this emptiness before he fell back on the crutch of the worldtrees. Not sure where else to turn, he decided to seek out Tery'l. Perhaps the old lens kithman could offer a different perspective. He always seemed so confident in his faith.

Though he searched in his usual meditation places, Kolker

could not find the ancient man. Growing increasingly worried, the green priest asked other Ildirans until he was finally directed into the damaged part of Mijistra, where a hastily erected infirmary held many of those who had been wounded in the explosions and collapsed buildings.

In the makeshift hospital, Kolker wandered among the cots where the injured were being tended by doctors. Young and determined lens kithmen hovered over those closest to death, helping them to see the soul-threads that would guide them as they passed to a plane of infinite light. Kolker expected to find Tery'l with his comrades caring for the wounded.

But his old friend lay by himself, on a cot, among the severely injured. Tery'l had sent the other lens kithmen away, instructing them to devote their attentions to those in greatest need. 'I am content,' he had told them. 'I know everything you could possibly say to me. I have nothing to fear.'

Kolker hurried forward to the battered old man. Tery'l's chest and head were bandaged and bloody, and his milky eyes stared into a bright, cloudless sky. Though Tery'l's eyesight was too weak to recognize the green priest, he seemed to know Kolker by instinct. 'Ah, my human friend! I am glad you came to speak with me.' His papery lips curled in a faint smile. 'But if you need more enlightenment, you had best listen quickly.' The ancient lens kithman could barely manage a laugh, and it came out as only a rattling breath.

Kolker knelt quickly. 'What happened to you? Where were you?'

'I was among the fountains where the prisms intensify the light. It was bright and warm and glorious.' Tery'l smiled. 'The people evacuated, but I could not run swiftly enough. When the warglobes crashed, I was struck by falling debris. Now only frayed ends of my soul-threads are left.'

Kolker touched his friend's forehead. 'You'll be fine. The hydrogues are defeated, and the doctors are taking care of you. There's no reason you can't get better.'

'*Time* is the reason. This body has simply lived too long. Ildirans have a greater lifespan than humans, but our bodies still have limits.' He stared upward again. 'I have done many good things in my life. As a lens kithman, I helped my people. I hope that our discussions have been at least interesting, if not thought-provoking.'

'Yes, they have.' In a rush, Kolker explained how he had finally been reunited through telink, how he'd let his mind sail through the connected trees. 'I wanted it so badly, but once I achieved it, even telink didn't seem adequate any more.'

'What happens to green priests when they die?' the lens kithman asked.

'When we know our time is at an end, we allow ourselves to be absorbed into the worldforest mind. We connect to a tree through telink, and then our body falls among the trees.' Kolker shook his head, and his voice became rough. 'If I had died here without my treeling, I would have been lost for ever – a meaningless death.

'At one time I pitied humans who weren't green priests. I knew that their verbal and written communications could not match my perfect sharing of thoughts through the trees. But now I see that even my blessed telink is exclusive. It doesn't unite humanity – only a handful of chosen green priests. That's not good enough.'

'Perhaps it is all you have,' Tery'l said.

'It doesn't need to be that way! If humans were linked to each other like Ildirans are through *thism*, then we could understand, cooperate, and grow stronger. We'd never have factions and enemies and civil wars.'

'Then you have truly learned from us, my friend. For millennia,

Ildirans had almost no internal struggle, except for the recent Hyrillka uprising – and that was due to flawed *thism*.'

'I wish I could be part of what you have, Tery'l.' Kolker felt desperation in his heart. 'I am so intrigued by your *thism*. I wish I could open myself to it . . .'

The lens kithman grasped Kolker's hand, squeezing with the power of a vice. 'You already understand more than you know. I am comforted that you are here, but comforted more that all my people are with me, all Ildirans together, sharing, thinking, supporting each other.'

'Right now you should be thinking of yourself – just be strong.'

'I am strong. And we all think for all of us. How else could I have survived and remained happy, even as my eyesight failed? It is the *thism*.' With his other hand, Tery'l reached for the shining, lens-etched medallion he always wore at his throat. As he picked it up, the prismatic disc caught the light and reflected rainbows. 'This . . . this may give you more to ponder.'

Not understanding, Kolker took the gift. 'What is it?'

'A symbol.'

The facets seemed full of light being sucked down into a gravity well, reflecting, sparkling with possibilities. 'So it doesn't do anything?'

'Symbols do many things. That depends on you.'

Kolker had seen the old lens kithman touch the medallion, claiming that it helped him to link to the Lightsource. 'Don't you need it yourself, Tery'l?'

As if knowing he was finished with life, *willing* himself to end, the ancient lens kithman simply died without releasing Kolker's hand.

The green priest remained at the old man's side for a long time. He passed through his grief thinking of everything Tery'l had said, clinging to a strand of hope and mystery. He looked down at the sparkling etched facets in the gift medallion, following lines of shattered light. What had the old lens kithman seen inside there? Had he used it to follow paths through the *thism*? Even in death, Tery'l had been comforted by his endless connections to his people.

Finally, Kolker climbed to his feet again and walked in a daze back towards the Prism Palace, toward Sullivan Gold, Tabitha Huck, and the other Hansa skyminers.

He had a mission now. Though he didn't know where he would begin, Kolker prepared for his new work.

PATRICK FITZPATRICK III

I n the space yacht he had 'borrowed' from his grandmother, Patrick stopped off long enough at a distant Hansa outpost to purchase hull paints, which he used to remove the prominent markings. He changed the registration numbers and automatic ID signal. Thinking of dark-haired Zhett, he renamed his yacht the *Gypsy*.

He was alone and far from anything else happening in the Spiral Arm. Patrick did not expect the Roamers to be easy to find, but he had a few obvious starting places.

It took him several lonely days to fly to Osquivel. He didn't expect to find anything useful at the ringed gas giant, however. Certainly not a secret message from Zhett. He'd already read the report of the EDF investigation team. Military engineers had combed over the rubble, finding useless debris, ejected machinery, and wrecked habitats. EDF investigators had collected every usable piece of equipment they could find, piecing together the Kellum operation. Patrick found it ironic. *Now who are the scavengers?*

As he flew through the rubble rings now, he experienced a wash of fearful memories. The Battle of Osquivel had been the most terrifying experience in his life – countless warglobes, EDF ships blasted into scrap metal, ships fleeing in panic and leaving damaged vessels and lifepods . . . including his own.

Strangely enough, Osquivel's cloud bands seemed different now, changed, as if lit from within. Brighter and less ominous. He couldn't imagine what might have happened to change a whole planet. It was as if the stain of the hydrogues themselves had disappeared.

He drifted among the rings, searching and thinking. Zhett had taken him out in a small grappler pod to tour the smelters and rubble prospectors, the small greenhouse domes, the recycling facilities, and the habitation complexes. Everything was silent and empty now. On one of the storage rocks he had tricked Zhett, strung her along. She had believed he was falling in love with her.

He couldn't imagine what she thought of him now. Zhett Kellum was a fiery young woman who had powerful feelings. He suspected she did not take humiliation well. How she must have cursed his name!

He had to be insane to steal a ship, escape from his powerful grandmother, and go AWOL from the Earth Defence Forces, just to find Zhett. And if he ever succeeded, how could he expect anything other than contempt from her? She would probably spit in his face – or worse.

Nevertheless, Patrick had to do it. He had no choice whatsoever.

Perhaps, if he could atone for his actions, make her see that he had changed and that he truly regretted what he had done, maybe then he'd have a chance.

*

Next, Patrick flew to the Roamer government centre of Rendezvous – or what was left of it. Admiral Stromo's battle group had done its work well.

He had seen surveillance images of the massive asteroid complex. The Roamers had made once-useless space rubble into a thriving trade and legislative centre. And the EDF's most powerful weapons had broken it all apart and scattered Rendezvous like a handful of gravel. In the short time since the pointless attack, the larger chunks had spread out, propelled on different trajectories by momentum imparted by explosions.

Patrick ached as he looked at the scene. This complex was the political equivalent of the Whisper Palace on Earth or the Hansa HQ. Roamers had never fired a provocative shot at any EDF vessel, as far as he knew. The clans had merely imposed sanctions after a legitimate grievance. Instead of trying to work out an adequate settlement, the Hansa Chairman had insisted on complete control instead of friendship. During her tenure, Maureen Fitzpatrick probably would have done the same.

No wonder all Roamers despised Eddies.

Patrick cruised slowly through the impossible rubble field, imagining how amazing this place had once been. Considering what had been done to them here, he couldn't believe the Roamers hadn't simply dumped their EDF captives right back out into space. Patrick supposed he should count himself lucky.

He drifted, following whatever course the mangled lines of gravity offered. He had a lot of time to think and a lot of thinking to do. He silently promised himself once again that he would find Zhett, that he would make things right. He didn't expect the task to be easy, but he'd had too many easy jobs in his life, thanks to his family. This was something he had to do for himself.

Patrick plotted his next course and flew off.

ONE HUNDRED AND FORTY-ONE

RLINDA KETT

The *Voracious Curiosity* drifted for days in open space. For Rlinda, it was the most enjoyable time in recent memory. 'I forgot just how much fun a person could have, given a little bit of privacy.'

BeBob wasn't complaining, either. They kept the *Curiosity* warm enough that the two of them could spend half the day without clothes on, if they chose – and they often chose just that. Rlinda preferred to keep the lights turned down low, for the mood. BeBob had seen her naked often enough, before, during, and after their brief and tempestuous marriage. She didn't qualify as one of those pheromone-enhanced models, but he never seemed to get tired of the view.

BeBob extricated himself from her and tried to move towards the *Curiosity*'s galley to get a snack, but she didn't let him get away so easily. 'Hey, I didn't say you were excused. I'd like a little more snuggling time here.' The two of them clung together again.

'Sure beats those crowded insulated huts on Plumas,' BeBob said.

'This beats just about everything on Plumas.' After a few minutes, though, she let out a long sigh. 'One of these days we really should get around to finishing these repairs.'

'All right, all right. As soon as you want to suit up, I'll help replace more components.'

'I didn't say I was in that much of a hurry.'

After escaping from the ice moon, the two had cooled their heels and relaxed. Fortunately, since the Tamblyn brothers had intended to keep the *Curiosity* as their own, they had gathered all of the parts for the anticipated repairs and stored them aboard. Working together, taking their time, Rlinda and BeBob finished fine-tuning her beloved ship, and testing it. They gave the *Curiosity* all the care it had needed for quite a while.

Most of the gourmet foods in the cargo hold were gone. She'd lost a lot of her best supplies and trading goods by dumping the main hold during their escape from the EDF, and then the greedy Roamers had ransacked the remaining boxes for delicacies. Speaking for herself, and almost certainly not for BeBob, she said, 'I'd rather just open my faceplate to vacuum than resort to living off standard-issue mealpax.'

'Oh, they're not so bad, once you get used to them.'

During their work, they frequently raised (and then avoided) the question of where to go from there. Their supplies were limited, and they would need to re-establish contact with civilization sooner or later. With their stardrive fuel starting to get low, they couldn't just flit from system to system. They talked about going to an asteroid and setting up a life for themselves, but they knew that couldn't last for ever.

Rlinda finished making some adjustments to the navigation console and, since the ship's gravity was set low, came over to him with dainty steps that would have made a ballerina proud. 'Process of elimination,' Rlinda said. 'We sure can't go back to the Hansa.

The EDF would snatch us both the moment we came within sensor range.'

'I didn't exactly care for Roamer hospitality, either,' BeBob said. 'And I don't know what we'd do in the Ildiran Empire.'

Rlinda ran a finger along her lower lip. When she finally thought of an alternative, the suggestion was so obvious she was surprised it hadn't been her first choice. 'Theroc is quite a nice place. Peaceful, full of fresh food and nice people. *And* they're independent from the Hanseatic League.'

'Seems we could do a lot worse,' BeBob said.

Rlinda checked their ekti levels, called up the star charts, and smiled. 'We've got enough fuel to get there. Want to try?'

BeBob gave her a boyish grin. 'As long as I'm with you, my dear, I'm happy.'

'Stop that nonsense and give me a straight answer.'

'All right, then. Yes.'

ONE HUNDRED AND FORTY-TWO

QUEEN ESTARRA

Within two days, the Therons had put together a transition ceremony. Estarra thought the people would give her time to rest and settle in, but Mother Alexa and Father Idriss had wanted to retire for years, and they were very pleased to have the opportunity.

After Reynald's death they had resumed their old leadership roles, always knowing it would only be temporary. Beneto had come back as a wooden golem, a spokesman for the worldforest, but not someone who could rule the Theron people. Sarein had expressed ambitions to be the next Theron Mother, but she was a puppet of the Earth government; when she couldn't keep up the pretence, she had hurried back to the Hansa.

Which left Estarra, Queen of the Hansa — now in exile — next in line.

Safely back home, she had not slept so well in years. The open fungus-reef windows let in breezes laden with the spicy-sweet scents of epiphyte flowers and the whispering lullabies of contented worldtrees. Holding each other, Peter and Estarra had

672

dozed until long after the bright sunlight flooded their room.

Celli awakened them, prancing with excitement for the up-coming ceremony. 'Today you two will become the new Mother and Father of Theroc! I was afraid you were going to sleep through the whole thing.'

'Shouldn't your people get to know me first? I'm still a stranger here.' Peter shook his head, still not understanding why Alexa and Idriss had simply assumed he would welcome the role. 'I was the mouthpiece for the Terran Hanseatic League. I had to issue some terrible orders, caused a lot of suffering. Does everybody know that it was really Basil behind the worst of it? I wouldn't think the Therons trust me yet.'

Estarra put her arms around his chest from behind, pressing her overlarge stomach against the small of his back. 'Nahton knows you very well, Peter, and all the green priests know what Nahton knows. He never let them be fooled about the things you hated to do.'

Celli let out a bright laugh. 'Besides, Estarra seems to think you're good enough. We're choosing *her* to be our next Mother, and you just happen to come along as part of the deal.'

Later in the day, they all gathered in the fungus-reef's large audience chamber. Feast tables crowded the rooms and platforms: a banquet of fresh fruits, edible flowers, and the most succulent insect steaks had been laid out from the bounty of the worldforest.

Estarra remembered her first taste of chicken and beef in the Whisper Palace's dining hall, though they had still been strangers, Peter had tried to make her feel at home. Now she reciprocated, though the King wasn't nearly as shy as she had been. She wondered if he would savour the tender morsels of pupating larvae cooked in their own cocoon casings. Her stomach growled, and she realized she'd been having strange cravings for Theron food.

First, though, they had their roles to play, and an extremely important announcement to make.

When she and Peter stepped up to the tall chairs in the throne room, Idriss and Alexa removed their headdresses and gave warm blessings to the King and Queen. Idriss boomed out to the people. 'I present to you your new rulers, Father Peter and Mother Estarra of Theroc!' The people cheered, and green priests used the interconnected trees to send the news and receive greetings from treelings on all the scattered planets.

Estarra knew their most important work was just beginning. Human civilization would have to change, starting with the government.

While flying to Theroc aboard the alien derelict, she and Peter had had many long discussions. Even if Earth survived the massive hydrogue attacks and the Soldier compy uprising, the Hansa was fatally flawed. Chairman Wenceslas had alienated his allies, provoked unnecessary confrontations, and withdrawn supplies and defences from colonies that depended on them. Basil was a divider, exactly the wrong sort of leader to bring humanity back from the edge of a terrible precipice.

'After everything that's happened, Peter, we've got to be as strong as a real King and Queen – not just showpieces.'

Peter considered all the opportunities he had lost. 'We'll be as strong as we should have been from the start.'

Together, they had developed a breathtaking scheme. While settling in on Theroc, they had discussed the idea with Estarra's parents, and they had already dispatched messages and proposals via telink to representatives on the orphaned Hansa colonies. Their suggestions had met with a great deal of support.

Now it was time to make it official.

With everyone gathered close for the coronation ceremony, Peter addressed all Therons. He was the Hansa's Great King and now the Father of Theroc. Yarrod waited near the flower-strewn stage, touching a small tree to report King Peter's message via telink; word would spread instantly.

'Earth has survived the attack by the hydrogues, but the Hanseatic League has fallen,' Peter announced. 'Even before the warglobes came, the Hansa was crippled from within by greed, arrogance, and corruption. Many of you saw it – especially those colonists who relied on Hansa support and the Roamer clans who were crushed simply because they demanded fair treatment.'

Beside him, Estarra added, 'All the colonies that signed the Hansa Charter agreed to certain things, and in return the Hansa had its own obligations. When Chairman Wenceslas abandoned those colonies, he breached the contract.'

Peter took her hand. 'In signing the Charter, those colonies swore allegiance to their King. I am the King. I may have left the Whisper Palace, and I may no longer be on Earth, but the centre of government resides with me, *wherever I am*. Therefore, here on Theroc with my Queen, I intend to establish a new seat of government.'

Some of the listeners were surprised. As Therons, they had never been part of the Hansa. 'But it will be a different sort of government from the failed example of the Terran Hanseatic League,' she assured them. 'This is a time for healing the rifts among the branches of humanity. Listen.'

Peter continued, 'We propose to form a new confederation that is *inclusive* and strong. We invite all Therons to join us, along with all of the orphaned Hansa colonies, and all of the unjustly persecuted Roamer clans. We will share skills and resources and help everyone rebuild after the past eight years of war. This is a dramatic change, but I know in my heart that it is the right thing for us all.'

Estarra could see some of the Therons nodding. She knew they would need time to absorb all the immense implications, but she wanted to give them plenty to think about. 'When the *Caillié* left Earth, we intended to be independent. After we formed our colony here, we reestablished ties with Earth, and King Ben granted us our sovereignty. For years now, the Hansa has been struggling to absorb Theroc, but we have refused.'

Peter swept his blue-eyed gaze across the room. 'The confederation we propose would allow the various colonies and groups to keep their independent identities, yet give us the strength in numbers we sorely needed in our recent battles. We will act together for the common good.'

'Shouldn't we worry about military reprisals?' someone called from the floor. Estarra knew the former Hansa colonies would be the most concerned about that.

'Not much of the EDF remains, and they certainly don't have extra ships for policing long-lost colonies.' Peter glanced out of the open balcony to the lush forest beyond. 'If we pull together and agree to certain terms of mutual aid, we will be stronger than the handful of battleships that survived the hydrogue war.'

Green priests passed along the messages. The people in the speaking hall seemed receptive to the idea.

Peter held out his hands. 'Obviously, there are many details to work out. All the clan leaders and colony governors will have their own concerns, legitimately afraid of being trampled by an overbearing government. But especially now, with humanity crippled and reeling, our greatest strength lies in unity. Estarra and I are offering a viable alternative to the Terran Hanseatic League.'

She took his hand. 'We invite representatives of the factions of humanity to come to Theroc, to discuss the fundamentals. If we are agreed, we can even draw up a constitution. We must be strengthened by our numbers, rather than crushed by them.'

Peter's expression grew hard, and he looked at Yarrod. 'Before we can move on, everyone must understand that the Hansa Chairman is no longer a legitimate ruler. Send the word out through telink. Tell every green priest what has taken place here. The King and Queen now rule from Theroc, not Earth. The Chairman no longer has any foundation of power.'

Surveying the room, Estarra saw faces full of heady idealism. Idriss and Alexa were extremely proud of their daughter. Even Celli applauded wildly.

Estarra felt a twinge in her belly – the baby kicking? An omen? She sat down in the ornate throne and put an arm across her abdomen, knowing now that their baby would be safe.

CHAIRMAN BASIL WENCESLAS

While grim assessments of death and destruction continued to roll in for days, Basil felt giddy with both euphoria and disappointment. For the time being, he had holed up in his penthouse office, from which he could look out at the bustling Palace District as the sun rose.

The population of Earth had survived. Basil never would have bet on that outcome.

He didn't yet know the real extent of the casualties, but he could look at the balance sheet and know that desperate times were still to come. The Terran Hanseatic League had never been so close to total obliteration. Since the beginning of his chairmanship thirty years ago, Basil had led the Hansa to its pinnacle of power and influence. Now, in a very short time, it had fallen to its most pathetic level.

While he waited for General Lanyan to shuttle down again from the remnants of his fleet, Deputy Cain joined him in the top-level offices, as did a browbeaten Sarein. Basil realized just how few people he actually trusted anymore, and even some of those were suspect.

When Sarein looked at him, he saw mingled love, fear, and something else in her eyes. She'd been acting strangely ever since the assassination attempt at Daniel's banquet. Or had he noticed odd behaviour even before? He had never completely understood the ambitious young woman, nor had he made a particular effort to do so. He was too busy – and *that* wouldn't change in the near future. Once again, he cursed the fact that Pellidor was dead. He doubted he'd ever find another expeditor so well-trained and trustworthy.

Eldred Cain was stony and unreadable as he took his seat. Basil didn't understand the ghostly deputy either. The human race needed Basil Wenceslas more than ever. That much was obvious.

Finally, guards escorted the General into the office. Lanyan looked exhausted, his uniform unkempt, his eyes bloodshot and baggy. He probably hadn't slept in the days of aftermath, dealing with hundreds of secondary and tertiary problems. *Just like all of us,* Basil thought.

The outlook for the Earth Defence Forces was not good. Despite the help of the Ildirans, the hydrogues and Klikiss robots had destroyed many of the assets the EDF had cobbled together for the last-stand defence. The battleships stolen by the Soldier compies were still out there, far outnumbering what remained of the Hansa military. The robots could return for a *coup de grâce* at any time.

And the damned Roamers. He didn't know what to do about them. Was he supposed to send them a thank-you card? A gift basket? If they had such effective weapons technology against the warglobes, why the hell hadn't they shared it with the Hansa a long time ago?

Even so, the General was charged with a strange sort of energy, as if his pride and indignation were enough to drive back the haggard edge of weariness.

Time to get down to business. Always business. That was what kept human civilization functioning, even more than strong political leaders ... even more than intractable kings and spoiled princes who disappeared in times of crisis. The Chairman would have been willing to ignore King Peter with a sneer of 'Good riddance!' – but Peter had *defied* him. That couldn't be forgiven.

The General manufactured a tired smile for Basil. 'Even considering the terrible cost, Mr Chairman, it is still a victory. The EDF is in a shambles, but the hydrogues have been crushed, perhaps even destroyed.' He shook his head. 'Who would have thought the Ildiran Solar Navy would do what they did? And thanks to the Roamers, dare I say it. We have inspectors trying to figure out what they did with those secret weapons, so we can duplicate them.'

'If the hydrogues are defeated, there's no need to duplicate the weapons,' Basil pointed out. 'Apparently, they will not be effective against any other target.'

'And those huge treeships from Theroc,' Sarein said in a strangely embittered voice. 'It's quite a surprise my people would go to such lengths to help Earth, after we did so little to aid *them* after the hydrogues attacked.'

'Again, the same could be said about the Roamers.' Cain seemed to be enjoying this.

Basil glared at his deputy and at Sarein. 'This is not the time to rehash petty feuds and differences.' He sat at his desk, put his hands in front of him, and straightened his back. 'We need to move swiftly. After this, whole populations will go into shock. There'll be chaos in the streets, anarchy. We must not allow that. We'll have to impose a severe crackdown to maintain control.

Getting the Hansa back up to full strength will require a tremendous amount of work.'

Cain cleared his throat. 'We already established priorities and the distribution of responsibilities based on our last meeting. Now we're ready to move on to the next step.'

Basil tried to drive back his persistent headache. 'In the following weeks, we will complete detailed damage assessments and strength projections – but they must be kept entirely confidential.' He looked meaningfully at Lanyan, then at Deputy Cain. 'Under no circumstances will the general population be allowed to know how badly we've been hurt.'

When they nodded, Basil was glad to see full cooperation for a change. If everyone he relied on had supported him all along, the Chairman could have led them safely through this mess from the beginning. 'We'll pull together the resources from our colonies. Across the Hansa, we need a full-scale effort to construct new battleships, encourage trade, strengthen bonds among the planets, and make the Hansa blossom again. And the effort will need to be far superior to what the human race has managed in recent years.'

They were fine words, but in his heart Basil realized that such an effort would also mean cripplingly high taxes and very lean years. And now Peter, Estarra, and Daniel had vanished. He narrowed his grey eyes, focusing on Sarein. 'Are you sure you have no idea where your sister or the King have gone? It's been days! We need a strong spokesman to prepare the people, to get back in touch with our orphaned colonies.' He thought he might have to haul out his unexpected alternative after all.

'I . . . I don't know where they are, Basil. I haven't spoken to Estarra since just after Daniel's banquet, when you made me show her the greenhouse you destroyed.' She was clearly trying to hide her distaste. 'As you well know, she was under tight guard – for her protection.'

Basil scowled. Was that sarcasm? Among the many unbeliev-able things that had happened during the attack, the hydrogue derelict had disappeared. He had assigned Deputy Cain the task of investigating the matter thoroughly, but with so much going on in the past several days, it wasn't Cain's highest priority.

A secretary appeared at the door of the penthouse office. 'A green priest to see you, Mr Chairman.'

'Send him in. Maybe he has news.' Basil took a seat at his desk. 'It's about time he decided to report to me.'

Nahton walked proudly into the chamber, tall, thin, and deter-mined. The high windows looked out into the bright morning. The green priest stared into the golden sunlight for a moment, then turned to face the Chairman.

'Well, what is it?'

'*As a courtesy*, Chairman Wenceslas, I have been asked to bring you a message from King Peter and Queen Estarra.'

Basil shot to his feet. 'Where are they? I demand that they return to the Whisper Palace immediately.'

'The King and Queen have relocated their throne to Theroc. From there, they will establish a human confederation and preside over a new seat of government.'

Basil could only bark a short, dry laugh. 'That's ridiculous! And it distracts us at a time when we must all pull together.'

'We are pulling together, Mr Chairman. We're just doing it without you.' Nahton's voice was emotionless, a delivery system for a formal proclamation. 'The Therons have endorsed this new confederation and have agreed to join it. The green priests who were dispersed to former Hansa colonies have also made the announcement to their settlers. Representatives are already being chosen.'

'What do you mean *former* Hansa colonies? They have never—'

Nahton interrupted him. 'Sixty-three orphaned worlds have

torn up the Hansa Charter and agreed to join the confederation.'

'That's a declaration of war!' Lanyan shouted.

'It is an appropriate and completely legal response. Since the beginning of the hydrogue conflict, the Terran Hanseatic League has cut them off from vital materials, denied them food and medical supplies. You withdrew the protection of the Earth Defence Forces. In other words, Mr Chairman, the Hansa failed to meet its obligations and thereby voided the Charter. For their own survival, most colonies now feel this is the best prospect.'

'They are *Hansa* colonies!' Basil insisted.

'Former Hansa colonies, Mr Chairman. Representatives from fifteen Roamer clans have also signed on. We are confident the Speaker will agree that such a confederation is in the best interests of humanity. While the Roamers still refuse to trade with the Hansa, to show their good faith they have announced that they will supply ekti to any orphaned colony that joins the new government.'

General Lanyan could make no comprehensible sounds. Only Deputy Cain seemed unruffled.

The Chairman glared into Nahton's implacable green face. 'Go get your treeling right now and send a message to King Peter. Tell him that I command him to return to Earth without delay!'

'I'm sorry, sir. Our telink communications services are no longer available to the Chairman or any Hansa representative.'

'You can't do that.' Basil's mind was ready to burst. His skin felt as if it were on fire. 'Send the message! You're supposed to be neutral. You're a green priest. You're—'

'I follow the instructions of King Peter and Queen Estarra, as do all green priests. We cannot be commanded. Neither you, nor any member of the Earth Defence Forces, nor any person from the Hansa government, will be able to send a message via telink.'

For a moment Basil thought about torturing the priest, even

executing him if he didn't follow instructions. Sarein sat stunned, shaking her head. 'He's right, Basil. No one can force a green priest to send a telink message.'

Lanyan fumed. 'But by the time we can send our own ships to enforce the Charter, this will all be sewn up!'

'That has already occurred.' Nahton smiled coolly. 'When Chairman Wenceslas resigns and the remnants of the Terran Hanseatic League are dissolved, the people of Earth will also be welcome to join us. All members of the new confederation must be loyal to the King.'

Basil wanted to spit the name. 'The King? Peter was never a real King!'

Sitting motionless, Sarein blinked and looked at the seething and helpless Chairman. 'Maybe he was, Basil. More than you knew.'

ONE HUNDRED AND FORTY-FOUR

DESIGNATE DARO'H

The last of the scorched buildings in the Dobro colony had been knocked down, the charred debris cleared away. The wildfires that ravaged the rolling landscape had burned out, leaving the surrounding hills blackened. Soon, the rains would come, and a fresh carpet of green would spring forth, a sign of rejuvenation just like the new buildings being erected in the Ildiran settlement.

The terrible revolt had not done fatal injury to Dobro. *All wounds heal, even if some of them leave scars*, Daro'h thought. He walked down the street, still smelling soot and blood in the air. The sour, scratchy odours would not go away for a long time.

As he'd promised, Daro'h offered the humans what they needed to rebuild their camp, but after many discussions, the survivors had decided to move elsewhere, perhaps down to the fertile southern continent. Benn Stoner and his followers wanted to set up their homesteads far from their former Ildiran captors. Later – maybe after a few years or a few generations – they might find sufficient forgiveness in their hearts to come back and join the others in the way the original *Burton* colonists had meant to live among the Ildirans.

For himself, Daro'h would soon go back to the Prism Palace. He was excited to take up his new duties as Prime Designate. Another person would serve in his role here. Unlike some of his brothers, Daro'h had no noble-born sons yet. Given the circumstances, Udru'h might even take back his former position, though Daro'h doubted the humans would ever allow it.

In his walk, he stopped in front of the former Designate's residence. Two guards were stationed outside the door, technically holding the man prisoner. That evening, the humans and Ildirans were scheduled to meet. Daro'h didn't know whether to call it a debate or a trial. Udru'h would speak in his own defence, the humans would air their grievances, and Daro'h would implement whatever terms they imposed. It was what the Mage-Imperator had decreed.

Udru'h, still looking bruised and battered, his skin discoloured, stepped past the guards to Daro'h. 'Tonight they decide my fate, and I will be done with this waiting. Perhaps the people will feel shame. Will they be afraid to impose a harsh retribution?' Strange ghosts seemed to be haunting him behind his eyes; memories of what he had done were not so easy to justify when those memories came from Nira's point of view. It wasn't clear to Daro'h if the former Designate wanted the people to forgive him anymore.

Daro'h shuddered. 'You are my mentor. I was the new Designate. Had this happened a few years later, it would be me instead of you.'

Udru'h shrugged. 'We will see if my good intentions outweigh bad memories. Crimes must be punished, one way or another. I know that now.'

Unexpectedly, Daro'h felt a sudden and unusual heat down his spine and in his mind. The air became crackling hot. The smell of smoke and scorched bones intensified around him. The normally stoic guards looked into the sky, alarmed.

A trio of shimmering ellipsoids encased in flame descended like comets towards the scarred settlement.

'Faeros,' Udru'h said. 'What are they doing here?'

Daro'h had never seen the flaming shapes up close before. He couldn't tell if they were ships or living elemental creatures. Many thousands of the faeros had been extinguished in their battles with the hydrogues. But why would they come to Dobro? What did they want?

The pulsing faeros drew closer, blazed brighter. Daro'h feared he might go blind if he stared, but he could not tear his eyes away. The fireballs loomed directly overhead, pausing as if they had come to the former Designate's residence on purpose. Udru'h flinched, as if he heard something loud inside his head.

The *thism* within Daro'h grew hot, like overheated wires burning through his nerves and his thoughts. He felt the strong and silky soul-threads being pulled and strained, knotted, melted . . .

A voice boomed through his mind, a roaring, skull-splitting shout that wasn't even directed at him. 'Udru'h, you betrayed me. Because of you, I lost everything. I failed.'

The former Designate reeled, as if his head might explode. The hammering molten voice continued its damning speech. 'But I am stronger than ever now. I no longer see the Lightsource – I *am* the Lightsource.'

In shock, Daro'h recognized the angry voice of the mad Designate. At the end of his defeated rebellion, Rusa'h had flown his ship into Hyrillka's sun. Now he was alive and intact . . . and with the faeros?

Unable to tear himself away, Udru'h shook his head against the thoughts, covered his eyes and ears, but the booming continued to rip through the *thism*. 'Many faeros have perished. Now you will spark a new one. Let your treachery consume you.'

Daro'h drew back in horror as Udru'h's face began to glow as if his very bones had grown incandescent. The former Designate opened his mouth to scream, and smoke gushed out. His flesh turned white-hot. Suddenly Udru'h burst into flames. Fire licked out of his eyes, his mouth, his ears, and finally cracked out of the bones in his fingers.

Daro'h watched, unable to run, unable to scream.

Udru'h was engulfed by a single flare that incinerated every speck of his physical being. The new curl of fire, rolling and braided, shot up like a spark into the nearest pulsating faeros fireball.

Nothing was left of the former Designate but a black mark on the ground, a smear of residue. Glassy footprints marked where the heat of his body had melted the dirt. Daro'h looked up, feeling his skin singe.

Six more faeros fireballs descended to join the others over Dobro.

ONE HUNDRED AND FORTY-FIVE

ORLI COVITZ

I t was Orli's turn to bring a delivery of home-made food to the EDF barracks near the Klikiss transportal wall. There was nothing wrong with being good neighbours to the fifteen soldiers still assigned to Llaro.

The Roamer detainees, Crenna colonists, and original settlers had decided to think of the stranded soldiers as 'protectors' instead of prison guards or babysitters. With the uproar and turmoil out in the Hansa, even the Roamer detainees were resigned to staying here for the time being. The EDF troops were not at liberty to leave either. They were all cut off, while the rest of the Spiral Arm went to hell.

From messengers passing through the transportal, the Llaro colonists had heard about how Soldier compies had seized much of the EDF fleet. Orli lived in fear that the robot-controlled battleships might attack here, just as they had wiped out Corribus. And no one had any explanation for why the eerie faeros ships had come here searching, destroying one of the patrol Remoras in the process. She did not feel particularly safe.

If anything bad happened now, Llaro had no defences at all – except for those fifteen soldiers. So, the colonists took turns making meals for the troops, sharing some of their fresh produce from the fields. Best to keep the options open. It was a good thing for everybody to get along, she thought.

Orli and Mr Steinman trudged uphill to the barracks, carrying the day's baskets. 'My legs are getting too stiff to make this walk every single day,' the older man said.

Orli was used to Mr Steinman's complaints. 'You don't make it every single day. And if you were all alone on a planet, like you wanted to be, you'd have a lot more work to do just to keep yourself alive. The house you're living in now is a thousand times better than the rickety shack the two of us built together.'

'I was proud of that shack.'

'So was I.' Orli grinned. The whole settlement seemed to have adopted her. She had rooms of her own in one of the large multi-family structures, a place where she slept and had private time to play her music synthesizer strips. Since the colonists liked to listen to her melodies, she often sat in the communal areas at night and played and played.

Seeing the two approach, the EDF soldiers waved a greeting. Orli and Mr Steinman were bright and cheery as they handed over the meals. The lonely troops ploughed through the baskets, making appreciative sounds as they saw fresh breads and vegetables.

'We're gonna have to go back to basic training,' said one of the soldiers. 'I never ate this well in the EDF! I'm bound to gain so much weight that I won't fit in my uniform anymore.'

'Just find a colonist wife,' his comrade chided him. 'Maybe she can let out some of the seams.'

'*These* colonist women? She'd make me do it myself.'

'And so you should,' Orli said. 'It wouldn't hurt you to be self-sufficient.'

The soldier guffawed. 'Would you listen to this girl?'

Behind them, a buzzing sound crackled through the air like static electricity. The guards snapped to their feet as the transportal wall thrummed. 'Something's coming through!'

'Nothing's scheduled that I know of — hey, maybe it's our replacements.'

'Keep dreaming.'

Other EDF soldiers rushed out of the barracks, eager for any change in the monotony. Anybody who came through the transportal wall might be bringing good news, or at least fresh supplies.

The trapezoidal sheet of stone grew murky, and two figures stepped through. It was not anybody they knew. The EDF soldiers grabbed their weapons and looked uncertainly at each other. 'Who are you? Identify yourselves!'

Orli saw an older woman with weathered features, tattered clothes, and bedraggled hair. Her face had a distant, haunted look. Beside her walked a silvery compy, a Friendly model with bright golden eye sensors. The little compy spoke, as if happy to make introductions. 'This is Margaret Colicos, and I am DD.' Orli thought the woman's name sounded familiar.

Weirdly disoriented and unearthly, Margaret focused her eyes, spotted Orli and Mr Steinman, then the EDF soldiers. 'It has been so long since I've seen other humans.'

'What happened to you, ma'am?' Orli said. 'Where did you come from?'

The transportal wall flickered again, and more shapes appeared behind her.

'I'm sorry. I did not want to do this.' Margaret's voice was hollow and devastated. 'Everything will change now ... everything.'

Behind her dozens of multi-legged creatures emerged from the trapezoidal wall, swarming through. The tall beetle-like shapes held sharp and sophisticated-looking weapons. Their leathery exoskeletons were black and segmented. Their smooth eyes burned with a strange intelligence. Behind the first ranks came another twenty creatures, then another rank, and another.

The EDF soldiers scrambled backwards, shouting to each other. Panicked, they drew their weapons, fell back, and took aim.

'Don't shoot!' one of the men cried. 'We're outnumbered a hundred to one!'

Mr Steinman held onto Orli's arm as if *she* might be able to protect him.

Margaret Colicos stood close to DD, as if in a daze. 'After thousands of years of breeding and recovery, the Klikiss are ready to swarm again. They want their planets back.'

Waves of Klikiss creatures exhibiting several different shapes or breeds continued to flow through the transportal. The giant insects seemed numberless. Already, hundreds had marched through the trapezoidal gateway, sweeping out into the Llaro colony.

Margaret continued, 'The Klikiss have returned with a vendetta against their treacherous robots, who brought about the end of their civilization ten thousand years ago.'

As the alarm spread, Llaro settlers ran about, shouting, trying to find ways to defend themselves. But the Klikiss had not attacked, Orli realized. Not yet.

Margaret turned to look behind her. 'At this moment, Klikiss are swarming through every transportal on every one of their worlds. They will reclaim their sovereign territory.'

Orli saw a larger shape emerge through the transportal, a giant Klikiss covered with enormous spines, curved spikes, and mottled armour. Its head crests were jagged and threatening, vastly more powerful than the rest of the Klikiss.

In a clicking and chittering language that was oddly musical, with notes that rose and fell in an alien melody, the giant Klikiss spoke to Margaret. The little compy DD translated, his brightness of his tone belying the dire message. 'The breedex is angered to see such widespread human habitation on these worlds.'

Margaret's unfocused gaze swept across the established colony on Llaro. 'Leave. Or the Klikiss will exterminate you all.'

GLOSSARY

ADAM, PRINCE – predecessor to Raymond Aguerra, considered unacceptable candidate.

ADAR – highest military rank in Ildiran Solar Navy.

AGUERRA, RAYMOND – streetwise young man from Earth, former identity of King Peter.

ALEXA, MOTHER – interim ruler of Theroc, wife of Father Idriss, mother of Reynald, Beneto, Sarein, Estarra, and Celli.

ANDEZ, SHELIA – EDF soldier, held captive by Roamers at Osquivel shipyards.

AQUARIUS – wental-distribution ship flown by Nikko Chan Tylar, damaged by Klikiss robots on Jonah 12.

ARCHFATHER – symbolic head of Unison religion on Earth.

AVILA – Roamer clan.

BATTLEAXE – nickname for former Hansa Chairman Maureen Fitzpatrick.

BEBOB – Rlinda Kett's pet name for Branson Roberts.

BEN – third Great King of the Terran Hanseatic League.

BENETO – green priest, second son of Father Idriss and Mother

Alexa, killed by hydrogues on Corvus Landing, but returned as a wooden golem to the forest.

BIG GOOSE – Roamer derogative term for Terran Hanseatic League.

BLAZER – Ildiran illumination source.

BLUE SKY MINE – skymine facility at Golgen, operated by Ross Tamblyn, destroyed by hydrogues.

BRIA'NH, TAL – legendary Ildiran commander who fought against the Shana Rei.

BRIGGS, SERGEANT JAMES – Security chief aboard Juggernaut *Eldorado*.

BRINDLE, CONRAD – Robb Brindle's father, former military officer.

BRINDLE, NATALIE – Robb Brindle's mother, former military officer.

BRINDLE, ROBB – young EDF recruit, comrade of Tasia Tamblyn, captive of hydrogues after Battle of Osquivel.

BURTON – One of the eleven generation ships from Earth, fourth to depart. Lost en route, captured by Ildirans and the colonists aboard were used as breeding subjects.

CAILLIE – One of the eleven generation ships from Earth, taken to settle Theroc.

CAIN, ELDRED – deputy and heir-apparent of Basil Wenceslas, pale-skinned and hairless, an art collector.

CARBON SLAMMER – new-design EDF weapon, effective at breaking carbon-carbon bonds.

CARGO ESCORT – Roamer vessel used to deliver ekti shipments from skymines.

CARRERA, ENSIGN FEDERICO – EDF trainee pilot, part of General Lanyan's 'cavalry'.

CELLI – youngest daughter of Father Idriss and Mother Alexa.

CHAN – Roamer clan.

CHARYBDIS – the first water world where Jess disseminated the wentals.

CHILDRESS, ENSIGN SANDRA – EDF trainee, part of General Lanyan's 'cavalry.'

CHRYSALIS CHAIR – reclining throne of the Mage-Imperator.

CITYSPHERE – enormous hydrogue habitation complex.

CLANKER – deprecatory term for either compies or Klikiss robots.

CLARIN, ROBERTO – former administrator of Hurricane Depot, now leader of POWs on Llaro.

CLOUD HARVESTER – ekti-gathering facility designed by Hansa.

CLYDIA – one of the nineteen green priest volunteers aboard EDF ships.

COHORT – battle group of Ildiran Solar Navy consisting of seven Maniples, or 343 ships.

COLICOS, ANTON – the son of Margaret and Louis Colicos, translator and student of epic stories, sent to Ildiran Empire to study *The Saga of Seven Suns*.

COLICOS, MARGARET – xeno-archaeologist, wife of Louis Colicos, specializing in ancient Klikiss artifacts, vanished through transportal during Klikiss robot attack on Rheindic Co.

COMPETENT COMPUTERIZED COMPANION – intelligent servant robot, called compy, available in Analytical, Friendly, Teacher, Governess, Listener, and other models.

COMPY – shortened term for 'Competent Computerized Companion'.

CORRIBUS – Klikiss colony world, obliterated by Klikiss robots.

CORVUS LANDING – Hansa colony world, obliterated by hydrogues.

COVITZ, ORLI – waifish survivor of Corribus massacre.

CRENNA – Hansa colony, evacuated when hydrogue–faeros battles extinguished the sun.

DANIEL – new Prince candidate selected by the Hansa as a potential replacement for Peter.

DARO'H – the Dobro Designate-in-waiting.

DD – Friendly compy, formerly owned by Margaret and Louis Colicos; taken captive by Klikiss robots, but recently escaped.

DESIGNATE – any pure-bred noble son of the Mage-Imperator, ruler of an Ildiran world.

DIAMONDFILM – crystalline parchment used for Ildiran documents.

DOBRO – Ildiran colony world, site of human-Ildiran breeding camps.

DOORBELLS – resonance mats invented by Kotto Okiah, capable of blasting open a hydrogue warglobe.

DROGUE – deprecatory term for hydrogues.

DUNSEL – slang term for token human commanders aboard EDF rammer ships.

DURRIS – trinary star system, close white and orange stars orbited by a red dwarf; three of the Ildiran 'seven suns', one of which was extinguished by faeros–hydrogue battles.

EA – Tasia Tamblyn's personal compy; her memory was wiped when she was interrogated by Basil Wenceslas.

EARTH DEFENCE FORCES – Terran space military, head-quartered on Mars but with jurisdiction throughout the Terran Hanseatic League.

EDDIES – slang term for soldiers in EDF.

EDF – Earth Defence Forces.

EKTI – exotic allotrope of hydrogen used to fuel Ildiran stardrives.

ELDORADO – Grid 5 flagship Juggernaut, captained by Admiral Kostas Eolus.

ELMAN, PRIVATE KEVIN – silver beret.

EOLUS, KOSTAS – Grid 5 admiral.

ESTARRA – daughter of Father Idriss and Mother Alexa. Current Queen of Terran Hanseatic League, married to King Peter.

FAEROS – sentient fire entities dwelling within stars.

FITZPATRICK, MAUREEN – former Chairman of the Terran Hanseatic League, grandmother of Patrick Fitzpatrick III.

FITZPATRICK, PATRICK, III – spoiled cadet in the Earth Defence Forces, General Lanyan's protégé, presumed dead after Osquivel but captured by Roamers in Del Kellum's shipyards.

FORREY, KARLTON – first Roamer to set up operations at Forrey's Folly, which ended in disaster.

FORREY'S FOLLY – Roamer outpost.

FRAK – slang term for fracture-pulse drone.

FREDERICK, KING – previous figurehead ruler of the Terran Hanseatic League, assassinated by hydrogue emissary.

FRICK, ANSELM – Palace District businessman.

FUNGUS REEF – giant worldtree growth on Theroc, carved into a habitation by the Therons.

GALE'NH – experimental half-breed son of Nira Khali and Adar Kori'nh, third oldest of her children.

GOFF, BORIS – Roamer skyminer.

GOLD, SULLIVAN – administrator of the Hansa's modular cloud harvester at Qronha 3, now held prisoner on Ildira.

GOLGEN – gas giant where Ross Tamblyn's Blue Sky Mine was destroyed, bombarded by comets targeted by Jess Tamblyn. Wentals have made it safe for skymining again.

GOLIATH – first expanded Juggernaut in EDF fleet.

GREEN PRIEST – servant of the worldforest, able to use world-trees for instantaneous communication.

GU – analytical compy assigned to work with Kotto Okiah.

GUIDING STAR – Roamer philosophy and religion, a guiding force in a person's life.

HALL OF REMEMBERERS – central building of the rememberer kith, where *The Saga of Seven Suns* is compiled and memorized.

HANSA – Terran Hanseatic League.

HAPHINE – gas giant.

HAPPINESS – former Klikiss world, colonized by neo-Amish group.

HUCK, TABITHA – engineer aboard Sullivan Gold's cloud harvester at Qronha 3, now held captive at Ildira.

HUYSTRA, JEREMIAH – leader of neo-Amish farmers on Happiness.

HYDROGUES – alien race living at cores of gas-giant planets.

HYRILLKA – Ildiran colony in Horizon Cluster, devastated by recent rebellion led by Designate Rusa'h.

IDRISS, FATHER – ruler of Theroc, husband of Mother Alexa, father of Reynald, Beneto, Sarein, Estarra, and Celli.

ILDIRA – home planet of the Ildiran Empire.

ILDIRAN EMPIRE – large alien empire, the only other major civilization in the Spiral Arm.

ILDIRAN SOLAR NAVY – space military fleet of the Ildiran Empire.

ILDIRANS – humanoid alien race with many different breeds, or kiths.

ISIX CATS – sleek feline predators native to Ildira; Jora'h's daughter Yazra'h keeps three of them.

ISPEROS – hot planet, site of Kotto Okiah's failed mining base.

JAZER – energy weapon used by Earth Defence Forces.

JORA'H – Mage-Imperator of the Ildiran Empire.

JUGGERNAUT – large battleship class in Earth Defence Forces.

KAMAROV, RAVEN – Roamer cargo-ship captain, destroyed with his cargo ship by Patrick Fitzpatrick.

KEFFA, SMITH – hydrogue prisoner and experimental subject.

KELLUM, DEL – Roamer clan leader, in charge of Osquivel shipyards.

KELLUM, ZHETT – daughter of Del Kellum.

KETT, RLINDA – merchant woman, captain of the *Voracious Curiosity*.

KITH – a breed of Ildiran.

KLEEB – derogatory term for an EDF cadet.

KLIE'F – senior member of Ildiran scientist kith.

KLIKISS – ancient insect-like race, long vanished from the Spiral Arm, leaving only their empty cities.

KLIKISS ROBOTS – intelligent beetle-like robots built by the Klikiss race.

KLIKISS TORCH – a weapon/mechanism developed by the ancient Klikiss race to implode gas-giant planets and create new stars.

KOLKER – green priest, friend of Yarrod, stationed on Sullivan Gold's modular cloud harvester at Qronha 3, now held captive on Ildira. He has lost his treeling.

KORI'NH, ADAR – leader of the Ildiran Solar Navy, killed in suicidal assault against hydrogues on Qronha 3.

KOSEVIC, BRION – executive officer aboard the *Goliath*.

KOWALSKI – Roamer clan.

KOWALSKI, OSCAR – head of operations at Forrey's Folly.

KR – analytical compy assigned to work with Kotto Okiah.

LANYAN, GENERAL KURT – commander of Earth Defence Forces.

LENS KITHMEN – philosopher priests who help guide troubled Ildirans, interpreting faint guidance from the *thism*.

LIGHTSOURCE – the Ildiran version of Heaven, a realm on a higher plane composed entirely of light. Ildirans believe that faint trickles of this light break through into our universe and are channelled through the Mage-Imperator and distributed across their race through the *thism*.

LLARO – abandoned Klikiss world, now used as a colony and also POW holding world for Roamer prisoners.

LORIE'NH, TAL – cohort commander in the Ildiran Solar Navy.

LOTZE, DAVLIN – Hansa exosociologist and spy on Crenna, now presumed dead and hiding on Llaro.

MAE, TERENE – EDF ensign.

MAGE-IMPERATOR – the god-emperor of the Ildiran Empire.

MANIPLE – battle group of Ildiran Solar Navy consisting of seven septas, or forty-nine ships.

MANTA – mid-sized cruiser class in EDF.

MARATHA – former Ildiran resort world, now infested with Klikiss robots.

MCCAMMON, CAPTAIN RICHARD – head of the royal guard in the Whisper Palace.

MIJISTRA – glorious capital city of the Ildiran Empire.

MUREE'N – experimental half-breed daughter of Nira Khali and a guard kithman, youngest of her children.

NAHTON – court green priest on Earth, serves King Peter.

NEMATODES – scarlet prehistoric worms living in underground ocean of Plumas.

NEMO, ALEXANDER – false name of Davlin Lotze.

NIALIA – plantmoth grown on Hyrillka, source of shiing.

NIRA – female green priest, lover of Jora'h and mother of Osira'h.

NODU'NH, TAL – commander of a Solar Navy cohort.

NOGALES, ROSAMARIA – biologist studying the hydrogue derelict.

OKIAH, JHY – former Speaker of the Roamer clans, now dead.

OKIAH, KOTTO – Jhy Okiah's youngest son, brash and eccentric inventor.

O'NH, TAL – second highest-ranking officer in Ildiran Solar Navy, has only one eye.

ORRYX – Ildiran splinter colony, first to be destroyed by the Shana Rei.

OSIRA'H – daughter of Nira Khali and Jora'h, possesses unusual telepathic abilities.

OSQUIVEL – ringed gas planet, site of secret Roamer shipyards, now abandoned.

OSSUARIUM – storage chamber in the Prism Palace for the glowing skulls of former Mage-Imperators.

OTEMA – old green priest, sent from Theroc to Ildira, where she was murdered by former Mage-Imperator.

OX – Teacher compy, one of the oldest Earth robots. Now instructor and adviser to King Peter.

PALACE DISTRICT – governmental zone around Whisper Palace on Earth.

PALAWU, HOWARD – Chief Science Adviser to King Peter, one of the dissectors of the Klikiss robot Jorax.

PALMER, BING – Roamer skyminer.

PASTERNAK, SHAREEN – chief of Welyr skymine, betrothed to Del Kellum but killed in an early hydrogue strike.

PAXTON, SERGEANT W.H. – leader of silver beret squad.

PELLIDOR, FRANZ – assistant to Basil Wenceslas, an 'expeditor'.

PERONI, CESCA – Roamer Speaker of all clans. Cesca was betrothed to Ross Tamblyn, but has always loved his brother Jess.

PERONI, DENN – Cesca's father, a Roamer merchant.

PERONI, LYRA – Cesca's mother.

PERY'H – the Hyrillka Designate-in-waiting, murdered at start of Rusa'h's rebellion.

PETER, KING – successor to old King Frederick.

PLUMAS – frozen moon with deep liquid oceans, site of Tamblyn clan water industry.

PRIME DESIGNATE – eldest son and heir-apparent of Ildiran Mage-Imperator.

PRISM PALACE – dwelling of the Ildiran Mage-Imperator.

QRONHA 3 – gas giant close to Ildira, site of first hydrogue attack on Ildiran cloud harvesters, then repeat attack on Sullivan Gold's skymine.

RAMIREZ, ELLY, COMMANDER – acting commander of Tasia Tamblyn's Manta cruiser.

RAMMER – kamikaze EDF ship designed to be crewed by Soldier compies, initial sixty lost at Qronha 3.

REMEMBERER – member of the Ildiran storyteller kith.

REMORA – small attack ship in Earth Defence Forces.

RENDEZVOUS – asteroid cluster, centre of Roamer government, destroyed by EDF.

REYNALD – eldest son of Father Idriss and Mother Alexa, killed in hydrogue attack on Theroc.

RHEINDIC CO – abandoned Klikiss world, site of major excavation by the Colicos team.

RIDEK'H – young boy, new Designate of Hyrillka.

ROAMERS – loose confederation of independent humans, primary producers of ekti stardrive fuel.

ROBERTS, BRANSON – former husband and business partner of Rlinda Kett, also called BeBob.

ROD'H – experimental half-breed son of Nira Khali and the Dobro Designate, second oldest of her children.

ROSSIA – eccentric green priest, survivor of a wyvern attack, now volunteer aboard EDF ships.

RUSA'H – Hyrillka Designate, leader of unsuccessful revolt against the Mage-Imperator; flew his ship into the sun before he could be captured.

SAGA OF SEVEN SUNS, THE – historical and legendary epic of the Ildiran civilization.

SAREIN – eldest daughter of Father Idriss and Mother Alexa, Theron ambassador to Earth, also Basil Wenceslas's lover.

SARHI, PADME – Grand Governnor of Yreka colony.

SEEDSHIP – Verdani battleship.

SEPTA – small battle group of seven ships in the Ildiran Solar Navy.

SEPTAR – commander of a septa.

SHADOW FLEET – legendary group of warliners destroyed by the Shana Rei.

SHANA REI – legendary 'creatures of darkness' in *The Saga of Seven Suns*.

SHIING – stimulant drug made from nialia plantmoths on Hyrillka, dulls Ildiran receptivity to the *thism*.

SHIR'OF – senior member of Ildiran engineering kith.

SHIZZ – Roamer expletive.

SILVER BERET – sophisticated special forces trained by EDF.

SIRIX – Klikiss robot, leader of insidious revolt against humans, former captor of DD.

SKYMINE – ekti-harvesting facility in gas giant clouds, usually operated by Roamers.

SKYSPHERE – main dome of the Ildiran Prism Palace. The skysphere holds exotic plants, insects, and birds, all suspended over the Mage-Imperator's throne room.

SOLIMAR – young green priest, treedancer and mechanic. Celli's boyfriend.

SOUL-THREADS – connections of *thism* that trickle through from the Lightsource. Mage-Imperator and lens kithmen are able to see them.

SPAMPAX – processed meat rations, designed to last for centuries.

SPEAKER – political leader of the Roamers.

SPIRAL ARM – the section of the Milky Way Galaxy settled by the Ildiran Empire and Terran colonies.

SPLINTER COLONY – an Ildiran colony that meets minimum population requirements.

STANNA, BILL – EDF POW, killed during a poorly planned escape attempt from Osquivel.

STEINMAN, HUD – old transportal explorer, discovered Corribus on transportal network and decided to settle there.

STONER, BENN – leader of human breeding captives on Dobro.

STROMO, ADMIRAL LEV – admiral in Earth Defence Forces, Grid 0 commander, derisively called 'Stay-at-home Stromo'.

SUNSHINE – Roamer settlement run by clan Tomara.

SWENDSEN, LARS RURIK – Hansa engineering specialist.

TABEGUACHE, PETER – Grid 1 admiral.

TAE'NH, TAL – commander of a Solar Navy cohort.

TAL – military rank in Ildiran Solar Navy, cohort commander.

TALBUN – Beneto's green priest mentor, died on Corvus Landing.

TAMBLYN, ANDREW – one of Jess's uncles, brother to Bram, killed by reanimated Karla Tamblyn.

TAMBLYN, BRAM – former scion of Tamblyn clan, father of Ross, Jess, and Tasia, died after his son Ross perished on the Blue Sky Mine.

TAMBLYN, CALEB – one of Jess's uncles, brother to Bram.

TAMBLYN, JESS – Roamer, second son of Bram Tamblyn, in love with Cesca Peroni, now infused with wental energy.

TAMBLYN, KARLA – Jess's mother, frozen to death in ice accident on Plumas.

TAMBLYN, ROSS – estranged oldest son of Bram Tamblyn, chief of Blue Sky Mine at Golgen, killed in first hydrogue attack.

TAMBLYN, TASIA – Jess Tamblyn's sister, currently serving in the EDF.

TAMBLYN, TORIN – one of Jess's uncles, brother to Bram, Wynn's twin.

TAMBLYN, WYNN – one of Jess's uncles, brother to Bram, Torin's twin.

TAMO'L – experimental half breed daughter of Nira Khali and a lens kithman, second youngest of her children.

TELINK – instantaneous communication used by green priests.

TERRAN HANSEATIC LEAGUE – commerce-based government of Earth and Terran colonies, run by Chairman Basil Wenceslas.

THEROC – forested planet, home of the sentient worldtrees.

THERON – a native of Theroc.

THISM – faint racial telepathic link from Mage-Imperator to the Ildiran people.

THOR'H – eldest noble-born son of Mage-Imperator Jora'h, traitor during Rusa'h's revolt, now held prisoner and drugged.

THUNDERHEAD – mobile weapons platform in Earth Defence Forces.

TOMARA – Roamer clan.

TRANSGATE – hydrogue point-to-point transportation system.

TRANSPORTAL – Klikiss instantaneous transportation system.

TREELING – a small worldtree sapling, often transported in an ornate pot.

TREESHIP – Verdani battleship.

TWITCHER – EDF stun weapon.

TYLAR, NIKKO CHAN – young Roamer pilot, son of Crim and Marla.

UDRU'H – Dobro Designate, in charge of secret breeding programme.

UR'NH, TAL – commander of a Solar Navy cohort.

VAO'SH – Ildiran rememberer, patron and friend of Anton Colicos.

VERDANI – organic-based sentience, manifested as the Theron worldforest.

VORACIOUS CURIOSITY – Rlinda Kett's merchant ship.

WAN, PURCELL – administrative engineer of Jonah 12, killed by Klikiss robots.

WARGLOBE – hydrogue spherical attack vessel.

WARLINER – largest class of Ildiran battleship.

WELYR – gas giant, site of Roamer skymine destroyed by hydrogues.

WENCESLAS, BASIL – Chairman of the Terran Hanseatic League.

WENTALS – sentient water-based creatures.

WHISPER PALACE – magnificent seat of the Hansa government.

WILLIS, SHEILA, ADMIRAL – commander of Grid 7 EDF battle group.

WORLDFOREST – the interconnected, semi-sentient forest based on Theroc.

WORLDTREE – a separate tree in the interconnected, semi-sentient forest based on Theroc.

WORM HIVE – large nest built by hive worms on Theroc, spacious enough to be used for human habitation.

WU-LIN, ADMIRAL CRESTONE – Grid 3 commander.

WYVERN – large flying predator on Theroc.

YAMANE, Dr KIRO – cybernetic specialist held captive by Roamers at Osquivel shipyards.

YARROD – green priest, younger brother of Mother Alexa.

YAZRA'H – oldest daughter of Jora'h, keeps three Isix cats, personal guard of the Mage-Imperator.

YREKA – fringe Hansa colony world, now site of thriving black market centre.

ZAN'NH – eldest son of Mage-Imperator Jora'h, Adar of the Ildiran Solar Navy.

ZIZU, ANWAR – EDF Sergeant, security chief on Tasia Tamblyn's Manta.

ZOLTAN – Roamer clan.

Out now in Simon & Schuster trade paperback

METAL SWARM

The Saga of Seven Suns

BOOK SIX